DEAD SOULS

NIKOLAI GOGOL was born in the village of Sorochintsy, Poltava province, in 1809. He began to write in his teens, studied painting at the Academy of Fine Arts, and entered the Civil Service as a scribe in 1830. He soon moved to a post as a history teacher, followed by a brief and unsuccessful stint as Assistant Professor of History at St Petersburg University. Working on *Dead Souls*, Part One, he travelled in Switzerland, France, Italy, and Germany in the late 1830s. He continued to travel and write in the 1840s; in his self-imposed exile he dedicated himself to recreating the land he had left behind. Gogol never married, although he proposed marriage to the sister of his dear friend Prince Vielgorsky, whom he had nursed through his last illness. In 1848 he moved back to Russia, living under a cloud of religious introspection. His last significant act as a writer was to burn the manuscript of *Dead Souls*, Part Two, on which he had worked during the 1840s and early 1850s. He died in 1852 and was buried in Moscow's Danilov Monastery; his remains were transferred to the Novodevichy Cemetery in 1931.

CHRISTOPHER ENGLISH is a translator based in Zimbabwe. He attended Oxford and Moscow universities and has worked as a translator and teacher in the USSR, USA, Zimbabwe, and Kenya.

ROBERT MAGUIRE is Bakhmeteff Professor of Russian Studies at Columbia University. His books include *Red Virgin Soil: Soviet Literature in the 1920's Gogol from the Twentieth Century: Eleven Essays*, and *Exploring Gogol*.

OXFORD WORLD'S CLASSICS

NIKOLAI VASILYEVICH GOGOL

Dead Souls
A Poem

Translated and Edited by
CHRISTOPHER ENGLISH

With an Introduction by
ROBERT MAGUIRE

OXFORD
UNIVERSITY PRESS

OXFORD

UNIVERSITY PRESS

Great Clarendon Street, Oxford OX2 6DP

Oxford University Press is a department of the University of Oxford.
It furthers the University's objective of excellence in research, scholarship,
and education by publishing worldwide in

Oxford New York

Athens Auckland Bangkok Bogotá Buenos Aires Calcutta
Cape Town Chennai Dar es Salaam Delhi Florence Hong Kong Istanbul
Karachi Kuala Lumpur Madrid Melbourne Mexico City Mumbai
Nairobi Paris São Paulo Singapore Taipei Tokyo Toronto Warsaw

with associated companies in Berlin Ibadan

Oxford is a registered trade mark of Oxford University Press
in the UK and in certain other countries

Published in the United States
by Oxford University Press Inc., New York

Translation, Biography, Note on Texts and Transliteration, Table of Ranks,
Chronology, Explanatory Notes © Christopher English 1998
Bibliography © Richard Peace
Introduction © Robert Maguire 1998

British Library Cataloguing in Publication Data

Data available

Library of Congress Cataloging in Publication Data

Gogol', Nikolai Vasil'evich, 1809–1852.
[Mertvye dushi. English]
Dead souls: a poem / Nikolai Vasilyevich Gogol; translated
and edited by Christopher English; with an introduction by
Robert Maguire.
(Oxford world's classics)
I. English, Christopher. II. Title. III. Series: Oxford world's
classics (Oxford University Press)
PG3333.M4 1998 891.73'3—dc21 98–10537

ISBN 0-19-281837-6 (pbk.)

5 7 9 10 8 6 4

Printed in Great Britain by
Clays Ltd, St Ives plc

TRANSLATOR'S FOREWORD

In 1972, as a student at Oxford University, I was approached by the Oxford Playhouse Company and asked whether I would prepare for them an English acting version of Gogol's *The Government Inspector*, to be worked on together with the then director, Gordon MacDougall. I agreed, and the production was successfully staged some nine months later.

Twenty-five years on, with the publication of this volume, I reach the end of a journey which, unwittingly, I began with that chance request in 1972. For, over those years I have almost constantly been occupied with some work or other by, or about, Gogol. First, as a staff translator with Progress Publishers in Moscow, I prepared a collection of Gogol's plays and stories. Some years later I returned to Gogol, to translate the critical study *Gogol and the Western European Novel*, by Anna Yelistratova; this I followed with a translation of *Dead Souls* for the Soviet publishing house Raduga, and, in more recent years, for Oxford University Press, I have reworked all those translations and translated other works, all of which are now collected in three World's Classics volumes, two of stories and plays and—finally—this, Gogol's great poem.

To thank those who have helped me in this long endeavour would be, quite simply, to list the names of my friends, my family, my colleagues, in various towns and countries—in Moscow, Ashkhabad, and Sukhumi; in Cape Town, Harare, and Nairobi; in New York, Oxford, and London. There have been few people with whom I have come into contact whom I have not wearied at one time or another with questions pertaining to these works—a technical enquiry about bird-calls, perhaps, or parts of carriage harness; a search for an English word, a *mot juste*, which I knew existed but had continued to elude me; a request to listen to three or four renditions and to state a preference. Some have helped with a word or a suggestion which, in turn, has sent me to the word I sought; others have read through entire stories and chapters and made countless valuable suggestions; others still have helped with encouragement and patience. They know who they are: I hope they will find in the pages that follow, and in the volumes that preceded this, evidence of their help and will be pleased with what they see. I can think of no better way to show my gratitude.

A translation will never be perfect: it can only reflect, with different degrees of distortion, the original. By the same token, a translator's work is never done: I could work and rework these chapters many, many more times and would do so, if it were not for such things as deadlines, publication plans, and, ultimately, human life expectancy. I have already tried the patience of my editors to its generous limit and I must stop now and offer up this text, with all its imperfections. I only hope they are fewer and lesser than those of previous translations.

To my knowledge, *Dead Souls* has been translated into English not less than eleven times. A number of those translations are still in print. Why then, as I am so often asked, translate it again?

The answers are various. First, no translation can be definitive: in a sense, a translation of a great work is like the performance of a work of music. The original is the work as composed, as it exists in the mind of the composer; the translations, into whatever language or idiom, are the performances. Each performer tries to get closer to that absolute, the work in the composer's mind; so, too, the translator.

Second, there is the nature of that original. 'Ah, but surely,' I am often asked, 'the closest—and therefore the best—translation will be one prepared closest in time to the original, using the same language and social values as the original?'

All other things being equal, this would probably be true, yes, but with the translation of Russian classics into English—and particularly Gogol—those other things are not equal at all. For a start, between 1840 and the end of the twentieth century, the English language has changed in a way that the Russian has not: the major changes in Russian occurred shortly before Gogol took up his quill, and one of his most striking legacies was to set down on paper a version of the Russian language so fresh and vital that it reads almost as if it had been written today. Many of Gogol's expressions circulate in the day-to-day speech of Russians, not as self-conscious quotations, but as living idioms, without any awareness on the speaker's part of their origin. Much of the dialogue in this book could be imagined in the mouths of modern-day Russians, without adjustment. As to the social values: these too differed greatly, and Gogol's

Russia was a much earthier, more robust place, without the decorum and gentility of nineteenth-century England. Thus, translations closer in time to the original are misleading to the modern reader, in the archaic cast of their language and decorum of their description, while—paradoxically—contemporary translations may do better justice to Gogol's language and world.

By some, Gogol is acclaimed as a realist, as a painter of Russian life as it was. Others maintain that Gogol knew nothing of Russia or its life, that his world is an imaginary construct which has nothing to do with the reality of Tambov or Ryazan. Thus Nabokov remarks: 'It is as useless to look in *Dead Souls* for an authentic Russian background as it would be to try and form a conception of Denmark on the basis of that little affair in cloudy Elsinor.' It may indeed seem ironic that a book so essentially Russian, about travel in the country's remoter regions, should have been written almost entirely outside its frontiers, in Austria and France, in the spas of central Europe, and in Italy, by a man of Ukrainian descent.

On one point, however, all are agreed: whether or not Gogol was interested in the reality of Russia, he was intensely interested in the words Russians used to talk about that reality. Thus, the Russia of *Dead Souls* is a land of the mind and not of historico-geographical reality, a Russia of words and not of flesh and blood. Perhaps, like the Ireland of James Joyce a hundred years later, Gogol's Russia could only have been created from self-imposed exile.

The words of which it is composed were painstakingly gathered by Gogol over the years and recorded in his notebooks: they were retrieved from his own memories and limited travels about the country, and also provided, at his request, by his friends in letters to him in his foreign residence. And, as a world of words, it is entirely, quint-essentially, *sugubo* Russian. I like to think Gogol would have reversed Johnson's dictum, and have averred that, where things are the sons of earth, words are the daughters of heaven.

Gogol's is a world not so much of things, as of the names of these things. For that reason he may be among the hardest of all writers to translate adequately and, accordingly, his translators have always received short shrift from critics. Only an intrepid—or foolish—translator would embark on Gogol after heeding Nabokov's warning: 'I see however no other way of getting to Gogol [than by learning the Russian language]', he writes. 'His work . . . is a

phenomenon of language and not one of ideas.' Of existing translations, his verdict (written in 1944) is brutal: with the exception of
the Guerney translation, which had just appeared, he declares that
translations of Gogol into English 'are absolutely useless and should
be expelled from all public libraries'; of the then highly regarded
Constance Garnett version, he writes that 'the English is dry and
flat, and always unbearably demure. . . None,' he concludes, 'but an
Irishman should ever try tackling Gogol.' Fifty years—and half a
dozen translations—later, Susanne Fusso complains that 'Published
translations of Gogol are normally smoothed out and sanitized for
general consumption'.

Aware of the challenge posed by Gogol, and of the deficiencies of
earlier versions, such as that pointed out by Fusso, I have endeavoured to preserve, as far as possible, the singularity of Gogol's language, even where this results in awkward phrasing which might
strike the English reader as a poor translation. A case in point is
Gogol's use of the word *dazhe* ('even'). In the course of some 300
pages, Gogol uses this word more than 400 times. His attachment to
the word was noted by, among others, the American writer Edmund
Wilson, who wrote to Nabokov on 23 November 1943: 'I don't think
dazhe exactly means *even* in Gogol, but, as we would say, *in fact*, or
as a matter of fact.' Nabokov replied (28 November 1943): 'You are
absolutely right about the *dazhe* business,—those possibilities had
not occurred to me—but there is one little methodological hitch in
this respect which I shall discuss with you.' Quite what this 'little
methodological hitch' was we never find out—and, despite Nabokov's
concurrence, he himself uses 'even'—rather than Wilson's alterna-
tives—when translating extracts from Gogol in his book.

I believe that if Gogol had meant 'in fact', or 'as a matter of fact',
he would have said so. Instead he said 'even'. Accordingly, the word
'even' occurs with comparable frequency in my translation. I have
tried to respect the author's choice with other favourite—although
less conspicuous—words of Gogol's, such as 'noble' and 'nobility',
'respectable' and 'respected' (and other derivatives), which I have
preserved in the same density as their Russian cognates in Gogol's
original; thus too with what Nabokov calls his 'disheveled grammar', which, similarly, I have endeavoured to reflect in the English
in the hope of more authentically reproducing his untidy, often
tormented world to the English reader. In this I share the view of

Maguire, stated in his book *Exploring Gogol*, that '*every* word in any text, Gogolian or not [is] meaningful'—even what he calls the 'verbal clutter'.

Gogol's taxonomic inclinations—particularly in the realm of words—also oblige me to resort extensively to endnotes. It is sometimes simply not possible to convey the meaning and the suggestion of words through mere translation and the reader's indulgence is craved. That Gogol himself has so carefully gathered many of these words, requesting his friends to note down unusual turns of phrase, dialect terms, any unusual names, and to send them to him in their letters, and has then collected them like a lepidopterist his specimens, pinning them to the cork board of his notebooks for future use in his fiction, is an indication of their rarity and often total obscurity: consequently, even Russian editions are often furnished with extensive endnotes, explaining many of the same terms that appear in the notes to this volume.

A few weeks of the summer of 1972, before being approached by Gordon MacDougall and the Oxford Playhouse, I spent holidaying in Morocco with a friend. One day, as we lay on a beach in Al Hoceima, we decided to list, in order, our ten greatest books—a leisure pastime familiar, I am sure, to many readers. I had not set myself such a task before, but without hesitation I put, at the head of my list, *Dead Souls*. Twenty-five years later—twenty-five years of intermittent, but frequent and often lengthy, habitation of Gogol's world, of exploration of his labyrinths of words, of his shambolic grammar—if I were to return to that beach and that task, *Dead Souls* would keep its place.

CONTENTS

INTRODUCTION

In 1834, Vissarion Belinsky, soon to become the most important literary critic in Russia, proclaimed: 'We have no literature.' This might have struck his contemporaries as provocatively inaccurate. Russian literature, though just arriving on the European scene, was growing into robust adolescence, and even boasted one unquestioned genius, Alexander Pushkin. For Belinsky, however, 'literature' was synonymous not with variety and quantity, but with the novel.

The celebrity of the novel was rather recent. Between 1790 and 1830 it had gradually displaced the drama as the most important form of high literature. Virtually all its major practitioners, whether English, French, or German, had been translated into Russian, and had prompted Russians to try their hand too. But these native productions were generally perceived as too beholden to European models, too badly written, and too frivolous to serve as worthy mirrors of the nation's mind and soul, as the enormously influential German theorists had insisted novels must be. Even the best of them, Pushkin's *Eugene Onegin* (1833), struck many readers as being too 'Byronic' or 'French'. Russia had become the largest and most populous country in Europe, a Great Power, in fact, ever since its defeat of Napoleon. But where was the great Russian novel that would not only match its political and military stature, but confirm its very vitality as a nation?

The publication of *Dead Souls* in 1842 seemed to lay the doubts to rest. A few critics hated it, and proclaimed it a slander on Russia; but most agreed, whatever their other reservations, that here at last was a novel of the kind so long awaited, serious in purpose, national in content, and brilliant in execution. The fact that, although written in prose, it was designated as a *poema*, or 'long poem', did not disturb most people. Pushkin, after all, had called *Eugene Onegin* a 'novel in verse'. Generic boundaries were shaky in the early nineteenth century, and mixes were common. Gogol had begun by referring to his work as a 'novel' (*roman*). As he characterized it to Pushkin, in a letter of 7 October 1835: 'I've begun writing *Dead Souls*. The plot has grown into a very long novel, and I think it will be extremely funny.'[1] This makes it sound no weightier than the hundreds of other Russian specimens of the genre that had earned the scorn of so many critics, including Belinsky. But as Gogol came to realize that his undertaking would amount to far more than an adventure-filled romp, he adopted the term *poema* to signal that he was creating something ambitious, serious, lengthy, even revolutionary in form, with its juxtapositions of unrelated phenomena, its mixtures of seemingly incompatible styles, dictions and genres, its relish of linguistic luxuriance, and its narrator spinning verbal arabesques with dazzling virtuosity. In these respects, *Dead Souls* would have met with the approval of the German Romantic critics.

Ironically, no Russian blood flowed in the veins of the creator of this quintessentially Russian novel. The Gogol-Yanovskys, as the full family name ran, were of Ukrainian and Polish provenance. Nikolai Vasilievich, the oldest child, was born on 20 March 1809, in the village of Greater Sorochintsy, near Vasilievka, the family estate. This was an establishment of 3,000 acres, with some 200 male serfs, or 'souls', located in the Ukrainian province of Poltava, not far from the small town of Mirgorod. Gogol's father was decently educated by the standards of the time, had literary leanings which found expression in plays written in Ukrainian, and died when his son was 16. His mother was uneducated, credulous, supersititious, but not unintelligent. Of his eleven siblings, five survived. None rose above the ordinary, and nothing in Gogol's early life indicated that he would either. In 1821 he went off to secondary school in Nezhin, some 100 miles away. There he did reasonably well in his studies, was regarded as an eccentric, showed some interest in amateur theatre, and tried his hand at poetry, which his classmates advised him to drop. By 1828 he had graduated and had moved to St Petersburg in search of an occupation. A low-level position in a minor branch of the civil service helped pay expenses. His ambitions reached higher, however: he was convinced that he was destined for something great. But what? Would he be an actor? A disastrous audition for the

---

[1] All translations from *Dead Souls* are taken from the present volume. For Gogol's other writings, I rely on the complete works in Russian (*Polnoe sobranie sochinenii*, 14 vols., Moscow and Leningrad: ANSSSR, 1937–52). The volume and page numbers will be indicated in the text. Letters are also taken from this source, but I indicate only the date. Unless otherwise specified, as 'New Style' (n.s.), all dates are given in so-called 'Old Style', that is, according to the Julian calendar, which remained in force in Russia until 1918.

imperial theatres made short work of that. A poet? In 1829 he published, under the pseudonym 'V. Alov', a long 'idyll' in verse entitled *Hanz Küchelgarten*. It garnered two reviews, which were so damning that he bought up all the copies he could find and burned them. Prose fiction, perhaps? As he noted in a letter to his mother, written on 29 April 1829, shortly after his arrival in the capital, 'everyone [is] so interested in everything Little Russian'. He set to work on eight short stories set in the Ukraine, or 'Little Russia'. They were collected under the title *Village Evenings Near Dikanka* and published in two volumes, the first in 1831, the second the following year. They made him immediately famous, and have become classics. They also opened the doors of the literary world of St Petersburg to him, including an introduction to Pushkin, ten years his senior and the most celebrated writer in Russia. Yet it was only in 1835, with the success of *Arabesques*—a mixed collection of essays and stories—and *Mirgorod*—four brilliant specimens of straight fiction—that he determined on writing as his true vocation. When Pushkin was killed in a duel, in January 1837, the mantle of Russia's greatest writer passed to Gogol. By then he had already begun work on *Dead Souls*.

The Origins of Dead Souls

Gogol always insisted that *Dead Souls* owed its origin to Pushkin. The most extensive account is found in 'An Author's Confession', a manuscript which dates from 1847 but was not published until after his death:

He had long been trying to persuade me to undertake a large work, and finally, on one occasion, after I had read him a short description of a short scene, which nonetheless made a stronger impression on him than anything I had previously read, he said: 'With such an ability to put your finger on a person and present him as a fully living human being in just a few strokes, with such an ability, and no large work undertaken! That's just sinful!' Then he began to remind me of my weak constitution and my ailments, which could bring my life to an early end. He cited the case of Cervantes, who admittedly had written several very good and outstanding stories, but if he had not undertaken *Don Quixote*, he would never have occupied the place among writers he now does. And in conclusion, he gave me a plot of his own, which he himself had wanted to make into something of a long poem [*poema*], and which, as he put it, he would not have given anyone else. This was the plot of *Dead Souls*. (The idea for *The Government Inspector* was also his.) (viii. 439–40)

How literally Gogol meant these statements to be taken has been the subject of much critical speculation for more than a century. We expect writers to be unreliable about artistic debts. They may not care, or know. They may conceal, evade, pass over in silence. Gogol is unusual for doing just the opposite. Whatever the reasons, it was vital for him, regardless of the facts, to present himself as the beneficiary of Pushkin. Perhaps he really did believe, as he had told a correspondent ten years earlier, that 'not a single line was written without [Pushkin's] being present before my eyes. I consoled myself with the thought that he would be satisfied, I tried to guess what would please him, and that was my greatest and highest reward' (letter to Mikhail Pogodin, 30 March 1837). Perhaps he was engaging in self-promotion, at which he was adept, perhaps responding to some compelling demand of his psyche. In any event, he certainly could have conceived his novel and discovered its 'plot' with no direct assistance from Pushkin. The 'plot' had been common currency for generations. It was not merely an amusing anecdote: many people claimed to know of sharp operators who had profited by a loophole in the tax laws. Every ten years the government required landholders to take a census of their 'souls,' or male serfs. But in the interval, those who had died were still carried on the rolls as living, and their owners had to pay taxes on them. If someone could buy enough of them up, the cheaper the better, he could use them as collateral to secure a mortgage on property. In *Dead Souls*, the 400 that Chichikov acquires are worth a total of about 20,000 roubles on the books, although he has paid far less than that. That is a large enough number to give substance to his dreams of an estate, a wife, and children.

Gogol's own earlier excursions into fiction tell us something too. Many of his stories contain themes, images, subjects, and character-types that would eventually migrate to *Dead Souls*. Many have a density of texture, a complexity of structure, and a variety of narrative strategies that give them a novelistic feel. Gogol was also thinking big along other lines. As early as 1830 he had tried his hand at a novel, *The Hetman*, whose single surviving chapter marks it as a specimen of the fictionalized history that had made Sir Walter Scott famous throughout Europe. With a slight shift of focus, Gogol then decided that he would become a historian, on the grand scale cultivated by Gibbon in the eighteenth century, and Karamzin in the early nineteenth. Despite his lack of academic qualifications, he sought an appointment as a professor of general history in Kiev University, which he did not obtain, and, in 1834, an adjunct professorship in medieval history at St Petersburg University, which he did. Predictably, his tenure was brief and disastrous. His publishing plans were equally ambitious. In 1833 he announced that he intended to write *The Earth and its Peoples* 'in three if not in two volumes'. Then he projected a history of Little Russia, or the Ukraine, 'in six small or four large volumes'. He did considerable reading for both projects; but its only fruits were some nine articles, which were brought together, along with three superb stories, in the collection *Arabesques* (1835). Very purple in style, these are really pieces of historical impressionism; yet they show evidence that here too Gogol was working out techniques that would later serve him well in the more congenial purlieus of prose fiction, particularly in 'Taras Bulba', a tale of seventeenth-century Cossack life, which was first published in 1835 as part of the *Mirgorod* collection, and subjected to major revisions in 1842.

Finally, we cannot discount the push of public pressure. A writer who aspired to greatness was expected to write a novel. It is hard to believe that a man with Gogol's thirst for recognition did not take note. Nor can we overlook his own acute sense of personal crisis at mid-decade. It seems to have been triggered by the first performance of his play *The Government Inspector*, on 19 April 1836. The reactions of the audience ranged from enthusiasm to outrage. As would prove the case throughout much of his career, Gogol's ear was tuned to the negative frequencies. Even after admitting to one correspondent on 29 April that 'people abuse me and go to the play: you can't get tickets for the fourth performance', he told another on 10 May that he had decided to leave Russia in order to 'rid myself of the anguish that is daily visited upon me by my fellow-countrymen'. The posture of victim and martyr was to become all too familiar to Gogol's correspondents in the years to come, but it was entirely sincere, as far as one can tell. Here it conveys his growing sense that, despite the enormous success he had achieved in just a few years, his writing had reached a dead end. In a letter written shortly after he had gone abroad, he announced that 'a great turning-point, a great epoch' was at hand. He registered a determination to change course and 'accomplish something that an ordinary man cannot. I feel the strength of a lion in my heart . . . if I take a hard and judicious look at things, what does all my writing up to this point amount to? I feel as if I am leafing through an old student notebook . . . The time has long since passed when I must get down to business' (to Vasily Zhukovsky, 28 June, n.s., 1836). This 'business' was *Dead Souls*.

For a while he travelled through Europe, but once he settled in Rome, he tackled his 'poem' in earnest. The stimuli were powerful: the warm sunshine, which he constantly contrasted to the icy gloom of Russia; the long tradition of northern artists and writers who had travelled to Italy for inspiration; the large Russian colony, from which he could draw sustenance whenever he felt the need. Particularly important was the very remoteness of Rome from his native country. We may wonder at the spectacle of a man who was writing about a Russian provincial life he had never experienced in any depth from the vantage-point of lodgings hard by the Spanish Steps. But distance had always been an essential ingredient of his creative psychology. His excursions into history never moved much beyond the seventeenth century, and focused on Asians and Western Europeans, to the virtual exclusion of Russians. His tales about the Ukraine had been written from the remove of St Petersburg. Though he used this same city in several of his stories while actually living there, it always struck him as an unreal and un-Russian place, from which he felt spiritually distanced.

The new work continued to grow and deepen in his mind. But he moved slowly, often in fits and starts. His letters from the late 1830s are filled with complaints about poor health and an inability to concentrate, which he attributed to vague nervous disorders. Still, by late 1839 he had completed at least the first four chapters, which he read aloud to friends during a visit to Russia, and by March of the following year, the next two. On his way back to Italy, in 1840, he stopped in Vienna, where he fell so ill—from what he described as 'anguish' and an unbearable restlessness—that he did not expect to survive. He even set down his last will. But not wishing, as he put it, to die among 'Germans', he forced himself to return to Rome, where he gradually recovered and finally reported that he was 'healthy'. The spring of 1841 initiated a period of extraordinary creativity. In some five months, he prepared an edition of his earlier works for publication, including completely new versions of 'The Portrait' and 'Taras Bulba'; he wrote his most famous story, 'The Overcoat'; and he completed *Dead Souls*.

Off it went to the censors in Moscow, where, after an initially smooth reception, it ran into serious opposition. As Gogol related to a friend, one member of the committee 'began to shout in the voice of an ancient Roman: "No, this I will never allow: the soul is immortal; there can be no such thing as a deal soul; the author is taking up arms against immortality."' When others explained that Gogol was using the term 'souls' in the sense of 'peasants', further objections surfaced: the book disapproved of the institution of serfdom, and its hero, Chichikov, was a criminal, who would inspire other potential lawbreakers; the 'souls' had been human beings, and the price set on them was so low as to be degrading. '"After this,"' Gogol reported one of the censors as saying, '"not a single foreigner will come to visit us"' (letter to P. A. Pletnyov, 7 January 1842). The committee ended by banning the book outright. Gogol was crushed. But he fought back, resubmitting the manuscript this time to the censors in St Petersburg and asking friends to intervene. It passed, with only a few changes required. The troublesome matter of the mortality of souls was resolved with a new title: 'The Adventures of Chichikov, or Dead Souls'. But he found one inflexible demand deeply disturbing: the elimination of the entire 'Tale of Captain Kopeikin' in Chapter 10, for its irreverent treatment of the higher reaches of the state bureaucracy. Gogol toned it down; the censor approved; and the book was published on 21 May 1842.

Chastened by his experience with *The Government Inspector*, Gogol began to voice apprehensions about the critical reception of *Dead Souls* even before it was completed. He took steps to defang hostile readers by asking friends to write favourable notices, and by insisting that he was aware of flaws in the forthcoming volume, which in any event could not be properly judged until the sequel had appeared. Indulging his fondness for architectural metaphors, he wrote to Vasily Zhukovsky: 'I cannot help but see its insignificance in comparison to the other parts that are to follow. In relation to them it strikes me as resembling a porch hastily attached by a provincial architect to a palace that has been planned on colossal lines but not yet built. I don't doubt that it has acquired a sizable number of defects that I can't yet see' (26 June, n.s., 1842). He need not have worried. Nearly all the critics understood that the book marked an important moment in Russian literature. Some set it on a level with Homer and Shakespeare. The negative reviews tended to be petty, in their disapproval of Gogol's relish for graphically sordid details of lower-class life, his odd, sometimes incorrect uses of language, and his failure to provide the kind of characters who would inspirit the reader; but even they were written against a high level of expectation. In any event, Gogol paid them little mind. Perhaps his capacity for outrage had been exorcised during the book's passage through the censorship, or perhaps his residence abroad provided a salubrious detachment. By now, too, he had decided, in what was to become an ever more insistent motif of his life and work, that unfavourable criticism had some justification, and that it could be turned to profit as he embarked on the continuation of his great work.

At various stages in the writing, Gogol had invoked Dante, Cervantes, Homer, and Sir Walter Scott as models. There is in fact much that looks familiar to us about *Dead Souls*. In adopting the adventure-tale structure, he of course invites comparison with a 2,000-year-old tradition that begins with the *Odyssey*. Fielding's *Tom Jones* has been proposed as the nearest source of the ironic narrator and the roguish character who meets a series of challenges with his wits. Some readers have been reminded of Laurence Sterne's obsession with meaningful trivia, as in his famous discourse on noses in *Tristram Shandy*, his deployment of multiple perspectives, and his assumption that 'truth' and 'reality', whether fictional or not, can never be absolute. Others have detected the voice of Balzac or of Thackeray. Readers who know their Russian literature will note the strong imprint of folklore, the puppet theatre, seventeenth-century rogues' tales, and Pushkin's *Eugene Onegin*. Fascinating as such detective work may be, however, the important question is ultimately what Gogol does with these materials. In every case, he bends them to his own purposes, and incorporates them into a far larger and more complex design, which defies ready paraphrase or analysis, as generations of critics have discovered. Probably no other work of Russian literature has opened itself to such a variety of readings. Is it a faithful picture of the manners and mores of provincial Russia at a particular time? A symbolist extravaganza? A satire, a moral tract? An instance of Rabelaisian carnival? An encoding of Gogol's own troubled psyche? One could easily organize a history of Russian literary criticism around the critical responses to *Dead Souls*. Non-Russian critics have been slower to appreciate its seemingly infinite possibilities, but, in recent years, first-rate studies have begun to appear, particularly in Britain, the United States, and Germany. The first of many translations into English came out in the 1850s, not long after Gogol's death. At least eleven are now in print. Some sense of the challenges that await anyone who ventures to turn *Dead Souls* into a foreign language is well conveyed by Christopher English, in his 'Translator's Foreword' to this volume.

Structure, Characters, Themes

To record the adventures of a traveller as he moves through the world is to employ a structural device that goes back to Homer. It had already served Gogol in some of his earlier works. There he posits a tightly enclosed society, bound together by custom and ritual against a presumably hostile outside world. Suddenly and unexpectedly it is invaded by a force from that world. It may be a traveller (as in *The Government Inspector*), a spouse ('A Terrible Revenge'), the weather ('The Overcoat'), a person who goes forth and then returns ('Old-World Landowners'), or the supernatural ('Viy'). The result is usually drastic and permanent change within the enclosure, sometimes total destruction, with the hostile agent departing unscathed.

This structure informs *Dead Souls* at many levels. Enclosures abound, ranging from town to landed estate, from palisades, houses and rooms to carriages, boxes, and codes of behaviour. All are violated in one way or another. The displacement of their components enables us to glimpse, if only for a moment, the larger issues which such enclosures have been designed to exclude, conceal, or regulate.

Chichikov enters the novel as a faceless nonentity, intent on pursuing his goal as affably and unobtrusively as possible, leaving behind him neither wreckage nor memories. His first few days in the anonymous town do not go unremarked; but ultimately, all that the local worthies can say of him, apart from his name and rank, is that he is 'honourable', 'civil', 'well-intentioned', and 'engaging'. No one knows anything about his past life, and the narrator does not provide even the reader with an accounting of it until the final chapter. But he does remark on the 'particular minuteness' of Chichikov's inquiries concerning the town officials and nearby landowners, describes the care with which he scrutinizes a theatre-poster and folds it away in his 'little box', and shows how under his gaze the governor's ball soars off into Homeric simile (a favourite device of Gogol's), with the guests turning into flies crawling over lumps of sugar. Anyone who has read Gogol's earlier stories is aware that insignificant details have a habit of turning significant, and must therefore be carefully watched. As yet we are ignorant of the real reason why Chichikov has appeared in this particular provincial town, but we do know that he leaves the first chapter as a character potentially more complex than the nonentity of the first paragraph. Gogol is already busy establishing the multiple perspectives that will carry through the entire novel, whereby Chichikov is usually unaware of the larger implications of what is happening, or at least does not give voice to them; the narrator moves between total submission to the events of the story or total control of them; and the reader is allowed to feel more privileged and enlightened than anyone else.

In Chapter 2 Chichikov sets out on his rounds of the landowners from whom he must acquire dead souls if he is to bring his scheme to completion. Their estates are the tightest enclosures in the novel, and are therefore highly susceptible to disruption from a dynamic outside force. Chichikov would prefer to treat the buying and selling of souls as a purely legal matter whose terms he can dictate, confident that natural human greed will yield a favourable outcome. But the very fact that the matter is illegal, and that the landowners either have some scruples or are more ruthless than he is, creates complications that require negotiation. In the process, both Chichikov and his hosts unwittingly reveal sides of themselves that make them fuller and more plausible characters.

Each estate is organized according to a particular ethos, which is epitomized in the name of the proprietor. Presiding over the first is Manilov, whose speech, deportment, and ideals represent an attempt to resuscitate the eighteenth-century idyll. When we understand that his name is derived from the verb *manit'*, meaning 'lure' or 'beckon', we more easily take Gogol's point that the desire to indulge private fantasies in a self-constructed world far removed from the cares and responsibilities of the present tempts us all now and then, but must be resisted if we are not to become Manilovs ourselves and join the large company of impractical dreamers who have populated Russian literature—in imitation, some would say, of Russian life—from that day to this. The detail of the 'little mounds' of ash that have been 'knocked out of the pipe and stacked with considerable care in most attractive little rows' on the window-sills of his study hints at the consequences of allegiance to a dead ideology. Chichikov is the kind of unscrupulous entrepreneur whom Gogol regarded as lamentably typical of the nineteenth century, but he is as much a dreamer as Manilov, and his goal, though set in the future instead of the past, amounts to the same thing: gentility, prosperity, and carefree comfort in the bosom of an adoring family.

As soon as we know that Korobochka means 'little box', we may wonder why Gogol attaches this name to the only woman among the five landowners. Of course, it is an admirable image of enclosure, especially for a house that is extremely difficult of access, and for a mistress who cherishes order and predictability. But it also serves as an image of female sexuality, as becomes evident the moment Chichikov arrives. In preparing him to take his rest in an enormous feather-bed, Korobochka offers to have his back rubbed and his heels tickled ('my dear departed could never go to sleep without it'), and has her maid-servant take his wet and muddy clothes, which the narrator calls 'this heap of dripping armour', as if Chichikov is a lovelorn knight. This comic scene is tinged with a menace conveyed by Chichikov's utter helplessness and by the old clock which hisses snake-like before it bangs out the time. All this makes the nocturnal Korobochka an older albeit more benign sister to the seductive witch-figures of some of the earlier stories. In the light of day, Chichikov regains his sense of controlled self-assurance until his hostess resists his proposal with the kind of housewifely logic which insists that if dead souls can be bought and sold, then they must be goods like honey or hay, and subject to the vagaries of the market-place. Because these two characters talk past each other in what has been called a 'dialogue of the deaf', another of Gogol's favourite devices, we doubt that they can have anything in common. But once again, a detail of language makes the point. Chichikov too has a 'box', which he carries with him on all his travels, and in which he deposits all manner of things, including the lists of the dead souls. It is but one of many boxes, or enclosures, that he has created in an attempt either to shut out or confer sense on a world he perceives as alien and hostile. His chaise is another, as are his hermetic persona and his rigid rules of deportment. But these enclosures avail him nothing in his dealings with Korobochka. The chaise overturns and dumps him in the mud; his integrity as a male is threatened; his well-practised patter makes no impression; and the box will not long hide the secret of the scheme that has consigned the names of the dead souls to it. Gogol's point is not simply to force Chichikov to lose his temper and reveal the passion and ruthlessness that lie very close to the surface of his cool exterior, but to suggest that the price Korobochka pays for efficiently managing her enclosure is permanent self-enclosure, where the boxes become coffins. Chichikov, who is destined to grow and develop, must learn to rely less and less on the boxes he has so carefully constructed.

Nozdryov's estate looks like anything but an enclosure, lacking as it does fixed boundaries in his mind, or the kind of order and purpose ideally provided by a wife and children. Yet it does have a distinctive character, which is conferred by its function not only as a storage-facility for indiscriminately collected junk, but as a virtual prison for Chichikov. Nozdryov's constant proclamation of undying friendship seems implausible until we reflect that Chichikov also lacks home and boundaries, is as passionate and ruthless a player of the game of swindling as his host is of cards and draughts, and is as much a liar too, albeit more genteel. Once again, names confirm the connection. If Nozdryov is a 'nostril' (*nozdrya*), then Chichikov is a 'sneeze' (*chikh*) or a 'hachoo' (*apchkhi*). A nostril is just a hole in one part of the face, and a sneeze is just a gust of wind. This looks like an obvious way of saying that there is less to these two characters than meets the eye, but in Gogol, it says more. Fragments that pass themselves off as wholes are always the mark of demonism for him; and he is well aware too that in folklore, sneezing is associated with the devil. The presence of this theme may invite our contemplation of the consequences of failing to direct enthusiasms and energies to worthy ends. If this is the lesson, then it is lost on Chichikov, who is interested only in escaping as quickly as possible before he is beaten up.

Every aspect of Sobakevich's estate is shaped by the dominant image of bearishness, from the clumsy design of the house to the heaviness and solidity of the structures in the yard, the sturdy furniture, the outsized portraits on the wall, even the thrush in the cage. The proprietor himself presents a 'powerful' and 'rough-hewn countenance', and an ungainly walk that threatens the toes of the people around him. His first two names are Mikhail Semyonovich, as Russians affectionately call bears. But his surname is curious. We would expect it to be a derivative of *medved'*, the Russian for 'bear'—something like 'Medvednikov' or 'Medvedsky'. Instead, it comes from *sobaka*, 'dog'. A bear is a good heraldic beast, whereas a dog is more suited to the signboards of country inns. Yet Sobakevich is endowed with qualities which most people would regard as heroic: cunning, energy, resourcefulnesss, ruthlessness, even eloquence of speech. In an earlier age, they would have made him a plausible *bogatyr*, or Russian epic hero. Now, however, their only purpose is to best Chichikov, who is certainly not an effective or worthy opponent. If a dog is no bear, then a sneezer is no Odysseus or Don Quixote. But this is only fitting for the representative of a century which, as Gogol saw it, offers narrowed horizons and diminished expectations, and has no room for the grand gestures and noble impulses of which a man like Sobakevich, and perhaps even Chichikov, is capable.

With Plyushkin, the last of the landowners, diminishment is about to play out its horrifying inevitability. The name finds no obvious correspondence in any dictionary; but if it derives from *plyushch*, 'ivy', or *plyush*, 'plush', it connotes a low stage of vegetative life verging on inanimation. Nowhere else in Gogol's work do we see a picture of such squalor and degradation, which is all the more graphic because it stands in shocking contrast to Plyushkin's prosperous past. Chichikov is appalled by this spectacle—'one such as this he had never before seen'—and even feels a twinge of compassion. From our privileged perspective we see that he is capable of a finer emotion, which must be present, albeit embryonically, in any hero-to-be; but, as usual, he dismisses it as he gets down to the cruder business at hand. Nor is he yet ready to heed the obvious lesson of *memento mori*, even though it is as vividly present here as it is concealed in the alluring world of Manilov.

These estates remain frozen in time and space, like the societies visited by Odysseus. But Chichikov, in accordance with the laws of the adventure-tale, moves on, equipped with the list of souls he has purchased and will now register with the authorities. To us he seems altogether more palpable than the virtual shadow who entered Chapter 1, and he will fill out even more. But his main business, in Chapters 7–10, is to work changes in the town. Gogol's business is to make this far larger enclosure as memorable and interesting as any of the estates, while using a very different set of techniques. Although he gives us the occasional brilliant portrait, as with the chief of police in Chapter 7, he is more interested in titles and functions than in names, and in types, often paired, rather than individuals: 'the fat men' and 'the thin men,' 'the Lady Pleasant in All Respects' and 'the Merely Pleasant Lady', 'the male' and 'the female'. He strives to create a collective character which will respond as one to the presence of Chichikov. Now it is not Chichikov who tries to bend people to his idea of what dead souls are, but a society which tries to bend him to its idea of how a wealthy landowner and eligible bachelor should behave. The classic comic devices of reversal and misunderstanding are exploited to the fullest. Some of the funniest passages in all of Gogol are found here. But, as usual, they have a far more serious purpose. For what Gogol is describing is the subsidence of an entire society into madness, a madness born of the ambiguities of language.

Language is one of the largest and most consistent themes in Gogol's works. Our natural tendency is to assume that words 'mean' what they 'say'. Gogol plays that assumption off against his demonstration, again and again, that words are slippery, tricky, deceptive, sometimes even lethal. Even at the very beginning of Chapter 1, the befuddled narrator—a fixture of Gogol's beginnings—can describe the figure who is riding through the town gate only in terms of what he is *not:* 'neither handsome, nor yet of an unpleasing aspect, neither too fat, nor too thin; not exactly old, nor yet what you would call over-young.' Nor can he hit on the proper term for the conveyance: is it 'chaise', 'carriage', or 'wheel'? Much of the novel, in fact, turns on the search for definitions. What are 'dead souls'? Who or what is 'Chichikov'? Why does Sobakevich have a 'dog' name instead of a 'bear' name? No comfortingly definitive answers are provided. Gogol deploys an enormous array of linguistic devices to create a sense of impalpability and elusiveness, which we can never shake as we move through the book. Transformations are perhaps the most spectacular, as cups on a waiter's tray turn into birds on the seashore (Chapter 1), or a man's face turns into a pumpkin, which then becomes a balalaika, and in turn conjures up a little scene of rural lads and lasses (Chapter 5).

These are more than games in Gogol's world. A word, once uttered or written, may begin to live a life of its own, quite beyond the ability of a speaker or writer to make it 'mean' what he wishes. Such a power can change people's lives, usually for the worse. When, for instance, the townsfolk are busy speculating about Chichikov's identity, they decide, on no evidence, that he is a 'millionaire'. This prompts the ladies in particular to discover 'other qualities' in him, and soon an elaborate ritual, verbal and behavioural, takes form. 'The fault', we are told, 'lay entirely with the word "millionaire"—not the millionaire in person, but the word itself: for the very sound of this word carries with it, beside the clinking of gold coins, something which affects equally people of a knavish disposition, people who are neither one thing nor the other, and also good people—in a word, it affects everyone.' When 'millionaire' does not satisfactorily account for Chichikov, other identities are devised: 'abductor of the governor's daughter', 'Captain Kopeikin', even 'Napoleon in disguise'. It is noteworthy that Chichikov is kept pretty much off the scene now, blissfully unaware of what the townsfolk are up to, as if to emphasize that it is the *word* 'Chichikov' that is at issue. Gogol makes good use of lessons learned in writing *The Government Inspector*, which also explores questions of true and false identities, as well as the power of a word, 'inspector', to deafen its hearers to the patently discrepant reality of the figure, Khlestakov, to whom it has been mistakenly attached. 'Chichikov' generates other words, which grow into whole stories. The 'Chichikov/abductor' story has originated in a remark by the Lady Pleasant in All Respects, and as it spreads through the town, 'everything swiftly acquired a vivid and definite aspect, was clothed in clear and manifest forms, was explained, and cleansed of clutter, so that a finished picture emerged.' The other ladies find it convincing, even though it is a complete fiction, whereas, ironically, the men, who have figured out what Chichikov is really up to, can persuade no one because they are incapable of creating interesting and logical narratives: 'Everything about them was somehow uncouth, awkward, inept, sloppy, and ugly, their thinking was muddled, incoherent, untidy, and contradictory.'

The most sustained and ingenious version of Chichikov's identity is 'The Tale of Captain Kopeikin', which is embedded in Chapter 10. Before we dismiss it as merely a funny story, we should note how Gogol reacted to its rejection by the censor: 'this is one of the best places in the poem, and without it there is a hole that I simply haven't the strength to patch and sew.' And so he rewrote it, while preserving the style. What kind of 'hole' did he mean? The piece is a linguistic *tour-de-force*, a brilliant instance of the first-person narrative manner known in Russian as *skaz*. If it were only that, he could surely have placed it elsewhere in the book, instead of insisting, as he seems to do, that it belonged precisely here. The language in which it is told diverges drastically from the standard Russian otherwise spoken by the postmaster who narrates it, or by any of the townsfolk, and Kopeikin bears no obvious resemblance to Chichikov. Yet the listeners accept it as 'true' until the moment when the postmaster slips and reminds them that it is *just* a story. Still, the point has been made that any well-told tale, however absurd, is 'true' in its own terms, and can compel listeners and readers to suspend disbelief and, in this case, even entertain lingering doubts after it has proved 'false' to the reality it purports to describe. So strong is the need to name, so acute the anxiety lest words no longer 'mean' anything, so rooted the conviction that Chichikov must be *something*, and that this 'something' must lend itself to verbal representation, that the listeners, 'inspired by the keen powers of induction displayed by the postmaster', offer 'suggestions that were even farther-fetched', and propose that Chichikov is 'Napoleon in disguise'. 'Not that the officials believed any of this', the narrator hastens to assure us; yet because the proposal is promptly fashioned into an interesting anecdote, they hear it through. They even believe Nozdryov's story of the dead souls, even though 'they knew only too well' that he 'was a liar and that they could not believe a word he said'. Ironically, his story is true. But once he begins embroidering, it becomes incoherent, and they cease to listen. When all conceivable labels have been tried and discarded, when, in other words, language has failed, the town disintegrates into chaos, with dire results: 'For some strange reason it was the poor prosecutor who suffered most from all these discussions, theories, and rumours. They had such an effect on him that when he arrived home he started to rack his brains and suddenly, for no earthly reason, as they say, he upped and died.' The 'reason' is certainly clear enough to us readers: words, however ludicrous, even the absence of words, can have an effect far beyond what anyone is capable of imagining.

Our obvious conclusion, though the narrator does not articulate it, is that people must use language to proper ends. Only three characters in the book are capable, potentially or actually, of doing so: Chichikov, his driver Selifan, and, of course, the narrator.

Chichikov has started unpromisingly enough. As a story-teller, he puts forth several versions of his scheme, and some skimpy details of his life, which are perhaps true, perhaps not, but in any event are designed to please and persuade his listeners. He is largely successful, but not wholly so, for his stories, like those of the townsfolk, are told for unworthy purposes. As he reveals more of the self that lies beneath the mask, however, he begins to blossom as a narrator. One of the first and most striking instances comes at the end of Chapter 6. He has left the last of the landowners, and is making his way back to town. To himself he is the same old unreflective Chichikov. But suddenly he is confronted with the spectacle of the town at dusk, so unfamiliar as to be quite new: 'Light and shade had merged completely and it seemed as if the objects themselves had blended into one another. The striped turnpike had taken on a strangely indeterminate colour; the moustache on the face of the soldier standing on guard appeared to grow on his forehead, high above his eyes, whilst his nose seemed to be missing altogether.' We cannot tell whether this surrealistic scene is observed by him or by the narrator; but it is clear that Gogol means us to read it as a correlative of changes that are under way in Chichikov. And when in the next chapter Chichikov begins to look over the names of the dead souls he has acquired, he is suddenly 'overcome by a strange sensation, one he himself could not comprehend', but one which confirms that he is now a different man. The names on the papers before him almost bring their possessors to life, and prompt him to create little biographies for them. Once bodied forth verbally, they become as real as any of the other characters in the book. Gone for the moment is the cold calculator; he gives himself over to pure fancy, which he manages to sustain for some five pages before he is interrrupted by the narrator, upon which he chides himself for 'talking a lot of nonsense' and falling 'into a reverie' instead of 'doing business'.

This excursion marks an important moment in the development

of the book. It is different from Sobakevich's enthusings over the wonderful qualities of his dead serfs because it springs from the imagination, and is not designed as a sales-pitch. It is different from the frenzied speculations of the townsfolk in having no purpose beyond itself, yet acknowledging, albeit fictionally, the worthiness of the humble individuals to whom the names were originally attached. From this point on, Chichikov is increasingly entrusted with duties which have hitherto been reserved to the narrator. His disquisition on the vanity of formal balls in Chapter 8 is just one instance. But where does that leave the narrator? Throughout the earlier chapters, he has shown himself under various aspects—bumbler, clever manipulator, all-seeing eye, pawn of the events of the story—but he is more a voice, or welter of voices, than a literary character. It is only with the disquisitions which open Chapters 6 and 7 that he begins to take on fictional flesh. Their subject-matter is conventional, even clichéd: youth is preferable to middle age, the dishonest writer who captures the plaudits of the crowd is inferior to the honest writer who is despised by his readers for revealing things they do not wish to see. What carries them is the very energy of the sentences, which do nothing to advance the story itself but show the narrator challenging himself to make something interesting out of tired old material, as if learning his craft in full public view.

From this point on he begins to refer to himself more and more as 'author' or 'writer', and lays claim to certain rights and powers. These may well include the right to be unoriginal, if he chooses, or the right to walk boldly on the brink of incoherence, as when he proclaims, in Chapter 7, that '[s]till far off is the day when the dread whirlwind of inspiration shall soar upward, resonating in an altogether different key, rising from a head wreathed in a radiant nimbus of sacred awe'. Chichikov, for all his budding linguistic prowess, is incapable of such transports. Lest we miss that point, the narrator often interrupts him when he is well launched into a passage of narrative, points out his inadequacy, and then tops him, as if to demonstrate how a real author works. The handling of the Abram Fyrov story in Chapter 7 is the first of several such instances. Or he may remind us, perhaps with a simple 'my hero', that Chichikov is a fictional construct, which implies, of course, that the narrator is not. By the time we reach Chapter 11 the narrator is exercising fully developed powers, as he presents an extensive account of Chichikov's life, and sets himself up as the authoritative commentator on Russia.

Chichikov is present in this last chapter too, as a silent companion of the narrator. So is Selifan, the driver of the chaise which has carried his master through all the adventures that now lie in the past. He has been a comically endearing character, entrusted with the function of mimicking and parodying the attitudes and language of his betters. Now, however, he is granted a loftier role, as with his 'thin, singing voice' he sets into motion the chaise which turns into the magic vehicle that bears all three characters into the future. We are undoubtedly bidden to recall the 'song' which the narrator, in his paean to Rus earlier in the chapter, identifies as the expression of the national essence, and tries to convey in euphonious outpourings, nowhere to better effect than in the final paragraph.

But why is it, we may ask, that the colourful characters who populate the first ten chapters and have been left behind as the final chapter begins are not vouchsafed the same lofty privilege as the three who remain? True enough, the estates and the town present a famously gloomy and moribund aspect. One reason, surely, is the virtual absence, as in all Gogol's work, of those traditional emblems of physical and spiritual renewal: children, members of the clergy, and, in particular, nurturing females. Yet the narrator has assured us, quite without irony, that the townspeople are good at heart, albeit suggestible and ridiculous. Although the landowners offer as full a catalogue of vices and tempers as has ever been seen in Russian literature, their strength as characters is that they are not mere caricatures. Manilov's vapidity is leavened by a genuine need for friendship. Through Plyushkin's miserly ways glimmers an uncomprehending sadness at the dreadful course his life has taken, relieved only by a flash of happy reminiscence about a childhood friend. Such touches endow these characters, even Korobochka and Nozdryov, with redeeming human qualities. But they will never be redeemed. As we read Homer, we may be moved by the plight of the lonely Calypso or even by the cruelty visited on the stupid Polyphemus, yet we understand that things are as they are in a world still ruled largely by the laws of myth. But in a society which, for all its exoticism, stands far closer to ours in concepts of justice, we may wonder, as we do about characters in Gogol's earlier works, why these people, without exception, are forever condemned to remain as they are. Do they bear personal responsibility for their condition? Are they victims of a pitiless fate? Above all, why is Chichikov, who is far less engaging than most of them, given a chance that they will never have?

In Chapter 11, the narrator identifies a tiny group of people who are invested with 'passions which are not of man's choosing. For they are born with him when he comes into the world, and he is not given the strength to reject them'. He obviously numbers himself among them. The vast majority of mankind is free to choose either base or lofty passions; most, mistakenly and irrevocably, choose the base. This rather chilling theology of the passions apparently explains the situation of the townsfolk and the landowners. Since the narrator is also a version of the Romantic poet, we are invited to conclude that one sign of election is the power of prophecy and a creative facility with language. It may seem preposterous of him to suggest that Chichikov is entitled to membership in this group as well: 'perhaps the passion that drives him is not of his choosing, and perhaps his own cold existence already contains within it that same element which one day will bring man to his knees before the wisdom of Providence and reduce him to dust.' But Chichikov has survived virtually all the other characters, and has already demonstrated a command of language that poses a challenge to the narrator here and there. Since the highest power granted a writer is prophecy, and the only power granted a prophet is language, perhaps he too might have become both artist and prophet in the volumes to come. Finally, Selifan, in his humble and non-verbal way, is also one of the elect, although the narrator does not tell us so. He is neither prophet nor artist. He is, however, the embodiment of the vital force without which there can be neither prophecy nor artistry, nor a Russia in which to exercise these gifts.

Russia has of course been there all the time. But now it emerges as the real hero of the novel. If it too is an enclosure, then it is different from the others, because it is so vast as to be virtually without bounds. It is also an unmistakably female Russia. Gogol takes full advantage of the fact that its name—whether registered as *Rossiya* or as the poetic *Rus*—is grammatically feminine in gender. But she is a female who bears no resemblance to the women in the earlier chapters of this novel, or in any other work by Gogol. She is neither evil, nor silly, nor even beautiful. She is seductive, but her power has nothing to do with sex and its consequences, which Gogol invariably sees as baneful. In fact, she is the sole instance of a healthy, life-affirming female in all of his writings. He might have called her 'Mother Russia', but he does not wish to limit her to any of the traditional gender roles. Rather, she makes herself known to the narrator as disembodied energy, conveyed in and through song. With Russia as hero, or heroine, *Dead Souls* attains to the capaciousness, high seriousness, and magnitude that are essential marks of the epic spirit.

Part Two

Even at an early stage, Gogol hinted that *Dead Souls* might develop into a longer work than he had originally planned. 'Colossally great is my creation,' he wrote to Vasily Zhukovsky on 12 November 1836, 'and its end is far distant.' By the early 1840s he clearly saw that a continuation would be necessary, and expressed the hope that he would be granted 'another three years' of inspiration to complete what he now knew would be two more parts, in which Chichikov would sin some more, and eventually be redeemed. The structure of Dante's *Divine Comedy* was never far from his mind. It was on the long return journey from Rome to Moscow, in the late summer and early autumn of 1841, that he apparently formulated a definite plan. Actual writing, however, began two years later. He had to endure many an arid spell, and by 1845 was so discouraged with what he had produced that he consigned it to the flames. Another three years passed before he took it up again. But he had not been sitting idle. Between 1845 and 1848 he wrote non-fiction, mostly on religious, social, and moral subjects, including an interpretation of *Dead Souls*. Serious work resumed on Part Two of *Dead Souls* only in October 1848, after he had returned to Russia for the last time. It went smoothly, despite his usual complaints about health and spiritual deficiencies. In July 1849 he read seven chapters to friends, and in the following months, a revised version of the first four. The two years 1850 and 1851 were devoted to further rewriting. But misgivings soon surfaced. As he confessed to one of his correspondents on 2 February 1852, 'I have had no luck with any of my new [works]. Their subject is so important that my weak capacities prevail over my indispositions with difficulty, and only in the event that someone

prays really, really hard for me.' Ten days later, on the night of 11–
12 February, he once again fed his manuscript into the fire. A day
later he began to refuse food; little more than a week after that, on
the morning of 21 February, he died.

Surprisingly, much of the ill-fated Part Two survived the flames,
enough at least to suggest what the whole might have been. There
are two versions, dating most probably from the mid-1840s and the
early 1850s. Some striking departures from Part One are immediately
apparent. For one thing, descriptions of nature abound, and in a lush
detail reminiscent of the early stories. For another, the ingeniously
exhibitionistic narrator has yielded to one who, except in the opening few paragraphs, cultivates self-effacement. The travel-structure
remains intact; but the personages Chichikov meets have greater
dimension, and are generally more admirable. If they are flawed, as
most are, the narrator sometimes explains why, as he does not in Part
One. For instance, Tentetnikov, the young landowner who is full of
plans to improve his estate but lacks the will to do so, is the product
of bad education. By contrast, Kostanzhoglo is the exemplar of an
effective landowner; and Gogol thinks that it is in the hands of such
people, not social planners in the central bureaucracy, that the future
of Russia rests. He seems to have forgotten about the Russian peasantry, or *narod*, that he had extolled in Part One. Indeed, we are
invited to wonder whether being Russian does not constitute an im-
pediment to healthy government. To be sure, Kostanzhoglo regards
himself as a Russian, and speaks no other language, yet we are told
that he is not 'a pure Russian', that his face bears 'the print of his
provenance from the fiery south' in its 'swarthiness', its crisp black
hair, and the 'lively expression in his eyes'. 'Southern', throughout
Gogol's works, is shorthand for vitality and creative energy, qualities
which he located variously in Italy, the Ukraine, the Near and Far
East, and ancient Greece, and rarely, if ever, in Russians, whom he
regarded as models of endurance, patience, and toughness. His ideal
is a combination of these qualities, as Kostanzhoglo's name suggests:
kost' is Russian for 'bone', and *-oglo* is a common Turkic suffix.
Gogol hereby contributes to the image of the Russian foreigner, who
has achieved almost mythical status in the national history and literature, whether embodied in Catherine the Great, a German, Insarov,
the Bulgarian in Turgenev's *On the Eve* (1860), Stalin, a Georgian, or
Nikolai Gogol himself, a Ukrainian Pole.

Many readers and critics, from Gogol's time to ours, have thought of Part Two, even allowing for its fragmentary nature, as a grotesque curiosity. More attentive readers may conclude that in many places it does speak in a powerful, compelling, and convincing manner, and bears many of the marks of the realist novel, which was just emerging in Russia during the 1840s and 1850s. Still, we have to contend with Gogol's own dissatisfaction, and with his decision to destroy the work of a decade. Some critics, like Mikhail Bakhtin, have attributed its failure to Gogol's desire to turn a fundamentally 'epic' gift into a 'novelistic' one. Others have argued that the introduction of so many 'positive' characters, like Murazov, created a moralistic tract which destroyed it as a work of fiction. It may be too that after the soaring paean to Russia which closes Part One, the reintroduction of an unredeemed Chichikov is anticlimactic, even jarring. But a more sinister possibility is contained in a question which is implicit in Gogol's handling of the theme of language throughout Part One. How do we distinguish an artful liar from an artful truth-teller, if both have access to the same language, techniques, and devices, and often can employ them equally well? What makes one form of discourse authoritative and veracious, and another merely sugar-coated fraud? This question appears to find resolution in the narrator's theory of the passions in Chapter 11, and in the lyric effusions that bring the 'poem' to a close. But it re-emerges in the 1840s, in Gogol's increasingly agitated musings on the nature of his vocation, and ends by destroying that vocation altogether. He came to believe that the only guarantee of authenticity, certainly in his own case, was spiritual purity. As he put it in *Selected Passages from Correspondence with my Friends* (1847): 'It is necessary to deal honestly with the word. It is God's highest gift to man. Woe unto the writer who utters it . . . before his own soul has achieved harmony: the word that emerges from him will be loathsome to all. And then, however pure his intention of doing good, he may well do evil. . . . It is dangerous for a writer to trifle with the word' (Letter IV, 'A Definition of the Word', viii. 231–2). As he took a closer look at himself, he saw dishearteningly scanty evidence of the necessary spiritual qualities, and concluded that his work was therefore deceitful and even dangerous. The final immolation of Part Two, and his lapse into silence and death are a terrible confirmation of his beliefs.

Yet much as we may regret the fragmentary nature of Part Two, and the absence of Part Three, and much as we may find tragedy, even at the remove of a century and a half, in Gogol's final torments, we can still enjoy Part One as a work that is complete in itself, rising to an artistically logical conclusion which needs no sequel.

ROBERT A. MAGUIRE

NOTE ON THE TEXT
AND TRANSLITERATION

As with the previous two volumes of Gogol's works published in the Oxford World's Classics series, *Village Evenings near Dikanka and Mirgorod* (1994), and *Plays and Petersburg Tales* (1995), this translation of *Dead Souls* is based on the fourteen-volume edition of Gogol's works published by the Academy of Sciences of the USSR and known as the 'Academy edition' (1937–52). The text of Part Two—following the Academy edition—is that found in the later version, or 'stratum', of the manuscript, with missing words and phrases supplied by the editors and, where they could not be supplied, marked hiatuses. Significant variant readings from the earlier strata of the manuscript have been included in an appendix to Part Two.

The Academy edition also contains extensive commentary on the text and the composition of the work, which has been of great value in the preparation of this translation and the notes which follow it. Among the other editions of *Dead Souls* which I have consulted for this purpose, I mention in particular the 1993 edition (containing Part One only) published by Shkola Klassiki, Moscow, edited by V. A. Voropaev, and the excellent 1994 nine-volume collected works, published by Russkaya Kniga, Moscow, and edited—once again—by Voropaev, together with I. A. Vinogradov. For further background material, critical and biographical, the reader is referred to the bibliography on pp. xxxviii–xxxix.

The present translation arises out of an earlier translation of *Dead Souls*, commissioned by Raduga Publishers, Moscow, and published in 1986, by whose kind permission it has been used in the preparation of this Oxford World's Classics edition. Here I have extensively reworked that earlier version, however, restored the later 'stratum' of Part Two, and added endnotes, and the text which follows is, essentially, a new translation.

The system used here for the transliteration of proper names is that generally followed in the Oxford World's Classics series, and is designed to be readable rather than academically precise. A more academic system has been used in the endnotes and bibliography, for the transliteration of Russian words and titles.

SELECT BIBLIOGRAPHY

Biography

Lindstrom, Thais S., *Nikolay Gogol* (New York, 1974).

Margarshack, David, *Gogol: A Life* (New York, 1960).

Setchkarev, Vsevolod M., *Gogol: His Life and Works*, trans. Robert Kramer (New York, 1965).

Troyat, Henri, *Gogol: The Biography of a Divided Soul*, trans. Nancy Amphoux (London, 1974).

General studies

Bely, Andrey, 'Gogol', trans. Elizabeth Trahan and John Fred Beebe in *Twentieth-Century Russian Criticism*, ed. Victor Erlich (New Haven, Conn., 1975).

Erlich, Victor, *Gogol* (New Haven, Conn., 1969).

Fanger, Donald, *The Creation of Nikolai Gogol* (Cambridge, Mass., 1965).

Gippius, V. V., *Gogol*, ed. and trans. Robert A. Maguire (Ann Arbor, Mich., 1981).

Karlinsky, Simon, *The Sexual Labyrinth of Nikolai Gogol* (Cambridge, Mass., 1976).

Maguire, Robert A. (ed. and trans.), *Gogol from the Twentieth Century: Eleven Essays* (Princeton, NJ, 1974).

——*Exploring Gogol* (Stanford, Calif., 1994).

Mersereau, John, jun., *Russian Romantic Fiction* (Ann Arbor, Mich., 1983).

Nabokov, Vladimir, *Nikolay Gogol* (London, 1973).

Peace, Richard, *The Enigma of Gogol: An Examination of the Writings of N. V. Gogol and their Place in the Russian Literary Tradition* (Cambridge, 1981).

Rowe, William Woodin, *Through Gogol's Looking Glass: Reverse Vision, False Focus, and Precarious Logic* (New York, 1976).

Shapiro, Gavriel, *Nikolai Gogol and the Baroque Cultural Heritage* (University Park, Pa., 1993).

Tertz, Abram [Andrei Sinyavsky], *In the Shadow of Gogol* (London, 1975).

Woodward, James B., *The Symbolic Art of Gogol: Essays on his Short Fiction* (Columbus, Ohio, 1982).

Zeldin, Jesse, *Nikolai Gogol's Quest for Beauty* (Lawrence, Kan., 1978).

On Dead Souls

Fusso, Susanne, *Designing Dead Souls* (Stanford, Calif., 1993).

——and Meyer, Priscilla (eds.), *Essays on Gogol. Logos and the Russian Word.* (Evanston, Ill., 1992).

Proffer, Carl R., *The Simile and Gogol's Dead Souls* (Paris, 1968).

Yelistratova, Anna, *Nikolai Gogol and the Western European Novel*, trans. Christopher English (Moscow, 1985).

Further reading in Oxford World's Classics

Gogol, Nikolai, *Plays and Petersburg Tales*, trans. Christopher English, introduction by Richard Peace.

——*Village Evenings near Dikanka and Mirgorod*, trans. Christopher English, introduction by Richard Peace.

A CHRONOLOGY OF GOGOL

1777   Birth of Gogol's father, Vasily Afanasievich Gogol, minor land-owner, possessing some 200 souls.

1791   Birth of Gogol's mother, Maria Ivanovna Kosyarovskaya.

1805   Vasily Afanasievich Gogol and Maria Ivanovna Kosyarovskaya marry (she is 14).

1809   Gogol born on 20 March,[1] in village of Greater Sorochintsy, Mirgorod province. His parents ask the village priest of Dikanka to pray for a safe delivery. Contemporaries remember him as a sickly, introspective child, serious beyond his years.

1821   Enters the Nezhin Lyceum.

1825   Shortly after the birth of his fourth daughter, Olga, Gogol's father dies. Gogol's first literary ventures can be dated to this period.

1827   *Hanz Küchelgarten* (an idyll, in verse).

1828   Completes studies at the Lyceum, gaining membership of the fourteenth (lowest) class in the Petrine Table of Ranks.

1829   First published work, a five-stanza poem 'Italy', appears anonymously in the review *Son of the Fatherland*. *Hanz Küchelgarten* published anonymously at the author's own expense. When the work is ridiculed by the critics, Gogol gathers up all the unsold copies and burns them. Leaves for Germany in July, returning in September.

1829–30   Works on literary reviews, publishing *St John's Eve* and other stories which are later to be collected in *Village Evenings near Dikanka*. Studies painting at the Academy of Fine Arts. Enters the Civil Service on 10 April, working as a scribe in the cadastral department.

1831   Publishes his first piece under his own name: an article entitled 'Woman'. Leaves the Civil Service and takes a position as an assistant history teacher in a girls' school. Makes the acquaintance of Alexander Pushkin. *Village Evenings near Dikanka*, Part One, published, and praised by Pushkin.

1832   *Village Evenings near Dikanka*, Part Two, is published.

1832–3   Works on *Mirgorod* stories.

1833   Completes *The Story of How Ivan Ivanovich Quarrelled with Ivan Nikiforovich*.

---

[1] Dates are given in the old style, according to the Julian calendar (to convert to the new style, or Gregorian, calendar, add twelve days).

1834   Appointed Assistant Professor of History at St Petersburg University; his lectures are lacklustre and ill prepared, and attendance declines rapidly.

1835   *Arabesques*, a collection including *Nevsky Prospekt*, *Notes of a Madman*, and *The Portrait* published (January). *Mirgorod* published (March). Completes *Marriage*, and works on *The Government Inspector*, developing an idea suggested to him by Pushkin. On 31 December leaves his position at St Petersburg University.

1836   More stories published, including *The Carriage*. *The Government Inspector* has its first performance on 19 April and is a sensational success. Tsar Nicholas attends the première, laughing often and loudly, which is fortunate for the other spectators, as etiquette prohibits them from laughing unless His Majesty laughs first. Leaves for Germany, spending the rest of the year there and in Switzerland and France.

1837   Works on *Dead Souls*. Rome, associating with Russian painters, and Baden-Baden.

1838   Continues work on *Dead Souls*, travelling between Rome, Naples, and Paris,

1839   Rome, Vienna, Hanau, and Marienbad, returns to Moscow in September. In May his friend Prince Vielgorsky, whom Gogol nursed in his final illness and to whom he is thought to have had a romantic attachment, dies.

1840   Travels to Rome, where he prepares the first volume of *Dead Souls* for publication.

1841   Rome, Frankfurt, and Hanau, then returns to Russia (mid-September).

1842   *Rome* published. First printing of *Dead Souls* (2,400 copies). Travels to Badgastein, then Venice. Winters in Rome. *Marriage* has its première on 9 December.

1843   Spends the summer in Germany and travels south to Nice for the winter. Works on *Dead Souls*, Part Two.

1844   Nice, Frankfurt, Ostend; continues working on *Dead Souls*, Part Two.

1845   Paris, Frankfurt, Hamburg, and Carlsbad. Gogol takes the waters, to recuperate from a serious illness. Develops a fear of death. Travels between Prague, Berlin, Rome, also visiting Badgastein, Salzburg, Venice, Florence, and Bologna. By the end of the year his health improves.

1846   Rome, Genoa, Paris; works on *Dead Souls*, Part Two, and on *Selected Passages from Correspondence with my Friends*. Moves to Naples.

1847   *Selected Passages from Correspondence with my Friends* published (January). Bad Ems, Ostend; works on *Author's Confession*.

1848   Visits the Holy Land, then travels on to Odessa, where he is quarantined for a time because of the cholera epidemic, and to St Petersburg.

1849   In May Gogol writes of a 'serious nervous disorder' and 'spiritual distress', complaining of his inability to write anything and of general listlessness. *Dead Souls*, Part Two, according to the memoirist I. Arnoldi, is virtually complete in manuscript at this time.

1850   After a correspondence lasting a number of years, proposes marriage to Prince Vielgorsky's sister, but is refused. Visits the religious community of Optina Pustyn, near Kaluga, and travels to Odessa for the winter.

1851   Makes the acquaintance of Ivan Turgenev, who had been one of his students during his disastrous year as a history lecturer. Conducts a correspondence with one of the coenobites in Optina Pustyn and visits other monastic communities.

1852   Informs Arnoldi that he has completed *Dead Souls*, Part Two. On the night of 10–11 February burns the manuscript of *Dead Souls*, Part Two. Dies on 21 February (4 March by the Gregorian calendar, or new style) and is buried in the Danilov Monastery in Moscow. In 1931 his remains are transferred to the Novodevichy Cemetery.

TABLE OF RANKS

The Table of Ranks was instituted by Peter the Great in 1722, modelled on the system of civil service ranks employed in Germany. Originally, membership of the 14th class brought with it personal gentry status and of the 8th class hereditary gentry status. The correspondence between the civilian and military ranks changed as reforms were carried out in the respective services; this table reflects the situation prevailing at the time Gogol was writing—the 1830s and 1840s. In addition to civil service and military ranks, there was also a system of courtiers' ranks corresponding to various levels of the Table; thus the Kammerherr, or chamberlain, mentioned in the final chapter of Part Two had the rank of an Actual State Councillor.

Class	Civilian rank	Military rank (land; naval)
1	Chancellor	Field Marshal; Admiral of the Fleet
2	Actual Privy Councillor (Class I and II)	General; Admiral
3	Privy Councillor	Lieutenant-General; Vice-Admiral
4	Actual State Councillor	Major-General; Rear-Admiral
5	State Councillor	Brigadier; Commodore
6	Collegiate Councillor	Colonel; Captain
7	Aulic (Court) Councillor	Lieutenant-Colonel; Commander
8	Collegiate Assessor	Major; Lieutenant-Commander
9	Titular Councillor	Captain; Senior Lieutenant
10	Collegiate Secretary	Staff-Captain; Lieutenant
11	Naval Secretary	Lieutenant; —
12	Gubernia Secretary	Second-Lieutenant; Midshipman
13	Provincial Secretary Senate Registrar Synodal Registrar Cabinet Registrar	Ensign; —
14	Collegiate Registrar	— ; —

The forms of address appropriate for the various ranks were also carefully determined and strictly adhered to; thus in the first chapter Chichikov is able to flatter an interlocutor by inadvertently using a salutation for higher ranks. It is also worth recording that, in order to get his book past the censors, Gogol was required to discard every mention of the word 'Excellency' from the 'Tale of Captain Kopeikin'.

I include below a list of these titles (secular only—there are many more for members of religious orders, which do not occur in this book), giving the Russian original, a literal translation, and an approximate English equivalent, as used in this translation. The English system of honorifics is less graduated than the Russian, and I have had to resort to some slightly awkward inventions to preserve the important distinctions of the Russian.

Princes and counts: *vashe siyatel'stvo*—(lit.) 'Your Radiance', rendered here, *selon le cas*, as 'Your Highness', 'His Majesty'.

Classes 1 and 2: *vashe vysokoprevoskhoditel'stvo*—(lit.) 'Your High Excellency', rendered here as 'Your Noble Excellency'.

Classes 3 and 4: *vashe prevoskhoditel'stvo*—(lit. and here) 'Your Excellency'.

Class 5: *vashe vysokorodie*—(lit.) 'Your High-bornness', rendered here as 'Your Worship'.

Classes 6–8: *vashe vysokoblagorodie*—(lit.) 'Your High-nobleness', not attested as a form of address in *Dead Souls*, although the third-person form is used to refer to one of the extravagantly dressed ladies in Chapter 8 (given here as 'her noble laydship').

Classes 9–14: *vashe blagorodie*—(lit.) 'Your Nobleness', given here as 'Your Honour'.

Map of Chichikov's Russia

DEAD SOULS

a Poem

PART ONE

CHAPTER ONE

Into the gates of the inn in the provincial capital NN there drove a small but rather handsome sprung chaise* of the kind affected by bachelors, such as retired lieutenant colonels, staff-captains,* land-owners possessed of some one hundred souls—in a word, by all those regarded as gentlemen of the middle estate. In the chaise sat a gentleman neither handsome, nor yet of an unpleasing aspect, neither too fat, nor too thin; not exactly old, nor yet what you would call over-young. His arrival caused absolutely no stir in the town, nor was it accompanied by anything out of the ordinary; only two Russian peasants, standing by the doors of a pothouse opposite the inn, made a few remarks, which, as it happened, pertained more to the conveyance than to the traveller seated within.

'Take a look over there,' said the one to the other, 'see that wheel! What do you reckon, with a wheel like that would you make it to Moscow if you had to?'

'Course you would,' answered the other.

'But not Kazan, would you?'

'No, not Kazan,' agreed the other. Whereupon the conversation came to an end. And then, when the chaise drove up to the inn, a young man happened by, dressed in white drabbet breeches, very short and tight, and a tailcoat with pretensions to fashion, beneath which could be seen a starched shirt-front secured with a Tula pin* in the shape of a bronze pistol. The young man swung round, surveyed the carriage, caught hold of his cap, which the wind was about to blow off, and continued on his way.

When the carriage drove into the courtyard the gentleman was met by the inn-servant, or 'floorman', as they are called in Russian inns, a character so lively and fidgety that his features were a permanent blur. He nimbly darted out, a napkin over his arm, his elongated form clad in an elongated demicoton tailcoat, the collar reaching almost to the back of his head, tossed back his hair, and nimbly led the gentleman upstairs and along the entire length of the wooden portico to show him the room God had sent him.

The room was of the familiar kind, for the inn was also of the familiar kind, that is to say, precisely the kind found in provincial capitals where for two roubles a day travellers are given a quiet room, complete with cockroaches gleaming like prunes in every corner, and a door—permanently blocked by a chest of drawers—leading to the adjoining room, which is occupied by another traveller, a taciturn and placid man, but exceptionally inquisitive, eager to learn every detail about his new neighbour. The outer façade of the inn matched its interior: it was very long and two storeys high; the lower storey was unplastered, leaving exposed the dark red bricks, already rather grubby and rendered even darker by the sharp changes in the weather, and the upper was painted the inevitable yellow; on the ground floor were little shops selling horse collars, ropes, and wooden harness rings. In the corner shop—or, to be more precise, at its window—a honey-tea vendor stood beside his copper samovar, his face as coppery as the samovar beside him, so that from afar one might well have thought there were two samovars standing in the window, had not the one samovar sported a pitch-black beard.

While the new arrival was surveying his room, his chattels were borne in: first his valise of white leather, its somewhat battered state indicating that it had been on the road often before. The valise was carried in by the coachman Selifan, a squat little character in a sheepskin coat, and the valet Petrushka, a surly looking fellow of about thirty with very thick lips and a big nose, wearing an oversized and antiquated frock-coat, clearly a hand-me-down from his master. The valise was followed by a box of mahogany inlaid with Karelian birch,* a pair of boot-trees, and a roast fowl wrapped in blue paper. When all this had been carried in, the coachman Selifan withdrew to the stables to attend to the horses, while the valet Petrushka settled in the little hallway, a dark kennel of a room, in which he had already installed his overcoat and, with it, his own special smell, which also clung to the sack he then lugged in, containing his valet's paraphernalia. In this kennel he propped a narrow three-legged bed up against the wall, covering it with a wretched palliasse, as flat as a pancake and—by all appearances—as greasy as the pancake he had wheedled from the inn-keeper.

While his servants attended to their business, our gentleman set off for the public room. Just what these public rooms are like every traveller knows only too well: the same oil-painted walls, which, higher up, had been stained brown by tobacco smoke and, lower down, rubbed smooth by the backs of various travellers, and even more so by the backs of the local merchants who, on market days, gathered here in their sixes and sevens for their customary round of tea: the same smoke-blackened ceiling; the same smoked chandelier with its multitude of glass pendants, which bounced and tinkled when the inn-servant hurried past along the shabby oil-cloth runners, deftly balancing his tray stacked with tea-cups as densely as birds on the sea shore; the same oil paintings stretching the length of the wall—in a word, everything just as it is everywhere, the sole difference being that one of the pictures depicted a nymph with breasts so enormous that the reader has probably never seen their like. Such freaks of nature can be seen, however, in some of those historical pictures which were brought to us here in Russia no one knows when, from where, or by whom, although some were even acquired by our own dignitaries, connoisseurs of the arts, who bought these *chefs-d'œuvre* in Italy on the advice of their coachmen.

The gentleman threw off his cap and unwound from his neck a brightly coloured woollen muffler of the type which, for husbands, are knitted by their wives, and presented with appropriate instructions on how to wrap themselves up in them, and, for bachelors— well, I cannot really say how bachelors come by them, it's a complete mystery to me: I myself have never worn such a muffler. Once the muffler was unwound, the gentleman called for his supper. In due course he was brought the fare usually served in such inns, to wit: cabbage soup with a meat pie—of the sort which is made specially for travellers, and can be kept for several weeks—calves' brains with peas, sausages with cabbage, roast capon, salt gherkins, and that faithful friend of travellers, the ubiquitous jam tart, and while all this was being served to him, some of it reheated, some of it cold, he prevailed upon the inn-servant—or floorman—to tell him this and that: who had kept the inn before and who kept it now, how much profit it brought, and was their master a great rogue; to which the inn-servant gave his customary answer: 'Oh, a great rogue, sir, a proper scoundrel.'

Just as in enlightened Europe, so too in enlightened Russia there are now a great many distinguished people who simply cannot dine at an inn without striking up a conversation with the waiter, and sometimes even pulling his leg. Admittedly, our guest was not merely asking idle questions; with particular minuteness he inquired after the names of the governor, of the president of the chambers, of the public prosecutor;* in a word, he did not overlook a single prominent official, and with even greater minuteness—almost as if inquiring after dear friends—he asked about all the prominent landowners: how many souls each of them owned, how far they lived from the town, even what sort of people they were and how frequently they visited the town; he also inquired intently into the state of the province: had there been any illnesses, epidemics, any deadly fevers, smallpox, and the like, displaying a thoroughness and attention to detail that betokened more than mere curiosity.

The gentleman's manner was that of a man of substance, and he blew his nose extremely loudly. It is unclear how he accomplished this, but his nose resounded like a trumpet. This seemingly quite innocent distinction did, however, earn him the considerable respect of the inn-servant, so that every time the latter heard this sound he would toss back his hair, stand more respectfully to attention, and, bowing his head on its elevated perch, ask whether the gentleman required anything. After dinner the gentleman drank a cup of coffee and sat down on the divan, wedging behind his back one of those cushions which in Russian inns are stuffed not with springy wool but with something uncommonly like bricks and cobblestones. At this point he began to yawn and asked to be conducted to his room, where he lay down and slept for two hours. When he had rested, he wrote down on a scrap of paper, at the request of the inn-servant, his rank and name in full for the information of the appropriate quarters, namely, the police. As the servant descended the staircase he haltingly read the following: 'Collegiate Councillor* Pavel Ivanovich Chichikov,* landowner, on private business.'

While the servant was thus deciphering the note syllable by syllable, Pavel Ivanovich Chichikov set off to view the town, with which he was, it appeared, satisfied, for he discovered that it was in no way inferior to the other provincial capitals: the stone houses dazzled the eye with their yellow paint, while the wooden houses were a modest and dingy grey. The houses were one, two, or one-and-a-half storeys high, with the inevitable mansard, a very elegant feature in the opinion of the local architects. Some of these houses appeared lost amidst the wide expanse of the street and the unending wooden fences; others were grouped in tight clusters, and here one saw more movement and colour. There were shop signs depicting breadrolls and boots, the pictures almost totally washed away by the rain, a sign with blue trousers painted on it and the inscription: 'Arshavsky, Tailor'; there was a shop with hats, peaked caps and headgear of various kinds, and written above it: 'The Foreigner Vasily Fyodorov'; in another place there was a sign showing a billiard table with two players in tailcoats like those worn in our theatres by the guest actors who appear on stage only at the finale. The players were depicted aiming their cues, arms twisted back slightly, legs poised in mid-air as after an *entrechat*. Beneath all this was written: 'Behold the Establishment'. Here and there tables had simply been set out in the street, purveying nuts, soap, and gingerbread that looked like soap; somewhere else there was an eating-house under a sign showing a fat fish impaled on a fork. And yet the most conspicuous and most frequent signs were those faded boards depicting the twin-headed imperial eagle, which have now been replaced by the laconic inscription: 'Drinking Establishment'.* The roadway was in poor condition throughout.

He also glanced into the town garden, consisting of a few spindly trees which had not properly taken root, their trunks propped up by triangular supports, most attractively painted a dark green. Moreover, although none of these trees stood any higher than a reed, the newspapers, reporting on the town's festive illumination, said of them that: 'Our town has been embellished, thanks to the solicitude of the city fathers, with a garden, consisting of shady, spreading trees, affording coolth on a sultry day', and that 'it was a joy to behold how the hearts of our citizens trembled from an overflow of feeling, and how the tears streamed down their faces, tears of gratitude to our honoured burgomaster.'

Having established, after detailed inquiry of a constable, the shortest route, should he need to visit the cathedral, the municipal offices, or the governor, he set off to have a look at the river, which flowed through the centre of the town. On the way he pulled a playbill off the post to which it was nailed, with the intention of reading it more closely when he got home, stared hard at a lady of not displeasing aspect who passed by on the wooden pavement, followed by a young boy dressed in military livery with a bundle in his hand, and, casting one last glance all round him as if to commit to memory the disposition of the place, he repaired home, making directly for his room, gently assisted up the stairs by the inn-servant.

After having his tea he seated himself at the table, called for a candle, took the playbill from his pocket, held it up to the candle and began to read it, slightly screwing up his right eye. As it happened, the playbill contained little of interest: a drama by Mr Kotzebue* was being performed, in which Rolla was to be played by Mr Poplyovin, Cora by Miss Zyablova, and the other parts were even less memorable; nevertheless, he read them all, right down to the price of a seat in the stalls, and ascertained that the playbill had been printed at the print shop of the provincial government offices; he then turned it over to see whether there might not be something on the other side, but finding nothing he wiped his eyes, neatly folded it, and placed it in his little box, into which he customarily placed everything that came his way. His day, it seems, was concluded by a helping of cold veal, a bottle of sour malt, and a deep sleep 'with his bellows full open', as the expression goes in far-flung corners of the Russian Empire.

The whole of the next day was devoted to visits; the newcomer set off to make his obeisances to all the local dignitaries. He paid his respects to the governor, who, as it turned out, like himself was neither fat nor thin, wore the order of St Anne on his collar, and, so it was rumoured, had even been nominated for a star;* for all that, he was a splendid fellow and was even not averse to doing a spot of embroidery on tulle. Next, he repaired to the vice-governor, then called upon the public prosecutor, the president of the chambers, the chief of police, the liquor concessionaire,* the superintendent of imperial manufactories...

Regrettably, it is hard to keep count of all the great men of this world; suffice it to say that our visitor evinced a remarkable assiduity in the matter of visits: he even went to convey his respects to the inspector of the medical board and the town architect. Thereafter he remained seated in his chaise for a long time, as he deliberated which other visits he might make, but there simply were no more officials to be found. In his conversations with each of these worthies he demonstrated great skill in the art of flattery. To the governor he remarked, as it were *en passant*, that entering his province was like entering Paradise, the roads were smooth as velvet, and that those administrations which appointed wise men to positions of authority deserved high approbation. To the police chief he said something most complimentary about the local constabulary; while in his conversation with the vice-governor and the president of the chambers, who had the rank of mere state councillors, he even mistakenly said, on at least two occasions: 'Your Excellency',* which pleased them no end. This brought the reward that the governor requested the honour of his company that same day at a private gathering, while the other officials also extended invitations, some to dinner, some for a little game of Boston,* some to take tea.

Our visitor appeared loath to divulge much about himself and if he did speak his discourse was somehow laden with clichés, and delivered in a markedly self-effacing way. On such occasions his speech acquired rather bookish turns of phrase: that he was but an unworthy worm of this earth, who merited not that others should be incommoded on his account; that he had endured much in his journey through life, had suffered for truth in his career, had many enemies, and attempts had even been made on his life; that now, in his quest for peace, he hoped at last to select a domicile and that, having arrived in this town, he considered it *de rigueur* to pay his respects to its leading dignitaries. This was all that became known in the town about the new arrival, who, for his part, lost no time in taking the governor up on his invitation.

Preparations for this event occupied rather more than two hours, and here our visitor displayed a punctiliousness in the matter of his toilet that was even quite unparalleled. After a brief after-dinner nap he called for hot water and spent an inordinately long time lathering both cheeks, pushing them out with his tongue; then, taking his towel from the shoulder of the inn-servant, he rubbed all over his fleshy face, commencing from behind his ears and first snorting twice directly into the servant's face. Then, standing before the mirror, he donned his starched shirt-front, plucked two little hairs which had peeped out of his nostril, and immediately thereafter was helped into a speckled, cranberry-red tailcoat. Thus attired, he drove forth in his own carriage along the endlessly wide streets, which were faintly illuminated by the dim gleam from an occasional lighted window.

The governor's house, however, was lit up as for a ball; a calèche with lanterns, two gendarmes* standing guard at the entrance, the cries of postilions in the distance—in a word, everything as it should be. Entering the hall, Chichikov had to screw up his eyes for a minute, so fierce was the glare from the candles, the lamps, and the ladies' gowns. All was bathed in light. The black tailcoats flashed and whizzed about, singly and in groups, like flies on a hot July day buzzing around a dazzling white sugar-loaf which the old house-keeper, standing before an open window, chips and divides into sparkling chunks, while the children gather round and gaze in fascination at the movements of her sinewy arms wielding the hammer, and the airborne squadrons of flies, buoyed up by the light air, swoop bravely in, like full masters of the house, and—taking advantage of the old woman's poor eyesight, made worse by the glare of the sun—scatter over the succulent morsels, either separately, or in dense clusters. Already sated with the richness of summer, which sets out such dainties at every step, they have come swarming in without the least intention of eating, but merely to flaunt them-selves, to promenade up and down the sugar-loaf, to rub their hind legs or forelegs together, or to scratch beneath their wings, or again, stretching forth their arms, to rub these above their heads, to turn around and take to the air once more, only to return with new squadrons of importunate aeronauts.

Chichikov had scarcely had time to get his bearings before his elbow was seized by the governor, who at once presented him to his lady wife. Here too our visitor was nothing discomposed: he deliv-ered a compliment most appropriate from a man of middle years, of a rank neither too high nor too low. When the dancing couples took the floor and pressed everyone else to the wall he put his hands behind his back and studied them for about two minutes with close attention. Many ladies were finely and fashionably dressed, others wore what God had sent to their provincial capital. The men here, as everywhere, fell into two types: those of the first type were slen-der men, forever hovering around the ladies; some could hardly be distinguished from their St Petersburg counterparts: they had the same neatly groomed whiskers, which had been combed back with taste and deliberation, or they merely had pleasant and very clean-shaven oval faces; they seated themselves just as nonchalantly beside the ladies, talking French and making the ladies laugh exactly as is done in St Petersburg.

The second type were the fat men, or those like Chichikov—that is to say, those who were not over-fat, nor yet exactly thin. These, by contrast, shied warily away from the ladies and kept glancing around to see whether the governor's footman had not anywhere set out green baize tables for whist. Their faces were full and round, some even had warts, and one or two were pockmarked; they wore their hair neither in tufts, nor in curls, nor in the *que diable* manner, as the French put it—no, their hair was either cut short or slicked down, and their features were mostly well-rounded and strong. These were the town's august dignitaries.

Alas! The fat are so much better able to conduct their affairs in this world than the thin. Thin men serve mostly on special assignments or have jobs that exist only on paper, whilst they flit about from place to place; their very existence is somehow too light, airy, and totally unreliable. Fat men, on the other hand, never occupy peripheral positions, but only central ones, and if they do take a chair somewhere, they will do so firmly and solidly, so that it may well crack beneath them and cave in, and yet they will still remain firmly ensconced. They disdain outward sparkle; their tailcoats are not so smartly cut as those of their thin brethren, yet their coffers are full of God's plenty. After three years a thin man will not possess a single unmortgaged soul; but before you know it the fat man will have acquired a house at one end of the town, bought in his wife's name, then another house at the other end of town, then a little hamlet near the town, then an entire village, too, complete with serfs and all its land and amenities. Finally, the fat man, having served God and Tsar and earned universal regard, leaves the service, moves to his new home and becomes a landowner, a Russian country squire of the best kind, convivial and hospitable, and there he lives and prospers. But then, after his demise, his thin heirs gallop through their patrimony in the true Russian manner.

We cannot conceal that reflections of almost precisely this nature occupied Chichikov while he observed the company, and in consequence he finally joined the fat men, among whom he encountered almost exclusively familiar faces: the public prosecutor with his beetling, coal-black eyebrows and a slightly drooping left eyelid, that seemed to wink and say: 'Here, old chap, let's slip into the next room and I'll tell you a story'—but who was, in fact, a serious and taciturn man; the postmaster, a squat fellow, but a wit and a philosopher; the president of the chambers, a most sagacious and congenial man—all of whom greeted him like an old friend, which honour Chichikov returned with a slightly oblique bow, delivered, it must be said, in a far from disagreeable fashion. Here he also made the acquaintance of the most courteous and obliging landowner Manilov and the rather ungainly looking Sobakevich,* who there and then stepped on his toes, saying, 'Beg your pardon.'

Here too he was presented with an invitation to whist, to which he acceded with an equally gracious bow. They sat at the green baize table and did not rise again until supper. All conversation totally ceased, as always happens when people at last get down to real business. Although the postmaster was a most garrulous man, even he, once the cards were dealt, promptly took on a pensive expression, covering his upper lip with his lower and retaining this disposition throughout the game. When making his play he would slap the card hard down on the table, exclaiming, if it were a queen, 'Off with you, you old priest's wife!' if a king, 'Go to it, you Tambov peasant!' while the president reiterated: 'You wait: I'll get him by the beard!' or: 'I'll get her by the beard!' Sometimes as the cards hit the table the players would exclaim: 'To hell with it! If you've nothing better, lead with diamonds!' or else: 'Hearts! Heartburn! Spade-face!' or: 'Spadelets! Spadrillo! Spadrango!' and even simply: 'Spads!' calling out the names with which, in their company, they had christened the various suits.

At the end of the game they argued heatedly, as was their custom. Our visitor argued too, but in such an adroit way that the others could see that he was arguing, and yet he argued pleasantly. He never said: 'You led', but: 'you were so good as to lead', or 'I had the honour to trump your deuce', and so forth. In order to propitiate his opponents still further, he would then invite them all to take a pinch from his silver enamelled snuff-box, at the bottom of which they noticed two violets, placed there for their aroma.

Our visitor's attention was particularly caught by the landowners Manilov and Sobakevich, whom we have mentioned above. He at once made enquiries about them, drawing the president and the post-master slightly to one side. The few questions he put were trenchant and to the point, and not just idle curiosity, for, first of all, he asked how many serfs each of them had, and what state their properties were in, and only then did he inquire after their first names and patronymics. In no time he succeeded in totally charming them both.

The landowner Manilov, a man still in the vigour of youth, with eyes as sweet as sugar, which he screwed up when he smiled, was quite in thrall to Chichikov. He shook his hand hard and long and implored him to honour him with a visit to his estate, which, in his own words, lay a mere fifteen versts* from the town limits. To which Chichikov retorted, most graciously inclining his head and sincerely squeezing Manilov's hand, that he was not only willing to comply, but would even regard it as his most sacred duty. Sobakevich also added rather brusquely: 'Come to my place too', scraping his foot, which was shod in a boot of such gigantic dimensions that it is most unlikely another foot could be found anywhere to fit it, particularly in this day and age, when legendary giants are becoming increasingly hard to find, even in Russia.*

The next day Chichikov repaired for dinner and a *soirée* to the home of the police chief, where after dining they sat down to whist, playing solidly from three in the afternoon until two in the morning. There, incidentally, he made the acquaintance of the landowner Nozdryov,* a man of about thirty, a dashing fellow, who after three or four words began addressing Chichikov in terms of the utmost familiarity. Nozdryov was also on the closest terms with the police chief and the public prosecutor, and was most affable towards them but, when they sat down to play for big stakes, the police chief and the public prosecutor studied his tricks with great suspicion and scrutinized practically every card he played. The following evening Chichikov spent at the home of the president of the chambers, who received his guests in a rather grubby dressing-gown, even though there were two ladies present. Then he attended a *soirée* at the vice-governor's, a large dinner at the concessionaire's, and a small dinner at the public prosecutor's, which in fact was as big as a large dinner; after the midday service he repaired to a light luncheon given by the chief guildsman, which was just as heavy as a dinner. In a word, he did not have to tarry at home for a single hour and he returned to the inn only to sleep.

Our visitor seemed able to find his feet everywhere, and proved to be an experienced man of the world. Whatever the topic of conversation, he was always able to hold his own: if the discussion turned to stud farms, he too would talk of stud farms; if they talked about hounds, here too he made highly apposite contributions; should they touch on a prosecution brought by the imperial revenue chamber*—he showed he was not altogether ignorant of legal chicanery either; if the subject raised was billiards—he was always on the ball; were they to deliberate on the subject of virtue, on virtue he too would discourse most movingly, with real tears in his eyes; if the topic was the distillation of spirits, in the matter of the distillation of spirits he proved to be no neophyte; if the talk turned to customs inspectors and officials—he held forth as if he himself had been both an inspector and an official. Most remarkable, however, was the gravity which he brought to bear on all these topics and the dignity with which he conducted himself. He spoke neither loudly nor quietly, but exactly as the occasion required. In a word, whichever way you looked at it he was a very respectable man.

All the officials were pleased with the arrival of a new person in their midst. The governor delivered himself of the opinion that Chichikov was a well-intentioned man; the public prosecutor that he was a practical man; the colonel of gendarmes declared that he was a man of learning; the president of the chambers that he was a knowledgeable and honourable man; the police chief that he was an honourable and civil man; and the police chief's wife that he was a man of the utmost civility and circumspection. Even Sobakevich, who rarely found anything good to say about anyone, returned late from town and, after throwing off all his clothes and lying down on the bed beside his spindly wife, announced: 'I spent the evening at the governor's, dear heart, and had dinner at the police chief's, and made the acquaintance of Collegiate Councillor Pavel Ivanovich Chichikov: a most engaging man!' To which his good wife retorted: 'Hm!' and gave him a kick.

Such was the opinion, most flattering to our visitor, that was formed of him in the town, and it remained in force until a singular feature of this visitor and the undertaking he launched—or, as they say in the provinces, a certain pretty pass—about which the reader shall learn forthwith, plunged almost the entire town into total bewilderment.

CHAPTER TWO

By now our visitor had been in the town for more than a week, attending *soirées* and dinners, and in general having a most congenial time, as they say. Finally he decided to extend his visits to the outlying areas and to pay the promised calls on the landowners Manilov and Sobakevich. Perhaps he was prompted here by some other more cogent reason, by a business graver and closer to his heart... But the reader will be apprised of all this gradually and in good time, if he only has the patience to read through the story we offer him, long though it be, which will grow in breadth and scope as it nears the end and culmination of the affair.

The coachman Selifan had received instructions to harness the horses early in the morning to the chaise, by now familiar to the reader; Petrushka was ordered to remain at home and keep an eye on the room and the valise. At this point the reader could do worse than to make the acquaintance of these two stout men in our hero's service. It is true, of course, that they are not such prominent characters, being of the genus termed secondary or even tertiary, and it is true that the main springs and gears of our poem do not repose on them and only brush lightly against them now and again—but the author is uncommonly fond of describing everything in the most minute detail, and in this respect, for all that he is himself a Russian, would be as punctilious as a German.

This will not take up much time, or space, however, because little need be added to that which the reader already knows, namely, that Petrushka sported an over-large brown frock-coat (one of his master's cast-offs) and, like all people of his calling, had a large nose and lips. By character he inclined more to the taciturn than to the loquacious; he even had a noble aspiration towards enlightenment—that is, towards the reading of books, the content of which bothered him not in the slightest: it was quite immaterial to him whether he read the adventures of an amorous hero, or a simple reading primer, or a prayer book—he read them all with equal attention; hand him a manual of chemistry and he would not demur. He enjoyed not so much what he read as the act of reading, or to be more precise, the very process of reading, the remarkable way those letters combined to produce some word or other, a word which sometimes meant the devil knows what. This reading was usually accomplished in a supine position in the hallway, on the bed, and on the palliasse, which had been worn by this exercise to the thinness and flatness of a pancake.

Besides his passion for reading he had two other habits, which constituted his two remaining characteristics: he did not undress to sleep, but lay down as he was, complete with frock-coat, and he carried about with him his own particular aura, a special miasma, somehow redolent of a well lived-in room, so that he only needed to roll out his bedding somewhere, even in a room that no one had ever lived in, and to lug in his overcoat and chattels, and it would at once seem as though it had been somebody's home for at least the last ten years. Chichikov, being a most pernickety, finicky man and on occasion even squeamish, on taking a fresh noseful of air in the morning would frown, shake his head, and say: 'What's the matter with you, damn you: have you been sweating again, is that it? I wish you'd go to the bathhouse sometimes.'

To which Petrushka would vouch no reply, but would instead make a sudden show of activity: he would either advance on his master's tailcoat with a clothes brush, or start tidying things up. There is no knowing what he was thinking while he thus remained silent—perhaps he was saying to himself: 'You're a fine one to talk, how come you're not sick of saying the same thing forty times over?'—God knows, it is hard to tell what thoughts pass through a house serf's head while his master is delivering an admonition. So this is all we can say about Petrushka for the time being.

The coachman Selifan was quite a different order of being... But the author feels somewhat ashamed to be occupying his readers at such length with people of low rank, knowing from experience how loath they are to acquaint themselves with the lower orders. For such is the Russian character: we have a passionate longing to rub shoulders with any man who stands at least one notch higher on the scale of ranks, and a nodding acquaintance with a count or a prince is worth more than any number of close friendships. The author even feels some anxiety on account of his own hero, who is a mere collegiate councillor. Aulic councillors may perhaps be pleased to make his acquaintance, but as for those who have already ascended to the rank of general,* they—Heaven help us—might even cast one of those contemptuous glances which a man casts haughtily on any-thing crawling at his feet or, worse still, might sail past without so much as a glance—which would be fatal for the author. However much we might deplore both such attitudes we must, in any event, return to our hero.

Thus, having issued the necessary instructions the previous evening and waking very early in the morning, he first sponged himself down from head to toe, something he did only on the Sabbath—for it was indeed Sunday—shaved so closely that his cheeks acquired the softness and lustre of satin, donned his speckled, cranberry-red tailcoat and over it a greatcoat lined with bearskin, and thereupon descended the staircase, supported by the inn-servant, now on one side, now on the other, and took his seat in his chaise. The chaise clattered out of the inn gates on to the street. A priest walking by doffed his cap;* a gaggle of urchins in grubby shirts stretched out their hands, intoning: 'Sir, alms for a poor orphan!' The coachman, observing that one of these was very adept at jumping on the run-ning-board, lashed out at him with his whip, and the chaise contin-ued on its way, bouncing on the cobblestones. The striped barrier in the distance was a joy to espy, for it proclaimed that this roadway, like all earthly torment, would soon come to an end; and after knocking his head a few more times fairly hard against the carriage roof Chichikov at last felt the carriage rolling along the soft ground.

No sooner was the town behind them than there appeared on both sides of the road the sort of useless vegetation that is the rule in our country: tussocks; a fir-grove; mangy, low clumps of young pines; the scorched stumps of old ones; wild heather and such-like rubbish. They drove through villages strung along the roadside, the houses like so many stacks of old firewood, topped by grey roofs whose intricately carved eaves hung beneath them like embroidered hand-towels. Groups of peasants wearing sheepskin coats sat yawn-ing, in their customary manner, on the benches in front of the gates. Country wives with fat faces and tightly swathed bosoms peered out of the upper windows; from the lower gazed the occasional calf, or a pig would thrust out its myopic snout. In a word, all the usual sights.

After covering fifteen versts Chichikov recalled that, by Manilov's reckoning, he should by now have reached his destination, but the sixteenth verst flew by too, and there was still no sight of the village.

Indeed, had they not come upon two peasants they probably would never have found their bearings. In response to the question whether it was far to the village of Zamanilovka, the peasants doffed their hats, and one of them, the more intelligent of the two, who sported a wedge-shaped beard, answered:

'Zamanilovka... Not Manilovka by any chance?'

'Ah yes, Manilovka.'

'Manilovka! Well, you go another verst, and there you have it, straight to the right, that is.'

'To the right?' repeated the coachman.

'Aye, to the right,' said the peasant, 'that'll be your way to Manilovka; there's no Zamanilovka round these parts. That's what they call it, you see, I mean, its name is Manilovka, but there's no Zamanilovka round here. You'll see the house there, right up on the hill, a stone house two storeys high, the manor house, the one the master himself lives in, that is. That's your Manilovka, but there's no Zamanilovka here, and never has been.'

They set off in search of Manilovka. After driving for two versts, they came to a turn on to a country track, but following it for what seemed a further two, then three, then four versts, they still could see no stone double-storeyed house. At this point Chichikov remembered that, if a friend invites you to call on him in his village fifteen versts from town, you can be fairly certain you will have a good thirty to travel. The village of Manilovka would have lured few by its setting. The manor house stood in isolation on the brow of a hill, exposed to all the winds that might ever chance to blow; the slope of the hill on which it stood was carpeted with closely mown turf. Scattered about it after the English manner* were clumps of lilac bushes and yellow acacia; half a dozen birch trees raised their mangy foliage aloft. Two of them shaded a pergola with a squat green dome, pale blue wooden columns, and the inscription 'Temple of Solitary Contemplation'; some way below there was a pond, covered with duckweed, something which, we should point out, is no oddity in the English gardens of Russian landowners. At the foot of this eminence and partly on the slope itself, a number of shabby log huts stood in higgledy-piggledy fashion, and our hero, for some obscure reason, at once set about counting them, arriving at a total of over two hundred; between them there was not a single tree nor scrap of greenery, the view was one of unrelenting log walls. The scene was enlivened by two peasant women, who, with skirts pictur-esquely gathered up and tucked in on all sides, waded knee-deep about the pond, carrying two wooden yokes, from which they pulled a tattered drag-net; in their net they had snared two crawfish and a stray shimmering roach; the women seemed to be quarrelling and bickering about something.

Afar off to one side lay the pine forest, a dark and dreary blue. Even the weather was somehow appropriate: it was not a bright day, nor exactly overcast, but a sort of pale grey colour, like that found only in the old uniforms of regular garrison soldiers—in point of fact, a peace-loving body of men, but somewhat inclined to drunk-enness on the Lord's day. To complete the picture the inevitable cockerel was also in evidence, that herald of changeable weather, who, notwithstanding the sorry state of his head, which the other cocks had thoroughly pecked—right through to the brain—in retri-bution for his philandering ways, crowed throatily and even flapped his wings, as tattered as two old bast mats. Chichikov now observed the owner himself standing on the porch in a green shalloon* frock-coat, his hand held to his brow to shade his eyes, the better to see the approaching conveyance. As the chaise rolled up to the porch his eyes sparkled with joy and a broad smile spread across his face.

'Pavel Ivanovich!' he exclaimed at last, when Chichikov clam-bered out of the chaise. 'So you did remember us, after all!'

The two friends embraced fervently and Manilov led his guest inside. Although the time it will take them to traverse the vestibule, anteroom, and dining-room is not extensive, we shall none the less try to make good use of it to say something here about the master of the house. But first the author must confess that such an undertak-ing is fraught with great difficulty. It is so much easier to describe characters larger than life: there you need only hurl the paints on to the canvas—gleaming black eyes, beetling eyebrows, a furrowed brow, a cloak, black or flame-red, thrown over the shoulder—and the por-trait is complete; but as for that great multitude of gentlemen who are so similar in appearance, yet who on closer inspection show many highly elusive and distinctive features—these gentlemen are the devil of a job to portray. Here you must make a supreme effort of mind to bring into clear focus all these subtle, almost impercept-ible features, and even eyes adept in the science of observation have to be strained to the utmost.

Perhaps only God could have said what Manilov's character was like. There is a certain type of person who is neither one thing nor the other, not fish nor fowl, neither town mouse nor country mouse, as the proverb has it. Perhaps we should rank Manilov among their number. To look at he was a presentable man; his features were not unpleasing, but this pleasantness seemed excessively saccharine: his mannerisms and turns of phrase seemed designed to court favour and affection. His smile was alluring, his complexion fair, with pale blue eyes. In the first minute of conversation with him you could not help thinking: 'What a pleasant and kind person!' In the second minute you would not think anything, but in the third you would curse inwardly: 'What the devil is all this!' and you would move further away, for if you did not move away you would be bored to death.

You would never hear from him a single lively or even slightly presumptuous word, of the sort you would expect to hear from any other man when you spoke on a subject so close to his heart. For everyone has such a pet subject: with one it is borzoi dogs; another will fancy himself a great lover of music, remarkably sensitive to its hidden profundities; a third is known for his fondness of good food; a fourth likes to play a role ever so slightly higher than that properly assigned to him; a fifth, whose desires are more limited, dreams of going for a stroll arm-in-arm with an aide-de-camp to the Emperor, in full view of his friends, acquaintances, and even strangers; a sixth was born with one hand afflicted with a diabolical itch to bend the corner on an ace of diamonds, or the two of diamonds*—while the hand of a seventh aches to enforce proper law and order, usually by addressing the physiognomy of a stationmaster* or a cab-driver—in a word, everyone has a pet subject, but Manilov had none.

At home he spoke very little and spent most of his time in thought and reflection, but as to what he was thinking, the Lord only knew. You could not exactly say he took an interest in running his estate: he never even drove out to his fields, and the estate more or less looked after itself. When his bailiff said: 'Well, master, it would be a good idea to do such-and-such,' he would usually respond, 'Yes, not a bad idea', drawing on his pipe, a habit he had acquired while still in the army, where he had been considered an officer of the utmost modesty, tact, and good breeding. 'Yes, not a bad idea at all,' he would repeat. When a peasant came shuffling up, scratching the back of his head, and asked, 'Master, will you release me so I can find a job somewhere to earn some tax money',* he would say: 'Off you go', pulling on his pipe, and it would never even enter his head that the peasant was going on a drinking spree.

Sometimes, as he gazed from the porch into the yard or on to his pond, he would announce how splendid it would be if they were to dig a subterranean passage from the house, or to erect a stone bridge across the pond, with little shops along both sides, where merchants could sit and ply those petty wares so essential to peasants. As he said this his eyes would take on an expression of extraordinary *tendresse* and his face a look of utter contentment; needless to say, all these hare-brained schemes began and ended with his words. A book always lay in his study with a bookmark at page fourteen, a book he had been reading continuously for the past two years. In his house there was permanently something lacking: his drawing-room was furnished with a fine set of furniture, upholstered in a stylish silk fabric which had clearly not been cheap, but it had not been sufficient for two of the armchairs, which remained covered in coarse matting; he would invariably warn his guests, year after year: 'Pray do not sit in those chairs, they are not quite ready yet.'

In one room there was no furniture at all, although it had been his habit to declare in the days immediately after his wedding: 'Sweet-heart, tomorrow we really must get down to it and have some furniture put in this room, if only temporarily.' In the evenings a most elaborate candelabra of dark bronze adorned with the three Graces of antiquity and an ornate, mother-of-pearl base would be set on the table, and beside it a crippled brass invalid of a candlestick, lopsided and covered in tallow-grease, and this would not be noticed by the master, nor by his lady, nor by the servants.

As for his wife... for all that, they were utterly content with each other. Although more than eight years of married life had elapsed, each would still bring the other some titbit: a piece of apple, a sweetmeat, or perhaps a little nut, and would say in a touchingly tender voice, expressive of perfect love: 'Open mouthies, sweetie, and I'll pop in this little morsel.' Needless to say, at this suggestion, mouthies would open most gracefully. For birthdays special surprise gifts were prepared: such as a miniature toothpick case sown with glass beads. And very often, as they sat on the settee, suddenly, and for no apparent reason, the one would lay aside his pipe and the other her work, if indeed these were in their hands at that moment, and they would plant upon each other's lips a kiss of such languor and duration that you could smoke a small cheroot from beginning to end while it lasted. In a word, they were what is known as a happy couple.

Of course, we might remark that there are many other things to do in a house besides exchanging lengthy kisses and surprise gifts, and there are many different questions we might ask. Why, for instance, was stupidity and waste the order of the day in the kitchen? Why was the larder so empty? Why have a thief for a housekeeper? Why were the servants slovenly and drunken? Why did all the household staff sleep all morning and spend the rest of the day carousing? But all these are lowly matters, and Madame Manilova had been properly brought up—a proper upbringing, of course, being that received in boarding schools for young ladies. In boarding schools for young ladies, as everyone knows, three main subjects constitute the basis of all human virtue: the French language, essential to the happiness of family life; playing the fortepiano, to provide pleasurable minutes for the husband; and, finally, the so-called domestic sciences, that is, the knitting of tiny purses and the preparation of other surprise gifts. The methods do change and improve, however, especially nowadays; all this depends more on the good sense and capabilities of the ladies who run the boarding schools. In some boarding schools playing the fortepiano may come first, then French, and finally the domestic sciences. And occasionally you find that they start with the domestic part, that is, the knitting of surprise gifts, then move on to French, and only after that to the fortepiano. Procedures differ. It would not go amiss to note here, too, that Madame Manilova... But I must confess I greatly fear talking about ladies and, besides, it is time I returned to our heroes, who have now been standing for several minutes before the doors of the drawing-room, each inviting the other to proceed.

'Pray, do not discommode yourself on my account, I shall follow,' said Chichikov.

'No, no, Pavel Ivanovich, you are my guest,' said Manilov, gesturing towards the door.

'I beg you, please do not trouble yourself. Please, after you,' said Chichikov.

'Now you must forgive me, I cannot allow such an agreeable and educated guest to enter behind me.'

'Why educated?... No, I insist: after you.'

'I must ask you to be so kind as to lead the way.'

'But why?'

'Well, because!' said Manilov with a pleasant smile.

Finally the two friends entered the doorway sideways, slightly squashing each other.

'Allow me to present my wife,' said Manilov. 'Sweetheart! It's Pavel Ivanovich!'

Chichikov did indeed see a lady, whom, while exchanging civilities in the doorway with Manilov, he had not noticed at all. She was not unattractive and was prettily dressed. She looked becoming in a pale silk morning-dress; with her small, slender hand she hastily tossed something on to a table, and in her fingers crumpled a batiste handkerchief with embroidered corners. She rose from the settee, and Chichikov stepped up to her and kissed her hand, not without pleasure. Madame Manilova averred, elegantly slurring her 'r's, that his visit was a source of great joy to them, and that never a day passed without her husband mentioning his dear friend.

'Ah, yes,' said Manilov, 'indeed she too is forever asking me: "Now why doesn't your friend come to see us?"—"Just wait, sweetheart," I say, "he'll come." And now at last you have honoured us with your visit. Why, it's such a delight for us... a May day... a celebration for the heart...'

Hearing that things had already reached the point where hearts were celebrating, Chichikov was somewhat embarrassed and modestly protested that he had neither an exalted name nor even a prominent rank.

'You have everything,' interrupted Manilov with the same pleasant smile, 'you have everything, even more than everything.'

'How did you find our town?' chimed in Madame Manilova. 'Did you have a pleasant time there?'

'A very fine town, an excellent town,' replied Chichikov, 'and I spent my time most pleasantly: the most charming society.'

'And what did you think of our governor?' asked Madame Manilova.

'Is he not the most extremely distinguished and most amiable of men?' added Manilov.

'Indeed he is,' concurred Chichikov, 'a most extremely distinguished man. How well he exercises his duties, how well he understands them! One could only wish there were more like him.'

'How ably he can receive anyone, you know, and conduct himself *avec délicatesse*,' adjoined Manilov with a smile, and from the sheer pleasure of it he screwed up his eyes, almost completely, like a cat that is being gently tickled behind the ears.

'A very charming and pleasant man,' continued Chichikov, 'and so skilful! I would never have imagined it. How well he embroiders those pretty things for the home! He showed me a purse he had made with his own hands: rare even are the ladies who can embroider with such skill.'

'And the vice-governor? Is he not a dear man?' asked Manilov, once again narrowing his eyes slightly.

'A very, very worthy man,' agreed Chichikov.

'But might I inquire: what were your impressions of the chief of police? Did you not think him a most pleasant man?'

'Extraordinarily pleasant, and such a clever, such a well-read man! We played whist at his house with the public prosecutor and the president of the chambers till cockcrow; a very, very worthy man.'

'Well, and what is your opinion of the police chief's wife?' asked Madame Manilova. 'A most delightful woman, would you not say?'

'Oh indeed, she is one of the most worthy women I know,' answered Chichikov.

Thereupon they proceeded to the president of the chambers and the postmaster, and in this manner worked their way through almost all the officials in the town, who all turned out to be the most worthy people.

'Do you spend all your time in the country?' Chichikov inquired, at last, in his turn.

'Mostly in the country,' answered Manilov. 'We do occasionally visit the town, but for the sole purpose of enjoying the society of well-educated people. You go to seed a bit, you know, living shut up here all the time.'

'How true, how true,' echoed Chichikov.

'Of course,' continued Manilov, 'it would be quite a different matter if one had a better class of neighbours, if one had the sort of person with whom, so to speak, one could talk about refinement, about good manners, with whom one could pursue some science or other, don't you know, that would stir the soul, so to say, and send it soaring upwards...' Here he was about to voice something more, but perceiving that he had rather let his tongue run away with him, he merely stabbed at the air with his hand and continued: 'It's true, the country and solitude would be very enjoyable then. But there is positively no one... All one can do is to read the occasional issue of *Son of the Fatherland*.'*

Chichikov expressed his full agreement with this sentiment, adding that nothing could be more pleasant than living in solitary retirement, delighting in the spectacle of nature and occasionally reading some book or other...

'But do you know,' adjoined Manilov, 'without a friend, with whom one can share things, all this...'

'Why, how true, how very, very true!' interjected Chichikov. 'What are all the treasures of the world worth in comparison! For, as one wise man has said, "Seek ye not riches, seek but the society of good men."'

'And then, you know, Pavel Ivanovich!' exclaimed Manilov, his face taking on an expression that was not merely sweet, but distinctly cloying, like cough linctus which a shrewd society doctor has mercilessly sugared, intending thereby to delight his patient. 'You feel something, in a manner of speaking, like spiritual delight... Such as, for example, now, when fortune has granted me the happiness, I might say, the exemplary beneficence of talking to you and delighting in your pleasant conversation...'

'Oh come, my pleasant conversation?... I am a man of utter insignificance, that's all,' replied Chichikov.

'Oh no Pavel Ivanovich! Permit me to be quite candid. I would gladly give up half my fortune in exchange for a portion of those merits which you possess!'

'On the contrary, I, for my part, would consider it the most extreme...'

We can only guess where this mutual effusion of sentiment by the two friends would have led, had not the footman entered to announce that dinner was served.

'Shall we go in?' said Manilov. 'You must forgive us if we do not serve the kind of dinner you will find in fine houses and in the capitals: we eat simple fare here, our Russian cabbage soup, to start with, but it's offered from the heart. Shall we go in?'

Here for a while they returned to their dispute about who would be the first to proceed, until finally Chichikov sidled past his host into the dining-room.

Two boys stood waiting in the dining-room: Manilov's sons, who were already old enough to eat at the table, but still on high chairs. Attending them was a tutor, who bowed politely and with a smile. The lady of the house took her place behind the soup tureen; the guest was seated between his host and hostess, and the footman fastened napkins round the necks of the children.

'What delightful children,' said Chichikov, taking a look at the two boys, 'and how old would they be?'

'The elder one is seven, and the younger had his sixth birthday only yesterday,' said Madame Manilova.

'Themistoclus!' said Manilov, addressing the elder, who was en-deavouring to free his chin from the napkin which the footman had tied round it.

Chichikov slightly raised his eyebrows, hearing this partly Greek name, to which, for some unknown reason, Manilov had appended the suffix '-us', but he immediately endeavoured to rearrange his features in their usual expression.

'Themistoclus, tell me, which is the best city in France?'

Here the tutor turned his full attention on Themistoclus and fixed him with a ferocious stare, but relaxed and nodded his head when Themistoclus said:

'Paris.'

'And which is our best city?' enquired Manilov further.

Once again the tutor fixed the boy with his stare.

'St Petersburg,' answered Themistoclus.

'And another?'

'Moscow,' answered Themistoclus.

'What a clever boy, what an angel!' exclaimed Chichikov, and, turning a look of amazement upon the Manilovs, continued: 'Really, I must say!... Such knowledge at such a tender age! I am bound to tell you that this child will display great abilities.'

'Oh, you do not know him yet,' replied Manilov, 'he has a remark-able wit. Now the younger one, Alcides,* he's not so quick, but as for this lad, when he sees something, a bug or a little beetle, his clever little eyes will start to dance at once; he'll run after it and watch it closely. I'm putting him down for the diplomatic service. Themistoclus,' he continued, turning to the boy, 'do you want to be an ambassador?'

'Yes,' replied Themistoclus, chewing a piece of bread and wagging his head from left to right.

At this moment the footman standing behind him wiped the ambassador's nose, and not before time too, for otherwise a sizeable foreign droplet would have fallen into His Excellency's soup. A conversation was now struck up at the table about the pleasures of a quiet life, interrupted by the hostess's remarks about the local theatre and its actors. The tutor watched the speakers with keen attention, and the moment he noticed they were about to laugh, he at once opened his mouth and laughed with gusto. In all probability, he was a grateful man and wished thereby to repay his employer for the good treatment accorded him. On one occasion, however, his face took on a severe look and he fiercely thumped the table with his fork, glaring at the children sitting opposite him. This intervention was well-timed, for Themistoclus had just bitten Alcides's ear, and Alcides, screwing up his eyes, had opened his mouth to emit a pitiful wail but, sensing that this action was very likely to cost him his dinner, recomposed his features and, with tears in his eyes, set about gnawing a mutton bone, which caused both his cheeks to glisten with fat.

The hostess repeatedly addressed herself to Chichikov with the words: 'You're not eating anything, you've taken too little.' To which Chichikov would invariably reply: 'I thank you most humbly, I'm quite sated, a pleasant conversation is better than any dish.'

They had already risen from the table. Manilov was extremely contented, and, placing his hand lightly on Chichikov's back, he was about to guide his guest into the drawing-room, when the guest suddenly announced with a look of great significance that he wished to discuss a most important matter with his host.

'In that case allow me to invite you into my study,' said Manilov, and conducted him into a smallish room, whose window looked out on to the darkening forest.

'This is my little den,' said Manilov.

'A pleasant little room,' said Chichikov casting his eyes around.

The room was indeed rather pleasant: the walls were painted a pale greyish-blue, there were four upright chairs, one armchair, a desk, on which lay the book with its trusty bookmark that we have already had occasion to mention, and some papers covered with writing, but what there was most of was tobacco. It was to be found in a variety of forms: in paper bags and in a tobacco jar, and, finally, poured in a heap on the desk. On both window-sills stood little mounds of ash, knocked out of the pipe and stacked with considerable care in most attractive little rows. Evidently this was something of a pastime for the master of the house.

'Do please seat yourself in this armchair,' said Manilov. 'You will find it more comfortable.'

'I'll sit on a chair if I may.'

'Please allow me not to allow you,' said Manilov with a smile. 'This armchair is specially assigned for my guests: you simply must sit in it, like it or not.'

Chichikov sat down.

'Please allow me to fill you a pipe.'

'Thank you, I do not smoke,' answered Chichikov affably, with a look of seeming regret.

'Why is that?' enquired Manilov just as affably and with a look of regret.

'I never formed the habit, I'm afraid; they say a pipe dries up the system.'

'Please allow me to point out that that is sheer prejudice. I would even submit that smoking a pipe is much more healthy than taking snuff. In our regiment there was a lieutenant, a most excellent and cultivated gentleman, who never removed his pipe from his mouth, not only at meals, but even, would you believe it, everywhere else too. And now he is already over forty, but, by the grace of God, remains in perfect health to this day.'

Chichikov observed that such things did indeed happen and there were many things in nature which were beyond the comprehension of even the most exalted intellect.

'But please allow me first to make one request...' he ventured in a voice in which a strange, almost furtive note could be heard, and for some obscure reason looked round. For the same obscure reason Manilov also looked round. '—How long ago did you submit your census list*?'

'Well, a long time ago. Truth to tell, I don't recall exactly.'

'And have many of your peasants died since that time?'

'Well, I couldn't say; for that I think we would have to ask my bailiff.' He called out to his manservant: 'Fetch the bailiff, he should be here today.'

The bailiff appeared. He was a man nearing forty, beardless, clad in a frock-coat and visibly enjoying a life of great tranquility, because his face looked well-filled and chubby, whilst the sallowness of his skin and his little piggy eyes betrayed his excessive familiarity with feather beds and soft pillows. It was at once evident that he had reached his position along the path followed by all estate bailiffs: he had started as a servant boy who could read and write, then he married the housekeeper, the mistress's favourite, was appointed steward and then bailiff. Once appointed bailiff, he naturally did as all bailiffs do: he hobnobbed with the wealthier villagers and stood godfather to their children, upped the rents of the poorer ones, slept late in the morning, until after eight o'clock, then called for the samovar and drank his morning tea.

'I say, my good man, how many of our peasants have died since we put in the census list?'

'How many? Well... Lots have,' replied the bailiff and thereupon hiccuped, half covering his mouth with his spade-like hand.

'I must admit, I thought so myself,' said Manilov, 'Yes, indeed, a great many have died!' Here he turned to Chichikov and added for good measure, 'Indeed, a great many.'

'But how many, would you say, in numbers?' asked Chichikov.

'Yes, how many in numbers?' repeated Manilov.

'How can I say? No one knows how many died, nobody counted them.'

'There, you see,' said Manilov, turning to Chichikov. 'Just as I thought: the mortality was high. It's quite unknown how many have died.'

'Count them up, will you,' said Chichikov to the bailiff, 'and make a detailed list of all their names.'

'Yes, of all their names,' said Manilov.

The bailiff said, 'Yessir!' and withdrew.

'And for what purpose might you want this?' asked Manilov, when the bailiff had left.

This question appeared to disconcert his guest; his face took on a somewhat strained expression and he flushed—from the strenuous effort to express something that could not easily be put into words. And, to be sure, Manilov was to hear such strange and extraordinary things as had never before been heard by the ear of man.

'You ask, for what purpose? My purpose is this: I would like to buy some peasants...' said Chichikov, stammering to an abrupt halt.

'But allow me to enquire,' said Manilov, 'how would you like to buy the peasants: with the land, or to take away, that is, without the land?'

'No, no, what I want are not exactly peasants,' said Chichikov. 'It's the dead ones I want...'

'I'm sorry? I beg your pardon... I'm a little hard of hearing, I thought I heard something very strange...'

'I propose to acquire the dead ones, but those who figure in the census as alive,' said Chichikov.

Manilov promptly dropped his pipe on the floor and gaped at Chichikov in wide-mouthed astonishment for several minutes. The two friends, who had been discoursing so pleasantly on the gratifications of a convivial life, were now frozen, staring into each other's eyes, like those portraits which in days gone by were hung opposite each other on the two sides of a mirror. Finally Manilov bent down to pick up his pipe and glanced up at Chichikov, to see if there was a smile on his lips, which would imply that he had been joking; but there was no shadow of a smile—on the contrary, Chichikov's features were even more composed than usual. Then Manilov wondered whether his guest might not suddenly have lost his wits and he peered at him in alarm; but his guest's eyes were perfectly clear, they did not burn with a wild, restless fire, such as dances in the eyes of a madman: in his mien all was as it should be. No matter how Manilov racked his brains, wondering how to react and what to do, he could think of nothing better than to exhale the remaining smoke from his mouth in a long, thin plume.

'So, I would like to know if you would transfer to me those serfs who are not in reality alive but are alive with regard to their legal form, if you would sell them to me, or make them over in whatever manner you think best?'

But Manilov was so taken aback and nonplussed, he could only gape.

'I believe you are in two minds about this?' observed Chichikov.

'I?... No, it's not that,' said Manilov, 'it's just that I can't quite grasp... I'm sorry... Of course, I did not receive such a brilliant education as, so to speak, can be seen in your every movement; I lack the lofty art of rhetoric... Perchance here... in the explanation which you have just vouchsafed... there is some hidden meaning... Perhaps you expressed yourself thus for the sake of eloquence?'

'No,' interjected Chichikov, 'no, I mean exactly what I said: I want precisely those souls which have already died.'

Manilov was utterly at a loss. He felt that he ought to do something, to ask something, but the devil only knew what. In the end, all he did was once again to exhale smoke, this time not from the mouth, but through his nostrils.

'Well then, since you have no objections, so be it: let's start the paperwork and draw up the deed of purchase,' said Chichikov.

'How do you mean, a deed—for dead souls?'

'Ah, no!' said Chichikov. 'We shall put them down as living men, just as it is stated in the census list. I make a rule never to deviate from the laws of the land, although I suffered for this in the service, but it is the way I am: an obligation is something sacred to me, and the law—I prostrate myself before the law.'

These last words were much to Manilov's liking, but he still could not fathom what was going on and instead of replying, puffed away at his pipe with such vigour that it finally started to wheeze like a bassoon. It was as if he were trying to draw from it an opinion pertaining to such an unheard-of circumstance; but the pipe only wheezed and nothing more.

'Perhaps you have some doubts?'

'Oh no! Heavens no, none at all! I say this not because I have any, so to speak, critical prejudice against you. Forgive me for suggesting it, but would not such an undertaking or, if I may put it more precisely, negotiation, be somewhat at odds with the civic decrees and other future prospects of Russia?'

Here Manilov, with a slight motion of his head, cast a very meaningful look at Chichikov, all his features and his pursed lips taking on an expression of such profundity as had perhaps never before been beheld on a human face, except perhaps for that of some excessively clever Minister of State, and even then at a moment of the utmost mental exertion.

But Chichikov declared quite simply that such an undertaking, or negotiation, would not be at odds with the civic decrees and future prospects of Russia, and a moment later added that the treasury would even derive a profit therefrom, for it would receive the legal dues.

'Are you quite sure about that?...'

'I am, I believe it will be a good thing.'

'Ah, if it is a good thing, that is another matter: I have no objections,' said Manilov, feeling completely reassured.

'It only remains now to agree on the price.'

'What do you mean: on the price?' Manilov began and stopped. 'Surely you are not suggesting that I would take money for souls which—in a certain sense—have finished their existence? If you are really set on this—shall we say—most extraordinary course, then for my part I shall simply give them to you and I shall pay the transfer fees myself.'

The historian of the events described would be greatly at fault if he omitted to say that our guest was overcome with delight when he heard these words uttered by Manilov. Rational and moderate creature though he was, he nearly leapt into the air like a goat, a reaction generally associated with only the most vigorous transports of joy. He twisted so violently in his seat that the woollen upholstery of the cushion burst; Manilov cast him a look of some bewilderment. Spurred by gratitude, Chichikov at once delivered himself of so many protestations of his indebtedness that his host was quite overcome with confusion, flushed deeply, made a gesture of disavowal with his head, and finally assured his guest that it was an absolute trifle, that he had in fact wanted to find some way of demonstrating his heartfelt affinity, the magnetism of the soul, so to say, and that, in a certain sense, dead souls were mere rubbish.

'Not rubbish at all,' said Chichikov, squeezing his host's hand. Thereupon a deep sigh escaped him. He appeared to be in the mood for an outpouring of the heart; not without emotion did he at last utter the following words: 'If you only knew what a service you render, with this so-called rubbish, to one who has neither kith nor kin! For indeed, what have I not suffered? Like a barque tossed on stormy seas...* What houndings, what persecutions have I not endured, what sorrow have I not tasted, and for what? For upholding the truth, for keeping my conscience clean, for reaching out my hand both to the helpless widow and to the sorrowing orphan!...' At this point he even dabbed at an escaping tear with his handkerchief.

Manilov was profoundly moved. The two friends squeezed each other's hands at great length and stared long and silently into each other's eyes, eyes which brimmed with tears. Manilov was most loath to relinquish the hand of our hero, and continued to squeeze it with such ardour that Chichikov had great difficulty disengaging himself. Finally, having gradually worked his hand free, he ventured that it would be as well if they drew up the purchase deeds as soon as possible, and that it would be excellent if Manilov himself would come into town. Then he took his hat and started to make his farewells.

'What? You want to leave so soon?' asked Manilov, suddenly coming to his senses with something close to alarm.

At this moment Madame Manilova entered the study.

'Lizanka,' said Manilov with a woebegone look. 'Pavel Ivanovich is leaving us!'

'We must have bored Pavel Ivanovich,' answered the good lady.

'Madam!' protested Chichikov. 'Here, right here,' he placed his hand on his heart, 'there will always remain the pleasant memory of the time I spent in your company, and believe me, there could be no greater bliss for me than to live with you, if not in the same house, then at least in the closest contiguity.'

'Why, you know, Pavel Ivanovich,' said Manilov, who found this idea greatly to his liking, 'indeed how excellent it would be to live thus together, under one roof, and to philosophize about this and that in the shade of an elm-tree, to delve into the very heart of things!...'

'Oh! That would be paradise on earth!' said Chichikov with a deep sigh. 'Farewell, dear madam!' he continued, stepping up to kiss his hostess's hand. 'Farewell, most honourable friend! Do not forget my request!'

'Oh, rest assured!' answered Manilov. 'We shall be parted for no more than two days.'

They all went out into the dining-room.

'Farewell, darling sparrows!' said Chichikov to Alcides and Themistoclus, who were playing with a wooden hussar, already missing both one arm and his nose. 'Farewell my little morsels. Please forgive me for not bringing you a present, because I must confess that I did not even know of your existence in this world, but now, when I come again, I shall certainly bring something. I shall bring you a sabre: do you want a sabre?'

'Yes,' answered Themistoclus.

Dead Souls

'And for you a drum—would you not like a drum?' he continued, with a bow towards Alcides.

'Dwum,' answered Alcides in a whisper, bashfully lowering his eyes.

'Good, I shall bring you a drum. An excellent drum, and you'll go: turum-tum, tra-ta-ta, ta-ta-ta... Farewell, my sweet child! Farewell!' He kissed him on the head and turned to Manilov and his spouse with the kind of little chuckle that is usually addressed to parents as an indication of the ingenuousness of their children's desires.

'Pavel Ivanovich, you really must stay!' said Manilov, after they had stepped out on to the porch. 'Just look at those thunderclouds.'

'They are only little thunderclouds,' answered Chichikov.

'But do you know the way to Sobakevich's?'

'I intended to ask you about that.'

'Allow me to explain to your coachman at once.'

Manilov thereupon explained everything to the coachman most obligingly, addressing him in terms of great courtesy.

The coachman, hearing that he had to pass two turnings and take the third, said: 'We'll get there all right, Your Honour', and Chichikov drove off, sped on his way with much bowing and waving of handkerchiefs by his hosts, who stood on tiptoes to watch their guest depart.

For a long time thereafter Manilov remained standing on the porch, watching the chaise disappear into the distance, and even when it was quite lost to sight he still remained there, smoking his pipe. Finally he went back indoors, sat down on a chair and fell into a reverie, rejoicing in spirit at the small pleasure he had been able to afford his guest. Then his thoughts imperceptibly strayed to other matters, and were borne off heavens knows where. He thought about the bliss of a life of friendship, about how agreeable it would be to settle down with his friend on the bank of some river, then in his imagination he started to build a bridge across this river, then a most enormous house with a roof-top belvedere so high that from it they could even see as far as Moscow; here they would sit in the evenings, drinking tea in the open air and discussing various pleasant subjects. Then he imagined himself and Chichikov arriving together in fine carriages at some social gathering, where they would charm all the guests with their pleasant manners, and the Tsar himself, learning of this great friendship, would promote them both to the rank of general, and then his thoughts became so hazy that Manilov himself could no longer make sense of them. Suddenly Chichikov's strange request intruded upon his reverie. Try as he might, he simply could not fathom its meaning; he turned it over this way and that, but he was quite unable to make any sense of it, and thus he sat, smoking his pipe, right until supper-time.

CHAPTER THREE

Meanwhile Chichikov sat contentedly in his chaise, which had by now travelled far along the highway. It is already apparent from the preceding chapter what constituted the primary object of his taste and inclinations, and it is therefore small wonder that he was soon thoroughly immersed in the contemplation of this object, both in body and in soul. The assumptions, estimates, and considerations which passed through his head were clearly most agreeable, for each successive thought left behind on his face the traces of a self-contented smile.

Thus occupied, Chichikov paid no attention to his coachman, who, well pleased with the treatment Manilov's servants had accorded him, was making extremely pertinent remarks to the dappled trace-horse harnessed on the right. This dappled horse was very cunning and made a mere show of pulling, while in fact the shaft-horse, a bay, and the other trace-horse—a light chestnut called Assessor because he had been bought from an assessor—toiled away for all they were worth, pulling with such gusto that even from the look in their eyes it was evident what great pleasure this gave them.

'You think you're smart! But I'll outsmart you,' said Selifan, rising from his coach-box and lashing the shirker with his whip. 'You do your job, you German pantaloon! The bay's an honourable horse, he does his duty, I'll gladly give him an extra bagful of oats, because he's an honourable horse, and Assessor's also a good horse... What's this? Shaking our ears, are we? Listen when I talk to you, blockhead! Don't think I'll let you learn bad habits, you dunce. Look at you, crawling along!'

At this he gave the beast another lash with the whip, crying: 'Barbarian! Damned Bonaparte!'

Then he shouted at them all: 'Giddyap, my beauties!' and cracked his whip across all three, not by way of chastisement, but to show that he was pleased with them. Having thus conveyed his pleasure, he resumed his admonition of the dappled trace-horse: 'You think you can fool me? Oh no, you do the job properly if you want to be shown respect. Now those were good people at that landowner's place. I'm always happy to talk to a good man. I always get on well with a good fellow, we're sure to hit it off: we can drink tea together or have a bite to eat—it's a pleasure, if he's a good man. Everyone respects a good man. Like our master now, everyone respects him, because, d'you hear, he's done his civil service, he's an allegiate consessor...'*

Deliberating thus, Selifan finally strayed into the farthest realms of abstraction. If Chichikov had lent an ear, he would have learnt many details pertaining to his own person; but his thoughts were so taken up with his pet subject that only a loud clap of thunder brought him to his senses and made him look round; the sky was entirely covered with thunderclouds and the dusty post-road was spattered with drops of rain. Then there was an even louder and closer thunderclap and the rain suddenly came pouring down in buckets. First it took an oblique path through one window of the carriage; next it lashed down through the other; finally, changing its angle to an exact perpendicular, it drummed on the roof; and now the spray blew full into his face. This obliged him to draw the leather blinds, with their two round little peepholes, designed for the enjoyment of the roadside views, and to bid Selifan to drive faster.

Selifan, thus interrupted in the very middle of his discourse, realized that this was indeed no time for lingering, promptly pulled out an ancient grey coat from under his coach-box, thrust his arms into its sleeves, seized up the reins in both hands, and urged on his troika, which had been languidly ambling along, lulled into a pleasant torpor by his admonitory speeches. But Selifan could not for the life of him remember whether they had passed two or three turnings. With a supreme effort of memory, he finally recalled that he must have gone past a great many turnings, all of which he had ignored. Since a Russian will always find a way out of any predicament without wasting time on lengthy deliberations, he turned right at the very next crossroads, shouted: 'Off we go, my honoured friends!' and whipped the horses into a gallop, giving little thought to where the road he had taken would lead.

The rain, however, seemed to be of the persistent kind. The dust on the road soon turned into mud and with every minute it became harder for the horses to drag the chaise forward. Chichikov was already becoming seriously alarmed that they had come this far without seeing Sobakevich's village. By his calculations, they should have arrived long ago. He peered to either side, but it was so dark he could not see the nose before his face.

'Selifan!' he called at last, leaning out of the chaise.

'What is it, master?' answered Selifan.

'See if there's a village in sight!'

'No master, can't see one anywhere!'

Whereupon Selifan, brandishing his whip in the air, launched into a song, or not exactly a song, but some long, apparently interminable incantation. It contained everything: all the exclamations and interjections used to spur horses on throughout the length and breadth of Russia, and adjectives of every kind, uttered at random, just as they came to his tongue. Continuing in this vein, he even started calling the horses secretaries.

Meanwhile Chichikov noticed that the chaise was throwing him violently from side to side; this suggested to him that they must have strayed from the road and were probably careering through a furrowed field. Selifan seemed to have made the same deduction, but he held his tongue.

'Hey, you rogue, what the devil is this road you've taken?' said Chichikov.

'But what can I do, master, it's this weather: it's so dark I can't see the whip!' Saying this, Selifan caused the chaise to list so far to one side that Chichikov had to hold on with both hands. Only then did he realize that Selifan had been imbibing.

'Watch out, you're going to tip us over!' he shouted.

'No, master, how could I do a thing like that,' said Selifan. 'It wouldn't be right to tip us over, I know that; I'd never tip us over.' He then started to pull the chaise round slightly, then more and more, until it finally flopped over on its side. Chichikov was left sprawling in the mud. Selifan, did, however, halt the horses, although they would have come to a stop anyway from utter exhaustion. This unforeseen eventuality left him quite flabbergasted. Clambering down from the box he stood before the chaise, arms akimbo, while his master floundered in the mud, in a vain endeavour to regain his footing, and after some deliberation declared:

'Well, what do you know, we did come a cropper after all!'

'Why, you're blind drunk!' said Chichikov.

'No, master, how could I be drunk? I know it's a bad thing to be drunk. I had a chat with a friend, because you can chat with a good man, there's nothing wrong in that; and we had a bite together. There's no harm in having a bite; it's not wrong to have a bite with a good man.'

'And what did I tell you last time you got drunk? Well? Have you forgotten?' said Chichikov.

'No, Your Honour, how could I forget? I know my business. I know it's not seemly to be drunk. I had a chat with a good man because...'

'You wait: I'll give you such a whipping that you'll soon find out how to chat with a good man!'

'As your worship sees fit,' answered the amenable Selifan, 'if you must whip, then whip you must; I'll not say a thing against that. And why shouldn't you whip me, if there's cause—that's for the master to decide. There has to be whipping, because we peasants get out of hand, and you've got to keep order. If there's cause, whip me: why shouldn't you?'

This line of argument left his master at a loss for an answer. But at this moment it seemed fate itself had decided to take pity on him. From afar they heard the sound of dogs barking. Overjoyed, Chichikov ordered Selifan to whip up the horses.

The Russian coachman has a keen sixth sense which serves him instead of his eyesight: with his eyes shut tight, he will tear along blindly and yet will always arrive somewhere. Quite unable to see a thing, Selifan took a route to the village so straight that he only stopped when the shaft of the carriage collided with a fence and they simply could go no further. All Chichikov could see through the thick blanket of pouring rain was something that looked like a roof. He sent Selifan in search of the gate, a quest that would certainly have been of long duration were it not for the Russian custom to keep, in place of porters and gate-keepers, packs of fierce dogs. These dogs announced his arrival so clamorously that he was forced to stop his ears with his fingers. A light appeared in a little window, casting a feeble beam as far as the fence, and revealing to our travellers the whereabouts of the gate. Selifan started knocking and shortly a little door in the gate opened. A figure emerged, draped in a coarse peasant caftan, and the master and his servant heard a hoarse female voice:

'Who's knocking? What are you up to?'

'We're travellers, my good woman. Let us in for the night,' said Chichikov.

'Well I never, what impudence!' said the old woman. 'Fancy arriving at this time of night! This isn't an inn, you know, this is a lady's residence.'

'But what can we do, we lost our way. We can't spend the night in the steppe in weather like this, can we?'

'Yes, the weather's too dark, too bad,' added Selifan.

'Shut up, fool,' said Chichikov.

'But who are you anyway?' asked the old woman.

'A nobleman, my good woman.'

The word 'nobleman' seemed to give the old woman pause.

'Just wait, I'll tell the mistress,' she announced and in about two minutes she was back again, bearing a lamp.

The gates were opened. Now a faint light could be seen in another window too. The chaise drove into the yard and pulled up before a small house which was hard to discern in the darkness. Only one half of it was illuminated by the light which spilled from its windows: they could also see a puddle in front of the house, directly in the path of that faint beam of light. The rain drummed noisily on the wooden roof and poured in rivulets into the barrel set out beneath the eaves. In the mean time the dogs struck up a varied and cacophonous chorus; one, craning his head upwards, howled so assiduously that you would think he was earning some enormous fee for his toil; another rapped out his responses impatiently, like a sexton; and between these two rang, like a post-chaise bell, the shrill and indefatigable descant of what was evidently a young puppy; all this was finally drowned by a deep bass, probably that of a doughty old canine patriarch, who barked with the husky voice of a choir contrabass when the concert is in full swing, when, in their anxiety to hit a high note, the tenors stand on tiptoe and everyone and everything around cranes upwards, with heads thrown back, while he alone, unshaven chin thrust into his cravat, crouches almost to the ground and from there gives utterance to his own particular note, which makes the very windows shake and rattle.

The barking of this choir, composed of such accomplished musicians, was sufficient to make any visitor think that this was a fair-sized village; but our drenched and frozen hero was oblivious of all this and could think only of bed. Even before the chaise came to a complete standstill he sprang out on to the porch, where he lurched and almost fell. Another woman stepped out on to the porch, younger than the first but in appearance very like her. She led him inside. Chichikov stole two glances about him: the room had shabby, striped wallpaper; there were pictures of birds; between the windows hung ancient little mirrors in dark foliated frames; a letter, an old deck of cards, or a stocking was stuffed behind each mirror; a wall clock, its face decorated with flowers... He lacked the strength to observe anything more. His eyelids seemed to stick together as if they had been smeared with honey.

A minute later the mistress of the house entered, a lady in her middle years, wearing some sort of night-cap, donned in haste, with a flannel shawl about her neck, one of those small landowners who are forever grumbling about poor harvests and losses, who hold their heads somewhat inclined to one side, but who constantly squirrel away little bits of money in small calico bags, which they then conceal in various chests of drawers. Into one bag they put all the silver roubles, into another all the fifty-copeck pieces, into a third the quarters, and they tuck the little bags away into the corners so that there appears to be nothing in the drawers besides undergarments and bed jackets, and skeins of yarn, and an unstitched old jerkin, which will one day do service as a dress, if ever a hole should be burned in the old dress during the festive baking of spicy cakes and sweetmeats, or if it simply wears out by itself. But the dress will not be burnt nor wear out by itself; the old lady is thrifty and the jerkin is destined to lie many a year in its unstitched state, then to be bequeathed in the deceased's will to the niece of a third cousin, together with all manner of assorted junk.

Chichikov apologized for troubling her with his unexpected arrival.

'Never mind!' said the good lady. 'To think of travelling in this weather! Roaring and blowing and what not... You should really have something to eat after your journey, but we can't start cooking at this time of night.'

His hostess's words were interrupted by a strange hissing noise, which caused our guest considerable alarm; it sounded as though the entire room was suddenly full of snakes; but, looking up, he saw to his relief that it was merely the wall clock deciding, on an apparent whim, to chime. The hissing was followed by a wheezing, and finally, with a mighty effort, the clock chimed two o'clock, making a noise like someone striking a broken pot with a stick, whereupon the pendulum resumed its quiet oscillation from right to left.

Chichikov thanked his hostess, avowing that he needed nothing to eat, begging her not to worry about anything, that all he wanted was a bed for the night, and he merely sought to know where he had strayed and how far it was from here to Sobakevich's estate, to which the old lady retorted that she had never heard the name and there was no such landowner.

'You do at least know Manilov?' ventured Chichikov.

'And who's Manilov?'

'A landowner, madam.'

'No, never heard of him, there's no such landowner.'

'And what landowners are there hereabouts?'

'Bobrov, Svinin, Kanapatiev, Kharpakin, Trepakin, Pleshakov.'*

'Are they wealthy people or not?'

'No, sir, none of them is any too wealthy. One may have twenty souls, and another thirty, but there's none would have as many as a hundred.'

Chichikov realized he had strayed into a real backwater.

'Well, is it far to the town, at least?'

'Must be sixty versts. How sorry I am that there's nothing to eat! But wouldn't you like a cup of tea, sir?'

'No thank you, madam. I need nothing, besides a bed.'

'That's true, after a journey like that you do need a good rest. Here, my good sir, make yourself comfortable, on this sofa, right here—Fetinya, bring a feather-bed, pillows, and a sheet. What weather the good Lord has sent us: such thunder—I've kept a candle burning before the icon all night long. Goodness gracious, sir, your whole back and side are covered with mud, just like a hog! How in heaven's name did you get yourself in such a mess?'

'Thank God it's nothing worse than a mess: I should be grateful I didn't break all my bones!'

'Saints above, what calamities! But would you not like something rubbed into your back?'

'Thank you, no. Please don't trouble yourself about it, only ask your girl to put my clothes out to dry and to clean the dirt off them.'

'Do you hear, Fetinya?' called the lady, turning to the woman who had stepped out on to the porch with a candle and who now brought a feather-bed, which she had plumped up on both sides with her hands, filling the entire room with an a blizzard of feathers. 'Take the gentleman's coat and his underclothes and first dry them out before the fire like you used to do for the late master, and then give them a good rub and beat the dirt out.'

'Yes, ma'am!' said Fetinya, spreading a sheet over the feather-bed and laying out the pillows.

'So there's your bed ready for you,' said the lady. 'Farewell, sir, I wish you a good night. But do you really need nothing more? Perhaps you're used to having someone tickle your heels at night? My dear departed could never go to sleep without it.'

But her guest declined the tickling of heels too. His hostess withdrew and he undressed, handing over all his clothes as he removed them, outer and under, to Fetinya, who, also wishing him a good night, bore away this heap of dripping armour. Left alone, he gazed not without pleasure at his bed, which reached almost to the ceiling. Fetinya, it appeared, was adept at the art of plumping up feather-beds. When, after pushing up a chair, he climbed on to the bed, it sank beneath him almost to the floor, while the feathers which his weight had squeezed through the seams flew all round the room. He blew out his candle, covered himself with the patchwork quilt, curled up tightly beneath it, and instantly fell asleep.

He awoke the following day late in the morning. The sun blazed straight into his eyes and the flies, which the night before had been peacefully sleeping on the walls and ceiling, now all turned their attention to him: one alighted on his lip, another on his ear, a third buzzed about, endeavouring to land on his eyeball, and one which had the lack of forethought to position itself close to his left nostril was promptly inhaled by its half-awakened owner, who thereupon sneezed violently—and it was this circumstance that finally brought him to full consciousness.

Casting his eyes about the room, he now noticed that the pictures did not only depict birds; among them hung the portrait of Field Marshal Kutuzov and an oil-painting of some old man with red lapels on his uniform, as was the fashion under Emperor Paul.* The clocks once again began their hissing and struck the hour of ten; a woman's face peeped in at the door and promptly disappeared, for, to ensure the deepest possible sleep, Chichikov had cast off every stitch of clothing. The face which peeped in seemed vaguely familiar. He wondered who on earth it might be—and at last remembered that it was his hostess. He put on his undershirt; his clothes, by now dry and clean, lay beside him. Once dressed, he walked up to the mirror and sneezed again so loudly that a turkey cock scrabbling about just outside the window, which was very close to the ground, gobbled something in response at great speed in its strange language, presumably on the lines of: 'And a very good morning to you, too!' and was called a fool by Chichikov.

Stepping up to the window, he inspected the views that unfolded before him: the window appeared to overlook a chicken-run; at any rate, the narrow yard before it seethed with poultry and all sorts of domestic creatures. There were turkeys and chickens beyond number; amongst them a cock strutted with measured strides, shaking his comb and tipping his head to one side, as if listening out for something; right under his nose a sow and her family rooted through a heap of rubbish; in the process, the sow devoured a young chicken without even noticing and went on consuming watermelon rinds* as before. This small yard, or chicken-run, was partitioned off by a deal fence, beyond which stretched extensive vegetable gardens with cabbages, onions, potatoes, beets, and other market produce. Scattered about the garden were a few apple trees and other fruit trees, covered with nets to protect them from magpies and also from the sparrows which swept in great flocks like massive, slanting storm-clouds, from one place to another. For the same purpose several scarecrows had been erected on long poles, with outstretched arms; one of them wore a lace bonnet that had once graced the mistress herself. Beyond the vegetable garden stretched the peasants' huts, which, although scattered helter-skelter and not arranged in regular streets, did, as Chichikov remarked, demonstrate the prosperity of their occupants, for they were properly maintained: dilapidated planks on the roofs had all been replaced with new ones; none of the gates hung askew, and in some of the covered sheds facing him he could see a spare cart, sometimes even two, and these too were virtually brand new.

'Well, this little village of hers is a fair size,' he said and promptly determined to become better acquainted with the lady herself. He peeped through the gap in the doorway, through which she had earlier poked her head, and seeing her sitting at her tea table, stepped in with a cheerful smile and most affable look on his face.

'Good-day to you, sir. Did you sleep well?' she asked, rising slightly from her chair. She was more neatly attired than on the previous night—in a dark dress and no longer wearing a night-cap, but she still had something wound around her neck.

'Very well, thank you,' said Chichikov, seating himself in an armchair. 'And yourself, madam?'

'Badly, badly.'

'Why so?'

'Couldn't sleep. My backbone's aching from top to bottom and my leg, just above the knee, is throbbing unbearably.'

'It'll pass, it'll pass. There's nothing to worry about.'

'I wish to God it would. I rubbed in some pig fat, then I dabbed it with turpentine. Will you have a little nip of something with your tea? There's some fruit vodka in the flask.'

'Now that's not a bad idea, madam, perhaps I'll try the fruit vodka.'

I expect the reader has already noticed that Chichikov, despite the affable look on his face, was speaking far more freely here than he had with Manilov, and was not standing on ceremony at all. I should point out that, whilst we in Russia may in certain respects still lag behind our foreign friends, we have far outstripped them in the art of comportment. It would be impossible to enumerate all the nuances and subtleties of our behaviour. In an entire lifetime, a Frenchman or a German will never fathom or comprehend all these particularities and distinctions; he will employ almost the same tone and language when speaking with a millionaire and with a tobacco peddler, although, of course, in his soul he will be inclined to fawn on the former. With us, it is not so: among us there are people of such cleverness that they will speak with a landowner who owns two hundred souls in a manner quite unlike that in which they speak with the owner of three hundred, while with the owner of three hundred souls they will again talk quite differently from the way they will talk with him who has five hundred, and with him who has five hundred quite differently from the way they will talk with him who has eight hundred—in a word, you could go up to a million, and still not exhaust the many different nuances.

Let us imagine, for example, a government office somewhere— not here, but in the back of beyond, and in this office let us suppose there sits the office chief. I invite you to look at him while he sits amongst his subordinates—why, you will be struck dumb from sheer terror! Pride, nobility, and heaven knows what else is expressed in his face! It is a countenance that begs to be painted: a Prometheus, a veritable Prometheus! He glowers like an eagle, he stalks with measured step. Yet this same eagle, the moment he leaves his office and nears that of his own superior, begins to scurry along for all the world like a partridge with papers tucked under its wing. In society and at a *soirée*, so long as no high rank is present, Prometheus remains Prometheus, but should there appear someone ever so slightly senior to him, Prometheus undergoes a metamorphosis such as Ovid himself could never imagine: he becomes a fly, less than a fly, he is reduced to a grain of dust!

'But that's not Ivan Petrovich,' you will say, looking at him. 'Ivan Petrovich is taller, and this man is short and puny; Ivan Petrovich talks in a deep, booming voice, and never laughs, while this fellow sounds nothing like him: he twitters like a bird and keeps cackling with laughter.' You go up a little closer and look, why—it is Ivan Petrovich after all!

'Dear, oh dear!' you think to yourself...'

But let us now return to our dramatis personae. Chichikov, as we have already seen, had decided not to stand on ceremony at all and accordingly, taking up his cup of tea and pouring in a tot of fruit vodka, embarked on the following discourse:

'Now, madam, you have a fine little village here. How many souls in it?'

'There must be, well now, nigh on eighty,' said his hostess, 'but times are bad, and last year there was such a terrible harvest, may God preserve us from another such.'

'Still, the peasants look a sturdy lot, their huts are good and strong. Might I ask your surname? Remiss of me not to have asked before, but it was so late when I arrived...'

'Korobochka, widow of a Collegiate Secretary.'*

'I thank you most humbly. And your name and patronymic?'

'Nastasya Petrovna.'

'Nastasya Petrovna? Now that's a nice name, Nastasya Petrovna. I have an aunt, sister to my mother, who's a Nastasya Petrovna.'

'And what would your name be,' asked his hostess, 'for I presume you must be an assessor?'*

'No, madam,' answered Chichikov with a chuckle, 'no, indeed,

I'm not an assessor; I am merely travelling on private business.'

'Ah, so you're a buyer! Dear me, it's such a pity I sold my honey so cheaply to the merchants, or you would have bought it from me, sir, I'm sure.'

'No: honey I wouldn't have bought.'

'But what then? Hemp perhaps? I'm afraid I don't have much hemp: no more than half a pood.'*

'No madam, my merchandise is rather different. Tell me: have any of your peasants died?'

'Oh, sir, eighteen of them!' said the old lady with a sigh. 'And they were such fine fellows, the ones who died, all good workers. After this, of course, more have been born—but what good are they: all such small fry; and then the assessor comes and says I've got to pay soul tax* on them. The men are dead, but I have to pay as if for live ones. Last week my farrier was burnt to a cinder, such a skilful soul, and he could turn his hand to plumbing too...'

'So did you have a fire, madam?'

'Heavens no, the Lord preserve us from such a disaster: a fire would have been even worse; no, my good sir, he burnt himself up. He just caught fire inside, somehow: he'd had too much to drink and suddenly a blue flame came spurting out of him, he glowed and smouldered away and then turned black like charcoal—and to think he was such a skilful farrier! And now I can't go for a drive: there's no one to shoe the horses.'

'It's all the will of God, madam!' said Chichikov, with a sigh. 'There's no gainsaying the wisdom of God... Why not let me have them, Nastasya Petrovna?'

'Have whom, sir?'

'All those that died.'

'How do you mean: let you have them?'

'Just like that. Or if you like, sell them to me. I'll give you money for them.'

'But how? I don't think I quite understand—surely you don't mean to dig them up out of the ground?'

Chichikov could see that the old lady had got quite the wrong end of the stick and that he would have to explain it all very carefully to her. So, in a few words he told her that the transfer or purchase would only figure on paper and that the souls themselves would be registered as if alive.

'But what do you need them for?' asked the old lady, her eyes popping out at him.

'Well, that's my business.'

'But they're dead!'

'So who's saying they're alive? And it's for that very reason that they're a liability to you, because they're dead: you have to pay for them, and now I'm going to take that trouble and expense away from you. Do you understand? And I'm not only going to rid you of them, I'm going to pay you fifteen roubles on top. Now is it clear?'

'I must say, I don't know,' declared his hostess, speaking slowly and deliberately. 'After all, I've never sold dead ones before.'

'I should think not! It would be nothing short of miraculous if you had—or do you think there really might be some profit in them?'

'No, I don't think that. What profit would there be in them—there's no profit. The only thing that troubles me is that they're dead.'

'The woman's a stubborn old mule!' thought Chichikov. 'Now, listen to me madam,' he said, 'you work it out for yourself: if you carry on paying tax for them just like for the live ones you'll only ruin yourself...'

'Heavens, don't I know it!' interrupted the old lady. 'Only a couple of weeks ago I handed over more than a hundred and fifty. And I had to grease the assessor's palm.'

'So you see? Now, just consider that you'll never have to grease the assessor's palm again, because I'll be paying for them; me, not you. I shall take all the dues and obligations upon myself. I'll even pay for the purchase deed out of my own pocket—do you understand now?'

The old lady fell to thinking. She could see that, on the face of it, the deal was very good, only there was something too novel and odd about it, and she couldn't help suspecting that this buyer was trying to trick her; after all, God only knew where he had come from, and at such an ungodly hour, too.

'Well, then, madam, do we shake on it?' said Chichikov.

'To tell the honest truth, I've never had occasion to sell deceased folk before. Living ones I've sold of course; only the year before last I let the archpriest have two strapping girls, one hundred roubles apiece, and he was very grateful, they turned into fine workers; they can even weave napkins.'

'Yes, but we're not talking about the live ones. Don't worry about them—I want your dead.'

'I must admit, it does worry me, being the first time—I wouldn't want to bear a loss. What if you're cheating me, my good sir, and they're... and somehow they're worth more.'

'Now listen, madam... I mean, for heaven's sake—what are you saying? How could they be worth anything? Just think about it: they're dust and ashes. Do you see? Dust and ashes. Take any old piece of rubbish, even an ordinary rag, and that rag will have its price; you can always sell it to the paper factory—but those souls are totally useless. I mean, you tell me, what use are they?'

'Well yes, that is true, of course. Of course they're no earthly use at all; but there's only one thing which troubles me: they're already dead, you see.'

'What a numbskull!' said Chichikov to himself, beginning to lose patience. 'It's impossible to do business with her! She's put me all in a sweat, the cursed old hag!' Thereupon he took his handkerchief from his pocket and mopped his brow, which was indeed beaded with sweat. Chichikov's anger was, however, unfounded: even highly distinguished people, men of state, are often no better than this Korobochka. Once people like that get an idea into their heads nothing will drive it out; no matter how carefully and clearly you reason your arguments all bounce off them, like an India-rubber ball off a flat wall. Mopping his brow, Chichikov resolved on a different tack.

'Now then, my dear madam,' he said, 'either you don't want to understand my words, or you're deliberately saying that just to be difficult... I'm offering you money: fifteen roubles in banknotes. Do you understand? That's money, you know. You won't find it growing on trees. Now tell me: how much did you sell your honey for?'

'Twelve roubles the pood.'

'A little sin on your conscience there, madam. You didn't sell it for twelve roubles.'

'As God's my witness, I did.'

'Well, now do you see? And then, that was honey. You'd been collecting it for a whole year, perhaps, with all sorts of effort and bother; you had to go and smoke the bees, then feed them in your cellar throughout the winter; but dead souls are not of this world. Here you have not had to expend any energy, for it was the will of

God that they should leave this world, to the detriment of your estate. There, for your work, for your effort, you received twelve roubles, but here you're getting money for nothing, and not twelve but fifteen roubles, and not in silver, but in nice, dark blue banknotes.'* After such persuasive arguments Chichikov had no doubt but that the old woman would give in.

'The truth of the matter,' answered Korobochka, 'is that I'm only an old widow who knows nothing of these things! It would be better if I waited a little; perhaps some other buyers will come along, and I'll be able to compare prices.'

'Shame on you, madam! Shame! Just think what you're saying! Who's going to buy them? What possible use could they be to any man?'

'Who knows, maybe they might come in useful round the farm...' objected the old lady, but did not finish her sentence. Her jaw dropped and she gazed at him almost fearfully, waiting to hear his reply.

'Use the dead round the farm! Whatever next! Do you mean to scare away the sparrows from your vegetable patch at night, is that it?'

'O Lord, have mercy on us! What terrible things you are saying!' muttered the old lady, crossing herself.

'But where else did you want to use them? Anyway, you can keep all the bones and the graves; the transfer will only take place on paper. So what is it to be? Well? You might answer me at least.'

The old lady again fell to thinking.

'What's on your mind, Nastasya Petrovna?'

'To be honest, I still can't decide what to do; rather let me sell you some hemp.'

'Hemp? Why hemp? For heavens' sake, I am talking about something else entirely, and you push your hemp at me! Hemp's all very well in its own way; the next time I come I'll take your hemp too. So what is it to be, Nastasya Petrovna?'

'Honest to God, it's such a strange thing to sell. I've never heard anything like it before!'

Chichikov had reached the end of his tether. In his anger he pounded a chair against the floor and threatened her with the devil.

The good lady harboured an uncommon fear of the devil. 'Oh no, you must not mention him, God preserve us from him!' she exclaimed, going quite pale. 'Only a couple of days ago I dreamt of the old fiend all night. I'd been setting out the cards to tell my fortune after saying my prayers, and God must have sent him to me as a punishment. He looked so horrible, with horns longer than a bull's.'

'I'm only surprised that devils don't haunt your sleep by the dozen. I was merely hoping to help you, out of a Christian love of my neighbour: here, I thought, was a poor widow suffering, undergoing hardship... but you can go rot and take your village with you!'

'Oh! What terrible curses!' gasped the old lady, staring at him in terror.

'You've driven me to them! You know, you're just like the dog in the manger, if you'll excuse me for saying so. I was even going to buy some of your farm produce, because I also buy in supplies for the government...' This revelation was in fact a little fib, which slipped out quite without any ulterior motive but—to his surprise— it proved most felicitous. The mention of government supplies had a powerful effect on Nastasya Petrovna, for she responded in an almost supplicatory voice:

'But why do you get so vexed? If only I'd known earlier how vexatious you are I would never have uttered a word to cross you.'

'I'm not in the least vexed! The whole deal isn't worth a pickled egg, so why should I get vexed about it!'

'Very well then! I'm ready to let you have them for fifteen roubles. Only remember about the supplies, sir: if you need any ryeflour, or buckwheat, or groats, or slaughtered bullocks, don't pass me over.'

'No madam, I shan't pass you over,' he said, wiping his hand across his face, down which the sweat poured copiously. He asked whether she had a solicitor in the town, or an acquaintance, whom she could authorize to draw up the purchase deed and so forth.

'Well yes, there's the son of Father Kiril, the archpriest, he clerks in the chambers,' said Korobochka.

Chichikov asked her to write him a letter of authorization and, to avoid further complications, offered to draw it up himself.

'It would be a fine thing for me,' thought Korobochka in the meanwhile, 'if he were to buy some flour and cattle from me for his supplies. I must talk him round somehow: there's some batter left over from last night, so I'll go and tell Fetinya to bake pancakes; and an egg-pie would also be a good idea: they always turn out very tasty

and they don't take long!' She went out to put into effect her plan
about the egg-pie and no doubt to supplement it with other home-
baked concoctions and sweetmeats; for his part, Chichikov returned
to the drawing-room where he had spent the night, in order to fetch
the necessary papers from his little box.

The drawing-room had long since been thoroughly tidied up, the
luxurious feather-bed had been borne away and before the settee
there now stood a table, covered with a cloth. Setting his box upon
it Chichikov rested for a moment, for he was drenched with sweat:
every scrap of clothing on his body, from his shirt to his stockings,
was wringing wet. 'That cursed old hag has me totally finished!' he
said, after resting for a moment, and opened his box.

The author is convinced that some of his readers are of such an
inquisitive disposition that they would like to know the design and
inner layout of the box. Very well, why not satisfy their curiosity! As
to the inner layout: at the very centre was a soap box; behind the
soap box there were six or seven narrow compartments for razors;
then rectangular recesses for blotting-sand and an inkwell, with a
boat-shaped groove cut between them to hold the quills, sealing-
wax, and other longer instruments; then there were all sorts of
compartments—with and without little lids—for the shorter objects,
crammed full of visiting cards, memorial cards, theatre tickets, and
so forth, which had been kept as souvenirs. The entire upper drawer,
with all its compartments, could be removed to reveal beneath it a
space crammed full of papers, and beneath this a small secret drawer
for money, cunningly fitted to one side of the box. It was always
opened and shut by its owner with such rapidity that it was impossible to say for certain how much money it contained.

Chichikov at once set to work, sharpening his quill and starting to
write. At this moment his hostess entered the room.

'That's a nice box you have,' she said, sitting down next to him.
'I suppose you bought it in Moscow?'

'Yes, in Moscow,' answered Chichikov, still busy writing.

'I knew it; you can tell by the quality. The year before last my
sister brought back from Moscow some warm boots for the children:
so solidly made they're still wearing them. My goodness, what a lot
of official crested paper* you have!' she continued, peeping into his
box. Indeed, there was a considerable quantity of crested paper.
'Couldn't you give me one little sheet? I'm so short of official paper;

sometimes you have to submit petitions to the courts and there's nothing to write them on.'

Chichikov had to explain to her that this was a different sort of paper, that it was intended for purchase deeds and not for petitions. To appease her, however, he gave her one sheet with a stamp value of one rouble. When he had finished his letter he passed it to her to sign and asked for a list of the peasants. It transpired that the old lady did not keep any records or lists, but knew practically every name by heart; so he prevailed upon her to dictate them to him there and then. Some of the peasants rather surprised him with their names and even more with their nicknames, causing him to pause each time before writing them down. He was particularly struck by one Pyotr Saveliev Neuvazhai-Koryto*—or 'Disdain-the-Trough'—and couldn't stop himself from commenting: 'What a long one!' Another had the tag attached to his name: 'Cow's Brick', a third was simply 'Ivan the Wheel'. When he had finished he took a deep breath and caught the tantalizing smell of hot food and melted butter.

'Be so kind as to partake of this humble fare,' said his hostess.

Chichikov looked round and saw the table already laden with mushrooms, pies, dumplings, doughnuts, muffins, pancakes, pastries with all sorts of fillings: onion pastries, poppy-seed pastries, cream-cheese pastries, sparling pastries, and the Lord knows what else besides.

'Have some egg-pie,' said his hostess.

Chichikov embarked on the egg-pie and promptly devoured the better half of it with extravagant expressions of praise. Indeed the pie was very tasty, and after all the fuss and bother he had had with the old lady it seemed all the tastier.

'How about some pancakes?' she asked.

In reply, Chichikov rolled three pancakes up together and, dunking them in melted butter, guided them into his mouth. He then wiped his lips and hands dry with a napkin. After repeating this procedure about three times he asked his hostess to order his carriage. Nastasya Petrovna at once dispatched Fetinya, directing her at the same time to bring some more hot pancakes.

'I must say, madam, your pancakes are very good,' said Chichikov, as he fell upon the hot ones that had just been brought in.

'Yes, my girls cook them well; the only trouble is, the harvest was poor, and the flour is not so good... But why are you in such a hurry, sir?' she asked, seeing Chichikov take up his cap. 'Your chaise has not been brought round yet.'

'Oh, they'll bring it round. It doesn't take long to get it ready.'

'But please, don't forget about the supplies.'

'No, no, I shan't forget,' said Chichikov, stepping out into the hallway.

'How about pork fat—would you like to buy some of mine?' asked his hostess, walking behind him.

'Yes, why not? I'll buy some, only later.'

'I'll have some pork fat ready for yuletide.'*

'We'll buy some, we will, we'll buy a bit of everything, and we'll buy some pork fat too.'

'Perhaps you need some feathers? I will have feathers too, by St Philip's fast.'*

'Fine, fine,' said Chichikov.

'There you see, your chaise is not ready yet,' said his hostess, when they were out on the porch.

'It'll be ready in good time. Just tell me how to get to the main road.'

'Now let me see, which is your best way?' asked Korobochka. 'It's hard to explain, there are so many turnings: it would be better if I gave you a girl to guide you. I expect there's room for her, up on the coach-box?'

'There is, of course.'

'Yes, I think I should give you one of my girls. She knows the way, only don't you drive off with her; some merchants did that once with a girl of mine.'

Chichikov assured her of the girl's safety and Korobochka, her mind set at rest, turned her attention to all the activity in her yard; she peered closely at the housekeeper, emerging from the cellar bearing a wooden cask full of honey, then at a peasant who appeared in the gateway, and little by little she became reabsorbed in her usual household cares.

But why do we spend so long on Korobochka? What do we care for Korobochka or Madam Manilova? What matters it to us how well—or badly—they run their households? Let us press on! What should cause us to marvel, on the other hand, is the way things are ordered in this world: joy will instantly turn into sadness if you linger too long before it, and then God only knows what manner of thing will stray into the mind. You might even start thinking: come now, does Korobochka really stand so low on the endless ladder of human self-improvement? Is there really such a vast chasm separating her from the grand lady, securely ensconced behind the walls of an aristocratic house with its fragrant wrought-iron balustrades, its gleaming brass, its mahogany, and its carpets, who yawns over an unfinished book as she waits for her next fashionable and witty visitor, when she will be able to display her own brilliance and give utterance to various hackneyed sentiments, sentiments which—in accordance with the laws of fashion—occupy the town for an entire week. These are not thoughts about the affairs of the house and the estate, which has been reduced to a state of neglect and disorder by incompetence and mismanagement, but speculation about the political upheavals imminent in France, or the latest trends in the fashionable religion of Catholicism.*

But let us press on, let us press on!—Why need we speak of this? Yet why is it that, amidst our most unthinking, carefree, and insouciant moments another, quite bizarre train of thought should suddenly flash past, entirely of its own accord; the laughter has hardly died on a man's face, yet he has become a stranger among his fellows and his face is now lit up by a different light...

'Ah, there's the chaise! There's the chaise!' exclaimed Chichikov, when at last he saw it drive up. 'What kept you so long, you dunderhead? I suspect you still haven't shaken off the effects of yesterday's binge.'

To this Selifan made no answer.

'Farewell, madam! And where's this girl of yours?'

'Come, Pelageya!' called the old lady to a girl of about eleven, loitering by the porch in a home-dyed dress and in bare feet which, from a distance, could have passed for boots, so caked were they with fresh mud. 'Show the master the way.'

Selifan helped the girl up on to the coach-box; planting one bare foot on the running board, she spattered mud all over it, and then clambered up on top and seated herself behind the coachman. After her Chichikov hoisted his own foot on to the running-board, and causing the chaise to tilt to the right because he was a little on the heavy side, finally installed himself, declaring:

'There now, we're all set! Farewell, madam!'

The horses moved off.

Selifan was moody throughout the journey and at the same time exceptionally attentive to his duties, as was his way when he had committed some peccadillo or had been on a binge. The horses had been splendidly groomed. The collar on one of them, which had always been very tattered, with oakum sticking out of the leather, had now been skilfully sewn together. He remained silent throughout the journey, only cracking his whip and delivering no admonitions to the horses, although the dappled trace-horse would of course have preferred to hear some words of edification, for at such times the loquacious driver would idly relax his hold on the reins and the whip would only play across the horses' backs for form's sake. But on this occasion the only sounds to issue from those sullen lips were monotonous and surly exclamations: 'Look at you, old crow, yawning away!'—and nothing further. Even the bay and Assessor were disgruntled never once to hear the words: 'My kind sirs' or 'Your Honours'. The dappled horse received some extremely nasty lashes across his broad, plump haunches. 'What's got into him!' he thought to himself, flattening his ears. 'He knows where to aim his whip all right! He doesn't flick you across the back, but finds the spot where it hurts most: he whacks you on the ears or lashes you under the belly.'

'Turn right, do we?' Selifan asked the girl sitting by his side, as he pointed with his whip to the rain-blackened road that led between the bright green, fresh-smelling fields.

'No, no; I'll tell you when,' answered the girl.

'So, which way do we go, then?' asked Selifan, when they had driven up closer.

'That way,' answered the girl, pointing.

'For heaven's sake!' said Selifan. 'We do turn right: she doesn't know her right from her left!'

Although it was a fine day, the ground had become so muddy that the wheels of the chaise were soon thickly caked as if with felt, and this considerably impeded their progress; furthermore, the soil was loamy and extraordinarily sticky. In consequence it was past noon before they were clear of the cart tracks. Without the girl they would not even have got that far, because roads forked off in every direction, like captured crawfish when they are shaken out of the sack, and, through no fault of his own, Selifan would have floundered about for hours. Soon the girl pointed at something looming darkly in the distance and announced:

'There's the highway!'

'And that building?' asked Selifan.

'That's the inn,' said the girl.

'Well, now we can go on by ourselves,' said Selifan. 'You run along home.'

He stopped and helped her alight, muttering through his teeth: 'Look at those filthy feet!'

Chichikov gave her a copper coin and she skipped off homewards. Just to sit on a coach box had been happiness enough.

CHAPTER FOUR

As they drove up to the inn Chichikov called a halt for two reasons. On the one hand he wished to rest the horses, and on the other he himself wanted a bite to eat and some liquid sustenance. The author is obliged to confess that he is most envious of the appetite and digestion of such people. He has no time at all for all the grand folk of St Petersburg and Moscow, who spend an age deliberating what they would like to eat tomorrow and what they might fancy for dinner the day after tomorrow, never embarking on these dinners without first swallowing a pill, after which they gobble down their oysters, sea spiders, and other horrors and then go off to Karlsbad or the Caucasus for a cure. No, these gentlemen have never excited his envy. But people of the middle estate, who at one post-house order ham, at the next, sucking pig, at the third, a collop of sturgeon or a spiced sausage fried with onions, and then, quite as if they had not eaten all day, will sit down at any time you like and tuck into a bowl of sterlet soup with burbot and soft roe, which hisses and sizzles between their teeth, followed by kedgeree pie or a sheat-fish pastry—just to watch them makes your mouth water. These people are truly blessed with a most enviable gift from heaven! Many a gentleman of quality would, without a moment's hesitation, sacrifice half his serfs and half his estates, mortgaged and unmortgaged, complete with all improvements in the foreign and the Russian manner, to have a digestion such as that of his less exalted brethren, but the sad truth is that no amount of money, nor estates, with or without improvements, can buy the kind of digestion generally enjoyed by people of the middle estate.

The well-weathered timber inn received Chichikov beneath its narrow but welcoming eaves, supported by chiselled wooden posts, which were not unlike antique church candlesticks. The inn was built somewhat in the manner of a Russian peasant house, only on a larger scale. The woodcarver's lace, fashioned from new wood, that surrounded the windows and ran along the eaves stood out brightly against the dark walls; the shutters were decorated with paintings of jugs of flowers.

As he climbed up the narrow wooden staircase into the wide

vestibule a door creaked open to reveal a fat old woman, clad in a gaudy cotton print, who announced: 'This way, please!' Inside he found all the old friends, familiar to anyone who has put up in small inns of this kind so common along our roads, to wit: a samovar, discoloured as if covered with hoar-frost; smoothly planed pine walls; a three-cornered dresser in the corner with teapots and cups; gilt porcelain eggs suspended below the icons on blue and red ribbons; a cat that has recently kittened; a mirror, reflecting not two, but four eyes and some sort of a pancake instead of a face; and, finally, little bunches of fragrant herbs and carnations tucked behind the icons, but so desiccated that anyone leaning forward to smell them would only sneeze and nothing more.

'Do you have sucking pig?' enquired Chichikov of the woman standing before him.

'We do.'

'With horseradish and sour cream?'

'With horseradish and sour cream.'

'Let's have some then!'

The old woman went off and brought out a plate, a napkin, starched so stiff that it was buckled like a piece of dried bark, then a knife with a yellowed bone handle and a blade as thin as a pen-knife, a two-pronged fork, and a salt cellar which refused to stand upright on the table.

Our hero, as was his wont, at once struck up a conversation with the old woman, inquiring whether she herself were the innkeeper, or if there was a landlord, and what sort of income the inn brought in, and whether her sons lived with them, and was the eldest son a bachelor or married, and what sort of wife he had taken, with a big dowry or not, and had the father-in-law been content, or had he been angry that he had received so few gifts at the wedding—in a word, he overlooked nothing. Needless to say, he also satisfied his curiosity as to the local landowners, and learnt that there were many: Blokhin, Pochitaev, Mylnoy, Colonel Cherpakov,* and Sobakevich. 'Ah! You know Sobakevich?' he asked, and thereupon learnt that the old woman knew not only Sobakevich, but also Manilov, and that Manilov was the more particular of the two: he would straight away demand a boiled chicken, and would also call for some veal; if she had lamb's liver he would order that too, but he would only nibble at all this, while Sobakevich would order only one thing, but would then eat the lot and even demand a second helping, refusing to pay extra for it.

Thus engaged in conversation, and in the consumption of his sucking pig, of which only the last morsel remained to be eaten, he heard the rattle of a carriage driving up outside. Looking through the window he espied a light chaise that had drawn up before the inn, pulled by three handsome horses. Two men alighted from the carriage. One was fair and tall; the other not quite so tall, and swarthy. The former was clad in a dark blue hussar's jacket, the latter more simply attired in a striped caftan. In the distance another carriage could be seen, heading for the inn: a small, scruffy calèche, empty and dragged along by a shaggy foursome with tattered collars and rope harness. The fair-haired gentleman at once ascended the staircase, whilst his swarthy companion remained behind, groping for something in the chaise, at the same time talking to the servant and waving to the carriage that had followed them. His voice struck Chichikov as somehow familiar.

While he was thus inspecting him, the fair-haired traveller managed to find the door and open it. He was a tall man, with gaunt features—or what they call a raddled face—and a small ginger moustache. From his bronzed complexion one could conclude that he was no stranger to smoke, of at least the tobacco, if not the gunpowder, variety. He made a courteous bow to Chichikov, which the latter returned in like manner. In all probability, they would have fallen into conversation and have become well acquainted in a matter of minutes, as the foundations had already been laid, with both almost simultaneously expressing their pleasure at the way the dust on the road had been completely laid by the previous day's rain and how cool and agreeable the weather was for driving, had not his swarthy comrade entered at precisely that moment, flinging his cap on to the table, and running his hand through his hair, ruffling it up in a devil-may-care manner. This was a well-built fellow of medium height, with full, ruddy cheeks, teeth white as snow, and whiskers black as pitch. From his vigour and the fresh look on his face, it was clear that he was in the very pink of health.

'Well, well, well!' he exclaimed suddenly, throwing out both arms on seeing Chichikov. 'What brings you here?'

Chichikov recognized Nozdryov, the very same Nozdryov whom he had met at the dinner given by the public prosecutor and who in the space of a very few minutes had assumed such close familiarity with Chichikov, although, for his part, Chichikov had done nothing to encourage this.

'Where've you been?' inquired Nozdryov, and, without waiting for a reply, continued: 'I've just come from the fair, old chap. Congratulate me, I'm cleaned out—clean as a whistle! Would you believe it, never in all my life have I been cleaned out like that! I even had to come home with hired horses. Take a look through the window!'

Here he wrenched Chichikov's head round with such force that he almost struck it against the window frame.

'Did you ever see such rubbish! Those old nags only just made it here, confound them, so I had to climb over into his chaise.'

As he said this, Nozdryov pointed a finger at his comrade. 'Oh—you don't know each other yet, do you? My brother-in-law Mizhuev! We've been talking about you all morning. "Just you wait," I said, "I bet we run into Chichikov." You should have seen how they cleaned me out, old chap! Would you believe it, I had to let them take my four trotters—and not only that: I even lost the shirt off my back. I've neither a chain, nor a watch to hang on it...' Chichikov looked and saw that he did indeed have neither watch nor chain. It even seemed to him that one of Nozdryov's whiskers was shorter and less bushy than the other. 'And yet if I had only had another twenty roubles in my pocket,' continued Nozdryov, 'not a copeck more, I would have won it all back and more, I tell you, as I'm an honest man, I would have come away with thirty thousand in my wallet.'

'But that's just what you said at the time,' objected the fair-haired traveller, 'and when I gave you fifty roubles, you promptly lost the lot.'

'But I shouldn't have! Honest to God, I shouldn't have lost that fifty! If I hadn't been so stupid, I wouldn't have lost it. I should never have raised on that confounded seven after we had doubled the stakes—if I hadn't I could have broken the bank.'

'But you didn't break it,' observed his fair-haired companion.

'I didn't break it because I raised too early. Do you really think that major of yours knows his cards?'

'Whether he knows them or not, he still beat you.'

'So what if he did?' said Nozdryov. 'But I'll beat him yet. No, next time he should go for double or quits and then we'll see what sort of a player he is! All the same, Chichikov, old man, those first few days we had terrific fun! I must say, that fair was one of the best ever. Even the merchants were saying they'd never had such a good crowd. All the stuff we brought from the village we sold at the very best prices. Brother, did we have fun! Even now, when I think back... Damnation! I mean, it's such a pity you weren't with us. Would you believe it, there was a regiment of dragoons stationed just out of town, only three versts away. Just imagine: all those officers—forty officers at least—were in town—the whole damn lot of them; and then, brother, the wine really started to flow... Staff Captain Potseluev... now there's a fine chap! Brother, you should see his whiskers! Bordeaux—he calls "bawdy slops!" "Hey, waiter, bring us a bottle of your bawdy slops!" he orders. Lieutenant Kuvshinnikov*... Ah, brother, now there's a first-rate fellow! A drinking man to the marrow of his bones! We were together the whole time.

'You should see the wine we bought off old Ponomaryov! Mark my words, he's a scoundrel and you mustn't buy anything in his shop; he puts all sorts of rubbish in the wine: sandalwood, burnt cork, and even elderberries, the rogue! But if you can get him to bring you a bottle from his little room at the back, his special store he calls it—now that, brother, will have you floating in the Empyrean fields. That fizz he brought us—after a sip of that the governor's champagne tastes like kvass! Just imagine, that was no mere Cliquot, but some sort of Cliquot Matradura—that means double Cliquot. And then he bought us another bottle of that French stuff called Bon-Bon. You should have smelt the bouquet—pure roses. Did we have fun!... After us some prince or other arrived, sent out for champagne, and there wasn't a bottle left in town, the officers had drunk the lot. Would you believe it, I alone flattened seventeen bottles of champagne during a single dinner!'

'Come now, you couldn't drink seventeen bottles,' objected his fair-haired companion.

'I swear it, on my word of honour: seventeen bottles,' insisted Nozdryov.

'Say what you like, but I'm telling you you couldn't even drink ten.'

'Will you wager that I can't?'

'Wager what?'

'That gun, for example, the one you bought in town.'

'No, not the gun.'

'Go on, take a chance on it.'

'Thank you, I don't wish to take any chances.'

'If you did, it'd be the last you saw of your gun. Damn it, Chichikov, my dear chap, I mean, what a pity you weren't there. I know you and Lieutenant Kuvshinnikov would have hit it off. Oh yes, you'd have got on like a house on fire. That Kuvshinnikov's not like our public prosecutor, he's no provincial skinflint like those penny-pinching officials of ours. This, brother, is a chap who'll take you on at bezique or faro,* or what you will.

'Damnation, Chichikov, why didn't you come? You're a real swine, you know that?—a pig-swiller, that's what! My dear chap, give me a kiss, you know how I love you! I say, Mizhuev, isn't it marvellous how fate has brought us together? I mean, what's he to me or I to him? He's come here from the back of beyond, and I live here too... And, brother, you should have seen the carriages, millions of them. I had a crack at the old lucky wheel: I won two jars of pomade, a china tea-cup, and a guitar; then I put it all back on for one more spin and lost the lot, damn and blast, plus six roubles on top. But that Kuvshinnikov fellow, you should see him, such a lady's man! He and I went to practically every ball in the place. There was one wench, dressed up like a doll, you know, all frills and flounces and God knows what else... There I was saying to myself: "Well, I'll be damned!" But that scoundrel Kuvshinnikov, he's such an old goat, he goes and sits next to her and spouts all these fancy compliments in French... Believe it or not, he couldn't even keep his hands off the peasant women. He calls it "sampling the local strawberries". The merchants brought in some marvellous fish, especially the smoked sturgeon. In fact I've brought some sturgeon with me; it's a good thing I thought of buying it while I still had the money. Where are you bound for now?'

'I have to go and see a fellow I know,' said Chichikov.

'To blazes with him! Come to my place!'

'No I cannot, I have business to do.'

'Ha! Business, is it now? What a pack of lies! Castor-oil Ivanovich!'*

'It's true, I do have business, and important business too.'

'I'll wager you're lying! Come, tell me: whom are you going to see?'

'Sobakevich, as it happens.'

Here Nozdryov burst into peals of ringing laughter, of the sort that could only be produced by a hale and hearty man such as he, with all his sugar-white teeth exposed to view and his jowls trembling and shaking, the kind of laugh that causes a fellow traveller sleeping somewhere behind double doors three rooms away to wake with a violent start, rub his eyes and mutter: 'Now what the devil's got into him!'

'What's so funny about that?' asked Chichikov, somewhat disconcerted by this hilarity.

Nozdryov only continued to roar with laughter, at intervals gasping:

'Have mercy on me, I can't bear it: I'm going to split my sides!'

'There's nothing funny about it: I gave him my word,' said Chichikov.

'You'll be sorry you ever lived to see the light of day when you get to his place: he's a thorough skinflint! Remember, I know the sort of chap you are, and you're grievously mistaken if you're hoping for a little game of bezique and a nice bottle of Bon-Bon when you get there. You listen to me, brother: to the devil with Sobakevich, come to my place! I'll treat you to some superb sturgeon! Ponomaryov, the old swine, started bowing and scraping and said: "This is specially for you", he said. "You can search the whole fair and you won't find another like it". But he's a terrible rogue. I told him so to his face: "You and that liquor concessionaire of ours," I said, "you're the biggest scoundrels in town." He just laughed, the swine, stroking his beard. Kuvshinnikov and I took our breakfast at his stall every morning. I say, old chap, I almost forgot: I know you'll never give up trying, but I won't let you have it, not even for ten thousand, I warn you in advance. Hey, Porfiry!'

Going to the window, he summoned his man, who in one hand was clutching a little knife and in the other a crust of bread and a chunk of the sturgeon which he had managed to purloin while unloading something from the chaise.

'Hey, Porfiry!' shouted Nozdryov, 'bring me that pup! This is no ordinary pup,' he continued, turning to Chichikov. 'Had to steal him, you know; the owner said he wouldn't sell him to save his own life. I even offered him my chestnut mare—you remember, the one I got in a swap from Khvostyryov...' Chichikov did not, however, know Khvostyryov from Adam, nor had he ever clapped eyes on the chestnut mare.

'Master! Nothing to eat or drink for you?' asked the old woman, entering at this moment.

'No, nothing. Brother, did we have fun! On second thoughts, you could bring me a glass of vodka; what kind do you have?'

'Aniseed,' answered the old woman.

'Bring me some aniseed then,' said Nozdryov.

'And a glass for me too!' called the fair-haired friend.

'In the theatre there was an actress, confound it, who sang like a canary! Kuvshinnikov was sitting next to me and you know what he said? "Brother," he said "wouldn't you like to sample that little strawberry!" I reckon there must have been a good fifty booths at that fair. Old Fenardi* turned cartwheels for four solid hours.' At this point he took his glass from the old woman, who handed it to him with a low bow.

'Aha, bring him here!' he cried, seeing Porfiry coming in with the puppy. Porfiry was dressed just like his master, in a sort of quilted, but somewhat grubby, caftan.

'Bring him here, put him down on the floor!'

Porfiry put the puppy down and it sprawled out on its four legs and started sniffing the floor.

'Now that's what I call a pup!' said Nozdryov, catching it by the scruff of the neck and hoisting it up. The puppy gave a rather plaintive squeal.

'But you didn't do as I ordered,' said Nozdryov, turning to Porfiry and carefully inspecting the puppy's belly. 'You didn't give him a brushing, did you?'

'Yes I did.'

'So where do all these fleas come from?'

'I couldn't say. Perhaps they jumped on to him from the chaise.'

'You're a lying scoundrel, you never brushed him; if you ask me you've given him some of yours as well. Now have a good look, Chichikov, look at those ears, just feel them with your hand.'

'No thank you, I can see them from here: a fine specimen!' answered Chichikov.

'No—I insist, take hold of an ear and feel it!'

To humour him Chichikov felt the puppy's ears and agreed: 'Yes, he'll grow into a fine dog all right!'

'Now feel his nice cold nose. Touch it with your hand.' Anxious not to offend, Chichikov felt the puppy's nose, declaring: 'He'll have a good scent.'

'He's got a good muzzle on him,' continued Nozdryov, 'I've always wanted one with big jowls like that. All right, Porfiry, you can take him away now!'

Porfiry picked up the puppy and carried it back to the chaise.

'Listen, Chichikov, you must leave with me immediately, it's only five versts, we'll get there in two shakes of a lamb's tail and then you can go on to Sobakevich's.'

'What the hell,' thought Chichikov, 'why not just go to Nozdryov's after all? He's no worse than any of the others, cast in the same mould, on top of which he's lost money. He seems game for anything, so who knows, I might be able to wheedle something out of him for nothing.'

'Very well, let's go,' he said, 'but I mustn't tarry long, my time is precious.'

'Now that's more like it, my dear chap! That's splendid—hang on a second, let me give you a kiss for it.' Whereupon Nozdryov and Chichikov embraced. 'Excellent: we shall drive on, all three together!'

'No, if you don't mind, I must excuse myself,' said the fair-haired companion, 'I'd better be getting home.'

'Stuff and nonsense, brother, I shan't let you go.'

'Honestly, my wife will be angry; and now you can travel in this gentleman's chaise.'

'No, no, no! I won't hear of it.'

The fair-haired companion was one of those men whose characters appear at first to show a stubborn streak. No sooner have you opened your mouth to speak than they are preparing to dispute what you say and will apparently never agree with anything that is manifestly contrary to their own manner of thinking, nor will they ever mistake stupidity for wisdom, and under no circumstances will they ever dance to another man's tune; but in the end they're no different from the rest: they always turn out to be soft, they agree to the very thing they have so vehemently opposed, they do mistake stupidity for wisdom, and they prove to be very good at dancing to someone else's tune: what at first looks like glory ends up the same old story.

'Nonsense!' barked Nozdryov in answer to some suggestion from his fair-haired friend, put on his hat for him—and the friend tagged along with them after all.

'Master! You haven't paid for the vodka,' said the old woman.

'Ah yes, of course. Listen, brother-in-law, settle up, will you? I haven't a copeck in my pocket.'

'What do we owe you?' asked the brother-in-law.

'A silver twenty will do.'

'Nonsense. Give her a copper fifty,* that's more than enough.'

'It's not enough, master,' protested the old woman, nevertheless accepting the proffered money with gratitude and eagerly bustling forward to open the door for them. She was not out of pocket as she had charged four times what the vodka cost.

The travellers took their places. Chichikov's chaise travelled alongside the chaise bearing Nozdryov and his brother-in-law, and thus all three were able to converse with one another the entire length of the journey. They were followed at a steadily increasing distance by Nozdryov's little buggy, pulled by its scrawny hired horses. In it sat Porfiry and the puppy.

Since the conversation between our voyagers would be of no great interest to the reader, we would do better to take a closer look at Nozdryov, who may be destined to play a not insignificant role in our poem.

People of Nozdryov's type are no doubt already fairly familiar to the reader. We have all had occasion to encounter a great many like him. They are called lovable rogues even as children and at school they are known to make good friends, although they are often subjected to quite painful thrashings. Their faces always display something open, direct, and devil-may-care. They make friends easily, and in no time are on the most intimate terms with them. Eternal friendship is declared, but somehow it invariably happens that the new friends quarrel that very same evening, on their first night on the town. They are past masters at spinning yarns, carousing, and cutting a dash; they like to be noticed and admired.

At the age of thirty-five Nozdryov was exactly the same as he had been at eighteen and at twenty: a great one for drinking and making merry. Marriage had not changed him one whit, the more so since his wife soon quit him for a better world, leaving behind two youngsters, for whom Nozdryov had no time at all. The children were, however, taken care of by a pretty young nursemaid.

He was quite incapable of sitting at home for more than one day at a time. His sharp nose could sniff out a village fair, with all its gatherings and balls, at a distance of twenty or more versts; in the twinkling of an eye he would be there, to enter the lines at the green baize tables, for, like all such men, he had a great passion for cards. His card playing, as we have already seen in the first chapter, was not altogether unimpeachable, since he knew many different little ruses and other subtle manœuvres, and therefore his evenings very often ended with a different sort of game: either he would be dealt a sound boot-inflicted drubbing, or his abundant and most impressive side-whiskers would receive such an energetic tugging that he sometimes returned home with one whisker only, and that rather bedraggled. But his full and healthy cheeks were so well constituted and had such growing power that a new side-whisker would soon grow back, even better than the old one. But strangest of all—and this is the sort of thing that could only be possible in Russia—after a little while he would be playing cards again with the very same friends who had thrashed him: they would meet as if nothing had happened; he would think nothing of it, and they would think nothing of it.

In a sense, Nozdryov was a history-making man, for no gathering at which he was present could proceed without an *histoire*. Either he was escorted out of the room by gendarmes, or kicked out by his own companions. If not this, then something else, the kind of thing that never happens to anyone else: he would either get so sozzled in the refreshment room that he could do nothing but giggle inanely, or he would tell such tall tales that he would shame even himself. He would tell the most pointless lies, suddenly announcing that he once had a horse with a pale blue or pink coat, and gradually drive away all his listeners, who would mutter as they retreated: 'For heaven's sake, old man, you do talk a load of rot!'

There are people who simply love to take unfair advantage of their fellow men, sometimes for no reason at all. Among them you can find high-ranking officials, upstanding citizens with the most noble bearing and stars on their chest, who will shake your hand, converse with you on matters profound and thought-provoking, and then—to your astonishment and right before your very eyes—will play some dirty trick on you. And they will do it just as if they were paltry collegiate registrars,* and not upstanding citizens with stars on their chest, capable of conversation on matters profound and thought-provoking, so that you can only stand in wonderment, and shrug your shoulders.

Nozdryov had this very same quirk. The closer his friendship grew with another man, the more he would single this same friend out for his malice: he would spread some unimaginably ridiculous slander about him, break up his betrothal or business deals and yet would not in any way regard himself as his enemy; on the contrary, if fate were to bring them together again he would treat him as a long-lost friend, even saying: 'You're such a scoundrel, you never call on me!'

Nozdryov was a man of many parts, by which we mean he could turn his hand to many things. At one and the same moment he would offer to accompany you anywhere you liked, even to the ends of the earth, to embark on any business venture under the sun, and to exchange anything at all for whatever you wished. His gun, dog, horse—to him they were all objects for barter with no thought at all of profit: the exchange would be prompted entirely by his quick wit and insuppressible high spirits. If he had the good fortune to come across a simpleton at the fair and clean him out at cards he would at once squander the money on the first thing he clapped eyes on: horse collars, incense sticks, kerchiefs for the nursemaid, a stallion, raisins, a silver wash-stand, Dutch sailcloth, wheaten flour, tobacco, pistols, salted herrings, pictures, a grindstone, pots, boots, crockery—until the money ran out.

These purchases rarely reached home, however; later that very same day they would probably all be lost to another, luckier player, sometimes with the addition of his pipe, complete with tobacco pouch and mouthpiece, or even his coach-and-four together with the coachman, leaving the bereft owner to set off in his short coat or caftan in search of some crony or other who would let him share his carriage. For such a one was Nozdryov! People may think his type extinct, and assert there are no Nozdryovs today. Alas! Those who say so are mistaken. Nozdryovs will be around in this world for a long time to come. They are everywhere amongst us, except perhaps wearing a different caftan; but people are careless and lacking in perspicacity, and to them a man in a different caftan is a different man.

In the mean time the three carriages had already rolled up to the porch of Nozdryov's house. In the house nothing had been prepared for their arrival. Two wooden trestles had been placed in the middle of the dining-room, and on these stood two peasants, who were whitewashing the walls to the lusty accompaniment of an interminable song; the floor was thoroughly bespattered with whitewash. Nozdryov at once told the men to make themselves scarce with their trestles and dashed into the next room to issue instructions. His guests heard him order the cook to make luncheon; realizing the implications of this, Chichikov, whose appetite had started to revive, calculated that it would be at least five o'clock before they sat down to table. Nozdryov meanwhile returned and took his guests on a conducted tour of his estate, but in a little over two hours he had shown them absolutely everything, as there simply was nothing more to show. First of all they went to inspect the stables, where they saw two mares, one a piebald dun, the other a chestnut, and then a bay stallion, not particularly prepossessing to look at, but for which Nozdryov claimed to have paid ten thousand.

'You never paid ten thousand for him,' remarked the brother-in-law. 'He's not even worth one thousand.'

'I swear to God, I paid ten thousand,' said Nozdryov.

'You can swear till you're blue in the face,' retorted the brother-in-law.

'Well then, let's take a wager on it!' said Nozdryov.

The brother-in-law declined this offer.

Then Nozdryov showed them some empty stalls, where previously there had been other fine horses. In this same stable they did, however, see a billy-goat which, in accordance with an old superstition, was kept with the horses, and which appeared to be on good terms with them, strolling about blithely beneath their bellies. Then Nozdryov took them to see a wolf-cub which he kept on a chain.

'Now there's a wolf-cub!' he said. 'I feed him raw meat because I want him to grow into a fierce beast!'

They went to view the pond in which, according to Nozdryov, there were fish of such great dimensions that it took two men to lift each one of them, and then only with extreme difficulty, another story about which his brother-in-law was quick to express reservations.

'Now Chichikov,' said Nozdryov, 'I shall show you a superb pair of borzoi hounds: the strength of their black haunches is simply incredible, and their muzzles—pointed like needles!'

He led the way to an elegantly constructed little house, surrounded on all sides by a large walled yard. Entering this yard they saw a great variety of dogs, shaggy-haired and smooth-haired, of every possible coat and colour: black and tan, black with white flecks, dun-skewbald, spotted-skewbald, brown skewbald, black-eared, grey-eared... All the known canine names were represented: Shooter, Scolder, Flapper, Blaze, Boaster, Blasphemy, Pesty, Scorcher, Jumpy, Dolly, Prize, Headmistress.* With them Nozdryov was like a father amongst his children; they all at once hoisted their tails—or 'rudders', as dog-fanciers call them—and dashed across to greet the guests. At least ten of them jumped up and put their paws on Nozdryov's shoulders. Scolder bestowed the same sign of favour on Chichikov and, standing on his hind legs, licked him full in the mouth, causing him to spit in disgust. They inspected the dogs, the strength of whose brawny black haunches provoked their incredulity—they were indeed fine dogs. Then they set off to view a Crimean bitch, which was already blind, and—according to Nozdryov—would soon die, although only two years ago she had been a fine bitch; they viewed the bitch, and the bitch, indeed, was blind. Then they set off to inspect the windmill, which was missing its 'jiggler'—the stone which supports the upper mill-stone as it whizzes round on its spindle and causes it to jiggle, in the marvellous expression of the Russian peasant.

'We shall soon be at the smithy!' said Nozdryov.

Walking on a little way they did indeed come to the smithy, and duly inspected it.

'Now in this field here,' said Nozdryov, pointing, 'there are so many hares you can't see the ground for them; I even caught one by its hind legs with my bare hands.'

'Come now, you could never catch a hare with your bare hands!' objected the brother-in-law.

'I did catch it, I did!' retorted Nozdryov and, turning to Chichikov, said: 'And now I shall take you to see the boundary, where my land ends.'

Nozdryov led his guests through a field which in places consisted of nothing but tussocks. The guests were obliged to make their way between strips of fallow and harrowed land. Chichikov was beginning to feel weary. In many places their feet squelched through water, so low-lying was the terrain. At first they tried to pick their way carefully over these areas, but then, realizing the futility of such caution, they ploughed on regardless, not bothering to ascertain where the mire was deeper and where shallower. After covering a considerable distance they did indeed see the boundary, consisting of a wooden post and a narrow ditch.

'There's the boundary!' announced Nozdryov. 'Everything you see on this side is mine, and even on the other side, that forest you can see over there in the distance, that's all mine, and everything beyond the forest, that's all mine too.'

'Since when has that forest been yours?' asked the brother-in-law. 'Do you mean you've recently bought it? It wasn't yours before.'

'Yes, I bought it recently,' said Nozdryov.

'How did you manage to do that so quickly?'

'It wasn't difficult, I bought it the day before yesterday, and paid a fortune for it too, confound it.'

'But you were at the fair then.'

'For heavens' sake, simpleton! Are you saying it's impossible to be at the fair and buy land at the same time? Yes, I was at the fair, and my steward bought it here in my absence.'

'Oh, I see—the steward! Of course!' said the brother-in-law, and shook his head in doubt.

The guests returned by the same filthy route to the house. Nozdryov led the way into his study, which, however, lacked any of the usual appurtenances of such places, to wit, books and paper; on the walls hung sabres and two guns—one costing three hundred, the other eight hundred roubles. The brother-in-law only shook his head as he inspected them. Then Nozdryov showed his guests some Turkish daggers, on one of which the words 'Craftsman Savely Sibiryakov' had been engraved by mistake. After these the guests were shown a barrel-organ. Nozdryov at once gave them a tune. The barrel-organ emitted a not unpleasant sound, but something must have come unstuck inside it, because what had begun as a mazurka somehow turned into the song *'Marlboro' s'en va-t-en guerre'*,* and this suddenly ended with a well-known old waltz. Nozdryov had stopped turning the handle, but one of the reeds inside the organ was particularly energetic and refused to fall silent, whistling away by itself for a long time. Then they were shown pipes—wooden pipes, clay pipes, meerschaum pipes, pipes that had been broken in and pipes not yet broken in, suede-covered and uncovered pipes, a *chibouk* with an amber mouthpiece which he had recently won at cards, a tobacco pouch, embroidered by a countess who had fallen head-over-heels in love with him at some post-house, and whose little hands—in his own words—were most sublimely *superflescent*— a phrase which for him appeared to signify the summit of perfection.

After an hors d'œuvre of smoked sturgeon they waited for dinner until five o'clock. Dinner, it appeared, was not the most important thing in Nozdryov's life; some of the dishes were burnt, others were sadly underdone. It was apparent that the chef followed some sixth sense and threw in the first ingredients that came to hand: if the pepper was near at hand, in would go a dash of pepper; if some cabbage was handy, he would stick in the cabbage, the same went for milk, ham, peas—in short, any old thing would do, so long as the dish was hot, for it was bound to have some sort of taste in the end.

Nozdryov did, however, set great store by his wines: even before the soup had been served he had already poured large glasses of port and similarly large glasses of Hauts Sauternes, for plain Sauternes is not to be had in our provincial and district capitals. Then he called for a bottle of Madeira, declaring that the Field Marshal himself had never drunk better. The Madeira did indeed have a slightly fiery taste, for the merchants who sold it, familiar as they were with the tastes of landowners, mercilessly laced it with rum, and sometimes even poured in a dash of aqua regis, on the assumption that the Russian constitution can withstand anything.

Then Nozdryov called for another special bottle of something or other, which according to him was a blend of 'Champagnon' and 'Bourgognon'. He lavishly dispensed it, right and left, into the glasses of his brother-in-law and Chichikov; but Chichikov noticed that Nozdryov did not pour much for himself. This encouraged him to be cautious, and whenever Nozdryov became absorbed in what he was saying or was busy filling his brother-in-law's glass, Chichikov would promptly empty his own into his plate. Before long some rowanberry vodka was served, which, according to Nozdryov, had the smoothness of cream, but which in fact startled them by tasting of rot-gut at its potent worst. Then they drank a balsam with a name far too difficult to remember, so that even Nozdryov called it something else the second time round.

Dinner was long over, and all the varieties of liquor had been sampled, but the guests remained seated at table. Chichikov found it impossible to broach his main subject in the presence of the brother-in-law. For the brother-in-law was after all an outsider, and Chichikov's subject demanded confidential and friendly discussion. In point of fact the brother-in-law would hardly have posed much of a threat; he must have sampled to his heart's content, for every few minutes, as he sat in his chair, his head would slump forward on to the table. Finally realizing that he was no longer entirely *compos mentis*, he started to make his excuses and prepared to go home, but in an extremely lethargic and listless manner, just like—as Russians say—a person pulling on a horse's collar with a pair of pincers.

'No, no, no! I won't hear of it!' said Nozdryov.

'No my friend, I really must go,' said the brother-in-law. I shall be most offended if you won't let me.'

'Nonsense, nonsense! We'll get out the cards and have a little game right away!'

'You go ahead and play, but I can't join you, the wife will be terribly annoyed, she really will, I have to tell her all about the fair. No I must, brother, I must give her that pleasure. No, no, don't detain me!'

'Well confound her, your wife, to hell with her! As if you could have any important business with your wife!'

'No, brother! She's a good woman, respectable and loyal! She does me such favours... Believe me, it's bringing the tears to my eyes. No, don't try and detain me; I swear, I must go. It's the honest truth.'

'Let him go, what use is he anyway?' interjected Chichikov quietly.

'Very true!' agreed Nozdryov. 'I can't abide wet rags like him!' And to his brother-in-law he said: 'Well, confound you, go and knit stockings with your wife, you thumbsucker'.[1]

'No, brother, don't you call me a thumbsucker,' answered the brother-in-law. 'I owe her my very life. She's truly so kind and sweet, she does such nice things... it brings tears to my eyes. She'll

---

[1] A particularly offensive name to call a man because of the letters 'th', considered by some to be indecent (*note by N. V. Gogol*).*

ask me what I saw at the fair, I must tell her everything. She's such a dear, truly she is.'

'Well go then, and tell her all your claptrap! Here's your hat.'

'No, brother, you really shouldn't talk of her in that tone; when you do that you hurt my feelings too, you know, she's such a dear.'

'Go and join her then, quickly!'

'Yes brother, I shall go, and forgive me for being unable to stay. I would be delighted if I could, but I cannot.'

The brother-in-law continued on and on in this apologetic vein, not even noticing that he had in fact long been seated in his chaise, had long since driven out of the gates and that before him there had long been only empty fields. We are bound to conclude that his wife did not get to hear many details about the fair.

'What a useless wretch!' said Nozdryov, standing at the window and gazing after the departing carriage. 'But look at the way he's bowling along! That trace-horse is a fine beast, I've wanted to get my hands on him for ages. But the man's quite impossible to deal with. A thumbsucker, that's what he is!'

Thereupon they returned inside. Porfiry set out candles, and Chichikov noticed that a pack of cards had mysteriously appeared in his host's hands.

'How about it?' asked Nozdryov, arching the pack so that the paper wrapping burst open. 'Just to pass the time, I'll hold the bank at three hundred roubles.'

But Chichikov pretended not to have heard the suggestion, and, as if suddenly remembering something, said: 'Ah! Before I forget: there's something I want to ask you.'

'What?'

'First give me your word that you'll do what I ask.'

'But what's the request?'

'First give me your word!'

'Very well.'

'On your word?'

'On my word.'

'This is my request: I dare say you have a great number of peasants who have died but have remained in the census lists?'

'I dare say I have; so what?'

'Transfer them to me, into my name.'

'What do you want with them?'

'Well, I just need them.'

'What for?'

'I just need them... it's my business, anyway... The long and the short of it is: I need them.'

'You're up to something, I can tell. Own up, what is it?'

'But what could I get up to? What could you get up to with worthless rubbish like that?'

'So why do you need them, then?'

'You're so inquisitive! You're the sort who has to pick up every bit of rubbish, finger it and give it a good sniff, too.'

'Why won't you tell me?'

'But what good is it to you if I tell you? Very well, I'll tell you: it's a pure whim.'

'I shan't go along with it until you tell me, and that's that!'

'There, you see, that's not honest of you: you gave your word and now you're trying to back out.'

'Have it how you will, but I won't play until you tell me what you're up to.'

'What can I tell him?' thought Chichikov and after a minute's reflection declared that he needed the dead souls to gain some weight in society, that he did not own any large estates, so for the time being he would at least like to have some souls.

'You lie! You lie!' said Nozdryov, cutting him short. 'You're lying, brother!'

Chichikov himself could see that the excuse he had come up with was not very convincing, and that his pretext was rather feeble.

'Very well; I'll be more frank,' he said, recovering his aplomb. 'Only I beg you not to breathe a word of it to anyone. I've decided to marry; but I must tell you that my betrothed's mother and father are extremely ambitious people. It's such a daunting task, you know— I'm sorry I started it in the first place. They insist that the husband-to-be should have no fewer than three hundred souls, and seeing that I am short by almost a hundred and fifty...'

'Liar! You lie!' shouted Nozdryov again.

'Oh no, this time I haven't lied even this much,' said Chichikov, showing the top joint of his little finger, which he had marked off with his thumb.

'I'll bet my life that you're lying!'

'This is really most offensive! Who do you think I am? What possible reason should I have to lie?'

'Ah, but I know you, you see: you're a terrible rogue, allow me to tell you that as a friend! If I were your superior I should hang you from the nearest tree!'

Chichikov took umbrage at this remark. Indeed, any remark that was ever so slightly coarse or injurious to good breeding was upsetting to him. He was not prepared to put up with any over-familiar behaviour unless perhaps it originated from a person of very high rank. For this same reason he now took great offence.

'I swear, I would hang you,' repeated Nozdryov. 'I'm telling you quite frankly, not to offend you, but simply as a friend.'

'There's a limit to everything,' said Chichikov with dignity. 'If you wish to flaunt such threats in your conversation, the barrackroom is the place for you.' And then he added: 'If you won't give them away, you might at least sell them.'

'Sell them! But I know you, you rogue, you won't give much for them.'

'You're a fine one to talk. Just listen to that! After all, it's not as if they were made of diamonds!'

'There you are. I knew you'd say something like that.'

'I beg your pardon, brother, but you reason like a Jew! You should simply hand them over to me.'

'Well, just to prove that I'm not a skinflint, I won't take a penny for them. Buy a stallion from me and I'll throw them in for nothing.'

'What on earth do I need a stallion for?' said Chichikov, genuinely astonished at this proposal.

'What for? You do realize I paid ten thousand for him and I'm letting you have him for four?'

'But I have no need of a stallion. I don't run a stud farm.'

'Listen, it seems you don't understand: all I'm asking for now is three thousand, and you can give me the remaining thousand later.'

'But I do not need a stallion, confound it!'

'Very well, buy the chestnut mare.'

'Nor do I need any mares.'

'For the mare and that dun horse I showed you I'd be prepared to accept a paltry two thousand.'

'I tell you, I do not need a horse at all.'

'You can sell them, you'll get three times as much at the very first fair.'

'In that case you would do better to sell them yourself, since you're so sure you'll get triple the price.'

'I know I'll make a profit, but I want you to benefit as well.'

Chichikov thanked him for his consideration and adamantly refused both the dun horse and the chestnut mare.

'In that case, buy some dogs. I'll sell you a breeding pair that'll send shivers down your spine! Handsome, shaggy beasts with big whiskers and thick, bristly coats. And their ribcages—firm and round like little barrels: beyond belief!—and such trim paws, they hardly touch the ground.'

'But what do I need dogs for? I'm not a hunter.'

'I'd like you to have some dogs. Listen, if you don't want any dogs, why don't you buy my barrel-organ? It's a wonderful organ, and I promise you, on my word of honour, I paid one and a half thousand for it: I'll let you have it for nine hundred.'

'But what do I need a barrel-organ for? I'm no German, to go lugging a barrel-organ around the streets begging for money!'

'But this is not the sort of barrel-organ that Germans use. This is the real thing; just take a close look: it's solid mahogany. Let me play it for you!'

Here Nozdryov seized Chichikov's hand and started to pull him into the next room, and despite the latter's resistance and remonstrances that he already knew what the organ was like, he still had to hear once again how Marlborough betook himself to war. 'If you don't want to pay money I have another idea, listen: I'll give you the organ and everything else I have, dead souls too, and you give me your chaise and three hundred roubles into the bargain.'

'Excellent idea! And in what, pray, am I to travel?'

'I'll give you another chaise. Let's go into the shed, I'll show it to you! All it needs is a coat of paint and it'll be a beauty.'

'What confounded ideas the devil has put into his head!' thought Chichikov and silently resolved at whatever cost to steer well clear of any chaises, barrel-organs, or dogs of whatever breed, notwithstanding the belief-surpassing and barrel-like roundness of their ribcages and trimness of their paws.

'But I'm offering the chaise, the barrel organ, and dead souls too, the whole lot.'

'I don't want them,' said Chichikov again.

'Why don't you want them?'

'Because I just don't want them, and there's an end to it.'

'You're a queer fish! I can see you're not the sort of fellow one can deal with like a decent friend or comrade, not you, oh no!... Now I can see how two-faced you are!'

'What sort of a fool do you take me for? Think for yourself: why on earth should I acquire something I have absolutely no use for?'

'No, I beg you, say no more. Now I see right through you. A thorough scoundrel! But I'll tell you what: why don't we have a little game of bank? We can play cards for them. I'll stake all my dead souls and the barrel-organ too.'

'Staking them on the cards means placing oneself in the hands of uncertainty,' said Chichikov with a sideways glance at the cards in Nozdryov's hands. Both packs looked very much as though they had been doctored and even the pattern on the back of the cards looked decidedly suspicious.

'What do you mean "uncertainty"?' demanded Nozdryov. 'There's nothing uncertain about it! You only need luck on your side and you can win the devil of a lot. That's the thing! It's all luck!' he said, dealing the cards and working himself up into a fever of excitement. 'It's all luck! Pure luck! You never know when it'll strike! Look—there's that cursed nine on which I blew the lot! I had a feeling that it would let me down, but I screwed up my eyes and thought: "All right, you swine, just you try and let me down, damn you!"'

While Nozdryov was saying this Porfiry brought in a bottle. But Chichikov firmly refused either to play or to drink.

'And why will you not play?' asked Nozdryov.

'Because I do not feel like it. And to be perfectly honest, I'm no great lover of cards.'

'Why not?'

Chichikov shrugged his shoulders and answered: 'I'm just not.'

'Good-for-nothing!'

'I can't help it. That's the way God made me.'

'A thumbsucker, that's what you are! I used to think you had some decency in you, but I was wrong: you have no idea of good behaviour. It's impossible to talk to you as a good friend... you've no honesty, no sincerity! You're just like Sobakevich, an out-and-out swine!'

'But why do you abuse me? Is it an offence not to play cards?

Why not just sell me the souls on their own, if you think rubbish like that is so valuable?'

'You'll get the devil and his bald pate, that's what you'll get! I was planning to give you them for nothing, I really was, but not now, oh no! I wouldn't let you have them now, not for all the tea in China! What a scabrous, double-dealing knave! Henceforth I shall have no further dealings with you. Porfiry, go and tell the stable boy not to give his horses any oats, they can make do with hay.'

This last instruction took Chichikov quite by surprise.

'I only wish I had never set eyes on you!' said Nozdryov.

Notwithstanding this heated exchange, the host and his guest sat down to sup together. True, this time there were no wines with exotic names on the table. There was only one bottle containing some sort of Cyprian concoction, of the kind customarily referred to as turpentine. After supper Nozdryov took Chichikov to a side room in which a bed had been prepared for him and said:

'That's your bed! And I shan't even wish you a good night!'.

Nozdryov departed and Chichikov was left in the worst possible mood. He was highly vexed and he scolded himself for having wasted valuable time by coming to this place. But he cursed himself still more for having even broached the subject of his business with Nozdryov, for having acted without discretion, like a child, like a fool: for this was no matter to be confided to Nozdryov... Nozdryov was a complete good-for-nothing, Nozdryov might talk, exaggerate, spread the devil knows what lies, all sorts of scandalous rumours would fly around—the situation was bad, very bad. 'I'm a total idiot,' he said to himself. That night he slept very badly. Some exceptionally nimble little insects attacked him and bit him so painfully that he lay awake, scratching at the bites with both hands and muttering: 'Damn and blast you—and that Nozdryov too!'

He awoke early on the following morning. Without further ado he donned his dressing-gown and boots and set off across the courtyard to the stables, to order Selifan to harness the chaise at once. On his way back across the yard he encountered Nozdryov, who was also in his dressing-gown, with his pipe between his teeth.

Nozdryov greeted him most cordially and asked if he had slept well.

'So-so,' answered Chichikov very drily.

'As for me, brother,' said Nozdryov, 'I had such horrible dreams all night, too sickening to recount, and my mouth tastes as if a squadron of horses had been camping in it. Just imagine: I dreamt I was being whipped. Whipped! And do you know by whom? You'll never guess: staff officer Potseluev and that Kuvshinnikov, the two of them together.'

'Indeed,' thought Chichikov, 'I only wish they'd do it in real life!'

'Honest to God! And let me tell you—it hurt! I woke up: and blow me down if I'm not really itching—sure enough, it's those cursed fleas. Well, you run along now and get dressed and I'll join you shortly. First I must go and give that scoundrel of a steward a piece of my mind.'

Chichikov withdrew to his room to dress and wash. When he entered the dining-room he found the table laid with tea things and a bottle of rum. The room retained traces of the dinner and supper the day before; it appeared quite untouched by any form of brush or broom. The floor was strewn with breadcrumbs, and there was tobacco ash even on the tablecloth. Our host himself, who promptly joined Chichikov, wore nothing but a dressing-gown open at the chest, over which grew a sort of beard. Clutching a long pipe in his hand and slurping tea from his cup he presented a fine subject for the painter who cannot abide the sort of gentlemen you see in barbershop signs, well-groomed and pomaded, with their hair swept up into elaborate cockscombs.

'Well now, what have you decided?' asked Nozdryov, after a brief silence. 'Shall we play for the souls?'

'I've already told you, my friend, that I never gamble; as for buying them, I'll buy them with pleasure.'

'I would not like to sell them, not to a friend. I'm not one to derive profit from worthless rubbish. But staking them on the cards—that's quite another story. Let us at least play one round!'

'I have already said no.'

'Will you not swap them?'

'I will not.'

'Very well, then, let's play draughts, and if you win they're all yours. After all, I have a lot of souls which should be removed from the census list. Hey, Porfiry, bring the draughts board.'

'You're wasting your time, I will not play.'

'But this is not like cards—there's no question of good or bad luck here: it's pure skill; for that matter, I'm a hopeless player, and you might even let me have a bit of a start.'

'What the hell: I'll give him a game of draughts!' thought Chichikov. 'I used to be pretty good at draughts, and it will be hard for him to pull a fast one here.'

'Very well,' he said, 'so be it: I'll play draughts.'

'The souls stand at one hundred roubles!'

'Why so much? Fifty would be quite enough.'

'Nonsense, what sort of a stake is fifty? If we put them at fifty I might just as well throw in a middling puppy or a gold watch-fob.'

'Very well, as you wish!' said Chichikov.

'What sort of start will you give me?' asked Nozdryov.

'Why on earth should I give you a start? None at all, of course.'

'At least let me make the first two moves.'

'Certainly not, I'm a poor player myself.'

'I know the sort of poor player you are!' said Nozdryov, moving a piece.

'It's ages since I held a draughts piece in my hand!' said Chichikov, also moving forward a piece.

'I know the sort of poor player you are!' said Nozdryov, moving a piece, and at the same time nudging forward another piece with the cuff of his sleeve.

'It's ages since I... I say, what's all this! Put it back!' protested Chichikov.

'Put what back?'

'That piece, of course!' said Chichikov and even as he said this he could see before his very nose another piece well on its way to becoming a king—God only knows where it had come from. 'No', he said, rising from the table, 'it's quite impossible to play with you! That's no way to play: moving three pieces at a time.'

'What do you mean, three pieces? That was a slip. One was pushed accidentally—look, I'll move it back.'

'Then where did the other one appear from?'

'Which other one?'

'This one, about to become a king.'

'I like that, as if you didn't remember!'

'I beg your pardon, I've been counting all the moves and I remember everything: you've only just slipped it in there now. That's where it should be!'

'What do you mean, where?' asked Nozdryov, flushing red. 'You have a fertile imagination, I see!'

'No, brother, you're the one with the fertile imagination, but it won't get you anywhere I'm afraid.'

'Who do you take me for?' cried Nozdryov. 'Are you saying I'm a cheat?'

'I do not take you for anyone, but one thing is for sure: I shall never play with you again.'

'No, you cannot refuse now,' said Nozdryov, incensed, 'the game has started!'

'I have the right to refuse because you are not playing as befits an honest man.'

'No, you lie, how dare you say that!'

'No, brother, you're the liar!'

'I was not cheating, and you can't pull out now, you have to finish the game!'

'You will never force me,' said Chichikov coolly and, stepping up to the board, scattered the pieces.

Nozdryov exploded in fury and bore down on Chichikov, advancing so close that the latter recoiled a couple of paces.

'I *will* force you to play! It makes no difference that you've scattered the pieces, I can remember all the moves. We'll set them out just as they were.'

'No, brother, the matter's closed; I shall not play any more with you.'

'Do you mean to say that you will not play?'

'You can see yourself that it's impossible to play with you.'

'Rubbish—just give me a straight answer: will you or will you not play?' said Nozdryov, advancing on him.

'I will not!' said Chichikov, and to be on the safe side he raised his hands to his face, for things were getting very hot indeed.

This precaution was, as it happens, very timely, because Nozdryov swung a fist—and one of our hero's agreeably plump cheeks might well have been branded forever with the mark of ignominy; but to his good fortune he parried the blow, gripped the irascible Nozdryov by both arms and held him firmly.

'Porfiry! Pavlushka!' Nozdryov yelled in a frenzy, struggling to free himself.

When he heard this, Chichikov, having no wish to make the servants witness to such an indecorous scene and at the same time sensing the futility of restraining Nozdryov any further, released his arms. At that very moment Porfiry appeared, accompanied by Pavlushka, a strapping fellow with whom it would have been most inadvisable to engage in such negotiations.

'So you do not wish to finish the game?' said Nozdryov. 'Give me a straight answer!'

'It's quite impossible to finish the game,' said Chichikov, with a glance through the window. He could see his chaise, which was all ready, with Selifan waiting—presumably for a signal—before driving up to the porch, but the presence of the two hefty idiot serfs, standing in the doorway, removed any prospect of escape from the room.

'So you do not wish to finish the game?' repeated Nozdryov, his face flushing a fiery red.

'I would if you played as befits an honest man. But now I cannot play.'

'The devil you can't play, you scoundrel! You're losing—that's why you won't play! Thrash him!' he roared in a transport of rage, turning to Porfiry and Pavlushka, while he himself reached for a long cherry-wood pipe. Chichikov went as pale as a sheet. He tried to say something, but he felt his lips move without making a sound.

'Go to it, thrash him!' shouted Nozdryov and, flushed and covered with sweat, he lurched forward, brandishing his pipe, as if mounting an assault on an unassailable fortress. 'Thrash him!' he shouted in the voice of a desperado lieutenant who shouts 'Forward, lads!' urging his platoon on to some great exploit, a lieutenant whose manic daring has already earned him such notoriety that special orders have been issued for him to be held back by the arms during the heat of battle. But the lieutenant is already fired with bellicose fervour, his head spins; the image of Suvorov* hovers before him, he longs for glory. 'Forward, lads!' he shouts in his delirium, quite unaware that he is upsetting the carefully plotted general plan of attack, and that, through the embrasures of the towering and unassailable fortress walls, millions of gun barrels are being trained upon him, and his helpless platoon is about to vanish into the air like dust, and that a fateful bullet is already whistling through the air, on its way to plug his clamorous throat once and for all.

But whilst Nozdryov may have resembled a desperate, madcap lieutenant storming a fortress, the particular fortress on which he marched seemed anything but unassailable. On the contrary, the fortress was stricken with such terror, that its heart was in its mouth. Even the chair, with which the fortress had prepared to defend itself, had been wrested from its hands by the servants, and, its eyes screwed shut in a dead funk, the fortress waited to be smitten by its host's Circassian pipe, and the Lord only knows what fate would have befallen it.

The fates, however, saw fit to preserve from injury the sides, shoulders, and other well-bred appurtenances of our hero. Suddenly, out of the blue, came the jingling of bells and the rattle of a vehicle careering up to the porch and even inside the room they could hear the heavy breathing and laboured snorting of the over-heated horses outside. All eyes at once turned to the window: a man with a moustache, in a half-military frock-coat, was alighting from the carriage. Making enquiries in the hall, he entered the room at the very moment when Chichikov, still beside himself with terror, was in the most pitiful state a mortal could possibly find himself in.

'Might I enquire which one of you gentlemen is Mr Nozdryov?' asked the stranger, looking with some bewilderment at Nozdryov, brandishing his pipe, and at Chichikov, who had barely begun to recover from his plight.

'Might I first make so bold as to enquire with whom I have the honour to speak?' asked Nozdryov, stepping closer to him.

'Captain of police.'

'And what can I do for you?'

'I have come to convey to you information that has been imparted to me, namely that you are under arrest until such time as a decision is reached in your case.'

'What's all this nonsense: what case?'

'You have been implicated in an affair, concerning the infliction on landowner Maksimov of personal injury with a birch rod when in a state of inebriation.'

'You're lying! I've never clapped eyes on landowner Maksimov!'

'Sir! Allow me to remind you that I am an officer. You may speak like that to your servant, but not to me!'

At this point Chichikov resolved not to wait for Nozdryov's reply, and reaching swiftly for his hat, slipped behind the police captain's back out on to the porch, climbed into his chaise and ordered Selifan to whip the horses on for all they were worth.

CHAPTER FIVE

Our hero had certainly been given a terrible scare. Although his chaise raced along like a bat out of hell and Nozdryov's village had long been lost from sight behind the fields, hills, and rolling countryside, he continued to cast fearful looks behind him, as if expecting at any moment to be overtaken. His breathing was laboured and when he pressed his hand to his heart he felt it fluttering like a quail in a cage. 'Goodness, what a close shave! What an abominable character!' At this point many unpleasant and heartfelt consequences were wished on Nozdryov; certain indecorous words could even have been heard. But who can blame him? He was a Russian, and an angry one to boot. And besides, this was no laughing matter. 'Whichever way you look at it,' he said to himself, 'if the captain of police hadn't pitched up in the nick of time I might have breathed my last in this world! I would have vanished without a trace, like a bubble on the water, leaving no descendants, with neither fortune nor honourable name to pass on to my future children!' Our hero was much preoccupied with the matter of his descendants.

'That Mr Nozdryov was a nasty gentleman!' Selifan was thinking. 'I've never come across a gentleman like him! I'd like to spit in his face! It's one thing not to give a man anything to eat, but you've got to feed a horse, because a horse loves his oats. That's his provisionals, see: what's tack to us is oats to him, that's his provisionals.'

The horses had also, so it seemed, formed a poor opinion of Nozdryov: not only the bay and Assessor, but the dappled horse too—all were out of spirits. Although the dappled horse usually got the worst share of the oats and Selifan could not fill his trough without first muttering: 'You shirker!'—all the same, it was still oats, and not plain old hay, and he would chew them with relish, frequently thrusting his long face into his comrades' troughs to check what sort of provisions they had been given, especially when Selifan had left the stable. But here all they had been given was hay... that was just not good enough; all three of them were highly disgruntled.

But soon the disgruntled wayfarers were interrupted in the midst of their perorations in the most sudden and unexpected manner.

Every one of them, not excepting the coachman himself, was brought rudely to his senses when a carriage drawn by a team of six horses bore down upon them and the air above their heads was rent by the shrieks of the ladies within, and the oaths and threats of its coachman: 'Hey, you there! Didn't you hear me yelling at you, you brigand, to get off the road, to keep to the right! Are you drunk or what?' Selifan knew perfectly well that he was to blame, but like all Russians he hated to admit to others that he was in the wrong and at once riposted, in high dudgeon: 'And what the devil do you think you're doing, galloping along at that speed? I suppose you drank yourself into a stupor at the last roadside tavern?' He then started tugging back his own team, to free them from the harnesses of the other horses, but it was not to be, for they were hopelessly entangled.

The dappled horse was sniffing with great curiosity at his new friends, who now stood on both sides of him. All the while the ladies seated inside the carriage beheld all this with a look of terror on their faces. The one was an old lady, the other a pretty girl, no more than sixteen, with golden tresses, deftly and charmingly smoothed down over her little head. She had a sweet oval face, like a fresh egg, which glowed with that same translucent whiteness that can be seen in a newly laid egg when the housekeeper holds it up against the light in her swarthy hands, to see whether it is fresh; the girl's little ears were also translucent, and rosy from the warm light that shone through them. All this, which contrasted so agreeably with the alarm on her parted lips and the tears in her eyes, made such a charming picture that our hero stared at her for some minutes, oblivious of the commotion being created by the horses and coachmen.

'Back your horses, do you hear, you Nizhny Novgorod half-wit!'* shouted the other coachman. Selifan tugged at his reins, the other coachman did likewise, the horses recoiled slightly and then collided once again, stepping over each other's traces. In the resulting configuration, the dappled stallion was so pleased with his new acquaintance that he had no wish to remove himself from the ditch in which he had landed in this unforeseen manner, and, placing his muzzle against the neck of his new friend, appeared to be whispering something right into his ear—foolish nonsense, no doubt, to judge by the way the newcomer kept twitching his ears.

This fracas drew a crowd of local peasants, whose village, fortunately, was in the vicinity. Since such a spectacle is manna from heaven to a Russian peasant, as great a source of joy as a newspaper or his club are to a German, soon such a multitude of them had gathered round the carriage that only the old women and small children were left in the village. They disentangled the traces; a few prods on the dappled horse's muzzle persuaded him to retreat; in short, they disengaged and separated carriages and horses. But whether from pique, because they had been parted from their friends, or from sheer stupidity, however much the other coachman whipped his horses, they refused to budge and remained rooted to the spot.

The peasants were by now totally embroiled. They vied with each other in offering advice: 'Go on, Andryushka, you take hold of the trace-horse on the right, and let old Mityai get up on the shaft-horse and ride it away! Up you get, Uncle Mityai!' The tall, lean, and ginger-bearded Uncle Mityai duly climbed up on the shaft-horse and, once mounted, looked like a village bell-tower, or, even better, like the long crook used to pull up the bucket from a well. The coachman whipped the horses, but to no avail: Uncle Mityai was unable to provide any assistance.

'Stop, stop!' shouted the peasants. 'You get on the trace-horse, Uncle Mityai, and let Uncle Minyai get up on the wheeler!' Uncle Minyai—a broad-shouldered peasant with a coal-black beard and a belly as round and full as one of those gigantic samovars from which they serve honey-tea for the entire frozen populace at a country market, brewing gallons at a time—happily mounted the shaft-horse, causing its back to buckle almost to the ground.

'Now things will start moving!' cried the peasants. 'Give him stick! And give that one a taste of your whip—that one over there, the light bay: look at him balk, just like a great gallinipper!'[1]

But when they saw that things were not moving and that no amount of stick helped, both Uncle Mityai and Uncle Minyai climbed on the shaft-horse's back and seated Andryushka on the trace-horse. Finally, the thoroughly exasperated coachman drove away both Uncle Mityai and Uncle Minyai, and it was just as well he did, for the

---

[1] A large, long-legged, lethargic mosquito; it occasionally flies into a room and perches alone somewhere on the wall. You can quite easily walk up to it and grab it by the leg, in response to which it will only resist by spreading wide its legs, or 'balking', as the people put it. (*Note by N. V. Gogol*).

horses were steaming as heavily as if they had galloped an entire stage without drawing breath. He gave them a minute to rest, whereupon they moved off by themselves.

Throughout all these proceedings Chichikov had remained gazing raptly at the pretty young girl. He attempted several times to engage her in conversation, but somehow nothing came of it. In the mean time the ladies drove off, the girl with the delicate features and the slender figure was lost from sight, like a vision, and once again there was only the road, the chaise, the equine threesome by now so familiar to the reader, Selifan, Chichikov, and the smooth expanse and emptiness of the fields on either side.

Everywhere, in all walks of life, whether amongst the callous, scraggily poor, unkempt, and mouldy lower orders or amongst the insipidly cold and tediously proper upper classes, everywhere a man is bound to encounter, at least once in his life, a phenomenon quite unlike any other he has seen hitherto, which—on at least this one occasion—will inspire in him a feeling quite surpassing any he has been fated to feel all the days of his life. Everywhere, despite all the sorrows from which our lives are woven, there will flash a glittering dream of joy, just like a brilliant carriage with gold trappings, fairy-tale steeds, sparkling windows which suddenly appears from nowhere and flashes past some wretched backwater village, which has never seen anything other than farm carts, and for a long time after the peasants remain standing, mouths agape and caps still doffed, although the wondrous carriage has long since passed from view. Thus too did the fair-haired beauty suddenly appear from nowhere in our story and just as suddenly vanish. Imagine if, instead of Chichikov, this had been some twenty-year-old youth, a Hussar, say, or a student, or merely some fellow just starting out on his chosen career—and heavens above! What turmoil, what fever would have raged within him! Long would he have stood insensate, rooted to the spot, his eyes fastened blankly on the distance, his journey quite forgotten, and with it all the reprimands that awaited him, and the severe scolding for being late—all forgotten: himself, his career, the world, and everything it contained.

But our hero was already a man of middle age and of a temperate and circumspect character. He also grew pensive and fell to thinking, but his thoughts were more positive, not so uncontrolled and in some respects even rather down-to-earth. 'A first-rate little wench!'

he said, opening his snuff-box and taking a pinch of snuff. 'Yet, come to think of it, what's so first-rate about her? The main point in her favour is that she's fresh from some boarding school for young gentlewomen, and has not yet acquired female affectations, in other words, none of that which is most unpleasant about ladies. She is still child-like, she does everything simply: she says whatever comes into her head and laughs when she wants to.

'She can be shaped into anything, she can become a creature of enchantment—or just as easily turn into worthless rubbish, which is precisely what will happen! Just wait until all those mamas and aunties get to work on her. In one year she'll be so crammed full of woman's stuff and nonsense that her own father won't recognize her. Suddenly, before you know it, she'll become all prim and haughty, blindly following the rules that have been drummed into her, forever calculating with whom, and in what manner, and for how long she should speak, whom she should look at, and, living in constant fear of saying more than she should, finally growing so confused that she spends the rest of her life telling bare-faced lies and turns into something quite frightful!'

At this point he fell silent for a little while before adding: 'All the same, it would be intriguing to know who her people are? Who's her father, I wonder; what's he like? Is he a rich and respectable landowner or simply some level-headed fellow with a bit of capital that he has acquired in the service? For if, let us suppose, this young girl has a tidy little sum of two hundred thousand or so settled on her as a dowry, she would make a very, very tasty morsel indeed. In fact it would be enough to secure the happiness of a decent man, you might say.'

The tidy little sum now started to assume such alluring proportions in his mind that he became quite vexed with himself for having omitted, during all the brouhaha with the carriages, to ascertain from either the postilion or the coachman the identity of the travellers. Soon, however, these vexatious thoughts were dispelled by the appearance of Sobakevich's village, and his mind involuntarily returned to its customary subject.

The village struck Chichikov as fairly large; two woods, one of birch and the other of pine, bounded it to left and to right, like two wings, the one darker, the other lighter; in the middle stood a wooden house with a mansard, a red roof and dingy grey—or, rather, unpainted—walls: a house like those built in Russia for military cantonments and German colonists.* It was evident that during its construction the architect had constantly warred with the owner's taste. The architect was a pedant and desired symmetry whereas the owner sought only convenience, and this had evidently caused him to board up all the matching windows on one side of the house, replacing them with just one small window, which—presumably— was necessary for the dark larder. The pediment also could not be fitted into the middle of the building, however hard the architect tried, because the owner had insisted that one of the side columns should be scrapped, with the result that there were not four columns, as intended, but only three.

The yard was enclosed by a strong and extraordinarily thick wooden trellis. The owner, it seemed, was greatly concerned with solidity. The stables, sheds, and cookhouses were constructed of bulky logs, designed to last a hundred years. The peasants' huts were also a wonder to behold: there were no planed walls,* carved ornamentation, or other fanciful touches but everything had been snugly and soundly joined. Even the shaft of the water well was made of the sort of strong oak that is normally only used for windmills and ships. In a word, everything Chichikov set eyes on was rugged and sturdy, ungainly but solidly built.

As they drove up to the entrance he saw two faces, which peeped almost simultaneously out of the windows: a female face, in a lace bonnet, long and narrow like a cucumber, and a man's face, broad and round like those Moldavian pumpkin gourds from which balalaikas are made in Russia—by which we mean those light, two-stringed balalaikas which are the pride and joy of every spry young lad of twenty or so, of every young blade and gallant winking and whistling at the lasses with their lily-white bosoms and necks, who have gathered round to listen to his soft-stringed strumming. After one glance both faces instantly vanished. A footman in a grey jacket with a stiff, pale blue collar came out on to the porch and conducted Chichikov into the hall, where he was joined by the master of the house. This latter, on seeing his guest, announced brusquely: 'This way please!' and led Chichikov inside the house.

When Chichikov stole a sidelong glance at Sobakevich he thought him remarkably like a medium-sized bear. To complete the likeness, the suit he was wearing was exactly bear-coloured, with coat-sleeves and trouser legs too long for his arms and legs; he walked with a lumbering, awkward gait, constantly treading on other people's toes. His complexion was a deep, burnished red, the colour of a copper coin. As we all know, there are many such faces in this world, faces on whose finishing touches Mother Nature has wasted little time or effort, disdaining the use of fine instruments such as files, gimlets, and so forth, but preferring instead to hack away: one swipe of the axe—and there's the nose; another swipe, and there's the mouth; sockets for the eyes she gouges out with a massive awl, and without any smoothing or polishing she pushes the product out into the world, saying: 'There—it lives!'

Such was the powerful and astonishingly rough-hewn counten-ance of Sobakevich: he held his head down more than up, never twisted his neck at all, and, as a result, rarely looked his interlocutor in the eye, staring instead at a corner of the stove, or at the door. Chichikov cast him another sidelong glance, as they walked through the dining-room: 'A bear! A perfect bear!' But imagine the strange coincidence: he was even called Mikhail Semyonovich.*

Knowing his host's tendency to tread on people's toes, Chichikov placed his own feet with great care and allowed him to lead the way. Sobakevich appeared to be aware of this deficiency in himself and at once enquired: 'Have I perhaps discomforted you?' But Chichikov thanked him and said that there had been no discomfort thus far.

Entering the drawing-room, Sobakevich pointed at a chair and said again: 'Please!' Chichikov sat down and glanced at the pictures hanging on the walls. They all depicted dashing warriors, illustrious Greek generals, portrayed full length: there stood Mavrocordato in his red trousers and uniform, spectacles on his nose, Miaulis, Kanaris.* All these heroes had such massive haunches and fabulous mous-taches that it sent a shiver down his spine. Squeezed between these redoubtable Hellenes, heaven knows how or why, was our own Bagration,* thin and scrawny, with a few small battle standards and cannon at his feet, and mounted in the narrowest of frames. Then came the Greek heroine Bobelina,* with legs so massive that one of them would have exceeded in its girth the entire trunk of any of those dandies who throng our drawing-rooms today. The master of the house, being a powerful and sturdily built man himself, seemed to wish his room to be adorned with similarly powerful and sturdily built people. Beside Bobelina, in the corner of the room, hung a cage, out of which peered a dark, speckled thrush, also very like Sobakevich. Host and guest had not been silent for more than two minutes together before the door to the drawing-room opened and the lady of the house entered, a personage of inordinate height, wearing a lace bonnet with home-dyed ribbons. She made a stately entrance, bearing her head up high, like a palm tree.

'This is my Feodulia Ivanovna!' said Sobakevich.

Chichikov stepped up to kiss Feodulia Ivanovna's hand, which she so good as thrust against his lips, affording him the opportunity to observe that her hands had been washed in cucumber brine.

'Dear heart,' continued Sobakevich, 'may I present Pavel Ivanovich Chichikov! I was favoured to make his acquaintance at the governor's and the postmaster's *soirées*.'

Feodulia Ivanovna asked him to be seated, also saying: 'Please!' with a motion of her head such as that made by actresses playing the parts of queens. Then she disposed herself on the settee, wrapped her merino wool shawl around her and made no further movement, of neither her eyes nor even her eyebrows.

Chichikov once again raised his eyes and once again saw Kanaris with his large haunches and formidable whiskers, Bobelina, and the thrush in its cage.

A general silence was maintained for almost a full five minutes; all that could be heard was the tap-tap of the thrush's beak against the wooden floor of the cage, on which it angled for grains of wheat. Chichikov cast another glance around the room and saw that everything in it was solid and exceedingly ungainly in design, bearing an uncanny resemblance to the master of the house himself; in the corner of the room stood a paunchy walnut bureau on four ridiculous legs: a perfect bear. The table, chairs, arm-chairs—all possessed this same cumbrous and peculiar quality—in a word, each piece, each chair, seemed to proclaim: 'I, too, am Sobakevich!' or 'I, too, am very like Sobakevich!'

'We were talking about you at the house of the president of the chambers, at Ivan Grigorievich's,' said Chichikov at last, seeing that no one was inclined to initiate a conversation, 'last Thursday, that is. We had a most agreeable time.'

'It's true, I was not at the president's on that occasion,' answered Sobakevich.

'What an excellent man!'

'Who's that?' asked Sobakevich, staring at the corner of the stove.

'The president.'

'Well, perhaps that's how he seemed to you: he may be a mason, but he's still the biggest fool the world's ever seen.'

Chichikov was somewhat taken aback by this rather harsh appraisal, but then, recovering himself, continued: 'Of course, we all have our failings, but then the governor is such an excellent man!'

'The governor—an excellent man?'

'Why yes, is he not?'

'The world's worst cutthroat!'

'What—the governor a cutthroat?' said Chichikov, quite unable to comprehend how the governor could be classed as a cutthroat. 'I must confess, I would never have thought it,' he continued. 'But with your permission I might point out that he does not act at all like one, on the contrary, there is something very gentle about him.' Here he cited in evidence the purses which the governor embroidered with his own hands, and added a few words in praise of the latter's affable expression.

'He has the face of a cutthroat too!' said Sobakevich. 'Give him a knife and let him loose on the highway and he'll cut your throat, he'll cut it for a copeck! He and the vice-governor together—they're a proper Gog and Magog!'*

'He's clearly not on good terms with them,' Chichikov said to himself. 'Let me try talking about the police chief: I believe he's a friend of his.'

'Anyhow, it's no concern of mine,' he said. 'I must admit I was most taken with the chief of police. Such an upright, honest character; somehow you can see real candour in his face.'

'The rogue!' said Sobakevich, in his usual imperturbable way. 'He'll hoodwink you, betray you and then eat dinner with you! I know them all: they're all rogues, the whole town's like that: rogue upon rogue, each trying to swindle the other. They're all Judases. There's only one decent man amongst them, the public prosecutor, and even he, if the truth be told, is a swine.'

After such eulogistic, if somewhat abridged, biographies Chichikov could see there was little point in bringing up any other officials, and he realized that Sobakevich was averse to expressing good of any man.

'Come, dear heart, dinner is served,' Sobakevich's wife said to him.

'Please!' said Sobakevich.

At the table, which had been set with *zakuski*, guest and host drank their statutory glass of vodka each, chased it down with the *zakuski*, just as vodka is chased down throughout the length and breadth of Russia, in towns and villages alike—that is, with an infinite variety of salty titbits and other appetite-whetting dainties—and then proceeded into the dining-room; the procession was led by the hostess, who sailed along like a water-borne goose. The small dining-table was set for four. The fourth place was soon taken, but by whom it is difficult to say exactly, whether a lady or a girl, a relative, housekeeper, or simply someone living in the house; a creature, around thirty years of age, and wearing not a starched cap but a brightly coloured kerchief* on her head. There are some characters who exist in this world not as objects in their own right, but as foreign blotches or blemishes on other objects. They remain sitting in one place, holding their heads in exactly the same way, so that one could easily mistake them for pieces of furniture, and it is hard to imagine that such lips could ever have uttered a human word; but get them somewhere like the maids' quarters or the pantry and then you will not believe the things you hear!

'The soup, dear heart, is very good today!' said Sobakevich, slurping his cabbage soup and helping himself to a massive chunk of 'nanny-pie', a dish served with cabbage soup and consisting of sheep's stomach stuffed with buckwheat, sheep's heart, and trotters. 'You won't find nanny-pie like this anywhere in town,' he continued, turning to Chichikov, 'the devil only knows what rubbish they'll serve you there!'

'Yet, the governor keeps a pretty good table, I must say,' said Chichikov.

'But have you any idea what goes into all that food? You wouldn't touch it if you knew.'

'I do not know how it is cooked, I would be no judge of that, but his pork cutlets and steamed fish were excellent.'

'That's what you thought. But I know the sort of stuff they buy at the market. That rascal of a cook, who was apprenticed to a Frenchman, he'll buy a cat, skin it, and serve it up as hare.'

'Ugh! How can you say such nasty things!' said Madame Sobakevich.

'It's true, dear heart, that's their way, and I'm not to blame for it. All the kitchen waste, the stuff our Akulka throws into the slop-pail, if you'll pardon me saying so, they'll put in the soup! Yes sir, in the soup!'

'Why must you always discuss these things at table?' objected his good lady again.

'Why not, dear heart,' said Sobakevich, 'it's not as if I were doing it myself; but let me tell you straight that I refuse to eat filth. You can coat a frog with sugar and I still won't stick it in my mouth, nor will I touch oysters: I know what oysters remind me of. Take some mutton,' he continued, turning to Chichikov, 'here we have a saddle of mutton with buckwheat! This isn't one of those fricassees which they serve up in fashionable households, using mutton that has been lying around at the market for at least four days! All those concoctions were dreamt up by a pack of French and German doctors and, if you ask me, they should hang the lot of them! Concocting that diet of theirs, to cure people by starving them! Just because they have that wishy-washy German constitution, they imagine they can get the better of a Russian stomach! No, it's all wrong, it's all a lot of stuff and nonsense, it's all...' At which point Sobakevich shook his head angrily.

'They are always on about their enlightenment: enlightenment this, enlightenment that—but what is this enlightenment?—Pshaw! I would have used another word, but it would not be proper at table. It's not like that in my house. What I say is: if you want pork—put the whole pig on the table; you want mutton—bring on the whole sheep; a goose—take the whole goose! I'd rather have only two dishes, but sufficient portions, so I can eat my fill.' Sobakevich proved as good as his word: he tipped half the saddle of mutton on to his plate, devoured all the meat, gnawed the bones, and sucked them clean.

'Yes,' thought Chichikov, 'this one certainly likes his grub.'

'It's not like that in my house,' repeated Sobakevich, wiping his hands with a napkin. 'I don't believe in living like that Plyushkin:* he owns eight hundred souls, but lives and eats worse than my goatboy.'

'Who is this Plyushkin?' asked Chichikov.

'A brigand,' answered Sobakevich. 'A worse skinflint than him you couldn't possibly imagine. Convicts in prison live better than him: he's starved all his serfs to death.'

'Is that so!' interjected Chichikov with enthusiasm. 'Do you mean to say that his serfs are really dying in large numbers?'

'Dying like flies.'

'Like flies! Goodness! Might I ask how far from you he lives?'

'Five versts.'

'Five versts!' exclaimed Chichikov, feeling his heartbeat quicken slightly. 'Now if one were to drive out of your gate, would one turn to the right or the left?'

'You wouldn't want to know the way to that cur's house!' said Sobakevich. 'It would be more pardonable to visit a house of ill-repute than to call on him.'

'Oh no, I'm not asking for any specific reason, but only because I always take an interest in learning the lie of the land,' countered Chichikov.

The saddle of mutton was followed by curd pastries, each much bigger than a dinner plate, then came a turkey the size of a calf, stuffed with all manner of good things: eggs, rice, liver, and goodness knows what else, all of which lay heavily in the diners' stomachs. With this the meal ended; as they rose from the table Chichikov felt he had gained an entire pood in weight. They proceeded to the drawing-room, where saucers of jam awaited them—not pear, nor plum, nor berry of any kind, but, in the event, neither guest nor host was to ascertain from what the jam was made. The hostess departed, in order to fill more saucers with jam. Availing himself of her absence Chichikov turned to Sobakevich, who, recumbent in his armchair, could do nothing after such a massive repast but wheeze and mutter indistinctly, crossing himself and covering his mouth with his hand every few seconds.

Chichikov addressed him with these words: 'I would like to discuss a small business matter with you.'

'Here's another jam,' said the hostess, returning with a dish. 'This is radish, stewed in honey!'

'We'll have some later!' said Sobakevich. 'You run along to your own room now, Pavel Ivanovich and I want to take off our coats and have a little breather!'

Their hostess offered to send for feather bolsters and pillows, but her husband said: 'No, no—no need, we'll stretch out in the arm-chairs,' and Madame Sobakevich withdrew.

Sobakevich bent his head slightly forward as he prepared to learn the nature of this small business matter.

Chichikov started in a most roundabout way, first touching on the entire Russian state in general, waxing lyrical about its great expanse, declaring that even the most ancient monarchy of Rome had not been so vast and that it was with good reason that foreigners were so impressed... Sobakevich listened intently, his head bent forward. And that by the existing statutes of this state, unequalled in its glory, registered souls who had departed the portals of this life, still continued to count, until the next census, alongside the living, lest the municipal offices be overwhelmed with a mass of trivial and useless reports which would only further complicate the already sufficiently complex machinery of state... Sobakevich still listened intently, head bent forward. And that, however justified this measure might be, it was none the less sometimes onerous for many landowners, obliging them to pay taxes just as they would for living serfs, and that he, out of a feeling of respect for his host, was prepared to take upon himself a portion of this truly burdensome obligation. As for the main subject itself, Chichikov tiptoed towards this very gingerly: he scrupulously avoided referring to the souls as dead, describing them merely as non-existent.

Sobakevich listened as before, inclining his head forward and displaying nothing that could remotely be described as an expression. You might have thought his was a body entirely devoid of a soul, or that if it did have one it kept it not where it should be, but like the miser of folklore, the deathless Koshchei,* somewhere very remote and covered with such a thick shell that, whatever stirrings there might have been deep within, they produced not the slightest tremor on the surface.

'Well?...' asked Chichikov, waiting with some trepidation for the answer.

'You want dead souls?' asked Sobakevich very simply, without the slightest surprise, as if they were discussing wheat.

'Er—yes,' answered Chichikov, and at once softened the expression, adding: 'the non-existent ones, that is.'

'Should be some, why not?..' said Sobakevich.

'And if there are, then you would surely... be pleased to disburden yourself of them?'

'Why not, I'll sell,' said Sobakevich, now lifting his head slightly as he tumbled to the fact that the buyer must surely derive some profit from his transaction.

'What the devil,' thought Chichikov, 'this one's already selling before I've even broached the subject!' and he continued aloud: 'Now what sort of price did you have in mind? Although, of course, with merchandise of this nature... to talk about price is rather strange...'

'I don't want to overcharge you, so we'll say a hundred roubles a piece,' said Sobakevich.

'A hundred!' exclaimed Chichikov, gaping wide-mouthed at Sobakevich, uncertain whether he had misheard or whether Sobakevich's unwieldy tongue had twisted the wrong way and blurted out one word in place of another.

'So you think that's too dear?' declared Sobakevich and added: 'What's your price then?'

'My price! I think we must have made a mistake, or be talking at cross-purposes, or perhaps we have forgotten the nature of the merchandise. For my part all I can suggest in all honesty is eighty copecks a soul, that's the best I can offer!'

'Eighty copecks? That's ridiculous!'

'Why, in my opinion, as I see it, you could not ask more.'

'We're not talking about bast sandals, I'll have you know.'

'But think about it: they're not people, either.'

'Do you think you'll find yourself some fool who'll sell you registered souls for twenty copecks a piece?'

'I crave your pardon: why do you call them registered when these souls have themselves passed away long ago, and all that remains is the impalpable sound of the word? However, to obviate further discussion of the subject I'm prepared to give you a rouble fifty each, but that's my last word.'

'You should be ashamed to mention such a sum! If you want to do business, name a proper price!'

'No, Mikhail Semyonovich, on my word of honour, believe me, I cannot: what cannot be done, cannot be done,' said Chichikov, but promptly added another fifty copecks.

'Why be so stingy?' asked Sobakevich. 'They're cheap at the price! Another scoundrel would cheat you, selling you a lot of dross, and not real souls at all; mine are the genuine article, the pick of the crop—they're all either skilled craftsmen or strapping peasants. See for yourself: take Mikheev the carriage-maker for instance! You know, he's never turned out a carriage that wasn't properly sprung. And this isn't any of your Moscow workmanship, which lasts for one hour only: this is good, solid work, he'll upholster them himself and put on the varnish too!'

Chichikov opened his mouth, intending to point out that Mikheev had, however, long since departed this life; but Sobakevich had now entered, as they say, the very power of speech, whence came the jog and the gift of the word:

'And Stepan Probka, the carpenter? I wager my own head you'll never find another to match him. The strength of that man! He could have been a guardsman with his build! He stood over three arshins* tall in his stockinged feet!'

Once again Chichikov was about to observe that Probka, likewise, had departed this life, but there was no stopping Sobakevich now: the words spewed forth in such a torrent that his guest could only sit and listen.

'Milushkin, the bricklayer! He could build a stove in any house. Maxim Telyatnikov, the cobbler: a few jabs of his awl and there's a pair of boots for you—good solid boots, too—and never a drop of liquor! And Yeremei Sorokoplyokhin! That fellow is a match for the best of them, he even plied his trade in Moscow and paid me five hundred roubles in quit-rent* alone. That's the sort of men they are! Not the rubbish that old Plyushkin would sell you.'

'But pardon me for saying so,' said Chichikov finally, somewhat nonplussed by this overwhelming and seemingly unending torrent of words, 'why do you enumerate all their merits when there is no use in them now anyway, as they are all dead? A dead man's only good for propping up a fence, as the proverb says.'

'Yes, of course, they're dead,' said Sobakevich, as if coming to his senses and suddenly realizing the truth of this, then added: 'But look at it this way: what about all the people who count as being alive? What sort of people are they? They're flies, not people.'

'None the less they do exist, whereas these are only imaginary.'

'Oh no, no—not imaginary! Allow me to inform you what a stout fellow that Mikheev was, you'll never find his equal anywhere: such an ox of a man, he wouldn't fit through this door; oh no: there's nothing imaginary about him! And in his shoulders he had the strength of a carthorse—stronger even; I'd like to know where else you think you can find someone imaginary like that!'

These last words he addressed to the portraits of Bagration and Kolokotroni hanging on the wall, as sometimes happens during conversations, when the speaker, for some unknown reason, suddenly addresses not the person to whom his words are directed, but someone else who has unexpectedly entered the room, perhaps even a total stranger, from whom the speaker knows he will receive neither reply, nor opinion, nor confirmation, yet on whom he fixes a stare as if asking him to be an intermediary; this stranger, somewhat bewildered at first, does not know whether to venture an answer on a matter about which he has heard nothing, or merely to stand there, preserving proper decorum, and then to take his leave.

'No, I cannot go higher than two roubles,' said Chichikov.

'Very well: since I would not wish you to claim that I had overcharged you, or that I refused to do you any favours, let us say seventy-five roubles per soul, but in banknotes, and even that price is only for the sake of our friendship!'

'Does he really take me for a fool?' Chichikov wondered, and added aloud:

'I must say this seems very odd to me: it is as if we were acting out some theatrical performance or comedy, I cannot see any other explanation... I do believe you to be a person of considerable intelligence, endowed with the knowledge conferred by education. After all, this merchandise is worthless. What is its value? What use is it to anyone?'

'Well, you're the one buying it, so it must be of use to you.'

Here Chichikov bit his lip, at a loss for an answer. He started to mention certain family circumstances and concomitances, but Sobakevich abruptly retorted:

'I have no wish to learn about your circumstances. I do not interfere in family matters, that's your own business. You require souls, so I'm selling them to you, and you'll regret it if you don't buy them.

'Two roubles,' said Chichikov.

'Listen to that: "two roubles, two roubles"—just like Jacob's magpie:* you've set your mind on two roubles and now nothing will shift you. Name a proper price!'

'The devil confound him,' thought Chichikov, 'I'll throw him his bone and give him another fifty copecks, the dog!'

'Very well, I'll offer another fifty copecks.'

'Then allow me also to say my last word: fifty roubles! I have to admit I'd be selling at a loss, you wouldn't get such fine serfs anywhere at that price!'

'What a money-grubbing koulak!'* said Chichikov to himself, and then continued aloud in some vexation:

'Now really, this is quite ridiculous, you cannot mean it; anywhere else I could get them for nothing. Indeed, most people would be only too glad to let me have them, if only to get rid of them the quicker. No one but a fool would wish to hold on to them and pay taxes for them!'

'But are you aware that purchases of this nature, and I say this just between you and me, out of friendship, are not always permissible, and if I, or someone else, happened to talk about such a matter, no one would trust the person thus implicated were he ever to try and make a contract or enter into a commitment for profitable purposes.'

'So, that's his game, the knave!' thought Chichikov, and thereupon announced with an air of the utmost nonchalance:

'Please yourself; I'm not buying them for any particular purpose, as you think, but for no particular reason at all, just as a whim. If you won't take two and a half roubles—I bid you farewell!'

'He won't give in, he's too stubborn!' thought Sobakevich, and said: 'Very well then, thirty a piece and they're yours!'

'No, I see you do not wish to sell, good-day!'

'Hold on a minute,' said Sobakevich, taking the hand Chichikov offered in farewell and leading him back into the drawing-room. 'Let me put something to you.'

'There's no need. I've said everything I wish to say.'

'Now, just a moment!' said Sobakevich, keeping hold of his hand and treading on his toes, for our hero had omitted to take precautionary action, in punishment for which he was forced to hiss in pain and hop about on one leg.

'I crave your pardon! I seem to have discomforted you. Please, take a seat over here!' He seated his guest in an armchair with even a measure of dexterity, just as a well-schooled bear can turn somersaults and perform various tricks in response to the commands: 'Now, Misha, show us how country-wives take their steam bath,' or: 'How do the little children steal peas, Misha?'

'Seriously, I am wasting my time here, I must press on.'

'No, stay another minute and I'll tell you something you'll be happy to hear.' Hereupon Sobakevich moved his chair up close and whispered into his ear, as if imparting a secret: 'How about a quarter?'

'You mean twenty-five roubles? Not on your life, I wouldn't offer even a quarter of that; I will not up the price by a single copeck.'

Sobakevich fell silent. Chichikov too lapsed into silence. This continued for about two minutes. From his perch on the wall Bagration gazed down his aquiline nose at this transaction with a look of keen interest.

'What then is your final price?' asked Sobakevich at last.

'Two fifty.'

'If you ask me, you must have a boiled turnip in place of a heart. You could at least make it three roubles!'

'I cannot.'

'Very well then, have it your own way. I'm losing money, but that's just the good-natured dog in me,* I just can't help giving pleasure to my fellow-man. And now, I suppose, I'd better make out the deed of purchase, so that everything will be above board.'

'Naturally.'

'Very well. Now I expect I shall have to go into town.'

And thus the deal was concluded. They agreed to meet the very next day in town and to settle the deed of purchase. Chichikov asked for a list of the serfs. Sobakevich acquiesced willingly, and promptly stepped over to his writing bureau, where he set about transcribing in his own hand not only the list of all their names, but even giving an indication of their laudable qualities.

Meanwhile Chichikov busied himself, as he stood behind Sobakevich, with an inspection of his host's massive frame. As he gazed at that back, as broad as that of a squat Vyatka carthorse,* and at those legs, as solid as the cast-iron bollards positioned along city pavements, he could not help exclaiming inwardly: 'Heavens: the potter certainly spared no clay when he made you! A true case of "roughly hewn but toughly sewn", as they say!... Were you born a bear, I wonder, or have you been turned into one by this rough backwoods life, with its digging and ploughing, its bother with peasants, which has made you so tough and tight-fisted?

'On second thoughts, no: you would be just the same even if you'd had a fashionable education and embarked on life in St Petersburg rather than in this God-forsaken corner of the empire.

The only difference is that now you wolf down half a saddle of mutton with buckwheat, polishing off a curd pastry the size of a dinner-plate as a mere side dish, while there you would have nibbled at dainty little cutlets with truffles. And now you have serfs under your authority: you get along well with them, and naturally, you do not maltreat them because they are your own property, and it would only make things worse for you; there, on the other hand, you would have lorded it over underlings, whom you would have bullied because they were clerks and not your own property, like serfs; or else you would have embezzled funds!

'No, no: once a koulak, always a koulak—an old pinchfist like you will never unclench his fingers. And if one did manage to prize open one or two fingers, it would only make matters worse. If he acquires the most rudimentary knowledge of any science or skill, and then gains some influence in life, he'll use it to get the better of all those who really do know their stuff. Eventually, he might decide to show them what he's really capable of and he'll cook up such an elaborate directive that many will be left licking their wounds... Just imagine if they were all koulaks like that!...'

'The list is ready,' said Sobakevich, turning round again.

'It is?—Let's have a look!' Chichikov ran his eyes over it and marvelled at its neatness and precision: not only had the trade, title, age, and family status of each been recorded in detail, but in the margin he had even put special comments on their conduct, sobriety, and so forth: in a word, it was a pleasure to behold.

'Now let's have a little something in advance!' said Sobakevich.

'What do you want an advance for? You shall receive all the money in a lump sum in town.'

'All the same, that is the way it's done, you know', objected Sobakevich.

'I don't know how I can pay you, I didn't bring any money with me. Well, I do have ten roubles.'

'Ten! Give me fifty at least!'

Chichikov began to remonstrate that he did not have the money, but Sobakevich was so insistent that he produced another banknote, saying:

'As you wish, here is another fifteen, making twenty-five in all. I shall need a receipt, though.'

'Why on earth would you want a receipt?'

'It's always better to have a receipt. You never know, anything might happen.'

'Very well, let's have the money!'

'What's the hurry? Here it is in my hand! Write out your receipt and I'll hand it over, right away.'

'Really now, how can I write a receipt before I've seen the money?'

Chichikov released the notes from his hand. Sobakevich stepped closer to the table, and placed the fingers of his left hand on the money, while with his other hand he wrote on a scrap of paper that he had received in full the deposit of twenty-five roubles in state banknotes in payment for souls. After writing the receipt he re-examined the notes.

'Look at this old note!' he declared, holding one of them up to the light, 'and it's pretty tattered, but since we're friends we need not worry about that.'

'The old koulak!' thought Chichikov again. 'And a thorough scoundrel into the bargain!'

'Don't you want females?'

'No, thank you.'

'I'd let you have them cheap. As a friend: a rouble a piece.'

'No, I don't need any females.'

'Well if you don't need them, then there's no point discussing it. There's no accounting for taste; some love the priest, others the priest's wife, as the proverb says.'

There is one more thing I wanted to ask you,' said Chichikov, taking his leave. 'I trust this transaction will remain strictly between ourselves.'

'Of course, that goes without saying. Why should anyone else know?—What happens between close friends in the sincerity of their hearts should remain within the bonds of their friendship. Farewell! Thank you for visiting us; please do not neglect us in the future: if you have a spare hour or so, come round for dinner, spend some time with us. Perhaps we'll be able to do each other a further good service.'

'Very likely!' mused Chichikov, as he took his seat in the chaise. 'To think he made me pay two roubles fifty per dead soul, the old skinflint!'

He was displeased with Sobakevich's conduct. After all, which-ever way you looked at it, the man was an acquaintance, they had met at the governor's, and at the police chief's, yet he had behaved like a complete stranger, taking money for worthless rubbish! As the chaise drove out through the gates, he turned round and saw Sobakevich still standing on the porch, peering after his guest, as if hoping to ascertain whither he was bound.

'Confound him, he's still standing there!' Chichikov muttered through his teeth, and ordered Selifan to turn towards the peasants' huts and drive off in such a way that the chaise would not be visible from their master's house. He wished to call on Plyushkin, whose serfs, if Sobakevich was to be believed, were dying like flies, but he did not wish this to be known to Sobakevich. Once the chaise had reached the very end of the village, he called out to a peasant who had found an enormous log somewhere on the road and was now lugging it home on his shoulders, like an indefatigable ant.

'You there, beardy! How do we get to Plyushkin's estate from here, without going past the master's house?'

The peasant appeared at a loss for an answer.

'Well, don't you know?'

'No, sir, I don't know.'

'Shame on you! An old greybeard like you! You're telling me you don't know the miser Plyushkin, the one who doesn't feed his serfs properly?'

'Oh—you mean old Patches!' exclaimed the peasant.

He also affixed another adjective to the word 'patches', a very appropriate epithet, but one not employed in fashionable conversation, and therefore we shall omit it here. That it was singularly well-chosen was evident, however, from the way Chichikov continued chuckling in his chaise, even after they had travelled some distance and the peasant had long since been lost from sight. What strong language the Russian people use! Once an epithet is bestowed on someone, it will stick to his kith and kin, he will take it with him to his office, and into retirement, and to St Petersburg, and to the four corners of the earth. And no matter how cunningly he might try to ennoble his sobriquet, even if he hires scribblers to derive its etymology from some ancient princely line, it will avail him nothing: the name will croak for itself at the top of its ugly raven's voice and will make it quite plain from where this bird has flown. A word aptly spoken is as good as a word written down: it cannot be cut out, not even with an axe. And nothing could be more apt than some of the expressions coined in the heart of Russia, where there are no Germans, nor Finns, nor any other tribes, but only the salt of the Russian earth, with that quick and artful native wit which does not have to search in its pockets for the right word, which does not need to hatch it, like a broody hen her chicks, but unhesitatingly slaps it on you, like a label to be worn for ever, and there's no point in adding later that in reality your nose or mouth are like this or like that: your likeness has already been drawn, from head to toe, in a single stroke!

Just like that numberless multitude of churches and monasteries, with domes, cupolas, and crosses, which lie scattered across the devout expanse of holy Russia, so, across the face of the earth, does a countless multitude of tribes, generations, and nations churn, surge, and jostle one another in colourful confusion. And each and every nation, endowed with its own strength and creative abilities, its own vivid individuality and other gifts of God, sets itself apart from each every other nation by its own special word, a word which, no matter what object it describes, also reflects a facet of that nation's own character. The word of the Briton will resound with worldly wisdom and knowledge of the human heart; the ephemeral word of the Frenchman will flash for a brief moment of brilliance like a frivolous dandy and then vanish in the wind; with deliberation the German will fashion his portentous but skeletal word, not understandable to all; but there is no word so pert and quick, which bursts from the heart with such spontaneity, which seethes and bubbles with such vitality, as the aptly spoken Russian word.

CHAPTER SIX

Long, long ago, in the years of my youth, in the years of my childhood, which flashed by never to return, it delighted me to drive up for the first time to an unfamiliar place: it mattered not whether this was a small village, a poor little provincial town, a hamlet, or a settlement—the child's inquisitive eye uncovered much of interest wherever it chanced to look. Every building, anything which bore the least trace of the peculiar or the remarkable—they all caught my attention and amazed me. It could have been a granite government building, built in the usual manner with half its windows false, towering in splendid isolation over the woodpile of plain, single-storeyed houses erected by the local citizenry, or perhaps a perfectly rounded onion dome, totally clad in sheets of zinc, rising proudly above a new, freshly distempered church, whose walls gleamed as white as snow; it could have been a market, or some provincial dandy, that I happened to see in town—nothing could escape my eager attention as, thrusting my nose out of the post-chaise, I would stare at a frock-coat cut in a style I had never before seen, or at the wooden boxes filled with nails, with sulphur, gleaming yellow from afar, with raisins, or with soap, which I glimpsed through the doors of greengrocers' shops, alongside jars of dried-up confectionery from Moscow.

I would stare too at the infantry officer who strolled by on one side, blown God knows from where into these provincial doldrums, and at the merchant, smart in his waisted Siberian coat, who whizzed by in a racing droshky, and in my thoughts I too would be borne off with them into their wretched world. Should a local official walk past, I would at once fall to thinking: where was he bound, to a *soirée*, perhaps, at a cousin's house?—or was he on his way home, where, after lingering for half an hour on the porch until the last glow of dusk had faded, he would sit down to an early supper with his dear old mother, his wife, his wife's sister, and all his family? And I would wonder what they would chat about at that hour, when, once they had finished their soup, a tallow candle in an ancient, home-made holder would be brought in by the housemaid, a serf-girl with her coin necklace, or the house boy in his padded jacket.

As we drove up to the village of some landowner or other, I would gaze with interest at the tall, narrow wooden bell-tower or the broad, dark form of the old wooden church. From afar, the red roof and white chimneys of the manor house would beckon enticingly to me through the leafy branches, and I would wait impatiently for the gardens which lay on both sides of the driveway to unfold before me and for the house to be revealed in all its splendour, a splendour which then—unlike today, alas!—was free of any vulgarity; and from the appearance of the house I would try to judge what the landlord was like: was he fat, did he have any sons, or was he blessed with a brood of six daughters, filling the house with their ringing, girlish laughter and games, and was the youngest girl, as always, the prettiest of all, and were they black-eyed, and was he a jovial fellow himself, or sullen as the last week of September, forever studying his almanac* and discoursing on subjects that are so tedious to young people, such as rye and wheat?

Today when I drive up to an unfamiliar village I do so with complete indifference, and with like indifference I survey its vulgar aspect; it holds no appeal for my now cold gaze, it fails to divert me, and what in earlier years would have brought animation to my face, arousing laughter and incessant chatter, now slips past me and my immobile lips preserve an impassive silence. Oh my youth! Oh my freshness!*

Chichikov was so busy chuckling over the nickname that the peasants had bestowed upon Plyushkin, that he failed to observe that they had driven into the centre of an extensive village, made up of a large number of little houses and streets. He was soon made aware of this, however, by a violent jolt, caused by the log paving, compared to which the cobblestones of a town are a delight. These logs jump up and down like piano keys, and the incautious traveller will be rewarded either with a bump on the back of his head, or a bruise on his forehead, or—most painful of all—he may even bite off the tip of his tongue.

He noticed something particularly dilapidated about all the buildings: the log walls of the cottages were old and dark; the roofs were threadbare and full of holes, some were in such disrepair that all that remained were the cross-piece and the rib-like side beams. It was as if the owners themselves had removed all the shingles and planks, reasoning—quite correctly, of course—that a house cannot be roofed while it rains and when it's fine there's no rain anyway, so why stay cooped up inside like an housewife, when there's plenty of space at the inn and outdoors—in a word, anywhere you like. The windows in the cottages were unglazed, some had been stuffed with rags or an old coat, while those little balustraded balconies beneath the roofs, which for some unknown reason are often built on to Russian peasant cottages, stood askew and had turned so sullenly black that they were no longer even picturesque. In many places huge ricks of corn, which had evidently stood there for a long time, stretched in rows behind the houses; they had taken on the colour of old, badly fired bricks, while a great variety of weeds sprouted on top of them and shrubs grew in their sides. The grain clearly belonged to the local master.

Two village churches, one beside the other, came into sight behind the ricks of corn and the dilapidated roofs, now on the right, now on the left, as the chaise negotiated the turns; the one was an abandoned wooden church and the other a brick church, with dingy yellow walls, cracked and stained. Then parts of the landowner's residence hove into view, and finally the whole building became visible at the point where the line of cottages came to an end, giving way to a large empty vegetable plot, perhaps a cabbage patch, encircled with a low, partly broken fence. This strange castle, immensely, inordinately long, looked like a vast, decrepit invalid. In places it had one storey; in others two; from its dark roof, which did not everywhere provide secure protection for its ancient interior, two belvederes protruded, one opposite the other, both lurching to one side and stripped of whatever paint had once covered them. The walls of this edifice, with the plaster crumbled away to reveal the bare stuccoed wattle beneath, had clearly suffered badly from every manner of storm, rain, whirlwind, and inclement autumn weather. Of the windows only two were open, the others being shuttered or even boarded up. And even these two windows were half-blind; a triangular dark-blue piece of sugar-paper had been stuck over one of them.

An old and spreading garden, overgrown and choked with weeds, which stretched away behind the house, beyond the village and eventually merged with the fields, appeared to be the only source of greenery in this vast village and was the single vivid feature in all its picturesque desolation.* The crowns of the untended trees merged together to form a mass of green clouds and trembling, asymmetrical arboreal cupolas along the distant horizon. The colossal white trunk of a birch tree, decapitated by violent winds or storms, towered above this mass of greenery like a gleaming, perpendicular marble column; where the capital to that column would have stood the trunk ended in a jagged, oblique fracture, which showed black against the snowy whiteness of the bark, like a cap, or a dark bird. A tangle of hops, which choked the bushes of elder, rowan, and hazel growing below, ran along the top of the entire palisade around the garden before meandering upwards to wreathe around the fractured birch. On reaching the halfway point the hops swung down again, either to catch on to the tops of other trees or to hang in the air, plaiting their slender, sticky tendrils into ringlets that swayed gently in the breeze. In places the green thickets, which caught the rays of the sun, fell apart to reveal between them a shadowy hollow, yawning like the dark maw of a beast; this was entirely enveloped in shadow, and only the faintest impression could be gleaned of the fuliginous depths within: a narrow, winding path, a broken balustrade, a sagging gazebo, the hollow trunk of an ancient willow, and, behind the willow, a grizzled and bedraggled underbrush, which thrust out its hoary stubble of tangled twigs and leaves, grown dry and brittle in that terrible, forsaken place, and finally, the bough of a young maple, reaching forth its leafy green fronds, one of which— miraculously transformed by a shaft of sunlight which had penetrated behind it into something translucent and fiery—glowed wondrously amidst this impenetrable gloom.

To one side, at the very edge of the garden, a group of tall aspens rose above the other trees, lifting enormous crows' nests aloft on their trembling summits. Boughs that had been broken, but not totally detached, dangled their withered leaves. In short, it was all somehow splendid, in a way that neither nature nor art alone could contrive, but as can only occur through their union, when the cumulative and often senseless labours of man are lent a finishing touch by nature's chisel, which lightens the heavy masses, sweeps away the crudely obvious symmetry and wretched rents and tears, through which the naked, unconcealed plan is revealed, and imparts a marvellous warmth to everything that has been created in the coldness of calculated cleanliness and propriety.

After following the road round one or two bends our hero finally found himself in front of the house, which now struck him as even more wretched. A green mould had already spread over the ancient timbers on the fence and gate. A profusion of buildings—cottages, barns, cellars, all visibly dilapidated—crowded the courtyard. Everything bespoke a former agricultural prosperity but now all wore an aspect of utter gloom. There was nothing in evidence to enliven the picture: neither the opening of doors nor the stir of people emerging from within—none of the lively hustle and bustle of a home. Only the main gate was open, and that merely to admit a peasant with a heavily laden cart, covered with bast matting, who entered this desolate scene as if with the deliberate intent of breathing a little life into it; at any other time the gate too would have been securely fastened, as was evident from the massive padlock hanging from an iron staple. By one of the buildings Chichikov soon espied a figure, squabbling with the peasant who had just driven up in his cart. For a long time he could not work out whether this creature was man or woman. Its garb was quite indeterminate, very like a woman's *capote* with a hood such as those worn by village serving-wenches—only the voice struck him as a little husky for a woman.

'Yes, a woman!' he said to himself and at once added: 'No, it's not!'—'A woman, of course!' he said at last, when he had had a closer look. For her part the creature stared back just as hard at him. Guests must have been rare here, for she scrutinized not only him, but also Selifan, and the horses, starting with the tail and continuing to the head. Judging by the keys hanging from her belt and the way she scolded the peasant in roundly abusive language Chichikov concluded that this must be the housekeeper.

'Listen, my good woman,' he said, alighting from his chaise. 'Is the master at home?'

'Not at home,' interrupted the housekeeper, without waiting for him to finish his question, and then, a moment later, added: 'And what do you want?'

'I have business!'

'Go inside!' said the housekeeper, turning her back on him, which he noticed was dusted with flour, while there was a great rent lower down in her *capote*.

He entered the large, dark hall, as cold and draughty as a cellar. From here he passed into a room, also very dark, although some faint light seeped in through a large chink at the bottom of the door.

Opening this door he at last found himself in the light, and was astounded by the disorder which he saw before him. Perhaps it was the day on which all the floors were scrubbed, so all the furniture had, for the time being, been stacked in here. On one table there stood a broken chair, and next to it a clock with a motionless pendulum, to which a spider had already affixed its web. Here too, turned sideways against the wall, stood a cupboard full of old silver, decanters, and Chinese porcelain. On top of a bureau, inlaid with mother-of-pearl, pieces of which had long since fallen out, exposing the glue-filled grooves in the yellow wood beneath, lay a mass of assorted rubbish: a pile of papers covered in a fine scrawl and held down by a marble paper-weight, shaped like an egg on top and green with mould, an ancient, leather-bound book with red edging, a dried-up lemon, which had shrivelled to the size of a hazelnut, the broken-off arm of a chair, a wine-glass containing some sort of liquid and three flies, over which a letter had been placed, a small lump of sealing wax, a scrap of rag picked up somewhere, two quill pens, stained with ink and as dried up as if victims of consumption, a tooth-pick, completely yellowed, which the owner had, in all probability, used to pick his teeth well before the invasion of Moscow by the French.*

The walls were crowded with pictures hanging in utter confusion: a long, yellowed engraving of some battle, with enormous drums, shouting soldiers in tricorns, and drowning horses, hung in a glassless mahogany frame with thin bronze strips along the side and little bronze discs at the corners. Alongside this an enormous, age-darkened picture occupied half the wall, painted in oils and depicting flowers, fruit, a watermelon cut in half, the head of a boar, and a duck hanging by its feet. From the centre of the ceiling hung a chandelier in a canvas sack, so layered with dust that it resembled an enormous silk cocoon around a giant worm. Heaped on the floor in the corner were various coarser items impossible to place on tables. What exactly was to be found in this heap it was hard to discern, for it was caked in a layer of dust so thick that any hand which touched it would at once have been encased in a brown glove; more conspicuous than the other items were a broken-off piece of a wooden spade and the sole of an ancient boot. One would never have thought that this room was inhabited by a living creature, had this fact not been proclaimed by an old and well-worn night-cap lying on the table.

While Chichikov was thus engaged in surveying these strange furnishings, a side door opened to admit the housekeeper he had seen outside. But now he observed that this creature was more likely the steward than the housekeeper: a housekeeper, at any rate, should not need to shave her beard, whereas this one did shave, and, it would seem, somewhat infrequently, for his entire chin from the cheeks downwards resembled one of those wire curry-combs that are used in a livery-stable to groom the horses. Chichikov, adopting an interrogative mien, waited with impatience for the steward to speak. For his part, the steward also waited for Chichikov to say something. Finally the visitor, somewhat nonplussed by this peculiar misapprehension, brought himself to ask:

'So where's the master? In his room, is he?'

'The master's here,' said the steward.

'Where "here"?' repeated Chichikov.

'For heaven's sake, are you blind or something?' asked the steward. 'Here in front of you! I'm the master!'

Whereupon our hero recoiled and stared closely at the figure before him. In his time he had seen many people of every imaginable type, even such as the gracious reader and I may never have occasion to see; but one such as this he had never before seen. There was nothing remarkable about the face; it was practically identical to that of many scrawny old men, except that the chin was extremely prominent, so much as that its owner had to keep covering it with a handkerchief lest he drool on it; his little eyes had not yet lost their gleam and darted about eagerly beneath his tufted eyebrows like mice poking their sharp little noses out of their dark mouseholes, with their ears pricked up and their whiskers twitching, on the lookout for a lurking cat or a mischievous small boy, lying in wait, as they suspiciously sniff the air.

Still more remarkable was his attire. By no exertion of the imagination could one possibly divine the material used to make his dressing-gown: the sleeves and upper skirts were shiny and greasy to the point where they shone like the Russian leather used for boots; at the back hung not two, but as many as four flaps, from which the cotton stuffing dangled in lumps. Wound round his neck was something similarly mysterious: a stocking, perhaps, or a knitted sash, or even a stomacher, but most definitely not a cravat. In a word, if Chichikov had met him thus attired somewhere by the doors of a church, he would probably have given him a copper coin. For, to our hero's credit, it must be said that his heart was compassionate and he would never walk past a beggar without giving him a copper coin.

Yet the person standing before him was no beggar but a land-owner. This landowner possessed more than a thousand souls, and you would be hard put to find another landowner with as much wheat in grain, flour, and stooks, or whose barns and drying sheds were so crammed with linens, bolts of cloth, dressed and tawed sheepskins, dried fish, and every kind of vegetable or preserve. Any-one glancing into his workyard, with its stores of timber and never-used pots and pans, would imagine that he had somehow landed up in the woodcraft market* in Moscow, to which the city's industrious mothers-in-law bustle each morning, cooks in tow, to do their house-hold shopping and where you find mountains of wooden utensils—jointed, chiselled, dovetailed, or wattled: barrels, vats, piggins, skeels, pitchers with spouts and without spouts, twin drinking cups, bast punnets, trugs, into which country women put their yarn and thread and other odds and ends, kists made from aspen slats, pyxes of plaited birch-bark, and much else besides, of the sort used by both rich and poor Russia. Yet what possible use could Plyushkin have had for such a mountain of these artefacts? In the course of an entire human life he could not have found employment for them all even on two estates like his—yet he still thought them insufficient. Not content with what he had, he patrolled the streets of his village every day, peering under the footbridges, and beneath the duckboards, and everything he saw—an old sole, a woman's rag, an iron nail, or a clay shard—he would carry home to add to the pile Chichikov had seen in the corner of the room.

'There goes the fisherman out to his nets!' the peasants would say, seeing him setting off in search of booty.

It was true: once he had passed through there was no need to sweep the streets; should a visiting officer happen to lose one of his spurs—this same spur would at once make its way to Plyushkin's pile; if a peasant woman stood gawking at the well and took her eyes off her bucket, he would squirrel away the bucket too. If, however, an observant peasant caught him in the act he would not argue and would promptly surrender the purloined object; but once it had found its way to the pile it was gone for good: he would swear till he was blue in the face that the thing was his own, bought at some time or other, from someone or other, or inherited from his grandfather. In his room he would pick up everything he saw on the floor: a lump of sealing wax, a scrap of paper, a quill pen, and all this he would place on his bureau or on the window-sill.

And yet there had once been a time when he had been merely a thrifty squire! He had had a wife and a family, and neighbours would come for dinner, to listen to his advice and learn from him the skills of farming and the prudence of thrift. Everything ran briskly and smoothly: the windmills and fulling mills, the clothmills, spinning wheels, and joiners' lathes all worked; nothing eluded the master's keen eye, and like the sedulous spider he scurried everywhither, finicky but effectual, to all four corners of the web of his husbandry. At that time his features bore no trace of excessive emotions, but his eyes revealed an astute mind; his conversation was imbued with experience and knowledge of the world and it was a pleasure to hear him talk; his affable and talkative spouse was renowned for her hospitality; guests would be met by two pretty daughters, both fair-haired and fresh as roses; his son would come running out, a lively young lad who would give everyone a welcoming kiss, whether they liked it or not.

All the windows in the house were kept open, and in the mansard lived the French tutor, a splendid exponent of the art of shaving and a fine marksman: he frequently brought home a brace of black-cock or wild duck for the table, or sometimes only sparrows' eggs, which the cook would fry for him, for no one else in the house would eat them. The mansard was shared by his country-woman, governess to the two girls. The master himself would appear at dinner in a frock-coat, a little worn perhaps, but still neat, with the elbows still intact and free of patches. But the good lady died; a portion of the keys, and with them certain petty chores, now devolved upon her husband.

Plyushkin became more fretful, and like all widowers, more suspicious and niggardly. He felt he could not rely in all matters on his elder daughter Aleksandra Stepanovna, and, as it happens, rightly so, because Aleksandra Stepanovna soon eloped with a staff-captain from some cavalry regiment or other—God knows which, with whom she concluded a hasty marriage in a village church, well aware that her father nursed a strange prejudice against officers, regarding them all as inveterate card-sharps and spendthrifts. For a valediction her father sent her his curses and did not bother to pursue her. The house became even emptier. He started to display more obvious signs of miserliness; and this developed further as the grey streaks which are the faithful friend of miserliness began to appear in his coarse hair; the French tutor was dismissed because the time had come for the son to enter the civil service; the governess was banished, because she proved to have been not entirely blameless in the abduction of Aleksandra Stepanovna; the son, having been dispatched to the provincial capital to prepare for what his father considered worthwhile service in the Civic Chambers, elected instead to join a regiment, and once he had received his commission wrote to his father with a request for money to buy his uniform; as might have been expected, he received what in common parlance is called a fig.

Finally, his youngest daughter, the last of his children to remain at home, died, and the old man was left alone as watchman, custodian, and proprietor of his riches. The solitary life provided ample nourishment for miserliness, which has the appetite of a wolf: the more it devours the more insatiable its hunger grows; all common human feelings, which in any case had never been deeply rooted in him, gradually faded and every day something more was lost in this worn-out wreck of a man. Then, as ill-fortune would have it, and as if to corroborate his views on officers in general, his son lost all his money at cards; he sent the lad his heartfelt paternal curse and never again sought to discover whether he was still alive or not.

Every year more and more windows were shuttered up in his house; finally only two were left, and one of these, as the reader has already seen, was papered over; with every year more and more important areas of his farm business were lost to his sight and his attentions became increasingly myopic, focusing on the papers and quill pens which he collected in his room; he became increasingly unyielding to the merchants who came to buy his farm produce; the buyers would haggle and haggle, but finally they abandoned him altogether, protesting that this was no man but a monster; his hay and wheat rotted, his bins and ricks of grain turned to compost, ideal for the cultivation of cabbages; the flour in his cellars hardened to stone and had to be chipped away; the cloths, linens, and other homespun textiles disintegrated at the touch. He had already forgotten exactly what he owned and how much and could only remember such matters as where and in which cupboard he had placed a small decanter containing the remains of some liqueur, on which he made a mark to prevent any pilfering; or where he had placed his quill pen and sealing wax.

Meanwhile income continued to accrue on the farm just as before: the peasants had to continue paying the same amount of quit-rent,* their womenfolk continued to render the same contribution of nuts as before, the weaver women had to weave for him the same quantity of linen;* all this was piled in storerooms, where it became mouldy, rotting away into shreds, and finally the owner himself rotted away into a mere shred of humanity.

Aleksandra Stepanovna visited on two occasions with her little son, in the hope of getting something out of him; evidently the peripatetic life with her officer husband was not so rosy as she had pictured it before their elopement. Plyushkin did in fact offer her his pardon and even gave his little grandson a button that was lying on the table to play with, but he would not part with any money. The next time Aleksandra Stepanovna came with both her children and brought her father an Easter cake she had baked him, and a new dressing-gown, because the one he wore was not merely embarrassing, but a disgrace to behold. Plyushkin caressed both his grandsons, and seating them one on his right knee and the other on his left, jigged them up and down as if they were on horseback; he took the cake and the dressing-gown, but he gave his daughter not a bean, and with that Aleksandra Stepanovna's visits ended.

This, then, was the landowner that Chichikov now confronted! It must be said that his is a rare breed in Russia, where one is more likely to encounter the open hand than the closed fist, and the very existence of such a landowner is all the more striking when one compares him to his neighbour, who in all likelihood is a man much given to carousing and who revels in the grand Russian manner, living life, as they say, to the full. This neighbour lives on an estate before which the uninitiated visitor will stop with amazement, marvelling that such a potentate should suddenly be encountered here, amongst such petty, parochial householders! His white stone houses look like palaces, with their profusion of chimneys, belvederes, and weather-vanes, surrounded by flocks of outbuildings and every type of housing for visiting guests. His life seems to lack nothing. He gives theatrical shows and balls, his gardens are illuminated from dusk till dawn with a riot of torches and lampions, and reverberate with thunderous music. Half the province gathers here in its finery, to carouse beneath the trees, and no one finds it odd or alarming to see, in this blaze of light, an artificially illuminated branch, stripped of its own leaves, which protrudes from the midst of this foliage like a stage property, while the night sky beyond appears somehow darker and grimmer and twenty times more menacing and, with their leaves rustling high above, almost lost in the impenetrable gloom, the stern crowns of the trees murmur their indignation at the tawdry brilliance that lights up their roots below.

Plyushkin had now stood for several minutes without saying a word, while Chichikov could not yet manage to initiate a conversation, so distracted was he both by the appearance of his host and by everything else in his room. For a long time he could not find the right words to explain the reason for his visit. He was on the point of declaring that, having heard much of his host's virtue and the rare qualities of his soul, he deemed it his duty to offer him the personal tribute of his respect, but he caught himself in time, realizing that this would be somewhat excessive. Casting another sidelong glance at everything in the room he sensed that such words as 'virtue' and 'rare qualities of the soul' could most appropriately be replaced by the words 'economy' and 'good order'; and thus, having revised his speech accordingly, he said that, having heard great things of his host's economy and rare abilities in the management of his estates, he considered it his duty to make his acquaintance and to pay his respects in person. It might of course have been still better to adduce another, more plausible reason, but nothing else came to mind.

In response Plyushkin mumbled something through his lips, as he had no teeth, and while the exact sense of his exact words are not known, their general drift was probably as follows: 'To the devil with you and your respects!' But since hospitality is so ingrained with us that even a miser is unable to defy its laws, he at once added, somewhat more distinctly: 'Please be seated!'

'I have not received guests for quite some time,' he continued, 'and, to be quite honest, I see little point in them. People have developed a most despicable custom of calling on one another whilst their estates go to rack and ruin... and you even have to feed their horses with your own hay! I have long since had my dinner, and my kitchen is in a wretched, filthy state—the chimney has completely collapsed, so when you start a fire you expect the whole house to go up in flames.'

'Listen to that!' thought Chichikov. 'It's just as well I had that curd pastry and helping of mutton at Sobakevich's.'

'And as ill luck would have it, there's hardly a tuft of hay on my entire farm!' continued Plyushkin. 'Besides, how could one store it? It's only a little place, the peasants are idle and work-shy, all they think about is slipping off to the inn... You mark my words: I shall end up begging for a living in my old age!'

'But I was told,' ventured Chichikov diffidently, 'that you have more than a thousand souls.'

'Now who told you a thing like that? Why, you should have spat in the eye of the man who said it! He must be one of those pranksome types, having fun at your expense. More than a thousand souls— just imagine!—you go out and count them for yourself and you'll see there are next to none! In the last three years the cursed typhus has carried off the best part of my peasants.'

'You don't say! So were many carried off?' exclaimed Chichikov with enthusiasm.

'I lost a good number, yes.'

'If I might make so bold as to enquire: how many, to be precise?'

'Some eighty souls.'

'Never!'

'I have no reason to lie, sir.'

'Allow me to put another question: I presume these are all the souls that you've lost since the last census?'

'If only they were,' said Plyushkin. 'The worst of it is that there's as many as a hundred and twenty bitten the dust since the census.'

'Good heavens! A hundred and twenty?' exclaimed Chichikov, gaping in amazement.

'I'm too old to start lying, sir: I'll be seventy soon!' said Plyushkin. He appeared to take umbrage at Chichikov's almost joyous response. Chichikov realized that such apparent insensibility to another's misfortune was indeed improper, so he promptly uttered a deep sigh and expressed his condolences.

'The trouble is, you can't put condolences in your purse,' said Plyushkin. 'Now take the captain who lives close to me; devil knows where he sprung from, but he calls himself a relative: "Uncle! Uncle!" he says, and kisses my hand, and when he starts on his condolences he makes such a song and dance that you have to block your ears. His face is as red as a beet: he must hit the bottle heavily. I dare say he squandered all his money while serving in the army, or he let himself be fleeced by some actress, so now he comes to me with his condolences!'

Chichikov endeavoured to explain that his own condolences were of quite a different kind from those of the captain, and that he was prepared to demonstrate them not through empty words but in action and, wishing to delay matters no further and without beating about the bush, at once expressed his readiness to take upon himself the obligation to pay the soul tax for all the peasants who had met such unfortunate deaths. This proposal appeared to leave Plyushkin quite nonplussed. His eyes started from his head and he stared long and hard at Chichikov before finally asking:

'Did you yourself serve in the army, by any chance?'

'No,' answered Chichikov in a rather evasive way, 'I was in the civil service.'

'The civil service?' repeated Plyushkin, and started to gnaw his lips, as if eating something. 'But how could you do it? It would mean a loss to you?'

'For your pleasure I am prepared to assume even a loss.'

'Ah, sir! Ah my benefactor!' exclaimed Plyushkin, in his delight failing to notice that a dollop of snuff was protruding in a most unpicturesque manner from his nose, like a smear of coffee-grounds, and that the skirts of his dressing-gown had parted to reveal underclothes that were not entirely suitable for public scrutiny. 'Now there's comfort for an old man! Praise the Lord and His saints above!...'

With that Plyushkin ran out of words. But scarcely a minute passed before this joy which had so suddenly transfigured his wooden features disappeared just as suddenly, as if it had never been at all, and his face once again took on its preoccupied look. He even mopped his brow with his handkerchief and, rolling it into a ball, fell to rubbing his upper lip.

'Allow me to enquire, without wishing to anger you in any way, do you intend to pay the tax on them every year? And are you going to give the money to me, or to the Treasury?'

'We shall do it like this: we'll draw up a deed of purchase, just as if they were alive and as if you had sold them to me.'

'Ah yes, a deed of purchase...' said Plyushkin, growing pensive and once again gnawing his lips. 'But deeds—they cost money, you know. Those chancery clerks have no shame! In the old days, you know, you could get away with half a rouble in brass and a bag of flour, but now you must hand over an entire cartload of grain, and a ten-rouble banknote into the bargain, they're such money-grubbers! I cannot understand why the priests don't do something about it; they should bring it up in their sermons: after all, whichever way you look at it, there's no going against the word of God.'

'Oh no, you'd never go against it, would you!' thought Chichikov, and promptly announced that, out of respect for his host, he was even prepared to take all these expenses upon himself.

Hearing these assurances, Plyushkin concluded that his guest must be a complete fool and was lying when he said he had been in the civil service; he had probably been an officer after all, and had spent his time chasing after chorus girls. Despite all this, he could not conceal his delight, and wished his guest every possible blessing and the same for his little children, without even ascertaining whether he had any or not. Stepping up to the window he rapped on the pane and shouted: 'Hey, Proshka!'

A moment later they could hear someone run panting into the anteroom, and fuss around in there for some time with a loud stamping of boots, before the door finally opened to admit Proshka, a lad of about thirteen, shod in such huge boots that they almost dropped off his feet whenever he took a step. Why Proshka had such big boots can easily be explained: for the use of all his domestic serv-ants, however many there were in the house, Plyushkin kept only one pair of boots, which always had to remain in the anteroom. Anyone summoned into the master's presence had to scurry bare-foot across the yard, put on the boots once inside the house and appear before the master thus shod. On his departure from the room he would leave the boots in the anteroom again and walk back on his own tender soles. If a visitor were to glance out of the window in autumn, and especially when the light morning ground-frosts had started, he would see the entire household staff performing leaps of which the most accomplished dancer in any theatre would have been justly proud.

'Just take a look at that mug!' said Plyushkin to Chichikov, pointing at Proshka's face. 'Stupid as a tree-stump, but leave anything lying around and he'll steal it in a flash! Well, fool, why have I called you?'

This he followed with a brief silence, which Proshka answered with a similar silence.

'Put on the samovar, d'you hear, and take this key to Mavra so she can go to the pantry: she'll find some dry Easter cake on the shelf in there, the one Aleksandra Stepanovna brought, for us to have with our tea!... Wait, where are you going? Numbskull! Fathead! Can you not stand still for two seconds, or is the devil in your legs?... First hear me out: the crust might be a bit mouldy, so tell her to scrape it off, but mind she doesn't throw away the crumbs, she can feed them to the chickens. And you'd better watch out, young fellow, don't you go poking your nose in the pantry or you'll get what for! If you want to taste something, I'll give you a taste of the birch rod! I know you've a fine healthy appetite, that'll sharpen it for you! Just you dare go into the pantry, I'll be watching all the while from the window here.

'You can't trust them with anything,' he continued, turning to Chichikov, after Proshka had removed himself and his boots. Having said this, he started to peer suspiciously at Chichikov too. This extraordinary show of magnanimity began to seem highly improbable to him and he said to himself: 'How the devil do I know, maybe he's just another loud-mouth, like all these spendthrifts and ne'er-do-wells; he'll tell you a lot of lies for his tea, and then make himself scarce.' And therefore, partly out of caution and partly wishing to test Chichikov a little, he suggested it would be a good idea to conclude the transfer as swiftly as possible, because human life is an uncertain thing: today a man may be alive and well, but God alone knows what the morrow will bring.

Chichikov declared himself ready to settle the matter that very minute if need be and requested only that he be given a list of all the peasants' names.

This set Plyushkin's mind at rest. He appeared first to consider some course of action, and there—sure enough—he took up his keys, walked across to a cupboard, opened the door, rummaged about amongst the cups and glasses, and finally announced:

'I can't seem to be able to find it, but I had a splendid liqueur in here somewhere, if someone hasn't drunk it already! The servants are such thieves! Ah yes, I think this is it!' Chichikov saw in his hand a decanter, covered in a thick layer of dust, like a padded jacket. 'This was made by my late wife,' continued Plyushkin, 'and that rogue of a housekeeper was all for throwing it away, and didn't even cork it up, the wretch! In no time it was full to the brim with bugs and weevils, but I cleared all the rubbish out and it's quite clean now; I'll pour you a little glass.'

But Chichikov declined the splendid liqueur, saying that he had already eaten and drunk.

'You've already eaten and drunk!' said Plyushkin. 'Yes, of course, you can always tell a man of breeding: he eats nothing, yet he doesn't grow hungry. Now take some thieving ne'er-do-well, no matter how much you feed him... Like that captain, he comes here and says: "Give us something to eat, Uncle!" And I'm no more uncle to him that he's grandpa to me. There's probably not so much as a crust of bread in his own home, so he comes to scrounge from me! Well, I suppose you want a list of all those idlers? Oddly enough, as if I knew you were coming, I wrote all their names down on a separate piece of paper, so that I could have them struck off the census at the very next opportunity.'

Plyushkin put on his eyeglasses and started to rummage through his papers. He untied countless bundles of documents and in the process treated his guest to such a helping of dust that the latter succumbed to a fit of sneezing. He finally extracted a scrap of paper, which had been scrawled all over. Peasants' names covered it as densely as midges. There were all sorts of names: Paramonov was there, and Pimenov, and Panteleimonov, and Chichikov even spotted some Grigory Doezzhai-ne-Doedesh—Go-But-Never-Get-There*—in all, more than one hundred and twenty names. Chichikov's face beamed at the sight of such abundance. Stuffing the list in his pocket he remarked to Plyushkin that to conclude the deal it would be necessary for him to travel into town.

'Into town? But how can I? How can I leave my house? My peasants are either thieves or rogues: in one day they'll pick this place so clean there won't be anywhere to hang my coat.'

'In that case, do you not have an acquaintance who could do it?'

'What acquaintance? All my acquaintances have either kicked the bucket or become unacquainted. But wait a moment, what am I saying, of course I have!' he exclaimed. 'The president himself is an acquaintance, in the old days he even used to drive out to visit me—how could I forget! We were trough-mates at school, we used to climb fences together! What do I mean, no acquaintances? When I have an acquaintance like that! Why not write to him?'

'Why not, indeed?'

'Fancy forgetting him, an acquaintance like that! We were such great friends at school.'

A ray of warmth suddenly glanced across those wooden features, as they expressed—not feeling—but a pale reflection of feeling, calling to mind the effect created by a drowning man who suddenly bobs back to the surface. This event is greeted with a shout of joy from the crowd standing along the bank, but it is in vain that the delighted brothers and sisters cast a rope from the bank and wait for his back, or his arms, exhausted by the struggle, to reappear: that appearance was the last. After this all is dark and silent and the now unruffled surface of the unresponsive element now seems all the more ghastly and desolate. Thus too did Plyushkin's face, after one momentary flash of feeling, become still more unfeeling and more crass.

'There was a quarter square of clean paper lying here on the table,' he said. 'I cannot think where it's got to: these servants of mine are such rogues!' He set about looking under the table and above the table, rummaging through everything, and finally shouted: 'Mavra! Come here, Mavra!'

His summons was answered by the entry of a woman bearing a plate. On this lay a piece of the dry cake with which the reader is already familiar. The following conversation ensued between them:

'Where did you put that paper, you thieving hag?'

'Honest to God, master, I never saw any paper, excepting a tiny little scrap which you used to cover the wine glass.'

'I can see by your eyes that you filched it.'

'Now why would I want to filch it? It's no good to me: I can't read or write.'

'You liar, you took it to the sexton's boy: he knows a few letters, so you gave it to him.'

'But the sexton's boy, if he wants, can get his own paper. He has no use for your piece of paper!'

'Just you wait: for this, on the Day of Judgement, the devils will give you a good thrashing with their steel rods! You'll see what a thrashing you'll get!'

'But why should they thrash me when I never even touched your piece of paper? Let them thrash me for some other woman's weakness, but no one's ever had reason to accuse me of stealing.'

'All the same, those devils will thrash you anyway! They'll say: "Take that, you scoundrel, for deceiving your master!" and they'll thrash you with red-hot rods too!'

'Then I shall say: "I've done nothing, honest to God, I've done nothing, I never took nothing..." Look, there it is on the table! You're always blaming me for no reason!'

Plyushkin saw that the quarter piece of paper was indeed on the table, and he paused for a moment, gnawing his lips, before announcing:

'So what's all the fuss about? What a quarrelsome old nag! Say one word to her, and she answers with ten! Run along and fetch a candle so I can seal the letter. No, wait: knowing you, you'll bring a tallow candle and that tallow melts too fast: once you've lit it that's the end of the candle, it burns to nothing—just bring me a taper!'

Mavra went off. Plyushkin seated himself in the armchair and took up a quill pen; for a long time he turned the quarter piece of paper round and round, wondering whether he might not make two eighths out of this one quarter, but he finally decided it couldn't be done; he plunged his pen into the inkwell, which contained some mould-covered liquid and a mass of dead flies on the bottom, and started to write, producing letters that looked more like musical notation, constantly having to restrain the eager motion of his hand, which skipped across the paper, and stingily cramming the lines close together, although this also made him realize with some regret that a lot of empty space would still be left on the paper.

To what a nadir of paltriness, pettiness, and squalor a man can sink! How could he change so! But is this really true to life? —It is, it's all true to life, for anything can happen to a man. Your ardent youth of today would recoil in horror if you were to show him his own portrait as an old man. Once you set off on life's journey, once you take your leave of those gentle years of youth and enter the harsh, embittering years of manhood, remember to keep with you all your human emotions, do not leave them by the wayside, for you will not pick them up again! Grim and terrible is the old age which awaits us, and nothing does it give in return! The grave itself is more merciful than old age, for at least on the gravestone you will find written the words: 'Here a man lies buried!' but in the cold, unfeeling features of inhuman old age you can read nothing.

'You don't happen to have a friend who might need some fugitive souls?' asked Plyushkin, folding the piece of paper.

'You have fugitives as well?' Chichikov asked quickly, awaking from his reverie.

'I'm very much afraid I do. My son-in-law made some enquiries, he reckons we've lost track of them now, but then he's a military man: an expert at jingling his spurs but when it comes to legal matters...'

'How many are there, precisely?'

'Could be as many as seventy.'

'You don't say?'

'There are, I swear! There's never a year passes without some of them giving me the slip. My peasants are a terribly greedy lot: for want of anything better to do they've developed the habit of guzzling, and I don't even have any food myself... I'd take anything I was offered for them. So this is my advice to your friend: even if he only tracks down a dozen of them, his money will be well spent. After all, a registered soul is worth a good five hundred roubles.'

'I'm afraid my friend will never get a sniff of this,' said Chichikov to himself, and then explained that such a friend would be impossible to find, and that the expenditure incurred in such a business would make it not worth while, for the legal costs alone one would have to sell the shirt off one's back and worse; still, if Plyushkin really was in such straitened circumstances, he was prepared to offer... but it would be such a trifle it was hardly worth mentioning.

'How much would you offer?' asked Plyushkin, with the eagerness of a Jew: his hands started to tremble like quicksilver.

'I would give twenty-five copecks per soul.'

'And how would you pay, in cash?'

'Yes, the money's here.'

'Out of pity for my poverty, would you make it forty copecks a piece?'

'My most respected sir!' said Chichikov. 'Not merely forty kopecks but five hundred roubles would I give! I should be delighted to pay so much, for I can see a respected and kind old man being forced by his own good nature to endure adversity.'

'Why yes, that's how it is! Honestly, that's the truth!' exclaimed Plyushkin, hanging his head and shaking it in desolation. 'It all stems from my own good nature.'

'There, you see, I comprehended your character at once. So why should I not give you five hundred roubles per soul—But alas... I lack the means; with your pardon, I might be prepared to put it up another five copecks, thereby bringing the price of each soul to thirty copecks.'

'As you wish, sir, but could you just add on another two copecks per soul?'

'Very well, another two copecks I shall add. How many of them do you have? You did say seventy, I seem to recall?'

'No, in all there are seventy-eight.'

'Seventy-eight, hm, let me see... at thirty copecks each, that will be...' Our hero deliberated for one second, no longer, and promptly declared: 'That will be twenty-four roubles and ninety-six copecks!' Chichikov was good at arithmetic. He at once made Plyushkin write a receipt and handed over the money, which his host received with both hands and carried across to his writing bureau as gingerly as if it were a bowl of liquid which he was afraid of spilling. On reaching the bureau he counted the money again and deposited it, still with extraordinary caution, in a drawer, where, no doubt, it was destined to lie until the day when Father Karp and Father Polikarp, the two priests in the village, would lay him to his earthly rest, to the un-bounded joy of his daughter and son-in-law, and perhaps also of the captain who claimed kinship with him. After stowing away the money Plyushkin seated himself in an armchair and appeared at a loss for a topic on which to discourse.

'What, are you going already?' he said, observing a slight move-ment made by Chichikov, who was only trying to take his handker-chief out of his pocket.

This question reminded our hero that there was indeed no pur-pose in lingering any longer.

'Yes, I must be away!' he announced, taking up his hat.

'And the tea?'

'Thank you, but I think perhaps we'll leave the tea for another time.'

'Oh dear, and I've called for the samovar. I myself, to be quite honest, am no great lover of tea: it's a costly beverage, and the price of sugar has gone up mercilessly. Proshka! We don't need the samovar. Take the cake back to Mavra, do you hear: tell her to put it back where it was—no, on second thoughts, bring it here, I'd better put it away myself. Farewell, kind sir, and may God bless you, and be sure to give my letter to the president. Yes! Let him read it, he's an old friend of mine. Imagine! He and I were school-fellows once!'

Thereupon this weird apparition, this shrivelled old ancient saw Chichikov off from the yard, after which he ordered the gates to be locked at once, and then toured his storerooms to check whether the guards were at their posts; they stood at every corner, drumming with wooden spoons on an empty barrel, rather than the customary iron bar.* After this he peered into the kitchen, where, on the pretext of ascertaining whether his servants were enjoying their supper, he ate his fill of their cabbage soup and porridge and, after scolding them all roundly for thieving and general misconduct, returned to his own room.

Once on his own again he started to consider how he could thank his guest for such truly unparalleled generosity. 'I shall present him my pocket watch. It is a good one, after all, real silver, and not some pinchbeck alloy or bronze; a little damaged, but then he can have it repaired; he is still a young man, he needs a pocket watch to please his betrothed! On second thoughts, no,' he added after a few moments' consideration; 'I would do better to leave it to him after my death, in my will, so that he remembers me.'

Even without a pocket watch, however, our hero was in the best possible spirits. This latest acquisition—so unexpected—had been a most fortuitous windfall. Imagine, not only did he have dead souls, but also fugitives—all told, some two hundred and more! True, even on the drive up to Plyushkin's estate some sixth sense had told him that there would be gain in his visit, but he had never expected to make such a killing. All the way he remained in uncommonly high spirits; whistling away, pursing his lips and putting his fist to his mouth as if blowing a trumpet, and finally bursting into a song so outlandish that even Selifan, after listening for some time, said, with a slight shake of his head: 'Heaven help us, listen to the master sing!'

The gloom of dusk had already set in by the time they reached the town. Light and shade had merged completely and it seemed as if the objects themselves had blended into one another. The striped turnpike had taken on a strangely indeterminate colour; the moustache on the face of the soldier standing on guard appeared to grow on his forehead, high above his eyes, whilst his nose seemed to be missing altogether. From the rattling noise and lurching motion it was apparent that the chaise was now driving on cobblestones. The street lamps had not yet been kindled, lights burned in only a few windows, while in the side-streets and alleys various scenes and dialogues were being played out, as they invariably are at this evening hour in all towns where there are large numbers of soldiers, cabmen, and day-labourers and where one can see, flitting across the streets and crossroads like bats, specimens of that particular female species that go about wrapped in red shawls and wear their shoes on stockingless legs.

Chichikov did not notice them and was even oblivious of the many slender young officials brandishing thin canes, who were probably homeward bound after taking the air outside town. Every now and again certain exclamations, apparently feminine in origin, reached his ears: 'You're lying, you drunkard! I never allowed him any such liberties!' or: 'Put your fists down, you churl: let's go to the police station and I'll show you what's what!' In a word, those utterances which suddenly descend like a thick fog to cloud the vision of some day-dreaming twenty-year-old youth, who, as he emerges from the theatre, still carries in his head a street in Spain, night, and a wondrous woman's image, with a guitar and with curly locks. There are no bounds to his flights of fancy: he has ascended to heaven and is paying his compliments to the great poet Schiller* himself—when suddenly the fateful words ring out above him, like thunder, and he is brought back with a rude bump to earth—or, more precisely, to Sennaya Square,* to a spot near an inn, even—and once again real life resumes its prosaic strutting before him.

Finally the chaise, with a sudden hefty lurch, plunged through the gates of the inn, as if into a deep pit, and Chichikov was met by Petrushka, who helped his master out with one hand, while with the other he held down one flap of his coat, for he did not like the flaps to separate. The inn-servant also came running out, bearing a candle in his hand and a napkin over his shoulder. Whether the arrival of his master was a source of joy to Petrushka we do not know, but he and Selifan did at least exchange winks and his normally dour expression seemed to brighten somewhat on this occasion.

'Your Honour was gone a long time,' said the inn-servant, lighting the way up the stairs.

'Yes,' said Chichikov, climbing the steps, 'and how are things here?'

'God be praised,' answered the inn-servant, with a bow. 'Yesterday a lieutenant from some regiment or other arrived, he took room number sixteen.

'A lieutenant?'

'I don't know the regiment, but he's from Ryazan, with bay horses.'*

'Good, good, keep up the good work!' said Chichikov, repairing to his room. As he crossed the entrance-hall he wrinkled his nose and said to Petrushka: 'You could at least have opened the windows!'

'But I did open them,' said Petrushka, which was a bare-faced lie. His master knew perfectly well he was lying, but he could not be bothered to object. After his journey he was overcome with fatigue. Having called for an extremely light supper, consisting only of some sucking pig, he swiftly undressed and, climbing under the quilt, fell fast asleep, sinking into that blissful sleep enjoyed only by those lucky people who are not disturbed by haemorrhoids, fleas, or excessive cerebral abilities.

CHAPTER SEVEN

Happy the traveller who, after a long, tedious journey with its cold and slush and mud, groggy station masters, jingling bells, roadside repairs, altercations, coachmen, blacksmiths, and highway rogues of every description, at last espies a familiar roof and lights rushing towards him, and then sees before him the familiar rooms, hears the joyous cries of the servants running out to greet him, the noisy excitement of the children, and his wife's soft, soothing words, interrupted by ardent embraces, so heartfelt as to efface even the most dismal memories. Happy the family man, who has such a nook, but pity the poor bachelor!

Happy the writer who bypasses those tedious and repulsive characters whose lives impress us only with their misery, to reach instead characters who embody the supreme merits of human creation, the writer who, out of the maelstrom of images that spin past him every day, has selected but those rare exceptions, who has never once departed from the sublime pitch of his lyre, who has never descended from his lofty heights to the level of his paltry and wretched fellow men, and whose feet never so much as touch the ground, so utterly absorbed is he by his remote and exalted images.

Such a writer is to be doubly envied: he abides among these elevated creatures as among his own family; yet at the same time his glory spreads far and wide. He has clouded men's eyes with his spellbinding smoke-haze; he has cast his spell upon them, concealing from them all that is wretched in life and displaying to them Man in all his splendour. He drives his triumphal chariot amidst a tumult of applause, with admiring crowds following in his train. He is acclaimed a great, universal poet, soaring high above all other geniuses of this world, as the eagle soars high above all other denizens of the upper air. At the very mention of his name, young and ardent hearts begin to flutter and all eyes glisten with responsive tears... In his power he is unrivalled: he is a god!

But this is not the lot, nor this the destiny of the writer who dares to expose for scrutiny the reality which is constantly before our eyes, yet which these eyes—if indifferent—do not see: the hideous and appalling mire of petty cares in which our lives are bogged down, the writer who dares, with bold and unforgiving strokes of his remorseless chisel, to carve out in depth and clarity, for all to see, those commonplace characters, so cold and fragmented, whom we encounter in such great numbers on our journey through life, a journey that is often so bitter and tedious! Not for him the tumult of popular applause; not for him the spectacle of tears of gratitude and unanimous rapture of the souls he has moved; not for him the veneration of the sixteen-year-old maiden who, giddy with extravagant rapture, flies to meet him; not for him the sweet sensation of losing himself in the bewitching sounds he himself has uttered; not for him, finally, to escape the judgement of his contemporaries— that hypocritical, unfeeling judgement which will condemn as paltry and base the creations he has lovingly nurtured, which will assign to him a contemptible corner among those writers deemed to have defamed mankind and will ascribe to him the qualities of his own heroes, which will deny him his heart, his soul, and the divine flame of his talent.

For the judgement of our contemporaries does not recognize that both the lenses through which we view the heavenly bodies and those through which we watch the movements of tiny insects are equally wonderful; for the judgement of our contemporaries does not recognize either that to take a scene from contemptible life and to fill it with radiance, thereby transforming it into a pearl of creation, requires great depth of spirit; for the judgement of our contemporaries does not recognize either that exalted, rapturous laughter has every right to stand beside the ebb and flow of high lyricism, and that there is an immense divide between such laughter and the clowning of a fairground buffoon!* None of this is recognized by contemporary judgement, which so misconstrues the work of the unrecognized writer that it can only rebuke and vilify him; denied compassion, response, and fellow-feeling, he is left alone on the road like a solitary wayfarer, without friends or family. Cheerless is his calling, and bitterly he bears his solitude.

For a wondrous power ordains that I shall walk hand-in-hand with my strange heroes for a long time yet, viewing the broad sweep and rapid flow of life, viewing it through the laughter that the world sees and the tears that it neither sees nor suspects! Still far off is the day when the dread whirlwind of inspiration shall soar upward, resonating in an altogether different key, rising from a head wreathed in a radiant nimbus of sacred awe, and when men shall pay heed in confusion and alarm to the magnificent thunder of new words and different speeches!...

But let us be off! Let us take to the road! And banish the frown that flits across our brow and the grim cloud that darkens our features! Let us take the plunge into life itself, with all its empty chatter and tinkling of bells, and let us see what Chichikov is about.

Chichikov awoke, stretched his arms and legs, and felt that he had had a good night's sleep. Remaining supine for a moment or two longer, he snapped his fingers and beamed all over his face as he recalled that he was now the owner of close on four hundred souls. He at once sprang from the bed without even pausing to examine his face, which he loved so well and whose most attractive feature he deemed to be its chin, for he would most frequently boast of it to his friends, particularly if at that moment he was shaving. 'See what a perfect rounded chin I have!' he would often say, stroking it with his hand.

On this occasion, however, he spared no glances for chin nor face, but, without further ado, pulled on his Morocco leather boots, with their many-coloured tooled design, the kind with which the town of Torzhok* does such a brisk trade thanks to the Russian's predilection for loafing and indolence, and clad only in his short nightshirt, forgetting all concern for decorum and middle-aged respectability, performed two leaps, Scottish-fashion,* across the room, adroitly kicking himself with his heel as he did so. Thereupon he got down to business: positioning himself before his little box, he rubbed his hands with all the relish of an incorruptible district magistrate who has travelled out to hear a case and is about to enjoy a good meal, and then removed some papers from within.

He was anxious to conclude everything as swiftly as possible and not defer it to some later date. He decided to draw up the deeds of purchase himself, writing down all the names and making copies, so as not to have to pay for the services of a scrivener. He was well versed in the necessary formalities and boldly inscribed in large letters: 'The Year One Thousand Eight Hundred and N', then after this in smaller letters: 'Landowner such-and-such', and all the rest according to accepted practice.

Within two hours all was ready. Afterwards, whenever he looked at these sheets of paper, at the names of peasants who had once been real, living peasants, toiling, ploughing, carousing, carting, thieving from their masters, or who perhaps had simply been decent peasants, he would be overcome by a strange sensation, one he himself could not comprehend. Each little list seemed to have its own special character, and through this the peasants themselves somehow acquired characters all of their own. Those peasants who belonged to Korobochka nearly all had appendages to their names, which in turn were accompanied by epithets and sobriquets. Plyushkin's list was remarkable for its terseness: frequently only the initials of the names and patronymics were given, followed by two dots. Sobakevich's roll was remarkable for its extraordinary fullness and circumstantiality of detail, with not one of the peasants' qualities overlooked: about one he had written: 'Good joiner', about another: 'Knows his business and doesn't touch liquor.' He also included detailed information about the identity of the mother and father and indicated how these latter had conducted themselves; of one fellow called Fedotov, however, he had written: 'Father unknown, born to the house-girl Kapitalina, but has good morals and not a thief.' All these details lent a particular air of freshness: it was as if the peasants had been alive only yesterday.

Gazing at length at the list, he felt spiritually moved and declared with a sigh: 'Heavens above, what a great number of you are crammed in here! Tell me, my dear fellows, what did you do in your lives? How did you make ends meet?' And his eyes involuntarily came to rest on one name: that of our old friend Pyotr Saveliev Neuvazhai-Koryto—'Disdain-the-Trough'—who had once belonged to Korobochka. Yet again he could not restrain himself from saying: 'Heavens, what a mouthful, sprawling across a whole line! I wonder, were you a master craftsman, or a simple peasant, and what manner of death bore you off? Did it come to you at the inn, or were you run over by an unwieldy baggage-train as you slept, sprawled in the middle of the road?

'"Probka Stepan, carpenter, of exemplary sobriety." Ha! So this is he, that Stepan Probka, that legendary giant of a man, who would have made a fine guardsman! You probably walked the length and breadth of all the provinces, your axe thrust in your belt and your boots slung over your shoulder, eating a groat's worth of bread and two groats' of dried fish, always coming home, no doubt, with a hundred silver roubles in your pouch, and perhaps with a two-hundred-rouble banknote sewn into your hempen breeches, or stuffed into your boot. So where did death overtake you? Did you climb high into the church dome, lured perhaps by the extra pay, perhaps you even clambered up on to the cross itself, only to slip from the crossbeam and crash to the ground, where only old Mikhey was around to see you fall and, scratching the back of his head, to sigh: "Well, Vanya, that was a smart thing to do!" before tying the rope around his own waist and climbing up in your place.

'"Maxim Telyatnikov, bootmaker." Huh, bootmaker, indeed! "Drunk as a bootmaker," goes the saying. Yes, I know all about you, my good fellow; if you like I'll tell your story: you were apprenticed to a German, who used to feed all his lads together, beating them across the back with a leather strap for turning out slipshod work and not allowing them out of the house to gad about the streets, and you would have made a marvel of a cobbler, and your German couldn't praise you too highly, when talking to his wife or his *Kamerad*. And I know how your apprenticeship ended: "Now it's time I started my own business," you said to yourself, "and I shan't do it like a German, saving my money copeck by copeck; I shall get rich right away."

'So, after paying your master a tidy sum in quit-rent, you set up a little shop, took in a pile of orders, and set to work. You got hold of some half-rotted old leather for a third of the price and—it's quite true—you made a double profit on each boot, but after a fortnight all your boots fell apart and you were cursed as an out-and-out swindler. No more customers came to your shop, and you took to drinking and loitering in the streets, complaining: "No, it's a rotten world! There's no life for a Russian, the Germans are always getting in the way."

'Now which peasant do we have here? Yelizaveta Vorobei. I'll be damned: a woman! How did she get in here? You old rogue, Sobakevich, sneaking this one in!'

Chichikov was right: this was indeed a woman. How she got on the list we do not know, but her name had been so skilfully written that from a distance she could be mistaken for a man, and it was even written without the usual feminine ending, so it read Yelizavet rather than Yelizaveta. Chichikov was not impressed by this amendment, however, and promptly scratched her off the list.

'Grigory Go-But-Never-Get-There! What sort of a man were

you? Were you a carrier by trade, and did you decide one day to harness your threesome to your bast-covered wagon, and turn your back for ever on your home, on your native hearth, setting off with the merchants on the long drive to the fair? Was it on the road that you gave up your soul to God, or did your own friends dispatch you, in a dispute over some plump, red-cheeked soldier's wife, or maybe a forest vagabond took a fancy to your leather gauntlets and your three squat, sturdy horses, or perhaps, as you lay on your stove-bunk,* you yourself fell to thinking and then suddenly, quite without warning, headed for the inn and from there slid straight into an ice-hole, and that was that! Ah yes, that's what you Russians are like! Not ones for dying peacefully in your beds!

'Now what about you, my little doves?' he continued, his eyes moving across to the list of Plyushkin's fugitive souls. 'You may still be alive, but what earthly use are you? You're as good as dead, and yet I still wonder where your swift legs have taken you? Was it that bad with Plyushkin or did you simply decide, on a whim, to take to the forests and rob wayfarers? Are you now languishing in prison somewhere or have you found new masters and new lands to till?

'Yeremei Karyakin, Nikita Volokita, his son Anton Volokita— these fugitives are fine fellows: you can tell by their names.* Popov, house-serf—you must have had schooling: I bet you never waved a knife about, but did all your thieving like a true gentleman. Then one day you got caught with no passport by a police captain. You face him boldly. "Who do you belong to?" asks the captain, prompted by the situation to use some rather strong language.

'"I belong to landowner so-and-so" you answer readily.

'"So what are you doing here?" asks the police captain.

'"Released on quit-rent," you answer without hesitation.

'"Where's your passport?"

'"With my master, the merchant Pimenov."

'"Fetch Pimenov!—Are you Pimenov?"

'"Yes, I'm Pimenov."

'"Did he give you his passport?"

'"No, he never gave me any passport."

'"So you're lying?" says the captain, appending a particularly strong epithet.

'"That's correct, sir," you reply boldly, "I didn't give it to him because I came home late, so I gave it for safekeeping to Antip Prokhorov, the bell-ringer."

'"Fetch the bell-ringer! Did he give you his passport?"

'"No, I never received any passport from him."

'"So you're lying again!" says the captain of police, embellishing his utterance with yet another strong epithet. "So where's your passport?"

'"I did have it," you reply adroitly, "but I must have dropped it somewhere on the road."

'"Then why," continues the captain, once again for good measure affixing a choice epithet, "did you steal a soldier's greatcoat? And a coffer full of coins from the priest?"

'"No, no," you say, without batting an eyelid, "not me: I've never been one for pinching and thieving."

'"So how come the greatcoat was found on you?"

'"I couldn't tell you: perhaps someone else brought it."

'"Huh, you lying, thieving devil!" says the police captain, shaking his head and standing with his hands on his hips. "Put him in stocks and march him to gaol."

'"Why certainly! With pleasure," you reply. And then, taking your snuff-box from your pocket, you hospitably proffer it to the two veteran soldiers busy fastening the shackles on your legs, and you enquire how long they have been in retirement and which war they fought in. And then you settle into prison life until your case comes up in court. The court decrees: you are to be transferred from Tsarevokokshaisk to such and such a gaol, and the court there decrees: you are to be transferred to some place called Vesyegonsk,* and so you travel from gaol to gaol complaining, as you inspect each new abode: "No, the Vesyegonsk gaol was a bit cleaner than this: there was enough space even for a game of knucklebones, there was plenty of room, and more company too!"

'Abakum Fyrov! And who might you be, brother? Where, in what corner of the land are you kicking your heels? Did you stray as far as the Volga and grow to love the free life, joining the Volga boat-men?'

Here Chichikov paused and fell to thinking. What was he thinking about? Was he thinking about the fate of Abakum Fyrov, or was he simply thinking for thinking's sake, as every Russian will, of whatever age, rank, and station, when his thoughts turn to the joys of a life of freedom and carousal? Indeed, where is Fyrov now? Pehaps he is carousing noisily and merrily at the grain wharf, after striking a bargain with the merchants. With flowers and ribbons in their hats, the gang of boatmen make merry, as they take their leave of sweethearts and wives, tall and slender, adorned with ribbons and necklaces; the revellers dance and sing; the entire wharf is a hive of activity, and all the while the stevedores continue about their business, shouting, cursing, and goading one another, with their hooks hoisting massive loads of nine poods apiece on their backs, noisily dumping the peas and wheat into the deep holds,* rolling massive sacks of oats and barley along the pier, while further off stand piles of sacks, stacked like cannon-balls into tall pyramids. To shift this massive arsenal of grain seems a hopeless task, but, finally, everything is loaded into the deep wheat barges, which then proceed in interminable single file through the spring ice-floes. Now is your turn to sweat, Volga boatmen! Toil together as before you caroused and went wild together, and haul your barges to the strains of a song as endless as Russia herself.

'Goodness me! Twelve o'clock!' said Chichikov at last, glancing at his watch. 'How can I have tarried so? It would be one thing if I had been doing business, but first I started talking a lot of nonsense, and then fell into a reverie. Really, what a fool I am!'

Having said this, he exchanged his Scottish costume for something more European, buckled his belt tighter to draw in his ample paunch, splashed himself with Cologne, picked up his winter cap, and, tucking his papers under his arm, set off for the Chambers to effect the transfer of souls. He hurried on his way not because he was afraid of being late—he had no fear of that, for the president was a personal friend and could extend or curtail receiving hours as he wished, after the manner of Homer's Zeus in antique times, who would lengthen the days and send down premature nights when he wished to cut short the hostilities of his favoured heroes or to enable them to fight to the finish, but he felt an inner compulsion to bring matters to their conclusion as swiftly as possible. Until this was done things would seem awkward and unsettled: he could not quite suppress the thought that the souls were not entirely real and that, with a business like this, the sooner one got clear of it the better.

No sooner had he set foot outside the inn, reflecting on all this while he pulled his brown coat with its bearskin lining around his shoulders, than, at the first turning into a side-street, he bumped into another gentleman wearing a brown coat, similarly lined with bearskin, and a winter cap with earflaps. The gentleman cried out in surprise: it was Manilov. They at once fell into each other's arms in the middle of the street and remained in this position for fully five minutes. The kisses they exchanged were so powerful that for the rest of the day they both suffered from aching front teeth. So great was Manilov's joy that only his nose and lips remained visible in his face, while his eyes disappeared completely. For a good quarter of an hour he clutched Chichikov's hand in both of his own, rendering it unbearably hot. Employing the choicest and most felicitous turns of phrase, he recounted how he had flown to embrace Pavel Ivanovich; this oration was concluded with a compliment fit only to bestow upon a lady with whom one is about to dance. Chichikov opened his mouth, still not knowing how to express his gratitude, when Manilov suddenly produced a document from inside his coat, rolled up and secured with a little pink ribbon, and handed it over, holding it most adroitly between two fingers.

'What is that?'

'Our little serfs.'

'Ah!' Chichikov at once unrolled the document, ran his eyes over it and marvelled at the neatness and beauty of the hand.

'Splendidly written,' he said, 'there's no need to write it out again. With a special border too! Who drew such an artistic border?'

'Heavens, how can you ask such a question?' said Manilov.

'You?'

'My wife.'

'My word! I must say, I feel somewhat ashamed to have caused so much trouble.'

'For Pavel Ivanovich nothing we do could ever be trouble.'

Chichikov bowed in gratitude. Hearing that he was bound for the Chambers to conclude the business, Manilov declared his willingness to accompany him there. The two friends linked arms and proceeded together. At every slight incline, or elevation, or little bump in the road, Manilov supported Chichikov, and practically lifted him up bodily, averring with a pleasant smile that he would in no circumstances permit Pavel Ivanovich to hurt his precious feet. Chichikov was greatly embarrassed and did not quite know how to thank him, for he was aware that he was a trifle on the heavy side.

Thus engaged in the performance of these mutual services, they finally arrived at the square where the government offices were situated: these took the form of a large, three-storeyed building, painted as white as chalk, presumably to reflect the purity of the souls of the officials within; the other structures around the square were dwarfed by this imposing brick building. These were: a sentry box, by which a soldier stood, holding a rifle; a couple of cabstands; and, finally, long fences adorned with the usual inscriptions and drawings, scratched on with a piece of charcoal or chalk; there was nothing more to be seen on this desolate—or, as we are wont to say, gracious—square. The incorruptible heads of the acolytes of Themis* sometimes poked out of the second- and third-floor windows, only to disappear the next instant: presumably, at that moment, their superior had entered the room.

The friends did not walk up the staircase, but ascended it at a run, because Chichikov, anxious to free himself from Manilov's so-licitous arm, had quickened his pace, while Manilov also flew ahead, endeavouring to prevent Chichikov from tiring, and thus they were both considerably out of breath when they finally entered the dark corridor. Neither the corridors nor the rooms themselves impressed them unduly with their cleanliness. In those days no one was much concerned about cleanliness, and when a thing became dirty it re-mained dirty, with no attempt at decorum. Themis received her guests informally—that is to say, in her negligee and dressing-gown.

We should now proceed to a description of the offices through which our heroes passed, but the author must confess to a great timidity with regard to offices of any kind. Even on those occasions when he chances to pass through gleaming and ennobled offices, with polished floors and tables, he endeavours to hurry through as swiftly as possible, his eyes humbly and modestly downcast, and for that reason he has no idea how the affairs conducted therein prosper and flourish so.

Our heroes saw much paper, both rough copies and fair copies, they saw bowed heads, broad necks, tailcoats, and frock-coats of a provincial cut. They even saw one plain, light-grey shortcoat, which stood out conspicuously, as, with its head inclined so far to one side that it rested almost on the paper, it transcribed in a bold and florid hand a report on the sequestration of land or the inventory of an estate, unlawfully seized by some peace-loving landowner, who happily lived out his days while the case continued, blithely begetting children and grandchildren under protection of the courts, and they overheard such snatches of dialogue, uttered in gruff and hoarse voices, as: 'Allow me, Fedosey Fedoseevich, to see case No. 368!' or: 'You're always taking the cork from the office ink-well and losing it!'

Sometimes more imperious voices, no doubt those of the superiors, would ring out in a peremptory manner: 'You there, copy this out again, or I'll have your boots taken away and you can sit here in the office for six days on end with nothing to eat!'

The scratching of the pens generated considerable noise, not unlike the sound of carts laden with brushwood crunching through the forest over a deep carpet of dry leaves.

Chichikov and Manilov approached the first desk, at which sat two still youthful officials, and enquired:

'I wonder if you could tell us where deeds of purchase are dealt with here?'

'What do you want?' asked both officials, looking around.

'I wish to submit an application.'

'So, what have you bought?'

'First I would like to know: where is the purchase desk—here, or somewhere else?'

'You tell us first what you've bought and for how much, then we can tell you where, otherwise there's no way of knowing.'

Chichikov could see at once that the officials were merely inquisitive, like all young officials, and that they wished to attach greater importance and weight to themselves and their activities.

'Listen, my good fellows,' he said, 'I know perfectly well that all purchase matters, at whatever price, are dealt with in one and the same place, and therefore I request that you show me the desk, and if you do not know what goes on in your office then we shall enquire elsewhere.'

To this the officials made no answer. Instead, one of them merely pointed to one corner of the room, where an old man sat at a desk, making marks on sheets of paper. Chichikov and Manilov made their way between the desks right up to him. The old man was intent on his work.

'Allow me to enquire,' said Chichikov with a bow, 'is this where purchase deeds are dealt with?'

The old man raised his eyes and, speaking in a slow and deliberate manner, said:

'No purchase deeds here.'

'Where then?'

'You must go to the purchase department.'

'And where is this purchase department?'

'That's Ivan Antonovich's section.'

'And where is this Ivan Antonovich?'

The old man pointed to another corner of the room. Chichikov and Manilov headed towards Ivan Antonovich. Ivan Antonovich had already peeped round and given them a sideways glance, but the moment they approached him he buried himself even more intently in his copying.

'Permit me to enquire,' said Chichikov with a bow, 'is this the purchase desk?'

Ivan Antonovich appeared not to hear and remained immersed in his papers, vouchsafing no reply. It was at once evident that this was a man of prudence and maturity, not some young loudmouth and scatter-brain. Ivan Antonovich, it appeared, was already well over forty years of age; his hair was black and thick; the entire middle part of his face protruded and somehow merged with his nose—in other words, it was one of those faces which in common parlance is known as a 'jug-snout'.

'Permit me to enquire, is this the purchase department?' said Chichikov.

'It is,' said Ivan Antonovich, turning his jug-snout back to his papers and applying himself once more to his copying.

'My business is as follows: I have purchased peasants for transfer from various landowners in this district: I have the deeds of purchase, they only need to be finalized.'

'Are the sellers present?'

'Some are present, others have given power of attorney.'

'Have you brought the application?'

'I have indeed. I should like to... I am in rather a hurry... Would it not, for example, be possible to conclude the matter today?'

'Today! Quite impossible,' said Ivan Antonovich. 'We shall need to investigate whether there remain any distraints.'

'In fact, with regard to speeding things up, I might say that Ivan Grigorievich, the president, is a close friend of mine...'

'But remember, Ivan Grigorievich is not alone: there are others,' retorted Ivan Antonovich severely.

Chichikov understood the innuendo and said: 'The others will have no cause for complaint either, I used to be in the service myself, I know the form...'

'Go and see Ivan Grigorievich,' said Ivan Antonovich in a slightly more amenable voice, 'let him issue a pertinent order, and we will speed things up all we can.'

Chichikov now produced a banknote from his pocket and placed it before Ivan Antonovich, who appeared not to notice it at all and promptly covered it with a book. Chichikov was on the point of bringing this to his attention, but with a movement of his head Ivan Antonovich gave him to understand that such action was unnecessary.

'He will take you to Ivan Grigorievich's office!' said Ivan Antonovich, motioning with a nod of his head to one of the acolytes sitting nearby, who had been rendering oblations to Themis with such zeal that both his sleeves had burst at the elbows and the lining had long since fallen out. For this service he had at the time been promoted to the rank of collegiate registrar. This zealous acolyte now waited upon our friends, as once Virgil had waited upon Dante, and conducted them into the office, where—occupying the only armchair in the room—the president sat in solitary splendour behind a desk on which stood a glass pyramid, displaying the imperial edicts of Peter the Great, and two hefty volumes. Our modern-day Virgil felt so overawed in this hallowed place that on no account would he presume to set foot within, and he turned around, revealing a back as threadbare as a bast mat and with a chicken feather stuck to it.

As Chichikov and Manilov entered the office, they discovered that the president was not in fact alone, for next to him sat Sobakevich, totally obscured by the pyramid. The entry of the visitors provoked an exclamation, and the presidential armchair was noisily pushed back. Sobakevich also half-rose from his seat and was now visible from all sides with his over-long sleeves. The president welcomed Chichikov into his embrace, and the office resounded with the noise of osculation; they enquired after each other's health; it transpired that they both suffered somewhat from lumbago and this was ascribed to a sedentary life. The president, it seemed, had already been apprised by Sobakevich of the purchase, because he set about offering his congratulations, and at first rather embarrassed our hero, particularly when he realized that Sobakevich and Manilov, two sellers with whom he had conducted his business in camera, so to speak, were now standing face-to-face. None the less, he thanked the president and, turning at once to Sobakevich, enquired:

'And how is your health?'

'Thank the Lord, nothing to complain about,' said Sobakevich.

And that, to be sure, was no lie: an iron bar would be more likely to catch a cold and start coughing than this astoundingly robust country gentleman.

'But then you've always been renowned for your good health,' said the president, 'and your late father was also a strong man.'

'Yes, he could take on a bear single-handed,' answered Sobakevich.

'I reckon, however,' said the president, 'that you also could wrestle a bear to the ground if you took one on.'

'No, I couldn't,' answered Sobakevich, 'the old man was stronger than me.' With a sigh, he continued: 'No, you don't get people like that any more; take my life, for example—what sort of a life is it anyway? Nothing to crow about...'

'But in what way is your life deficient?' asked the president.

'It's no good, no good at all,' said Sobakevich, shaking his head. 'Judge for yourself, Ivan Grigorievich: I'm nearing fifty years of age, and I've never once been ill, not so much as a sore throat, or a boil or an abscess... No, it's not a good sign! Sooner or later I shall have to pay for it.' Thereupon Sobakevich sank into melancholy.

'Listen to that,' thought Chichikov and the president at the same time, 'imagine grumbling about that!'

'I have a little note for you here,' said Chichikov, taking Plyushkin's letter from his pocket.

'From whom?' asked the president and, opening the letter, exclaimed: 'Ha! It's from Plyushkin. So he's still dragging out his miserable existence? Talk about the vagaries of fate—to think what a brilliant, wealthy man he was! And now...'

'A cur,' said Sobakevich, 'a scoundrel, he's starved all his serfs to death.'

'Why, of course, of course,' said the president, reading the letter, 'I'm quite happy to be his attorney. When would you like to formalize the transfer, now or later?'

'Now,' said Chichikov, 'in fact, if possible I would even request that we do it right away, because I was hoping to leave town tomorrow; I've brought both the transfer deeds and the application.'

'All that can be done, but—like it or not—we shall not let you leave us so soon. The transfer deeds will be completed today, but you will have to stay on with us for a while. I shall give the order right away,' he said, opening a door into the chancery office, which was packed with clerks, exactly like a swarm of industrious bees buzzing round their hives, if one might presume to liken chancery affairs to the workings of a bee-hive.

'Is Ivan Antonovich here?'

'He's here,' answered a voice from within.

'Send him in!'

The jug-like snout of Ivan Antonovich, with which the reader is by now familiar, appeared in the office, and its owner bowed deferentially.

'Here, Ivan Antonovich, take all these transfer deeds...'

'Now don't forget, Ivan Grigorievich,' interrupted Sobakevich, 'we need witnesses, at least two on each side. Send for the public prosecutor: he's a man of leisure and is probably sitting at home while all his work is being done for him by that scrivener Zolotukha, the world's worst money-grubber. The medical inspector is another gentleman of leisure and also at home, no doubt, unless he's off somewhere playing cards, and there are plenty of others even nearer at hand—Trukhachevsky, Begushkin—all useless ballast on life's journey!'*

'Quite so! Quite so!' said the president and promptly dispatched the messenger to fetch them all.

'Could I also ask you,' said Chichikov, 'to send for the attorney of a certain gentlewoman, with whom I also did some business, the son of the archpriest Father Kiril; he works here in your department.'

'Why, of course, we'll send for him too!' said the president. 'All will be done, and, I beg you, please do not give the officials any money. My friends should not have to pay.' Having said this he at once gave some instruction to Ivan Antonovich, which appeared not to please the latter. The purchase deeds seemed to have a highly salutary effect on the president, especially when he saw that the transactions amounted to a total of almost one hundred thousand roubles. For several minutes he gazed into Chichikov's eyes with a look of genuine delight and finally declared: 'Well, what about that!

So that's how it is, Pavel Ivanovich! You've made some acquisitions, I see.'

'I have indeed,' answered Chichikov.

'An excellent thing, to be sure, an excellent thing!'

'Quite so: I can see myself that I could not have embarked on a more excellent undertaking. Say what you will, but man's purpose in life remains uncertain unless he plants his feet firmly on solid ground and does not cling to some frivolous youthful dream.' At this point he roundly castigated all young people for their liberalism—and with very good reason. But oddly enough, even as he spoke a lack of conviction could be sensed in his words, as if at the same time he were saying to himself: 'Tush, brother, what lies you tell: you should be ashamed of yourself!' He even avoided Sobakevich's and Manilov's eyes, lest he read something in their expression. He had nothing to fear, however: Sobakevich's face was utterly impassive, whilst Manilov was so enchanted by the sentiments Chichikov had expressed that he could only rock his head from side to side in approbation and pleasure, sinking into that position assumed by a music lover when the soprano outdoes even the violin, in her endeavour to reach a note so high and shrill as to be beyond the range of any songbird.

'Yes, why do you not tell Ivan Grigorievich,' rejoined Sobakevich, 'exactly what it is you've bought; and you, Ivan Grigorievich, why do you not ask what acquisition has been made? Let me tell you, these are first-class men! Solid gold. Would you believe it, I sold him my coach-builder Mikheev.'

'No—surely you haven't sold Mikheev?' said the president. 'I know Mikheev, your coach-builder: a splendid craftsman, he refurbished my droshky. But—hold on a second, surely... Did you not tell me he had died?'

'What, Mikheev dead?' said Sobakevich, not batting an eyelid. 'No, it's his brother who died, but he's alive and kicking, and even healthier than before. The other day he knocked together a britzka better than any you would find in Moscow. A fellow like that should really work for the Tsar.'

'Yes, Mikheev's a fine craftsman,' said the president, 'I'm amazed you could part with him.'

'And Mikheev's not the only one! There's Stepan Probka, the carpenter, Milushkin, the bricklayer, Maxim Telyatnikov, the cobbler—they've all gone, I've sold them all!' But when the president asked how he could have sold all those serfs when they were so indispensable for the house and workshops, Sobakevich answered with a wave of his hand: 'Ah! It's simple, a moment of folly: "Why not sell them?" I said, "I'll sell them!" And, like the fool I am, I sold them!' Then he hung his head, as if repenting of his deed, and added: 'You see, wisdom does not come with grey hairs.'

'But allow me to ask, Pavel Ivanovich,' said the president, 'how can you be buying peasants without land? Are they to be transferred?'

'Yes, to be transferred.'

'Ah well, that's a different matter. And where to, might I ask?'

'To, er... to Kherson province.'*

'Ah yes, there's some excellent land there!' said the president and proceeded to speak admiringly of the flourishing tall grass in those parts. 'And is the property sufficiently large?'

'It is, yes: there's plenty of land for the peasants I have bought.'

'Does it have a river or pond?'

'A river, yes. In fact, there's a pond too.' Having said this, Chichikov inadvertently caught Sobakevich's eye, and although Sobakevich was as impassive as ever, Chichikov seemed to read in his face: 'Shame on you, you liar! I bet there's no river, nor pond, nor any land at all!'

While this conversation was in progress the witnesses were gradually assembling: the readers' old friend, the winking prosecutor; the inspector of the medical board; Trukhachevsky; Begushkin and those others who, in Sobakevich's words, were all useless ballast on life's journey. Many of them were quite unknown to Chichikov; to make up the necessary numbers reserves were promptly pressed into service then and there, from the ranks of the department clerks. They had also summoned not only the son of the archpriest Father Kiril, but even the archpriest himself. Each witness signed his name complete with all his ranks and distinctions, some writing in a back-slanting hand, others slanting forward, and others still writing practically upside down, inserting letters the like of which have never been seen in the Russian alphabet. Our friend Ivan Antonovich dispatched his functions most expeditiously: the transfer deeds were recorded, dated, entered in a register and all other necessary places, and stamp duty of one half of one per cent was charged, together with a fee for publication in the *Gazette*,* all of which entailed only

minimal expenditure for Chichikov. The president even gave instructions that he should only be made to pay half the assessed
amount, while the other half, by some sleight of hand, was charged
to the account of another petitioner.

'So,' said the president, when all was completed, 'there remains
only the matter of celebrating your little purchase.'

'It will be my pleasure,' said Chichikov. 'You need only set the
time. It would be a serious transgression on my part if I were not to
uncork two or three bottles of fizz in such delightful company.'

'No, no, that would not do at all!' said the president, 'that is our
duty, our obligation. You are our guest: we must treat you. Gentlemen, I have a proposal! This is what we shall do: let us all go, just
as we are, to the chief of police; he's a true miracle-worker: he need
only wink as he walks past a fish-stall or a wine-cellar and we shall
all have a feast to remember! And while we're about it we can have
a little game of whist!'

This was a proposal no one could decline. The witnesses could
feel an appetite stirring within them at the very mention of the
words 'fish-stall': they all at once reached for their hats and caps and
the official business was over. As they passed through the chancery
office Ivan Antonovich—he of the jug snout—gave a most respectful
bow and said to Chichikov, *sotto voce*:

'You've bought peasants to the value of one hundred thousand,
and all I get for my hard work is a measly twenty-five rouble note.'*

'But you should see the peasants,' replied Chichikov, also *sotto
voce*, 'a useless and worthless lot—they're not worth half what I
paid.'

Ivan Antonovich understood that this client was a man of resolve
who would give no more.

'How much did you pay for Plyushkin's souls?' whispered Sobakevich in his other ear.

'And why did you slip Vorobei on to your list?' whispered Chichikov
in reply.

'Which Vorobei?' asked Sobakevich.

'Some serf woman, Yelizaveta Vorebei, and you even dropped the
-*a* off her name.'*

'No, I never added any Vorobei,' said Sobakevich and went to
join his other companions.

The company eventually arrived *en masse* at the home of the police chief. This good man was, indeed, a miracle-worker: no sooner did he hear what was afoot than he summoned his constable, a nimble young fellow in patent leather jackboots, and whispered what seemed to be no more than two words in his ear, then added: 'Is that clear?' and—lo and behold! in the next room, while the guests were settling down to a game of whist, a table was laid with dishes of beluga, sturgeon, salmon, pressed caviare and fresh-salted caviare, salted herring, morsels of sevruga, cheeses, smoked tongue, and cured *balyk*—all this contributed by the fish-stalls. These delicacies were followed by domestic offerings from the host's own kitchen: fish-head pie, made of the gristle and cheeks of a nine-pood sturgeon,* another pie stuffed with milk mushrooms, then meat patties, dumplings, and berries stewed in honey.

To a certain extent the chief of police acted as father figure and benefactor to the town. He regarded his citizens as members of his own family, and dropped in on the shops and market-place as if calling into his own pantry. He kept a firm grip on the reins, as they say, and knew his job inside out. It was even hard to say whether he had been created for the job or the job for him. He performed his duties with such wisdom that he drew twice as much profit as all his predecessors, and at the same time earned the affection of the entire town. The merchants loved him dearly because he was not a proud man; to be sure, he stood godfather to their children, he fraternized with them, and although at times he fleeced them mercilessly it was always done with great adroitness: with a slap on the back, a friendly laugh, a shared glass of tea, a promise to come and play draughts, and an enquiry about business and his victim's general welfare. And if he learnt that a child had fallen ill he could recommend the right medicine—in a word, he was an excellent fellow! Proceeding through the town in his droshky he would issue instructions and, as he drove, he would hail his acquaintances: 'Ah, Mikheich! There you are! You and I must get together sometime to finish that game of ours.' 'Yes, Aleksei Ivanovich,' Mikheich would reply, doffing his cap, 'we must.' Or: 'I say, brother, Ilya Paramonich, you must come and see that new trotter of mine: I wager he'll beat any of yours, so get out your racing harness and let's try him out.' The merchant, who was also a passionate devotee of buggy racing, would grin and welcome the suggestion, stroking his beard and saying: 'Let's try him out, Aleksei Ivanovich!' Even the stall-keepers usually doffed their caps at such moments, and exchanged glances as if to say: 'He's a good man, that Aleksei Ivanovich.' In other words, he managed to make himself universally popular, and the merchants were of the opinion that Aleksei Ivanovich—as they put it—'might help himself to a bit here and there, but then he'll never play you false.'

Observing that the food was ready, the chief of police suggested to his guests that they resume their whist after luncheon, whereupon they all proceeded into the next room, from which an interesting aroma had for some time been wafting and assailing the guests' nostrils. This had already caused Sobakevich to poke his head through the door, and there, in the distance, he had espied an entire sturgeon, laid out on a large platter. After downing a glass of vodka of a dark olive colour, like that found only in the translucent Siberian stone from which seals are cut in Russia, the guests gathered round the table, and here each revealed his own character and predilections, one going for the caviar, another for the salmon, a third for the cheese. Scorning all these trifles, Sobakevich addressed himself to the sturgeon, and while the others drank, conversed, and ate, he, in the course of little more than a quarter of an hour, polished off the entire fish. As a result, when the chief of police suddenly remembered about the fish and, enquiring of his guests: 'Now tell me, gentlemen, what is your esteemed opinion of this masterpiece of nature?' approached the platter, fork at the ready, he saw that of this masterpiece of nature there remained only the tail. Sobakevich pretended, however, that he had had nothing to do with it, and, moving across to another serving dish, as far from the sturgeon as possible, started to prod a small dried fish with his fork.

Having thus indulged himself with the sturgeon, Sobakevich sat down in an armchair and neither ate nor drank any more, apparently capable only of half-closing and blinking his eyes. The chief of police, it appeared, was not one to stint his guests of their wine: the toasts were without number. The first was drunk, as the reader might already have guessed, to the health of the new Kherson landowner, then they drank to the welfare of his serfs and their successful resettlement, then to the health of his future wife, a lady of great beauty—which brought a pleasant smile to the lips of our hero. Well-wishers pressed up on all sides and entreated him to remain in the town at least for another fortnight: 'It's no good, Pavel Ivanovich!

We simply will not take no for an answer! You know what they say: a welcome guest stays long in the nest! No, you must spend some time with us! You'll see, we shall find you a wife: we shall marry him off, Ivan Grigorievich, shall we not?'

'We'll marry him off, all right!' echoed the president. 'No matter how hard you dig in your heels, we'll get you to the altar! No, my good sir, you brought yourself here, so don't you complain. We take these things seriously round here.'

'Well—why not? Why should I dig in my heels?' said Chichikov with a chuckle. 'I've nothing against marriage, you know, provided there's a bride.'

'We'll find you a bride, never fear, everything will be just as you wish!'

'Well, in that case—'

'Bravo, he's staying,' they all chorused. 'Hooray, three cheers for Pavel Ivanovich! Hooray!' And they all crowded round to clink glasses with him.

Chichikov clinked everyone's glass. 'Again, again!' shouted the more adventurous among them, and they all clinked again; then they called for a third round, and they clinked glasses a third time. Before long everyone felt decidedly merry. The president, a most charming man when in his cups, embraced Chichikov several times, exclaiming in an excess of emotion: 'My dear soul! My dearest soul!' and even danced a little jig around him, clicking his fingers and singing the well-known song: 'Oh you little so-and-so, Kamarinsky laddy-o!'* After the champagne they uncorked some Tokay, which infused even greater energy and still higher spirits into the company. The game of whist was totally forgotten; they argued, shouted, talked about anything and everything: about politics, even about military matters, expounding the sort of free-thinking ideas for which at another time they would have birched their own children. There and then they reached agreement on a great number of highly vexatious issues. Chichikov had never before felt so jolly, and already imagined himself a real Kherson landowner, as he described the various improvements he planned for his estate: the three-field system of agriculture,* the happiness and blissful coexistence of two conjoined souls, and he began to recite to Sobakevich the verses which Werther writes to Charlotte.* Sobakevich's only response to this recitation, which he received sitting in his armchair, was to blink his eyes, for after his encounter with the sturgeon he felt a strong inclination to sleep.

At last Chichikov sensed that he had started to unwind a little too much, so he called for a carriage and accepted the offer of the prosecutor's droshky. The prosecutor's coachman, as was soon apparent, once he got under way, was a sturdy fellow of some experience in these matters, for he was able to drive with only one hand, leaving the other free to support the gentleman behind him. Thus Chichikov arrived back at the inn in the prosecutor's droshky, and here for a long time he continued to prattle all sorts of nonsense: about a fair-haired bride with a rosy complexion and a little dimple on her right cheek, the villages in Kherson province, capital investment, and so on and so forth. Selifan was even given certain administrative instructions: to assemble all the newly resettled peasants and to take a roll-call. Selifan listened in silence for a long time and then left the room, saying to Petrushka: 'In you go and undress the master!' Petrushka set about tugging off his master's boots and, in the process, nearly pulled their occupant down on to the floor with them. At last the boots were removed; the master threw off his clothes and, after tossing and turning for a while on the bed, which creaked unmercifully, he finally fell asleep and slept the sleep of a real Kherson landowner.

Meanwhile Petrushka took the Kherson landowner's breeches and speckled cranberry tailcoat out into the corridor, hung the coat on a wooden hanger, and pounded it with a stick and brush, filling the corridor with clouds of dust. As he was about to take the garments down he glanced down from the gallery and saw Selifan on his way back from the stables. Their eyes met and an unspoken message passed between them, to wit: the master is dead to the world, we can make a little visit to you-know-where. So Petrushka promptly put the coat and breeches back in the room, then hurried downstairs, and the two set off together, saying not a word about the purpose of their journey and chatting away as they walked about totally unrelated matters. They did not have far to go: to be precise, only across the street, to a building directly opposite the inn, which they entered through a low, smoke-blackened, glass-paned door. This led into a low room, almost a cellar, in which a great variety of people were already sitting at the wooden tables: men with and without beards, some in coarse sheepskin coats and others in their shirt-

sleeves, and one or two even in frieze greatcoats.* What exactly
Petrushka and Selifan did once inside, God alone can say, but they
emerged an hour later, arms linked, preserving a total silence, showing great solicitude for each other's welfare, each taking care to draw
attention to any obstacles in the other's path. Gripping each other
firmly by the hand, they took at least a quarter of an hour to scale
the porch steps, finally made it to the top, and entered the inn.
Petrushka paused for a moment before his wretched pallet, deliberating how most decorously to install himself in it, and then flopped
down right across the top, with his feet propped against the floor.
Selifan also lay down on the same bed, resting his head on Petrushka's
belly and quite forgetting that under no circumstances was he allowed to sleep here, but was supposed to make his bed in the servants' quarters, if not in the stables next to his horses.

   They both fell asleep instantly, snoring with a sonority never
hitherto witnessed, to which their master in the adjacent room responded with a thin nasal whistle. Soon everything around them fell
quiet too, and the entire inn was enveloped in a deep slumber; light
still burned in the window of but one room, occupied by the lieutenant newly arrived from Ryazan, clearly a great amateur of boots,*
for he had already ordered four pairs, and was repeatedly trying on
a fifth. Several times he walked up to the bed, firmly intending to
pull them off and lie down, but he simply could not do it: the boots
were so well made, that for a long time he kept raising his foot in the
air and admiring the adroitly fashioned and superbly cobbled heel.

CHAPTER EIGHT

Chichikov's purchases became the talk of the town. The air buzzed with discussion, speculation, and opinions on the advisability of buying peasants for transfer. From these debates there emerged many accomplished experts on the subject. 'Of course,' reasoned some, 'it is true, one cannot deny it: the land in the southern provinces is fine and fertile; but how will Chichikov's serfs fare without water? There is not a single river there.'

'That's not the worst of it, I say, not the worst, at all, Stepan Dmitrievich; the truth of the matter is that resettlement as such is a risky business. You know our peasant: the area is new to him, on top of which he has to till the fields, and the man has nothing of his own—no hut, no farmyard, nothing, so what does he do? He takes to his heels, as sure as eggs is eggs, he runs so fast you won't see him for dust.'

'No, no, Aleksei Ivanovich, forgive me, but I cannot agree with you that Chichikov's peasants will run away. The Russian peasant is capable of anything, and he will adapt to any climate. You can send him to Kamchatka* and you need only give him a pair of warm mittens: he'll spit into his hands, grab his axe, and go and chop himself a new hut.'

'But, Ivan Grigorievich, you overlook an important consideration: you have not sought to discover what sort of serfs Chichikov has. You have forgotten that a landowner will not sell a good man; I would wager my own head that Chichikov's serfs are thoroughgoing thieves and drunkards, vagabonds, and trouble-makers of the blackest hue.'

'Yes, yes, I agree, it's true, no one will sell a good man, and Chichikov's peasants are drunkards, but you must bear in mind that this is the whole point, this is where the moral lies: scoundrels they may be today, but only resettle them in new lands and they could suddenly become excellent, loyal subjects. There are many such cases on record: you'll find them all over the world, and all through history.'

'Never, never,' said the superintendent of imperial manufactories, 'believe me, this can never happen. For Chichikov's serfs will now have two powerful enemies. The first is the proximity of the Little Russian provinces,* where, as you know, vodka is freely on sale. Let me assure you: within two weeks they will all have drunk themselves into a stupor. The other enemy is the predilection for the nomadic life which the peasants will inevitably acquire during the process of resettlement. The only way is for Chichikov to keep a sharp eye on them constantly and to rule them with a rod of iron; he must punish them for the slightest misdemeanour. Nor must he rely on anyone else: he must do it himself, and when necessary step in and give them a good slap in the face and clip on the ear.'

'But why should Chichikov have to go about slapping people himself, when he can find a bailiff to do it for him?'

'Huh!—you try finding a bailiff: they're all thieves!'

'They're thieves, because their masters don't know their own business.'

'That's true,' chimed many others. 'If the squire himself knows something about farming and is a good judge of people, he will always have a good bailiff.'

To which the superintendent retorted that for less than five thousand you would never find a good bailiff. The president maintained that you even could find one for three thousand. But the superintendent said: 'So where do you think you'll find him: somewhere up your nose?'

But the president said: 'No, not up my nose, but in our own district, and his name is Pyotr Petrovich Samoilov: there's the bailiff Chichikov needs for his peasants!'

Many of them felt strongly for Chichikov, and the arduous task of resettling such an enormous number of peasants scared the wits out of them; they even began to fear lest there might be a riot amongst men as unruly as Chichikov's peasants. This the chief of police countered with the assurance that a riot was nothing to fear, that for the suppression of riots they had the local police captain and his authority, that the police captain did not even have to go himself, he need merely send his peaked cap along in his place, and the cap alone would drive the peasants to their new place of residence. Many debated how to eradicate the rebellious spirit that had so gripped Chichikov's peasants. There were views of every kind: some smacked all too strongly of military severity and a cruelty that was, perhaps, excessive; some, on the contrary, were imbued with mildness. The postmaster observed that Chichikov faced a sacred obligation, that he could become something of a father to his peasants, that he could even, in the postmaster's phrase, introduce the benefits of enlightenment, and he took the opportunity to lavish praise on the Lancaster school of mutual instruction.*

Thus did the townsfolk talk and deliberate, and many of them, prompted by their fellow-feeling, took it upon themselves to convey certain of these counsels to Chichikov in person, even recommending a convoy as the safest means of transporting the peasants to their new place of residence. Chichikov thanked them for their advice, assuring them that he could not miss an opportunity to avail himself of their wisdom, but he rejected the idea of a convoy most resolutely, saying that this was quite unnecessary, that the peasants he had purchased were of a markedly submissive character, were themselves well-disposed to the idea of resettlement, and that there was simply no possibility of a riot amongst them.

All these debates and deliberations did, however, have the most fortuitous consequences for Chichikov. To be precise, rumours started to circulate that he was nothing less than a millionaire. The inhabitants of the town had already, as we have seen in the first chapter, quite lost their hearts to Chichikov, but now, after such rumours, they lost their hearts still further. If the truth be told, they were all good souls, they lived in concord amongst themselves, addressing each other in the most cordial terms, and their discourse was remarkable for its extreme good nature and intimacy: 'My dear friend, Ilya Ilyich!'—'Listen, brother, Antipator Zakharievich!'—'You're talking through your hat, my dear heart, Ivan Grigorievich.' When addressing the postmaster, who was called Ivan Andreevich, they would invariably add: 'Sprechen Sie deutsch, Ivan Andreich?'—in a word, they were like one big family.

Many of them were men of some erudition: the president of the chamber knew Zhukovsky's *Lyudmila** by heart, a poem which was then still fresh off the presses, and he could masterfully declaim many passages, particularly: 'The forest sleeps, the vale reposes', and pronounce the word 'Hush!' in such a way that one could actually see the vale reposing; for greater verisimilitude he would even squeeze his eyes shut at this point.

The postmaster had devoted himself more to philosophical pursuits and was a most assiduous reader, even at night, of Young's

Night Thoughts and Eckartshausen's *Key to the Mysteries of Nature*,* from which he would copy out very long extracts, each several pages in length, but exactly what all these meant no one could ever say; he was a witty fellow, however, florid in his speech and fond, as he put it himself, of embellishing his language. These embellishments took the form of parenthetical phrases, such as: 'Allow me, my good sir... if I may say so... you know... you understand... you can imagine... relatively speaking... so to say... in a manner of speaking', which he would liberally sprinkle about his speech. He would also rather felicitously embellish his words with sly winking, a crinkling of one eye, which lent a most caustic expression to many of his satirical innuendos.

The others were also to a greater or lesser extent men of enlightenment: one read Karamzin,* another the *Moscow Gazette*,* some even read nothing at all. One was a sluggard, that is to say a man who had to be kicked into action; another no better than a marmot— such a lie-a-bed that it was useless even trying to rouse him, for nothing in the world would make him stir. As far as respectability is concerned, we have already seen that they were all solid, good men and that there was not a single consumptive amongst them. All were the sort of men to whom their wives, in moments of tender intimacy, give pet-names such as tubby, fattykins, blacksy-wacksy, chi-chi, jou-jou, and so forth. But on the whole they were good folk, full of hospitality, and any man who had once shared their repast or spent an evening with them at whist was already regarded as a friend. So much greater a friend, therefore, was Chichikov, with his enchanting qualities and manner, a man possessed of the great secret of pleasing others. They grew to love him so dearly that he could see no way of escaping from their town; on all sides he heard their entreaties: 'Do stay with us a week, one little week more, Pavel Ivanovich!'—in brief, he was, as they say, lionized.

Yet this was nothing in comparison to the impression (cause for utter amazement!) that Chichikov made on the ladies. To explain this at all, it would be necessary first to dwell at some length on the ladies themselves, on their society—to paint, as they say, their spiritual qualities in vivid colours; but this is very difficult for the author. On the one hand he is inhibited by his unbounded respect for the spouses of dignitaries, and on the other hand... on the other hand it is simply very difficult. The ladies of the town of N were...

no, I am quite unable to proceed: I am too faint-hearted. What was most remarkable about the ladies of the town of N was their... It's most peculiar, I simply cannot lift my pen: it's as if it were filled with lead. So be it: we shall have to leave the painting of their characters to one whose colours are more vivid and more abundant on his palette, while we shall confine ourselves to a word or two about their appearance and more superficial aspects.

The ladies of the town of N were what is known as presentable, and in this respect they could boldly be held up as an example to all others. In such matters as deportment, *bon ton*, etiquette, and many other fine nuances of decorum, in particular the observance of fashion in the minutest detail, here they surpassed even the ladies of St Petersburg and Moscow. They dressed with great taste, drove about the town in a calèche, as the latest fashion dictated, with a footman, resplendent in gold-braided livery, perched up behind them.

A visiting card, even one scribbled on the back of a playing card—a two of clubs, say, or an ace of diamonds—was also a *sine qua non*. It was over such a card that two of the ladies, the greatest of friends and even kinswomen, had irreconcilably fallen out, because one of them had somehow neglected to return a courtesy call. No matter how hard their husbands and relations tried to reconcile them, the outcome was negative: for all things are possible in this world, except to reconcile two ladies who have quarrelled over an omitted *contre-visite*. Thus, the two ladies remained mutually ill-disposed, to borrow the expression of the local *beau monde*. Issues of precedence also prompted a great many rather strong scenes, which sometimes inspired in their menfolk a genuinely chivalrous and magnanimous conviction of the need to intercede on their ladies' behalf. There were of course no duels between them, because they were all civilians, but instead one husband would endeavour to play a dirty trick on another—something which, as we all know, can be far more injurious than any duel.

On questions of morality the ladies of the town of N were very strict and full of righteous indignation against any manifestation of vice and all temptations, and they castigated all weaknesses quite without mercy. If any jiggery-pokery took place in their midst, it did so in such a covert manner that no one was the wiser; all decorum was maintained and the husband himself was so well schooled that even if he did notice some jiggery-pokery was afoot or got to hear of it he would respond succinctly and sensibly with the proverb: 'Whose business is it, if godmother shares her bench with god-father?'

We should also remark that the ladies of the town of N, like many ladies of St Petersburg, were distinguished by the circumspection and decorum they exercised in their choice of words and expressions. They would never say: 'I blew my nose', 'I sweated', or 'I spat', but would say: 'I relieved my nose', 'I had recourse to my handkerchief'. Under no circumstances could a lady say: 'This glass or that plate stinks', or even anything which might hint at this, but instead they would say: 'This glass is behaving badly', or something on those lines. In order still further to ennoble the Russian language, almost half of its vocabulary was simply jettisoned from their conversation, and they were therefore frequently compelled to have recourse to the French language, because in French a different order prevailed: one could safely use words that were far blunter than those we have already mentioned.

So, this is what we can say about the ladies of the town of N, after a somewhat superficial glance. If we look a little deeper, however, much else will of course be revealed; but it is a most perilous occupation to gaze too deeply into the hearts of ladies. For that reason, we shall continue as we are, on the surface.

Until now the ladies had not spoken much about Chichikov, although giving him due credit for his agreeable manners; but the moment rumours that he was a millionaire started to circulate, other qualities were uncovered. The ladies were not, however, after his money; the fault lay entirely with the word 'millionaire'—not the millionaire in person, but the word itself; for the very sound of this word carries with it, beside the clinking of gold coins, something which affects equally people of a knavish disposition, people who are neither one thing nor the other, and also good people—in a word, it affects everyone. A millionaire has the advantage of being able to see baseness in its pure, disinterested state, not founded on any considerations of gain: most people know only too well that they will get nothing out of a millionaire, and have no right to expect anything, but they will still run ahead of him to catch his eye, they will still smile and doff their hats, they will still strive to get themselves asked to a dinner to which the millionaire has been invited.

It would be wrong to say that this tender predilection for baseness was shared by our ladies; none the less, one did start hearing in many drawing-rooms that, while Chichikov was not, of course, the most handsome of men, he was all that a man should be, and should he have been a little more portly it would have been most unbecoming. In the process, it was stated, apropos of thin men—and even rather unflatteringly—that they were really more like toothpicks, and not men at all. The ladies' *toilettes* started to acquire a variety of embellishments. The shopping arcade became so crowded that there was almost a crush, and so many carriages congregated outside that it started to look like a cavalcade. The merchants were amazed to see that certain bolts of cloth which they had bought from the fair and had been unable to dispose of, as the price was considered exorbitant, suddenly became fashionable and sold like hot cakes. During Sunday morning service one of the ladies was observed to be wearing a gown fitted with a whalebone hoop so wide that it spread halfway across the church, with the result that an inspector of police who happened to be standing nearby had to order the congregation to stand back, that is, closer to the porch, lest they crush her noble ladyship's regalia.

At times even Chichikov was not insensible to the inordinate interest he aroused. Once, on returning home, he found a letter on his table; whence it came and who brought it was impossible to ascertain; the inn-servant would only vouchsafe that it had been brought and that those who brought it had ordered him not to tell from whom it came.

The letter began with these very resolute words: 'No—I must write to you!' It then went on to declare that there is a secret affinity between souls; this truth was reinforced with a series of dots, occupying nearly half a line; there followed several sentiments so remarkable for their veracity that we feel almost duty-bound to reproduce them here:* 'What is our life?—a vale where sorrows dwell. What is the world?—a crowd of people without feelings.' Then the lady writer remarked that she was bathing these lines in tears, tears shed for a loving mother, who had departed this life twenty-five years before; Chichikov was invited into the wilderness, to leave for ever the confines of the city, within whose walls people had no air to breathe; the letter was concluded on a distinct note of despair and closed with the verses:

> *Two turtle-doves will show you*
> *My cold remains.*
> *With languid coos they'll tell you*
> *She died in tears.* *

The last line did not rhyme, but this was of no consequence: the letter was composed in the spirit of those times. There was no signature: neither Christian name nor surname, not even the month and day. There was a postscriptum which merely added that his own heart must tell him the identity of the writer and that the lady would be present in person at the governor's ball, to be held the following day.

This greatly intrigued him. The anonymous letter contained so much mystery and so inflamed his curiosity that he reread it a second and a third time and finally declared: 'It would be most interesting to know who wrote it!' In a word, matters were clearly taking a serious turn; for more than an hour he pondered this problem, before finally concluding, with outspread hands and lowered head: 'A most florid style! Most florid!' Then, we need hardly add, the letter was folded and stowed away in his box, alongside a theatre notice and an invitation to a wedding which had been preserved for seven years in the very same arrangement and position. Sure enough, a little later he was brought an invitation to the governor's ball—a common enough event in the life of provincial capitals: where you find a governor, there too you will find a ball, otherwise he would never win the appropriate love and respect of the local gentry.

All extraneous business was at once set aside and all his energies directed towards preparations for the ball; indeed, he had a great many persuasive and exciting reasons to look forward to this event. It is quite possible that, never before in all the history of the world, had so much time been lavished on a person's toilet. An entire hour was devoted exclusively to the inspection of his face in the mirror. A multiplicity of diverse expressions was essayed: the grave and dignified, the deferential—but with a slight smile, then the simply deferential without a smile; several bows were executed in the direction of the mirror to the accompaniment of certain indistinct utterances, somewhat resembling French, although Chichikov was totally ignorant of the French language. He even gave himself a number of pleasant surprises, raising an eyebrow and twitching his lips, and even performing some manœuvre with his tongue; for, when all is said and done, there is no end to the things a man might do when he finds himself alone, particularly when he believes he is rather handsome and is also quite certain that no one is peeping through the keyhole.

Finally he chucked himself affectionately under the chin, said: 'Now that's what I call a handsome mug!' and began to dress. He remained in a mood of the utmost contentment throughout this operation: as he pulled on his braces or knotted his cravat he scraped his foot and executed the most adroit of bows and, though not a dancer, performed an *entrechat*. This *entrechat* had one slight, in-nocuous consequence: the chest of drawers shook and a hairbrush fell from the table.

His arrival at the ball created an extraordinary commotion. All those present turned to face him, some clutching cards, others inter-cepted at a most interesting juncture in their conversation, having just uttered the words: 'So the lower court* said in reply—', but what exactly the lower court said in reply was promptly forgotten as the speaker hurried to greet our hero. 'Pavel Ivanovich! Heavens above, Pavel Ivanovich! My dear Pavel Ivanovich! My most re-spected Pavel Ivanovich! My dear, dear, dearest Pavel Ivanovich! So there you are, Pavel Ivanovich! There he is, our Pavel Ivanovich! Allow me to embrace you, Pavel Ivanovich! Just bring him here, so I can give him a big kiss, my dear Pavel Ivanovich!' Chichikov felt himself clasped in several embraces at one and the same time. No sooner had he extricated himself from the president's embrace than he found himself in the arms of the chief of police; the chief of police surrendered him to the inspector of the medical board; the inspector of the medical board to the liquor concessionaire; the concessionaire to the architect... On seeing him, the governor, who at this time was standing beside the ladies, holding a bon-bon card* in one hand and a lap-dog in the other, at once dropped both card and lap-dog on the floor, which brought a yelp from the latter; in a word, his arrival occasioned extraordinary delight and good cheer.

There was not a face that did not wear an expression of pleasure, or, at least, a reflection of the general pleasure. Such an expression appears on the faces of officials when a superior charged with the supervision of their offices arrives to conduct an inspection: after the first spasms of fear have passed they observe that he is pleased with much that he sees, and he finally deigns to drop a little *bon mot*, that is, to deliver himself of a few words with a pleasant little chuckle. The officials gathered close round him respond to this by laughing twice as loudly; roars of laughter are emitted by those who, in point of fact, have not been able to hear his words properly, and, finally, a police officer standing far away by the doors next to the exit, a man who has never laughed in his life before and who, prior to this, has just been shaking his fist at the crowd—he too is forced by the immutable laws of reflection to arrange his features into a semblance of a smile, although this smile is more akin to the grimace of a man preparing to sneeze after an inhalation of potent snuff.

Our hero returned the compliments of all and sundry and felt remarkably at ease: he bowed to right and to left, inclining in his customary manner somewhat to one side, but in an entirely effort-less manner, in a way that quite entranced everyone present. The ladies at once gathered round him in a glittering garland, bringing with them veritable clouds of fragrance of every kind: from one wafted the scent of roses, from another spring and violets, a third was drenched in the aroma of mignonette: Chichikov had only to lift his nose in the air and sniff.

Their gowns displayed no end of taste: there were muslins, satins, and chiffons in shades so fashionable and so unutterably delicate as to defy description (such was the refinement of their taste). Bright ribbons and sprays of flowers were scattered about their raiment in the most picturesque disorder, although much careful thought had gone into the creation of that disorder. On the tips of one pair of ears an ethereal head-dress rested precariously and appeared to say: 'Ah, I would fly away, if only I could take this beauty with me!' The bodices were close-fitting and their contours firm and most pleasing to the eye (we should note that in general the ladies of the town of N were a little on the plump side, but they laced themselves so skilfully and possessed such agreeable manners that their corpulence was quite unnoticeable).

Every detail of their *toilette* had been thought out with the most studied care; the neck and shoulders were uncovered just as far as was necessary and no further; each lady exposed her charms to pre-cisely that point where she was convinced she could cause the perdi-tion of any man, and the rest was concealed from view with exquisite taste: either a gossamer-like ribbon, or a scarf, lighter than one of those meringues commonly known as 'kisses', ethereally embraced the neck, or crinkly little ruffs of fine lawn, known by the name of 'modesties', edged the neckline. These 'modesties' concealed areas in front and behind which, in point of fact, would have been quite unable to ruin any man, but they still gave rise to the suspicion that possible ruination lurked beneath. Their long gloves were drawn up almost to meet their sleeves, but deliberately left bare those provocative and—in the case of many ladies—alluringly plump sections of arm above the elbow; some had actually split their kid gloves when attempting to pull them up further; in a word, everything seemed to proclaim: 'No, this is not the provinces, this is the capital, this is Paris itself!' Only here and there was the eye suddenly assailed by an outlandish starched bonnet or even a peacock feather in violation of all fashion, but in accordance with the wearer's own taste. Such things are inevitable, however, for that is the nature of the provincial capital: somewhere it is bound to fall flat on its face.

As he stood before the ladies, Chichikov thought: 'Which one, I wonder, wrote that letter?'—and he made as if to prod the air with his nose, but past that same nose swept an entire procession of elbows, cuffs, sleeves, ribbon trains, fragrant chemisettes, and gowns. The gallopade was in full swing: the postmaster's wife, the captain of police, a lady with a blue feather, a lady with a white feather, the Georgian prince Chipkhaikhilidzev, an official from St Petersburg, an official from Moscow, the Frenchman Monsieur Coucou, Perkhunovsky, Berebendovsky*—all swirled about and rushed past him...

'By Jove! Look at that—the provinces at play!' muttered Chichikov to himself, stepping backwards, and as soon as the ladies had resumed their seats he began studying them again, hoping to identify the letter-writer by the expression on her face and in her eyes; but it was quite impossible to tell, either from the expression on their faces or from the expression in their eyes, who the writer was. And yet in every face he could read the tiniest hint of something, the most elusive nuance, oh so very, very subtle!

'No,' said Chichikov to himself, 'women—now, women are the sort of thing...' He gave a dismissive wave of his hand. 'No—it's pointless even talking about them! Just try and recount or describe all that flits across their faces, all those little twitches, those hints— and you'll end up saying nothing. Their eyes alone are a boundless kingdom in which, once a man strays inside, he's lost for ever! You will never pull him out again, neither with a hook nor any other device. Try, for example, to describe their sparkle: it's moist, velvety, sugary—and the Lord only knows what else besides! It's harsh and soft and even quite languorous, or, as some would say, voluptuous—or not exactly voluptuous, but worse than voluptuous; once it hooks on to your heart, you will feel it stroke the strings of your soul like a violin bow. No, there are no words for it: women are the frills and fal-de-lals of the human race—you can say no more than that!'

I beg forgiveness! it would seem that a word normally associated with the street has escaped the lips of our hero. But what can one do? Such is the lot of the writer in Russia! In fact, when you think about it, if a word from the street occurs in a book it is not the writer who is guilty, but the readers, and primarily those readers belonging to the upper classes: for they are the ones who will never utter a single decent Russian word; their speech is so abundantly stuffed with every manner of French, German, and English words that you want to block your ears, and these words are employed, furthermore, with the observance of every possible rule of pronunciation: the French spoken through the nose and the 'r' gargled; the English spoken as befits a bird, with the adoption even of an avian physiognomy, and they would even make fun of those who cannot assume this bird-like expression. The only thing lacking is anything Russian, although— on a patriotic impulse—they may perhaps build themselves a little cottage *à la vieille Russie* at their summer residence. Such are the readers from high society, and they are followed by all those with aspirations to high society... And yet they are so exacting! They insist that everything should be written in the strictest language, purified and noble—in a word, they want the Russian language to descend suddenly from the clouds of its own accord, beautifully polished, and to alight right on to their tongues, so that they need do no more than open their mouths to utter it. Of course, the female half of the human race is unfathomable, but then our respected readers, you must agree, are sometimes more unfathomable still.

Meanwhile Chichikov had reached a complete impasse in his endeavours to identify the authoress of his letter. When he fixed his gaze on one or another of the ladies he observed that this attention was met on their part by something which could excite both hope and sweet torment in the heart of a wretched mortal, so that he finally sighed: 'No, I shall never guess!'

This did not, however, detract in any way from his good spirits. He exchanged pleasantries with some of the ladies in an easy and relaxed way, stepped up to kiss their hands with small, staccato steps, or, as the expression goes, with a mincing gait, like that affected by those foppish old men strutting about on high heels, the type called grizzled old mules, who can be seen prancing so adroitly around the ladies. After thus mincing about and executing rather dexterous turns to right and left, he would perform a little bow, raising his foot behind him like a little tail, or a comma. The ladies were delighted, and not only discovered in him a wealth of charm, but began to discern a majestic expression in his face, something martial and warlike, a quality which, as we all know, is very attractive to ladies. They even started to quarrel a little over him: noticing that he tended to stand by the doors some of them hurried to occupy the chairs closer to these doors, and when one of them was fortunate enough to get there first, a most unpleasant incident almost occurred, and this audacity now seemed quite abominable to the many others who had wished to do the same themselves.

Chichikov was so engrossed in conversation with the ladies, or rather, the ladies had so overwhelmed and giddied him with their conversation, besprinkling their speech with a multitude of the most convoluted and refined allegories, all of which had to be deciphered, in the process even causing a sweat to break out on his brow, that he quite forgot to observe the rules of decorum and to pay his respects first of all to his hostess, the governor's wife. He realized this lapse only when he heard the voice of the good lady herself, who had already been standing before him for some minutes. She announced in a caressing and rather sly voice, with a gentle shake of her head, 'Aha, Pavel Ivanovich, so this is how it is!...'

I cannot reproduce the good lady's words exactly, but she gave utterance to something very gracious in the style in which ladies and their cavaliers express themselves in the tales of our fashionable writers, those writers who are so fond of describing drawing-rooms and showing off their familarity with *le meilleur ton*, in phrases such as: 'Surely they have not so taken possession of your heart that there remains in it no place, not even the tiniest corner, for those you have so pitilessly forgotten?'

Our hero at once turned to face his hostess, and was on the point of delivering his reply, no doubt every whit as gallant as those delivered in fashionable stories by those Zvonskys, Linskys, Lidins, Gryomins,* and all such smart military men, when, raising his eyes, he froze, as if suddenly struck dumb.

The governor's wife was not alone: she held on her arm a pretty girl of sixteen or so, a sweet blonde, with fine and well-proportioned features, a pointed little chin, a face rounded into an enchanting oval shape, such as an artist might take as his model for the Madonna— indeed, a face that is all too rare in Russia, which in all things favours the grand scale, in all things without exception: mountains and forests and steppes, as well as faces and lips and feet. This was the very same blonde he had encountered on the road from Nozdryov's estate, when, whether through the coachman's or the horses' stupid- ity, their carriages had collided so strangely in a tangle of harnesses, from which the good uncles Mityai and Minyai had vainly toiled to extricate them. Chichikov was so abashed that he could not utter a single coherent word, muttering instead all sorts of rubbish and certainly nothing that would ever issue from the lips of a Gryomin, or a Zvonsky, or a Lidin.

'I do not think you know my daughter, do you?' asked the gov- ernor's wife. 'She has just finished school.'

He replied that he had already had the good fortune to meet her in a most unexpected manner; he tried to add something to this but nothing was forthcoming. The governor's wife added a few more words and moved off with her daughter to join the guests at the other end of the room, leaving Chichikov rooted to the spot like a man who has gaily stepped outside to take a stroll, his eyes dancing about, looking at everything around him, and who suddenly freezes as he realizes that he has forgotten something. At that moment he cuts a figure that could not be more comic: in an instant the carefree expression vanishes from his face; he strains to recall what it is he has forgotten—was it perhaps a handkerchief? But his handkerchief is in his pocket; his money, then? But the money is also in his pocket: he has everything on him, it seems, and yet some mysterious spirit whispers in his ear that he has forgotten something. Now he gazes distractedly and in confusion at the moving crowd before him, at the carriages flying past, at the shakos and rifles of the regiment marching by, at an *affiche*—and he sees nothing properly.

Thus, too, did Chichikov suddenly become abstracted from everything going on around him, while there floated to his ears from the fragrant lips of the ladies a swarm of enquiries, all of them imbued with refinement and courtesy. 'Might we, wretched inhabitants of this earth, make so bold as to venture to enquire whither your fancy has borne you?' 'Where are those happy regions over which your thoughts are hovering?' 'Might we seek to know the name of her who has plunged you into this sweet vale of reverie?'

Yet he was deaf to all these entreaties and the pretty phrases vanished like stones cast into a lake. He was even so inconsiderate as to walk away from the ladies to the other side of the room, wishing to establish whither the governor's wife had taken her daughter. But the ladies, it seemed, were not prepared to let him go so soon; each resolved inwardly to use all the devices at her disposal, all those weapons so perilous to our hearts.

We should note that some ladies—I am speaking here of some only, and not all—have a slight weakness: if they notice something particularly attractive about themselves—be it their brow, or mouth, or hands—they assume that this, their best feature, will be at once evident to everyone, and that all will say as one man: 'Just look, just look, what a lovely Grecian nose she has!' or 'What a charming, perfect brow!' A lady who has elegant shoulders is convinced that all the young men will be quite enraptured and will repeat to one another whenever she walks past: 'Lord, what heavenly shoulders that one has,'—and will not even glance at her face, hair, nose, or forehead, or—if they do glance at them—they do so as if at something quite unrelated. That's just how some ladies think.

Each of these ladies vowed inwardly to be as fascinating as possible on the dance floor and to display in all its splendour that feature which in her was most splendid. The postmaster's wife, as she waltzed, inclined her head to one side with such langour that the impression she gave could only be described as out of this world. One most charming lady—who had come to the ball with no intention of dancing because of a small '*incommodité*', as she herself put it, in the form of a bunion on the right foot, which compelled her to wear velveteen boots—proved unable to resist the challenge and danced a few turns of the waltz in her velveteen boots, just to take the postmaster's wife down a peg or two.

But all this totally failed to have the desired effect on Chichikov. He did not even look at the waltzing ladies, but spent the whole

time rising on tiptoe and craning his neck to peer over the heads of
the other guests in the hope of spotting the captivating blonde; he
also crouched down, to peer between people's shoulders and arms,
and at last he caught sight of her, sitting next to her mother, attired
in some sort of plumed Oriental turban, which swayed majestically
above her head. Chichikov responded as if he meant to take them by
storm: whether because he was impelled forward by the effect of
spring in the air, or whether he was being pushed from behind, but
he thrust his way decisively forward, oblivious of anything in his
path; the concessionaire received from him such a shove that he
recoiled and barely kept his balance, teetering on one foot, failing
which he would most certainly have brought down with him an
entire row; the postmaster also stepped back and regarded him with
a look of amazement, tempered with subtle irony, but Chichikov did
not so much as look at them; he had eyes only for the blonde, at that
moment drawing on long gloves and doubtless burning with desire
to launch herself on to the parquet floor. Four couples were already
executing a dashing mazurka; their heels pounded the floor, while
the army staff captain had thrown himself body and soul—not to
mention arms and legs—into the dance and was cutting capers more
outlandish than any you could see in your wildest dreams.

Chichikov slipped past the mazurka, practically stepping under
the heels of the dancers, and headed straight for that spot where the
governor's wife sat with her daughter. He approached them, however, with great diffidence, no longer mincing in so nimble and
debonair a fashion—in fact, he even stumbled a little, for all his
movements had become awkward and stiff.

It is hard to say for certain whether this marked the awakening in
our hero of a feeling of love—it is even doubtful whether gentlemen
of his ilk, that is to say, not exactly fat, nor yet what you would call
thin either, are even capable of love; all the same, there was something strange about him at this moment, something which he could
not explain to himself: it seemed to him then, as he was to realize
subsequently, that the entire ball, with all its hubbub and chatter,
had somehow, for the space of several minutes, receded into the
distance; the violins and trumpets scraped and tooted away somewhere far off, and all was cloaked in a mist, like a carelessly painted
field in a picture. Out of this murky, crudely sketched field there
emerged with clarity and definition only the fine features of the

enticing blonde: her delightfully oval face, her so very slender figure, a figure such as those which young girls rejoice in for the first
few months after leaving school, her white, almost austere gown,
which so softly and nimbly embraced every part of her shapely,
youthful limbs, clearly showing the purity of their lines. In every
way she seemed to resemble some sort of toy, minutely carved from
ivory; with her whiteness and translucence she alone radiated light
from amidst the turbid and opaque throng about her.

It would seem such things can happen in the world, after all; even
the Chichikovs among us can become poets for a few minutes—
although the word 'poet' is perhaps excessive here. At the very least
he felt practically a young man, in every way almost a Hussar.
Spotting an empty chair beside them he at once occupied it. At first
their conversation was halting, but then things warmed up, and he
even started to get into his stride, but... Here, to our immense
regret, we are forced to remark that gentlemen of a staid disposition
who hold important offices tend to be somewhat ponderous in their
conversation with ladies; the experts in these matters are lieuten-
ants—and certainly no one with a rank higher than captain. How
they do it God alone knows: they do not appear to say anything of
any particular interest, and yet the young ladies laugh so much they
almost fall off their chairs; your state councillor, however, will endeavour to bend her ear with all sorts of discourses: either he will
embark on a disquisition about the immensity of the Russian state,
or he will deliver himself of a compliment which has, of course,
been conceived not without *esprit*, yet has a heavy, bookish stamp on
it; and if he does permit himself a *bon mot*, he will laugh immeasurably louder and longer than she for whose delectation it is intended.

This has been pointed out here so that the reader might comprehend why the blonde started to yawn during our hero's earnest
declamations. Our hero, however, remained quite oblivious of this
and proceeded to recount a great many agreeable things which
he had already had occasion to recount in similar circumstances
in different places, to wit: in Simbirsk province* at the house
of Sofron Ivanovich Bespechny, in the presence of the latter's
daughter Adelaida Sofronovna and her three sisters-in-law: Maria
Gavrilovna, Aleksandra Gavrilovna, and Adelheida Gavrilovna; at
the house of Fyodor Fyodorovich Perekroev in Ryazan province; at
Frol Vasilievich Pobedonosny's in Penza province, and at his brother

Pyotr Vasilievich's in the company of his sister-in-law Katerina Mikhailovna and her second cousins Rosa Fyodorovna and Emilia Fyodorovna; in Vyatka province at the house of Pyotr Varsonofievich, in the company of his daughter-in-law's sister Pelageya Yegorovna and her niece Sofia Rostislavna and her two step-sisters Sofia Aleksandrovna and Maklatura Aleksandrovna.*

All the ladies were most put out by Chichikov's conduct. One of them deliberately walked past him to indicate her displeasure, and even rather carelessly caused the broad hoop of her gown to bump into the blonde maiden, and so manœuvred the scarf which fluttered lightly across her shoulders that its tip flicked the unfortunate young lady in the face; at that same moment an unmistakably caustic and venemous observation wafted across on a cloud of violets from the lips of a lady standing behind him. Either Chichikov did not hear this observation, or he pretended not to hear it, but this was an omission on his part, for the good opinion of ladies must be treasured: he repented of his lapse, but only afterwards, when it was too late.

Righteous indignation was writ large across many faces. However august Chichikov's standing in their society, be he even a million-aire, with majesty in his bearing and a martial and warlike mien, there are certain things which ladies will forgive no man, whoever he might be, and when that happens—woe betide him! There are occasions when a woman, however frail and feeble she might be in character in comparison to her male counterparts, will suddenly grow stronger not only than any man, but than anything in the world. Chichikov's more or less inadvertent neglect of the ladies had the effect of restoring among them even that harmony and concord which had been almost entirely destroyed by the battle for occupa-tion of the chair. The few dry and commonplace remarks he heed-lessly let slip were now found to contain acerbic innuendos. To cap all these disasters, one of the young gentlemen present composed some impromptu satirical verses about the dancers—the sort of verses which, as everyone knows, are an almost inevitable feature of all provincial balls. These verses were at once attributed to Chichikov. Indignation mounted, and the ladies gathered in the corners of the room to discuss him in most ungenerous terms; the poor *pensionnaire* was totally annihilated, and her sentence signed and sealed.

In the mean time a surprise of the most unpleasant kind was being prepared for our hero: while his blonde interlocutrice was yawning as he narrated to her various *petites histoires* that had taken place at different times, even touching upon the Greek philosopher Diogenes, there appeared from the end room the figure of Nozdryov. Whether he had emerged from the buffet, or from the small green drawing-room, where a game of whist with stakes rather higher than usual was in progress, and whether he emerged of his own free will or had been forcibly expelled we cannot say; we know only that he emerged joy-ful, in high spirits, grasping the prosecutor by the arm, in which position he had evidently held him for some time, for the wretched prosecutor was turning his beetling eyebrows in all directions, as if seeking a means of escape from this companionable, linked-arm prom-enade. Without a doubt the situation was past endurance.

Meanwhile, to muster Dutch courage, Nozdryov had gulped down two mugs of tea liberally laced with rum, and was now spouting his usual farrago of nonsense. Spotting him from afar, Chichikov even resolved to make a sacrifice, that is, to surrender his much-coveted seat and to beat as hasty a retreat as possible: this encounter boded no good for him at all. As ill luck would have it, however, at this very moment the governor suddenly loomed before him, declaring his unbounded joy at having run Pavel Ivanovich to earth, and stopped him in his tracks, pleading that he adjudicate in an argu-ment he was having with two ladies as to whether a woman's love was an enduring thing or not; in the mean time Nozdryov had already spotted him and was bearing down upon him.

'Aha, the Kherson landowner, the Kherson landowner!' he shouted, as he advanced on Chichikov and bellowed with laughter, which caused his cheeks, fresh and pink as a spring rose, to shake merrily. 'So, how's business? Bought a lot of dead bodies, have we?—For I am sure you were unaware, Your Excellency,' he continued, in a booming voice, turning to the governor, 'that he deals in dead souls! As God's my witness! Listen, Chichikov, you know what—and I tell you this as a friend, for we're all your friends here, and His Excellency will bear me out—I'd have you strung up, honest to God, I would!'

Chichikov was horror-struck.

'Would you credit it, Your Excellency,' continued Nozdryov, 'this is what he says to me: "Sell me your dead souls", he says, and I split my sides laughing. So I drive into town and people tell me that he's bought up three million roubles' worth of peasants for resettlement: for resettlement, I ask you! And it was dead ones he was trying to buy off me. Listen, Chichikov, you know what?—You're a swine, a real swine, honest to God. And His Excellency will bear me out—isn't that so, Prosecutor?'

But the prosecutor, and Chichikov, and the governor himself, were by now in a state of such bewilderment that they were quite at a loss for a reply; meanwhile Nozdryov, totally undeterred, continued his half-drunken diatribe:

'Now, brother, you watch out... I shan't leave you in peace until I find out why you've been buying dead souls. Listen, Chichikov, you know what?—You should be ashamed: you know you have no better friend anywhere than me, and His Excellency will bear me out, isn't that so, Prosecutor? You simply would not believe it, Your Excellency, how attached we are to each other, I mean, if you were to say: "Nozdryov! Tell me in all honesty, who is dearer to you: your own father or Chichikov?" I would say: "Chichikov", honest to God I would... Allow me, my dear chap, let me give you a big kiss, a real lip-smacker. Please will you permit me, Your Excellency, to give him a kiss. Yes Chichikov, there's no point in resisting, just let me plant one *petit baiser* on that snow-white cheek!'

Nozdryov and his *petit baiser* were so heftily repulsed that he almost went flying: at that point, the others all drew away from him and stopped listening; all the same, his words about the dead souls had been uttered with such stridency and accompanied with such loud laughter that they had attracted the notice even of those in the farthest corners of the room. This news struck them all as so extraordinary that they stood still in amazement, with wooden expressions of idiotic wonder on their faces. Chichikov noticed many of the ladies exchanging winks with a sort of malicious, sarcastic sneer, and the expression on some faces held something so ambiguous that it only increased the general bewilderment.

That Nozdryov was an inveterate liar was something they all knew, and it was nothing unusual to hear him spout the most outrageous nonsense; but we mortals are a peculiar breed and the way the human mind works quite defies comprehension: however vulgar an item of news, it matters only that it should be news and our fellow mortal will at once communicate it to the next mortal, if only to be able to say: 'Just imagine the lies some people tell!' and the next mortal will lend him his ear with pleasure, after which he himself will declare: 'What a shocking lie, no one should pay it the least heed!' and will immediately set off in search of a third mortal to whom to impart this slander, so that they may then exclaim together in righteous indignation: 'What a vulgar fabrication!' The news will most certainly make the rounds of the entire town, and all the mortals, as many of them as there are, will discuss it *ad nauseam* and then declare that no one should give it the slightest attention and that it is not even worth discussing.

This apparently trivial incident visibly discomfited our hero. However stupid the words of a fool may be, they are sometimes sufficient to throw a clever man into a state of confusion. He felt out of sorts and ill at ease—just as if he had inadvertently stepped with a beautifully polished boot into a filthy, stinking puddle; in a word, things were bad, very bad indeed! He tried not to think about this and, hoping to distract himself with other pursuits, to amuse himself, sat down to whist, but everything went awry, like a crooked wheel: twice he led with his opponents' suit and, forgetting that the third hand does not trump, slapped down his trump with all his might and made a fool of himself by picking up his own card. The president simply could not understand how Pavel Ivanovich, who played so well and had, one might say, a refined mastery of the game, could make such gaffes, placing in jeopardy the president's own king of spades, the card on which, to borrow his own phrase, he had been relying as he relied on the Lord Himself. Naturally enough, the postmaster and the president, and even the chief of police himself, poked gentle fun at our hero, as was customary, wondering whether he might perhaps have fallen in love and saying that they knew that Pavel Ivanovich's poor heart had sustained a wound, and they knew, too, from whose bow the arrow had been released; but, however much he tried to smile and laugh off their innuendos, none of this could bring him any consolation.

At supper he was still quite unable to recover his composure, despite the fact that the company at table was pleasant and that Nozdryov had long since been shown the door, for even the ladies had finally pronounced that his behaviour had become *un peu trop scandaleuse*. In the middle of the cotillion Nozdryov had plumped down on the floor, from where he lunged at the skirts of the dancers, antics which were, in the ladies' expression, really too much. The supper was very gay, and all the faces Chichikov glimpsed between the three-stemmed candelabra and assorted flowers, sweetmeats, and bottles, were radiant with a free and easy contentment. Officers, ladies, tailcoats—everything exuded courtesy to such an extent that it even became rather cloying. The gentlemen leapt from their chairs and ran to take the dishes from the footmen so that they could themselves serve the food to the ladies, which they did with a most extraordinary dexterity. One colonel balanced a sauce-boat on the end of his unsheathed sabre and proffered it to a lady guest. The men among whom Chichikov was sitting, who were of a more sedate age, argued noisily, following each portentous utterance with a mouth-ful of fish or beef which had been mercilessly doused in mustard, and they argued on subjects about which he would normally be quick to express his views; but he was like a man wearied by a long journey, who can take nothing in and lacks the energy to join in any discussion. He could not even wait until the end of the meal and made his departure far earlier than was his wont.

There, in that little room, so familiar to the reader, with one door blocked by the chest of drawers, and the occasional cockroach peek-ing from the corners, his state of mind and spirit was as uncomfort-able as the armchair in which he sat. His thoughts were unpleasantly troubled, and there was a gnawing emptiness in his heart. 'The devil take the lot of you for devising these confounded balls!' he thought angrily. 'What do they have to celebrate, the fools? The harvests have failed, prices are soaring in the province—so they throw a ball! It's such a farce, the way they dress up in all that silly finery! It's absurd: the rags on some of them must be worth thousands of roubles! And to think that all that rubbish is paid for by the peasant, with his quit-rent, or, even worse, by the likes of us, at the expense of our own honesty and integrity. We all know why people take bribes, and bend the rules a little: so that there's enough to buy the wife a shawl or some of those confounded bustle things, whatever the devil they're called! And for what? So that some strumpet Sidorovna won't start moaning that the postmaster's wife has a better gown than her—and it's good-bye to a thousand roubles.

'They all shout: "A ball, a ball, what fun!"—but a ball is a lot of nonsense, it's not in the Russian spirit, not in the Russian nature; it's quite absurd: a big, grown-up man, pinched and squeezed into his tight black evening coat like a puppet-show goblin, suddenly leaps up, and starts capering around. Sometimes you will even see one man discussing a business matter with another, dancing nearby, while their feet continue hopping, now to the right, now to the left, like a pair of young goats... It's all aping and parroting. Just because a Frenchman at the age of forty is as much a child as he was at fifteen we have to be the same!

'No, honestly... After every ball you feel ashamed, as if you've committed some sin; you don't even like to remember it. Your head becomes totally empty, as if you've just had a conversation with one of those fashionable types: they talk on and on, jumping from one topic to another, regurgitating everything they've dredged out of books, speaking colourfully, eloquently, but without making the faintest impression on your mind, and afterwards you realize that even a conversation with a simple merchant, who knows only his own business—but knows it well and from experience—is better than all this empty prattle. What earthly benefit can you squeeze from it, from this ball? Let us suppose that some writer or other decided to describe this entire scene exactly as it is: even in a book it would be as absurd as in real life. What does it all mean, anyway: is it moral or is it immoral? The devil only knows! You would say: "The devil take it!" and clap the book shut.'

Such were Chichikov's censorious thoughts about balls in general; but it seems that there was another, deeper reason for his indignation. His chief annoyance was directed not at the ball, but at the fact that he had come a cropper, so to speak, that he had suddenly shown himself to all and sundry in a most unbecoming light, that he had found himself playing a strange, ambiguous role. Of course, viewing all this with the eye of a sensible man, he could see that it was all nonsense, that a few stupid words could do no real harm, particularly now, when the main business had already been properly concluded. But man is a strange creature: Chichikov was most distressed to be in the disfavour of those very people whom he heartily despised and about whom he had expressed such harsh views, vilifying their vanity and their finery. This was all the more vexatious to him as, once he properly analysed the situation, he could see that he himself was largely to blame.

He did not, however, turn his anger on himself, and he was right not to do so. We all share the little foible of wishing to spare ourselves, and venting our spleen instead on someone nearby, for example, a servant, or a subordinate who happens to be on hand at that moment, or a wife, or, failing all else, a chair, which is sent flying through the air, landing right by the door and losing its arms and back in the process: 'Take that!' you say, wreaking your anger on the harmless object. Thus, too, did Chichikov soon find a whipping-boy nearby to bear the brunt of his exasperation. This whipping-boy was Nozdryov, and sure enough, he received a lashing no less thorough than that which might be administered to a thieving village elder or coachman by a much-travelled, experienced army captain, or perhaps even a general, who, in addition to the many objurgations which are now part of the classical repertoire of such occasions, will add many new ones of his own devising. Nozdryov's entire genealogy was investigated, and many members of his family in the ascendant line suffered badly in the process.

But at this very moment, while he sat in his hard armchair, troubled by his thoughts and afflicted with insomnia, heaping further abuse on Nozdryov and all his kith and kin; while before him the tallow candle flickered weakly, as wax built up around its wick and threatened at any moment to extinguish it; while the impenetrable, dark night stared in at him through the window, shortly to lighten with the blue haze of approaching dawn, as the cocks crowed in the distance; and while through the slumbering town there perhaps wandered a frieze greatcoat, a miserable wretch of unknown class and rank, who knew no other path in life than that (alas!) trodden by the hapless drunks of Russia—at this very moment at the other end of town an event was taking place which was to aggravate still further the unpleasantness of our hero's situation.

For at this very moment, through the distant streets and alleys of the town there rattled a most extraordinary equipage, a name for which it would be hard to find. It was quite unlike a tarantass, or a calèche, or a britzka,* but was much more like a bulging, fat-cheeked watermelon on wheels. The cheeks of the watermelon, that is to say, the doors, which bore traces of yellow paint, were very difficult to close properly because of the dilapidated state of the handles and catches, which were barely held together with bits of string. The melon was crammed full of calico print cushions, which came in a variety of shapes and sizes—pouches, bolsters and ordinary pillows—and was stuffed with sacks full of bread loaves, calatches, doughnuts, egg-rolls, and plaited sourdough buns. Poking out from above all these were a chicken pie and an egg-and-pickle pastie.* On the back-board behind the melon stood a person of flunkeyish provenance, clad in a shortcoat made of striped homespun drabbet, unshaven, his hair lightly streaked with grey: the sort of character who goes by the sobriquet 'laddie'.

The clatter and squealing given off by all the iron catches and rusty bolts awakened the town gatekeeper, and he, brandishing his halberd and still befuddled with sleep, shouted at the top of his voice: 'Who goes there?', but seeing that no one was going there, and that the clatter came from afar, apprehended a bug crawling on his collar and, stepping closer to the lamp, summarily executed it there and then on his fingernail. Whereupon, setting aside his halberd, he resumed his slumbers, in accordance with the code of his chivalric order. Every now and again the horses stumbled on their front legs, because they were not shod, and evidently had little familiarity with the quiet paved streets of the town. After executing a number of turns from one street into another, this juggernaut at last turned into a dark side-street next to the small parish church of St Nicholas on Nedotychki* and halted before the gates of the house of the archpriest's wife. A peasant girl wearing a scarf on her head and a padded jacket climbed down from the carriage, and banged on the gate with her two fists as powerfully as any man (the laddie in the drabbet shortcoat later had to be dragged off by his feet, for he was sleeping the sleep of the dead). The dogs started to bark, and the gates finally opened their jaws and swallowed up—albeit with great difficulty—this lumbering engine of peregrination.

The carriage drove into the cramped courtyard, cluttered with stacks of firewood, chicken coops and all manner of little sheds, and a gentlewoman alighted. This gentlewoman was Madame Korobochka, landowner and widow of a Collegiate Secretary. Soon after the departure of our hero the old lady had been thrown into such a state of agitation at the thought that she might let herself be swindled by Chichikov, that for three nights in succession she was unable to sleep. She then resolved to travel into town, despite the fact that the horses were unshod, in order to ascertain for herself the going price for dead souls and to determine whether—God forbid—she had not slipped up by selling them for next to nothing. As for the consequences of her visitation, these the reader may learn from a certain conversation which took place between a certain two ladies. This conversation... but let us rather save this conversation for the following chapter.

CHAPTER NINE

In the morning, at an hour even earlier than that appointed in the town of N for calls, the doors of a wooden house, painted orange, with an attic and blue columns, opened and a lady flitted out, clad in a fashionable plaid cloak and accompanied by a flunkey in a greatcoat with several collars and a shiny round hat edged with gold galloon. The next instant and with uncommon haste the lady flitted up the steps, which had been lowered in readiness, of the chaise standing at the entrance. The flunkey at once slammed the door after the lady, threw back the steps, and, seizing the straps at the back of the carriage, shouted to the coachman: 'Off you go!' The lady was in possession of a freshly garnered piece of news and felt an irrepressible compulsion to pass it on as swiftly as possible. Every few seconds she looked out of the window only to see, to her unutterable vexation, that half her journey still remained. Every building seemed longer than usual, the white stone almshouse with its narrow windows crawled past for an intolerably long time, until she could bear it no longer and exclaimed: 'Cursed building—is there no end to it?' The coachman had already been instructed twice: 'Faster, Andryushka, faster! You're driving unbearably slowly today!'

Finally they reached their destination. The chaise drew up before a dark-grey single-storeyed house, also of wood, with little white bas-reliefs above the windows, a tall wooden fence right in front of the windows, and a narrow little garden, home to a few spindly little trees, caked white by accretions of the ubiquitous and ineradicable dust which accumulates in all towns. In the windows could be seen flower pots, a parrot in its cage, swinging by its hooked beak from a ring, and two little dogs dozing in the sun. In this house lived the dear friend of the lady who had just arrived.

The author is at a complete loss as to how to name these two ladies without once again incurring the general wrath, as has happened all too often in the past. To use an invented surname would be dangerous. Whatever name you think up, you will most certainly find that somewhere, in some corner of our so very vast Empire, there is someone with precisely that name, and that someone will most certainly become a mortal enemy of the author, and will say that the author has made secret visits for the express purpose of gathering intelligence, to find out what kind of person he is, what sort of a sheepskin coat he wears, which of the ladies called Agrafena Ivanovna he calls on, and what his favourite dishes are. Now, Heaven forbid that you should call them by their rank—that is more dangerous still. Nowadays all those of a certain rank or class are so prickly that everything they find in a printed book they take as a personal affront: such, it seems is the prevailing attitude. You need merely say that there is a stupid person in a certain town, and that is already a personal slight; suddenly a gentleman of the most respectable appearance will leap to his feet and shout: 'Well, I'm a person too, so that means I'm also stupid!'—in other words he will instantly put two and two together.

For that reason, to avoid all this, we shall refer to the lady on whom our visitor has called exactly as she was referred to by virtually everyone in the town of N, to wit: a lady pleasant in all respects. This appellation she had acquired quite legitimately, for it was true that she spared no effort in her anxiety to make herself amiable to a fault, although, of course, through this amiability there shone an occasional streak of that—ouch!—needle cunning so typical of the female character! And sometimes each of her pleasant utterances would carry—ouch!—such a stinging dart! And God have mercy on the woman who dared to rouse her fury by stealing a march on her in any thing. But all this would be cloaked in the most refined genteelness, of the sort encountered only in provincial capitals. Her every movement was performed in the best of taste, she even liked poetry, she was sometimes even able to incline her head at an angle suggestive of reverie—and all were unanimous that she was indeed a lady pleasant in all respects.

By contrast, the other lady—that is to say, our visitor—did not have such versatility of character, and therefore we shall call her the merely pleasant lady. The arrival of the visitor awoke the dogs dozing in the sun: shaggy Adèle, who was forever getting entangled in her own fur, and lanky Pot-Pourri with his skinny legs. With tails held high both Adèle and Pot-Pourri rushed barking into the hall, where the visitor was divesting herself of her cloak, to reveal beneath it a gown of fashionable design and colour and, around her neck, a long fur scarf; the fragrance of jasmine filled the entire room. No sooner had the lady pleasant in all respects learnt of the arrival of the merely pleasant lady, than she dashed into the hall. The ladies grasped each other's hands, kissed and shrieked just as boarding school inmates shriek when they see each other again after the holidays, before their mamas have found an opportunity to explain to them that the father of the one is poorer and lower in rank than that of the other. The kisses had to be performed loudly, because the little dogs had resumed their barking, for which importunity they were slapped with a handkerchief. Thereupon both ladies repaired to the drawing-room, which was pastel blue, of course, with a sofa, an oval table, and even little screens entwined with ivy; they were followed—at a run and with little growls—by shaggy Adèle and tall, spindly Pot-Pourri.

'Come over here, into this little corner!' said the hostess, seating her guest in a corner of the sofa. 'That's right! That's right! Here's a cushion for you!' As she said this she thrust behind her guest's back an embroidered woollen cushion depicting a knight who looked like all cross-stitch, embroidered knights: his nose was like a little staircase and his mouth a perfect rectangle. 'How delighted I am that you... I heard someone driving up and I wondered who it could be, so early. Parasha said: "It's the Vice-Governor's wife!" and I said: "Oh no, not that crashing old bore again", and I was just going to say that I was not at home...'

The visitor was anxious to get down to business and impart her piece of news, but an exclamation uttered at that moment by her hostess suddenly turned the conversation in quite another direction.

'What a jolly print!' exclaimed the lady pleasant in all respects, gazing at the gown of the merely pleasant lady.

'Yes, isn't it? Praskovya Fyodorovna finds, however, that it would be better if the little checks were a bit smaller and the dots pale blue and not brown. Her sister has just been sent a piece of material: it's so charming, too delightful for words; just picture it to yourself: teeny-weeny little stripes, thinner than anything the human mind could imagine, a pale blue ground, and along every second stripe tiny little eyes and paws, eyes and paws, eyes and paws... It's quite exquisite! One can say quite positively that there's nothing like it anywhere else in the world.'

'But darling, that's awfully garish.'

'Garish?—it's not garish at all!'

'Oh but it is!'

We should note that the lady pleasant in all respects was something of a materialist, inclined towards negation and doubt, and there was much she rejected in life.

Hereupon the merely pleasant lady explained that it was by no means garish, and exclaimed: 'Oh, by the way, congratulations: flounces are out.'

'What do you mean: "they're out"?'

'Everyone's wearing scallops now.'

'Oh, but I don't like the sound of that—not scallops!'

'It's scallops, nothing but scallops: scalloped pelerines, scallops on the sleeves, teeny scalloped epaulettes, scallops below, scallops everywhere you look.'

'It's not very nice, Sofia Ivanovna, to have scallops everywhere.'

'But it's delightful, Anna Grigorievna, delightful beyond words. Everything is stitched in two ribs, with very broad arm-holes, and above... And now I'll tell you something that will really astound you, and then you'll say... You'll never believe it: just imagine, bodices have become even longer, coming down to a point in front, and the front stays are ridiculously long; skirts are now gathered all round, like farthingales in the old days—they even put in a bit of padding at the back to give you the look of the true *belle femme*.'

'Well that is all simply too, too... *je ne sais quoi*!' said the lady pleasant in all respects, tossing her head in a dignified manner.

'Quite so, it's too, too *je ne sais quoi*!' answered the merely pleasant lady.

'Well, you may say what you like, but I shall not start imitating that, not for anything in the world.'

'No, neither shall I... Really, when you think to what lengths some people will go for the sake of fashion... it's quite absurd! Just for a laugh, I took a pattern from my sister; my Melanya has started making it.'

'Do you mean to say you actually have a pattern?' shrieked the lady pleasant in all respects, not without a perceptible quickening of the pulse.

'I do indeed, my sister's brought one.'

'Darling Sofia Ivanovna, in the name of all that is most sacred, give it to me!'

'Oh dear, I've already promised it to Praskovya Fyodorovna. Perhaps you can have it after her.'

'Now, who would want to wear something after Praskovya Fyodorovna? I must say, I am most surprised at you, that you should prefer outsiders to your own nearest and dearest.'

'But she is also my aunt, once removed.'

'She's removed a lot more than once, might I tell you: and on your husband's side, too... No, Sofia Ivanovna, I wish to hear no more, this can mean only one thing: you want to wound me deeply... It is quite clear that I have already grown tedious to you, and you now wish to sever all ties of friendship with me.'

Poor Sofia Ivanovna did not know what to do. She now saw that she was steering a course between Scylla and Charybdis. So much for her bragging! She would gladly have cut out her own tongue for its stupidity.

'Well, and what of our Prince Charming?' asked the lady pleasant in all respects, after a pause.

'Merciful God! Look at me, sitting here and not so much as a word! Shame on me! You can probably guess, Anna Grigorievna, why I've come to see you?' At this point the visitor took a deep breath and the words were ready to come flying forth in rapid succession, like hawks, and only someone as inhuman as her own dear friend would have had the heartlessness to arrest her.

'I don't care how much you sing his praises,' she said with greater animation than usual, 'but I will tell you frankly, and I'll say it to his face, that he is a worthless man, worthless, worthless, worthless...'

'But just listen to what I'm about to reveal to you—'

'The word went round that he's so handsome, but he's not hand-some at all, and as for his nose... it's the most disagreeable nose.'

'Please, I beg you, just hear me out... My dear, sweet Anna Grigorievna, I beg you to hear me out! For this is a real story, do you see: a story, *c'qu'on appelle "histoire"*,' declared the visitor with a look almost of despair and with a note of real supplication in her voice. It would be apposite to remark here that a great number of foreign words were interpolated into both ladies' conversation, and sometimes entire, long sentences in French. Yet however great the author's veneration for the salutary benefits brought by the French tongue to Russia, however great his veneration for that most praise-worthy custom of our high society, which chooses to express itself in this language at all hours of the day, motivated, undoubtedly, by its deep love for our mother country, yet for all this he cannot bring himself to insert a sentence of any alien tongue whatsoever into this, his Russian poem. Thus, let it proceed in Russian.

'But what *histoire*?'

'My dear, dearest Anna Grigorievna, if only you could imagine the position in which I found myself! Just picture the scene: today the archpriest's wife comes to see me—you know, Father Kiril's wife—and what do you think? Our bashful newcomer—what do you think he is?'

'What—surely to goodness he didn't pay court to the archpriest's wife?'

'Oh, Anna Grigorievna, if only it were that, it wouldn't be so bad; but just listen to what the archpriest's wife told me: Madame Korobochka arrives at her house, she says, scared out of her wits and as pale as death, and she tells her such a story—and what a story! Listen, my dear, it's just like a novel: suddenly, in the dead of night, when everyone is fast asleep in the house, she hears knocking at the gate, the most dreadful racket you could possibly imagine, and voices shouting: "Open up, open up, or we'll break down the gates!" Now what do you think of that? What do you think of our Prince Charming after that?'

'Tell me about this Korobochka—is she young and pretty?'

'Not at all, she's an old crone.'

'Well, I like that! Going after an old crone. I must say, after that you really have to admire the taste of our ladies: there's a fine one for them to fall in love with.'

'But no, no, Anna Grigorievna, it's not what you're thinking at all. Just picture him to yourself, he comes armed to the teeth, like Rinaldo Rinaldini,* and demands: "Sell me all your souls who have died," he says. Korobochka answers very sensibly, she says: "I cannot sell them, because they're dead." "No," he says, "they are not dead; that," he says, "is for me to decide, whether they're dead or not; they're not dead, not dead," he shouts, "not dead!" In a word, he caused a terrible rumpus: the entire village came running to see, the children were crying, everyone shouting, no one could understand anything anyone was saying, it was quite simply *horreur, horreur, horreur*!...

'You simply cannot imagine, my dear Anna Grigorievna, the alarm I felt when I heard all that. "My dear madam," Mashka says to me, "just take a look in the mirror, you're quite pale." "I've no time for

mirrors now," I say, "I must go and tell all this to Anna Grigorievna."
I order the carriage that very instant: Andryushka the coachman
asks me where I want to go, but I am dumbstruck, I just stare back
at him like an idiot; he must have thought I had gone mad. Oh dear,
Anna Grigorievna, if only you could picture the alarm I felt!'

'It is rather strange, I must say,' said the lady pleasant in all
respects, 'what exactly might these dead souls mean? I must confess I understand absolutely nothing. This is now the second time
I've heard mention of these dead souls; but my husband assures me
that Nozdryov was lying; all the same, it seems there is something
to it.'

'But just imagine, Anna Grigorievna, the position I was in when
I heard all this. "And now," says Korobochka, "I simply do not
know," she says, "what to do. He forced me," she says, "to sign
some false document, and he threw down fifteen roubles in banknotes;
I'm just a helpless, inexperienced widow," she says. "I know nothing about these things..." Such goings on, imagine! My dear, just
imagine my utter alarm.'

'If you ask me, this is more than just dead souls, there's something else behind all this.'

'My very own thoughts,' declared the merely pleasant lady with a
certain measure of surprise, at once seized with a powerful urge to
discover what precisely could be behind all this. She even enquired
in an offhand way: 'So what do you suppose there is behind it all?'

'Well, what do you think?'

'What do I think?... I must confess, I'm completely at a loss.'

'All the same, I should still like to know your views on the whole
affair.'

But the pleasant lady could think of nothing to say. She was
capable only of deep alarm, while to draw some clever inference was
quite beyond her, and therefore, more than any other lady, she felt
the need for tender friendship and counsel.

'In that case, let me tell you what these dead souls are,' said the
lady pleasant in all respects and, on hearing this, her guest was at
once all attention: her ears pricked up of their own accord, she half
rose from the sofa, and, although she was rather on the stout side,
she suddenly became much thinner, and as light as a feather about
to be borne away by the first puff of wind.

In this she could be likened to the Russian squire, dog-fancier and intrepid huntsman, who, as he nears the forest into which the hare has been driven by the whippers-in so that at any moment it might dash out into his path, is transformed, together with his mount and his raised whip, frozen in time, into a stack of gunpowder, to which a flame is about to be applied. He gazes intently into the turbid air, and you may be sure he will overtake the hare, he will get his quarry, no matter how violently the whole snow-covered steppe might rise to oppose him, shooting its silvery stars into his mouth, his moustache, his eyes, his eyebrows, and his beaver cap.

'The dead souls...' began the lady pleasant in all respects.

'Yes, yes?' her guest urged her, greatly agitated.

'The dead souls...'

'Oh for pity's sake, do go on!'

'All that dead souls stuff has merely been concocted as a cover, but the truth of the matter is: he plans to elope with the governor's daughter.'

This conclusion, to be sure, was totally unexpected and in all respects extraordinary. The merely pleasant lady, on hearing it, froze, went pale—as pale as death—and was indeed most deeply alarmed.

'Good Lord!' she exclaimed, flinging up her hands. 'Now *that* I could never possibly have guessed.'

'While I, to be perfectly honest, guessed it the very moment you opened your mouth,' answered the lady pleasant in all respects.

'Well, so much for the boarding-school upbringing, Anna Grigorievna! That's innocence for you!'

'Innocence, indeed! I've heard her come out with things which, I must confess, I could not bring myself to repeat.'

'You know, Anna Grigorievna, does it not simply break one's heart to see how rife immorality has become?'

'And the men are out of their minds about her. Personally, I must confess, I can see nothing in her... She's intolerably affected.'*

'Oh, but my dear Anna Grigorievna, she has as much life in her as a statue, with never the slightest expression on her face.'

'And she's so affected! So affected! Goodness, so affected! Who taught it to her I do not know, but I have never yet seen a woman with such airs and graces.'

'But dear heart! She's like a statue and as pale as death itself.'

'Heavens no, Sofia Ivanovna: it's scandalous the way she rouges her cheeks.'

'But my dear Anna Grigorievna, what are you saying: she's chalk, the purest, whitest chalk!'

'My dear, I sat right beside her: the rouge was caked on her face, a finger thick, and it was flaking off like stucco, in chunks. She learnt it from her dear mama, who's also a coquette, but daughter will soon put mother in the shade.'

'I must disagree. You may ask me to swear by whatever you will, I'm prepared to forfeit my children, my husband, my entire fortune, this very moment, if she has the smallest little speck, the tiniest grain, or even the slightest shadow of colour!'

'Heavens, what are you saying, Sofia Ivanovna!' exclaimed the lady pleasant in all respects, flinging up her hands in exasperation.

'Really, Anna Grigorievna, how can you! You quite astonish me!' said the pleasant lady and also flung up her hands.

Now let it not seem strange to the reader that the two ladies should fail to agree on something that they had both seen at almost the same time. There really are things in the world which have this remarkable property: when one lady looks at them they will appear completely white, but let another look and they will be quite, quite red, like cranberries.

'Well, here's further proof for you that she has no colour,' continued the pleasant lady, 'I can remember, as if it happened only today, sitting next to Manilov and saying to him: "Just look how pale she is!" I must admit, it only goes to show how dull-witted all our menfolk are, that they should admire her so. And as for our Prince Charming... Ugh, what a nasty man! You simply cannot imagine, Anna Grigorievna, how nasty I thought him.'

'All the same, there were certain ladies who were not entirely indifferent to him.'

'I trust you're not referring to me, Anna Grigorievna? No, Anna Grigorievna, you cannot say that of me—never, never!'

'Oh, but I am not speaking of you—do you imagine there are no others besides you?'

'Never, never, Anna Grigorievna! Allow me to inform you that I happen to know my own mind very well; this might be true of certain other ladies who make themselves out to be unapproachable.'

'I beg your pardon, Sofia Ivanovna! Allow *me* to inform *you* that I have never been guilty of anything so shocking. Others have, perhaps, but not I: please allow me to point this out to you.'

'But why do you object so strongly? After all, there were other ladies there too, there were even some who rushed to occupy the chairs by the door, that they might sit closer to him.'

Well, it seemed inevitable that, after these words uttered by the pleasant lady, a storm should erupt, but—*mirabile dictu*—both ladies suddenly cooled down and absolutely nothing ensued. The lady pleasant in all respects recollected that the pattern for the fashionable gown was not yet in her hands, and the merely pleasant lady realized that she had yet to learn details of the discovery made by her dear friend; thus a truce was struck between them. To be sure, it cannot be said that either of the ladies harboured an inner compulsion to cause any unpleasantness, and on the whole they were not malicious by nature, it was simply that in the course of conversation each quite spontaneously felt a tiny urge to needle the other; thus, simply for the small satisfaction it gave them, they could not resist the temptation to make the occasional little jibe, as if to say: 'There, take that!' Such are the different urges that move the male and the female hearts.

'Yet there is still one thing I cannot quite understand,' said the merely pleasant lady, 'and that is how Chichikov, a visitor in our midst, could contemplate such an audacious *aventure*. It's quite unthinkable that he had no accomplices.'

'You surely do not think he had none?'

'But who, do you think, might have assisted him?'

'Well, Nozdryov, for one.'

'Not Nozdryov, surely?'

'Why not? He certainly has it in him. Do you know, he wanted to sell his very own father or, worse still, to stake him at cards.'

'Goodness me, what fascinating things one learns from you! I should never have guessed that Nozdryov could be mixed up in this affair!'

'But I have always suspected as much.'

'When you come to think of it, it's astonishing the things that go on in the world! I mean, who would have supposed, when Chichikov first arrived in the town, that he would cause such an extraordinary *mêlée* in our little *monde*? Oh, Anna Grigorievna, if you could only picture my alarm! If it were not for your kindness and friendship... there I was, I assure you, on the very brink of perdition... where was I to turn? My Mashka could see I was as pale as death. "My dear madam," she says to me, "you're as pale as death." "Mashka," I said, "I haven't the time to worry about that now." What a turn of events! So Nozdryov's in it too—well I never!'

The pleasant lady was most anxious to ascertain further details concerning the abduction, to wit: at what time it was set for, and so forth, but she wanted too much. The lady pleasant in all respects claimed complete ignorance. She could not tell a lie: making a surmise, yes, that was a different matter, but even then one only did it when the surmise rested on inner conviction; now, if she did happen to feel such inner conviction then she could stand up for herself, and let some foxy lawyer, famed for changing people's minds, try out his skills on her—he would soon find out what inner conviction meant.

That both ladies finally believed beyond any doubt something which had originally been pure conjecture is not in the least unusual. We, intelligent people though we call ourselves, behave in an almost identical fashion, as witness our scholarly deliberations. At first the scholar proceeds in the most furtive manner, beginning cautiously, with the most diffident of questions: 'Is it not perhaps from there? Could not such-and-such a country perhaps derive its name from that remote spot?' Or: 'Does this document perhaps not belong to another, later period?' Or: 'When we say this nation, do we not perhaps mean that nation there?' He promptly cites various writers of antiquity and the moment he detects any hint of something—or imagines such a hint—he breaks into a trot and, growing bolder by the minute, now discourses as an equal with the writers of antiquity, asking them questions, and even answering on their behalf, entirely forgetting that he began with a timid hypothesis; it already seems to him that he can see it, the truth, that it is perfectly clear—and his deliberation is concluded with the words: 'So that's how it was, that's how such-and-such a nation should be understood, that's the angle from which this subject should be viewed!' This is then publicly declaimed *ex cathedra* for all to hear—and the newly discovered truth sets off on its travels round the world, gathering adherents and disciples as it goes.

While the two ladies were so successfully and astutely unravelling this tangled skein, the prosecutor himself entered the drawing-room, his face, with its beetling eyebrows and blinking eye, wearing its usual impassive expression. The ladies began vying with each other to impart all these events to him, recounting the story of the buying of dead souls, the planned abduction of the governor's daughter, and confusing him so utterly that he stood rooted to the spot, twitching his left eyelid and flicking snuff out of his beard with his handkerchief, quite unable to understand a thing that they said. This was how the ladies left him, as they set off on their various ways to rouse the town to mutiny.

They succeeded in accomplishing this undertaking in little over half an hour. The town was decidedly roused: mutiny was fomented, but no one had the least idea what it was all about. The ladies were so adept at sowing confusion that everyone, and most particularly the officials, remained stunned for quite some time. In the first moments their position was like that of the schoolboy, who, while still asleep, has a 'hussar'—a paper cone filled with snuff—inserted in his nostril by his school-fellows, who have risen earlier.* Taking the deep breath of a sleeper, he inhales the entire twist of snuff, awakes, leaps out of bed, staring about him like an idiot, eyes popping out of his head, and is quite unable to understand where he is or what has happened to him. In a little while he starts to make out the walls, illuminated by the oblique rays of the morning sun, then hears the laughter of his fellows, hiding in the corners of the room, and becomes aware of the dawning day peeping through the window, bringing with it the awakened forest, ringing with the chorus of a thousand birds, and the glistening river, disappearing and reappearing as it twists and turns between the slender reeds, a river teeming with naked boys, noisily urging their fellows to join them in the water—and then, finally, he feels the 'hussar' lodged in his nose.

Exactly such was the situation in which the inhabitants and officials of the town found themselves in those first moments. Each froze in his tracks, like a sheep, with eyes popping. Dead souls, the governor's daughter, and Chichikov were all mixed together in the most extraordinary fashion; and only after the first wave of stupefaction had passed did they begin to distinguish one from the other, then demanded an explanation and grew angry when they realized that the matter simply defied all explanation. What did it all mean, when all was said and done: what was all this dead souls nonsense, anyway? There was no logic in dead souls, how could one buy dead souls? Was anyone fool enough to do so? What ill-gotten gains would he use to buy them with? And to what earthly purpose could he put these dead souls? And why was the governor's daughter mixed up in all this? If he was planning to abduct her, then why was he buying up dead souls? And if he was buying up dead souls, then why abduct the governor's daughter? Did he intend these dead souls as a present for her, was that it? What was all this poppycock being bandied around town? Things had come to such a pass that, before you could say procurator-general, another story was being put about, without a scrap of sense in it...

All the same, as they say, there's no smoke without fire. But where was the fire here, what reason would there be for these dead souls? No reason at all. The answer was simple: it was a lot of twaddle, flap-doodle, hogwash, and hard-boiled boots! In short: the devil knows what!... Thus, tongues flapped away and soon the whole town was busy talking about the dead souls and the governor's daughter, about Chichikov and the dead souls, about the governor's daughter and Chichikov, and there was commotion everywhere. It was as if a whirlwind had swept through this hitherto slumbering town! All the sloths and lie-abeds came crawling out of their nests, all those creatures who had spent the last few years loafing at home in their dressing-gowns, blaming their indolence by turns on the boot-maker, who had made their boots too tight, or on the tailor, or on that drunkard of a coachman. They all emerged: all those who had long since ceased all acquaintance and only kept company, as the saying goes, with Polezhaev and Zavalishin (these well-known terms, derived from the verbs for lying down and lolling about, are as widely used here in Russia as the phrase: 'paying a call on Sopikov—old Wheezer—or Khrapovitsky—the Snorer', which signifies any sort of log-like sleep on the back, the side, and in every other imaginable position, to the accompaniment of snorts, nasal whistling, and other similar embellishments);* all those who could not be lured out of their homes even by an invitation to join their friends around a 500-rouble tureen of fish soup with five-foot-long sterlets and all sorts of tasty, spicy meat-pies*— in short, it became clear that the town was large and its population most varied. Some fellow called Sysoi Pafnutievich suddenly popped up, as did a Macdonald Karlovich,* and neither had been heard of before; among the usual salon habitués there appeared an immensely tall character, with a bullet-hole in his arm, a man of a height never seen in these parts before. The streets were thronged with covered droshkies, unfamiliar brakes, rattle-traps, and shandrydans—total chaos reigned.

At another time and in other circumstances such rumours might perhaps have attracted no interest; but for so long the town of N had been starved of news of any kind. For three long months on end the town had not had even a single scandal of the kind known in our capital cities as a *commérage*, which, as we all know, is as essential to the well-being of a town as the timely arrival of fresh provisions. Suddenly, in these municipal deliberations, two entirely antithetical schools of thought emerged and two opposing camps were formed: the male and the female. The male camp, which was extremely dull-witted, concentrated on the dead souls. The female dealt exclusively with the abduction of the governor's daughter. This latter camp, we should note to the credit of the ladies, was conspicuous for its incomparably greater degree of orderliness and circumspection. For such, evidently, is their appointed purpose in life: to be good house-keepers and manageresses. In their hands everything swiftly ac-quired a vivid and definite aspect, was clothed in clear and manifest forms, was explained and cleansed of clutter, so that a finished picture emerged. It transpired that Chichikov had long been in love, that the sweethearts had held moonlight trysts in the gardens; that, since Chichikov was as rich as a Jew, the governor would even have even given him his daughter in marriage, had there not been the problem of the wife he had abandoned (how they had discovered Chichikov was married was something no one knew); that his wife, whose hopeless love caused her much suffering, had written a most moving letter to the governor; and that Chichikov, seeing that the governor and his wife would now never give their consent, had resolved to abduct their daughter.

In other houses a slightly different version was told: that Chichikov had no wife at all, but that, being a man of subtle ways and no scruples, he had commenced his undertaking—with the eventual aim of winning the daughter—by wooing the mother, and had es-tablished a secret liaison with her, and had then asked for the hand of the daughter; but the mother, alarmed lest a crime against reli-gion be committed here, and suffering the pangs of conscience in her own soul, had given a flat refusal, and that that was why Chichikov had come down in favour of abduction. This was amplified by many elucidations and amendments as the rumours finally percolated through to the more remote back-streets. For Russian folk of the lower estate are very fond of discussing scandal that originates in the upper: accordingly, tongues started to wag in the sort of disreputable houses in which Chichikov had never been seen and was not even known, and the story was embroidered and its details further elaborated.

Its plot became more fascinating by the minute, acquiring more definite contours every day, until, at last, in this embellished state, with all its new contours, it was delivered into the ears of the governor's wife herself. The governor's wife, as a materfamilias, as the first lady of the town, and as a lady who had never suspected anything of the sort, was mortally offended by these stories and filled with righteous indignation. The poor blonde was subjected to the most unpleasant *tête-à-tête* ever endured by a sixteen-year-old girl. She had to undergo a veritable torrent of questions, interrogations, reprimands, threats, reproaches, admonitions, with the result that she finally burst into floods of tears, sobbing and unable to understand a word that was said; the porter was given the strictest instructions not to admit Chichikov at any time or in any disguise.

Having disposed of the governor's wife, the ladies now turned their attention to the men's camp, attempting to win them over and maintaining that the dead souls were an invention, created to deflect any possible suspicion and to increase the chances of a successful abduction. A number of the men were thus seduced into the ranks of the ladies, despite the violent disapprobation of their comrades, who called them old women and petticoats, names which, as we all know, are most offensive to the male sex.

Yet, however robustly the men armed themselves, however valiantly they resisted, their camp altogether lacked the orderliness of the women's camp. Everything about them was somehow uncouth, awkward, inept, sloppy, and ugly, their thinking was muddled, incoherent, untidy, and contradictory—in short, in every respect they manifested their worthless male nature, coarse and ponderous, incapable either of home-building or of heartfelt convictions, incredulous, indolent, assailed by unremitting doubts and constant fear. The men declared that all this was rubbish, that the abduction of the governor's daughter was more likely to be undertaken by a hussar than by a civilian, that Chichikov would not do such a thing, that the women were lying, that a woman was like a sack: whatever you put in her she will carry; that their attention should in fact be focused on the dead souls, although the devil only knew what they signified, but that, none the less, there was clearly something unsavoury and iniquitous behind them.

Why the men should have thought there was something unsavoury and iniquitous behind the dead souls we shall ascertain directly, for a new governor-general had been appointed to the town, an event which—understandably—throws officials into a state of alarm: there would be enquiries, reprimands, shake-ups, and all those other ceremonial titbits to which a superior treats his subordinates. 'Just imagine if he finds out that certain foolish rumours are circulating round town,' thought the officials. 'Why, for that alone he's sure to haul us over the coals, to within an inch of our lives.' The inspector of the medical board suddenly paled, struck by the most awful thought: did the word 'dead souls' not perhaps refer to those patients who had died in great numbers in infirmaries and other places from the epidemic of fever against which proper measures had not been taken, and might Chichikov not be an official dispatched from the governor-general's staff to conduct a secret investigation? He confided his fears to the president of the chambers. The president retorted that this was poppycock, and then turned pale himself, as he asked himself the question: 'What if the souls which Chichikov has bought really are dead?' For was it not he that had arranged the purchase deeds for them and had he not even acted as Plyushkin's attorney—and what if all this came to the ears of the governor-general, what then? No sooner had he conveyed these apprehensions to one or two others, than these others suddenly paled too; for fear is more catching than the plague and spreads like wildfire. They all discovered in themselves sins that they had not even committed. There was something so elusive, so indefinable, about the words 'dead souls' that they even made people wonder whether there might not be some allusion here to two recent incidents, involving the over-hasty burial of two bodies.

The first incident concerned some merchants from Solvychegodsk, who came to town for the fair and after concluding their business threw a little feast for their friends the merchants of Ustsysolsk,* a feast in the true Russian style with German embellishments: orgeats, punches, balsams, and so forth. The feast, as is customary, ended in a fight. The Solvychegodsk contingent beat the men of Ustsysolsk

Dead Souls

to death, although they themselves received a thorough pounding beneath their ribs and in their bellies, testimony to the monstrous fists with which their deceased adversaries had been endowed by nature. One of the victors had his conk knocked off, as the gladiators put it, which is to say, his nose was completely pulped, so that it barely protruded from his face. In the ensuing court case, the merchants pleaded guilty and admitted that the party had been a bit wild. It was rumoured that each guilty member of the group had had to shell out four big, two-hundred-rouble notes; the exact circumstances of the case proved to be too obscure, however; from official inquiries and investigations it transpired that the fellows from Ustsysolsk had been suffocated by charcoal fumes, and so they were buried as victims of asphyxiation.

The other incident, more recent, was as follows: the state peasants of the little village of Vshivaya-Spes joined forces with other state peasants from the village of Borovki, known by some as Zadirailovo,* and had allegedly wiped the local police force—in the person of the district assessor, one Drobyazhkin—from the face of the earth, because this district police force—that is to say, assessor Drobyazhkin—had taken to visiting their village rather too frequently, and these visits were about as welcome as the bubonic plague. The reason for these visits was that the district police force, who suffered from a certain frailty in matters of the heart, had his eye on the village wives and wenches. Nothing, however, was established for certain, although in their depositions the peasants stated that the district police force was as lecherous as an old goat, and that on numerous occasions they had been constrained to detain him for his own protection, and once had had to chase him naked out of a hut into which he had poked his nose. Of course, the district police force fully deserved to be punished for this frailty in matters of the heart, but the peasants of both Vshivaya-Spes and Zadirailovo could not be excused for taking the law into their own hands, if indeed they really had participated in the murder. It was hard to get to the bottom of the matter: the district police force was found in the road, the force's uniform or tunic was torn to shreds, and its facial features were battered beyond recognition.

The case duly went through the courts and finally reached the Chambers, where at first it was considered in camera, in accordance with the following reasoning: since it was impossible to tell exactly which of the peasants had taken part, and there were so many of them, and since Drobyazhkin was dead anyway, winning the case would do him little good, while the peasants were still alive, and therefore a decision in their favour was extremely important to them; thus it was decided that assessor Drobyazhkin had himself been the cause of it all, by unjustly oppressing the peasants of Vshivaya-Spes and Zadirailovo, and that he had in fact died from a fit of apoplexy while driving home in his sleigh. With that the case seemed to be nicely wrapped up, but the officials, for some unknown reason, now began to think that these dead souls were somehow mixed up with it all.

As ill luck would have it, at a time when the officials were already in a quandary, the governor simultaneously received two letters. The first was to inform him that, according to evidence received and the testimony of informers, there was a forger of banknotes at large in their province, hiding under various aliases, and he was instructed to mount a most thorough investigation, without delay. The second was addressed to him by the governor of the neighbouring province, informing him that a bandit had escaped from prison, and warning him that, should any suspicious character appear in their province, lacking documents or a passport, he was to be detained forthwith. These two letters left everyone quite stunned. All their previous conclusions and conjectures were totally confounded. Of course, it could not possibly be surmised that any of this bore any relation to Chichikov; nevertheless, they all, once they had thought it over, realized that they still did not know exactly who this Chichikov was, and recalled that he had always been extremely vague about his own background, and that while he had told them that he had suffered in his service for the truth, it was still rather vague, and when they remembered that he had even admitted to having many enemies who had made attempts on his life, then they started to give the matter even more serious thought: so, his life was in peril; so, he was being pursued; so, he must have done something which... But who exactly was he? Of course, no one believed he could be a forger of banknotes, and still less a bandit: he had such a respectable appearance; but despite all this the question remained: just who the devil was he, anyway?

Thus the officials finally asked themselves the question which should have been asked right at the outset, that is, in the first chapter of our poem. It was decided to make certain enquiries of those from whom the souls had been bought, to ascertain at least what sort of purchases they were, and what exactly was to be understood by these dead souls, and to find out if he had revealed to anyone, perhaps inadvertently, or somehow in passing, what his real intentions were, and if he had told anyone exactly who he was. First they addressed themselves to Korobochka, but they did not get much out of her: they were told he had bought souls for fifteen roubles, and that he was also buying feathers, and had promised to buy much else besides, that he also procured lard for the government and for that reason was most probably a rogue, for once before she had had dealings with a man who had bought feathers and procured lard for the government, and he had pulled the wool over everyone's eyes and had swindled over a hundred roubles out of the archpriest's wife. After this all she did was to repeat what she had said before, and the only thing the officials discovered for sure was that Korobochka was a stupid old woman.

Manilov replied that he was always prepared to vouch for Pavel Ivanovich, as he would for himself, that he would gladly sacrifice his entire estate to have but a hundredth part of Pavel Ivanovich's sterling qualities, and in general spoke of him in the most flattering terms, and then, contemplatively closing his eyes, appended several observations on the nature of friendship and the sympathy of souls. These observations did, of course, satisfactorily account for the tender motions of his heart, but they shed no light on the case in hand.

Sobakevich replied that, in his opinion, Chichikov was a good man and that he had sold him first-class peasants and men who were in every respect very much alive, but that he would not vouch for what might happen subsequently, that if they were to die off on the road during the rigours of resettlement, it would not be his fault, that it was all in God's hands, and that, as for fevers and other mortal illnesses, there were plenty of those in the world, and there were even cases when entire villages were wiped out.

The officials then had recourse to an artifice which—though not entirely honourable—is, none the less, employed on occasion: that is, they sought clandestinely, through various contacts among the serving folk, to find out from Chichikov's servants whether perhaps they knew any details about the earlier life and circumstances of their master, but this too left them little the wiser. From Petrushka they discovered only the odour of his living quarters, and from Selifan the information that Chichikov had been in government service and had previously served in the customs, and nothing more. The servant classes have an extremely odd custom. If you ask them directly about something, they will never remember anything, they will be unable to take in your question properly and will answer flatly that they do not know; but if you ask about something else, they will somehow drag in the other matter too and will tell you all about it, with so many details that you will soon wish you had never asked. From all the inquiries conducted by the officials they discovered only that they positively did not know what Chichikov was, but that, none the less, Chichikov had to be something. They finally resolved that they had to get to the bottom of the matter and that they should at least decide exactly what they were to do and how, and which measures were to be taken, and what exactly he was: was he the sort of person who should be seized and detained as malevolent and undesirable, or was he the sort of person who could seize and detain all of them as malevolent and undesirable? To this end it was suggested that they gather in the house of the chief of police, a figure already familiar to the reader as the father and benefactor of the town.

CHAPTER TEN

Gathering at the house of the chief of police, already familiar to the reader as the father and benefactor of the town, the officials had occasion to remark to one another that they had even lost weight in consequence of these troubles and anxieties. And in truth, the appointment of a new governor-general, the receipt of those two letters of such grave import, and these rumours of God knows what—this had all left an unmistakable mark on their faces, and the tailcoats on many of them had become perceptibly looser. They had all suffered: the president had lost weight, the inspector of the medical board had lost weight, and the prosecutor had lost weight, and a certain Semyon Ivanovich, who was never called by his surname and who wore on his index finger a signet ring which he liked to show to the ladies—even he had lost weight. Of course, as one would find anywhere, there were among them a handful of intrepid men who still had not lost their presence of mind, but these were very few in number—to be precise, one only: the postmaster. He alone preserved his permanently equable temperament and in such cases was wont to say: 'We know these governor-generals! Governor-generals are here today and gone tomorrow, but I've been here a good thirty years, my good sir, and I'm staying put.'

To this the other officials would usually retort: 'It's all very well for you, Sprechen-Sie-Deutsch Ivan Andreich: you just deal with the post, receiving and dispatching the mail, the worst you can do is to pull an occasional fast one by closing your office half an hour early so you can charge a tardy merchant the extra fee for accepting a letter after hours, or you might slip up by sending some parcel which should not be sent—let's face it: in your job anyone could be a saint. I'd like to see what you'd do if you had the devil sneaking up every day to tempt you: you may think you wouldn't want to take the money but he'd keep thrusting it into your hand. It's easy for you, of course, you only have one son, but take me and my Praskovya Fyodorovna: God has blessed her with such bounty that she has a baby every year—one year a Praskushka, the next a Petrushka;* you'd sing a different tune then, brother.'

This was the drift of the officials' deliberations, and it is not for the author to say whether or not the devil's temptation could be resisted. The council which met on this occasion conspicuously lacked one essential property: that which common folk call horse sense. In general, we Russians are somehow not cut out for official meetings. All our convocations, from the humblest gathering of villagers to every kind of committee, scholarly included, are characterized by the utmost chaos and disorder, unless there is one person in full control of everyone. There is really no telling why this should be so; apparently, we are simply the kind of people who only cope successfully with gatherings that are called for the purpose of feasting and carousing, such as clubs and pleasure-gardens in the German manner. And yet, we are always ready to undertake anything. Whichever way the wind blows, we will be there, setting up societies of every kind: benevolent, charitable, progressive—take your choice. The intention will be quite admirable, but nothing will ever be achieved. Perhaps this is because we are contented with too little, too soon, and delude ourselves that everything possible has been done. For example, if we set up a philanthropic society to aid the needy, and contribute considerable sums to it, we begin by giving a dinner for all the senior dignitaries of the town to mark this praiseworthy undertaking, and this—it goes without saying—uses up half the monies contributed; with what remains we rent a magnificent suite of offices for the committee, complete with heating and commissionaires, and when the funds for the needy have been reduced to about five and half roubles, the question of how to distribute this sum causes discord among the committee members, each claiming the money for some kinsman of his own.

The meeting called here was of quite a different kind, however; it rose from necessity. No one here was concerned with needy folk or other outsiders; this matter was one which touched each official personally, it concerned a disaster that threatened them all equally, and one might have expected them to show a greater unanimity, a closing of the ranks, so to speak. Not a bit of it: instead, the outcome was infernal chaos. Quite apart from the disagreements characteristic of all councils, the opinions of those gathered together here were remarkable for the indecision they revealed: one said that Chichikov was a forger of banknotes and, in the next breath, added, 'On second thoughts, perhaps he's not a forger'; another insisted that he was an official from the governor-general's chancellory, and at once qualified this assertion: 'But there again, the devil only knows if that's what he really is. After all, it's not written on his face.' The surmise that he might be a bandit in disguise met universal opposition; they found that besides his appearance, which was of the most respectable kind, there was nothing in his conversation to indicate a man of a violent disposition. Suddenly the postmaster, who had been lost in reverie for several minutes, perhaps brought on by a momentary flash of inspiration or by some unknown cause, exclaimed to everyone's surprise: 'Do you know who he is, gentlemen?'

There was something so arresting about the tone in which he said this, that all the officials cried out in one voice: 'Who?'

'That, gentlemen, that, my good sir, is none other than Captain Kopeikin!'

And when, as one man, they all asked: 'And just who is this Captain Kopeikin?' the postmaster said: 'You mean to say you do not know who Captain Kopeikin is?' To which they all replied that, indeed, they did not have the slightest idea who Captain Kopeikin was.*

'Captain Kopeikin,' said the postmaster—and cautiously prised open his snuff box, fearful that one of his neighbours might thrust his fingers inside it, since he had serious misgivings about the cleanliness of all such fingers and was even fond of repeating: 'We know what you're like, my good friends: heaven knows where you go visiting with your fingers: but snuff is something which requires cleanliness'—'Captain Kopeikin?' he repeated, taking a pinch of snuff, 'Well, you know, if that story were to be told, some writer fellow could turn it into something most entertaining, something like a whole poem.'

All those present expressed their desire to hear the story—or, as the postmaster put it, a story which some writer fellow could turn into something most entertaining, like a whole poem—and he began as follows:

The Tale of Captain Kopeikin

'After the campaign of 1812,* my good sir,' began the postmaster, although there were no fewer than six 'good sirs' in the room, 'after the campaign of 1812, a certain Captain Kopeikin was sent back home with the wounded. It was either at the battle of Krasny, or perhaps at Leipzig,* but—well, you know how it was—he lost an arm and a leg. And in those days, you know, there were no special arrangements for the wounded; the invalid pension fund which we have now was only started one way or another, as you can probably imagine, some time later. Captain Kopeikin saw that he would have to work for a living, the problem was that the only arm he had, you see, was his left one. He goes home to see his father and his father says: "I have nothing to feed you," he says—just imagine—"I've hardly enough food for myself barely."

'So my Captain Kopeikin decides to set off, my good sir, for St Petersburg, to petition the Tsar for imperial favour, saying to him: "That's how it is, you see, this and that, in a manner of speaking, so to say, I sacrificed my life, spilt my blood and so on and so forth..." Well, somehow or other, my good sir, you know how it is, he eventually gets himself to St Petersburg, travelling on official wagons and baggage-trains. Now, you can imagine the scene: there you have some fellow or other, this Captain Kopeikin, that is, and there he is suddenly in the capital city, a city unlike any other in the world! Suddenly he sees the big wide world before him, so to say, a certain sphere of life, the fabled Sheherazade. Suddenly there's this something or other, you can just imagine, this Nevsky Prospect, or, you know, some Gorokhovaya Street or other, damn it all! Or some sort of Liteinaya Street* or other; over there he sees some spire or other sticking up in the air; bridges hanging over the river somehow or other, the devil knows how, you can just imagine, without any of those support things—in a word, my good sir, Semiramis* pure and simple! He's about to rent himself some digs, but all that stuff costs an arm and a leg, you know how it is: curtains, drapes, the devil knows what nonsense, carpets—it's just like Persia; as you walk, your feet—so to speak—trample over money. You walk along the street and you feel your nose twitching because it can smell money, it smells thousands and thousands; as for my Captain Kopeikin now, his store of banknotes, you understand, added up to about a dozen blue fivers.

'Anyway, somehow or other he gets lodgings in an inn—the Revel*—for a rouble a day; dinner is cabbage soup and a lump of beef. He takes a look around: his money won't last long here. He asks whom he should go and see about his business. They tell him

that there is this sort of supreme commission, some kind of board—
you know the sort of thing—and the chairman is this General-en-
chef such-and-such. Now the Tsar, I should tell you, wasn't back in
the capital at that stage; the army still hadn't returned from Paris—
you know how it is—they were all still abroad.

'My Kopeikin gets up good and early, shaves off his beard with
his left hand, because paying a barber to do it costs money—you
know the way it is—then he pulls on his old uniform and heads off
to see the chairman, the top man himself, clomping along on his
wooden stump—you can imagine the scene. He asks for the address.
There it is, they tell him, pointing to a house on the Palace Embankment. It's a handsome little shack, let me tell you: glass in the
windows—you can just imagine it—ten-foot-high mirrors, so that
the vases and everything else inside the rooms look as though they're
outside—you think you could just poke in your hand and help
yourself; the walls are faced with precious marble, fancy metal fal-
de-lals, and the kind of door handles that will send you at full haste
to the nearest roadside stall to buy a copeck's worth of soap, and
then you'll spend a good two hours scrubbing your hands, before
you dare touch any of those handles—to put it in a nutshell, all that
polish and varnish on everything—in a manner of speaking it's enough
to make the mind boggle. Even the commissionaire looks like a field
marshal, with a glittering gold mace, a face on him like a duke's,
standing there like a sleek, overfed pug dog; and he even has those
little lawn collars, damn it!...

'My Kopeikin somehow manages to drag himself on his wooden
peg up into the reception room, squeezes himself into a corner,
fearful of knocking his elbow into one of those gilded porcelain
vases, you can imagine the sort of thing, with pictures of America or
India. Well, sure enough, he has his fair share of waiting because, as
you can imagine, he arrived at an hour when—in a manner of speaking—the general had barely risen from his bed and his valet had
only just brought him his little silver basin for all those ablutions
they have, you know the sort of thing. My Kopeikin waits about
four hours before the adjutant or some other duty officer finally
makes an appearance. "The General", he says, "will shortly enter
the reception room." By this stage the crowd in the reception room
is packed as tight as beans on a plate. And these are not the likes of
us simple folk either, these are all personages of the fourth and fifth

class,* colonels and that, and some of them have those shining wads of silver macaroni sitting on their epaulettes—in a word: grandees.

'Suddenly a faint buzz runs through the room, hardly noticeable, like a fine breeze. Here and there people say: "Shh, shh!" and finally a fearful silence fills the room. The great man enters. Well... You can imagine: a man of state! And appearing in person, so to speak... well, in conformity with his title, you understand... with his high rank... the right sort of expression, you understand. At once everyone in the room, naturally enough, is as tense as a bowstring, hoping, trembling, waiting for a decision about his fate, in a manner of speaking. The minister, or grandee, goes up to one, then to another: "Why are you here?" he asks, "And you—why are you here? What do you want? What's your business?" And finally, my good sir, he arrives at Kopeikin. Kopeikin plucks up his courage: "It's like this and that, Your Excellency: I spilt my blood, lost, in a manner of speaking, an arm and a leg, unable to work, and make so bold as to seek imperial favour." The minister can see for himself: the man has a wooden leg and his right sleeve is pinned empty to his uniform: "Very well," he says, "call again in a few days' time."

'My Kopeikin leaves in a state of near rapture: first—he has gained an audience, so to speak, with a dignitary of the highest order; and second—at long last a decision will be reached, in a manner of speaking, about his pension. He is in such high spirits, you understand, that he fair jumps for joy on the pavement. He calls into the Palkin Inn to drink a glass of vodka, he has lunch, my good sir, at the London,* orders cutlet with capers and roast capon with all sorts of fancy trimmings, calls for a bottle of wine, and in the evening he heads for the theatre—in short, you understand, he goes on a spree. And then he sees her, walking along the pavement, this slender English miss, graceful as a swan, you can just imagine it, a real swan. Now my Kopeikin—the blood really rushing through his veins, you know how it is—sets off in hot pursuit, running along on his stump, clop, clop, clop... "But no," he thinks, "better wait till later, when I get my pension, I've already blown rather a lot."

'So, my good sir, my Kopeikin pitches up at the minister's rooms three or four days later and waits for him to appear. "It's like this," he says, "I've come," he says, "to hear what Your Noble Excellency has decreed with regard to the infirmities inflicted upon me and the wounds sustained..." and so on and so forth, you know, in all the right jargon. The grandee, just imagine, recognizes him at once: "Ha!" he says. "Excellent," he says, "but right now I have nothing more to say, except that you shall have to await the arrival of His Majesty; then, you can be quite sure, certain instructions will be issued regarding the wounded, but," he says, "without his, so to speak, monarchic approval there's nothing I can do." A bow, you know the sort of thing, and farewell.

'Kopeikin, you can imagine, leaves in a state of great uncertainty. He was convinced they would give him his money the very next day: "There you are, my good fellow, get drunk and make merry", but instead he's instructed to wait and not even told when to come back. So here he is, walking down the steps miserable as a dog, you know, when the cook has thrown a pail of slops over it; his tail between his legs and his ears flat against his head. "No, no," he thinks, "I'll go again and I'll explain, I'll say: 'I'm eating my last scrap of food, and if you don't help, I shall starve to death, in a manner of speaking.'" And so, my good sir, he goes back to the Palace Embankment; there they tell him: "No, he's not receiving today, come back tomorrow." The next day it's the same story; and the commissionaire hardly deigns to look at him. Meanwhile, of all those blue notes he had in his pocket at the beginning there's now only one left. Up to now he's been having cabbage soup and a big lump of beef for his dinner, but now he goes to a stall and buys a piece of herring or a pickled cucumber and a heel of bread for two copecks—in short, the poor fellow is starving and, to make matters worse, he has an appetite like a wolf. He goes past some fancy restaurant, and the chef—as you can imagine—is some sort of foreigner: a Frenchman or something with a big wide face, all decked out in Holland linen, an apron white as the driven snow, preparing some sort of *fines herbes*, or veal cutlets with truffles—in short, the kind of mouth-watering delicacies that give you such an appetite that you could quite simply, so to speak, feast on your own flesh. He goes past the Milyutin shops,* and there he sees this big salmon staring at him out of the window, and such cherries—five roubles a piece, a monster watermelon, the size of a carriage, poking out of the window and, so to speak, waiting for some idiot to come along and pay a hundred roubles for it*—in a word, at every turn there's such temptation that his mouth waters, and all the while he keeps hearing this word "tomorrow, tomorrow" ringing in his ears. So you can well imagine his position: on the one hand, so to speak, there's all this salmon and watermelon, and on the other, the one and only dish he gets served is this "tomorrow".

'Finally it's more than the poor fellow can stand, and he decides to take the place by storm, in a manner of speaking, and the devil take the consequences. He waits at the entrance until another petitioner arrives, and then slips past, you understand, going through with some general or other, and clomps into the reception room on his peg leg. In accordance with his custom the grandee emerges: "What do you want?—And you, what do you want? Ha!" he exclaims, seeing Kopeikin. "Have I not already explained to you that you will have to await a decision?"—"But I beg you, Your Noble Excellency, I do not have a crust of bread to eat."—"But what can I do about that? I can do nothing for you; for the time being try to do something for yourself, look for a way to earn some money."—"But, Your Noble Excellency, you can judge for yourself, so to speak: what money can I earn, when I am missing an arm and a leg?"—"But," says the dignitary, "you must agree: I cannot be expected to maintain you, as it were, at my own expense, can I? I have many wounded petitioners, they all have an equal right... Fortify yourself with patience. His Majesty will soon be back; I can give you my word of honour, that his imperial favour will not be denied you."—"But, Your Noble Excellency, I cannot wait," says Kopeikin, and he says it quite rudely, you might say. The great man, you understand, is already vexed. And with good reason: when you think that there are generals all round awaiting decisions, instructions; that there are matters of importance, so to speak, affairs of state, requiring the most expeditious action—a moment's delay might be crucial—and here some importunate insect comes along to pester him. "I am sorry," he says, "I have no time... I have more important matters to attend to than yours."

'He lets Kopeikin know—in this refined way, we might say—that it is finally time for him to make himself scarce. But my Kopeikin—it's the hunger, you know, spurring him on—stands his ground: "As you will, Your Noble Excellency. I shall not leave this spot until you give me your decision." Well! You can imagine: talk back like that to a dignitary, a man who has only to say the word and you'll be sent flying, you'll be sent to hell and gone. If an official only one rank below speaks to his superior like that, it already counts as serious impertinence. But look at the difference here—what a divide: a General-en-chef, and some Captain Kopeikin or other! Ninety roubles and nought!

'The general, you understand, only glares in answer, but his glare is worse than any firearm—enough to scare the living daylights out of the bravest man. Yet my Kopeikin, would you believe it, stands his ground, he doesn't budge an inch. "How dare you!" roars the general and grabs him, so to speak, by the scruff of the neck. Still, to tell the truth, he got off pretty lightly; in the general's place another man would have raised such hell that the entire street would have spun round in his head for the next three days, but he only says: "Very well," he says, "if you cannot afford to live here in the capital and you cannot wait quietly for your fate to be decided then I shall have to deport you at the state's expense. Call the sergeant-at-arms! Take him to his place of residence!" Next thing the sergeant-at-arms, you understand, is standing there: a giant of a man, standing seven foot tall in his stockinged feet, with massive great fists, as you can imagine, specially equipped by nature for admonishing coachmen—in a word, a dental surgeon...

'So, my good sir, they grab him, poor wretch, and bundle him into a cart, with the sergeant-at-arms. "Well," thinks Kopeikin, "at least I shan't have to pay my own post-fare, there's that to be grateful for." So there he is, my good sir, riding at the sergeant-at-arms's expense, and as he rides with his sergeant-of-arms, he reasons to himself, if you know what I mean: "So," he thinks, "the general tells me I must find some way to help myself: very well," he says, "I'll find a way all right!" Well, how they eventually arrived at their destination, and where precisely this was, no one has any idea. So, you see, all news of Captain Kopeikin sank for ever in the river of oblivion, in some Lethe or other, as the poets call it. But this, gentlemen, this is only the beginning, so to speak, of the thread, this is where the plot starts to thicken. Thus, we have no idea of Kopeikin's whereabouts, but—what do you know?—less than two months later a band of robbers appears in the Ryazan forests,* and who do you think, my good sir, is the robber chief? Why, none other than...'

'Forgive me for interrupting, Ivan Andreevich,' the chief of police broke in suddenly, 'but surely Captain Kopeikin, as you said yourself, is missing an arm and a leg, while Chichikov...'

Here the postmaster cried out and gave his forehead a hefty slap, calling himself a lump of veal, in the full hearing of all. He simply could not comprehend how this detail had not struck him at the very commencement of his tale, and he confessed that there was much truth in the proverb: 'The Russian is at his wisest only after the event.' The very next minute, however, he regained his cunning and tried to save face by pointing out that in England great advances had been made in mechanics, as could be seen from the newspapers, and someone had invented wooden legs that were so fashioned that the wearer needed only touch a hidden spring and his legs would carry him off so far that no one would ever see hide nor hair of him again.

Still, they all remained highly sceptical that Chichikov might be Captain Kopeikin, and agreed that the postmaster's story was a little too far-fetched. All the same, not to be outshone, and inspired by the keen powers of deduction displayed by the postmaster, they made suggestions that were even farther-fetched. Of the many surmises, all equally ingenious in their own way, one was particularly bizarre: might Chichikov not perhaps be Napoleon in disguise?* For the English had always envied Russia her vast territories and her power, and there had even been cartoons depicting a Russian speaking with an Englishman: the Englishman stands holding a dog behind him on a leash—and the dog is meant to be Napoleon—'You look out,' says the Englishman, 'you step out of line and I'll let my dog loose on you!'—so now, perhaps, they had indeed let him loose from the island of St Helena and he had made his way to Russia, pretending to be Chichikov, when in fact he wasn't Chichikov at all.

Not that the officials believed any of this, of course, but it did set them thinking, just the same, and when they each of them went over the matter on their own, they found that Chichikov's face, if he were to turn and stand sideways, was very like the portrait of Napoleon. The chief of police, who had fought in the 1812 campaign and had seen Napoleon in the flesh, had to admit that in height he was no taller than Chichikov, and that if you looked at the shape of him, Napoleon was also not what you could call overfat, nor yet was he exactly thin. Perhaps some readers will regard all this as improbable, and, out of deference to them, the author would dearly like to dismiss it all; but, whether we like it or not, everything took place precisely as we have recounted, and it is all the more astonishing since this town was not out in the backwoods but, on the contrary, quite near both capitals.

We should bear in mind, however, that all this took place shortly after the glorious expulsion of the French. At that time all our landowners, officials, merchants, shop-assistants, and every other class of literate and even illiterate persons became, at least for the period of eight years, passionate politicians. The *Moscow Gazette* and the *Son of the Fatherland** were avidly devoured and reached their last reader in shreds, no longer good for anything. Instead of the questions: 'How much did you get for your oats, old man?' or 'Did you make good use of yesterday's snowfall?' they would ask: 'What's new in the papers—they haven't let Napoleon off his island again, have they?' The merchants greatly feared such an eventuality, for they implicitly believed the prediction of a certain prophet, who had been incarcerated for the last three years; he had arrived among them from heaven knows where, clad in bast shoes and an uncured sheepskin coat that stank to high heaven of rotten fish, and he went about proclaiming that Napoleon was the Antichrist and was being held by a stone chain, behind six walls and seven seas, but that he would eventually break his chains and take possession of the entire world.* The prophet was thrown in gaol for his prophecy, as was right and proper, but the deed had been done and the merchants were now thoroughly rattled. For a long time thereafter, even during the most profitable transactions, when they would repair to the inn to finalize the deal over a glass of tea, the merchants' conversation would inevitably turn on the Antichrist. Many officials and even members of the nobility also found their thoughts involuntarily drawn to this subject and, infected by the mysticism which, as everyone knows, was then greatly in vogue, they ascribed special significance to each letter of the word 'Napoleon'; many even discovered in them the apocalyptic numbers.* Small wonder, then, that our officials should also have entertained this idea in their minds; they soon came to their senses, however, realizing that their imaginations had run away with them and that the whole business had got out of hand. They thought and thought, talked and talked, and finally decided that it would be no bad thing to question Nozdryov about it all. Since Nozdryov had been the first to bring up the story of the dead souls and since he and Chichikov were, as the saying goes, as thick as thieves, it would seem that he must surely know something of the circumstances of his life, and it was worth trying again, therefore, to see what Nozdryov had to say.

Officials are strange folk, as are all other professions: after all, they knew only too well that Nozdryov was a liar and that they could not believe a word he said, not even on trifling matters, yet he was the very one to whom they turned. What a strange creature man is! He does not believe in God, but he does believe that if the bridge of his nose itches he is surely going to die; he disdains to read the creation of a poet, as clear as day and imbued with harmony and the lofty wisdom of simplicity, yet he pounces eagerly on a book in which some know-all has churned everything up, spun a lot of nonsense, bent and twisted nature inside out. He thinks this book is marvellous and he shouts from the rooftops: 'This is it, these are the true facts of the mysteries of the heart!' All his life he despises doctors, and he ends up going to some old crone who treats people by whispering spells and spitting curses, or, worse still, he devises some concoction of his own out of all sorts of rubbish, which—God knows why—he imagines will cure his illness.

Of course, to some extent the officials can be forgiven because of the real difficulty of their position. A drowning man, as the saying goes, will clutch at a straw, and he does not have the presence of mind at such a moment to realize that, whilst a straw might just sustain the weight of a fly, he weighs almost four poods, if not five,* but in his plight he does not reason clearly and he clutches at the straw. Thus too did our gentlemen now clutch at Nozdryov. The chief of police at once wrote him a note, inviting him to a *soirée* that evening, and the constable, a handsome, ruddy-cheeked fellow in topboots, promptly ran off at full gallop, steadying his sword with his hand, to Nozdryov's lodgings.

Nozdryov was occupied with a most important matter; for four entire days he had remained closeted in his room, admitting no one and receiving his meals through the hatch; he had even lost weight and his skin had taken on an unhealthy, greenish hue. It was a matter which demanded the closest attention: he had to work through dozens of decks of cards to select one pair of two decks on which he could depend as on the most loyal of friends. There was still enough work to keep him busy for at least two more weeks; throughout this period Porfiry was under instructions to keep the mastiff puppy groomed by brushing his tummy with a special brush and cleansing his coat with soap three times a day. Nozdryov was furious at the invasion of his privacy; his first reaction was to send the constable to

the devil, but when he read in the governor's note that there might
be some profit in the evening, because they were expecting a fresh
new guest at the gathering, he at once relented, briskly locked up his
room, threw on the first clothes that came to hand, and set off as
summoned.

The evidence, depositions, and hypotheses furnished by Nozdryov
were so completely at odds with those arrived at by the officials, that
even their latest theories were confounded. This was a man who did
not admit even the possibility of doubt; the shakiness and timidity
of their own surmises were matched by the firmness and certainty of
his. He had an answer for every question, responding without a
moment's hesitation: he declared that Chichikov had bought up
dead souls to the value of several thousand roubles and that he
himself had sold him some, seeing no reason not to; to the question
whether Chichikov might be a spy seeking some piece of intelligence, Nozdryov replied that he was indeed a spy, that even while
they had been at school together, he had been called a tell-tale and
had been given such a hiding by his school-fellows, including
Nozdryov, that afterwards they had had to apply two hundred and
forty leeches to his temples alone—actually, he had meant to say
forty, but the two hundred somehow came out by itself. To the
question whether he might be a forger of banknotes Nozdryov replied that he was, and he took the opportunity to recount an anecdote about Chichikov's extraordinary dexterity: how, when it was
discovered that there were counterfeit notes to the value of two
million in his house, the house had been sealed off and placed under
guard, with two soldiers at each door, and how Chichikov had sub-
stituted them all overnight so that the very next day, when they
unsealed the house, they found that all the notes were genuine. To
the question whether it was true that Chichikov was plotting to
abduct the governor's daughter and whether it was true that he
himself had undertaken to lend a hand in the plot, Nozdryov replied
that he had helped, and that had it not been for him, nothing would
have come of it—here he suddenly realized that he was lying quite
without purpose and that he could easily land himself in serious
trouble, but it was too late, he was unable to stay his tongue. With
good reason, in fact, because such interesting details were coming to
light, emerging quite spontaneously, that it was simply impossible
to resist them: he even named the village in whose parish church the

wedding was to take place, namely the village of Trukhmachovka;* the priest—Father Sidor—was to be paid seventy-five roubles for the service, but even at that fee he would never have agreed had Nozdryov not put the fear of God in him, threatening to denounce him for having married the corn-chandler Mikhail to his own kins-woman,* and he had even offered Chichikov the use of his own carriage and arranged fresh horses at all the posting stations. He went into such detail that he started naming the coachmen.

The officials tried to bring up the Napoleon theory, but at once regretted it, because in response Nozdryov spun such a preposter-ous yarn, which contained not one iota of sense, let alone any truth, that in the end the officials merely sighed and withdrew. Only the chief of police persevered, and sat on for a long time listening in the hope that he might hear something interesting, but at last he too shrugged and said: 'What cock-and-bull!' Whereupon they all agreed that you can push a bull as hard as you like, but it's still no good for milking. Thus the officials were left in an even worse position than before, and they ended up agreeing that there was no way of ascer-taining exactly what Chichikov was. One thing had become clear, however, and this concerned human nature in general: a person might be prudent, sagacious, and sensible in all matters concerning other people, but not as concerns himself. How judicious, how de-cisive the advice he gives others in difficulties! 'What a quick thinker!' cries the crowd. 'What a strong character!'—But let some disaster befall this quick thinker, let him find himself in difficulties, and you will soon wonder what happened to that strong character of his, the pillar of strength is gone completely and in its place there is a wretched little coward, a puling infant, or simply a thumbsucker, as Nozdryov would say.

For some strange reason it was the poor prosecutor who suffered most from all these discussions, theories, and rumours. They had such an effect on him that when he arrived home he started to rack his brains and suddenly, for no earthly reason, as they say, he upped and died. Perhaps it was an apoplectic fit or something else which carried him off, but suddenly, as he was sitting in his chair, he just keeled over. After the usual wringing of hands and shrieks of 'Oh my God!' the doctor was sent for to bleed him, but it was obvious to all that the good prosecutor was no more than a soulless corpse. In fact it was only then, as they offered their condolences, that people realized that the dead man had indeed had a soul, for in his modesty he had never displayed it. And yet the appearance of death was just as awe-inspiring in this little man as it is in a great one: a man who so recently had been walking around, moving, playing whist, signing various documents, and frequently seen amongst the officials with his beetling eyebrows and twitching eye, was now laid out on a table, and the twitch was quite gone from his left eye, although one eyebrow was still raised in an interrogative arch. As to what the deceased was asking, whether he sought to know why he had died or why he had lived—that only God can say.

But all this is absurd, it really is! It's quite at odds with everything! It is impossible that the officials could have so frightened themselves, that they should have dreamt up so much nonsense and strayed so far from the truth, when even a child could have seen what was going on! This will be the verdict of many readers, who will reproach the author for his absurdities or call the poor officials fools, for man is generous with the word 'fool' and is happy to bestow it on his neighbour twenty times a day. If, out of ten aspects of your character, there is but one that is stupid, you will be branded a fool, despite the nine good ones. It is easy for readers to pass judgement, as they gaze from their serene heights, which command a full view of everything happening below, where man can see only the object immediately before him. And in all the history of mankind there are entire centuries which, so it seems, man has simply wiped out and forgotten, as having served no purpose. Many have been the blunders made in the world, blunders which, it seems, even a child would not commit today. How crooked, dark, narrow, impassable, and misleading are the paths which mankind has followed in its striving after the eternal truth, when it had only to take the straight road which lay open before it, like the road leading to the splendid temple, appointed as a palace for the Tsar! It is broader and more splendid than all the other roads, bathed in sunlight by day and illuminated by torches at night, yet people ignored it and streamed past in the Stygian darkness. And however often they were redirected by the good sense that descends from heaven, still they managed to fall by the wayside and wander from the true path, to stray once again in broad daylight into the impenetrable gloom, to lead one another astray, and then, as they dragged themselves onwards in pursuit of the will-o'-the-wisps, and finally reached the edge of the abyss, they turned to one another in horror and asked: where is the way out, where is the road? The new generation sees everything with perfect clarity, marvels at the blunders of its ancestors, and pours scorn on their folly—failing to observe that the pages of this chronicle are illuminated by a light from heaven itself, that every letter in it cries out in warning, that from all sides accusing fingers point at this new generation; but its members merely laugh in their usual cocksure way and arrogantly embark on an entire series of new blunders, at which future generations will also laugh one day.*

As for Chichikov, he knew absolutely nothing about all this. As ill luck would have it, at this very time he had developed a slight cold—accompanied by gumboils and an inflammation of the throat—of the kind so liberally dispensed by the climate of many of our provincial capitals. Lest his life might be ended somehow—which God forbid—without leaving heirs, he decided it would be best to stay indoors for about three days. During this confinement he repeatedly gargled with a mixture of milk and figs, afterwards eating the figs, and keeping a little bolster of camomile and camphor tied to his cheek. To pass the time he compiled several new and detailed lists of all the peasants he had bought, read some pages of his novel *La Duchesse de la Vallière** which he found in his valise, re-examined the various objects and notes in his little box, ran through some of them once more, and found it all intolerably wearisome. He simply could not understand what it might portend that not one of the town officials had called on him, not even once, to ask after his health, when until recently their droshkies had so frequently stood outside the inn—either the postmaster's or the prosecutor's or the president's. He could only shrug his shoulders in utter incomprehension as he paced about the room.

At last he began to feel better and was delighted beyond words at the prospect of stepping out into the fresh air. Without further delay he set about his toilet: opening his little box, he poured some hot water into a glass, took out his brush and soap and arranged his face for shaving, an operation which, if the truth be told, was long overdue, because, as he stroked his chin with his fingers and stared into the mirror, he exclaimed: 'Heavens, what thickets do we have growing here!' Indeed, his jowls were covered—if not by thickets—at least by a fairly dense undergrowth. After shaving, he dressed swiftly and briskly, all but leaping out of his breeches in his haste. At last he was dressed and, dousing himself with eau de Cologne, and wrapping his coat warmly about him, he ventured forth into the street, with his face prudently enveloped in a scarf. His emergence, like that of any person who has recovered from an illness, was, in its way, a sort of celebration. Everything his eye lit upon seemed to smile back at him—the houses, and the passing peasants, who in reality were rather morose, and some of whom had already boxed their neighbours' ears. Chichikov decided to pay his first call on the governor. As he drove, all sorts of thoughts crowded into his head: an image of the blonde damsel danced before him, his imagination started to play mild pranks, and he even started to jest and poke gentle fun at himself. Such was his mood when he drew up before the governor's house. He was on the point of casting off his overcoat in the entrance hall, when he was astonished to hear the porter announce:

'I have instructions not to admit you!'

'What, what do you mean?—clearly you do not recognize me! Take a close look at my face!' said Chichikov.

'I recognize you, of course: I've seen you often enough before,' said the porter. 'But you're the very one I'm ordered not to admit, all the others can come in.'

'What on earth! Whyever not? For what possible reason?'

'That's my orders, so I suppose there's a reason,' said the porter, and then added: 'Yes.' After this he struck a relaxed pose before Chichikov, dropping the obsequious look which his face had invariably worn on previous occasions, as he hastened forward to take the visitor's coat. From his expression he seemed to be thinking, as he looked at Chichikov: 'Well, well, well! If the master's decided to chase you off his porch, you really must be some sort of riff-raff!'

'I cannot understand it!' said Chichikov to himself, and promptly betook himself to the house of the president, but the latter was so embarrassed on seeing this visitor that he was unable to string two words together, and babbled such rubbish that they both felt quite ashamed. Chichikov took his leave. As he drove away, he racked his brains in an effort to grasp what the president may have meant and to what his words may have referred, but in vain; he remained quite baffled. He then called on the others: the chief of police, the vice-governor, the postmaster, but they all either would not receive him or did so very strangely, speaking in such a stilted and incomprehensible manner, with such obvious embarrassment, and prattled such senseless drivel that he began to doubt their very sanity. He attempted to make a few more calls if only to ascertain the reason for all this, but no reason was forthcoming. Like one in a stupor, he wandered aimlessly about the town, quite unable to decide whether he had lost his mind, or the officials had lost theirs; whether all this was a dream, or whether this madness—worse than any nightmare— was in fact real. It was already late, almost dusk, when he returned to his room, which he had left in such excellent spirits, and in a state of dejection he called for some tea. Musing incoherently about the peculiar position in which he now found himself, he started to pour the tea—when the door was suddenly thrown open, and there to his astonishment stood Nozdryov.

'As the proverb says: "To a true friend seven versts is but a stone's throw!"' he proclaimed, taking off his cap. 'I was walking past and saw the light in the window, so I said to myself: "Why don't I pay a little call—he's probably not asleep." Aha! Drinking tea, are we? Excellent! I'll gladly have a cup: I ate so much rubbish for dinner today I can feel a riot stirring in my stomach. Be a good fellow and order a pipe for me! Where's your pipe?'

'But you know I do not smoke a pipe,' answered Chichikov drily.

'Nonsense, I know perfectly well that you smoke like a chimney! Hey, you there! Tell me again, what's your man called? Hey you, Vakhramei, listen!'

'It's Petrushka, not Vakhramei.'

'What? But how come you had a Vakhramei before?'

'I have never had a Vakhramei.'

'Of course, it's Deryobin who had a Vakhramei. That Deryobin's a lucky so-and-so—just imagine: his aunt fell out with her son because he married a serf-girl, so she's now made her entire estate over to him. I keep thinking how I'd like to have an aunt like that—how handy it would be for future contingencies! But tell me, brother, why are you being so stand-offish and not calling on anyone? Of course, I know you are sometimes busy with your learned pursuits, you like to read and so on—' (as to why Nozdryov should have concluded that our hero was busy with his learned pursuits and liked to read, to be perfectly honest, we have no idea, and Chichikov even less). 'Why, Chichikov, brother, if you could only have seen...

now that would have been food for your satirical mind—' (why Chichikov should have had a satirical mind is also a mystery). 'Just imagine, brother, we were playing a little game of whist at Likhachov's, the merchant's, and what a laugh we all had! That old Perependev, who was playing with me, says, "If only Chichikov were here, I'd really show him!.." ' (yet Chichikov did not know Perependev from a bar of soap). 'But you must admit, brother: that was a dirty trick you played on me that time—do you remember?—when we were playing draughts, because I'd won the game, you know... Yes, brother, you hoodwinked me, plain and simple. But I'm like that, dammit, I really can't nurse a grudge. The other day at the president's house... But wait—while I think of it, I must tell you that everyone in the town has turned against you; they think that you make counterfeit money, they even started pestering me about it, but I stood by you, firm as a rock: I told them that we were at school together and I knew your father; well, I have to admit it, I spun them one hell of a yarn.'

'Me? Making counterfeit money?' exclaimed Chichikov, rising from his chair.

'All the same, why did you have to do that, scaring them like that?' continued Nozdryov. 'The devil knows, they are beside themselves with terror; they have you down for a brigand and a spy... The prosecutor went and died of fright, his funeral's tomorrow. Won't you be there? To tell the truth, they're all scared stiff of the new governor-general, in case there's some trouble because of you; but I'm of the opinion that if the new governor-general starts looking down his nose and giving himself airs and graces he won't be able to do a blind thing with the local gentry. Gentlefolk require a cordial approach, isn't that so? Of course, he can always shut himself away in his office and never throw a single ball, but what's the good of that? He'll gain nothing that way. But all the same, Chichikov, truth be told, that's a dicey plan you've hatched.'

'What dicey plan?' asked Chichikov uneasily.

'Why, abducting the governor's daughter. I must admit, I was expecting it, honest to God, I was! The very first time I saw the two of you together at the ball—"Well, I said to myself, old Chichikov's up to something, all right..." But I don't think much of your choice, I must say, I can't see anything special about her. There's this one girl, mind you, a relative of Bikusov's, his sister's daughter—now there's a nice filly for you! You might even say: a card from a very superior deck!'

'But what is all this, what are you talking about? Abducting the governor's daughter—what on earth are you talking about?' said Chichikov, his eyes starting from his head.

'Oho, brother, you're a dark horse! I must confess that's the real reason I called on you: if you wish, I'm even prepared to give you a hand. If you like, I'll be your best man, I'll provide the carriage and change of horses—only, on one condition: you'll have to lend me three thousand. I'm sorry, brother, but I need that money—it's a matter of life and death!'

Throughout Nozdryov's blather Chichikov repeatedly rubbed his eyes, to make quite sure that he was not dreaming. Forging of banknotes, abduction of the governor's daughter, death of the prosecutor—allegedly caused by him—arrival of the new governor-general: all this threw him into a state of great alarm. 'Well, seeing this is the turn events have taken,' he thought, 'there's no point in tarrying here any longer, it's time I made myself scarce.'

He got rid of Nozdryov as quickly as he could, and at once summoned Selifan and ordered him to be ready at dawn, so that they could make their departure from the town no later than six in the morning. He gave instructions that everything should be pre-pared, the chaise greased, and so on and so forth. Selifan declared: 'Yessir, Pavel Ivanovich!' but remained by the door for several min-utes, standing stock-still. The master then ordered Petrushka to pull his valise out from under the bed, where it had already gathered a thick layer of dust, and together they threw in everything as it came to hand, in no particular order: stockings, shirts, clean and dirty linen, boot trees, a calendar... All this was packed in any old how: he was determined to have everything ready that same evening, so that nothing would delay them in the morning. After standing a while by the door, Selifan very slowly withdrew from the room. Slowly, un-imaginably slowly, he descended the stairs, leaving the prints of his wet boots on the dilapidated steps and protractedly scratching the back of his head. What did this scratching signify? Indeed, what does scratching signify in general? Could it have been regret that he would not now make that planned rendezvous the following day in the local roadhouse, with his new friend, the one with the unsightly sheepskin coat, belted with a sash? Or had he already found himself a sweetheart in this new place, and would there now be no more standing at her gate and discreet holding of her dainty white hands at an hour when the town pulls the mantle of night over its weary shoulders, when a hefty fellow in a red tunic sits before the assembled household serfs strumming his balalaika, and a mixed crowd of working folk gather to exchange quiet gossip at the end of the day's labours? Or was it merely regret at having to leave his nice warm spot in the bustling kitchen, where he sat tucked up in his sheepskin next to the stove, the cabbage soup, and the tasty, town-baked pies, in order to head off once more in the rain, and the slush, to endure all the adversities of the road? God alone knows, we can but conjecture. Many and various are the things signified when the Russian serving man scratches the back of his head.

CHAPTER ELEVEN

Nothing worked out as Chichikov had planned, however. To begin with, he awoke later than he had intended—that was the first unpleasantness. Upon rising, he at once sent to inquire if the chaise was harnessed up and everything ready; but he was informed that the chaise was not yet harnessed and that nothing was ready. This was the second unpleasantness. He quite lost his temper and even resolved to administer something in the nature of a thrashing to our friend Selifan as he waited impatiently to hear what excuse the man would give him. Soon Selifan appeared in the doorway and his master had the pleasure of listening to one of those speeches which are customarily delivered by servants when a hasty departure has to be made.

'Well, you see, Pavel Ivanovich, the horses still need to be shod.'

'What!—you dolt! Dunderhead! Why didn't you mention it before? I suppose you didn't have the time?'

'Well, yes, there was time... And there's also the wheel. See, Pavel Ivanovich, the rim will have to be pulled good and tight, because the road's so bumpy now, and you find such big potholes everywhere... And also, if I may say so, the front of the chaise is all rickety, so I doubt it'll even make two stages now.'

'You scoundrel!' shouted Chichikov, flinging up his hands in exasperation, and stepping up so close to Selifan that the coachman recoiled somewhat and then moved to one side, afraid he might receive a token of his master's appreciation. 'Are you trying to kill me? Huh? Trying to cut my throat? Planning to cut my throat somewhere on the highway, you brigand! Worthless rodent! Sea monster! Huh? Huh? We've been sitting here in this same spot for three whole weeks! And never a peep, you reprobate! Now you tell me about it, at the last moment! When everything else is almost ready: we have only to get in and drive away. Huh? And you have to play your dirty trick, don't you? Huh? Because you knew it before, didn't you? Huh? Answer me! You knew, didn't you?'

'I did,' answered Selifan, hanging his head.

'So why didn't you say so then?'

To this question Selifan found no answer, but merely hung his head still lower and seemed to be saying to himself: 'It's funny how these things happen: I did know, but I never said!'

'Now go and fetch the smith, and make sure everything's ready in two hours. Do you hear? In two hours, and no more, or else I'll... I'll... I'll bend you in a hoop and tie you in a knot!' Our hero was beside himself with rage.

Selifan was about to go and carry out his master's order, when he stopped and said: 'There's one other thing, sir, it's that dappled stallion: it'd be better to sell him, you know, sir, because, Pavel Ivanovich, he's a complete rogue: a terrible horse that one, he's nothing but a hindrance.'

'Fine! So I'll run straight to the market and sell him!'

'As God's my witness, Pavel Ivanovich, he only looks useful, but in truth he's a most cunning horse; with a horse like that you'll never...'

'Fool! When I want to sell it, I'll sell it. Who asked for your advice? You listen to me now: if you don't bring me the blacksmiths right away and if everything isn't ready in two hours, I'll give you such a thrashing... You won't be able to see the nose on your own face... Off with you! Go!'

Selifan departed.

Chichikov was by now in a vile mood and he threw down the sabre which he carried with him on his travels to instil fear in the right quarters. For a quarter of an hour and more he did battle with the blacksmiths before coming to an agreement, because the black-smiths, as is customary, were thoroughgoing scoundrels and, once they had caught on that the work was urgent, stuck out for precisely six times the normal rate. No matter how Chichikov fumed and seethed, calling them swindlers, brigands, highway robbers, even alluding to the Day of Judgement, he could not beat them down: they stood as firm as a rock—and not only did they stick to their price, they dragged their feet so that the work took not two hours, but no less than five and a half.

All this time Chichikov had the pleasure of savouring those agree-able moments, familiar to any traveller, when everything is packed away in his valise and all that remains in the room are bits of string, scraps of paper, and other assorted rubbish, when a man is not yet on the road, but no longer settled, when he looks out of the window at the passers-by plodding along, discussing their paltry affairs, and raising their eyes in a sort of foolish curiosity to glance at him before continuing on their way, and all this only makes the poor, marooned traveller feel still more ill-at-ease. Everything around him, everything he sees—the little stall opposite his window, and the head of the old woman living in the house across the road, who comes up to her window with its short little curtains—everything is loathsome to him, yet he cannot tear himself away from the window. He remains standing there, either lost in reverie or once again turning his numbed attention to all that moves and does not move before him, and with vexation he squashes a fly, which buzzes and pounds its wings against the window as his finger presses down upon it.

Still, all things come to an end, and at last the long-awaited moment was at hand: everything was ready, the front of the chaise had been fixed, the wheel fitted with a new rim, the horses watered, the rapacious blacksmiths had departed, after counting their silver roubles and wishing the travellers Godspeed. The chaise was harnessed up, two hot loaves were put in with the luggage, Selifan stowed something away in the pocket attached to his coach-box, and, at last, our hero himself took his seat in the carriage, watched by the 'floorman', in the obligatory demicoton topcoat, who waved his cap, and by various flunkeys and coachmen from the inn and elsewhere, who stood about gawping as the gentleman visitor took his departure and as the other circumstances which attend all departures unfolded before them—and the chaise, of the kind affected by bachelors, which had stood in the town for so long, and which, quite possibly, has by now sorely tried the reader, finally drove out through the inn gates.

'Thank the Lord!' thought Chichikov and crossed himself.

Selifan cracked his whip; Petrushka, who until then had been standing on the step, now climbed up next to Selifan, and our hero settled himself more comfortably on his Georgian rug, tucking a leather cushion behind his back, squashing the two hot loaves as he did so. Thus the carriage was on its way again, lurching and bouncing along, thanks to the well-known successive effect of the cobble-stone paving.

A strange, inscrutable feeling filled Chichikov as he beheld the houses, walls, fences, and streets, which in turn also seemed to move slowly away, lurching up and down, and which God only knew if he would ever be destined to see again in the course of his life. At the turning into one of the streets the chaise was forced to an abrupt stop, because the entire length of the street was occupied by an endless funeral procession. Thrusting his head out of the window, Chichikov ordered Petrushka to ask who was being buried, and learnt that it was the prosecutor. Filled with disagreeable sensations, he at once hid from view in one corner, pulling up his leather coverlet and drawing down the blinds.

While the carriage was thus delayed, Selifan and Petrushka piously doffed their caps and studied the scene with interest to see who was there, how they were turned out, and what they were driving, and counted how many were on foot and how many in conveyances, while their master, who had ordered them not to acknowledge or greet any of their lackey friends, also peeked nervously through the little glass peep-holes fitted into the leather blinds: there, walking bareheaded behind the coffin, were all the town's officials. He was afraid lest they recognize his carriage, but their minds were on other things. They did not even engage in the sort of small talk customary with mourners walking behind a hearse. All their thoughts were turned in on themselves: they wondered how they would find the new governor-general, how he would go about his business, and how he would treat them. After the officials, proceeding on foot, came the carriages bearing the ladies in their mourning bonnets. From the movement of their lips and hands it was apparent that they were engaged in lively conversation; perhaps they too were talking about the arrival of the new governor-general, imagining the kind of balls he would give, and fussing as ever about their flounces and scallops.

The rear of the procession was brought up by several empty droshkies, proceeding in single file, then, at last, there was nothing and our hero could continue on his way. Opening his leather blinds, he sighed and declared from the bottom of his heart: 'So there you go, prosecutor! You lived and lived, and then you died! Now they'll say in the newspapers that he passed away to the grief of his subordinates and of all mankind; a respected citizen, an unparalleled father, an exemplary husband, and they will write all sorts of nonsense; probably adding that he was accompanied to the grave by the weeping of widows and orphans; but, if we are to be perfectly honest, the only remarkable thing about you was the bushiness of your eyebrows.' At that he ordered Selifan to go faster and, in the meantime, thought: 'Still, it's a good thing we bumped into a funeral procession like that: they say it brings good luck.'*

By now the chaise had turned on to more deserted streets; soon only the long wooden fences stretched on both sides, presaging the end of the town. Then the cobbled road ended too; the turnpike and the town were behind, and nothing lay ahead but the road, once again the road. And along both sides of the highroad it was the same old story: the usual succession of milestones, station-masters, wells, waggon trains, dreary villages with their samovars, countrywomen, and a spry, bearded inn-keeper, running out of his coachyard to meet them, bearing oats for the horses; a wayfarer who had trudged some eight hundred versts in his worn-out bast shoes; small, wretched towns with the houses arranged haphazardly, with their ramshackle wooden shops, flour barrels, bast shoes, calatches, and other trifling wares; striped turnpikes; bridges under repair; fields stretching as far as the eye could see on both sides of the road; the landaus of local landowners; a mounted soldier, carrying a green box of lead shot, which bore the legend: 'Artillery Battery such-and-such'; the steppe, with its stripes of green, and gold, and freshly turned black earth; a song borne from afar; the tops of pine trees seen through the mist; the peal of church bells ringing, and fading, in the distance; crows clustered as thick as flies, and a horizon without end...

Rus! Rus! I see you now, I see you from my wondrous, beautiful distance: I see you, mired in poverty and mess, unwelcoming, with no arresting wonders of nature, crowned by further arresting wonders of art, to delight the eye or to startle, no cities with lofty, many-windowed palaces, clinging like moss to rocky crags, no pictured trees and spreading ivy, growing over houses lost in the roar and eternal spray of waterfalls; no need to crane back and look up at massive granite slabs, towering high, immeasurably high above; no dark arches piled one above the other, and choked with vines, ivy, and numberless millions of wild roses, through which eternal contours of radiant mountains might be glimpsed in the distance, soaring upwards into the silvery skies above. Everything within you is open, desolate, and flat; your squat towns barely protrude above the level of your wide plains, marking them like little dots, like specks; here is nothing to entice and fascinate the onlooker's gaze. Yet whence this unfathomable, uncanny force that draws me to you? Why do my ears ring unceasingly with your dreary song, that carries across your length and breadth, from sea to sea? What is there in it? What is in it, in that song? What is it that so beckons, and sobs, and tugs at the heart? What sounds are these that sting as they caress, that irrupt into my soul and twine about my heart? Rus! What is it you want of me? What is the hidden, unfathomable bond that holds us fast? Why do you gaze like that, and why is it that everything in you has turned to look at me with eyes full of expectation?... And while I stand, baffled and motionless, there suddenly falls across my head the shadow of a thundercloud, heavy with imminent rain, and my mind is benumbed in the face of your vastness. What does this immense expanse portend? Is it not here, in you, that some boundless thought should be born, since you yourself are without end? Is not here that the hero of legend is to appear, where there is space for him to unfurl his limbs and stride about? Menacing is the embrace in which your mighty expanse enfolds me, terrible the force with which it strikes me to the very core, unnatural the power with which my eyes burn bright—Oh! What a glittering, wondrous distance, vaster than any there is on earth! Rus!...

'Whoa, whoa! You fool!' Chichikov shouted at Selifan.

'You wait, I'll give you a taste of my broadsword!' shouted an army courier with moustaches two feet across, galloping up towards them. 'Have you no eyes in your head?—the devil flay your soul: this is an official carriage!' and like a mirage, the troika thundered and vanished in a cloud of dust.

What a strange, enticing, enthralling, marvellous sound there is to the word: 'the road!' And what a wondrous thing, this road: a bright day, autumn leaves, a nip in the air... Wrap your travelling coat tighter about you, pull your cap down on your ears, and huddle more snugly into your corner! One last shudder of cold runs through your limbs before a delightful warmth envelops you. The horses gallop on... How irresistibly drowsiness creeps over you and knits together your eyelids, and you are already dozing as you hear the coachman sing 'The snows are white no more',* and the horses wheeze and the wheels rattle, and then you start to snore, as you squash your neighbour into his corner. You awake: five stages have passed; the moon, an unfamiliar town, churches with ancient wooden onion domes with their sharp points standing out darkly against the sky, and dark-timbered and white stone houses. Here and there gleam patches of moonlight, as if white linen kerchiefs have been hung about the walls, along the highroad, and laid down in the streets; these are criss-crossed by oblique, coal-black shadows; in the slanting shafts of light wooden roofs glint like shining metal; nowhere is there a soul to be seen, all is asleep. Perhaps somewhere, in one little window, a solitary light glimmers: perhaps some local citizen stitching a pair of boots, or a pastrycook busy in his bakery— who cares? But the night—Glory of heaven! What a night is unfolding in the firmament above! And the air, and the heavens—so distant, so high, so unimaginably deep, their broad expanse unfurled above us, so boundless, harmonious, and clear. But the cold of the night breathes its freshness right into your eyes and lulls you to sleep, and you are soon dozing and lost in your slumbers, and snoring, and your hapless neighbour, already squashed into his corner, fidgets in annoyance, as he feels your body press against him. You awake— and now once again before you there are only fields and the steppe, and nothing more: on all sides there are treeless plains, wide open vistas. A milestone with a number flashes by; morning is breaking; a pale, golden swathe stretches across the cold white horizon; the wind grows fresher and harsher: wrap that greatcoat more tightly about you!... What glorious cold! How wondrous to sink once more into the embrace of sleep! A jolt—and you awake once more. The sun stands high in the sky. 'Easy now, easy!' shouts a voice, the carriage makes its way down a steep incline: below is a broad weir and a wide, clear pond, gleaming like a copper plate in the sun; a village, cottages scattered across the hillside; the cross of the village church glinting like a star; the chitter-chatter of peasants and unbearable pangs of hunger assailing your belly... O Lord! How wondrous it is on occasion to set forth down the distant, open road! How often, like a drowning, dying man, have I clutched at you, and every time you have magnaminously borne me aloft and brought me to safety! And what an abundance of wonderful designs, of poetic fancies have you conjured forth in me, what magical impressions have you brought me!...

But on this occasion too our friend Chichikov was enjoying fancies that were far from prosaic. Let us take a little look at his innermost feelings. At first he did not feel anything at all, and merely kept looking back, anxious to convince himself that he had finally left the town behind him; but when he saw that the town had long since been lost from sight, that no smithies, nor mills, nor any

of those things that are found around towns were visible, and that
even the white domes of the stone churches had long since vanished
from sight, he turned his attention wholly to the road, looking only
to right and to left, as if the town of N was no longer even in his
memory, as if he had travelled through it long ago, in childhood.
Finally even the road ceased to hold his attention; his eyelids began
to droop and his head sank against the cushion. The author must
confess that he is quite glad of this, as it gives him an opportunity to
say a few things about his hero; for hitherto, as the reader has seen,
he has constantly been hindered either by Nozdryov, or by balls, or
by ladies, or by the town gossip, or by thousands of those trifling
occurrences which only strike one as trifling when one puts them in
a book, but which, when they come to pass in real life, are deemed
matters of great importance. But let us now set all this completely
aside and get down to business.

It is most unlikely that the hero we have selected will please our
readers. He will not please the ladies, that we can state with certainty, for ladies require a hero to be the summit of perfection, and
if he should have the smallest spiritual or physical blemish, then
woe betide him! However deeply the author may pry into his soul,
however faithfully he reflect his image, more clearly than any mirror—they will still reject him as quite worthless. The very fullness
of Chichikov's figure, the very maturity of his years, will already
work greatly to his disadvantage: under no circumstances can fullness of figure ever be forgiven a hero, and a great many ladies will
turn up their noses, protesting: 'Ugh, what a toad!'

Alas! The author is quite aware of all this, yet he still cannot
choose for his hero a virtuous man. All the same... It may come to
pass that in this very story different strings resound, strings which
have not yet been touched, the incalculable wealth of the Russian
spirit may yet be displayed, there may appear a man endowed with
godlike virtues, or perhaps a wondrous Russian maiden, such as
cannot be found anywhere else in the world, with all the miraculous
beauty of the female soul, alloyed of magnanimous impulses and
selfless virtue. Then all those upstanding members of other clans
will seem as dead men beside them, just as a book is dead beside the
living word! Russian souls will stir... and it will be seen how deeply
rooted in the Slav nature are those qualities which, with other
peoples, merely skim over the surface... But why and to what pur-

pose should we talk of things that are yet to come? It is unseemly for the author, who has long since entered manhood, who has been tempered by a stern inner life and the invigorating sobriety of solitude, to forget himself, like a callow youth. Everything has its proper turn, and place, and time!

The fact remains: we have not taken a virtuous man for our hero. We can even say why we have chosen not to do so. For the time has come, at last, for us to give the poor virtuous man a rest; for the words 'virtuous man' have lost all meaning on our lips; for the virtuous man has been turned into a beast of burden, and there is no writer who does not willingly climb on his back, urging him forward with his whip or anything else that comes to hand; for the virtuous man has been worn so thin that he no longer retains even a shadow of his virtue, and of his body there remain only skin and bones; for it is pure hypocrisy to introduce the virtuous man; for no one respects the virtuous man. No, it is time at last to put the rogue in harness too. So, let us put the rogue in harness!

Modest and obscure are the origins of our hero. His parents were gentlefolk, but whether they were noblemen of hereditary lineage or through personal merit,* God only knows. To look at, he was not at all like them: at least, a female relative who was present at his birth, a short, squat woman of the type usually called a peewit, took the child in her arms and exclaimed: 'He doesn't look anything like I expected! He should have taken after his old grandmother on the mother's side, that would have been better, but with this one it's just like the saying: "Not like father, not like mother, looks more like the blacksmith's brother."'

At first, life looked on him in a sour and unwelcoming way, as through a gloomy, snow-encrusted window: a childhood without friends or playmates! A poky little room with poky little windows, opened neither in winter nor in summer, a father in poor health, who always went about in a long frock-coat with a lambskin lining and knitted slippers, which he wore on his bare feet, who was forever sighing as he walked about the room and spitting into a sandbox standing in the corner; an eternity of sitting at his writing table, quill in hand, ink stains on his fingers and even on his lips; an eternity of copying such texts as: 'Do not lie, be obedient unto your elders and foster virtue in your heart'; an eternity of scraping and shuffling of slippers around the room, the familiar but invariably stern voice saying: 'Playing the fool again!' every time the child, to relieve the tedious monotony of his task, added a little hook or tail to a letter; and that eternally familiar, always disagreeable sensation caused by the excessively painful tweaking of the miscreant's ear, inflicted from behind by the nails of long fingers, which followed these words. Such is the wretched picture of his earliest childhood, of which he retained only the very faintest of memories.

But in life all things change swiftly and briskly: and one fine day, in the first rays of spring sunshine, when the rivers burst their banks, the father took his son off in a cart, pulled by a piebald mare, of the kind known by horse traders as a 'magpie'; the driver was a small, hunched peasant, paterfamilias of the one and only serf family on the Chichikov estate and responsible for performing virtually all the duties in the house. They trundled along behind their 'magpie' for something over a day and a half, slept by the roadside, forded a river, fed on cold pie and roast mutton, and only reached town on the morning of the third day. The boy was dazzled by the unexpected magnificence of the streets, which caused him to gape open-mouthed for several minutes. At that point, magpie and cart plunged into a deep pothole at the uphill end of a steep and narrow alley, deep in mud; here the beast toiled away at length with all her might and main, hooves sliding in the mire, whipped on by both the hunchback and the master himself, until finally she hauled them up the side of a hill into a small courtyard before a ramshackle old cottage, with two blossoming apple trees in front, and a little garden at the back, a wretched plot, comprising only a single rowan-tree, and some elder bushes. At the far end of this garden stood a small, shingle-roofed wooden shack, with one narrow, dark window.

Here lived a relative of theirs, a decrepit old woman, who still walked to market every day and then spread her stockings before the samovar to dry; she patted the boy on the cheek and admired his chubbiness. Here he was to remain and to attend lessons every day at the local school. The father stopped only the night and in the morning set off on his homeward journey. On their parting no tears were shed by the parental eyes; a fifty-copeck coin was given the boy for expenses and sweetmeats and—far more important—a wise admonition: 'Mind you learn your lessons, Pavlusha, don't play the fool and don't get into scrapes, but spare no pain to please your teachers and superiors. So long as you please your superiors it does not matter if you are no good at learning and God has not endowed you with talent: you will still go far and outstrip the others. Do not keep company with your schoolfellows; they will teach you no good; but if you must, then choose those that are richer so that when the occasion arises they may be useful to you. Do not open your purse too freely to others, but rather conduct yourself in such a manner that others will open theirs freely to you, and, most important, husband your money and save every copeck: of all things in the world, money is the most dependable. A playmate or friend will lead you a merry dance and will be the first to betray you in times of trouble, but a copeck will never betray you, whatever trouble you might be in. With that copeck you can do everything and achieve everything in this world.'

After delivering this admonition, the father took his leave of the son, mounted his cart, and the magpie plodded off homewards. Chichikov never saw him again, but his words and admonitions remained deeply etched in his soul.

The very next day Pavlusha started attending classes. He revealed no particular aptitude for any subject and was distinguished mostly by his assiduity and neatness, but then he did display great intelligence in another respect: in matters practical. He was quick to see the lie of the land and his conduct towards his fellows was carefully designed to ensure that they opened their purses freely to him, while he not only kept his purse firmly closed, but sometimes, after concealing the delicacies he had thus obtained, would even sell them back to them afterwards. While still a child he learnt how to deny himself everything. Of the half-rouble given him by his father he did not spend a single copeck; on the contrary, that same year he even increased his capital, demonstrating an almost uncanny resourcefulness: he moulded a bullfinch from wax, painted it, and sold it for a very good price. For some time thereafter he embarked on other speculative ventures, to wit: he would buy various comestibles at the market and choose a seat in class near the richer boys, then, as soon as he observed that a classmate was becoming uneasy—the first sign of approaching hunger—he would, as it were, accidentally pull out from under his desk the corner of a gingerbread cake or a sugar bun and, having thus excited his neighbour's desires, would name a price commensurate with his appetite. For two months he toiled away tirelessly in his room with a mouse, which he had confined to a small wooden cage, and he finally succeeded in getting the mouse to stand on its hind legs, to lie down, and get up again on command; then he sold it for a tidy sum. When he had amassed a total of five roubles he sewed the money up in a little bag and started to fill another bag.

With respect to his superiors he behaved even more astutely. No one could sit in class more quietly than he. We should note that his teacher was a great lover of silence and good behaviour and could not abide precocious boys; he always suspected them of being too sharp-witted. It was sufficient for any boy, who had suffered a reprimand for sharpness of wit, to make the slightest movement or even accidentally to twitch an eyebrow, at once to receive the full brunt of his rage. He would persecute and punish the boy mercilessly. 'I shall thrash the arrogance and disobedience out of you, my young friend!' he would say, 'I know you through and through, better than you know yourself. I'll have you here, down on your knees! And there you can starve!' And the poor innocent would get callouses on his knees and go hungry for days on end. 'Talents and gifts? That's all poppy-cock,' the teacher would say, 'I look only at behaviour. I will give full marks in all subjects to a fellow who doesn't know chalk from cheese but behaves himself commendably; but if I detect a rebellious or mocking attitude in a boy I shall give him nought, even if he makes Solon* look like a complete ignoramus!'

Such were the words of their teacher, who passionately hated the fabulist Krylov for saying: 'But as for me, I'd let them drink all day, if only they could play,'* and he loved to tell, with a look of relish on his face and in his eyes, how, in his old school, such silence had reigned that you could hear the beating of a fly's wings; how not one of his pupils had ever once, throughout all the years he had taught there, coughed or blown his nose in class; and how it had been impossible to tell, until the bell rang, whether there was anyone in the class or not. Chichikov swiftly got the measure of this teacher and understood how he must comport himself. He never moved an eye nor twitched an eyebrow throughout the entire lesson, however much the boys seated behind pinched him; as soon the bell rang he would dash forward to hand the teacher his hat with its earflaps (for such was the headgear affected by this teacher) before anyone else could get there; having given him his hat, he would be the first to leave the classroom and would endeavour to cross paths with the teacher at least three times on the latter's way home, never failing to doff his cap. This stratagem proved an unqualified success. Throughout his time at the school he was considered an exemplary pupil, and when he left he was given full marks in every subject, a certificate, and a book prize with the words 'For Exemplary Assiduity and Auspicious Conduct' engraved in gold letters.

Once out of school he was, it transpired, a rather attractive youth, with a chin that already needed the attentions of a razor. At this time his father died. His inheritance consisted of four irreparably worn-out jerkins, two old frock-coats lined with lambskin, and a small sum of money. His father, it transpired, had only been good at advising others to save their copecks, and had saved very few for himself. Chichikov at once sold the dilapidated old house with its miserable patch of land for a thousand roubles, and moved his family of serfs to the town, planning to establish himself there and enter the civil service. At this same time their poor teacher, the lover of silence and commendable behaviour, was thrown out of the school for stupidity or some other failing. This misfortune drove the teacher to the bottle until, finally, he no longer had the money even to buy drink; sick, helpless, and starving, he languished somewhere in an abandoned, unheated hovel. When they learned of his plight, his former pupils—the same precocious lads whom he had always suspected of disobedience and arrogance—at once had a whip-round for him, even selling many of their own essentials. Alone among them Pavlusha Chichikov pleaded poverty and offered a silver five-copeck piece,* which his schoolfellows at once threw back at him, saying: 'Skinflint!' The poor teacher hid his face in his hands when he learnt of his former pupils' kindness; the tears gushed from his dimmed eyes as from those of a helpless infant. 'The good Lord has brought me to tears on my deathbed,' he said in a feeble voice and, when he was told about Chichikov, he sighed deeply and added: 'For shame, Pavlusha! See how a person can change! To think what a well-behaved boy he was, nothing wild about him, as smooth as silk! He had me fooled, he really had me fooled...'

We cannot, however, say that our hero was by nature so harsh and severe, and that his feelings were so blunted as to admit neither pity nor compassion; he felt them both, he would even have liked to help, but only provided the sums involved were not too substantial, so that he would not have to touch the capital he had set aside; in a word, his father's admonition, 'husband your money and save the copecks', had not fallen on deaf ears. But he was not attached to money for its own sake; he was not possessed by miserliness and stinginess. No, these were not the impulses that drove him: he nursed the dream of a life of pleasure, a life with all the luxuries; carriages, an excellently appointed house, delicious dinners—such were the images that inhabited his mind. To ensure that eventually, in the fullness of time, all this might become reality, he saved the copecks so carefully, stingily denying them both to himself and others until that time should come. When a rich man flew past him in a handsome racing droshky, pulled by richly caparisoned trotters, he would stand rooted to the spot and then, as if suddenly waking from a long sleep, would say: 'To think that man was once a mere ledger clerk, wearing his hair in a pudding-basin cut!' Everything redolent of wealth and luxury made an impression on him which he himself could not quite fathom.

On leaving school he did not rest for a moment: such was his impatience to enter service and to set to work. Yet, notwithstanding his glowing school reports, he had great difficulty finding a place in the civil service. Even in a remote backwater one needs connections! The only position he could find was quite paltry, at a salary of some thirty or forty roubles a year. But he resolved to throw himself zealously into his work, to vanquish and surmount all obstacles. And to be sure, his zeal, patience, and self-denial were quite without parallel. He remained at his desk from early morning to late at night, succumbing neither to physical nor to mental fatigue, as he copied away, buried deep in his official papers, even preferring not to go home, but sleeping on the tables in the office, often taking his dinner with the night watchman and yet still managing to preserve his neat appearance, to dress tidily, to impart to his face a pleasant expression, and even to project a certain nobility in his movements. We should point out that clerks of this department were especially noted for their nondescript and unprepossessing appearance. Some had faces that were exactly like badly baked loaves of bread: on one side a bloated cheek protruded, on the other the chin pointed askew, the upper lip sported a blister which—to make matters worse—had burst; in short, a far from pretty sight. They always spoke in a gruff voice, as if about to fly off the handle; they often worshipped at the

altar of Bacchus, thereby demonstrating that the Slav character still
retains many traces of its pagan origins; sometimes they even came
to work pickled, as the expression goes, making things quite unpleasant in the office and filling the air with a miasma that was far
from fragrant.

In the company of such clerks Chichikov could not but stand out
and be noticed, in every way their exact opposite, with his prepossessing mien, his personable voice, and his total abstention from all
alcoholic beverages. Yet, despite all this, his road was a hard one; his
head clerk was a dotard, the very personification of stony insensibility and imperturbability: always remote and unapproachable, his
face never crossed by even the shadow of a smile, a man who never
once greeted anyone with an enquiry after their health. No one had
ever seen him in any other guise, whether outside or at home; never
once had he displayed any strong feeling about anything; never had
he got drunk and laughed in his drunkenness; or at least abandoned
himself to the boisterous hilarity of a ruffian in his cups; but no,
there was not even a shadow of such things in him. There was quite
simply nothing in him at all: nothing malevolent nor benevolent,
and this total absence was in itself quite terrifying. His cold, marble
features, unrelieved by any abrupt irregularity, resembled no other
person one had ever seen; his features were of the severest symmetry. Only the abundant bumps and pock-marks with which his
skin was pitted had given him one of those faces on which—as
country folk say—the devil grinds his peas at night.

It seemed as though mere earthly powers were insufficient to
reach inside such a man and win his favour, yet Chichikov set
himself precisely such a task. He began by obliging him in all sorts
of imperceptible trifles: he carefully noted how the old man liked his
quills to be sharpened and, having prepared several like them, was
always quick to proffer one when needed; he swept and blew the
dust and snuff from his desk; he provided new rags for his ink-well;
unearthed the old clerk's cap—the filthiest old tarboosh you could
possibly imagine—and always set it down beside him one minute
before the office closed; he dusted the plaster off his back if the old
fellow had been leaning against a wall—but all this went entirely
unacknowledged, as if he had done nothing at all.

Finally he started to sniff out the old man's private, domestic life,
ascertaining that he had a grown-up daughter with a face that, if

appearances were to be believed, had also served as a floor for the nocturnal grinding of peas. It was from this flank that he decided to mount his assault. He found out which church she attended on Sundays and always took up a position where she could see him, immaculately turned out, with a stiffly starched shirt-front—and his ploy worked: the severe autocrat weakened and invited him to tea! And before his clerks realized what had happened, Chichikov had moved into his superior's house, where he applied himself to domestic chores, making himself quite indispensable, buying the flour and sugar, treating the daughter like his betrothed, calling the old man 'dear papa', and kissing his hand; in the office it was generally assumed that the wedding would take place at the end of February, before the beginning of Lent. The stern head clerk even pulled strings to get a promotion for Chichikov, and before long the latter was himself appointed head clerk to fill a recently vacated position in another office. This, apparently, was the chief object of his relations with the old man for, without further ado, he secretly dispatched his trunk home and the very next day moved into new quarters. He ceased addressing his old superior as 'dear papa' and no longer kissed his hand, while all talk of a wedding stopped as abruptly as if it had never arisen. Nevertheless, whenever they chanced to meet, he would always warmly shake the old man's hand and invite him to tea, which would cause the old head clerk, despite his eternal impassivity and harsh indifference, to shake his head and mutter through his teeth: 'That young devil led me a proper dance!'

That was the hardest obstacle Chichikov had to surmount. Thereafter things progressed more smoothly. He became a man of some distinction. He proved to have all the qualities necessary for this world: an agreeable turn of phrase, pleasant manners, and a keen nose for business. By these means he managed in a short time to secure what is called a soft option, and he made excellent use of it. We should point out that this was the very period when the authorities launched their toughest ever campaign against bribery and corruption; nothing daunted, he even turned these measures to his own advantage, thereby demonstrating that resourcefulness which the Russian only shows when he finds himself in a corner. Matters were arranged thus: as soon as a petitioner entered his office and put his hand in his pocket in order to bring out those well-known 'letters of recommendation from Prince Khovansky',* as the expression goes here in Russia, he would protest: 'No, no!' smiling and staying the petitioner's hand. 'Surely you do not think that I... No, no! It is our duty, our obligation, to assist without any recompense! In this regard you may set your mind at rest: by tomorrow all shall be done. Be so good as to give me your address and you need trouble yourself no further, everything will be brought directly to your house.'

The delighted petitioner returns home almost in a state of rapture, thinking: 'Now that's the sort of man we need—if only there were more like him: a gem, a real gem!' But the petitioner waits a day, then another—nothing is brought to his house. Nor does it come on the day following that. He calls at the office: the matter has not even been started. He goes to see the 'gem' himself. 'Ah, do forgive us!' says Chichikov with great civility, taking him by both hands, 'we've been so terribly busy; but tomorrow everything shall be done, tomorrow, without fail! I am really quite ashamed!' All this is accompanied by charming gestures. If, in the process, the petitioner's coat should pop open, a restraining hand will at once appear and close the coat again. But neither tomorrow nor the day after, nor the day after that are the papers brought to the petitioner's house. The petitioner starts to smell a rat: 'There's something going on here, I'm sure.' He makes enquiries; they tell him that he must grease the copy-clerks' palms.

'Well, why not?' he says, 'I'm quite willing to give them a quarter rouble or two.'

'No, not twenty-five copecks, twenty-five roubles.'

'Twenty-five roubles each—to the copy-clerks!' exclaims the petitioner.

'But why are you so shocked?' they ask him. 'It comes to the same thing: twenty-five copecks each for the clerks and the rest goes upstairs.'

The slow-witted petitioner slaps himself on the forehead and rains curses on the new order of things, on the campaign against bribe-taking, and the courteous, ennobled conduct of the officials. 'In the old days at least you knew where you stood: you slipped the head clerk a ten-rouble note and the cat was in the bag; now you dish out twenty-five roubles, having wasted a whole week before you tumbled to it. To hell with all these new officials with their integrity and nobility!'

The petitioner is right, of course, but at least now there are no more bribe-takers: all head clerks are the most honest and noble-minded of people, and it's only the secretaries and scribes who are thieves and rogues.

Soon a much wider field was opened up to Chichikov: a commission was set up for the erection of some very substantial government building.* He managed to get himself on this commission and proved to be one of its most energetic members. The commission set to work without delay. For six years it busied itself with matters relating to the building; but either the climate was unsuitable, or perhaps the materials were faulty, but whatever the reason the government building rose no higher than its foundations. In the mean time handsome new homes, of a non-governmental design, arose in different parts of town: clearly the ground there was more suitable for building. The members of the commission now began to prosper and to raise families. It was only at this juncture that Chichikov began to depart somewhat from his strict regime of abstinence and unrelenting self-denial. Only now did he allow himself to break his long-enduring fast, and it transpired that he had at no time been insensible to those various pleasures from which he had been able to refrain in the years of ardent youth—that time of life when no man has complete mastery of his passions. One or two excesses were committed: he engaged a rather good cook, and took to wearing shirts of fine holland linen. For his coats he now ordered cloth of a quality unmatched anywhere in the province, and thenceforth favoured browner and more reddish shades with a speckled weave; he acquired an excellent pair of horses and would ride holding one rein himself, forcing the trace horse to prance in circles; he had already formed the habit of sponging himself down with a mixture of water and Cologne; he now bought, at considerable expense, a special kind of soap, which imparted a particular smoothness to his skin; he now started...

Then, quite suddenly, the old tortoise who had been in charge was replaced by a new director, a military man, stern and authoritarian, an enemy of all bribe-takers and a stickler for the rules. The very next day he put the fear of God in the entire commission, demanding balance sheets, at every step spotting discrepancies and sums of money that had gone missing, at once noticing the handsome houses and their non-governmental design—and an inquiry was ordered. Commission members were removed from office; the non-governmental houses became governmental after all and were converted into various charitable institutions and schools for the sons of soldiers; the fat was in the fire and Chichikov's worse than the rest. For some reason the new director took exception to his face, despite its agreeable aspect; God alone knows quite why it should have so displeased him—such things sometimes happen for no reason—and he conceived a mortal loathing of his subordinate. But, being a military man, and therefore not familiar with all the fine nuances and machinations of civilian life, in due course other officials wormed their way into his favour thanks to their upright appearance and ability to ingratiate themselves with any man, and the general soon found himself in the hands of even greater thieves and rogues, whom he regarded as thoroughly honest men; indeed, he was delighted that he had at last chosen the right men, and solemnly boasted of his skills as a judge of character.

The new officials quickly got the measure of his character, however. To a man, every one of his subordinates became an implacable foe of improbity; they hunted it out everywhere, in all transactions, just as a fisherman hunts out a plump beluga sturgeon with his gaff-hook, and they hunted it out with such success that within a short time they had all amassed nest-eggs of several thousand roubles each. During this period many of the former officials returned to the path of righteousness and were reinstated. But, try as he would, Chichikov was quite unable to worm his way back, notwithstanding all the efforts made on his behalf by the general's chief secretary, whose intercession was prompted by the usual letters from Prince Khovansky. The secretary had fully mastered the art of leading his general by the nose, but even he was quite unable to do a thing for Chichikov. The general was the sort of man who—quite unwittingly, of course—let others lead him by the nose but when he did get an idea of his own, it would lodge in his head like an iron nail and nothing could shift it. All the artful secretary could achieve was the destruction of Chichikov's sullied service record, and this he persuaded the director to do by appealing to his compassion, with a vivid description of the lamentable plight of Chichikov's family—a family which, to their own good fortune, Chichikov did not have.

'Ah, well!' said Chichikov. 'I hooked it, played it a little, and lost it—these things happen. No point in crying over spilt milk: there's work to be done.' And he resolved then and there to begin a new career, again to arm himself with patience, again to limit himself in all things, regardless of the gay abandon with which he had indulged himself before.

He had to move to another town and there make a new name for himself. Somehow nothing seemed to go right. He was forced to change his job two or three times within a short space of time. The work was somehow grubby and demeaning. It should be borne in mind that Chichikov was the most decorous man the world has ever seen. Although even he had been constrained to begin his career in most indecorous company, inwardly he had always remained clean and pure, he liked to have polished writing desks in the offices and wanted everything to look smart and noble. In his speech he never permitted himself to use an indecorous word, and was always affronted if he remarked in the words of others a lack of due respect for rank or position. The reader will, I believe, be pleased to learn that he changed his linen every two days, and in summer, during the hot weather, even daily: any odour that was ever so slightly unpleasant was offensive to him. For this reason, whenever Petrushka came to undress him and to pull off his boots he would insert a clove in each nostril, and on many occasions his nerves proved to be as sensitive as a young girl's; that is why it was so hard for him to return once more to those walks of life where everything reeked of cheap vodka and indecorous behaviour.

However much he fortified his spirits, he none the less grew thin and, during these times of adversity, his skin even took on a greenish hue. And this at a time when he had begun to fill out and acquire respectable, rounded contours, like those in which the reader found him at the time they became acquainted; a time when, as he gazed into the mirror, he would often muse on many pleasant things: a little woman and a nursery, a children's room, and these thoughts would be followed by a smile. But now, when he chanced to see himself in the mirror, he could not forbear to cry out: 'Holy Mother of God! How repulsive I have become!' And for days thereafter he could not bring himself to have a closer look.

Still, our hero endured it all, endured it stoically, patiently... and at last he secured a position in the customs service.* We should remark here that this service had long formed the secret object of his highest aspirations. He saw what flashy foreign merchandise fell into the hands of the customs officers, the fine porcelain and cambrics they sent to their aunts, sisters, and other kinswomen. Many was the occasion on which he had said to himself with a sigh: 'Now that's where I should like to work: the frontier is close by, the people are enlightened, and just imagine the fine holland shirts I shall acquire for my wardrobe!' We should add here that his thoughts touched also on a particular brand of French soap, which promised to impart an extraordinary whiteness to the skin and a freshness to the cheeks; it matters not what it was called, but he felt it safe to assume that it was most certainly to be had at the border.

Thus, he would have long since sought a post in the customs, but he had been delayed by the various advantages he derived from the construction commission, and he had understandably reasoned that the customs, for all its merits, was still only a bird in the bush, while the commission was very much a bird in the hand. Now, however, he resolved to use all means at his disposal to enter the customs service, and enter it he did. He applied himself to his duties with an extraordinary zeal. It appeared that destiny herself had decreed he should be a customs officer. Such dispatch, perspicacity, and acumen had not only never before been seen, they had never been heard of. In the space of three or four weeks he had become so adept in his work that he knew the customs business inside out: he no longer even weighed or measured anything, he could tell from the mere feel of a bolt of cloth how many yards of material it contained; by lifting a package in his hands he could at once tell how many pounds it weighed. And when it came to searches, here, as his colleagues put it, he had the nose of a bloodhound: they marvelled at his infinite patience as he inspected every little button, and carried out these minute tasks with a combination of impeccable courtesy and devastating imperturbability. And while his victims were fuming with rage, seized with a malevolent urge to rain blows on his pleasant physiognomy, Chichikov would merely repeat, without the least change of expression or departure from his courteous manner: 'Might I ask you to be so very kind as to stand up?' Or: 'Might I request, Madam, that you repair to the next room? There the lady wife of one of our officers will explain matters to you.' Or: 'Pray allow me to make a teeny incision in the lining of your coat with my little knife.' And, as he said this, he would be pulling out from this lining shawls and scarves as nonchalantly as if lifting them from his own trunk. Even his superiors declared that this was no human being but the devil incarnate: he would poke around and find smuggled goods inside wheels, carriage shafts, horses' ears, and God knows where else, in the sort of places where no author would dream of venturing and in which only customs officers are permitted to look. After crossing the border the poor traveller would be unable to recover his composure for several minutes and, as he mopped the sweat from his brow, could only cross himself and repeat: 'Dear, oh dear, oh dear!' His state of mind would be like that of a schoolboy emerging from the holy of holies to which the headmaster had summoned him, expecting to receive a verbal admonition, but where—to everyone's surprise—he had been caned instead.

Before long he made life quite impossible for smugglers. He was the scourge and despair of all the Jews in Poland. His integrity and incorruptibility were unassailable, almost superhuman. He even resisted the temptation to set aside for himself a little nest-egg of those assorted confiscated goods and personal items which would have caused unnecessary paper-work had they been forfeited to the State. Such zeal and disinterest could not fail to provoke general amazement and to come finally to the notice of his superiors. Chichikov was promoted in rank and thereupon submitted a master-plan for the apprehension of all smugglers, requesting only that he be granted the funds to carry this out himself. He was at once put in command of the project and given unlimited powers to carry out any searches he required. This was exactly what he had sought. At around this time a carefully planned, highly effective band of smugglers had gone into operation; their daring enterprise held the promise of millions in profit. He had long been party to information about these smugglers, and had even refused the bribes offered by their emissaries, commenting drily: 'The time for that has not yet come.'

No sooner did he gain his unlimited powers than he sent word: 'The time has now come.' His calculations proved sound: now in a single year he could make more than in twenty years of the most zealous service. Hitherto he had not wished to enter into any relations with the smugglers, because—as a mere pawn—he would have received too little, but now... Now it was quite a different story: he could set whatever conditions he wished. To ensure that things went as smoothly as possible he enlisted the connivance of a fellow officer, who proved unable to resist the blandishments offered, although at his venerable age he should have known better. The terms were agreed and the band went to work. At first, matters proceeded splendidly: the reader must surely have heard the oft-repeated story of the Merino sheep which were sent across the border in false coats, under which they carried a million roubles worth of Brabant lace.* This cunning ploy was engineered during Chichikov's term of office in the customs service. No Jew in the world could have carried out such an undertaking, had Chichikov not been acting as an accomplice. After three or four such flocculent border crossings both officers increased their capital by some four hundred thousand roubles. It is said that Chichikov even hit the half-million mark, because he was rather more dexterous.

God only knows to what astronomical heights these already copious sums would have grown had matters not been fouled up by the intervention of a mischievous goblin. This goblin utterly confounded the two officers, with the result that they fell out and started quarrelling over the merest trifles. Once, in a heated discussion, and perhaps when slightly the worse for drink, Chichikov called the other officer the son of a priest, and the latter—although he really was a priest's son—for some obscure reason took mortal offence and at once hit back in strong and uncommonly sharp words, namely: 'No, you lie, I'm a state councillor and not the son of a priest, it's you who's the son of a priest!' And then, to add insult to injury, continued: 'That's what you are!' Although in this manner he had soundly rebuffed Chichikov, by hurling his own insult back at him, and although the taunt 'That's what you are!' was already quite forceful, he was still not content and even wrote an anonymous denunciation of Chichikov. It is rumoured, besides, that they had also fallen out over some young wench, fresh and lusty as a juicy turnip, to borrow a favourite expression of the customs officers; the story even goes that men had been hired to apprehend our hero under cover of night in a dark alley and to give him a beating; but that both officers had been made to look utter fools by one Shamsharyov, a staff-captain, for he it was that won the favours of the pretty wench.

The true story no one knows; the curious reader would be best advised to complete it for himself. The main point is that their secret dealings with the smugglers were now revealed. Although it also meant his own ruin, the state councillor at least dragged Chichikov down with him. The officers were hauled before the judge, all their

ill-gotten gains were seized and confiscated, and all this burst over
their heads like a mighty thunderbolt. They finally came to their
senses like men awakening from a stupor and saw with horror what
they had done. The state councillor followed the Russian custom
and found solace in the bottle, but the collegiate councillor weath-
ered the storm. Notwithstanding the keen scent of the sleuths who
came to conduct the inquiry, he had managed to conceal some of his
profits. He used all the cunning and guile of his resourceful mind,
drawing on his rich experience as a man who knew his fellow men
only too well; with some he relied on his agreeable turn of phrase,
with others he pleaded for compassion; he knew where to employ
flattery—something which never goes amiss—and when to grease a
palm—in short, he so managed things that at least he escaped the
utter ignominy of his accomplice and he avoided criminal charges.
But he was now left with no capital, with no fancy articles of foreign
manufacture, with nothing; it had all passed to eager new owners.
He retained a paltry ten thousand or so, set aside against just such
an unlucky day, a dozen or two fine holland shirts, a smallish chaise
of the kind affected by bachelors, and two serfs, his coachman Selifan,
and his valet Petrushka. The customs officers, out of the kindness of
their hearts, let him keep five or six bars of soap to safeguard the
freshness of his cheeks—and that was all.

Such was the sorry state in which our hero again found himself!
Such was the torrent of misfortune that had fallen on his head! This
is what he meant when he spoke of suffering in the service of the
truth. Now one might conclude that after such tempests, such ordeals, such vicissitudes of fate and tribulations in life, he would
withdraw with his vital ten thousand roubles to the sleepy backwater of some small provincial town, there to fritter away his remaining days sitting in a cotton-print dressing-gown by the window
of a low-slung cottage, and, on Sundays, intervening in the fights
that flared up outside his window between the local peasants, or
stepping out to his chicken run to take a breath of fresh air and
personally to choose the next hen destined for his soup-pot, for
good measure giving the bird a squeeze, and in this way live out an
uneventful, but in its way not unrewarding, life.

Yet this was not to be. We must give due credit to the insuppressible strength of his character. After all this, which would have been
sufficient, if not to kill a man, then at least to subdue him and cool

his ardour forever, his extraordinary zest for life remained unquelled. He was vexed and aggrieved, he railed against the entire world, raged at the injustice of fate, berated the injustice of his fellow men—and yet was unable to resist new enterprises. In a word, he demonstrated a forbearance against which the wooden forbearance of the German, the product of the slow, sluggish circulation of his blood, is as nothing. Chichikov's blood, on the contrary, coursed strongly through his veins and he had to use all his will power and common sense to curb the energy that strained to escape and range freely abroad. He reasoned, and there was a certain justification in his reasoning: 'But why me? Why should this calamity have befallen me? Which official, these days, would let such an opportunity slip by? They all have their noses in the trough. I brought misfortune on no one: I neither robbed the widow nor did I cause anyone's ruination; I helped myself to the surpluses, I took where every man would have taken; had I not helped myself, others would have taken it instead. And why should others prosper, why must I perish like a worm? What am I now? What am I good for? How can I now look any respected husband and father in the face? How can I not suffer the pangs of conscience, knowing that I am but a worthless encumbrance on this earth? What will my children say when they find out? "Look," they'll say: "our father was such a swine, he never left us a bean!"'

We already know how preoccupied Chichikov was with the matter of his posterity. This was his most sensitive spot! Another man might not, perchance, have thrust his hand in so deep, had it not been for the question, which, in some obscure manner, posed itself, quite unbidden: 'But what will the children say?' Here the future paterfamilias may be likened to the cautious tom-cat, which squints warily from one eye, lest his master is watching from somewhere, and swiftly snatches up whatever lies within his reach: soap, candles, pork fat, or even a canary, if he can get his paws on it—he misses nothing. Thus did our hero weep and lament his fate, yet all the while the cogs of his brain kept turning; his mind teemed with half-formed schemes and projects and all that was needed was a master-plan. Once again he tightened his belt, once again he embarked on a life of hardship, once again he denied himself everything, once again he turned his back on cleanliness and decency and descended into the filth of lowly life. And in the hope of better things to come he was even forced to take up the calling of solicitor, a calling that with us has yet to gain its citizenship, that is scoffed and scorned by all and sundry, reviled by the most pettifogging clerks, and even by those who engage the solicitor's services, and was condemned to grovelling in antechambers, to enduring rude treatment and similar indignities, but dire necessity forced him to put up with anything.

Of his commissions there was, however, one that suited him: he was to arrange the mortgaging of several hundred peasants to the Board of Trustees.* The estate had been utterly and totally ruined. It had been brought to ruin by cattle murrains, by scoundrelly bailiffs, by failed harvests, by epidemic fevers that had carried off the best workers* and, finally, by the incompetence of the land-owner himself, who had furnished himself a house in Moscow in the latest fashion and had squandered his entire fortune, to the very last copeck, on this wasteful enterprise. Starvation stared him in the face, thus he was obliged to mortgage his last remaining estate. Mortgaging was a new idea in those days, a territory into which people ventured with trepidation. Acting in his capacity as solicitor, Chichikov first gained everyone's favour (for without such preliminary gaining of favour it is, as we all know, quite impossible to obtain the simplest form or document—instead, every throat must first be lubricated with at least one bottle of Madeira)—and, having gained the favour of all those who mattered, he explained that there was, however, a certain problem: half the peasants had died, so... lest there should be any complications afterwards...

'But they do still figure on the census list, don't they?' said the secretary.

'They do,' said Chichikov.

'So what are you worried about?' said the secretary. 'One dies, another's born, it's all the same in the end.' As we can see, the secretary was something of a rhetorician.

But while speaking with the secretary, our hero had been struck by an idea more inspired than any that has ever entered the portals of the human mind. 'What a numskull I am, what a village idiot!' he said to himself. 'Here I am, hunting for my mittens, when all the time they're stuck in my belt. Now let's suppose I were to buy up all the peasants that have died before they take a new census, let's say I bought a thousand of them, and let's say the Board of Trustees gave me two hundred per soul: why, that would give me a capital of two hundred thousand roubles! And now's a good time, there was an epidemic recently, and the numbers of peasants that kicked the bucket, God be praised, are considerable. The landowners have been gambling, carousing, and throwing their money about as usual; so they've all upped stakes and decamped to St Petersburg to get jobs in government; their estates are abandoned, they're left to manage themselves; every year it gets harder to find money for the soul tax, so they'll all be only too glad to let me have their dead serfs, if only so that they no longer need to pay the soul tax on them; who knows, I might even be able to squeeze the odd copeck out of some of them for doing them the favour. It'll be hard, of course, a great deal of bother, there's the danger that someone might blow the gaff. But then man was not given his brain for nothing. The best thing about this is that the very idea will seem so incredible, no one will believe it. Admittedly, without land one can neither buy nor mortgage. But then I shall be buying them for transfer, to take them somewhere else: these days land in Tavrida and Kherson provinces* is being given away, just so long as you come and settle it. So that's where I'll take them! Off to Kherson with them! Let them live there! The resettlement can be done quite legally, according to the rules. If they should require certificates of inspection of the peasants: with pleasure, I shall not object, why should I? I shall even present a certificate of inspection signed by the captain of police himself. I can call my village Chichikov Hamlet, or after my Christian name: the village of Pavlovskoe.' Thus it was that, in the mind of our hero, there took shape this strange design, for which the readers perhaps may not thank him, yet for which the author is more grateful than words can express. For, say what you will, had this idea not entered Chichikov's head, this poem would not have seen the light of day.

Crossing himself, as Russians are wont to do,* he set about putting his design into effect. Ostensibly for the purpose of selecting a place to settle in and under other such pretexts he undertook to visit various corners of our empire, primarily those which had suffered most from calamities, failed harvests, high mortality, and so on and so forth—in short, where the peasants he needed he could be procured most easily and at least cost. He did not approach all the landowners indiscriminately, but selected those who were more to his taste or those with whom he could strike such deals with the least difficulty, endeavouring first to make their acquaintance and to gain their favour, so that he might, if possible, acquire peasants through friendship rather than by purchase. Let our kind readers therefore not be indignant with the author if those characters who have appeared thus far have not been altogether to their liking: blame for this must be laid at Chichikov's door, for here he rules supreme, and whither he decides to go, there too must we follow. And, for our own part—if, indeed, accusations are made that the characters are humdrum and nondescript—we shall only rejoin that it is never possible at the outset to see the full scope and compass of any venture.

The entry into any town, be it even a provincial capital, is always rather humdrum; initially all is grey and monotonous: endless lines of soot-blackened factories file past, and only after them do you see the angular forms of six-storeyed buildings, shops, signboards, broad streets stretching before you, jammed with bell-towers, colonnades, statues, and spires, with the brilliance, the noise, and the clatter of the city, and every other wonder produced by the hand and mind of man. How his first purchases were made the reader has already seen; as for how things shall proceed from here, what successes and failures await our hero, how he will encounter and surmount still more daunting obstacles, what colossal figures shall arise before him, how this rambling tale shall be driven forward by its hidden levers, how its horizons will reach ever further into the distance and how it will take on a majestic, lyrical flow—all that he shall see in due course. Many versts have yet to be traversed by this equipage of ours, consisting of a gentleman of middle years, a chaise, of the kind affected by bachelors, a valet Petrushka, a coachman Selifan, and a threesome of horses, already familiar to us by name, from Assessor to the rascally dappled bay.

Thus our hero stands revealed before us, as large as life. To complete the portrait, however, one final detail might be required: what sort of a person is he with regard to moral qualities? That he is not a hero, replete with every perfection and virtue, is manifest. So what is he then? A rogue? But why a rogue, why should we be so hard on our fellow man? There are no real rogues among us nowadays, there are only well-intentioned people, agreeable people, while of that breed of men prepared to risk public disgrace and opprobrium you would be hard put to find more than two or three specimens and even those are now starting to talk about virtue. No: fairest of all would be to call him an owner, an acquirer. The acquisitive instinct lies at the root of all evil: it gives rise to deeds which the world has termed 'not very clean'. True, there is already something repugnant about such a character, and that same reader who in his own life will be friendly with such a man, happily hobnobbing and passing the time of day with him, will start to look askance at him if he pops up as the hero of a play or poem. But wise is he who does not disdain any man, but instead fixes him with a deep, searching look, and plumbs the very depth of his soul. Swift are the transformations in man; before you can blink a terrible, despotic worm has grown up within him, and has sucked up all his vital juices. Only too often does some caprice—no great passion this, but the merest of foibles—take root and grow in a man destined for fine achievements, and cause him to forget his great and sacred duties and instead to see something great and sacred in worthless baubles.

Numberless as grains of sand are the passions of man, and no one of them is like another. Initially, they all—whether base or noble—submit to man's will and only later do they exercise such fearful tyranny over him. Blessed is he who, from all their multitude, has selected the noblest passion; his immeasurable bliss grows and increases tenfold by the hour and minute as he plunges ever deeper into the boundless paradise of his soul. But there are passions which are not of man's choosing.* For they are born with him when he comes into the world, and he is not given the strength to reject them. They are directed by some higher design, and there is in them something eternally beckoning, something which never falls silent all the days of his life. They are destined to achieve great things here on earth: it matters not whether this be in dim obscurity or in a blaze of light that flashes by to delight the world—in equal measure are they summoned forth for some good unknown to man. And perhaps it is so with our very own Chichikov, perhaps the passion that drives him is not of his choosing, and perhaps his own cold existence already contains within it that same element which one day will bring man to his knees before the wisdom of Providence and reduce him to dust. It remains a mystery why this particular image should have taken shape in this poem which we present here to the world.

What troubles us, however, is not that our readers will be displeased with the hero but the irresistible conviction that, on the contrary, they might have been pleased with this same hero, with this very same Chichikov. Had the author not peered so deeply into his soul, had he not stirred in its lower depths all those things which slither away and shun the light, had he not revealed those innermost thoughts which a man will entrust to no other, but had he instead shown him as he appeared to the whole town, to Manilov and the other citizens, they would all have been delighted and would have regarded him as an interesting man. No matter that neither his face nor his entire person would have come alive before the reader's mind; instead, when he finished reading, his soul would not have been in any way troubled and he could have gone back to the card-table—the solace of all Russia. Yes, my good readers, you would prefer not to see the wretchedness of man in all its nakedness. Why, you ask, what's the use of this? Do we not already know that there is much in life that is despicable and stupid? As it is, we often happen to see things that leave us quite disturbed. Rather offer us something splendid and diverting. Let us rather forget ourselves for a while! 'Listen, brother, why do you tell me that business is going badly?' says the landowner to his bailiff. 'I don't need to be told, I know it already, brother, so is there not something else you could tell me? Could you not let me forget about that for a little while, could you not keep it from me, and then I would be happy.' Thus the money that could have gone some way towards setting matters right is spent instead on various means of inducing this amnesia. Thus sleeps a mind which might otherwise have uncovered a hidden source of great wealth; there the estate crashes beneath the auctioneer's hammer and the landowner sets off with his begging bowl in search of oblivion, his soul, in extremity, quite ready now to plumb depths of baseness before which in earlier times it would have recoiled in horror.

Reproaches will also be levelled at the author by those so-called patriots,* who sit quietly in their corners and attend to quite unrelated matters, amassing small fortunes and lining their own nests at the expense of others; but should something happen which to their mind is injurious to the mother country, should some book appear which dares to state the occasional bitter truth, they at once come scurrying from their corners like spiders seeing a fly caught in their web, and they all exclaim together: 'Is it such a good thing to bring all this to light, to proclaim it from the rooftops? After all, everything described here is all ours—is that such a good thing? What will the foreigners say? Will they not wonder whether we enjoy hearing a bad opinion of ourselves? Will they not wonder how it can fail to cause us pain? Will they not think we are not patriots?'

In answer to such wise remarks, particularly with regard to the opinions of foreigners, I must confess that nothing comes to mind. Except perhaps this: in a distant corner of Russia there lived two men. One was a husband and father, by name Kifa Mokievich, a meek and inoffensive man who lived his life in a slipshod way. He did not attend to his family's needs; his existence was directed more towards contemplative pursuits and taken up with the following, as he termed it, philosophical question: 'Take for example a beast,' he would say, striding about the room, 'a beast is born naked into the world. Yet why should it be naked? And why is it not born like a bird, why does it not pop out of an egg? It's a funny thing: you simply cannot understand nature, however deep you delve into it!'

Thus reasoned the one inhabitant, Kifa Mokievich. But this is still not the main point. The other inhabitant was Mokiy Kifovich, his own son. This latter was cast in a heroic mould, that of the *bogatyr** of Russian legend, and, while his father was preoccupied with the origin of beasts, this strapping youth of some twenty summers sought breadth and scope for his natural energies. If he put his hand to something he could not do so lightly: a fellow's arm would be sure to crack or a bump would spring up on another's nose. In the house and neighbourhood everyone, from the backyard wench to the backyard dog, would flee at the sight of him; even the bed he slept on he broke into small pieces. Such was Mokiy Kifovich, and yet he was a good soul.

But this is not the main point either; the main point is this: 'Begging your pardon, master, Kifa Mokievich,' the servants—both his own and others'—would say to the father, 'but what's the story with this lad of yours, this Mokiy Kifovich? He gives none of us any peace, he's such a bone-crusher!'

'Yes, he's a playful lad, full of pranks,' the father would usually reply, 'but what can I do? It's too late to thrash him, and if I did everyone would accuse me of cruelty; but he's an ambitious fellow, and if I told him off in the presence of two or three others he would cool off for a little while, but the story would get out, that's the trouble! The whole town would hear about it and call him a rotten cur. Do they think it causes me no pain? Am I not his father? Just because I dabble in philosophy and on occasion I may have no time to spend with him, does that mean I'm no longer a father? Not a bit of it! I'm a father all right, a father, may the devil take them all, a father! This is where I keep my Mokiy Kifovich, here in my heart!' At this Kifa Mokievich would violently thump his chest and become quite carried away. 'And if he wants to be a rotten cur, then I shan't be the one to spread it abroad, I shan't be the one to give him away.'

Having thus demonstrated his paternal concern he would leave Mokiy Kifovich to continue his heroic endeavours, while he returned to his own favourite pursuit, addressing some such question as: 'Now let us suppose that an elephant was hatched from an egg, just consider how thick the shell would have to be: a cannon ball wouldn't break it; we'd have to invent some new sort of fire-arm.'

Such were the lives led in their peaceful little corner by these two inhabitants, who have so unexpectedly popped up at the end of our poem in order to furnish a modest reply to the accusation of certain ardent patriots, who hitherto have been quietly occupied with some philosophical pursuit or the amassing of wealth for the good of their dearly beloved country, who are concerned not that they should do no wrong, but only that no one should say they are doing wrong. No, it is not patriotism, not some basic instinct, which lies behind these accusations, there is something else concealed there. And why should we not admit it? Who, if not the author, is to utter the sacred truth? You fear the deeply searching stare, you are loath to gaze too deeply into things yourself, you prefer to glance over the surface of things with unquestioning eyes. You will even laugh heartily at Chichikov, perhaps you will even praise the author, saying: 'You have to give him his due, he has a good eye for these things, he must have a good sense of humour, this writer fellow!'

And after these words you will turn to yourself with redoubled pride, a self-satisfied smile will play across your lips, and you will add: 'There's no getting away from it: you do find some mighty strange and comical customers in the provinces, and the damnedest scoundrels to boot!' But is there any one among you who, full of Christian humility and alone, in a moment of solitary self-examination, will direct this disturbing question, not aloud, but in silence, deep into your own soul: 'But might there not be some little bit of Chichikov in me too?' Why, you think, God forbid! Yet let some acquaintance happen by at this moment, a man of rank, not too high nor yet too low, and you will at once nudge your neighbour's arm and say, almost snorting with laughter: 'Look, look, it's Chichikov, there goes Chichikov!' Then, like a child, forgetting all the decorum consonant with your rank and years, you will set off in pursuit of him, taunting him from behind, and chanting: 'Chichikov! Chichikov! Chichikov!'

But we have started to speak rather loudly, forgetting that our hero, who has been asleep throughout the narration of his story, has already awoken and might easily hear his name being repeated so often. For he is quick to take offence and does not like to be spoken of in a disrespectful manner. It is all one to the reader whether or not Chichikov flies into a rage at him, but not so with the author, he must not under any circumstances quarrel with his hero: there still remains a long road for them to journey together hand in hand; two big parts still lie ahead, and that is no trifling consideration.

'Hey! What are you doing?' shouted Chichikov to Selifan, 'Hey, you!'

'Wha-at?' said Selifan in a slow drawl.

'What d'you mean—"wha-at?" You stupid gander! Have you forgotten how to drive this thing! Come along now, get cracking!'

Indeed, for quite some time Selifan had been driving with his eyes shut tight, only every so often—in his somnolent state—lightly flicking the reins against the flanks of the likewise dozing horses; as for Petrushka, his cap had long ago flown off heaven knows where, and he himself was reclining with his head firmly wedged against Chichikov's knee, so that the latter was forced to give him a thump. Selifan perked up and gave the dappled horse a few lashes across the back, causing the beast to break into a trot. He then cracked his whip above all three horses and called out in a thin, singing voice: 'Shake a leg, you lot!' The nags bestirred themselves and lunged forward, pulling the light chaise along like a ball of fluff. Selifan kept swinging his whip and shouting: 'Hey! Hey! Hey!' as he bounced rhythmically up and down on the box, while the troika flew up and plunged down the humps and dips of the highroad, which ran almost imperceptibly downhill.

Chichikov smiled contentedly as he swayed gently on his leather cushion, for he loved to drive fast. Indeed, which Russian does not thrill to the sensation of speed? And the Russian soul, which longs to roister and whirl about, to throw caution to the wind and say: 'To hell with it all!'—how can the Russian soul not thrill to the sensation of speed? How can it not thrill to that sensation when it can hear in it something rapturous, something wondrous? It is as though some unknown force has gathered you up on to its wing, and you are flying, and everything flies with you: the versts fly past, the traders perched high on the coachman's seats of their kibitkas fly towards you, the forest with its dark rows of firs and pines, with the knocking of axes and cawing of crows, flies by on both sides, the road itself flies away into the unknown, fading distance, and there is something terrifying in this flashing by of objects, so swift that they fade from sight before they can be distinguished—and only the sky above, and the wispy clouds, and the moon glinting through them, appear motionless. Ah, troika, bird troika, who dreamed you up? Surely you could only have come into being among a spirited race, in that land which has no truck with half measures, but which has spread in a vast, smooth plain over half the earth, so far that you would go cross-eyed before you could count all the verst-poles. Nor is this conveyance some cunning piece of work, held together with iron nuts and bolts—no, it has been hastily hewn to life with a rude axe and chisel and assembled by a nimble-fingered Yaroslavl peasant. No German topboots for our coachman: a beard, a pair of mittens, and a rough perch to sit on; but let him rise a little, let him crack his whip, let him strike up a song—and the horses swirl together like a whirlwind, the wheelspokes blur into a single smooth disc, the very road quakes beneath them, and a terrified passer-by cries out as he stops in his tracks—and it's off and away! Off and away! Off and away!... Very soon, all that can be seen in the distance is the dust raised as something cleaves the air.

And you, Rus, do you not hurtle forward too, like some spirited troika that none can catch? A trail of smoke marks your passage, the bridges rumble, everything falls back and is left behind. On seeing this miracle of God the onlooker stops in his tracks: what is this?—a bolt of lightning hurled from the heavens? And this terrifying onrush—what does it portend? And what unearthly power lies hidden in these unearthly steeds? And the steeds—what steeds, what steeds! Are there whirlwinds caught in your manes? Is there some eager, sensitive ear burning in every fibre of your being? You hear the familiar song ring out from high above, in unison you tense your bronze chests, and, your hooves skimming the ground, you are transformed into taut, elongated forms, flying through the air, and you hurtle forward, inspired by God!... Rus, where are you racing? Give an answer! No answer comes. With a wondrous jingling the carriage bells ring out; torn into shreds, the air rumbles and turns to wind; every thing on this earth flashes by as, with an oblique look, other peoples and empires step aside to let her fly past.

PART TWO

[Throughout Part Two, pairs of daggers (†) enclose passages
for which variant text is given in the Appendix. Angled brackets (⟨ ⟩)
indicate doubtful words or lacunae.]

CHAPTER ONE

But why expose to view the poverty and more poverty, the sad imperfection of our life, dredging people up from the backwater, from the remote nooks and crannies of our empire? There is nothing for it, if the author is of such a cast and if he is so sick at heart with his own imperfection that he can no longer portray anything but the poverty and more poverty, the sad imperfection of our life, dredging people up from the backwater, from the remote nooks and crannies of our empire! So here we are, once again, lost in the backwater, once again stuck in some remote cranny.

But then—what backwater and what a cranny!

For a thousand versts and more there stretched a range of mountains like the gigantic rampart of some endless fortress, with complete battlements and barbicans. The mountains towered majestically over the endless expanse of the plains, in places forming sheer walls, half-clay and half-lime, slashed with ruts and gulleys, in others softening into prettily rounded, green protuberances, swathed, as in lamb's wool, with the young undergrowth springing from felled trees, in yet others disappearing into dark thickets of forest, which—by some miracle—had as yet escaped the ravages of the axe. A river, holding true to its banks, followed them round their swerves and bends and at times flowed off into the meadows, there to meander in a series of loops, flashing like fire in the sun, before hiding in a copse of birch, aspen, and alder and emerging therefrom in triumph, with an entourage of bridges, mills, and weirs, which seemed to pursue it round every turn.

In one place the steep mountain slopes were more densely coiffured with the green tresses of the abundant trees. By the skilled hand of the gardener, and thanks also to the unevenness of the craggy terrain, north and south of the vegetable kingdom here communed. Oak, fir, forest pear, maple, cherry tree and acacia, yellow acacia and rowan, enmeshed in hops, in places encouraging one another's growth, in others choking their neighbours—they all scrabbled their way to the very top of the mountains. At the top, however, at the very peak, the red roofs of farm-buildings, the ridge-trees of peasant cottages behind them, and the upper storey of the manor house itself, with its carved balcony and a large, semicircular window, peeped out from amidst these leafy green crowns. Above all this confusion of trees and roofs an ancient village church raised aloft its five glinting, gilded onion domes. Each was crowned by a golden filigree cross, fastened to its dome by golden filigree chains, so that from afar it seemed as if this glitter of gold was suspended in the air and attached to nothing, scintillating like a multitude of incandescent pieces of gold. And all this—trees, roofs, church, and crosses—was prettily reflected upside down in the river, into which the hideously gnarled willows, some standing on the bank, others right in the water, dipped their dropping branches and leaves, as if admiring their own wondrous reflection, except where this view was occluded by the slimy waterweed and the bright, floating leaves of the yellow lilies.

The view was splendid, but the view from above, from the uppermost storey of the house across the distant plain was more splendid still. No guest or visitor standing on the balcony could remain unmoved. Catching his breath with amazement, he would only exclaim: 'Lord, how spacious it is here!' Endless vistas, boundless expanses stretched away before him: beyond the meadows, dotted with groves and watermills, forests stretched in long green bands; beyond the forests the yellow of sands showed through the hazy air. And then came more forests, now deep blue, like the waters of the sea, or a mist spreading in the far distance; then more sands, paler even than those before, yet still bright yellow. Rising like a crest on the distant horizon lay a line of chalk hills, which sparkled a brilliant white even in the most inclement weather, as if illuminated by an eternal sun. In the foothills, misty-grey dots stood out against the dazzling whiteness like puffs of smoke. These were distant villages, but too far away for the human eye to make out. Only the flash of a golden church cupola caught in the sun's rays betrayed that these were large, populous settlements. All this was enveloped in an imperturbable stillness, undisturbed even by the barely audible cries of the nightingales hovering in the distant sky. No guest standing on the balcony and contemplating that scene for two hours could fail to exclaim, quite simply: 'Lord, how spacious it is here!'

Who, one might ask, was the resident and proprietor of this village, which, like some impregnable fortress, could not even be approached from this side but could only be reached from the other, where the guest would be welcomed by oak-trees scattered picturesquely across the sward, spreading wide their branches like arms to receive him into their embrace, and guiding him to that house, the roof of which we had observed from behind. The house now stands before us, open to view, flanked on one side by a row of cottages proudly displaying their roof-trees and carved crests, and—on the other—by a church with its glinting gold crosses and intricately wrought golden chains, suspended in the air above? To which lucky man did this lost cranny belong?

To a landowner of Tremalakhansk district,* one Andrei Ivanovich Tentetnikov—a fortunate young fellow of some thirty-three years, and as yet an unmarried man.

But what manner of man, of what disposition, qualities, and character was he?—Ah, my lady readers, it is the neighbours, the neighbours, to whom you should put those questions. One neighbour, who came from that now disappearing line of retired, fire-breathing staff-officers, delivered himself of the following dismissive verdict: 'The most consummate swine!' A general, who lived ten versts away, declared: 'That young man is far from stupid, but he is too opinionated. I could be useful to him, because I have connections in St Petersburg, and even at...' The general did not complete his sentence. The local captain of police remarked: 'Him?—Ah yes, I shall be calling on him tomorrow to collect his tax arrears!' A peasant from his village, when asked what their master was like, found no answer. We may thus conclude that opinion of him was not favourable.

Speaking dispassionately, though, Andrei Ivanovich was not a bad man, he was simply what they call a fritterer: he frittered his life away. When there are already so many people in this world frittering away their lives, why should Tentetnikov not fritter his away too? Here, by way of illustration, is a day from his life, that the reader may judge for himself what his character was like and whether his life matched the beauty amidst which it was lived.

In the morning he awoke very late, and propping himself up, remained for a long time sitting on his bed, rubbing his eyes. These eyes, as ill luck would have it, were small, and therefore this rubbing operation continued for an uncommonly long time. Throughout this procedure his manservant Mikhailo stood at the door holding a wash-basin and a towel. The poor wretch would stand there an hour, even two, before retreating to the kitchen, and would then return to find his master still rubbing his eyes and sitting on the bed. Finally he would rise from the bed, wash his face, put on a dressing-gown and proceed to the drawing-room to drink tea, coffee, cocoa, and even milk fresh from the cow, sipping a little of everything, scattering breadcrumbs with gay abandon and shamelessly strewing pipe ash over everything. For two whole hours he would sit over his breakfast; as if this were not enough he would even take a cup of tea, by now quite cold, and move over to the window that faced the yard. The following scene was invariably played out before the window.

First of all Grigory, the house serf who served as pantryman, addressing himself to Perfilievna, the housekeeper, would bellow something along these lines:

'You despicable wretch, you piece of offal—you'd better keep your mouth shut, you vile creature.'

'How would you like one of these!' Perfilievna—or the piece of offal—would shout back, making a rude sign, for this wench was tough in her dealings with others, notwithstanding her fondness for fruit jellies and all manner of sweetmeats, which she kept carefully locked away.

'Huh!—you'll even lock horns with the bailiff, you worthless piece of chaff!' Grigory would bellow.

'Of course I will—the bailiff's as big a thief as you! Do you think the master doesn't know about you? Look—there he is: he hears everything.'

'Where's the master?'

'There he is, sitting by the window; he sees everything.'

True enough, the master was sitting by the window and could see everything.

To complete the mayhem, the urchin child of one of the servants, who had just been cuffed by its mother, would be bawling at the top of its voice; a borzoi hound, cowering in the corner, would start yelping and whining, after being scalded with boiling water which the cook had just flung out through the kitchen door. In a word, there was the most intolerable cacophony. The master saw and heard everything. And only when the din became so unbearable that it obstructed him even in his pursuit of idleness did he send to tell them to shout, bawl and yelp more quietly...

Two hours before luncheon Andrei Ivanovich would withdraw to his study to apply himself to a most serious project. This was a composition, which was to embrace the whole of Russia from all aspects: the civic, the political, the religious, and the philosophical, it was to solve the most complex tasks and problems posed by the age, and it was to determine with clarity its great future: in short, the very sort of undertaking so beloved of all men of the modern age. But for the time being this colossal undertaking went no further than mere contemplation; the pen was chewed, little drawings appeared on the paper, and then all this would be pushed to one side, a book would be taken up instead and it would remain in his hands right until luncheon was served. The reading of the book would continue throughout the meal—through the soup, the sauce, the roast, and even the dessert—so that some dishes grew cold while others remained quite untouched. After this he would sip a cup of coffee while smoking a pipe, and then play a game of chess against himself. As for how he passed the time until supper time—that, we must confess, is hard for us to say. It seems, simply doing nothing.

And that is how he spent his time, quite alone in the whole ⟨world⟩, this young man of thirty-two years, sitting at home in his dressing-gown, without a necktie. He did not feel like going for a stroll or a walk, he did not want to climb the stairs, he had no urge even to throw open the windows to let fresh air into the room, and the beautiful view of the village, on which no visitor could gaze with indifference, seemed not to exist for the owner.

From this the reader can see that Andrei Ivanovich Tentetnikov was a member of that tribe who are legion in Russia, and who go by the name of marmots, lie-abeds, lazybones, and the like.

Whether such characters are born like this or are formed later in life, as a consequence of the lamentable circumstances in which man finds himself, it is hard to say. I believe that, instead of seeking an answer, we should recount instead the story of the childhood and upbringing of Andrei Ivanovich.

It seemed that everything had conspired to ensure that great things would come of him. As a twelve-year-old boy, keen-witted, somewhat pensive, somewhat sickly, he wound up in a school whose then headmaster was a most exceptional man. The idol of his young charges, a wonder among pedagogues, the incomparable Aleksandr Petrovich* had the gift of being able to fathom the inner nature of men. How well he understood the different properties of his fellow Russian! How well he understood children! How he could move them! There was no mischief-maker who, upon wreaking some malefaction, did not appear before him of his own will and make a clean breast of everything. And it went further still: he would receive a stern ⟨reprimand⟩, but emerge from the headmaster's study not crestfallen, with his head held high. There was something about this man that said: 'Onwards! Get to your feet, quickly—it doesn't matter that you've stumbled.' He was wont to say: 'I ask you to use your mind, nothing more. Any boy who takes the time to determine how to use his mind will have no leisure for pranks: mischief must disappear by itself.' Indeed: the boys' inclination to mischief did just that. Any boy who made no effort to ⟨improve himself⟩ earned the contempt of his fellows. The most senior asses and fools were obliged to endure the most offensive names hurled at them by the most junior boys and dared not raise a finger in revenge.

'This is going too far!' objected many, 'You'll turn clever boys into arrogant men.'—'No, it's not too far,' he would say, 'I do not keep the useless ones for long; one year usually suffices for them. But for those who have promise I have quite another course.' It was quite true: all the more capable boys stuck with him for another year. There were many pranks he did not discourage, seeing in them the first stirrings of character and declaring that they were as necessary to him as rashes to a doctor: they enabled him to determine precisely what lay concealed within.

How all the boys loved him! No—not even their parents do children hold in such loving regard. No—not even in the years of mad infatuation does passion burn so intensely as that love which they bore ⟨him⟩. Until the end of their days, until the grave itself, his grateful wards would raise their glasses to their wondrous teacher— by then long in his own grave—on his every birthday, and they would pause, with eyes shut, and weep in his memory. The least word of encouragement from him would make them tremble with joy and anxiety, and fill them with ambition to outshine all their fellows. Those of limited ability did not stay long with him: for them the course he offered was a short one. But the talented were required to undergo from him a twofold education. His top class, which was for the chosen few, was quite unlike any class in any other school. Only here did he ask of his pupil what others so unjustly ⟨demand⟩ of young children: that high level of intelligence which is able not to mock and yet to endure every mockery, to suffer a fool without irritation and not to lose one's temper, never, on any ⟨account⟩, to seek revenge and to preserve a proud tranquility and imperturbability of spirit. Every known technique capable of turning boys into men was here applied in practice and he constantly experimented with new techniques. How well he knew the science of life!

He engaged few teachers: most of the subjects he taught himself. He was able, without recourse to pedantic terminology, to bombastic constructions and opinions, to convey the very essence of a science, so that even the youngest pupil could grasp precisely why he needed to study it. †Of the sciences he selected only those which could shape a person into a responsible citizen of his country. In most of his lectures he told his listeners what lay in store for a young man and he was able ⟨so vividly⟩ to describe the full scope and compass of their future careers that, as they sat there on the school bench, they were transported heart and mind to the service that still awaited them. He kept nothing from them—all the disappointments and obstacles that could possibly lie in a man's path, all the temptations and blandishments which faced him: he displayed them in their nakedness, concealing nothing. He knew it all, just as if he himself had served in all professions and offices. And how strange! Whether because their own ambition was so fiercely kindled, or whether because there was something in the eyes of this extraordinary tutor that exhorted these youths: 'Forward!'—a word so familiar to the Russian ear, working such wonders on the sensitive mind within—but, from the very beginning, that youth would seek out only the hardest challenges, eager to act only where things were difficult, where the obstacles were more daunting, where he had to display greater strength of spirit.† Few completed this course, but these few were men properly tempered in the smoke of battle. Once in the service they were able to hold the most precarious positions where many others, far cleverer than they, either quit their jobs altogether because of some trifling personal unpleasantness, or, having grown torpid and dull-witted, wound up in the clutches of bribe-takers and knaves. His alumni did not stumble, however: made wiser by their knowledge of man and his soul, they were able to exercise a strong moral influence even on their dissolute fellows.

The ardent heart of our ambitious young hero beat more eagerly at the mere thought that one day he would find himself in this select company. For what, indeed, could have been better for our Tentetnikov than to have such a tutor. But—as ill luck would have it—just as he had been transferred to this elite group—the very thing he had so fervently desired—when their extraordinary tutor suddenly ⟨died⟩. What a bitter blow this was to him, what a terrible first loss! He felt as if ⟨. . .⟩. Everything changed in the school: †Aleksandr Petrovich's place was taken by a certain Fyodor Ivanovich. He at once instituted a kind of superficial order; he started requiring of the children what should only realistically be expected of adults. He imagined he saw something unbridled in their free and easy manner and, almost as if to spite his predecessor, he declared on his very first day that to him intelligence and achievement meant nothing, that he would have regard only for good ⟨conduct⟩.† Oddly enough, good conduct was the one thing Fyodor Ivanovich had never achieved: the pupils engaged in secret mischief. By day all was decorous and orderly, but by night they went on wild sprees.

Something went awry in the classrooms as well. New teachers were engaged, with new opinions and new points of view on things. They dizzied their listeners with a mass of new words and terms; in their expositions they demonstrated the logical connection and their own enthusiasm for the subject, but—alas!—there was no life in the study itself. On their lips dead sciences remained so much dead matter. In short, everything was turned on its head. All respect for authority and power was lost: the pupils mocked the tutors and masters, they started to call the headmaster Fedka,* Bun-face, and various other names. Matters got so out of hand that many boys had to be suspended and expelled. In two short years the school changed beyond recognition.

Andrei Ivanovich was of a quiet disposition. He was not tempted by the nocturnal orgies of his fellows, who had secured the services of a young lady right beneath the windows of the headmaster's residence, nor by their blasphemy of everything holy simply because the school chaplain was not the brightest of priests. No: even in his sleep his soul heeded its heavenly origins. None of this could tempt him—still he lost heart. His ambition had been aroused, but he was offered neither vocation nor career to pursue. Better that it had never been aroused at all! He listened to the new professors ranting on their rostrums, and he recalled their departed tutor, who had been able to talk intelligibly, without ranting. He attended lessons in every imaginable subject—medicine, chemistry, philosophy, even law, and the universal history of mankind, addressed on such a vast scale that in three years the professor had merely covered the introduction and the growth of the *Gemeinde* in one or two German towns— the Lord only knows what lectures he heard! Yet all this remained in a hideous jumble in his head. His own native wit told him at least that this was not the way to be taught—yet he knew not how it should be done. He often recalled Aleksandr Petrovich, and such sadness overcame him that he became quite disconsolate in his misery.

But youth is lucky in that it has before it a future. As the day of graduation drew near, his heartbeat quickened. He would say to himself: 'After all, this is not life—not yet, this is only the preparation for life: real life begins in the service. That's where you can achieve great things.' And, without so much as a glance at the beautiful view which so astounded every guest and visitor, without even paying his last respects at his parents' grave, he charged off, like all ambitious men, to St Petersburg, the city to which our ardent youth flock from all four corners of Russia—thither they flock to serve, to shine, to seek promotion, or merely to scratch at the surface of society and the deceptive education, pallid and cold as ice, that it seems to offer. Any stirrings of ambition in Andrei Ivanovich were, however, arrested at the very outset by his uncle, Actual State Councillor Onufry Ivanovich.* He declared that the most important thing was a good hand, and that a man's career must begin with the study of calligraphy.

With great difficulty, and with his uncle's patronage, he finally secured a position in a government department. When he was first ushered into the brightly lit hall, with its gleaming parquet floor and varnished desks, which looked for all the world as if those seated within were the supreme dignitaries of the empire and that the destiny of this empire lay in their hands, and ⟨he⟩ saw the legions of handsome gentlemen scribbling and scratching away with their quills, their heads inclined to one side, and when he himself was thus seated and then and there instructed to copy a document—as ill luck would have it, of a rather insignificant tenor: the correspondence concerned a sum of three roubles, and had been continuing for some six months—he, callow youth that he was, felt himself overcome by a most singular sensation, just as if, for some misdeed, he had been demoted from the uppermost to the very bottommost class. The gentlemen sitting around him looked so like schoolboys. To complete the similarity, some were reading stupid foreign novels, concealed between the large sheets of the files on which, purportedly, they were working, and they would give a start every time their supervisor appeared. It all struck him as so odd: that the work he had done at school had been so much more meaningful than this, that his preparation for the service had been better than the service itself. †He began to wish he had never left school, and suddenly he saw in his mind's eye Aleksandr Petrovich, as clearly as if he stood before him in the flesh, and the tears welled up in his eyes.† The room started to spin, desks and officials swam together, and, in his sudden dizziness, he almost fell off his chair. 'No,' he said to himself, returning to his senses, 'I shall apply myself to my work, however pettifogging it might at first seem.' Thus, with a heavy heart and spirit, he resolved to serve after the example of others.

Yet is there any place where no pleasures are to be found? They exist even in St Petersburg, notwithstanding its severe and gloomy aspect. An angry, thirty-degree frost may lash the streets, a witch-like snowstorm may wail the fiendish howls of the icy north, sweeping across the pavements, blinding the eyes of passers-by, dusting the fur collars of their coats, powdering the moustaches of the men and the muzzles of beasts, but somewhere high up, through this welter of snowflakes, a little window shines welcomingly, even if it is on the fourth floor; in a cosy little room, lit by thin, stearin candles, to the hissing of a samovar, a conversation is in progress, warming both heart and soul, a radiant page of the work of an inspired Russian poet is being read, of one of those poets with which God has so richly endowed His beloved Russia, and a youthful heart palpitates with an exalted ardour, unsurpassed even by those warmed by the southern sun.

Soon Tentetnikov grew accustomed to the service, only it did not become the main activity and purpose of his life, as he had originally supposed it would, but something of secondary importance. It served to divide up his time, causing him to cherish more dearly the minutes which remained. His uncle, the actual state councillor, was already beginning to think that some good might come of the nephew after all, when the nephew suddenly went and ruined everything.

Andrei Ivanovich's abundant circle of friends included two men who were what one would describe as embittered people. They were specimens of that strange, restless genus who not only cannot bear injustice with equanimity, they cannot bear anything at all that appears to them as unjust. Essentially kind men, but disorderly in their own conduct, they demand the indulgence of others but are themselves filled with intolerance. Their fiery speeches and their image of noble indignation against society had a most pronounced effect on our young man, arousing his impatience and irritability, and causing him to remark all those trifles to which previously he had paid no heed. He suddenly took a dislike to Fyodor Fyodorovich Lenitsyn, chief of one of the departments accommodated in those magnificent halls. He discovered in him a multitude of faults. He imagined that, in conversation with his own superiors, Lenitsyn would be all sweetness and sugar, and then, as he addressed a subordinate, pure vinegar; that, like all petty-minded people, he singled out for reprimand anyone who forgot to offer him their congratulations on feastdays, that he exacted petty revenge on those whose names were not to be found on the commissionaire's list of those who had called to pay him their respects.* All this led him to develop an entirely irrational loathing for the man. An evil spirit urged him to do something nasty to Fyodor Fyodorovich and, with a particular relish, he sought the opportunity for this. One day, at last, such an opportunity came and he spoke to him so abruptly that he was ordered by his superiors either to apologize or to resign from the service. He tendered his resignation.

His uncle, the actual state councillor, called on him in a state of alarm and pleaded with him: 'In the name of all that's holy, my dear Andrei Ivanovich! What are you doing? To resign from a career in which you have made such a good start just because your chief wasn't entirely to your liking! My dear fellow! What do you think you're doing? Let's face it, if such things really mattered, no one would remain in the service. Think again, my boy, have some sense! Put aside your pride and your vanity, go and make your peace with him!'

'That is not the point, Uncle,' said the nephew. 'It's not hard for me to ask his pardon. I'm in the wrong: he is my superior and I should not have spoken to him thus. But the point is this: you have forgotten that I have another service; I have three hundred souls, an estate in complete disrepair, and a manager who's a fool. It is small loss to the state if my place in the chancellery is taken by another, to sit there copying out papers, but it is a great loss if three hundred men do not pay their taxes. You may think what you like, but I am a landowner: and that, I might say, is no idle calling. If I can improve the lot of the peasants in my charge, can look after them and keep them from misfortune, and can offer the state three hundred of its fittest, most sober, and hard-working subjects—will my service be less worthy than that of some department chief by the name of Lenitsyn?'

The actual state councillor stood there gaping in disbelief. He had not expected such an oration. After a few moments' thought he ventured as follows: 'But all the same... all the same, how can you?... How can you bury yourself in the country? What sort of society will you find amongst ⟨peasants⟩? Here at least, as you walk down the street, you may encounter a general or a prince. If you wish you may stroll past some sort of... well... you know, and there's gas lighting, this is industrial Europe; but down there all you will encounter will be the odd peasant, or his wench. Why condemn yourself to that, why condemn yourself to a lifetime of ignorance?'

†But the uncle's arts of persuasion were wasted on his nephew.† He now saw his village as a carefree refuge, inspiring thought and reflections, and the sole arena of purposeful activity. He had already unearthed all the latest books on agriculture. A week or two after this conversation he found himself nearing those places where he had spent his childhood, in the vicinity of that enchanting corner which no guest or visitor could praise too highly. A new feeling awoke ⟨within him⟩. Old sensations, which had long lain suppressed, stirred anew in his breast. Many of the places he had utterly forgotten and he now regarded them curiously, like a stranger beholding a splendid view for the first time.

And then, for no apparent reason, he felt his heartbeat suddenly quicken. When the road plunged through a narrow ravine into the thick of a huge, overgrown forest and he saw above and below, towering above his head and stretching away beneath his feet, those 300-year-old oaks, with a girth it would take three men to reach round, growing hugger-mugger with silver-firs, elms, and black poplar, taller than the highest poplar, and when to his question 'Whose forest is this?' the answer came: 'Tentetnikov's'; when, as they emerged from the forest, the road swept through meadows, past aspen groves, young and old willows and osiers, with a view of high ground stretching away in the distance, then bridged one and the same river twice in different places, leaving it now to the left, now to the right, and to his question 'Whose pastures and water-meadows are these?' the answer came: 'Tentetnikov's'; when then the road soared uphill and ran across an elevated tableland with—on the one side—unharvested fields of wheat, rye, and barley, and—on the other—all those places through which they had already driven and which were now seen in the foreshortened distance, and when, as darkness gathered around them, the road entered and then ran along beneath the shade of spreading trees, scattered here and there over the green carpet right up to the village itself, and the carved peasant cottages and the red-roofs of the stone farm buildings, the large manor house, and the ancient church flashed before them; when his ardently beating heart knew even without asking in which place they had arrived, the sensations which all this time had been mounting up within his breast finally burst from him in these words: 'Well, have I not been a fool until now? Fate appointed me the proprietor of an earthly paradise, and I chose instead the vile bondage of scribbling dead papers! After studying, acquiring education and enlightenment, amassing a store of the very knowledge which is necessary for the dissemination of good deeds among my subordinates, for the improvement of an entire region, for the performance of the many varied duties of a landowner, who is at one and the same time judge, and steward, and guardian of the peace—to entrust this domain to an ignoramus of a bailiff! And to prefer for myself the position of proxy for people I have never clapped eyes on, settling their administrative affairs, when I knew nothing of their character, nor of their qualities—to prefer to the task of administering my own real estate the fantastical, paper administration of provinces thousands of versts away, in which I had never set foot and where I could hope only to accomplish untold blunders and idiocies.'

In the mean time another spectacle awaited him. When they learnt about the arrival of their master, the peasants gathered by the porch. †The bonnets, headscarves, kerchiefs,* homespun coats, caftans, and picturesque spade beards sported by the colourful populace crowded around him. When the words rang out: 'Our provider! You've remembered us...' and the old men and women wept without restraint as they recalled his own grandfather, and his great-grandfather before him, he too could no longer restrain his tears. 'So much love! And for what?' he asked himself. 'For having never visited them, having never attended to their needs!' And he made a solemn vow to share with them their toil and their occupation.†

Thus Tentetnikov took up the reins of his estate. He at once reduced the corvée,* cut the number of days the peasants worked for their owner, and increased the time they had for their own work. †He sacked the fool of a bailiff.† He took an interest in everything himself, and showed his face in the fields, on the threshing floor, in the barns, at the flour-mills, on the wharf, and at the loading and casting off of the barges and wherries, until finally even the more slothful peasants grew disquieted. But this did not continue for long. His peasants were canny and they soon caught on that, although their master might be alert and eager to take on as much as he could, he still had not worked out where to start or how to do it, and he spoke in too highbrow a fashion, quite above the peasants' heads. The upshot was that, while master and peasant did not exactly fail to understand each other, they were unable to get attuned, they simply could not hit one and the same note. Tentetnikov started to observe that on the estate lands the crops somehow did not do as well as on the peasants' own. They were sown earlier and ripened later, and yet the serfs seemed to be working well: he supervised them in person and even gave orders that they each receive a mug of vodka for their hard work. The peasants' rye had long been ready for the scythe, their oats were dropping from the stalk, their millet clustering thickly, while in his fields the stalks of the wheat were only beginning to thicken, the buds of the future ears scarcely visible. In a word, the master started to notice that, despite all their new privileges, his peasants were quite simply cheating him.

He tried to reproach them, but he received the following reply:

'Your honour, how could we not care for our master's good? You could see for yourself how hard we worked when we were ploughing and sowing—and you gave us a mug of vodka each.' How could he argue against this?

'But then why has it turned out so badly?' he persisted.

'Heaven knows! Maybe worms ate through the roots, and then, it's been that sort of summer: no rains at all.'

But the master could see that on the peasants' plots the worms had not eaten through the roots, and even the rain seemed to be falling in a strange, piecemeal pattern: plenty for the peasants and nary a drop on the master's fields.

He had an even harder job sorting things out with the women. They kept asking to be excused from field work, complaining that the corvée was excessively onerous. It was so strange: he had abolished all contributions of flax, berries, mushrooms, or nuts, he had cut their other labours by half, thinking that the women would employ this time to good purpose in the house, making clothes for their menfolk and tending their vegetables. Nothing of the sort. Idleness, brawling, scandal-mongering, and quarrelling became so much the order of the day among the fair sex that their husbands came pleading to him: 'Master, please—get that devil woman off my back! She's a demon—she'll be the death of me!'

Sometimes, with sinking heart, he steeled himself to take severe measures. But how could he be severe? The woman herself would appear before him, employing all her woman's guile, whimpering and wailing, sickly and diseased, and wrapped in such wretched, filthy rags, God knows where she had found them. 'Go away, go away, just get out of my sight, for God's sake!' poor Tentetnikov would say, only to see how the sick woman, once she had passed through the gates, grappled with a neighbour over something like a turnip and pummelled her oppenent's sides with heftier blows than many a strong man could deliver. He had the idea of setting up a sort of school for them, but this proved such a fiasco that he quite lost heart and wished he had never even thought of it. A school, imagine! No one had the time for schooling: from the age of ten the boys were already helping out in most trades and that was where they received their schooling.

In the settlement of disputes and other matters of arbitration all those subtle points of jurisprudence through which he had been guided by his philosophically inclined professors availed him precisely nothing. The one party lied and the other party lied and the devil alone could tell who was right and who was wrong. Soon he saw that simple understanding of his fellow-man was of far more use than all the subtleties of his textbooks of law and philosophy; and he also saw that there was something lacking in himself, but the good Lord only knew what this was.

And there came to pass what frequently occurs in such cases: the peasant no longer knew his master, nor the master his peasant; the peasant showed his worst side to his master, and the master his worst side to the peasant; finally, ⟨he lost⟩ all his zest for management of his estates. He now stood by and gazed at the farmwork with a vacant stare. Regardless what activity was in progress before his very eyes—whether it was the quiet swish of the scythes, or the stacking of haystacks, or the gathering of wheat into sheaves, or some other rustic task—these eyes sought objects further afield; if the work was afoot in the distance, they sought objects near at hand, or gazed to one side, at a bend ⟨in the river⟩, along the banks of which strutted a red-billed, red-legged wader—we mean the bird, of course, not a man. He would watch intently as ⟨this wader⟩ caught a fish and held it crossways in its bill, as if debating whether or not to swallow it—and all the while staring fixedly a little way down the river, where another wader could be seen, as yet with no prey, but staring back just as fixedly at the wader which had caught the fish. Or, with deeply furrowed brow and head raised slightly aloft, gazing at the vault of the sky, he would surrender to his sense of smell, breathing in the fragrance of the fields, and to his hearing, marvelling at the voices of that airborne, singing populace, when from all sides, from the skies above and the earth below, it blends into a single mellifluous choir, not one note clashing with another. The quail taps in the rye; the corncrake crakes in the grass; above, the soaring linnet twitters and chatters; a young lamb raises its bleating into the air; a skylark trills* as its disappears into the bright light; and, like the peal of trumpets, the air fills with the cries of cranes, sweeping by in long, V-shaped formations, high in the heavens above. Everything around turns to sound and sends back its response. O, Creator! How splendid is Your world, deep in the countryside, far from the vile highroads* and towns.

Yet even this palled in the end. Soon he stopped visiting the fields at all, and instead would remain sitting in his rooms, refusing even to receive the bailiff with his reports. Previously a neighbour would occasionally call on him, perhaps the retired lieutenant of Hussars, an inveterate pipe-smoker and smoke-cured to the bone, or the superannuated student with his radical views and wisdom garnered from pamphlets and newspapers of the day. But this too grew tedious to him. He thought their conversation superficial; their breezy European manner, accompanied by slaps on the knee and other marks of familiarity, now seemed to him too bold and in rather bad taste.

He resolved to break off his acquaintance with them, and did so in a fairly abrupt manner. To be precise, when Varvar Nikolaevich Vishnepokromov,* representative of that now dying breed of fire-breathing colonels, a man skilled in conducting the most pleasant conversations on all matters superficial, and at the same time a leading exponent of the latest schools of thought, called on him for the express purpose of talking to his heart's content about everything under the sun, touching on politics, and philosophy, and literature, and morality, and even the state of the economy in England, he sent word that he was not at home, and at the same time was careless enough to show himself at the window. The eyes of guest and host met. The one, naturally enough, muttered through his teeth: 'Swine!' The other responded with some similar epithet. And there the acquaintance ended.

From that day on no one called on him again. He was quite content with this and devoted his time to fashioning in his mind his great composition on Russia. The reader has already had occasion to see the manner in which this composition was fashioned. A strange, disordered order was established. It would not, however, be true to say that there were no moments when he seemed to bestir himself from his slumbers. When the post brought newspapers and journals, and he saw in print the name of some former comrade, who had already gained advancement in a prominent area of government service or had contributed splendidly to the cause of science and universal education, a quiet, secret sadness crept upon his heart and a remorse, unspoken, sorrowful, silent, at his own inactivity forced its way into his mind. At such moments his life seemed repellent and quite odious to him. With remarkable vividness his lost schooldays reappeared before him, and he suddenly saw Aleksandr Petrovich as in real life... The tears burst from his eyes ⟨and he continued to sob all day.⟩

What did this sobbing mean? Was this how his ailing soul manifested the mournful secret of its ailment?—that the high-minded, inner man that had begun to form within him had failed to develop and grow strong; that, untested in his youth by struggle against adversity, he had not attained that higher state where he could rise and gain strength through the surmounting of barriers and obstacles; that, by melting like heated metal, his rich store of lofty feelings had not been properly tempered and hardened, and that his remarkable tutor had died too early for him, so that there was now no one in this world capable of rousing and stirring to action his forces, shattered by incessant vacillation, and his weak will, bereft of its resilience, no one to call out in a loud, rousing voice: 'Forward!'—the command that the Russian longs to hear everywhere, at every level of life, whatever his rank or estate or ambition?

Where is that man who in the native tongue of our Russian soul could utter to us that all-powerful word: 'Forward'?—who, knowing all the resources and properties and the full depth of our nature, with one magical wave of his hand could direct us to a higher life? With what tears, with what love would the grateful Russian repay him! †But one century succeeds another and all succumbs to the shameful indolence and mindless occupations of the callow youth, and yet God deigns not to give us a man capable of uttering that word!†

There was, however, one circumstance that nearly roused Tentetnikov and nearly wrought a complete transformation of his character. There occurred something akin to love, but here, too, all somehow came to naught. In the vicinity, some ten versts from his village, lived a general, who, as we have seen, expressed a less than totally favourable opinion of Tentetnikov. The general lived as befits a general, entertaining on the grand scale, always pleased when the neighbours called to pay their respects, whilst he himself did not pay visits, spoke in a hoarse voice, read books, and had †a daughter, a strange and most unusual creature. There ⟨was⟩ something vital about her, like life itself. Her name was Ulinka. Her upbringing had been most singular. She had been tutored by an English governess, who knew no word of Russian. She had lost her mother while still a child. Her father had no time to spend with her. This was perhaps just as well for, loving his daughter to distraction, he might only have spoilt her. It is uncommonly difficult to paint her portrait.† A child reared at liberty, she was the very embodiment of wilfulness. Any person seeing how she knitted her fair brow in sudden anger, or how hotly she argued with her father, would have thought her the most capricious creature alive. Her anger was aroused, however, only when she heard of someone being treated unjustly or with malice. But she would never grow angry, or pick quarrels on her own account, and never sought to justify herself. Furthermore, her anger would pass at once if she saw that the person against whom it was directed was himself suffering, †and she would readily throw him her purse, with all it contained, without giving it a moment's thought.†

She was so impulsive that, when she spoke, everything in her— her face, the tone of her voice, the movements of her hands— seemed to fly after her thoughts; even the very folds of her dress seemed to move in the same direction, and it was as though she herself would at any moment fly off in the wake of her own words. There was nothing secretive about her. She had no fear of speaking her mind before anyone, and when she resolved to speak no power on earth could stop her. She had such a blithe and carefree walk, so charming and unusual, unique to her alone, that everyone would involuntarily step aside to let her pass. The malevolent became meek in her company, and held their peace; in her presence, the uninhibited and glib would become tongue-tied, while the most diffident would chatter away with her as never before with anyone else, and from the first minutes of conversation they would feel that they had known her once somewhere before, that they had seen these features before, perhaps in the distant days of their childhood, at home, on a cheerful evening, as they had frolicked happily among a crowd of children, and afterwards, for a long time to come, this stage of life, this time of sobriety and good sense would seem tedious to them.

†This was precisely how it happened between her and Tentetnikov. A new, inexplicable feeling entered his soul. His tedious life was brightened for a moment.†

At first, the general received Tentetnikov fairly well, and with courtesy; but they were quite unable to get along with each other. Their conversations always ended in an argument that left an unpleasant feeling on both sides. The general did not like to be contradicted and opposed, while Tentetnikov, for his part, was also touchy by nature. But for the sake of the daughter he forgave the father much, and the peace was kept between them until two female relations came on a visit to the general, †the Countess Boldyreva and the Princess Yuzyakina, both former ladies-in-waiting under the previous tsar,† yet ladies who had preserved certain connections in that area and, accordingly, before whom the general was somewhat inclined to grovel.

It seemed to Tentetnikov that, from the very day of their arrival, the general's attitude towards him became somehow colder, he barely noticed him or treated him as if he were a person of no consequence; addressing him in a rather disdainful manner: 'I say, young chap', and 'Listen here, my good fellow', and even employing terms of great familiarity. In the end Andrei Ivanovich burst with indignation. Gritting his teeth and forcibly restraining his wrath, he still had the presence of mind to say, in a most respectful and soft voice, while angry blotches rose on his face and his blood seethed within him:

'I must express my gratitude to you, general, for the favour you bestow on me. By addressing me with such familiarity, you invite me into the most intimate friendship, obliging me to address you with equal familiarity. But permit me to observe that I cannot ignore the difference between our ages, which prohibits such familiar intercourse between us'.

The general was discomfited. Gathering his thoughts and words, he started to say, albeit in rather an incoherent way, that Andrei Ivanovich had misunderstood him, that an old man could sometimes be permitted to address a young man thus, in such familiar terms (he did not say a word about his own rank).

Naturally enough, their acquaintance ended there and then, and the romance was nipped in the bud. The light which had flashed for a brief moment before Andrei Ivanovich grew dim and faded and the twilight which took its place became ever more gloomy. The life of utter inactivity and lying abed, observed by the reader at the beginning of our chapter, returned. Disorder and filth reigned in his house. The floor brush lay for entire days on end in the middle of the room, together with the sweepings. His breeches found their way into the drawing-room. On the ornamented table before the settee lay a filthy pair of braces, as if set out as refreshment for a guest. His life became so insignificant and somnolent that not only did his own house servants lose all respect for their master, even his chickens were ready to start pecking him. Taking up his quill, he would spend hours on end listlessly fashioning little floral designs, houses, huts, carts, or troikas. But sometimes, in moments of total oblivion, his pen would move of its own will, without the owner's knowledge, and trace the outline of a small head with delicate features, with a quick, searching gaze and a wave of upswept hair—and to his astonishment there would appear before his eyes a portrait of that creature whose portrait could be painted by no living artist. Then his heart would grow still sadder and, confirmed in his belief that there was no happiness on this earth, he would remain taciturn and still more out of sorts for the rest of the day.

Such was the state of Andrei Ivanovich Tentetnikov's soul when, one day, in accordance with his custom, he took his seat by the window to gaze vacantly into the distance, but heard neither Grigory nor Perfilievna; in the yard outside there was a certain amount of commotion and activity. The kitchen boy and the scullery maid ran to open the gates, and in the gateway there appeared an equine ensemble exactly like those sculpted or painted on triumphal arches: a muzzle to the right, a muzzle to the left, and a muzzle in the middle. Above these, on the coach-box, sat a coachman and, behind him, a lackey in a loose frock-coat, fastened round the waist with a handkerchief.* Behind them sat a gentleman in a peaked cap and greatcoat, with a particoloured muffler round his neck. When the carriage swung round before the porch it transpired that it was nothing other than a light sprung chaise. A gentleman of an exceptionally respectable mien leapt on to the porch with the alacrity and agility almost of a military man.

Andrei Ivanovich was stricken with alarm. He took the visitor for an official from the government. We should say here that, in his youth, he had been implicated in a certain imprudent affair. A couple of philosophically inclined hussars, their heads crammed with ideas from pamphlets, in consort with a student who had abandoned his studies and a bankrupt gambler, founded some sort of philanthropic society, under the administration of an old rogue, a man who was at once a freemason and gamester, but also the most silver-tongued of orators. The society was formed with the broadest purpose: to secure lasting happiness for the whole of mankind, from the banks of the Thames to the shores of Kamchatka. An enormous sum of money was required for this, and the donations which flowed in from their generous members were astounding in their magnitude. The final destination of all this money was something known only to the head administrator. Andrei Ivanovich was drawn into this society by two friends who belonged to that genus of men disappointed by life; at heart they were kind people but they had drunk so many toasts to science, enlightenment, and progress, that they had become inveterate drunkards. He soon regretted his rash decision and removed himself from their company. But the society had already become enmeshed in certain other activities, of a kind not altogether seemly for a member of the landed gentry, so that subsequently the interest of the police was aroused... It is therefore small wonder that, although he had broken off all ties with the great benefactors of humankind, Tentetnikov still could not quite recover his peace of mind. His conscience was not entirely easy. Thus it was not without some trepidation that he now stared at the opening door.

His fear subsided at once, however, when the guest gave a low bow, executed with astounding adroitness, all the while preserving a respectful attitude with his head slightly inclined to one side. He explained in a few short but purposeful words that, for a long time, he had been travelling about Russia, urged on both by his needs and by curiosity; that our nation abounded in remarkable objects, not to mention the abundance of its trades and the variety of its soils; that he had been attracted by the picturesque setting of Tentetnikov's village; that, notwithstanding the picturesque setting, he still would not have presumed to disturb his host with his untimely visit had there not been a slight accident with his chaise, occasioned by the spring torrents and poor roads. That, despite all this—and even if there had been no accident with the chaise—he still would not have been able to deny himself the pleasure of calling in person to pay his respects.

When he finished his speech, the guest scraped his foot in a most charming and agreeable manner; the foot was shod in a fashionable patent-leather ankle-boot; then, notwithstanding his corpulence, he at once skipped backwards a little way with the lightness of an India-rubber ball.

Feeling greatly reassured, Andrei Ivanovich concluded that the visitor must be some scholarly professor of enquiring mind, travelling the length and breadth of Russia in search of certain plants or even minerals. He at once announced his willingness to assist in every possible way; he offered the services of his craftsmen, wheelwrights, and blacksmiths to repair the chaise; he besought him to make himself comfortable and to feel quite at home; he seated him in a large Voltaire ⟨chair⟩* and prepared to listen to his discourse on matters scholarly and scientific.

The guest, however, touched more on events of the inner world. He likened his life to a barque tossed on the seas and buffeted everywhither by treacherous winds; he mentioned that he had often been forced to change his position and duties, that he had suffered much for the truth, that even his very life had, on numerous occasions, been in danger from his enemies, and he recounted much else in the same vein, from which Tentetnikov could see that his guest was more of a practical man. By way of concluding his account he took out a white lawn handkerchief and blew his nose more loudly than Andrei Ivanovich had ever heard any nose blown before.* It sometimes happens that, in an orchestra, there is a rogue of a trumpet like that, and when it emits its blast you imagine the noise comes not from the orchestra but from inside your own ear. It was precisely such a sound that rang out through the newly awakened rooms of the slumbering house, and this was immediately followed by the fragrant aroma of eau de Cologne, invisibly diffused by an adroit flick of the lawn handkerchief.

The reader has perhaps already divined that the guest was none other than our honoured friend Pavel Ivanovich Chichikov, whom we abandoned so long ago. He had aged a little: evidently, the intervening time had not passed for him without its storms and upheavals. Even the tailcoat on his back appeared to have aged and grown shabby, and the chaise, the coachman, the manservant, the horses, the harness—they were all somehow a little battered and worn. It seemed that his finances, too, were in an unenviable state. But the expression on his face, his decorum, and courtesy were all perfectly intact. He had grown even more agreeable in his gestures and turns of phrase, he tucked one leg even more adroitly behind the other when seating himself in an armchair, there was still greater softness in the delivery of his speeches, more circumspection in his words and expressions, more skill in the way he held himself, and more tact in all respects. His collars and shirt-fronts were purer and whiter than the driven snow and, although he had just disembarked from his travels, no speck of dust had alighted on his tailcoat: he could have been dressed for a birthday dinner! His cheeks and chin were so smoothly shaved that only a blind man could have failed to marvel at their agreeable plumpness and rotundity.

A transformation took place in the house. That half of it which hitherto had languished in a state of blindness, behind shuttered windows, suddenly regained its sight and was filled with light. The visitor's things were set out in the newly lighted rooms and soon everything was arranged as follows: the room that was to be his bedroom accommodated those items essential for his night toilet; the room designated to be his study... But first it should be known that this room contained three tables: the first a writing table, facing the settee; the second a card table, before a mirror; the third a corner-table, in the corner, positioned between the door to the bedroom and the door to a room no longer lived in and used for storing broken furniture, a room which now served as an antechamber but which, for above a year, no one had entered. It was on this table that the clothes removed from the valise had been placed, to wit: a pair of trousers to go with his tailcoat, a pair of new trousers, a pair of greyish trousers, two velvet waistcoats and two satin waistcoats, and a frock-coat. All this was heaped into a pyramid and covered with a silk kerchief. In another corner, between the door and the window, †his boots were set out in a row: boots that were not quite brand-new, boots that were still brand-new, patent-leather ankle-boots, and bedroom slippers. These were also modestly curtained off with a silk kerchief—just as if there were no boots there at all.

On the writing table the following disposition of effects could, very shortly, be observed: first, the little box, then a jar of eau de Cologne, a calendar and two novels, both volume two.† The clean linen was stowed away in the chest of drawers already in the bedroom; but the linen that needed laundering was tied into a bundle and stuffed under the bed. The valise, once it had been emptied, was also shoved under the bed. The guest's sabre, which had accompanied him on his journey to instil fear into highway robbers, was likewise borne into the bedroom, and there it hung on a nail within reach of the bed. Both rooms now looked extraordinarily clean and tidy. Nowhere was there a scrap of paper, or a feather, or a speck of dust to be seen. The very air had been somehow ennobled: it was filled with the pleasant odour of a healthy, fresh man, who did not wear the same linen too long, visited the bathhouse regularly, and rubbed himself down with a wet sponge on Sundays. A short-lived attempt had been made by the odour pertaining to his manservant Petrushka to establish itself in the vestibule, but Petrushka was promptly banished to the kitchen, as was right and fitting.

For the first few days Andrei Ivanovich feared for his independence, lest his guest should somehow or other fetter him and inhibit him by making changes to the manner of his life, and lest the happy routine of his day be disrupted—but his fears were unfounded. Our Pavel Ivanovich displayed remarkable flexibility in his capacity to adapt to everything. He expressed approval of his host's life of philosophical leisure, declaring that it would ensure him a very long life. On the question of seclusion he acquitted himself most felicitously, averring that it nourished great ideas in a man. Casting a look at the library and expressing his praise of books in general, he went on to observe that they saved man from indolence. He remarks were laconic, but always to the point.

As far as his actions were concerned, he conducted himself still more appositely. His appearances were timely and so were his departures; he did not weary his host with questions when the latter was in an uncommunicative mood; it gave him pleasure to play chess, it gave him equal pleasure to sit in silence. When host diverted himself with the production of billowing clouds of pipe smoke, guest, who did not smoke a pipe, devised for himself a corresponding pastime: he would, for example, retrieve his black and silver snuff-box from his pocket and, holding it firmly between the thumb and finger of his left hand, spin it swiftly round with a finger of his right hand, just like the earth spinning on its axis, or he would simply drum on its lid with his fingers, whistling in accompaniment. In short, he did not in any way impose on his host. 'This is the first time I have met a man,' Tentetnikov would say to himself, 'with whom it is possible to live. It is an art which few of us possess. There is amongst us a sufficiency of clever men, well-educated men, good men, but as for men who are constantly agreeable, constantly equable in character, men with whom one can live one's entire life and never quarrel—I very much doubt you would find many like that!' Such was Tentetnikov's assessment of his guest.

Chichikov, for his own part, was delighted to sojourn for a while with so serene and peaceable a host. He had grown weary of the gypsy life. To have a little rest, if only for a month, in a gracious village, with a view of fields and, in the air, the advent of spring, was of benefit even from the haemorrhoidal point of view. A better haven of rest would be hard to find. Spring, delayed so long by the severe cold, at last burst on the land in all its beauty and on all sides life stirred afresh. The forest glades were bright with the blue of the spring sky, and the dandelions glowed yellow against the fresh emerald green of the new leaves; the lilac-pink anemones gently dipped their tender heads. Swarms of midges and clouds of insects hovered above the marshes; water spiders skated after them in swift pursuit; birds of every hue and feather gathered in the dry rushes beyond. All these creatures crowded together, ⟨to gaze⟩ more closely at one another. Of an instant, the earth was filled with life, the forests and meadows awoke. The villagers danced and sang in celebration and gave free rein to their revelry. What brightness there was in the greenery! What freshness on the air! What melodious birdsong in the orchards! The paradise, joy, and exultation of all things! The countryside reverberated and sang as if at a wedding feast.

Chichikov took many walks. There was boundless scope for these walks, endless grounds to explore. Sometimes he directed his steps along the flat tableland that overlooked the valleys stretching beneath, in which there still remained great lakes from the floodwaters, among which the still leafless forests loomed darkly, like islands; at other times he would stray deep into the wilds, plunging into the wooded ravines, where the trees, weighed down with the heavy nests of birds, grew densely together †and where the sky was darkened by great flocks of ravens, cawing as they flew hither and thither.† Once the ground dried underfoot, he was able to make his way to the quayside, from which the first boats, laden with peas, barley, and wheat, were being launched on the spring waters, while the water crashed down on the mill wheels with a deafening roar and compelled them back into operation. ⟨He⟩ set out for the fields to watch the first spring labours, to see the first furrows being cut in a black swathe through the green sward, or to admire the skilful sower, tapping the sieve hanging from his chest with his hand and casting handfuls of seeds evenly and precisely, without spilling a single seed to one side or the other. Chichikov betook himself everywhere. He chatted and exchanged views with the bailiff, the peasants, and the miller. †He enquired into everything, asking about this and that, and how the farm was doing, and all the while he thought to himself:† 'What a swine that Tentetnikov is, honest to God! Imagine letting his estate go to rack and ruin like that, when it could bring in at least fifty thousand a year!'

Often, during these walks, he wondered whether he himself might not one day—that is, not now, of course, but later, when his great undertaking was completed and he was in funds—whether he himself might not become the peaceful proprietor of just such an estate. Whereupon—quite understandably—he usually pictured a young wife, a healthy, fair-complexioned wench, from the merchant class or some other wealthy estate, †who had even learnt to play a musical instrument†. He also saw the younger generation, destined to perpetuate the name of Chichikov: a sprightly scamp of a boy and a beautiful little daughter, or even two boys, and two or even three little girls, so that everyone would know that he really had lived and existed, that he had not merely passed across the earth like a shadow or phantom—so that he would have no cause for shame before his country either. It also occurred to him that it would be no bad thing to gain a certain advancement in rank: to state councillor, for instance, an honourable and respected rank*... For such are the thoughts that occupy a man on his walks, bearing him away from the dreary reality of his present life, teasing, stirring, and rousing his imagination, and welcomed by him even when he knows perfectly well that none of it will ever come true.

Pavel Ivanovich's servants also found the village much to their liking. Like their master, they soon felt quite at home. Petrushka quickly made friends with the butler Grigory, although at first they both put on airs and showed off insufferably to each other. †Petrushka bragged to Grigory about his travels far and wide;† Grigory promptly countered with St Petersburg, which Petrushka had never visited. The latter now attempted to regain the upper hand by vaunting the great distances he had travelled to reach the places he had visited; but Grigory named a town which you would find on no existing map and cited a distance of some thirty thousand versts* or more, so that Chichikov's manservant could only goggle owl-like and gape in astonishment, which was greeted with howls of laughter from the assembled household staff. This rivalry ended, however, with the most intimate friendship: one of the peasants, known as 'Baldy' Pimen and uncle to half the village, kept a pothouse at the end of the village called the Akulka.* The two were to be found here at all hours of the day. Here they became fast friends, or what country folk call 'pothouse regulars'.

Selifan found another kind of lure. Never an evening passed in the village without the singing of songs, and the winding and un-winding of spring round-dances. The local girls, comely and statu-esque, of a beauty hard to find in larger villages, would cause him to stand entranced for hours on end. It was hard to tell which of them was the fairest: they were all white-breasted, white-necked, all with eyes as round as turnips,* with eyes that beckoned, with plaited braids reaching to their waists, and the proud gait of peahens. When he took their white hands in his own, and moved slowly with them in a round-dance or stood facing them, in a line with the village lads, and the girls swept toward them in a similar line, singing in loud, resonating voices: 'Come boyars, show us your bridegroom!'* as dusk settled softly over the surrounding fields, and the melan-choly echo of the refrain was wafted back to them from far beyond the river—at such moments he himself no longer knew what was happening to him. Afterwards, in his sleeping and his waking hours, in the morning and at dusk, he would continue to imagine that he held those white hands in his own †and that he was moving with them in the round-dance.†

Chichikov's horses also found their new habitat to their liking. The shaft-horse, and Assessor, and even the dapple bay, all found their sojourn on Tentetnikov's estate anything but tedious, the oats excellent, and the stables extraordinarily well-appointed. They each had their own stall, and though they were separated from one an-other it was still possible for them to see the other horses over the partitions, so that, if any of them, even the one standing furthest off, felt a sudden urge to neigh, he could be answered immediately in like manner.

In a word, they all felt perfectly at home. As for the business which had caused Chichikov to traverse the length and breadth of Russia, namely, his pursuit of dead souls, he had become very cir-cumspect and tactful in that regard, even when he was constrained to have dealings with utter fools. But Tentetnikov, for all his faults, read books, indulged in philosophical speculation, endeavoured to solve all mysteries—to plumb the whys and the wherefores. 'No,' he thought to himself, 'perhaps I should try approaching it from the other side.' Often, when passing the time of day with the household servants, Chichikov would gather pieces of intelligence, such as that their master used to make fairly frequent visits to his neighbour the general, that the general had a daughter, that the master seemed not indifferent to the young lady, and the young lady to the master, too... But then they had suddenly fallen out over something and their ways had parted. He himself noticed that Andrei Ivanovich was forever drawing little heads in pen or pencil, each exactly like every other. One day after luncheon, as he pursued his customary pastime of spinning his silver snuff-box round its axis, he ventured to remark:

'You have all you require, Andrei Ivanovich, except only for one thing.'

'What might that be?' asked his host, emitting a spiral of smoke.

'A companion in life,' said Chichikov.

Andrei Ivanovich made no reply. There the conversation ended.

Chichikov was not abashed, he merely chose another moment, this time shortly before supper, and, in the course of a general conversation about nothing in particular, suddenly said: 'But you know, Andrei Ivanovich, you really ought to marry.'

Not a word did Tentetnikov say in reply to this, as if the subject itself was disagreeable to him.

Chichikov was not put off. A third time he chose his moment, on this occasion after supper, and spoke as follows:

'All the same, the more I look at your situation the more convinced I am that you must get married: otherwise you will succumb to hypochondria.'

Either Chichikov's words on this occasion were especially convincing, or perhaps on that day Andrei Ivanovich ⟨was⟩ particularly disposed towards candour, but he sighed and said, blowing a cloud of pipe smoke towards the ceiling: 'For all things in life one must be born lucky, Pavel Ivanovich.' Then he told him all that had happened, the entire story of his acquaintance with the general and their rift.

When Chichikov heard the full story, word for word, and learnt that such a débâcle could have been caused by a single over-familiar word, he was dumbfounded. For several minutes he stared fixedly into Tentetnikov's eyes, wondering whether the man was really a complete fool, or merely somewhat touched, and finally spoke:

'But Andrei Ivanovich, my dear fellow,' he said, taking hold of both his hands. 'What's insulting about that? After all, what is so insulting about a little familiar word?'

'There's nothing insulting in the word itself,' said Tentetnikov, 'it's the tone of voice in which it is said: that's what contains the insult. It implies: "Now don't you forget that you're worthless rubbish; I've only been receiving you because there was no one better around, but the moment some Princess Yuzyakina or other arrives, make sure you know your place: go and stand by the door." That's what it implies.'

As he said this the meek and humble Andrei Ivanovich's eyes flashed with fire and his voice trembled audibly with outrage.

'Well, even if it was in that sense—so what?' asked Chichikov.

'So what?' said Tentetnikov, staring at Chichikov in amazement. 'You expect that ⟨I⟩ could continue calling on him after such an action?'

'After what action? It wasn't even an action!' said Chichikov.

'What do you mean—not an action?' repeated Tentetnikov in amazement.

'That is no action, Andrei Ivanovich. It is no more than a habit with generals: they are familiar with everyone. After all, why should familiarity not be permitted a distinguished, high-ranking man?...'

'That's a different matter,' said Tentetnikov. 'If he had been an old man, a poor man, not proud or haughty, not a general, then I should have accepted his familiarity and would even have taken it with deference.'

'He is a complete fool,' thought Chichikov. 'He'd accept it from a poor wretch but not a general!'—'Very well,' he declared aloud, 'let us suppose that he insulted you, but then you and he are now quits: he slighted you and you slighted him. As for falling out, abandoning your own personal... your... that, forgive me, is... Once you have chosen your goal you must stop at nothing. Pay no heed to the boorishness of others! People will always be boorish: that is the way they're made. You will not find a single man anywhere in this wide world who is not sometimes boorish.'

Tentetnikov was quite nonplussed: 'What a peculiar character this Chichikov is!' he thought, quite taken aback by Chichikov's words.

'All the same, this Tentetnikov is a queer fish!' thought Chichikov meanwhile. 'Andrei Ivanovich, let me talk to you as one brother to another,' he said. 'You have little experience of the world—allow me to try to sort ⟨this matter⟩ out. I shall call on His Excellency and I shall explain that all this came about through a misunderstanding on your part, by reason of your youth and your ignorance of people and the ways of the world.'

'I do not intend to abase myself before him,' said Tentetnikov, taking umbrage, 'and I cannot authorize you to act thus on my behalf.'

'I am not capable of abasement,' retorted Chichikov, also taking umbrage. 'I may be guilty of other failings, by my human nature, but of such base conduct—never... Forgive me, Andrei Ivanovich, for my good intentions, I never thought you would put such an offensive construction on ⟨my⟩ words.' All this was delivered in a tone of high dudgeon.

'Forgive me, Pavel Ivanovich, I am in the wrong!' hastily exclaimed Tentetnikov, deeply moved, and he seized hold of both Chichikov's hands. 'I never meant to offend you. Your kind concern is most dear to me, I swear it! But do let us leave this matter, let us never talk of it again.'

'In that case I shall just call on the general, for no particular reason,' said Chichikov.

'But whatever for?' asked Tentetnikov, staring at Chichikov in bewilderment.

'To pay my respects,' said Chichikov.

'What a strange fellow this Chichikov is!' thought Tentetnikov.

'What a strange fellow this Tentetnikov is!' thought Chichikov.

'I shall call on him tomorrow, Andrei Ivanovich, at about ten o'clock. In my view, the sooner one pays one's respects, the better. Since my chaise is not yet in a fit ⟨state⟩,' he continued, 'permit me to take your calèche.'

'My dear fellow, what a request! Everything here is yours now: my carriages, anything you like—they are all at your disposal.'

Thereupon they took their leave of each other and went their separate ways to bed, but not without reflecting upon each other's strangenesses.

A funny thing happened, though: the next day, when the horses were harnessed up and Chichikov, clad in a new tailcoat, white cravat, and waistcoat, sprang into the calèche with the agility almost of a military man and rattled off to pay his respects to the general, Tentetnikov was thrown into a state of excitement such as he had not experienced for a very long time. The entire course of his thoughts, grown rusty and somnolent, was galvanized into a frenzy of activity. A nervous agitation suddenly gripped all the emotions of this slug-gard, who had hitherto languished in a state of carefree torpor. He sat down on the settee, then jumped up and went to the window, then he took up a book, tried to think—it was all futile! Thought simply refused to come into his head. Then he tried to think of nothing at all—wasted endeavour! Snatches of something akin to thought, scraps and candle-ends of thoughts crowded into his head and refused to budge. 'What a peculiar state of mind!' he said and stepped closer to the window to gaze out at the road, which cut through the oak grove, and at the end of which there still lingered the cloud of dust thrown up by the departing carriage. But let us now leave Tentetnikov and hasten in pursuit of Chichikov.

CHAPTER TWO

In a little more than half an hour the horses had transported Chichikov a distance of some ten versts—first through the oak grove, then through wheatfields, where the young crop was starting to show green against the freshly ploughed earth, then along the crest of a hill, from which, with every successive moment of the journey, new vistas unfolded before him, and, finally, down a broad avenue of lime trees, just beginning to bud, deep into the general's estate. Here the avenue of limes swung to the right and, suddenly transformed into a colonnade of ⟨oval⟩ poplars, protected at their base with wicker cages, led to wrought-iron gates, through which could be seen the magnificent rococo façade of the general's house, supported by eight columns with Corinthian capitals. The air was filled with the smell of the oil paint which was constantly being applied throughout the house to prevent it from growing shabby. The courtyard was as clean as a parquet dance-floor. With a deep feeling of respect, Chichikov alighted from his carriage, asked to be announced, and was conducted directly into the general's study.

The general impressed him with his majestic appearance. He was clad at that time of day in a quilted satin dressing-gown of a magnificent purple hue. He had an open face, manly features, moustaches, and copious, grey-streaked whiskers, wore his hair closely cropped at the back, revealing a neck that was thick and fleshy, with three folds—what they call a three-storey neck—and a single vertical crease; in short, this was one of those colourful generals whose number was so legion in that illustrious year of 1812. General Betrishchev, like most of his fellow men, was endowed with both many virtues and many shortcomings. Former and latter, as is the way with the Russian character, were mixed together in him in colourful disarray. He had a capacity, at decisive moments, for magnanimity, courage, boundless generosity, unfailing wisdom, but these sterling qualities came with a generous admixture of caprice, vanity, ambition, egotism, and many other petty, personal foibles of the sort which no Russian can ever entirely shed when he leads a life of idleness. He loathed all those who had surpassed him in the service, and spoke splenetically of them, in sardonic, biting epigrams. The one who came off worst was his former friend and colleague, whom he considered his inferior both in intelligence and abilities, and yet who had gone ahead of him and was already the governor-general of two provinces. To make matters worse, these were the very provinces in which the general's own estates were situated, so that he found himself in some respects in a position of dependency *vis-à-vis* this man. By way of revenge, he vilified him at every opportunity, criticizing his every administrative disposition and declaring his every measure and act the very last word in ineptitude.

†Everything about the general was somehow strange, starting with his attitude to education, of which he was an impassioned zealot;† he loved to know things others did not know, and took against people who knew things that he did not. Having received a half-foreign education, he wished at the same time to play the role of the Russian squire. With such an inequable character and such massive, glaring contradictions in his nature, it was only inevitable that he would come up against all sorts of unpleasantnesses in his service, and it was this, in the end, which precipitated his retirement. He blamed it on a hostile conspiracy against him, and lacked the good grace to accept any of the blame himself. In retirement he preserved his same colourful, magisterial bearing. Whether wearing a frock-coat, a tailcoat, or a dressing-gown, he would always be the same general. Everything about him, from his voice to the slightest movement of his hands, bespoke authority and imperiousness, and instilled in all those of lower rank if not respect, then at least timidity.

Chichikov experienced both sensations—respect and timidity. Inclining his head deferentially to one side and reaching forward as if to offer a tray of tea-things he began as follows:

'I deemed it my duty to present myself to Your Excellency. Nourishing, as I do, a profound esteem for the valour of those brave men who defended our fatherland on the battlefield, I considered myself duty-bound to present myself in person to Your Excellency.'

This overture was not, as could be seen, altogether displeasing to the general. With a motion of his head that unmistakably betokened his favour, he said:

'Delighted to make your acquaintance. Please be seated. Where did you serve?'

'The route of my service,' said Chichikov, sitting down not in the middle of the chair, but perched on the edge and clutching its arm

with one hand, 'commenced in the Imperial Revenue Chamber,*
Your Excellency; its course then led through a diversity of offices: I
served in the Aulic Council,* on the Construction Commission, and
in the customs. My life may be likened to a barque tossed on the
waves, Your Excellency. I was reared, you might say, on forbearance—I was suckled on forbearance, was swaddled in forbearance,
and am myself, so to speak, the very embodiment of forbearance. I
have suffered more at the hands of enemies than is within the power
of words, or paints, or the skill, so to speak, of the artist's brush, to
convey. Now, however, in the evening, as it were, of my life I go in
search of a little haven in which to live out my remaining days. For
the time being I am sojourning with a close neighbour of Your
Excellency...'

'Who is that?'

'Tentetnikov, Your Excellency.'

The general frowned.

'He, Your Excellency, is most repentant for having neglected to
show due respect...'

'For what?'

'For the merits of Your Excellency, Your Excellency. Words fail
him. He says "If only there were some way in which I could...
because, to be sure," he says, "I know how to value the brave men
who have saved our fatherland," he says.'

'Heavens above, what does he mean!... But I'm not angry with
him,' said the mollified general. 'In my heart I formed a most sincere fondness for him and I am convinced that in time he will
become a thoroughly useful man.'

'Excellently well put, Your Excellency. Yes, indeed: a thoroughly
useful man, who has a flair for the spoken word and also great
mastery of the pen.'

'But I expect he writes a lot of rubbish, verses and the like?'

'Why, no, Your Excellency, not rubbish at all... He is writing a
work of substance... a history, Your Excellency.'

'A history? A history of what?'

'A history...' Here Chichikov paused and, whether because the
person sitting before him was a general or because he simply wished
to impart a greater significance to the topic, he continued: 'A history
of generals, Your Excellency.'

'What do you mean: of generals? What generals?'

292 *Dead Souls*

'Of generals in general, Your Excellency, as a generality... that is, properly speaking, of Russian generals,' said Chichikov, all the while thinking to himself: 'God—what rubbish I'm talking!'

'I'm sorry, but I do not quite understand... Does that mean a history of some period or other, or individual biographies, and is it then of all generals, or merely those who participated in the 1812 campaign?'

'Exactly so, Your Excellency, those who participated in the 1812 campaign.' As he said this, Chichikov thought: 'I'll be hanged if I know what I'm saying!'

'But then why doesn't he come to see me? I could gather together a mass of interesting material for him.'

'He does not dare, Your Excellency.'

'Stuff and nonsense! All because of some trifling thing. What happened between us, after all? And I'm not that sort of man at all. I think I shall call on him myself.'

'He will not let you take the trouble, he'll come himself,' said Chichikov, and thought at the same time: 'All that stuff about generals did the trick after all; and to think my tongue blurted it all out in sheer folly.'

A faint rustling sound could be heard in the general's study. The carved walnut door leading to the closet press swung open of its own accord, and on the other side there appeared a living statuette, its lovely hand clasping the brass door-handle. If a translucent tableau, illuminated by a lamp from behind, had suddenly lit up the darkened room, it could not have so amazed the onlooker as did this figure, which seemed to have appeared before them for the express purpose of filling the room with radiance. It was as if, with her arrival, the rays of the sun had suddenly flooded into the general's sombre, scowling room, causing it to burst into a radiant smile. At first, Chichikov could not understand what it was that stood before him. It was hard to say which land she was native to. A face of such pure and noble features could not have been found anywhere, except perhaps painted on antique cameos. Light-limbed and straight as an arrow, she seemed so tall that she towered above him. But that was an illusion: she was anything but tall. The illusion of height was created ⟨by⟩ the extraordinarily harmonious proportion of all the parts of her body. Her dress fitted her so well, it seemed as if the very best dressmakers had conspired among themselves as to how best to adorn her. This, too, was illusory. She dressed in whatever came first and easiest to hand: in two or three places an uncut and plain-coloured piece of cloth had been roughly tacked together and this was then gathered up and draped around her with such graceful tucks and folds that, had this ensemble of folds and wearer been depicted on canvas, next to her all the young ladies dressed in the latest fashion would have appeared like gaudy dolls, garishly attired in motley from the market. †And if she were to be depicted in marble, in this dress with its folds enveloping her limbs, it would have been declared a copy of the work of a great master.†

'Allow me to present the apple of my eye,' said the general, turning to Chichikov. 'Forgive me, I still don't know your full name and patronymic.'

'Is there really any need to know the name and patronymic of a man who has not distinguished himself with deeds of valour?' said Chichikov modestly, inclining his head somewhat to one side.

'Well, nevertheless, one should know...'

'It's Pavel Ivanovich, Your Excellency,' announced Chichikov, bowing with the agility almost of a military man and springing back as lightly as an India-rubber ball.

'Ulinka!' said the general, turning to his daughter, 'Pavel Ivanovich has just told me a most interesting piece of news. Our neighbour Tentetnikov is not such a stupid man as we supposed. He has embarked upon a project of some considerable importance: a history of the generals of the 1812 campaign.'

'But who thought he was a stupid man, anyway?' she retorted swiftly. 'Only that Vishnepokromov could have thought that, and you went and believed him, Papa, such an empty-headed and odious man!'

'Why do you say odious? Mind you, he is rather empty-headed, I must admit,' said the general.

'He's mean and repulsive, and not just rather empty-headed. Anyone who could so offend his brothers and banish his own sister from his house must be an odious man.'

'But those are only stories about him.'

'There's no smoke without a fire. I fail to understand, Papa, how †you, who have the kindest of souls and an uncommonly soft heart, can receive a man who is as unlike you as night is to day and who you know to be a good-for-nothing.'†

'There, you see,' said the general to Chichikov with an amused chuckle, 'that's the way she and I always quarrel.' Turning back to his adversary, he continued:

'My dear heart! You surely don't expect me to drive him away?'

'No—why drive him away? But why show him such attention, why be so fond of him?'

†At this point Chichikov deemed it appropriate to make a small contribution.

'All men need to be loved, Mam'selle,' he said. 'There is nothing for it. The lowly beast loves to be stroked: it thrusts its nose out at you from its stall and asks: please stroke me.'

The general guffawed loudly. 'That's exactly what it does: it thrusts out its nose and says: "Go on, stroke me." Ha, ha, ha! And yet not only the beast's snout, but its whole body is covered in soot, yet it still seeks attention, it still needs encouragement, as the saying goes... Ha, ha, ha, ha!' As he said this, the general's entire upper body shook with laughter. His shoulders, which had once been weighed down by heavy epaulettes, trembled, as if bearing the weight of those epaulettes still.

Chichikov also permitted himself an interjection of laughter. In deference to the general, however, he articulated his laughter not as 'Ha, ha' but as 'He, he, he, he, he!' His upper body also shook with mirth, although his shoulders did not tremble, because they had never borne heavy epaulettes.

'A creature like that will pinch whatever he lays his hands on, he'll clean out the Treasury, and expect a reward for his services, the swine. "You can't expect me to work without encouragement," he says, "and I've done my work"... Ha, ha, ha, ha!'

A pained expression took possession of the young girl's sweet and noble features. 'Oh papa, I don't understand how you can laugh. These underhand dealings fill me with dejection, and nothing more. When I see deceit perpetrated openly and for all to see and the perpetrators not punished with universal contempt, I feel quite overcome, at times like that I become angry, I even feel ill, I think and think...' Whereupon she all but burst into tears.

'Only, I beg you, don't be vexed with us,' said the general. 'We are not to blame in any way for all this.† Is that not so?' he asked, turning to Chichikov. 'Give me a kiss and go to your room, because I am now going to dress for dinner. I do hope,' he continued, looking again at Chichikov, 'you shall join us for dinner?'

'But only if Your Excellency—'

'No ceremonies please. I'm still able to feed my fellow man, thank God. There's plenty of cabbage soup!'

Adroitly stretching forward both his hands, Chichikov bowed his head in a manner that was both honorific and grateful, so that for a time everything in the room was obscured from his view, and all he could see were the stockings protruding from his own ankle-boots. When, finally, after spending some time in this position of respect, he raised his head again he could no longer see Ulinka. She had disappeared. In her place there stood a giant of a valet, with a bushy moustache and whiskers, bearing in his hands a silver basin and pitcher.

'Would you permit me to dress in your presence?' asked the general.

'Why of course, and not only to dress, but in my presence Your Excellency may do anything he sees fit,' said Chichikov.

Throwing off his dressing-gown and rolling up the shirtsleeves on his massive arms, the general started to wash, splashing and spluttering in the water like a duck. Water and suds flew about the room.

'Encouragement, encouragement—they all want encouragement,' he said, mopping down his neck with the towel. '"Please stroke me, please stroke me," it says! And it won't even bother to steal anything without encouragement. Ha, ha, ha!'

Chichikov was in exceptionally fine mettle; he felt himself inspired. 'The general is quite a wag and an uncommonly good fellow—perhaps I should give it a try?' he thought and, when he saw the valet leave the room with the basin, he exclaimed:

'Your Excellency! Since you are so kind to everyone and so attentive to their needs, I have a tiny favour to ask of you.'

'What?'

Chichikov gazed nervously around.

'I have an uncle, Your Excellency, a doddery old boy, a dotard. He has three hundred souls and a fortune of two thousand... and, besides myself, not a single heir. In his senility he's unable to manage his estate himself, neither will he hand it over to me. And he gives such a strange reason. "I don't know my nephew," he says; "maybe he's a spendthrift. Let him prove to me that he's a reliable man, let him first acquire three hundred souls of his own, and then I shall give him my three hundred."'

'Heavens—is ⟨the man⟩ a complete fool?' asked the general.

'If he were only a fool, it wouldn't matter: he could have kept his folly to himself. But just picture to yourself my own predicament, Your Excellency. The old fellow has taken some sort of housekeeper into his menage, and this housekeeper has produced children. Before I know it he'll bequeath the lot to them.'

'The old duffer's off his rocker, that's all there is to it,' said the general. 'Only I don't quite see what I could do to help,' he continued, looking with surprise at Chichikov.

'I've thought of a way out. If, for example, Your Excellency were to make over to me all the dead souls on your estate just as if they were alive, by drawing up a deed of purchase, I could then present this deed to the old man and he would hand his estate over to me.'

At this the general burst into gales of hearty laughter, heartier, in all likelihood, than any man had ever laughed before. He collapsed into his armchair; he threw back his head, and all but choked on his guffaws. The entire house was thrown into commotion. The valet appeared. The daughter came rushing in, alarmed.

'Papa, what's happened to you?' she asked anxiously, gazing with bewilderment into his eyes.

But for a long time the general was unable to make any reply.

'Nothing my dear, nothing. Ha, ha, ha! Run along to your room, we shall be coming to dinner shortly. Don't be alarmed. Ha, ha, ha!'

Whereupon he almost lost his breath several times, and then his guffaws rang out with renewed vigour, resounding through the house from the vestibule to its furthest room.

Chichikov began to grow anxious.

'Poor old uncle! What a fool you'd make of him! Ha, ha, ha! Instead of live bodies he'll be getting carcasses! Ha, ha!'

†'There he goes again: will the man never stop laughing!' ⟨fretted Chichikov to himself.⟩†

'Ha, ha!' continued the general. 'What an ass. Where did he get such a stupid idea: "First let him get three hundred souls by himself, out of the thin air, and then I'll give him my three hundred." What an ass.'

'An ass, Your Excellency.'

'But as for you, and your idea of fobbing the old boy off with dead ones—ha, ha, ha! I'd give anything in the world to see his face when you bring him a deed of purchase for dead souls. But what's he like? What sort of man is he? Is he very old?'

†'Eighty, Your Excellency.'†

'Yet he still gets around, he's a sprightly old boy? He must be pretty tough, if he still shares his bed with his housekeeper?'

'Tough—not a bit of it! He's starting to dote, Your Excellency.'

'What a fool! He is a fool, you say?'

'He's a fool, Your Excellency. The old chap's completely off his head.'

'And yet he still gets around, he goes visiting, he's still steady on his pins?'

'He's steady, but only just.'

'What a fool! But tough, you say? Still got his teeth?'

'Only two left, Your Excellency.'

'What an ass! Don't take it to heart, my dear chap... He may be your uncle, but he really is an ass!'

'Indeed, an ass, Your Excellency. Although he is my relative and it pains me to admit it, but what can I do?'

Chichikov was lying, of course: it was not at all difficult for him to admit, all the more so because in all probability he had never had an uncle in his life.

'So, if Your Excellency would be so kind—'

'As to let you have some dead souls? Why, for an idea like that I'll let you have them complete with land and dwellings! You can take the entire graveyard! Ha, ha, ha, ha! The poor old boy! Ha, ha, ha, ha! What a fool you'll make of him! Ha, ha, ha, ha!...'

And martial laughter once again reverberated through the martial apartments.*

CHAPTER THREE

†'If Colonel Koshkaryov is indeed off his rocker, so much the better,' said Chichikov, finding himself once more surrounded by open fields and spaces, with everything else lost from sight, leaving only the empty vault of the sky, with two clouds on one side.

'I say, Selifan, did you get good directions to Colonel Koshkaryov's house?'

'Me, Pavel Ivanovich?—Well, sir, seeing as how I was busy the whole time with the carriage, I didn't really have the time, so Petrushka asked the coachman.'

'You stupid fool! I've told you before, not to rely on Petrushka: Petrushka's a dolt, Petrushka's an idiot and, no doubt, Petrushka's now drunk, into the bargain.'

'But it doesn't take brains to work it out,' said Petrushka, turning round and giving his master a sidelong look. 'All you need to know is that, when you come down the hill, you have to stick to the meadow, and that's it.'

'I suppose nothing's passed your lips all day except that rot-gut vodka!? You're a fine one! No doubt you brought all Europe to its knees, as they say, with your good looks!' On saying this, Chichikov stroked his chin and thought to himself: 'All the same, what a remarkable difference there is between an educated citizen and a footman with his coarse physiognomy!'†

In the mean time the carriage had started to go downhill. Once again, meadows and open vistas unfolded before them, dotted here and there with aspen groves.

Bouncing gently on its firm springs, the comfortable carriage continued its smooth descent down the almost imperceptible slope until, finally, it reached the meadows below and flew on, past millhouses, clattering lightly over the bridges and swaying a little over the soft and uneven ground of the valley road. And with never so much as a jolt or a judder to assail the tender sides of the traveller within. It was balm to the senses, ⟨not⟩ a carriage. Afar off they saw the glint of sandy banks. In swift succession there flew past them clumps of osier, slender alders, and silvery willows, whose twigs slapped the faces of Selifan and Petrushka, up high on their coach-box. Every few minutes the cap of one or the other would be sent flying, whereupon the surly owner would leap down from the box and abuse the stupid tree and the farmer who had planted it, but would still refuse to tie the cap down or even to hold it on with his hand, preferring to hope that this was the last time and that it would not happen again. The trees, however, were becoming denser, as their ranks were swelled first with birch, and then firs. Around their trunks the undergrowth grew thickly; the ground was carpeted with blue sweet-flag and yellow forest tulips. The forest darkened and prepared itself for the embrace of night. Then suddenly bright shafts of light pierced the gloom on all sides, like so many flashing mirrors. The trees grew sparser, the shafts of light brighter, and there appeared before them a lake. It was a broad expanse of water, some four versts across. On the far shore, scattered on the slopes above the lake, stood the grey timbered cottages of the village.

Shouts rang out from the water. Some twenty men, waist-deep, shoulder-deep, and neck-deep in the lake, were dragging a net across to the opposite shore. There had been an accident: together with the fish, the net had somehow ensnared one of the fishermen, a man who measured no more in height than in girth, in shape exactly like a watermelon or a barrel. He was beginning to panic, and shouted at the top of his lungs: 'Denis, you blockhead, pass the line to Kozma! You, Kozma, take the end of the line from Denis! Stop pulling like that, Big Foma! Go and stand next to Little Foma! The devil take you all, you're going to tear the net!'

The watermelon was evidently not concerned for his own safety: because of his fatness he couldn't drown anyway, and however hard he might thrash about, trying to dive under the water, it would only have borne him up to the surface again; if two men had sat on his back he would still have remained afloat with them, like a huge, stubborn bladder, only grunting a little beneath their weight and emitting bubbles from his nose. But he was seriously afraid that the net might be torn and the fish allowed to escape, and, for that reason above all others, he had himself secured with ropes and dragged along by several men standing on the shore.

'Now that must be the master, Colonel Koshkaryov,' said Selifan.

'Why do you think that?'

'Because, if you'd like to take a look, sir, his body is whiter than the others, and he's more respectable, with more flesh on him, like a master should have.'

In the mean time the ensnared master had been dragged much closer to the shore. Once he could touch bottom with his feet he stood up and at that moment caught sight of the carriage, which had descended from the weir, and observed Chichikov sitting within.

'You had lunch?' shouted the master, wading up to the shore with the netted fish. He was still entangled in the toils, like the hand of a *belle dame* in summer, encased in its lace glove, and shaded his eyes from the sun with one hand, holding the other a little lower— à la Venus de Medici* emerging from the bath.

'No,' said Chichikov, doffing his cap and continuing to bow from his seat in the carriage.

'Then thank the Lord! Little Foma, show him the sturgeon. Chuck the net over here, Trishka, you blockhead', he shouted in his loud voice, 'and give us a hand lifting the sturgeon out of the tub. You, Kozma, blockhead, come and lend a hand!'

The two fishermen lifted the head of a great monster from the tub. 'What a prince! He swam in from the river,' shouted the rotund master. 'Drive up to the house. Coachman, take the lower road through the kitchen garden! You there, Big Foma, blockhead, run and take down the barrier; he'll show you the way and I'll join you right away.'

The long-legged, bare-footed Big Foma headed off, just as he was, clad in nothing but his shirt, running in front of the carriage through the entire village. Here, a variety of nets—drag-nets, bag-nets, and casting-nets—hung before every cottage: all the peasants were fishermen. Then he removed the barrier before one of the kitchen gardens and the carriage passed through the gardens into a square before a wooden church. Some distance off, beyond the church, Chichikov could see the roofs of the manor house and farm buildings.

'The Colonel's a bit of a queer fish,' he thought to himself.

'And look—here I am,' announced a voice beside him.

Chichikov looked round. The master was now driving along beside him, fully clad: he wore a grass-green nankeen frock-coat, yellow trousers, a shirt with an open collar and no cravat, just like a cupid! He sat sideways in his droshky, filling all the available space. Chichikov was about to say something to him, but the fat man had disappeared. He glimpsed the droshky fleetingly as it passed the ⟨spot⟩ where they had hauled the fish out of the lake. Once again voices rang out: 'Big Foma and Little Foma! Kozma and Denis!' But when Chichikov drove up to the porch of the house, he found to his astonishment that the fat master was already standing there, poised to receive him into his embraces. How on earth he had managed to fly ahead like that was quite beyond comprehension. They exchanged three kisses, according to the old Russian custom, first on one cheek, then on the other: in such matters the master belonged to the old school.

'I bring you regards from His Excellency,' said Chichikov.

'From which Excellency?'

'From your relation, General Aleksandr Dmitrievich.'

'Who's this Aleksandr Dmitrievich?'

'General Betrishchev,' answered Chichikov, somewhat surprised.

'Don't know him,' said his host, also surprised.

Chichikov's surprise increased.

'But how can that be?... I do trust, at least, that I have the pleasure of addressing Colonel Koshkaryov?'

'No, trust no further. This is not his place, it belongs to me, Pyotr Petrovich Petukh. Petukh, Pyotr Petrovich,'* repeated his host.

Chichikov was stunned.

'What on earth?' he turned to Selifan and Petrushka, who gawked and goggled back, one sitting on the coach-box, the other standing by the doors of the carriage. 'See what you've done, you fools? Didn't I tell you: we're going to Colonel Koshkaryov... But this is Pyotr Petrovich Petukh's place...'

'The lads have done splendidly! Take yourselves to the kitchen and they'll give you each a mug of vodka,' said Pyotr Petrovich. 'Unharness the horses and make yourselves at home in the servant's quarters!'

'I am so terribly sorry,' said Chichikov, 'such an unexpected mistake...'

'No mistake. First sample the lunch, then tell me: was it a mistake? Please, be my guest,' he said, taking Chichikov's arm and leading him into ⟨the house⟩. †From within two young lads came out to meet them, wearing summer frock-coats†—both as slender as willow saplings; they towered a full arshin* ⟨above⟩ their father.

'My sons, students at the gymnasium, here for the holidays.

Nikolasha, you look after our guest, and you, Aleksasha, come with me.'

Saying this, his host vanished.

Chichikov occupied himself with Nikolasha. The youngster appeared to have the makings of a good-for-nothing. †He wasted no time in telling Chichikov that there was no profit in studying at the local gymnasium, that he and his brother were planning to go to St Petersburg because there was no future for them in the provinces...†

'I see,' said Chichikov to himself, 'this road is going to lead to coffee-shops and boulevards...'—'And tell me,' he asked aloud, 'in what sort of condition is your old man's estate?'

'Mortgaged,' replied the old man himself, having reappeared in the drawing-room, 'mortgaged.'

'That's too bad,' thought Chichikov. 'The way things are going, soon there won't be a single estate left. I must get a move on.'—'Perhaps it was a mistake, all the same,' he said aloud, with a look of compassion, 'to be in such a hurry to mortgage it?'

'No, it didn't matter,' said Petukh. 'They say it's a good idea. Everyone's mortgaging these days: why should I lag behind? And besides, I've always been stuck out here: now I shall find out what it's like to live in Moscow. My sons here are constantly pressing me to move, they want some of that big city education and enlightenment.'

'The fool, the fool!' thought Chichikov, 'he'll squander everything and even turn his boys into wastrels. And it's a handsome property. As far as one can see, the peasants are happy enough and they themselves don't live badly. But once they start enlightening themselves with those restaurants and theatres it'll all go to the devil. You should stay where you belong, you clodhopper, in the country.'

'I bet I know what you're thinking,' said Petukh.

'What?' asked Chichikov, in some embarrassment.

'You're thinking: "What a fool, what a fool this Petukh is! He invites me to lunch, but there's still no lunch." It'll be ready soon, my most respected sir. It'll be served sooner than a crop-haired wench can plait her braids.'

'Daddy, Platon Mikhailovich is coming!' said Aleksasha, looking through the window.

'Riding his bay!' said Nikolasha, leaning across to the window.

'Where, where?' cried Petukh, hastening up.

'Who's this Platon ⟨Mikhailovich⟩?' Chichikov asked Aleksasha.

'He's our neighbour, Platon Mikhailovich Platonov, an excellent man, an outstanding man,' ⟨Petukh⟩ answered for him.

In the mean time Platonov himself entered the room: a handsome man, tall and slender, with lustrous, chestnut curls. He was followed into the room by a fearsome monster of a hound, called Yarb,* with a huge muzzle and a clanking brass collar.

'Have you lunched?' asked Pyotr Petrovich Petukh.

'I have.'

'So why have you come then, to mock me? What use are you to me after lunch?'

The visitor laughed and said: 'I can console you by assuring you that I did not eat a single bite: I have no appetite at all.'

'What a catch we had, if only you had seen it! You should have seen the monster sturgeon which swam into our nets! And such huge carp, such enormous crucians!'

'It's annoying even to listen to you. What have you got to be so cheerful about all the time?'

'But why should I be gloomy, pray tell!' said his host.

'Why should you be gloomy?—Because life's gloomy, that's why.'

'You don't eat enough, that's your problem. Just try and eat a good lunch. All this gloom business has only been invented recently, you know. In the old days no one was gloomy.'

'Enough of your bragging! Are you trying to tell us that you've never been gloomy?'

'Never! Anyway, I wouldn't have the time to be gloomy. You wake up in the morning—and there's the cook come to see you, and you have to order luncheon, and then your tea is brought, and there's the bailiff, and then you go fishing, and then it's time for lunch. After lunch you hardly have time to get up a good snore and there's the cook again: time to order supper; there comes the cook again, time to order lunch for the next day. When is there time to be gloomy?'

Throughout this conversation Chichikov studied the visitor, who amazed him with his extraordinary physical beauty, with the picturesque, harmonious proportion of his body, the still unspent, youthful freshness of his face, the innocent purity of his features, unblemished by even a single pimple. No vigorous passions, nor sorrows, nor even anything akin to agitation and anxiety had dared touch his virginal face and disfigure it with the merest wrinkle, but then neither had they lent it any vitality. There was something lethargic about it, despite the look of wry derision which sometimes enlivened it.

'I must confess,' declared Chichikov, 'I cannot understand it either, if you pardon my saying so, how a handsome young fellow like you could be gloomy. Unless of course, it's lack of money, or enemies—one sometimes comes across people who are prepared even to make an attempt on one's life...'

'Believe you me,' their handsome visitor interrupted, 'at times I honestly wish there was some upheaval like that in my life, to make it more interesting. If only someone would make me angry, at least! But no: utter gloom, that's all there is.'

'Do I take it, then, that your estate is insufficient, with too few souls?'

'Not at all. My brother and I have ten thousand dessiatines* and more than a thousand souls.'

'It's strange, I don't understand at all. But perhaps the harvest failed, epidemics? Have many of your male peasants died?'

'On the contrary, everything is in perfect order and my brother is a most excellent landlord.'

'And still you are gloomy! I fail to understand!' said Chichikov, and shrugged his shoulders.

'Well, now we shall drive away all that gloom,' said their host. 'Aleksasha, run to the kitchen and tell the cook to send in those little fish pies double quick. Now where's that dunderhead Yemelian and that thief Antoshka? Why are they not serving the *zakuski*?'

The door opened. The dunderhead Yemelian and the thief Antoshka appeared with napkins, laid the table, and bore in a tray with six decanters filled with homemade brandies of different colours. Soon a garland of plates was set around the trays and decanters, laden with all sorts of mouth-watering delicacies. The servants hastened hither and thither, constantly bearing in more good things, which arrived from the kitchen in covered dishes, under which the butter could be heard sizzling. The dunderhead Yemelian and the thief Antoshka were good and efficient men. These names had been given to them simply to encourage them. Their master was not given to abuse and insults, he was a good-natured soul. But the

Russian does like his speech a little spicy, it works on him as a glass of vodka works on the digestion. There's nothing for it, that's his nature: he doesn't like anything too bland.

The *zakuski* were followed by lunch. Here their good-hearted host became an out-and-out tyrant. The moment he noticed that a guest was down to a single helping of food, he would at once help him to another, declaring: 'No man nor bird can live in the world without a mate.' If the guest had only two helpings, he would heap on a third, declaring 'What sort of number is two? God loves a trinity.' Should the guest be addressing three—he would say: 'Show me a cart with three wheels! Who ever builds a hut with three corners?' For four he would have another saying, and for five yet another. Chichikov consumed something like twelve helpings and thought: 'Well now our host cannot possibly put anything more on my plate.' But not so: without saying a word, their host deposited on his plate a portion of veal ribs, spit-roasted and complete with kidneys—and excellent veal it was too!

'I reared it for two years on milk,' said their host, 'I nursed it like my own son!'

'No more!' said Chichikov.

'Just try it first, and then say: no more!'

'It won't go in. There's no room.'

'Why, there was no room in the church either. In came the Mayor—and room was found. Yet the congregation had been packed in so tight there wasn't room for an apple to drop. Just try it: that piece there is the Mayor.'

Chichikov tried—and, sure enough, the piece was like the mayor. Room was found for it, even though it had seemed that nothing more could go in.

'How can someone like this move to St Petersburg or Moscow?' wondered Chichikov. 'With hospitality like his he'll be reduced to penury in three years.' What he failed to realize, however, was that the process of ruination had been much improved: Petukh could be brought to penury in three months, not years, and even without recourse to hospitality.

†He kept topping up their glasses—what the guests did not finish he handed over to Aleksasha and Nikolasha, who knocked back glass after glass; ⟨it was⟩ quite obvious to which aspect of human science they would turn in their quest for enlightenment once they moved

to the capital.† The guests did not fare so well: with difficulty, with great difficulty they dragged themselves to the balcony, and with great difficulty they lowered themselves into armchairs. No sooner had their host ensconced himself on his four-seater dais, than he fell asleep. His corpulent mass was transformed into a blacksmith's bellows and through its open mouth and nostrils it started to emit noises such as even our modern composers could not imagine: there was a drum, a flute, and a sort of staccato yelping, much like a dog's bark.

'Listen to that whistling and wheezing!' said Platonov.

Chichikov laughed heartily.

'Of course, if one lunches like that,' said Platonov, 'how can gloom set in? Sleep comes first, is that not so?'

'Of course. Yet I still—and forgive me for saying so—I still cannot understand how one can be gloomy. There are so many remedies for gloom.'

'Such as?'

'Well, especially for a young man! You can dance, play some instrument or other... or get married, even.'

'To whom?'

'Do you mean to say there are no nice, wealthy young girls in the area?'

'There aren't.'

'Well then, seek them elsewhere, travel around.' Here a fertile thought suddenly planted itself in Chichikov's head. 'Now there's an excellent remedy!' he said, staring into Platonov's eyes.

'What?'

'Travel.'

'But where can one go?'

'Well, if you're free, come with me,' said Chichikov, and thought to himself as he looked at Platonov: 'That wouldn't be a bad arrangement: we could share the expenses and repairs to the carriage could be entirely to his account.'

'Where are you going?'

'I travel, for the time being, not so much on my own business as on commission for another. General Betrishchev, a close friend, and, I might say, benefactor, has asked me to visit his relations... Of course, relations are all very well, but in a sense, so to speak, it's also for myself; for, to see the world, the circumfluence of people—say what you will, it's like a living book, a second science.' As he said this, Chichikov found himself thinking: 'It's true, it wouldn't be at all bad. Perhaps he could cover all the expenses; we might even travel with his horses and put mine out to fodder in his village.'

'It's true: why not do a bit of travelling?' thought Platonov at the same time. 'There's nothing for me to do here at home, the farm business is all taken care of by my brother anyway; so it wouldn't cause any upheaval. Yes, why not do some travelling?'—'But you do agree,' he said aloud, 'to stop for a day or two as my brother's guest? Otherwise he would never let me go.'

'With great pleasure! Even three.'

'Well, in that case, let's shake on it! Travel we will!' said Platonov, at once livening up.

They slapped each other's hands. 'We'll travel!'

'Where? Where?' exclaimed their host, waking up and goggling at them in amazement. 'No, my good sirs, I have ordered the wheels to be removed from your carriage, and your stallion, Platon Mikhailovich, is fully fifteen versts from here by now. No, you shall stop the night here, and tomorrow after an early luncheon you may set off on your travels.'*

There was no arguing with Petukh: they had to stay. They were rewarded, though, with a remarkable spring evening. Their host organized an outing on the river. Twelve rowers, wielding twenty-four oars, bore them with songs across the smooth, mirror-like surface of the lake. From the lake they sped along a vast river, with gently sloping banks on both sides. †Not so much as a ripple disturbed the water; instead, a succession of vistas unfolded, in mute splendour, before them, and grove after grove comforted their gaze with the variety and disposition of its trees. The rowers, rhythmically plying their four and twenty oars, suddenly raised them all aloft and the boat glided like a light bird over the still, glassy surface of the water. The chorus-leader, a broad-shouldered young lad sitting third from the stern, struck up a song in a pure, ringing voice, sending forth the notes of his solo line from a throat as sweet as that of a nightingale; five others took up this melody, and then the last six joined in—and the song, as infinite as Russia herself, spilled out into the air. Petukh was infected with the spirit and bellowed his descant where he felt that the choir was lacking in volume, and, as he listened, Chichikov felt proud to be Russian. Platonov alone

⟨thought⟩ to himself: 'What's so good about this dreary singing? It only fills the soul with even greater melancholy.'

Dusk had already fallen as they returned home. In the dark the oars slapped on water that no longer reflected the sky. They put in to the bank in darkness. Lanterns had been set out to light their way; fishermen sat huddled over their tripods, boiling up fish soup from ruffs and other freshly caught fish. All living creatures had already settled for the night. Birds and beasts had long since been driven into their pens and stables, and the dust they raised had settled, and the herdsmen who had brought them in now stood by the gates, awaiting their jugs of milk and the invitation to share the fish soup. Here and there could be heard the chatter and hubbub of voices, and the barking of dogs carried from distant villages. The moon rose and the darkness began to recede before its radiance; finally everything was illuminated. Wondrous were the views, but their beauty passed unnoticed. Instead of racing up and down before this fine spectacle on two spirited stallions, Nikolasha and Aleksasha lay thinking about Moscow, about the pastry-shops and theatres which the visiting cadet had painted so vividly in their minds. Their father mused about how he would feed his guests. Platonov yawned. Chichikov was, apparently, the most alert. 'Yes, really I must get my own little village one day!' he thought. And, in his mind's eye, he started to see his comely wife and their little Chichlings.†

At dinner they gorged themselves once more. When Pavel Ivanovich had retired to the guest bedroom he lay on the bed and prodded his belly: 'Taut as a drum!' he said, 'No Mayor would squeeze in here!' It so happened, however, that his host's study was on the other side of the wall. The wall was thin, and everything that was said next door could be heard. The host was giving his cook instructions for a huge dinner to be served under the guise of an early breakfast the following day. And what an order he gave! A dead man's mouth would have watered.

'And bake us a four-cornered fish pie,' he said, sucking the air through his teeth and inhaling deeply. 'In one corner I want you to put the sturgeon cheeks and the gristle cooked soft, in another throw in some buckwheat, and then some mushrooms and onions, and some sweet milt, and the brains, and whatever else, you know the sort of thing. And make sure that on the one side it's—you know—a nice golden brown, but not so much on the other side. And the pastry—make sure it's baked through, till it just crumbles away, so that the juices soak right through, do you see, so that you don't even feel it in your mouth—so it just melts like snow.' As he said all this, Petukh kept smacking and sucking his lips.

'The devil take him, he's keeping me awake,' grumbled Chichikov, wrapping the blanket round his head to shut out the noise. But through the blanket he could still hear: 'And mind that the sturgeon is properly garnished, with sliced beetroot arranged around it in a star pattern, and with sparling and milk mushrooms, and that sort of thing, you know—some turnips, and carrots, and beans, and whatever else, you know the sort of thing, any vegetables, just make sure there's plenty of it. And put some ice inside the stuffed pig stomach-bag, so it swells up nicely.'

Many more were the dishes that Petukh ordered. The instructions continued, like a refrain: 'Fry some of this, and bake some of that, and make sure that this one simmers for a long time.' Chichikov finally fell asleep as they reached a roast turkey.

The next day the guests so gorged themselves that Platonov could no longer ride on horseback; the stallion was dispatched home with Petukh's stable-boy. They took their seats in the carriage. The big-jowled hound followed sluggishly behind: he had also gorged himself.

'No, that really was too much,' said Chichikov, once they had driven out of the yard.

†'And yet he's never gloomy, that's the annoying thing,' ⟨thought⟩ Platonov.

'Now if I had your income of seventy thousand a year,' thought Chichikov, 'I wouldn't let gloom through the door. And look at that liquor concessionaire Murazov—it's no problem for him:* ten million... A tidy little sum.'†

'Would you object if we drop in for a moment? I'd like to take leave of my sister and her husband.'

'With the greatest pleasure,' said Chichikov.

'If you're interested in estate management,' said Platonov, 'you'll be very interested to meet him. You won't find a better-run estate anywhere. In a mere ten years he has brought this estate, which used to yield barely thirty thousand a year, to the point where it now brings in two hundred thousand.'

'Indeed, he must be a most estimable man! It would be most interesting to make the acquaintance of such a one as he. After all— I mean, when you think of it... What is his name?'

'Kostanzhoglo.'

'And his first name and patronymic?'

'Konstantin Fyodorovich.'

'Konstantin Fyodorovich Kostanzhoglo! I shall be delighted to make his acquaintance. It will be most instructive to get to know such a man.'*

Platonov took it upon himself to guide Selifan, which was just as well, since this latter could barely keep his seat on the coach-box. Petrushka twice tumbled off the carriage like a log, so that, in the end, they had no choice but to tie him with a piece of rope to the coach-box. 'What an ass!' Chichikov muttered to himself.

'Look, over there, you can see where his land starts,' said Platonov, 'it looks quite different.'

It was quite true: the entire field was planted with trees—as straight as arrows; behind this forest lay another, taller than the first, also planted with young trees; and behind this, a forest of old trees, taller still. And beyond stretched yet more fields, planted first with young trees, then older ones beyond. Three times did they drive through such belts of forest, as through the gates in a city wall.

'He grew all this in some eight or ten years, when another farmer couldn't produce trees like these in twenty.'

'How does he do it?'

'You must ask him. He's that sort of farmer: with him, nothing goes to waste. Not only does he know what soil is best for what crop, he even knows what should be grown next to what, which grain should be planted next to which trees. In his system, everything performs three or four different functions. Like the forest: apart from timber, he needs it to ensure there's the right amount of moisture in certain parts of the field, or the right amount of leaf-cover, the right amount of shade. When all the other farms are cracking with drought his is not affected, his harvests do not fail. †It's a pity I don't know much about these things myself, I can't explain it to you, but he has these special ways. They call him a wizard.'†

'He does sound like an astonishing man,' thought Chichikov. 'It's a pity this young fellow is so superficial and can't explain any of it.'

Finally the village came into sight. It looked like an entire city, with countless cottages spread over three hills, at the crest of which stood three churches, and with a rampart of gigantic ricks of corn and haystacks surrounding it on all sides. 'Yes, indeed,' thought Chichikov, 'one can see that this is no ordinary landowner.' The cottages were all sturdily built; the streets were packed hard; every cart that they passed was solid and shining new; the peasants they met had the appearance of intelligent people; the cattle were the best pedigree; even the farmyard pigs had an aristocratic look to them. It was thus apparent that the peasants living here were precisely those who, in the words of the song, dig up silver by the spadeful. There were no *jardins anglais* here,* no manicured lawns with all the usual follies; instead, in the old-fashioned way, an avenue of barns and workyards stretched right to the manor house, so that the master could see everything going on around him, and, to complete the picture, a large lantern was mounted on the roof, illuminating everything for some fifteen versts around.

As they drove up to the porch they were met by bustling servants, quite unlike the drunkard Petrushka, although they were not kitted out in tailcoats, but wore simple Cossack tunics cut from dark blue homespun cloth.

†The lady of the house herself came running out to greet them. She was as fresh as peaches and cream, as pretty as a sunny day; she and her brother were as alike as peas in a pod but with one major difference: she had none of Platonov's listlessness, but was lively and talkative.†

'Good-day to you, brother! Oh, I'm so happy you've come. Although Konstantin's not at home—but he'll be back soon.'

'Where's he gone?'

'He has business to settle in the village with some buyers,' she said, escorting her guests into the house.

Chichikov inspected with interest the dwelling of this remarkable man, who brought in an income of 200,000 roubles, hoping to discover in its furnishings the key to his host's character, as one studies an empty shell and imagines the oyster or snail that once inhabited it and left there its imprint. But he was disappointed. The rooms were all simple, even bare: no murals, no pictures, no bronzes, no flowers, no pretty stands with porcelain ornaments, no books, even. In short, everything bore witness that the man who lived here spent the great part of his life not within the four walls of this room, but in the fields outside, and that even his thinking was not conducted at leisure, in sybaritic fashion, reclining in a soft armchair before a blazing hearth, but out there, where his ideas were to be brought to life—that was where the thoughts came into his mind, and that too was where they were put into effect. Only here and there, in the appointments of the rooms, could Chichikov detect a woman's touch: clean limewood boards had been placed on the tables and chairs and flowers spread out on them to dry.

'What's all this rubbish lying around, sister?' asked Platonov.

'What do you mean: rubbish?' said their hostess. 'That's the best cure for a fever. We used it last year to cure all our peasants. These here are for liquors, and these for syrups. You may laugh at any mention of making jam and pickles, but when you taste them you'll be full of praise.'

Platonov stepped up to the fortepiano and started tapping at the keys.

'Heavens, what an old cronk!' he exclaimed. 'Aren't you ashamed of it, sister?'

'You must forgive me, brother, but it's been a very long time since I had the time to spend on music. I have an eight-year-old daughter whom I have to teach. You might think I should hand her over to a governess so that I can have the leisure to play music—but no, forgive me, brother, that I shall not do.'

'Really, how tedious you've become, sister,' said her brother, and walked across to the window.

'Aha! There he is! He's on his way here!' said Platonov. Chichikov also hurried over to the window. Walking towards the porch was a man of some forty years, lively, and swarthy in appearance, wearing a camel-hair coat. He had no thought for his attire. He wore a velveteen peaked cap. Two men of a lower class, their caps doffed, walked along on either side of him, discussing something as they walked. One was a simple countryman; the other, in a dark blue caftan, apparently a visiting koulak, looked like an out-and-out knave. They came to a stop by the porch, so their discussion could be heard inside.

†'This is what you had better do: buy your release from your master. I could perhaps lend you the money; afterwards you could pay it back by working for me.'

'No, please, Konstantin Fyodorovich, why should we buy our release? Just take us. With you, any man would learn clever things—nowhere in this wide world is there another man as clever as you. But our problem is that, these days, we can't take proper care of ourselves. The innkeepers have started selling such potent liquors that one small glass gives you cramps in your stomach and you want to drink a whole bucket of water. And before you come to your senses you've blown all your money. There are too many temptations. If you ask me, it's the devil's work, he's running the shop, that what it is! Everything is arranged to throw us simple folk off the track: tobacco and all these ⟨. . .⟩ There's nothing for it, Konstantin Fyodorovich. People are people—you won't hold them back.'

'But listen, this is what you must understand: even with me, you won't be free. It's true that, to start with, you'll get everything: a cow and a horse; but then you've got to remember that I expect much more from my peasants than anyone else. For me, work comes first; whether you work for me or for yourself, it doesn't matter, but I don't let any man loaf about. I work like an ox myself, and, brother, my peasants do the same, because I know from experience that when a man stops working, that's when his head fills with nonsense. So you think about all this in your village and discuss it among ⟨yourselves⟩.'

'But we've already discussed it, Konstantin Fyodorovich. We've heard it from the old men, too. There's no getting away from it—all your peasants are rich men, and that's no accident; even your priests are the milk of human kindness. Meanwhile they took all our priests away and there's no one to bury our dead.'

'All the same, go back and talk it over.'

'As you say, sir.'†

'So, how about it, Konstantin Fyodorovich?—Be so kind... bring your price down a little,' said the visiting koulak in the blue caftan, walking on his other side.

'But I've told you already: I don't like to haggle. I'm not the sort of landowner you can descend on the very day he has to make his interest payments to the loan bank. I know you lot. You people have lists of all the landlords, you know exactly who has to pay how much, when, and to whom. There's no great mystery to it. You think: they're putting pressure on him, so he'll let me have it for half the price. But what's your money to me? I can hold on to my stuff for three years if I like! I don't have any loans to pay off.'

'Quite true, Konstantin Fyodorovich. But then I'm just... it's only for the pleasure of your company in the future, you see, and not for any personal gain. Won't you accept three thousand in advance?'

The koulak took out a wad of greasy banknotes from inside his caftan. Kostanzhoglo accepted the money very casually and, without bothering to count it, stuffed the wad in the back pocket of his frock-coat.

'Look at that!' thought Chichikov. 'Just as if it were a handkerchief.'

†Then Kostanzhoglo appeared in the doorway of the drawing-room. Chichikov was still more amazed by the swarthiness of his face, the crispness of his black hair, prematurely grizzled in places, the lively expression in his eyes, and a suggestion of bitterness, the print of his provenance from the fiery south. He wasn't a pure Russian. He himself did not know whence his ancestors hailed; he had never pursued his genealogy, considering this a futile occupation and of no use in the running of an estate. He was even quite convinced that he was Russian for he knew no language other than Russian.†

Platonov presented Chichikov. They embraced.

'Well, I've decided to go travelling around different provinces,' said Platonov, 'it might cure me of my melancholy.'

'Excellent idea,' said Kostanzhogolo. 'To which places, precisely,' he continued, turning affably to Chichikov, 'might you be thinking of directing your path?'

'I must confess,' said Chichikov, inclining his head to one side in a genial manner and, at the same time, stroking the arm of his chair with one hand, 'I travel, for the moment, not so much on my own behalf, as on that of another. General Betrishchev, a close friend, and, I might say, benefactor, has asked me to visit his relations. Relations, of course, are all very well in their own way, but it is partly, so to speak, for myself too; because, to be sure, not to mention the benefit that can be derived in haemorrhoidal respects, merely to see the world, the circumfluence of people, is ... er, so to speak, a living book, a science in itself.'

'Yes, it does no harm to look around.'

'You do put it most excellently,' remarked Chichikov, 'it is, indeed, just so. You see things you would not have seen otherwise; you meet people you would never have met. Conversation with them is its own reward: take, for example, our present encounter... I appeal to you, my most esteemed Konstantin Fyodorovich, teach me, teach me, slake my thirst with the waters of your wisdom. I await your sweet words like manna from heaven.'

'But what, though?... Teach you what?' said Kostanzhoglo, visibly embarrassed. All the education I received was that which could be bought for a few brass coins.'

'Wisdom, my most esteemed sir, wisdom! The wisdom to stand at the helm of the unruly barque of agriculture, the wisdom to reap sound profits, to accumulate property that is not a figment of the imagination, but real and substantial, and thereby to fulfil my duty as a citizen, to earn the respect of my fellow countrymen.'

'Do you know what?' said Kostanzhoglo, gazing at him pensively, 'just spend the day with me. I'll show you all my management and tell you about everything. There's no secret wisdom here, as you'll see, none at all.'

'Of course you shall spend the day here,' said his wife and, turning to Platonov, added: 'Brother, stop a while with us, why go rushing off?'

'It's fine by me. What about Pavel Ivanovich?'

'I too, with great pleasure... But there's one small circumstance— I have to call on a relation of General Betrishchev. There's a certain Colonel Koshkaryov...'

'But he's... he's a lunatic.'

'That's what I've heard: a lunatic. I have no business with him myself. But since General Betrishchev is a close friend, and even, so to speak, a benefactor...'

'In that case, you know what,' said Kostanzhoglo, 'call on him right away: he's less than ten versts away and my trap is standing ready. If you set off now, you'll be back in time for tea.'

'Capital idea!' exclaimed Chichikov, taking up his hat.

The trap was brought up and in half an hour it swept him to the colonel's. The colonel's whole village was in a state of total disarray: new buildings going up, old ones being rebuilt, heaps of lime, bricks, and logs all over the streets. Some buildings had been put up in the style of government offices. Emblazoned in gold letters across one was the legend: 'Agricultural Implements Depot'; across another: 'Chief Paymaster's Department', then 'Committee for Rural Affairs' and 'School for the Proper Enlightenment of the Villagers'—in a word, the devil only knows what!

†He found the colonel standing at a lectern, holding a quill between his teeth. He received Chichikov exceptionally warmly. To look at he was the most kind-hearted, the most considerate of men:† he started recounting to his visitor how hard he had laboured to raise the village to its present level of prosperity; with great fellow-feeling he lamented how difficult it was to convince a peasant that there were higher joys which a man derives from enlightened splendour and the arts; how, to that day, he had failed to persuade any of the women to wear corsets, †while in Germany, where he had been stationed with his regiment in 1814, the miller's daughter had even been able to play the fortepiano;† how, notwithstanding all this, despite all the stubbornness and ignorance, he would finally succeed in getting the peasants on his village, as they walked behind the plough, to read Benjamin Franklin's book about lightning conductors, or Virgil's *Georgics*, or *The Chemical Analysis of the Soil*.*

'He'll be lucky!' thought Chichikov. 'And to think that after all this time I still haven't read *La Duchesse de la Vallière*: there simply isn't the time.'

And the colonel continued to expatiate at length on how to steer people towards a life of prosperity. He attached great significance to the Parisian mode of dress. He was prepared to wager his life that one need only to put half the peasants in Russia into German trousers and the arts and sciences would soar to new heights, commerce would flourish and a Golden Age would dawn in Russia.

After gazing intently at him for a few moments, Chichikov reflected: 'No point in standing on ceremony with this one.' And, without further ado, he announced that there was a need for certain souls and for the effecting of certain purchases, with all the necessary formalities.

'As far as I can tell from your words,' said the colonel, without turning a hair, 'you're making a request, are you not?'

'I am indeed.'

'In that case put it in writing. It will go before the Office for Incoming Reports and Depositions. The Office will record it and send it on to me. From me it will proceed to the Committee for

Rural Affairs, and thence, once the necessary amendments have been introduced, to the Senior Steward. The Senior Steward, in consultation with the Secretary...'

'Hold on a second,' exclaimed Chichikov. 'In that way, the matter will drag on God knows until when. And then—how can this be dealt with in writing? After all, this is the sort of matter... The souls, you see, are, in a certain sense... dead ones.'

'And a very good thing too. Write it down, like that, that the souls are in a certain sense dead ones.'

'But how can we put that—"dead ones"? You can't write things like that. They might be dead, admittedly, but we have to make it seem as if they were alive.'

'Fine. Just write it like that: "but it is necessary, or required, or desirable, that they should appear to be alive." The matter cannot be dealt with without going through the paperwork and formalities. Take England, and even Napoleon himself, as an example. I shall dispatch the Commissioner to escort you to the necessary offices.'

He rang a bell; a man appeared.

'Ah, Secretary! Tell the Commissioner I wish to see him.' The Commissioner appeared, some fellow who was not entirely a peasant, nor yet a functionary. 'He will escort you to the proper offices.'

Chichikov decided to go with the Commissioner, out of sheer curiosity, and see for himself all these terribly important offices. The Office for the Submission of Reports and Depositions existed only on its sign, and its doors were locked. Its chief of staff, one Khrulev, had been transferred to the newly established Rural Construction Committee. His place had been taken by the valet Berezovsky; but he too had been dispatched somewhere else by the Construction Commission. They plied their suit at the Department of Rural Affairs—but some reconstruction was in progress there; they shook awake a drunk peasant, but they could get no sense out of him.

'The place is a mess,' the Commissioner finally said to Chichikov. 'We don't know if we're coming or going. They all lead the master by the nose. The Construction Commission rules the roost here; it takes all the men away from their work, and sends them wherever it likes. That's the only place worth working, for us, on the Construction Commission, I mean.' It was clear he was displeased with the Construction Commission. And it was true, as Chichikov could see:

everywhere construction work was under way. He decided to look no further, but, returning to the house, informed the colonel how things stood, that his place was a mess and it was impossible to get anything done and that, as for the Commission for the Submission of Reports,* it didn't even exist.

The colonel boiled up with noble indignation and, as a sign of his gratitude, gripped Chichikov's hand tight. Without further ado, he reached for pen and paper, and wrote down eight inquiries which were to be pursued with the utmost severity: by what right did the Construction Commission give orders to officials from departments over which it had no authority? How could the Chief Steward have permitted the Deputy to depart on an investigation without first giving up his post? And how could the Committee for Rural Affairs remain unconcerned that the Commission for the Submission of Reports and Depositions did not even exist?

'This is really too ridiculous,' thought Chichikov and started to make his farewells.

'No, I shall not let you go. My self-esteem is now at stake. I shall demonstrate what the organic and correct organization of a business should be. I shall now entrust your affairs to a man who is worth more than the rest of my staff put together: he is a graduate of the university. For such is the stuff of which my serfs are made... So as not to lose any more valuable time, I ⟨implore⟩ you: just sit a while in my library,' said the colonel, opening a side door. 'Here you will find books, paper, pens, pencils—everything. Please use whatever you like—feel quite at home. The path to enlightenment should be open to all.'

Such were Koshkaryov's words as he led Chichikov to his book repository. This was an enormous chamber, lined with books from floor to ceiling. There were even some stuffed animals too. †The books were on every subject under the sun—on arboriculture, boviculture, swiniculture, horticulture; special journals of every kind, of the sort which can only be obtained by subscription—but which no one ever reads. Once he was sure there was nothing here that could be called light reading, he turned to another bookcase. Out of the frying pan into the fire. These were all books of philosophy. Six massive tomes stood directly before his eyes, bearing the title: *Propaedeutics to the Theory of Thought in its Communality, Conjunctivity, and Essentiality and in Application to the Comprehension of the Organic*

Principles of Social Productivity.† Whichever book Chichikov leafed through, on every page he would encounter such words as 'manifestation', 'development', 'abstract', 'exclusivity', and 'conclusivity', and the devil knows what else besides. 'This is not my sort of stuff,' said Chichikov, and turned to a third case, which held books on the arts. Here he pulled out a large, fat volume embellished with immodest mythological illustrations, which he started to peruse. Pictures of this kind are to the liking of middle-aged bachelors, and sometimes even to spry old men of the sort who have a predilection for the ballet and other spicy entertainments. Having finished his perusal of this book Chichikov was on the point of pulling down another in the same vein, when Colonel Koshkaryov suddenly entered, beaming radiantly and clutching a piece of paper.

'All has been done and done most excellently. The man I was telling you about is an undeniable genius. For that I shall promote ⟨him⟩ above all the others: I shall institute a special department, just for him. You shall see for yourself what a brilliant mind he has and how he was able to settle everything in a matter of minutes.'

'Well, the Lord be praised,' thought Chichikov and prepared to listen. The Colonel started to read:

' "Embarking upon the deliberation of the commission assigned to me by Your Worship, I have to report thereupon as follows: First. The actual petition submitted by Collegiate Councillor and Cavalier Pavel Ivanovich Chichikov Esq. contains a certain misconception, for, through an oversight, the census souls are described as deceased. Hereunder, it is presumed, that what the aforesaid gentleman had in mind were those close to death, and not those already dead. Indeed, the very use of the epithet betrays a study of the sciences that is merely empirical, probably limited to the parish school, for the soul is immortal." '

'The rogue!' said Koshkaryov, pausing and smiling contentedly. 'Here he's had a bit of a jab at you. But you have to hand it to him: he knows how to wield a pen.

' "Second. Of the aforementioned registered souls, whether close to death, or any others, for that matter, there are none on the estate which are not already mortgaged, and re-mortgaged, with a supplementary loan of one hundred and fifty roubles per soul, with the exception of the small village of Gurmailovka, which, owing to our litigation with the landowner Predishchev, is in a disputatious position and which cannot therefore be entered into either sale or mortgage, as promulgated in the 42nd issue of the *Moscow Gazette*".'*

'Now why in God's name did you not tell me all this before? Why waste my time with all this nonsense?' said Chichikov heatedly.

'There, you see: we had to do it so ⟨you⟩ could see it set out on paper. Now you can see it's a serious matter. Any fool could work it out without thinking, but this had to be set out in a deliberate fashion.'

Enraged, Chichikov seized up his cap and stormed out of the house, disregarding all courtesies and proprieties: now he was truly angry. The coachman was standing ready, with the trap still in harness; he knew that it was pointless to unharness the horses since a request for fodder would have to be submitted in writing and the resolution to issue oats to the horses would only have been adopted the following day. The colonel, nevertheless, came running out, all tact and consideration. He vigorously squeezed Chichikov's hand, pressed it to his heart, and thanked his guest for affording him the chance to see the system of paperwork in operation; he assured him that he would have to issue a few drubbings and dressings-down, because the pall of lethargy could settle over everything and the springs of rural management would rust and weaken; that as a result of this incident he had had a bright idea: to set up a new commission to be called the Commission for the Supervision of the Construction Commission, so that then no one would dare steal a thing.

Chichikov returned, angry and disgruntled, late in the evening, long after the candles had been lit.

'What kept you so late?' asked ⟨Kostanzhoglo⟩, when he appeared in the doorway.

'What have you been discussing with him for so long?' said Platonov.

'In all my life I've never seen such a fool,' said ⟨Chichikov⟩.

'You've seen nothing yet!' said ⟨Kostanzhoglo⟩. 'Koshkaryov is a reassuring phenomenon. He is necessary because he reflects in caricature and more vividly the foibles of those people who think themselves so clever, those smart fellows who, without trying to understand what they see here at home, cram their heads full of stupid foreign ideas. That's the sort of landowner you find nowadays; they've set up offices and manufactories and schools and commissions and the devil knows what else besides. That's what they're like, these clever chaps. They've only just recovered from the visit by the Frenchman in 1812* and they're off rearranging everything again. They've managed to do more damage even than the Frenchman, so that now some Pyotr Petrovich Petukh passes for a good landowner.'

'But he's also mortgaged his property,' said Chichikov.

'Of course, he's mortgaged everything, everything gets mortgaged.' As he said this Kostanzhoglo started to get more and more angry. 'Now you'll find hat factories and candle factories, they bring skilled candlemakers from London—they've all turned into petty tradesmen. To be a landowner is such a respected calling—but they've all turned into peddlers and costermongers. Spinning machines—to make muslins for the local wenches and trollops.'

'But you have factories too, don't you?' observed Platonov.

'And who set them up? They set themselves up: there was a surplus of wool—it was impossible to get rid of the stuff—so I started to weave cloth, plain, thick cloth; I sell it cheaply right here in the markets—it's what the peasants need, what my peasants need. For six years the fish merchants used to dump the fish scales on my river banks; what else could they do with the stuff? So I started to boil it up into glue and it's brought in forty thousand. That's the way everything is with me.'

'The clever devil!' thought Chichikov, staring at him in wonderment, 'what grasping paws!'

'But the reason I started these businesses was that I had so many workmen, many would simply have starved to death. It was a year of famine, all thanks to those clever manufacturers, who had let their fields go to rack and ruin. In time, I'll have a lot more factories here, on my place, brother. Every year I set up a new one, depending on what surpluses and discarded produce I have. Just take a close look at your farm and you'll find all sorts of rubbish which can bring in a profit, so much that in the end you cast it aside and say: "Enough—I don't need any more." After all, I don't need to build palaces with colonnades and porticos for these factories.'

'That's astounding! But the most astounding thing is that any rubbish can bring in a profit!' said Chichikov.

†'It can indeed. But you have to take things exactly as they are and keep them plain and simple; with the way things are ordered today, however, everyone wants to show that he's some sort of engineer and, as in the fable, he wants to open a simple box with his

fancy tools, not just by lifting the lid.* And to do so he takes himself specially to England, that's the stupid thing. The idiots!' As he said this Kostanzhoglo spat in disgust. 'And yet he's a hundred times more stupid when he returns from his trip abroad.'

'Now, now Konstantin, you've got yourself all worked up again,' interjected his wife anxiously. 'You know it's not good for you.'

'How can I help getting worked up? It would be all very well, if it was something that didn't concern me, but these are all matters close to my heart. What is most vexing is that the Russian character itself is being ruined. These days there's a Quixotic streak in the Russian character that was never there before. Once he gets a little education in his head, he at once becomes the Don Quixote of enlightenment, setting up schools that even an idiot wouldn't dream of. The sort of men that these schools produce are good for nothing, neither on the farm nor in the town. All they're good for is getting drunk and feeling proud of themselves. Once they turn their hand to philanthropy—they become Don Quixotes at that too: they spend a million roubles on the erection of completely pointless hospitals and grand edifices with colonnades, they ruin themselves and turn everyone else into beggars; that's their philanthropy for you.'

Chichikov wasn't interested in anyone's education. He wanted to question his host closely about how any old rubbish can be turned to profit, but Kostanzhoglo wouldn't let him get a word in edgeways. The bile seethed within him and the words came pouring out in an unstoppable flow.

'They start wondering how to enlighten their peasants. First you should turn him into a wealthy and capable farmer, then he'll go out and get his own education. But look at the way things are today, the whole world has grown more stupid than you could possibly imagine. You should see the rubbish some of these scribblers write! Some idiot, still wet behind the ears, publishes a book and every-one goes mad about it. This is the sort of thing they're saying: "The peasant leads too plain, too simple a life; one should acquaint him with luxury, and instil in him desires beyond the means to which he can aspire."† Yet it is precisely this luxury which has made them soft and turned them into worthless rubbish, and caused them to contract the devil knows what diseases; among them even eighteen-year-old youths have tried their hand at everything: they have no teeth left in their mouths and their heads are as bald as blown up bladders—and now they want to infect the peasants too! But we should thank the Lord that we still have at least one healthy class left among us, which has not yet acquired a taste for those pursuits. We really should thank the Lord for that. Yes, for me the tiller of the soil is the most respected of men: why should you want to change him? I would to God we were all tillers of the soil!'

'So would you hold that tilling the soil is the most profitable occupation?' asked Chichikov.

'The most legitimate, not the most profitable. As it is said: "In the sweat of thy brow shalt thou till the land."* There's no argument about it. For it has been proven with the experience of centuries that the man who tills the land for a living is superior in his morals, purer, more noble, more exalted. †I do not mean that he should have no other calling, but tilling the land should be the basis for all others, that's what. Factories will rise up by themselves, and these shall be legitimate factories—the sort that are right there where they are needed, and not this kind, pandering to every whim, which have made our people go soft. Nor are they the sort of factories which, later on, to keep up supply and demand, resort to all kinds of underhand tricks, and corrupt and deprave the hapless Russian people. No: say what you will in their defence, but I won't set up any of those enterprises which excite these so-called higher needs, such as tobacco, or sugar, even if it means I lose millions. No, if corruption is to enter the world, let it not be through my doing. Rather may I stand without shame before God... I have lived with my peasants for twenty years; I know what consequences all this may have.'

'Yet the thing which most amazes me is how, following a sound management method, you can make a profit from left-overs, from cast-off produce, from all sorts of rubbish.'

'Ha! Political economists!' exclaimed Kostanzhoglo, not listening to Chichikov, with a look of bilious sarcasm on his face. 'A fine lot, those political economists. One fool sits on another fool's back and uses a third fool to goad him forward. They can see no further than their stupid noses. Take your political economist: he's a donkey, but he'll stick eyeglasses on his nose and be up at the blackboard, to lecture the likes of you and me... What idiots!' And he spat again in his rage.

'That's all quite true and no one's disputing it, but there's no need to get so angry about it,' said his wife, 'it seems you cannot talk about all this without falling into a rage.'†

'As one listens to you, my most respected Konstantin Fyodorovich,' said Chichikov, 'the deeper one delves, so to speak, into the meaning of life, the closer one draws to the very kernel of the matter. But if one might leave aside the universal issues for a moment, and turn one's attention to those close at hand, might I ask if, should we say, one were to become a landowner, and should one conceive the ambition to amass a sufficient fortune in a relatively short ⟨time⟩, in order thereby, so to speak, to be able to fulfil one's duty as a citizen, in such an event, how should one proceed?'

'How to amass a fortune?' repeated Kostanzhoglo. 'This is what you should do...'

'Let's go in to supper!' said the lady of the house, rising from the settee, and, wrapping a shawl round her chilled young shoulders, she led the way into the middle of the room.

Chichikov sprang from his chair with the agility almost of a military man, held out his arm to her like a yoke and ceremoniously escorted her through two rooms into the dining-room, where the soup tureen stood ready on the table and, with its lid removed, filled the air with the agreeable aroma of a potage of fresh greens and the first root vegetables of spring. They all took their places at table. The servants efficiently set the remaining courses on the table, in covered dishes, together with the necessary condiments, and at once withdrew. Kostanzhoglo did not like to have his house servants eavesdrop on their master's conversations and, still less, to stare at his mouth while he ⟨ate⟩.

After dispatching his soup and chasing it down with a glass of some excellent liquor, not unlike a Tokay, Chichikov addressed his host in the following terms:

'Permit me, my most esteemed sir, to return once more to the subject of our earlier discussion. I was asking you how to act, what to do, what best to undertake... ⟨. . .⟩*

'It's such a fine estate that even if he were to ask forty thousand for it, I would pay him on the spot.'

'Hm!' Chichikov grew pensive. 'But then,' he continued with a certain timidity, 'why don't you buy it yourself?'

'You have to know where to call a halt. As it is, I have enough bother with my estates. Besides, the local gentry are already raising hell, complaining that I'm taking advantage of the sorry state of their affairs to buy up their land for a song. I'm sick to death of hearing them moan about it.'

'Ah yes, people are so prone to malicious talk!' said Chichikov.

'Quite so, and right here, in our own province... You simply couldn't imagine the things they say about me. They actually call me a moneygrubber and skinflint of the first order. They won't accept the blame for anything. "Of course, I frittered it all away," they say, "but only because I followed the nobler aspirations of life, and because I gave encouragement to industrialists—or rather, swindling rogues, who ⟨. . .⟩ otherwise, of course, one could live swinishly, like Kostanzhoglo."'

'How I should like to live so swinishly!' said Chichikov.

'And it's all lies and poppycock. What nobler aspirations? Whom do they think they are fooling? They might lay in large stocks of books, but they never read them. All that matters to them is cards and drinking. And it's all because I don't give great dinner parties or lend them money. I do not give dinners because I would find them tedious and anyway I'm not accustomed to them. But if you wish to come and take pot-luck with me—I shall be only delighted. To say I do not lend money is nonsense. If you are in real need, come and explain in detail how you intend to make use of my money. If I see from what you say that you are going to use it wisely and that the money will bring you a clear profit, I shan't refuse you and I shall not even charge interest.'

'Hm, that's something worth noting,' remarked Chichikov to himself.

'In such a case, I shall never refuse someone,' continued Kostanzhoglo. 'But I am not going to throw money to the four winds. I beg humble forgiveness, but I shall not do it! Some fellow—the devil take him!—wants to throw a fancy dinner for his mistress, or furnishes his house in an absurdly extravagant manner, or goes to a masked ball with a trollop—or to some festive gathering, to celebrate a wasted life on this earth—and I'm expected to lend him money...'

At this point Kostanzhoglo spat and very nearly uttered one or two indecorous and abusive words in the presence of his spouse. The severe shadow of melancholy darkened his face. Wrinkles gathered across and down his forehead, betraying the angry upsurge of bile within him.

'Allow me, my esteemed sir, to return you once again to the subject of our interrupted conversation,' said Chichikov, drinking a glass of the raspberry liqueur, which was, indeed, excellent. 'If, let us suppose, I were to acquire that same estate which you have mentioned, in how much time and how quickly could I get sufficiently rich to...'

'If you wish,' interjected Kostanzhoglo abruptly and in a stern voice, still very ill-humoured, 'to get rich quickly, then you will never get rich at all; if, however, you merely wish to get rich, without asking when, you will get rich quickly.'

'Oh,' said Chichikov, 'I see.'

'Yes,' Kostanzhoglo said brusquely, as if he were actually angry with Chichikov himself. 'You have to love work; nothing would be achieved without that. Yes, you have to love running your estate. And believe me, it's not in the least bit tedious. They would even have one believe that life in the country is a bore—and yet I would die, I would hang myself from boredom, if I had to spend even a single day in the town living like them, with their stupid clubs, inns, and theatres. They're all fools, halfwits, a breed of jackasses! A landowner cannot be bored, he has no time for boredom. There is not a single patch of emptiness in his life—everything is fullness. You only have to consider the great variety of his work—and what splendid work it is! This is work that elevates a man's spirit. Whatever you may say, on the farm a man walks side-by-side with nature, with the seasons of the year, he is both participant and interlocutor in all the processes of creation.

'Consider only the yearly cycle of his work, how, even before spring has broken everything is in place and waiting for its arrival: the seed has to be prepared; there is the sifting and the weighing of the grain in the barns, and the drying; the new levies to be set. Costs for the entire ⟨year⟩ must be determined and all expenditure planned in advance. When the ice breaks on the rivers and the water flows once again, the land dries out and the fields must be dug: in the vegetable gardens the spade is hard at work and in the fields—the plough and harrow. Then there is the planting, sowing, and winnowing. Do you know what that means? You think it a small matter? Sowing the future harvest! Sowing the bounty of all God's earth! Sowing the nourishment for millions.

'Next it's summer—scything and haymaking. Then, before you know it, it's time to reap: rye followed by more rye, then wheat, followed by barley, and then oats. Everything is ripe, bursting with ripeness; no minute is to be lost. You could have twenty pairs of eyes and they would all be kept busy. And once it has all been taken in it must be stored in the drying barns and stacked into ricks, and then the winter planting begins, and the barns, the threshing floors, and the animal pens must be repaired, the women's work has to be done, then you take stock and see all that has been done, and it's quite simply...

'But then it's winter! Threshing on all the floors, carting the grain from the threshing sheds to the barns. You have to call at the mill, at the manufactories, you must take a look at the workyard, and also at your peasants, to see how they're doing their own work. For me it's a thing of joy to watch a carpenter who knows how to wield an axe; I can stand watching him for two hours on end, it so delights my heart. And then, you must also remember to what purpose all this work is done, how everything around you grows and multiplies, bringing forth fruit and profit! No, I couldn't begin to describe the pleasure it gives you. And it's not because the money increases—after all, money is not the be-all and end-all—but because it is all the work of your own hands; because you can see that you are the progenitor and creator of everything, and that you dispense goodness and abundance like some sort of magician. Where else can you find me pleasure to equal that?' said Kostanzhoglo, his eyes gazing upwards and all the wrinkles vanishing from his face. He was happy as a tsar on the day of his coronation; he was aglow and his face seemed to shine with its own radiance.

'No, nowhere in the whole world will you find another such pleasure! It is here, precisely here, that man works in God's image: God has reserved to Himself the task of creation as the supreme delight, and He demands of man that, like Him, he too should be the creator of prosperity and beneficence all about him. And some people call that boring work!'

Chichikov listened, enraptured, to his host's mellifluous speeches, as to the singing of a bird of paradise. His mouth watered. His eyes took on an expression of the utmost sweetness and he felt he could listen to Kostanzhoglo's discourse for ever.

'Konstantin! It's time to get up,' said their hostess, rising from her chair. They all rose. Holding out his arm like a yoke Chichikov led his hostess back to the drawing-room. But his movements had lost their erstwhile adroitness, because his thoughts were occupied with more essential matters.

'Say what you will, it's boring all the same,' said Platonov, walking behind them.

'Our guest, it seems, is a far from stupid man,' thought the host, 'moderate in his words and not a braggart either.' And these reflections made him still more cheerful, as if warmed by his own words and, as it were, rejoicing at having found a man willing to listen to wise counsel.

When afterwards they had all taken their seats in the candle-lit drawing-room, a small and cosy room with a French window, through which they looked out on to a balcony and the garden outside, and beheld the night sky, where the myriad stars, suspended high above the slumbering trees, twinkled back at them, Chichikov felt more content than he had for a very long time. It was as if after long peregrinations he had at last reached hearth and home and, now his work was done and all his desires fulfilled, he had declared, casting aside his wayfarer's staff: 'No more!' This sense of enchantment, this spell had been cast on his soul by the sagacious words of his hospitable host.

For every man there are certain subjects of conversation which are somehow dearer and closer to him in spirit than any other. And it often happens that, in some God-forsaken backwater, in a desert of desolation, you unexpectedly meet a man whose warming conversation makes you forget the impassable state of the roads, the discomfort of your billet, the vanity of the modern world, and the deceitfulness of the false illusions which lead man astray. An evening thus spent will remain vivid in your mind forever after, and your memory will faithfully preserve all that has passed: who was present, who sat in which seat, and what he held in his hands; you will remember the walls, the corners, and every little trifle.

Thus too did Chichikov's memory record everything that evening: not only that small and unpretentiously furnished room, the good-natured expression which remained constantly on the face of his host, but also the pattern on the wallpaper, the pipe with the amber mouthpiece given to Platonov, the smoke which he blew into the fat jowls of the dog Yarb, Yarb's snorting, and the laughter of their pretty hostess, interrupted by her words: 'Enough, stop tormenting the dog', and the cheerful candles, the cricket singing in the corner, the French window, and, gazing back in at them, the spring night, studded with countless stars, seemingly propped high above the tops of the trees, and filled with the music of the nightingales lustily giving voice from deep within the dense green foliage below.

'Your words are sweet to me, my most esteemed Konstantin Fyodorovich,' announced Chichikov. 'I can say that in all Russia I have not met a man equal to you in wisdom.'

Kostanzhoglo smiled. He could sense that these words were not entirely without validity.

'No, Pavel Ivanovich,' he said, 'if you really wish to meet a wise man, there is one such among us, someone of whom you can, in all truth, say: "Now this is a wise man, whose shoelace I am not fit to tie".'

'Who is that?' asked Chichikov in amazement.

'That's our commissionaire,* Murazov.'

'This is the second time I've heard that name!' exclaimed Chichikov.

'Now that is a man capable of managing not just a landowner's estate, but an entire empire. If I had a state of my own I would at once make him my minister of finance.'

'I've heard of him. They say he is a man whose capabilities surpass all comprehension; he has amassed ten million, they say.'

'Ten—that's nothing! He has well in excess of forty! Soon half of Russia will be in his hands.'

'You're not serious!' gasped Chichikov, his eyes starting from his head and his mouth agape.

'Without a shadow of doubt. It's plain for all to see. It is only those whose fortunes are measured in hundreds of thousands who grow rich slowly; he that has millions has a far greater range: whatever he puts his hand to will at once increase two or threefold. His field, his scope is too extensive. He simply has no competitors. There is none that can contend with him. Whatever price he fixes will stand: there is no one to outbid him.'

'Lord God in heaven above,' repeated Chichikov, crossing himself. He stared into Kostanzhoglo's eyes, breathless with excitement. 'Why, it's simply beyond belief! It's terrifying to think of. People marvel at the wisdom of Providence when they contemplate a tiny insect; but what I find more astounding is that such immense sums can be held in the hands of a mere mortal! Permit me to put one question to you with regard to a certain circumstance: tell me, surely— in the beginning at least—these sums must have been acquired in a not entirely unimpeachable manner?...'

'In the most irreproachable manner and by the most regular means.'

'Incredible. If it had been thousands, then perhaps, but millions...'

'On the contrary, with thousands it would be hard to proceed in a blameless manner, but millions are easy to amass. There is no need for a millionaire to have recourse to crooked methods. He need only follow the straightest possible road and grab everything lying in his path! No one else can pick it up: no one else has the power, he is without competitors. His scope is vast, I tell you: whatever he sets his hand to will multiply two or threefold. But what can you get from a paltry thousand? Ten, perhaps twenty per cent.'

'But what most defies comprehension is that all this must have started with a single copeck!'

'It cannot happen any other way. That is the proper order of things,' said ⟨Kostanzhoglo⟩. 'The man born with thousands, reared on thousands, will never acquire anything: he already has ingrained whims and caprices and all that nonsense. You have to start from the very beginning, and not from the middle, from the copeck, and not the rouble, from the very bottom, not from the top. Only there will you properly get to know the people and the milieu in which later you will have to make your way. When you have felt the blows of adversity on your own skin, when you have learnt that every one-copeck piece is held fast by a three-copeck nail, when you have undergone every imaginable ordeal, then you will be so well-schooled and wise to the ways of the world that you will never make any blunder in any transaction and never let anything slip from your grasp. Believe me, it's the truth. You must begin at the beginning and not in the middle. If a man tells me: "Give me a hundred thousand, I'll get rich immediately," I won't believe him: he's banking on luck and not on certainty. You must start with a copeck!'

'In that case I shall grow rich,' said Chichikov, involuntarily re-calling his dead souls, 'because I really am beginning with nothing.'

'Konstantin, it's time to let Pavel Ivanovich rest and have a little sleep,' said their hostess, 'but you keep rabbiting on.'

'You will most definitely grow rich,' said Kostanzhoglo, not listening to his wife. 'Rivers will flow into your hands, rivers of gold. You will not know what to do with the profits.'

Pavel Ivanovich sat spellbound, his thoughts spinning in a golden sphere of fancies and wild imaginings. Giving free rein to his imagination, he wove still richer golden patterns into the golden tapestry of his future enterprises, and he heard, ringing in his ears, the words: "Rivers, rivers of gold will flow."

'Really, Konstantin, it's time for Pavel Ivanovich to retire.'

'Why are you fussing? Why don't you run along, if you're tired!' said the host and suddenly stopped in mid-word, because the entire room reverberated to the loud noise of Platonov's snoring, accompanied by the even louder snores of Yarb. Kostanzhoglo realized that it was, indeed, time for bed. He nudged Platonov, saying: 'Enough of your snoring,' and bade Chichikov a good night. They all withdrew to their respective rooms and were soon fast asleep.

Chichikov alone was unable to sleep. His thoughts refused to quiesce. He was pondering how to become the owner of a real, and not an imaginary, estate. After his conversation with his host everything had become so clear; the possibility of growing rich seemed now so real. The arduous task of managing an estate appeared so simple and comprehensible, and so suited to his own nature! He needed only raise a loan on these dead souls of his, and he could become the owner of an estate that was in no way imaginary. He could already see himself acting and managing affairs just as Kostanzhoglo had instructed—efficiently, prudently, introducing nothing new without first learning the old through and through, inspecting everything himself, becoming personally acquainted with all his peasants, renouncing all luxuries, and dedicating himself utterly to his labours and management. He could already savour the pleasure he would experience when a harmonious order had been established and all the mainsprings of his administrative machine moved swiftly and smoothly, efficiently setting one another in motion. His estate would be a hive of activity and, just as the flour is swiftly ground from grains of wheat by the spinning millstone, so in his mill would money—real, hard cash—be ground from all manner of rubbish and refuse. The image of his wondrous host stood constantly before his eyes. This was the first man in all Russia whom he respected as a person. Hitherto he had respected a man either for his high office, or for his great wealth. There had not been a single man whom he had respected for his wisdom alone. Kostanzhoglo was the first.

Chichikov understood, too, that this was not the sort of man with whom he could broach his shady enterprise. His mind was now engaged by a new project: to buy Khlobuev's estate. He had ten thousand: he reckoned to borrow fifteen thousand from Kostanzhoglo, since the latter had himself declared his willingness to help any man who wished to grow rich. †As for the rest—he could manage somehow or other, either by mortgaging his souls, or simply by making them wait for the money. That would be easy enough: let them waste their time taking him to court, if they wished.† For a long time his thoughts continued to turn on all these matters. Finally the sleep which for the last four hours and more had held the entire house, as the saying goes, in its embrace, at last folded Chichikov too into its arms. He fell sound asleep.

CHAPTER FOUR

The next day everything turned out in the best way imaginable. Kostanzhoglo was delighted to lend him ten thousand without interest, without security—merely against a signed I.O.U. Thus was he prepared to help any man on his road to the acquisition of property. He showed Chichikov all the workings of his estate. It was all so simple and so sensible. Everything was so arranged, that it ran itself. Not a single minute was wasted, nor was there the slightest possibility that any of the peasants might become lax and slovenly. Should one be about to slip, his master, as if all-seeing, would at once lift him back on to his feet. Nowhere were there any idlers to be found. As they harrowed, sowed and ploughed, all the peasants wore on their intelligent faces looks of utmost contentment.

Chichikov could not fail to be astounded by the amount of work accomplished by this man, quietly and without fuss, without fashioning grandiose projects and treatises on the propagation of prosperity to all mankind. He was similarly struck by the futility of the life of the city dweller, one of those scrapers of parquet floors and habitués of salons, or of the architect of grand projects, sitting in his cramped little office and dictating instructions for the far-flung corners of the state.

Chichikov was quite enraptured, and the ambition to become a landowner strengthened in him by the minute. As for Kostanzhoglo, not only did he show him all round his own estate, he even undertook to accompany him to Khlobuev's,* in order that they might inspect the property together. After a filling breakfast they all set off, the three of them sitting together in Pavel Ivanovich's carriage: Kostanzhoglo's cabriolet followed behind, empty. Yarb ran on ahead, chasing birds from the road. For an entire fifteen versts Kostanzhoglo's forests and pastureland stretched along both sides of the road. Everywhere they looked there were forests alternating with meadows. No plant here grew without design, everything had its purpose, as in God's world. But, involuntarily, ⟨. . .⟩ as soon as they entered Khlobuev's land: here, instead of forests, they saw scrawny bushes, gnawed and eaten away by the hungry animals, and spindly stalks of ⟨rye⟩, barely poking above the weeds which choked them. Finally they caught sight of some dilapidated huts, with no hedge or palisade around them and, in their midst, a half-built stone house, as yet uninhabited. Clearly the money had run out before the roof was laid and thus its now blackened walls had remained under a temporary thatch. The owner lived in another, single-storeyed house. He ran out to meet them clad in an old frock-coat, his hair dishevelled and with his boots full of holes. He looked still half-asleep and had a somewhat dissipated air.

He was delighted beyond all measure at the arrival of his visitors, and welcomed them like long-lost brothers.

'Konstantin Fyodorovich! Platon Mikhailovich! How good of you to visit me! Let me rub my eyes! To be honest, I thought no one would ever visit me again. They all shun me like the plague: they think I'll ask for a loan. Oh it's hard, it's hard, Konstantin Fyodorovich! I can see I'm to blame for everything! What can I do? A pig deserves to live in a pigsty. Forgive me, gentlemen, for receiving you in such attire: my boots, as you see, are full of holes. But what can I offer you, tell me?'

'Let us not stand on ceremony. We've come to you on business,' said Kostanzhoglo. 'I've brought you a buyer, Pavel Ivanovich Chichikov.'

'Delighted to make your acquaintance. Let me shake your hand.' Chichikov held out both hands.

'I should have very much liked, my most respected Pavel Ivanovich, to show you an estate that merited your attention... But first tell me this, gentlemen: have you eaten?'

'We've eaten, we've eaten,' said Kostanzhoglo, wishing to press ahead. 'Let's get going without further ado.'

'Indeed, let's go.' Khlobuev picked up his cap. 'Let's go and view the disorder and dissipation I've sown.' The guests also donned their caps and the party set off down the road through the village. On both sides stood wretched hovels, their tiny ⟨windows⟩ blocked with rags.

'Come and see my disorder and dissipation,' said Khlobuev. 'Of course, you did well to eat first. Would you believe it, Konstantin Fyodorovich, there's not a single chicken in the house—that's what things have come to.' He sighed and, as if sensing that little sympathy would be forthcoming from Konstantin Fyodorovich, he put his arm through Platonov's and walked ahead with him, pressing him now and then to his chest. ⟨Kostanzhoglo⟩ and Chichikov were left behind and, walking arm in arm, followed at some distance.

'It's hard, Platon Mikhailych, it's hard!' said Khlobuev to Platonov. 'I can't tell you how hard it is! No money, no grain, no boots! And these are alien problems to us here in Russia! It would have been small worry if I were young and single, but when all these misfortunes strike as you approach old age, with a wife to support and five children—you do feel sad, you can't help feeling sad...'

'Well now, if you sell your estate, will that set you right?' asked Platonov.

'How can it set me right!' said Khlobuev, with a hopeless wave. 'It will all go to pay off my debts and after that I shan't even have a thousand left.'

'So what are you going to do?'

'God knows.'

'But why do you not try to do something to get out of this predicament?'

'Like what?'

'Well, why not take up some position or other?'

'But my rank is only Gubernia Secretary*. What sort of position would that get me? It would be something quite paltry. How could I live on a salary of five hundred? After all, I have a wife and five children.'

'In that case, find a post as a manager.'

'But who would entrust his estate to me! I've ruined my own.'

'Look: when starvation and death stare you in the face, you've got to do something. I'll ask my brother, he may be able to secure an appointment for you through someone or other in town.'

'No, Platon Mikhailovich,' said Khlobuev, with a sigh, and squeezing his arm tight, 'I'm no longer any good for anything. I have grown old before my time, my back aches from the sins of my youth and I have rheumatism in my shoulder. Where can I go? Why ruin the Treasury! As it is, there are hordes of civil servants looking for lucrative appointments. God forbid that, because of me, because of the need to pay me a salary, the taxes on the poor should be increased.'

'Now that's where dissolute conduct gets you,' thought Platonov. 'It's even worse than my lethargy.'

In the mean time, as they pursued this discussion, Kostanzhoglo and Chichikov walked behind them, and Kostanzhoglo started to open up to his guest:

'See how he's let everything go to rack and ruin!' said Kostanzhoglo, pointing about him. 'Reduced his peasants to such poverty! They haven't a cart or a horse between them. If the cattle plague strikes you, you shouldn't be too concerned about your own property. You should sell everything and buy your peasants some cattle, so they won't remain for a single day without the means of productive work. But all this you could not put right in years: the peasants have grown lazy and taken to drink and debauchery. It takes only a year of indolence and unemployment and a peasant is ruined for life: he'll have a taste for rags and vagrancy. And yet look at the land! Just look at it!' he said, pointing at the meadows which had just come into sight beyond the huts. 'It's all water-meadow. I'd plant flax, and I'd take in a good five thousand from the flax alone: I'd plant turnips, and they'd bring me in another four. And look over there—see the rye growing along the slope of the hill?—It's all self-seeded, you know. He's sown no grains, I know that. And see those ravines down there?—There I would raise such forests that the ravens couldn't fly higher than the trees. Such priceless land—and he lets it go to rack and ruin. If he has nothing to plough with he should at least have the soil dug up for vegetables. It would be fine for vegetables. He could take a spade in his own hands, and give one to his wife, his children, his house servants—there's nothing to it! The swine—he should get back to work, he should kill himself working! That way he would at least die with his duty done, and not from overeating, like a pig at a banquet.'

As he said this, ⟨Kostanzhoglo⟩ spat, and his brow clouded with rancour.

When they drew closer and could look over the sheer ravine, whose slopes were choked with broom, and in the distance the bend in the river glinted and the mountain spur loomed darkly, while in the middle distance they could discern General Betrishchev's house, part of which was hidden in the thicket, and beyond it a crisp, densely wooded hill, hazy blue in the distance, which Chichikov suddenly realized must be on Tentetnikov's land, he said: 'Now, if one were to plant forests here, the view would be quite exquisite...'

'So, are you fond of views?' asked Kostanzhoglo, suddenly looking at him severely. 'Take heed: if you go chasing after nice views, you'll end up with no food and no views. It's the use of a thing you should look out for, and not its beauty. Beauty will come of itself. Towns are a good example: the best and most handsome towns are those which have grown up by themselves, where each was built according to its own needs and taste. On the other hand, those which were built in a long thin strip are no better than army barracks... Leave beauty aside and look for the essential things.'

'It's a pity, though, that one should have to wait so long. If one could only see everything as one wished it, right away.'

'For heaven's sake, you talk like a twenty-five-year-old youth! A weather-cock, a Petersburg official! Absurd! It takes patience. You have to work for six long years: first planting, then sowing, digging the soil, never resting for a minute. It's hard, it's hard. But then afterwards, when you turn up the soil, it will start to help you—and we're not talking here about a paltry million roubles; no, old chap, you will have, in addition to your own seventy serfs, another seven hundred that you cannot see. Everything is multiplied tenfold. Take my farm now, I don't need to lift a finger: everything happens by itself. Yes, nature loves patience: this is a law ordained by God Himself, who gave his blessing to the patient.'

'As one listens to you, one can feel the strength mounting within oneself. And the spirit rises too.'

'Just look how that land has been ploughed!' exclaimed Kostanzhoglo in a tone of bitter resentment, pointing at the slope of the hill. 'I cannot remain here any longer! I hate to see all this disorder and neglect! You and he may now conclude your business without me. Take this priceless treasure away from its fool of an owner as soon as you can. He is only dishonouring a gift from God!'

And, with these words, a sullen cloud settled over Kostanzhoglo's features, as the bile rose within him; he took his leave of Chichikov and caught up with his host, to whom he also made his adieux.

'But my dear Konstantin Fyodorovich,' said his astonished host 'you've only just arrived—and you're off!'

'I can't stay. I have to be at home urgently,' said ⟨Kostanzhoglo⟩. He bade farewell, climbed into his cabriolet, and drove off.

Khlobuev seemed to have understood the reason for his departure.

'Konstantin Fyodorovich couldn't take it,' he said. 'It's no pleasure for a good farmer like him to view such slovenly management.

Would you believe it, Pavel Ivanovich: I didn't even sow any grain this year! Honest to God: there was no seed, not to mention horses or ploughs. It disgusts him to look at me, at my ⟨. . .⟩ Your brother, Platon Mikhailovich, is reputed to be an excellent landowner and, as for Konstantin Fyodorovich, there's no question about it: in his own way he is a Napoleon. I must admit, I often think: "But how can there be so much wisdom in a single head? If only a drop of it had fallen into my own addled pate!" Careful here, gentlemen, as you go over the bridge, take care that you don't step in a puddle. I told them to fix the planks way back in the spring. But it's my peasants I'm most sorry for: they need an example, someone to look up to— but how can they look up to me? What would you advise me to do? You take them, Pavel Ivanovich, you take charge of them. How can I teach them to be orderly when I'm so disorderly myself! I would long ago have given them their freedom, but it would have been no use to them. I realize that they must first be brought to a state where they can live by themselves. They need a strict and fair owner, who would spend a great deal of time with them and would set them an example of selfless and untiring endeavour... The Russian, as I can see from my own example, has to be constantly goaded on, otherwise he sinks into indolence and apathy.'

'It really is very strange,' said Platonov: 'why indeed is the Russian so prone to indolence and apathy, why is it that, if you don't keep a careful eye on him, your simple man will turn into a drunkard and ne'er-do-well?'

'From lack of enlightenment,' observed Chichikov.

'God only knows why,' said Khlobuev. Look at us: We're enlightened, we studied at the university—and how do we live? What good was all my education, what did I learn? Not only did I fail to learn the proper way to live, I became even more skilled in the art of squandering as much money as possible on every manner of new refinement and luxury, and I became more intimately acquainted with the sort of articles that require money. Was it because I was a poor student? Far from it. My fellow students were the same, you know. Perhaps two or three derived some real benefit from their education, and that was only because they were clever enough to start with, while the rest of us only learned how to ruin our health and throw away our money. It's God's truth! You know, sometimes I even think—honestly I do—that we Russians are a lost cause. We want to do everything—and we're capable of nothing. We keep thinking: tomorrow we'll turn over a new leaf, start our lives afresh. Tomorrow we'll go on a diet—but nothing of the sort: the very next evening we gorge ourselves so full that we can do no more than sit there and goggle like stuffed owls, blinking and unable to utter an articulate word. We're all like that.'

'Yes,' said Chichikov with a chuckle, 'you do get people like that.'

'We simply weren't cut out for sensible living. I do not believe that any one of us has ever been sensible. Even if I did see another man living in a decent manner, making and saving money—I still wouldn't trust him! He too will be led astray by the devil in his old age—and then he'll blow the lot! We're all like that, we are: the enlightened and the unenlightened. Somewhere we have something missing, but what exactly, I couldn't tell you.'

Discoursing in this manner, they walked past all the huts and then mounted the chaise and drove across the meadows. It would have been good land had not all the trees been felled. Before them vistas opened up: on high ground to one side, a hazy blue in the distance, were those places which Chichikov had so recently visited. But neither Tentetnikov's, nor General Betrishchev's village could be seen: they were obscured by the hills. They drove down to the meadows, where all that grew were scrawny willows and stunted poplars, all the tall trees had been cut down. They visited a dilapidated water-mill and inspected the river, which could have been plied with boats, had there been boats to ply it with. Here and there a scrawny beast could be seen grazing in the fields. Having viewed everything, without even alighting from the chaise, they returned to the village, where, on the road before them, they encountered a peasant who first scratched his hindquarters and then gave such a huge yawn that he even alarmed the headman's turkeys. Gaping yawns were visible in all the buildings; the roofs also yawned. As he looked at them, Platonov yawned. The buildings were nothing but holes and patches. One cottage even had an entire gate on top of it instead of a roof. In short, they seemed to have introduced the Trishka's caftan system into their farming methods: you cut off the coat-tails and lapels to make patches for the elbows.*

'That's the sort of place I have,' said Khlobuev. 'Now let's see the house,' and he led his guests into the inner rooms. Chichikov imagined he would encounter rags and yawn-inducing objects, but, to his surprise, the living rooms were very neat and tidy. As they passed through the different rooms, they were struck by the signs of poverty hugger-mugger with glittering knick-knacks in the very latest and most luxurious fashion. A bust, seemingly of Shakespeare, was mounted on the ink-well, and on the table lay a fashionable ivory back-scratcher. †They were welcomed by Khlobuev's wife, who was elegantly dressed, in the very height of fashion. There were four children, also well dressed, and even with their own governess;† they were all pretty, but it would have been better had they been dressed humbly, in plain homespun skirts and shirts, and had run around the yard by themselves, not differing in any way from the little peasant children! A lady friend of their hostess arrived, a twitter-brain and chatterbox. The ladies withdrew to their part of the house and the children ran after them, leaving the men to themselves.

'Now what would your price be?' said Chichikov. 'I only ask, I should add, because I expect you to name your very lowest price. The estate is in a much worse condition than I had thought to find it.'

'The most deplorable state, Pavel Ivanovich,' said Khlobuev. 'And that's not all. I shan't conceal it from you: of the hundred souls listed on the census, only fifty are still alive; that was the toll exacted by our cholera epidemic. The others have run away without their papers, so they're also as good as deceased. And if you try and get them back through legal process, you'll end up losing the estate to the courts as well. For that reason I'm only asking thirty-five thousand, no more.'

Naturally enough, †Chichikov decided to bargain.

'Come now, how can you ask thirty-five thousand—thirty-five thousand for this place! Let's make it twenty-five.'†

Platonov felt quite ashamed. 'I say, Pavel Ivanovich,' he said, 'buy the place. It's well worth the price. And if you're not prepared to give thirty-five thousand for it, my brother and I will go halves and buy it ourselves.'

'Very well, very well,' said Chichikov, taking fright. 'I'll buy it, only on condition that I can give you half the money in a year's time.'

'No, Pavel Ivanovich, I couldn't possibly agree to that. Give me half the money right now, and the balance in a fortnight. After all,

I could raise that amount by mortgaging the place and it would only be enough to feed my blood-sucking creditors.'

'Well, I don't know what to say... The problem is, I only have ten thousand on me at the moment,' said Chichikov, lying through his teeth: he had twenty thousand, counting the money he was borrowing from Kostanzhoglo; but he was loath to hand over so much all at once.

'No, please, Pavel Ivanovich: I insist that I really must have fifteen thousand.'

'I can lend you the five thousand,' offered Platonov.

'Very well, if you can!' said Chichikov, thinking: 'It suits me very well, that he should make me a loan.' The box was brought from the carriage, and ten thousand taken out and handed then and there to Khlobuev, while the remaining five thousand were promised for the morrow: that is to say, five were promised but Chichikov meant to bring only three; the rest would come a little later, in two or three days perhaps, and if possible later still. Pavel Ivanovich was not overfond of letting money out of his hands. And if it was absolutely essential to do so, then he still thought it possible to hand the money over tomorrow rather than today. In this he was like the rest of us, for we all like to lead our creditors a merry dance. Let them cool their heels a little while in the hall! As if it's impossible for them to wait! What do we care that every hour may be dear to them and that waiting causes their business to suffer! 'Drop by tomorrow, brother, I haven't the time today.'

'But where will you live now?' Platonov asked Khlobuev. 'Do you have another little village?'

'No, I shall have to move into town: I have a small town-house. I'd have to move anyway, for the children's sake: they need tutors. You could just about find a divinity tutor here, but not one for music or dancing, ⟨not for⟩ all the tea in China.'

'He hasn't a crust of bread, yet he wants to teach his children dancing!' marvelled Chichikov.

'Very odd!' thought Platonov.

'Well now, this calls for a little celebration,' said Khlobuyev. 'I say, Kiryushka: bring us a bottle of champagne, there's a good fellow.'

'There isn't a crust of bread, but there is champagne!' thought Chichikov.

Platonov did not even know what to think.

In fact, it was because he could get nothing else that ⟨Khlobuev⟩ had champagne. He had to send to town for it: he had no choice, since the local shop would not even sell him kvass* on credit, and he had to have something to drink. Meanwhile, the Frenchman who had recently arrived from St Petersburg and set up shop in town sold to everyone on credit. So there was nothing for: he had to produce a bottle of champagne.

The champagne was brought in. They drank three glasses each and grew merry. The wine loosened Khlobuev's tongue and he became witty and charming. *Bons mots* and anecdotes tumbled from his lips. His words displayed such knowledge of people and the world! He saw things so clearly and so accurately; he summed up his landowner neighbours in a few words, so succinctly and so adroitly; he saw their errors and shortcomings so exactly; he knew so thoroughly the history of those local squires who had been ruined—he knew the how, the why, and the wherefore of their ruination; and he imitated their minutest mannerisms with such originality and accuracy, that both his listeners were utterly entranced and ready to declare him quite the wittiest of men.

'I am amazed,' said Chichikov, 'that you, with all your intelligence, cannot find the means to extricate yourself from your own predicament?'

'Well, the means are there,' said Khlobuev, and at once disburdened himself of a great series of projects. These were all so absurd, so outlandish, so far removed from any knowledge of people and the world, that all his listeners could do was to shrug their shoulders and say to themselves: 'Heavens above! What an immense gap there is between *knowledge of the world* ⟨and the ability to make use of this knowledge!⟩' Practically all the projects were based on first obtaining from somewhere or other the sum of one or two hundred thousand roubles, after which, so he believed, everything would come right, the farm would run smoothly, the holes would all be patched up, profits would be quadrupled, and he would soon be in a position where he could repay all his debts. And he concluded his speech: 'But what would you advise me to do? There is no benefactor who would risk a loan of two hundred or even one hundred thousand! It seems God Himself does not wish it.'

'I should think not,' thought Chichikov. 'Fancy God sending a fool like that two hundred thousand roubles!'

'I do, as a matter of fact, have an aunt who's worth three million,' said Khlobuev, 'a pious old lady: she donates generously to the churches and monasteries, but when it comes to helping her nearest and dearest she keeps her fist tightly closed. She's a true member of the old school: you should see her for yourselves. For a start, she has about four hundred canaries. And pug-dogs, hangers-on, and servants the likes of which you no longer see these days. The youngest of the servants must be sixty if he's a day, though she still calls him "young fellow"! If a guest should somehow displease her she'll instruct the butler to miss him out when serving dinner. And sure enough: he won't be served. That's the sort of character she is.'

Platonov chuckled.

'What's her name and where does she live?' asked Chichikov.

'She lives right here in town: Aleksandra Ivanovna Khanasarova.'

'Why don't you go to her for help?' asked Platonov with genuine concern. 'It seems to me that if she were only acquainted a little more closely with the predicament of your family she would not be able to refuse you.'

'Oh no, she'd refuse all right! My aunt is a tough old bird. That old lady's as hard as flint, Platon Mikhailovich! Besides, apart from me there are all sorts of sycophants and toad-eaters hanging around her. There's one amongst them, a chap who aspires to being a governor, claims some sort of kinship with her... †I say, do me a favour,' he said suddenly, turning ⟨to Platonov⟩, 'next week I'm throwing a dinner in town for all the local dignitaries...'

Platonov's eyes started from his head.† He did not yet know that in Russia, in the big cities and in the capitals, there exists a breed of smart fellows whose life is an inexplicable puzzle. A man appears to have squandered everything, he is up to his ears in debt, without two copecks to rub together, and he throws a dinner; all his guests privately say that this must surely be his last, the very next day he will be dragged off to gaol. Ten more years pass, and the smart fellow is still going strong, he is now head-over-heels in debt and once again he throws a dinner, at which all the diners imagine this must be his last and are all convinced that their host will be hauled off to gaol the very next day.

†⟨Khlobuev's⟩ house in town was in itself a remarkable phenomenon. One day you'd find there a priest in full vestments conducting a thanksgiving service; the next a troupe of French actors would

give a dress-rehearsal of their play. Some days there would not be a crumb of food in the house; on others, tables would groan with a lavish banquet for all the local actors and painters and every guest would be splendidly provided for.† At other times, things looked so hopeless that anyone else would long since have hanged or shot himself, but he was saved by his religious fervour, which in him somehow went hand-in-hand with his dissolute life. In these bitter, painful moments ⟨he⟩ would read the lives of martyrs who had trained their spirit to transcend all suffering and adversity. At such times his soul would be quite softened, his spirit deeply moved, and his eyes would fill with tears. And—*mirabile dictu!*—help would almost invariably arrive from some quite unexpected quarter: either one of his old friends would remember about him and send him some money; or some lady travelling through town, a total stranger to him, would chance to hear someone talking about him, and in the impetuous magnanimity of her female heart would send him a generous gift; or somewhere or other a lawsuit he was quite unaware of would be settled in his favour. With piety he would then acknowledge the unbounded mercy of Providence, would order a thanksgiving service, and instantly return to his dissolute and improvident ways.

'I pity him, really I do!' said Platonov to Chichikov when they had taken their leave and driven off.

'The prodigal son!' said Chichikov. 'There's nothing to pity in people like that.'

And soon they both stopped thinking about him altogether: Platonov—because he observed the predicaments of others with just as much indolence and lassitude as he observed everything else in the world. The sight of suffering wrung his heart, but somehow no deep impressions were left in his soul. After a few minutes he no longer thought about Khlobuev. He no longer thought about Khlobuev for the same reason that he did not think about himself, either. Chichikov, however, did not think about Khlobuev because his thoughts were fully occupied with the purchase he had just made. †He thought how, whatever else might have happened, he had suddenly been transformed from an imaginary to a real, flesh-and-blood landowner of an estate that was also no longer imaginary, and he grew pensive, as the various considerations and thoughts passing through his head became increasingly grave and lent a significant expression to his face.

'Patience! Toil! There's nothing difficult about them: I made their acquaintance, so to speak, in my swaddling cloths. They hold no surprises for me. But shall I have the same reserves of patience now, at my present station of life, as in my youth?'

And he thought how, come what may, he would now sow and reap, how he would rid the estate of all those foolish schemes, how he would rise early in the mornings, how he would make the necessary dispositions even before sunrise, how it would warm the heart to behold the resurrection and flowering of the estate; he thought how heart-warming it would be, too, to behold little children.

'Ah yes, that's real life. Kostanzhoglo is right.'

And Chichikov's face itself seemed to grow more handsome from thinking these thoughts. Thus it is that the mere thought of righteousness ennobles man. But—as always happens with man—hard on the heels of every thought comes the contrary thought. 'I wonder if I mightn't even try something like this,' thought ⟨Chichikov⟩: 'first I could sell off the best land, in sections, then I could mortgage the rest of the estate together with the dead souls. I could even slip away without bothering to pay back Kostanzhoglo.'

This was a strange notion and not exactly one of Chichikov's own devising; rather, it appeared before him by itself, unbidden, to tempt and tease him, leering and winking at him. Importunate hussy! Busybody! And who was behind these thoughts that suddenly swept into his head? Without a doubt, whichever way he looked at it, the purchase ⟨was advantageous⟩. He felt a sense of pleasure—pleasure because he had now become a landowner, and not an imaginary landowner, but a real one, a landowner who really owned land, and pastures, and peasants. Not chimerical peasants, confined to the realm of the imagination, but ones that actually existed. And little by little he started to bounce on his seat, and rub his hands, and wink to himself.

'Stop!' his companion suddenly shouted to the coachman. The command brought him rudely to his senses and he looked about him:† they were driving through a splendid grove; a gracious colonnade of birches stretched away to right and left. The white ⟨trunks⟩ of forest birch and aspen, gleaming ⟨like⟩ the towering posts of a massive white palisade, stretched graciously and delicately aloft, through their soft green foliage of newly unfurled leaves. In the dense thickets, the nightingales sang noisily, as if in competition.

Scattered through the grass was the bright yellow of the forest tulips. He found it hard to comprehend how he had suddenly found his way into such a beautiful place when so recently they had been driving though open fields. Through the trees he caught a glimpse of a white stone church and, on its far side, through the copse, a trellis could be discerned. A gentleman appeared at the end of the avenue, wearing a peaked cap and walking towards them, with a knobbly stick in his hand. A sleek, long-legged English hound ran before him.

'Look—there's my brother,' said Platonov. 'Stop, coachman.' He alighted from the chaise, followed by Chichikov. The dogs had already managed to lick each other all over. Long-legged, lively Azor licked Yarb's nose with her swift, darting tongue and then licked Platonov's hand, and finally jumped up on Chichikov and licked his ear.

The brothers embraced.

'My dear Platon! What are you doing to me?' asked the brother, who, it transpired, was called Vasily.

'What do you mean?' answered Platonov nonchalantly.

'Now, really, I ask you: not a word from you for three whole days! The stable-boy brought your stallion across from Petukh's. "He went off with some gentlemen," he says. Well, you could at least have left word: where, why, for how long? I ask you, brother, is that any way to behave? I've been worried sick these last few days!'

'Well, I'm sorry: I forgot,' said Platonov. 'We called on Konstantin Fyodorovich. He sends his greetings, and to our sister too. Allow me to introduce Pavel Ivanovich Chichikov. Pavel Ivanovich—my brother Vasily. Vasily, this is Pavel Ivanovich Chichikov.'

The new acquaintances shook each other's hand and exchanged kisses, having first removed their caps.

'Now just who might this Chichikov be?' wondered brother Vasily. 'Brother Platon is none too choosy in his friendships.' He stole a glance at Chichikov, staring as hard as decorum permitted, and observed that, to all appearances, this was a man of the very best intentions.

For his part, Chichikov also tried, as far as decorum permitted, to size up brother Vasily and observed that the brother was shorter than Platon, with darker hair, and not nearly as good-looking, but that his face had in it far more life and animation, and seemed to betoken a more generous heart. But Pavel Ivanovich paid scant heed to this side of him. It was clear that this man was not so given to daydreaming.

'Well, Vasya, I've decided to travel around holy Russia, together with Pavel Ivanovich here: who knows, it might help me rid myself of my spleen.'

'How can you have decided so suddenly?...' began Vasily, in astonishment, and he was on the point of adding: 'And, to make it worse, you would travel with a man you've clapped eyes on for the first time, who may be a worthless scoundrel, and the devil knows what!' †And, full of mistrust, he gave Chichikov a sidelong look and saw a person of the utmost respectability.†

They turned right, and passed through the gates. The courtyard belonged to an earlier era, as did the house, which was of a kind that is no longer built, with eaves beneath a tall roof. Two immense limes, growing in the middle of the yard, spread their shade over practically half its area. Beneath the limes stood a large number of wooden benches. The courtyard was surrounded by blossoming lilac and bird-cherry trees, whose blossoms and foliage completely hid from sight the perimeter fence. The manor house was also quite hidden from view, with only its door and windows peeping prettily through the blossom-laden branches. Through the poker-straight stems of the trees glinted the white walls of the kitchen outhouses, pantries, and cellars. Everything had become part of this dense coppice. Nightingales trilled noisily, filling the trees with their singing. Involuntarily they felt an agreeable serenity invade their souls. Everything seemed somehow redolent of those carefree days when all people lived together in goodwill and everything was so simple and straightforward. Brother Vasily invited Chichikov to sit. They sat down on the benches beneath the limes.

A young lad of about seventeen, clad in a handsome pink shirt of Egyptian cotton, brought out and set before them carafes of fruit-flavoured kvasses of every kind and colour, some as thick as oil, others which fizzed like carbonated lemonades. After setting out the carafes he walked up to a tree, picked up the spade leaning against it, and headed off into the garden. On the Platonov brothers' estate, as on that of their brother-in-law Kostanzhoglo, there were no household servants as such: they were all gardeners, or, to be more precise, there were servants, but their duties were performed by all the household serfs in turn. Brother Vasily constantly averred that there was no such thing as a servant class. Anyone could serve up food, and it was quite unnecessary to train people specially for that purpose. He believed that the Russian peasant would be honest, efficient, and hard-working, just so long as he wore a shirt and a homespun coat, but that, as soon as he donned a German frock-coat, he became clumsy, inefficient, and slothful: furthermore, he would never change the frock-coat and altogether stop visiting the bathhouse; he would even sleep in it and lice would take up residence, in untold multitudes, under the German frock-coat. In this he may well have been right. In their village the peasants were somehow particularly attractive in their dress: the women's headdresses sparkled with gold, and the sleeves on their blouses were as richly decorated as the borders on Turkish shawls.

'These are fruit kvasses, for which our house has long been famous,' said brother Vasily.

Chichikov poured himself a glass from the first carafe—it was just like *lipec** he had once tasted in Poland: it sparkled like champagne and the bubbles churned in a pleasant commotion from mouth to nose. 'Nectar!' he said. He drank a glass from another carafe—it was better still.

'The drink *par excellence*!' he exclaimed. 'I might say that, at the house of your most esteemed brother-in-law, I had the good fortune to drink his first-class liqueur, and now this is kvass of the very first class.'

'Ah yes, and the liqueurs also come from here. After all, it's our sister who makes them. Our mother came from Little Russia, from near Poltava.* Nowadays people have all forgotten how to make these things themselves. But tell me: in which direction and to which places are you proposing to travel?' asked brother Vasily.

'I travel,' said Chichikov, swaying gently on the bench and rubbing his knee with his hand, 'not so much for my own needs as for those of another. General Betrishchev, a close friend and, I might say, benefactor, has asked me to visit his relations. Relations, of course, are all very well in their own way, but it is partly, so to speak, also for myself, for—not to mention the benefits in the haemorrhoidal respect—to see the world and the circumfluence of people is in itself, so to speak, already a living book and a second science.'

Brother Vasily grew pensive. 'This man speaks in a rather florid way, but there is truth in his words,' he thought. After a few moments' silence he said, turning to Platon: 'I'm beginning to think, Platon, that travel may, indeed, rouse you. You suffer from spiritual lethargy, that's your problem. You have simply fallen asleep, and fallen asleep not from any surfeit or fatigue, but from a lack of vivid impressions and sensations. Now I am quite the opposite. I would dearly love not to feel everything so keenly and not to take everything which happens so close to heart.'

'But no one forces you to take everything so close to heart,' said Platon. 'You go looking for worries yourself and invent causes for concern.'

'Why should I invent them when, as it is, there is some unpleasantness at every step?' said Vasily. 'Have you heard what a dirty trick Lenitsyn played on us while you were away? He's occupied that piece of empty ground. For a start, I would not have ⟨sold⟩ that piece of land for love or for money. Added to which, our people have always used it for their Red Hill festivities.* The village memories are tied up with it. For me tradition is a sacred matter, and I'm prepared to make every sacrifice for it.'

'He doesn't know that, that's why he's occupied it,' said Platon. 'He's new to these parts, he's only just come from St Petersburg. Someone should explain it to him, put him in the picture.'

'He knows, he knows very well. I sent to tell him, but he was just abusive.'

'You should have gone and explained it to him yourself, in person. Go and talk it over with him.'

'No, no. He has far too high an opinion of himself. I shan't go to him. If you feel like that, go and see him yourself.'

'I would go, but then I don't want to interfere. He'd lie to me too and I'd be taken in.'

'Well, perhaps I could be of help—why don't I go?' suggested Chichikov. 'Just tell me what it's about.'

Vasily looked at him and thought: 'This one certainly likes to travel!'

'Just give me an idea of what sort of man he is,' said Chichikov, 'and the nature of the problem.'

'I feel ashamed to burden you with such an unpleasant commission. In my view, he's an utterly worthless man: I should tell you he comes from a family of smallholding landowners here in our province, married somebody's natural daughter, wormed his way up in the service, and started to put on airs. Now he sets the tone here. But our local people are no fools. The dictates of fashion cut no mustard with us, and St Petersburg is not the Church.'

'Of course,' said Chichikov, 'but what is the problem?'

†'Well, you see, he does in fact need ⟨land⟩. And if he hadn't behaved like that I would gladly have given him land somewhere else, for nothing, and better than that waste plot. But now... He's a cantankerous fellow: he'll probably start thinking...'

'If you ask me, it's better to talk things over: you never know, the matter ⟨could be settled⟩. I've been given commissions like this before and people have not regretted it. Take General Betrishchev, for example...'

'Still, I'm ashamed you should have to talk to such a man.'† ⟨. . .⟩*

'⟨. . .⟩ and taking particular care that it remains a secret,' said Chichikov, 'for it is not so much the transgression itself as the temptation which is so harmful.'

'Ah yes, quite so, quite so,' said Lenitsyn, inclining his head completely to one side.

'How agreeable it is to find another in such complete agreement with oneself!' said Chichikov. 'Now I too have a certain piece of business, something both legal and illegal at the same time: on the face of it, it seems illegal, but in essence it's perfectly legal. I find myself in the need of a mortgage, but I am loath to cause anyone the risk of paying two roubles per live soul. If, let's say, I end up bankrupt—which God forbid—it would be most unpleasant for the owner, so I have resolved to use only fugitive and dead souls which have not yet been removed from the census list, with a view both to performing a Christian deed, and to relieving their poor owner of the burden of paying taxes for them. We would just agree between ourselves to draw up a formal deed of transfer, just as if they were alive.'

'Now this really is most peculiar,' thought Lenitsyn and even shifted his chair back a little. 'It's just that it's the sort of business, you see...' ⟨he⟩ began.

'But there will be no scandal, because the deal will be kept secret,' explained Chichikov, 'and, furthermore, it will be conducted between people of the most honourable intentions.'

'All the same, it's just that it's the sort of business which...'

'As I say, there shall be no scandal,' answered Chichikov in the most forthright way. 'It's precisely the sort of thing we've just been discussing: between people of the most honourable intentions, people of a prudent age and, it would seem, of a respectable rank, and, furthermore, conducted in secret.' †As he said this, he gazed into his interlocutor's eyes with a look of the utmost candour and nobility.

For all Lenitsyn's resourcefulness, for all his knowledge of the conduct of negotiations, he now found himself quite nonplussed, and his predicament was made all the worse because he appeared to have been ensnared in his own nets. He was utterly incapable of any fraudulent act, and was most unwilling to do anything fraudulent, even in secret. 'What an unexpected turn of events,' he thought to himself. 'You strike up a close friendship even with upstanding people, and this is what you get—it's all such a puzzle!'†

But it was as if fate and circumstances had conspired together to boost Chichikov's fortunes. For at that very moment, as if to rescue him from his predicament, Lenitsyn's wife entered the room. She was a pale, thin young woman, short in stature, but dressed in the latest St Petersburg fashion, a great devotee of *comme il faut* people. She was followed by the wet-nurse, bearing in her arms their first-born child, fruit of the tender love of this recently wedded pair. With the nimble spring in his stride and his way of holding his head inclined to one side, Chichikov totally enchanted first his St Petersburg hostess and then the infant. At first this latter was about to start howling, but with the words: 'Coo-coo-coo, my little sweetheart,' and by clicking his fingers and displaying the beauty of his cornelian watch-fob, Chichikov somehow managed to entice it into his own arms. He then began lifting it high in the air, thereby causing the young child to chuckle most agreeably, which greatly delighted both parents. But then, whether through the sudden surfeit of pleasure or for some other reason, the infant unexpectedly committed an indiscretion.

'Oh my God!' shrieked Lenitsyn's wife: 'He's utterly ruined your tailcoat!'

Chichikov looked down: the sleeve of his nice new tailcoat was indeed quite ruined. 'May Satan take you to hell, you cursed little devil!' he muttered angrily to himself.

Host, hostess, and wet-nurse all rushed off in search of Cologne and then set about rubbing at him from all sides.

'It's nothing, it's nothing, it's nothing at all,' repeated Chichikov, frantically trying to arrange his features in a cheerful expression. 'What harm can an innocent child do at this, its most golden age?' All the while he was thinking: †'He certainly has a good aim, the nasty little brat—may he be thrown to the wolves!'

This seemingly insignificant circumstance quite won Chichikov into Lenitsyn's favour. For how could one refuse a guest who had shown such affection for his child and had so magnanimously paid for it with his own tailcoat? So as not to set a bad example, they resolved to conclude the matter in secret, for it was not the matter itself, so much as the possible scandal, which was so harmful.

'Now allow me, by way of rewarding you for your services, to render a service in return. I would like to act as your intermediary in the matter between you and the Platonov brothers. You need land, do you not?'†*

FINAL CHAPTER*

†In this world, people always find a way of doing what they want.†
'God helps those that help themselves', as the saying goes. The
odyssey through the various trunks proved quite fruitful, and the
odd trophy from this expedition made its way into the already familiar little box. In other words, everything worked out satisfactorily. It wasn't exactly that Chichikov stole: let us say, rather, that he
availed himself of things. After all, every one of us occasionally
avails himself of things: for one man, this might be government
timber, for another, sums of money, a third might rob from his own
children for some visiting actress, while a fourth might rob from his
peasants to buy Hambs furniture* or a new carriage. How can we
help it, when there are so many wonderful, tempting things in the
world? Such as fashionable restaurants charging outrageous prices,
and masked balls, and public festivities, and music and dancing with
Gypsy women. After all, it is hard to hold yourself in check, when
around you everyone is doing what they wish and following the
dictates of fashion—it is asking too much of any man that he should
hold himself back. It's simply not possible to hold oneself constantly
in check.

Man is no god. Thus Chichikov, too, like an increasing number of
people with a propensity for comfort in its various forms, turned
matters to his own advantage. He should, of course, have driven out
of town, but the roads were in bad condition. At the same time,
another fair was about to start in town, and this was a fair for the
landed gentry. The previous such event had been more of a horse-
trading affair, with livestock, raw materials, and an assortment of
peasant wares, bought up by stockjobbers and koulaks.* But everything at this fair had been bought at the fair in Nizhny Novgorod,
by dealers in linen and stuffs, and brought here. Gathered here were
all those intent on emptying Russian purses—Frenchmen with
pomades and French ladies with pretty bonnets, out to relieve the
Russian of his hard-earned money, like the plague of locusts in
Egypt, as Kostanzhoglo put it, which not only eat everything in
their path, but then lay eggs behind them as they go, and bury them
in the ground.

It was only the bad harvests and, in fact, their unlucky ⟨. . .⟩ which kept many of the landowners on their estates. The officials, on the other hand, being quite untroubled by bad harvests, were all out on display, as—to everyone's misfortune—were their wives. These ladies, having crammed their heads full with various recently published books, intended to arouse in the human race all sorts of new longings, were now afflicted with an unslakable thirst for new pleasures of every kind. A Frenchman opened a new business: a pleasure garden of a kind hitherto unheard of in that province, offering supper at a purportedly extraordinarily low price, with half the cost offered on credit. This in itself was sufficient to ensure that ⟨not only⟩ all the office supervisors, but even all the chancery clerks ⟨. . .⟩ in the hope of future bribes from their petitioners. In each of them the desire was aroused to cut a dash before his friend with his new horses or coachmen. The things that happen when the different classes foregather for the purpose of entertainment!... Despite the foul weather and the mire, smart calèches flew back and forth. Whence they all came, God alone knew, but they would have turned heads even in St Petersburg. Merchants and shop assistants deftly doffed their hats and named preposterous prices. Bearded men with shaggy fur caps were few and far between. Instead the European look was favoured, with clean-shaven chins, they were all wasted-looking, with rotten teeth.

'Step this way, sir, step this way. Please, just be so kind as to look inside my shop. Sir, sir!' young boys called out by some of the shops.

Yet those dealers who were more *au fait* with Europe regarded the public with a look of contempt, only occasionally pronouncing, in a dignified voice: 'Pinstripe,' or '*Argent, claire* and black cloths here.'

'Do you have any cranberry shades with a speckled weave?' asked Chichikov.

'First class fabrics,' said the merchant, raising his cap with one hand and with the other pointing to his shop. Chichikov stepped inside. The merchant adroitly raised the hinged top of the ⟨counter⟩ and reappeared on its other side, facing his customer and with his back to his wares, which were stacked in a heap from floor to ceiling. Skilfully balancing on his two hands and gently swinging his entire upper body, he enquired:

'What kind of cloth were you looking for?'

'A speckled weave, of an olive, or bottle-glass colour, verging, if you know what I mean, on cranberry.'

'I'm happy to tell you that we can offer you cloth of the very best quality, better than which you could only find in the world's most cultured capital cities. You lad, pass me that bolt there, on top, ⟨number⟩ 34. No, no, not that one, my good lad. You fellows are such typical proletarians, always trying to get above your proper station! That's the one—throw it here. Now this is what I call a cloth.' And, unrolling it from the other end, the merchant held the cloth right up to Chichikov's nose, so that he was able not only to appraise its silky sheen with his hand, but even to sniff at it.

'It's very nice, but it's not what I want,' said Chichikov. 'I should tell you that I once worked in the customs service, so I must have the very best there is. I want one more on the reddish side, not that bottle colour, but with more cranberry in it.'

'I quite understand: you're after the sort of colour which is so *à la mode* right now in St Petersburg. Now, I have one cloth of the most exceptional quality. I must warn you, though, that it's not cheap, but it is worth the price.'

The European climbed back up the shelves and the bolt of cloth came tumbling down. The merchant unfurled it with a flourish reminiscent of bygone times, forgetting for the moment that he now belonged to the modern generation, and brought it up to the light, even stepping out of the shop with it, squinting as he held it up to the light and said: 'An excellent colour. Navarino smoke-grey shot with flame-red.'*

The cloth was to the customer's liking; a price was agreed upon, although the cloth came with a *prix fixe*, as the merchant kept asserting. Thereupon a length was torn off with an adroit, two-handed manœuvre. It was wrapped in paper, after the Russian manner, with a quite improbable speed. The package was secured with a slender piece of twine, fastened with a quivering knot. The twine was cut with a pair of scissors and parcel and customer were soon installed in their chaise. The merchant doffed his cap. He had good reason to doff his cap: ⟨. . .⟩ his customer had taken the money out of his pocket.

†'Let me see your black cloth,' commanded a voice.

'Good heavens, it's Khlobuev,' said Chichikov to himself and promptly turned round, hoping not to be seen, deeming it most inadvisable to enter into any discussions with Khlobuev on the subject of inheritance. But he had already been spotted.

'Well, look who it is: Pavel Ivanovich—you surely weren't thinking to slip away from me? You have been nowhere to be found, and this business is one we need to discuss most urgently.'

'My most, most respected friend,' said Chichikov, squeezing his hand, 'please believe me: I too have been wanting to have a talk with you, but I simply have not had the time.' All the while he was thinking to himself: 'May the devil take you to hell.' Then he suddenly saw Murazov entering the shop. 'Well I never, if it isn't Afanasy Vasilievich. How are you, sir?'

'And how are you?' asked Murazov, raising his hat. The merchant and Khlobuev also took off their hats.†

'Having problems with the old back and some difficulty sleeping. No doubt, because I don't get enough exercise.'

But instead of ⟨delving⟩ further into the reasons for Chichikov's ailments, however, Murazov turned to Khlobuev: 'As soon as I saw you go into the shop, Semyon Semyonovich, I followed you in. I need to talk something over with you, so I wonder if I could invite you round to my place?'

'Why, of course, of course,' said Khlobuev hastily, and the two left the shop together.

†'I wonder what it is they have to talk about?' thought Chichikov.

'Afanasy Vasilievich is a respected and clever man,' said the merchant: 'and he knows his business, but he is quite lacking in enlightenment. After all, a merchant must know how to strike a deal, or he's no good as a merchant. His budget and the reaction of his clients, are all tied up with this, and if he doesn't attend to it, he'll end up a pauper.' Chichikov could only shrug.

'Ah, Pavel Ivanovich, I've been hunting everywhere for you,' said a voice behind him: it was Lenitsyn. The merchant respectfully doffed his cap.

'Ah yes, Fyodor Fyodorovich.'

'I beg you, let's go to my place. I need to discuss something with you,' he said. Chichikov looked at him: he looked terribly out of countenance. Settling his bill with the merchant, he left the shop.†

'I've been waiting for you, Semyon Semyonovich,' said Murazov, seeing Khlobuev enter. 'Please come with me to my little room.' He led Khlobuev into the little room already familiar to the reader, more spartan than even the wretched cubby-hole of an official earning seven hundred roubles a year.

'Now tell me, I imagine your circumstances must have improved somewhat? You must have inherited something from your old aunt.'

'How can I explain it, Afanasy Vasilievich? I really don't know whether my circumstances are any better. All I got was fifty serfs and thirty thousand roubles, which I had to use to settle a portion of my debts, and I'm back with nothing again. And the worst of it is that there was something very fishy about this whole will business. I tell you, Afanasy Vasilievich, you wouldn't believe the roguery and skulduggery that went on. When I tell you about it you'll be astounded at the things you hear. That Chichikov—'

'But wait, Semyon Semyonovich, before telling us about that Chichikov, let's talk about you yourself. Tell me, in your estimation, how much would you consider entirely sufficient to extricate you from your predicament?'

'My predicament is unenviable,' said Khlobuev. 'If I am to extricate myself, to settle all my debts and be in a position to live a modest life, I would need at least one hundred thousand, perhaps even more—in other words, my situation is quite impossible.'

'And just suppose you had this sum, how would you order your life thereafter?'

'Well, I would rent a small apartment, and devote myself to the education of my children. But there's no point even thinking about what I would do, my career is finished, I'm no use for anything now.'

'But like this your life would be one of idleness, and in this idleness there appear temptations which are quite unknown to a man who has work to do.'

'It's no good: I'm no use for anything. My eyes have grown dim and I am troubled with lumbago.'

'But how can you live without work? How can you face life without a position, without a job? I ask you: just take a look at any of God's creatures. Each of them serves some purpose, it has its own function. Even the humble stone, which is there that it may be put to some useful purpose, and here we have a man—the wisest of all creatures—unfit for anything. So how can that be possible?'

'But I shall not be entirely idle. I can take up the education of my children.'

'No, Semyon Semyonovich, no, that's the hardest thing of all. How can you teach your children something you haven't learnt yourself? After all, children can only learn from the example of our own lives. Do you think your life is a suitable example for them? Do you really want them to learn how to spend their time ⟨in⟩ indolence and playing cards? No, Semyon Semyonovich: let me have your children, you will ruin them. Think about it seriously: your idleness has been your undoing. Now it's time for you to put this life of idleness behind you. How can one live in this world with no firm attachment? There must be some duty you can perform. Even a day-labourer has his role in life. He may eat the very cheapest bread, but then he earns it himself and he gets satisfaction from the work he does.'

†'Honest to God, Afanasy Vasilievich, I've tried, I've tried to pull myself out of it. But what can I do?—I'm old now, I'm no longer capable. So what can I do? Surely I am not to seek a position in government service? How could I, at my age of forty-five, sit at the same desk with young clerks just beginning their careers? Added to which, I'm unable to handle bribes, I'd stand in the way of my own advancement, and ruin the career of others. And these new civil servants have their own caste system now. No, Afanasy Vasilievich, I've thought about it, I've considered all the different jobs, I wouldn't fit anywhere. Only in the workhouse...'

'The workhouse is for people who've worked in their lives; but to those who've frittered away their youth having fun we can only say, as the ant says to the dragonfly in the fable: "Now you're free to dance out there."* Besides, even in the workhouse they keep on working, and working hard; they don't play whist. Semyon Semyonovich,' continued Murazov, looking closely into his face, 'you're trying to fool me and yourself.'

Murazov continued to stare intently at him, but poor Khlobuev was quite at a loss for a reply. Murazov started to feel sorry for him.†

'Listen, ⟨Semyon Semyonovich⟩,' he said, 'after all, you're a God-fearing man, you go to church; you never miss matins or vespers, I know. You may not feel like getting up early, yet up you get and off you go to church, even at four in the morning when no one else has risen.'

'That's different, Afanasy Vasilievich. I know that that is something I'm doing, not for my fellow man, but for Him Who set us all here on this earth. What can I do? I believe that He is merciful to me, that, however rotten I might be, however loathsome, He can still forgive me and take me unto Himself, while people will thrust me away and even the best among them will betray me and then will aver afterwards that he did it for a worthy cause.'

A look of distress spread across ⟨Khlobuev's⟩ features. As he listened, tears even formed in the old man's eyes, but there was nothing ⟨. . .⟩

'So you should serve Him, Who is so merciful. Your toil will be as pleasing to Him as your prayers. Take up any occupation—any one at all, but do it as if you did it for Him, and not for your fellow man. Pass water through a sieve, if you will—but as you do so, remember that you are doing it for Him. The advantage at least would be that you would have no time left over for mischief, for losing money at cards, for gluttonous feasts and drinking orgies, for social high jinks. Dear me, Semyon Semyonovich... Tell me, do you know Ivan Potapych?'

'I do and I greatly respect him.'

'Ivan Potapych was a fine trader: worth half a million. But the moment he started making a profit on everything, he went to the dogs. He spent every penny he owned. He had his son taught French, married his daughter off to a general. And he no longer spent his days in the shop or on the bourse, but would be forever looking up his friends and dragging them off to an inn to drink tea. He spent days on end drinking tea with his friends and ended up bankrupt. And then the good Lord visited misfortune on His son Ivan Potapych. Now he works for me, as a shop assistant. He started again, from scratch and his affairs came right again. Once again he could have done deals for half a million, but instead he says: "I was a shop assistant before and I will die a shop assistant. Now," he says, "I am healthy and fresh again but, before, I had developed a paunch and dropsy was setting in. No thank you," he said. And now he never touches tea. Cabbage soup and buckwheat porridge, and nothing more, that's his way. And he prays with greater devotion than any man alive. He helps the poor more generously than we could ever do; many of us would like to help the poor, but we've squandered all our money.'

Poor Khlobuev fell to thinking.

The old man took his hands in both of his. 'Semyon Semyonovich! If you only knew how I pity you! I have been thinking of you constantly. So listen to this. You know that here in our monastery there is a recluse, a man who sees no other men. This recluse is a man of great intelligence—an intelligence that we cannot even imagine. Now, if he ever decides to give advice... I started to tell him that I have such-and-such a friend, without naming names, a friend who has such-and-such a disorder. He listened to me and then suddenly interrupted with the words: "Put God's work before your own. They're building a church and there is not enough money: you must collect the money for the church." Then he slammed the door.

'I wondered to myself: what does this mean? Clearly he does not wish to give advice. So I went to see our archimandrite. I was no sooner through the door than he asked me whether I knew anyone who could be entrusted with collecting money for a new church, someone from the landed, or merchant classes, more educated than the others, who might see this as his salvation? I at once thought to myself: "Good Heavens! It's Semyon Semyonovich—that's who the anchorite wants to perform this task. This will be a good way of ridding him of his ailment. As he travels from landowner to peasant and from peasant to burgess, with his book in hand, he will see how different men live and what their particular needs are. So when he finally returns home, after having travelled the length and breadth of several provinces, he will have come to know the area and its people better than all those of us who live in the towns... And people like that are what we need nowadays." Just as the prince told me the other day that he would give anything to find a secretary who knew his business not from the books and papers, but from life itself, from the way things actually are, because, as they say, you'll never see anything clearly from papers, everything is so jumbled up.'

'You totally confound me, Afanasy Vasilievich, I am quite at a loss,' said Khlobuev, gazing ⟨at him⟩ in astonishment. 'I can hardly believe that you're saying all this to me: for an undertaking like that you need an energetic, indefatigable man, and besides—how could I abandon my wife and my children, who would have nothing to live on?'

'You need not concern yourself about your wife and children. I shall take on the task of looking after them and the children will have tutors. Rather than go about with your begging bowl seeking alms for yourself, it will be so much better and more noble to seek these alms for God. I shall give you a simple ⟨trap⟩, and you must not be concerned about the bumpy rides: this will be good for your health. I shall give you money for the journey, so that, as you travel, you can give some to those whose need is the greatest. In this way you can do a great deal of good. You're not likely to err in your judgement, and those whom you help will be fully deserving of your help. As you travel about, you will learn what people are like, and how they live. You will not be like those officials who are universally feared and from whom people run and ⟨hide⟩; people will be happy to talk to you, knowing that you're collecting for a church.'

'It's a fine idea, I can see, and I would earnestly ⟨wish⟩ to be able to put at least part of it into effect, but I honestly think it is beyond my capability.'

'How do you mean—beyond your capability?' said Murazov. 'Nothing is really within our capability, you know. Everything is beyond it. We can do nothing without assistance from on high. But through prayer we can gather strength. As he makes the sign of the cross, the believer says "Lord, have mercy", and he takes up his oars and rows to the shore. You need not waste time thinking about all this: you need only accept it as the will of God. My trap will be ready for you at once; in the mean time, go quickly to the archimandrite to collect the book and to get his blessing, and then you can set on your way.'

'I submit to your will and I accept this as nothing less than the bidding of God.'

'Lord, give me your blessing,' he said to himself and at once felt spiritual strength and vigour flowing into his soul. Even in his mind he felt the stirrings of hope that he might find some way out of his miserable and dire predicament. In the distance a light shone beckoningly...

†But let us leave Khlobuev a while and return to Chichikov.†

In the mean time one petition after the other was indeed submitted to the courts. Various relations came out of the woodwork, about whom no one had ever heard before. As birds of carrion descend on a carcass, so did they all swoop down on the vast estate left by the old lady: denunciations poured in—denunciations against Chichikov, denunciations attesting to the spuriousness of the most recent will, and even to the spuriousness of the first will, as well as evidence of theft and embezzlement. Depositions were even made accusing Chichikov of buying up dead souls and alleging that he had smuggled contraband during his years in the customs service. Everything about him was dug up and every detail of his previous life was exposed to scrutiny. The Lord only knows where they sniffed it all out. Evidence even came to light of activities which Chichikov firmly believed were known only to him and the four walls. For the time being all this was confidential and *sub judice* and did not come to his attention, although a confidential memorandum from his jurisconsult, which he shortly received, made him realize than the fat was about to hit the fire.

The memorandum was very terse: 'I hasten to inform you that the case will cause something of a commotion but remember that there is no cause for alarm. The main thing is to remain calm. We shall sort it all out.'

This set his mind at rest. '⟨This chap⟩ really knows his onions,' said Chichikov. Then, to make things better still, the tailor arrived with his new outfit. ⟨Chichikov⟩ was filled with the desire to admire himself in his new tailcoat of Navarino smoke and flame. He pulled on the trousers, which clung closely to him on all sides in the most superb way—indeed, he could have had his portrait painted then and there. The cloth was pulled so splendidly tight on his thighs, on his calves too, it embraced every little contour, imparting an even greater elasticity to his limbs. When he tightened the buckle at the back, his paunch became as taut as a drum. He tapped it with a brush and said: 'Call me a fool if you like, but it does make a handsome picture!'

The tailcoat, it appeared, was an even better fit than the trousers: no wrinkle anywhere, close fitting all round, moulded to show off his supple figure. When Chichikov observed that it was a little tight under the right arm, the tailor only smiled: this meant it would hug him all the tighter round the waist. 'Rest assured,' he said, with undisguised triumph, 'this side of St Petersburg you will find nothing to match it.' The tailor was himself from St Petersburg and his sign read: 'Foreigner from London and Paris.' He was not a man to jest with, and by yoking together these two great cities, he intended once and for all to put all the other tailors in their place, so that henceforth none would dare lay claim to such capitals but would have to be content with such lesser towns as 'Karlseru' or 'Copenhara'.

Chichikov magnanimously settled the tailor's account and, once alone, started to inspect himself in the mirror at leisure, like an actor, with an aesthetic sensibility and *con amore*. It transpired that everything was somehow even better than before: his plump cheeks more interesting, his chin more alluring, his white collar tips lent tone to his cheek, the dark blue satin cravat lent tone to the collar tips; the highly fashionable pleats in his shirt-front lent tone to his cravat, the sumptuous velvet ⟨waistcoat⟩ lent ⟨tone⟩ to the shirt-front, and the tailcoat of Navarino smoke and flame, which shimmered like silk, lent tone to everything. He turned to the right—excellent! He turned to the left—better still! His supple figure was that of a Kammerherr at court* or of those gentlemen who rattle away in French and yet who, even in moments of anger, will be unable to utter a single oath in the Russian language and will have to give vent to their rage in the French dialect instead. Such refinement! He attempted, by slightly inclining his head to one side, to strike the pose of one addressing himself to a lady *d'un certain age* and of the utmost enlightenment: the result was quite exquisite. Artist, take up your brush and paint! In his pleasure he performed a little leap, not unlike an entrechat. The chest of drawers shook and a phial of eau de Cologne tumbled to the floor; but this did not in any way discompose him. He called the stupid phial a fool, as was quite befitting, and thought: 'Now to whom should I pay my respects first? Best of all...'

When suddenly from the hall came the clatter of boots with jingling spurs, and there appeared a gendarme in full armour, and wearing an expression of such severity he could have been an entire army. 'You are ordered to present yourself at once to the Governor-General.'

Chichikov was stupefied. Before him towered a hideous ogre, with moustachios, a horse's tail on his head, a bandoleer across one shoulder, a bandoleer across the other shoulder, and a monstrous cutlass lashed to his side. Chichikov was quite ready to believe that a rifle—and God knows what else besides—hung from his other side: the man was an entire army in one person! He opened his mouth to object, but the ⟨ogre⟩ declared roughly: 'Orders are to go at once.' Through the open window he saw another ogre in the hall, he looked through the window—and there was a carriage. What could he do? Just as he was, in his tailcoat of Navarino smoke and flame, he had to take a seat in the carriage, and, trembling from head to toe, was forthwith driven and escorted by the ogre-gendarme to the Governor-General.

In the antechamber he was not even given the chance to compose himself. 'In you go, the prince is waiting for you,' said the duty official. As in a fog, Chichikov saw before him the antechamber, filled with couriers receiving packages, then a hall through which he walked, thinking only: 'They're going to seize me and send me straight to Siberia, just like that, without a trial or anything!' His heart pounded harder than that of the most ardent lover. Finally, the fateful door opened before him: he saw an office with portfolios, cabinets, and books, and the prince the very embodiment of wrath.

'My destroyer!' said Chichikov to himself. 'He will destroy my soul, he'll tear me to shreds like a wolf slaughtering a lamb!'

'I spared you,' said the prince, 'I permitted you to remain in town, when you should have been cast into the dungeon; but again you have sullied yourself with the most heinous skulduggery that has ever sullied the honour of man.'

His lips trembled with rage.

'Which heinous act and skulduggery, Your Highness?' asked Chichikov, shaking from head to toe.

'The woman,' declared the prince, stepping up a little closer and staring straight into Chichikov's eyes, 'the woman who, at your bidding, signed the will has been apprehended and will be brought face-to-face with you.'

Chichikov felt his eyes cloud over.

'Your Highness! Let me tell you the full truth of the matter. I am guilty, it's true, I am guilty; but not that guilty. I have been slandered by my enemies.'

'It is not possible for anyone to slander you, for there is more vileness in you than could be ⟨invented⟩ by the most accomplished liar. In all your life, I believe, you have not done a single deed that is not dishonest. Every copeck you have gained has been gained through the utmost dishonesty, you have committed the sort of robbery and vile perfidy for which there is only the knout and Siberia. No, this is the end! You will be taken from this place to gaol this minute and there, together with the vilest scoundrels and cut-throats, you will have to ⟨await⟩ your verdict. And even that is merciful, considering that ⟨you⟩ are incomparably more vile than those criminals: they come in rough peasant coats and sheepskins, while you...'

He glared at the tailcoat of Navarino smoke and flame and tugged at the bell-cord.

'Your Highness,' cried Chichikov, 'have mercy! You are a husband and father. I plead not for myself. Spare my old mother!'

'You lie!' shouted the prince wrathfully. 'Before, you implored me in the name of children and a family you never had, and now it's a mother!'

'Your Highness, I am a blackguard and the worst of rogues,' said Chichikov in a voice ⟨. . .⟩ 'I did indeed tell a lie, I have neither children nor a family; but, as God is my witness, I have always wanted to have a wife, to fulfil my duty as a man and a citizen, so that I would properly earn the respect of my fellow citizens and the authorities... But circumstances so calamitously conspired against me! With my lifeblood, Your Highness, with my lifeblood I was forced to earn my daily bread. At every step I encountered blandishments and temptation... enemies, and destroyers, and usurpers. My whole life has been... like a tempestuous whirlwind or a barque, tossed on the waves at the mercy of the winds. I am a mere mortal, Your Highness!'

The tears suddenly gushed from his eyes in torrents. He fell at the prince's feet just as he was—in his tailcoat of Navarino smoke and flame, in his velvet waistcoat and satin cravat, in his superbly tailored new trousers, with his carefully groomed hair from which there wafted the sweet aroma of the very finest eau de Cologne.

'Get away from me. Call the soldiers to take him away,' said the prince to the men who hastened into the room.

'Your Highness!' shrieked ⟨Chichikov⟩, clutching the prince's boot with both hands.

A shudder of aversion shook the ⟨prince's⟩ entire body.

'Get away, I tell you!' he said, endeavouring to wrest his foot from Chichikov's embraces.

'Your Highness, I shall not move from this spot until I receive your pardon!' said ⟨Chichikov⟩, without releasing the prince's boot and sliding with it across the floor, in his tailcoat of Navarino smoke and flame.

'Get away, do you hear!' the prince said with that inexpressible feeling of revulsion which fills us when we see a most hideous insect, one so hideous we cannot bring ourselves to crush it under-foot. He kicked out so sharply that Chichikov felt the boot hit his nose, lips, and well-rounded chin, but still he did not release the boot and clenched ⟨it⟩ all the tighter in his arms. Two strapping gendarmes forcibly dragged him away, and taking him by the arms frogmarched him through all the rooms. He was pale, broken, in that terrible insensible state that a man enters when he sees before him the inescapable, black shadow of death, that dread spectacle so repugnant to our nature...

There, in the doorway leading to the staircase, was Murazov. A ray of hope flashed before Chichikov. In an instant, with super-human strength, he wrenched himself free from the grip of the two gendarmes and threw himself at the feet of the astonished old man.

'Heavens above, Pavel Ivanovich, what ever is the matter?'

'Save me! They're taking me to gaol, to my death...'

The gendarmes seized hold of him and led him away, without letting him finish.

A dank, musty lumber room, smelling of the boots and footcloths of garrison soldiers, a bare wood table, two wretched chairs, a win-dow with iron bars, a decrepit old stove wheezing smoke through a narrow crack but giving off no warmth—such was the residence in which our ⟨hero⟩ was installed, a man who had already begun to savour the sweetness of life and to attract the attention of his fellow countrymen, in his fine new tailcoat of Navarino smoke and flame. They did not even permit him to take his bare necessities with him, to take the little box in which he kept his money, money which might now have been sufficient. The papers, the deeds of purchase for the dead ⟨souls⟩—all that was now in the hands of officials. He collapsed on the ground, and the sarcophagous worm of terrible, hopeless grief coiled itself around his heart. It gnawed, ever more ravenously, at this heart, reft of all protection. Another such day, a day of such grief and Chichikov would have departed this world. But Someone had kept vigil, had kept His all-protecting hand stretched out even over Chichikov. An hour later the doors of the gaol opened to admit old Murazov.

Even a wayfarer, enfeebled by a searing thirst, into whose dust-dry throat someone has poured a stream of spring water, could not have been so refreshed, so revived as wretched ⟨Chichikov⟩ was now revived.

'My saviour!' he cried, and leaping from the ground, on to which he had prostrated himself in his inconsolable grief, seized hold of Murazov's hand, swiftly kissed it and pressed it to his heart. 'May the Lord reward you for visiting this poor soul!'

He burst into tears.

The old man gazed at him with a look of sorrow and pain and said only: 'Oh, Pavel Ivanovich, Pavel Ivanovich, what have you done?'

'What was I to do! That cursed woman ruined me! I lost all sense of proportion: I was not able to stop myself in time. Cursed Satan led me astray, he clouded my reason and human good sense. I transgressed, I know it. But how could they behave like that? A nobleman, a nobleman, and I am cast into this dungeon, without a trial, without an investigation. A nobleman, Afanasy Vasilievich. And how could they refuse me the time to call at my apartments, to sort out my things? I have had to leave everything there, unattended. My little box, Afanasy Vasilievich, my little box, it contains all my valuables. Earned by the sweat of my brow, by the blood of my veins, over years of toil and privation... My little box, Afanasy Vasilievich. They will steal everything, they will take it all away... Oh, my God, oh my God!'

And unable to suppress another uprush of grief to his heart, he started to howl loudly in a voice which penetrated the thick walls of the gaol and gave off dull, distant echoes, he ripped off his satin cravat and, seizing his tailcoat of Navarino smoke and flame by the collar, rent it asunder.

'Oh dear, Pavel Ivanovich, how you have been blinded by these valuables of yours. It is because of them that you have been unable to see your own terrible situation.'

'Benefactor, save me, save me!' groaned the wretched Pavel Ivanovich in despair, falling at Murazov's feet. 'The prince loves you, he will do anything for you.'

'No, Pavel Ivanovich, I cannot, much as I would have wished to help. You have fallen beneath the inexorable blade of the law, and not beneath the power of any man.'

'I was tempted by that satanic rogue, by that monster of the human race!'

He beat his head against the wall and pounded the table with such force that his fist was covered with blood, but he felt neither the pain to his head nor the severity of the blow with his hand.

'Pavel Ivanovich, compose yourself, consider how you will make your peace with God and not with other people; think of your own poor soul.'

'But it was all fate, Afanasy Vasilievich. Has such misfortune ever befallen any other man? Did I not earn every copeck with forbearance—with the forbearance of sweat and blood, you could say, with my toil?—And not by robbing my fellow man or plundering the public coffers, as others do. And why did I earn those copecks? So that ⟨I could live out the remainder of my days in contentment; that I could leave something for my children, for the children I intended to beget for the good of my country, to serve the fatherland⟩. I fiddled a bit, I'll not deny it, I fiddled a bit. But what of it? After all, I only fiddled when I saw that you could get nowhere on the straight road, and that a crooked road reaches its goal much more directly. But I did work hard, I did use my brains. And if I took anything, I took it from the rich. Not like those scoundrels who use the courts to swindle thousands from the Treasury, they rob people with little money, they snatch the last copeck from those who have nothing. But tell me, was it not a terrible misfortune that, every time, whenever I was just beginning to reap the fruits of my labour and, so to speak, to touch these fruits with my hand... suddenly a storm would break, a hidden rock would wreck my vessel, smash it into smithereens. My capital had grown to close on three ⟨hundred⟩ thousand. I had a three-storeyed house. On two separate occasions I had bought villages. No, Afanasy Vasilievich, why should ⟨fate⟩ treat me thus? Why these bitter blows? Even without all this my life has been as a barque tossed on the waves, has it not? Where is the justice of heaven? Where is the reward of patience, of the most exemplary steadfastness? And to think that I started afresh three times; after losing everything, I started again with a single copeck, when another man would long ago have drunk himself to death in a pot-house, in his despair. If you only knew how hard I battled, and what I had to endure! For every copeck I earned, you might say, with all the might of my soul... To others such bounty might come easily, but for me every ⟨copeck⟩, as the proverb says, was nailed to the floor with a three-copeck nail, and I earned each of these copecks with their three-copeck nails through my iron will and perseverance, as God is my witness.'

He did not finish what he was saying, and began to sob noisily from the unbearable pain in his heart. He fell on to the chair, ripped the now shredded tails from his coat, and flung them from him, then, thrusting both hands into his hair, which he had previously taken such care to secure, he mercilessly tore at it, relishing the sharp pain which he hoped would deaden the unbearable anguish in his heart.

For a long time Murazov sat before him in silence, contemplating this extraordinary ⟨suffering⟩, the like of which he had never before seen. And this wretched, obdurate man, who until so recently had flitted about with the ⟨unfettered⟩ ease and adroitness of a man of the world or a military man, now flung himself from side to side in ⟨a state⟩ of utter dishevelment and indecorous disarray, in his tattered tailcoat and unbuttoned ⟨breeches⟩, brandishing a bloody, battered fist, venting his fury on the inimical forces that thwart mankind.

'Oh, Pavel Ivanovich, Pavel Ivanovich. To think what a man you could have been, if you had applied such strength and perseverance, if you had lent such toil to the service of good and to a better purpose! Heavens above, how much good you might have done! If any philanthropic person had so exerted himself in the exercise of his good causes as you have in the earning of your copecks, and if they had been able so to sacrifice their self-esteem and ambition for good, and had worked without sparing themselves just as you have not spared yourself in pursuit of those copecks—holy God, how our land would have prospered! Pavel Ivanovich, Pavel Ivanovich! What makes me sorry is not that you have betrayed your friends, but that you have betrayed yourself—you have betrayed those rich forces and gifts which fell to your share. Your destiny was to be a great man, but you have fallen by the wayside and ruined yourself.'

The soul has its own secrets. However far a man may stray from the straight and narrow path, however hardened he may grow in his criminal heart, however obdurately he may cling to his depraved ways, should you but reproach him with his own character, pointing out those of his own merits which he has disgraced, despite himself he will recoil and be shaken to the very core.

'Afanasy Vasilievich!' said the wretched Chichikov and seized Murazov's hands in his own. 'Oh, if only I could be set free, if I could recover my valuables! I swear to you, I would lead a quite different life! Save me, my benefactor, save me!'

'But what can I do? You want me to fight against the law. Assuming

I did presume to do this, the prince still would not go back on his decision: he is a just man.'

'Benefactor! You can do everything. It is not the law I fear—I shall find a remedy for the law—but the fact that I have been thrown guiltless into this dungeon, that I shall perish here, like a dog, and that my valuables, my papers, my box... Save me!'

He threw his arms around the old man's legs and rained tears on his feet.

'Oh, Pavel Ivanovich, Pavel Ivanovich!' said old Murazov, shaking his head. 'How you have been blinded by these valuables! They have deafened you even to the entreaties of your own poor soul!'

'I shall also think about my soul—just save me!'

'Pavel Ivanovich!' said the old man, and paused... 'It is not in my power to save you, that you can see for yourself. But I shall do my utmost to alleviate your fate and to obtain your release. I do not know whether I shall succeed, but I shall try. 'If, however—contrary to my expectation—I do succeed, I shall ask you for a reward for my services, Pavel Ivanovich: abandon all this seeking after gain. I tell you in all honesty that if I were to lose my fortune—and mine is bigger than yours—I should not shed a tear. No, no, what matters is not the valuables which can be confiscated from me, but that which no one can steal or take away. You have lived long enough in this world to understand. You yourself liken your life to a barque tossed on the waves. You already have the wherewithal to live out the remainder of your days. Settle down in some quiet little corner, close to a church and to simple, good folk; or, if you have set your heart on leaving descendants, find a nice girl of modest means to marry, a girl accustomed to moderation and simple housekeeping. Forget this clamorous world and all its seductive whims; and let it forget you too. There is no peace in it. You can see: everyone in it is either an enemy, a tempter, or a traitor.'

'I shall, I shall! I was already planning it, I firmly intended to live a decent life, I had resolved to take up farming, to moderate my habits. That devil-tempter led me astray, he threw me off the track, the cursed Satan, creature of hell!'

Something strange, feelings he had never known before, inexplicable feelings filled his heart: it was as if something was struggling to awake in him, something from afar, something which in childhood had been stifled by harsh, stultifying admonitions, by the miserable, disconsolate years of his childhood, by the bleakness of his home, by his bachelor loneliness, by the poverty and wretchedness of his earliest impressions of life, as if that something, which had been ⟨stifled⟩ by the stern regard of fate staring so tediously at him through a dingy, wintry, snow-bespattered ⟨window now strained to break out and be free⟩. A dull moan escaped from his lips and, covering his face with his two hands, he declaimed in a voice full of sorrow: 'It's the truth, the truth!'

'All your knowledge of people and their ways, all your experience failed to help you in your nefarious ways. And yet, if you had brought these to bear on lawful undertakings... Dear, oh dear, Pavel Ivanovich, why have you ruined yourself? Come to your senses: it's not too late. There's still time.'

'No, it's too late, it's too late,' he wailed in a voice which tore at Murazov's heart. 'I am beginning to sense that things are not right, that I have taken the wrong path and that I have strayed far from the right ⟨way⟩, but I can no longer help myself. No, it is my upbringing that is to blame. My father instilled moral precepts in me, he thrashed me, he forced me to copy out these moral precepts, and all the while he stole timber from neighbours before my very eyes and even forced me to be his accomplice. I saw him pursue an unjust case through the courts; he depraved a girl orphan who had been entrusted into his care. Example speaks louder than any precepts. I see, I feel, Afanasy Vasilievich, that I am not living my life correctly, but I have no great revulsion for vice: my nature has grown coarse, I have no love of good, I have none of that fine inclination for deeds which are pleasing to God, an inclination which becomes part of your nature, a habit of life. I have no longing to exert myself in the name of good, such as I have for the acquisition of property. I am telling the truth—I cannot help myself.'

The old man sighed deeply.

'Pavel Ivanovich, you have such will-power, such patience. Medicine is bitter, but the patient still takes it, knowing that without it he will not recover. You have no love of good—so force yourself to do good, without the love of it. This will be counted an even greater service than the good deeds of him who does good for the love of doing good. You need only force ⟨yourself⟩ one or two times—then the love will come to you too. Believe me, everything can be done ⟨. . .⟩ The kingdom suffers violence, it is written.* But you must force yourself to approach it, you must drive yourself forward and take it by storm. Yes, Pavel Ivanovich, you have the strength to do this, something others do not have, you have your iron will and perseverance—why should you not vanquish in the end? If you ask me, you could have been a hero, a knight of legend. Nowadays people are so weak, so lacking in will-power.'

It was evident that these words struck deep into Chichikov's soul and there, at its bottom, they stirred feelings which longed for glory. A look—if not of determination, then of something firm and akin to determination—burned in his eyes.

'Afanasy Vasilievich,' he said resolutely, 'if you would only plead on my behalf for a pardon and the means of departing from this place with a small amount of property, I give you my word that I shall start a new ⟨life⟩: I shall buy a small village, I shall become a farmer, I shall save money not for myself but in order to help others, I shall exert myself to do good. I shall turn my back on my own needs and put behind me all my big city feasting and dining and shall lead a plain and sober life.'

'May God strengthen you in this resolve,' said the delighted old man. 'I shall do everything in my power to persuade the prince to release you. Whether or not I shall succeed only God can say. In any event, things will, in all likelihood, be made easier for you. Dear God! Come, let me embrace you. How delighted I am to hear what you say! Now I bid you adieu and I shall go at once to the prince.'

Chichikov remained ⟨alone⟩.

His entire person had been deeply shaken and somehow softened. Even platinum, the hardest of metals, and that which withstands fire the longest, will melt: the flame is fanned up in the furnace, the bellows applied with force and the intolerable heat of the flames carried upwards, and then the obdurate metal glows white and turns at last to liquid; thus too will the strongest of men succumb in the furnace of misfortune, when, with each blow stronger than the last, his hard-tempered character is finally consumed by the inexorable flames of adversity.

'I myself am incapable of good and I have no sense of it, but I shall do all in my power to enable others to feel it; I am worthless and utterly incapable, but I shall do all in my power to direct others to the right path; I myself am a bad Christian, but I shall do all in my power not to set temptation before others. I shall labour, I shall toil in the sweat of my brow in my village, so that I may also exercise a good influence on others. After all, am I so utterly worthless? I have some affinity for a farmer's work; I have the qualities of thrift, and efficacy, and prudence, and even perseverance. I need only set my mind to it.'

Thus did Chichikov muse and, it seemed, with the half-awakened impulses of his soul he began to sense something. It was as if a shadowy awareness stole upon him, a realization that there is a particular duty which man must fulfil in this world, a duty which may be fulfilled anywhere, in any corner, regardless of the circumstances, of the upheavals and commotion which surround him. And a life of industry, far from the hubbub of the cities and from those delusions conjured up by man in his idleness, in his estrangement from toil, took shape so vividly in his mind's eye that he almost completely forgot all the unpleasantness of his present circumstances and he might even have been prepared to thank Providence for this hard-learnt ⟨lesson⟩, provided he could first be released and a portion of his possessions be returned to him...

But, instead, the narrow door of his squalid cell opened to admit an official personage—Samosvistov,* Epicurean, man-about-town, broad-shouldered, athletic, boon companion, debauchee and thoroughgoing rogue, in the words of his own comrades. In time of war such a man would have performed miracles: he could have been dispatched on a mission across hazardous, impassable ground, to steal a cannon from under the very nose of the enemy—that was the sort of task he should have been set. But in the absence of any martial arena, in which he might have become an honest man, he applied all his energies to skulduggery. It was quite baffling! He had the oddest convictions and rules of conduct: with his friends he was a trusty fellow, he would never betray them and was always as good as his word. Any superior authority, however, he regarded as some sort of enemy battery through which he had to fight his way, to which end he would seek out any weak spot, any breach or omission...

'We know all about your sorry plight, we've heard all about it!' he said, after verifying that the door was firmly closed behind him. 'It's nothing, it's nothing! Have no fear: it will all be set right. We shall

all start to work for your benefit, we are all your servants! Thirty thousand for the lot of us—that's all we ask.'

'Is that true?' exclaimed Chichikov. 'And I shall be completely acquitted?'

'Totally and utterly! And you'll receive compensation for your losses.'

'And for your work?'

'Thirty thousand. That's for everyone—for our chaps, and for the Governor-General's men, and for the secretary.'

'But, pray, how can I do it? All my things... my little box... it's all being kept under seal, heavily guarded...'

'In an hour's time you'll get the lot. Shall we shake on it?'

Chichikov held out his hand. His heart pounded and he could not believe this was really happening.

'Farewell for now! Our mutual friend has asked me to ⟨tell you⟩ that the main thing is to remain calm and keep your presence of mind.'

'Aha!' thought Chichikov, 'I know who that is: the jurisconsult!'

Samosvistov vanished... Alone again, Chichikov still could not believe what he had heard; then, no more than an hour after this conversation, his box was brought in: complete with papers and money—with everything in perfect order. Samosvistov had appeared at Chichikov's lodgings as though he were in charge: he had roundly scolded the guards on duty for their lack of vigilance, he had demanded extra soldiers to step up surveillance, he had collected not only the box, but also any papers which could in any way compromise Chichikov; all this he had tied together and sealed up and he had ordered a soldier to take the package at once to Chichikov himself, as it ostensibly contained his essential night things and sleeping attire.

Thus, together with his papers Chichikov received all the warm clothing he needed to cover his frail limbs. This swift delivery delighted him beyond words. His hopes soared, and once again he began to dream of various blandishments: theatre in the evening, a *danseuse* to whom he was paying his addresses... The village and its life of quiet started to fade, the town and its tumult were again more vivid, more bright... Oh, life!

Meanwhile in the courts and judicial chambers his case had swelled to unprecedented proportions. The scriveners' pens scratched and scribbled, and, snuffboxes always at the ready, the juris-prudential hacks toiled away, pausing only to admire their spidery depositions, as artists admire their creations. Like a concealed magician, the jurisconsult operated the entire mechanism from behind the scenes: before anyone realized quite what was afoot, he had sown total confusion on all sides. This confusion mounted. Samosvistov surpassed himself in valour and unheard-of audacity. Having ascertained where the arrested woman was being held under guard, he betook himself there directly and cut such a dashing and authoritative figure that the sentry leapt to attention and saluted.

'Have you been standing here long?'

'Since morning, Your Honour.'

'How long till you're relieved?'

'Three hours, Your Honour.'

'I'm going to need you. I'll tell the officer to detail someone in your place.'

'Yessir, Your Honour.'

He then drove home and, without a moment's delay—taking care to involve no one else so that none should be any the wiser—dressed up as a gendarme, putting on false sideburns and moustache, and the devil himself would not have recognized him. He returned to the house where Chichikov was being held and, grabbing hold of the first woman he saw, handed her over to two doughty accomplices, both crooked lawyers like himself, and then—suitably kitted out with moustaches and rifle—marched up to the sentries:

'You run along, the commanding officer's sent me to finish the shift.'

He took the sentry's place and stood there with his rifle. This was all that was needed. The detained woman's place was taken by the new woman, who had no idea what was going on. The first woman was hidden away so successfully that even afterwards they never found out what had become of her.

While Samosvistov was acting armed guard, the jurisconsult was working miracles in the civil arena: the governor was informed in close confidence that the public prosecutor was preparing a denunciation against him; the chief of gendarmes was informed that an official living amongst them incognito was writing denunciations against him; the incognito official was assured that an even more incognito official was writing denunciations of *him*—and everyone was reduced to such a state of bewilderment that they were forced to turn to him for advice. The end result was one of unholy confusion: the denunciations poured in thick and fast and chicanery and she-nanigans were uncovered such as had never before seen the light of day, and even such as did not exist at all. Every bit of dirt was dragged out and put to good use: who was whose illegitimate son, and what his rank and calling were; who kept a mistress; and whose wife had set her heart on whose husband. The scandals, imbroglios, and everything else got so stirred together with Chichikov's own story and with the dead souls that it was quite impossible to say which of all these reported goings-on was the greatest nonsense: they all seemed of equal merit. When at last the papers started to arrive on the Governor-General's desk, the poor prince could not make head nor tail of them. The exceptionally clever and efficient official charged with making a résumé all but went stark staring mad.

At this same time the prince was concerned about a great number of other matters, each more disagreeable than the last. In one part of the province famine had struck. The officials dispatched to the area to distribute grain had failed to organize things properly. In another part of the province the schismatics were stirring. Someone had spread among them the rumour that the Antichrist had come among them, that he would not even let the dead alone, and was buying up some dead souls or other. They repented and they sinned and, under the pretext of catching the Antichrist, bumped off many a non-Antichrist. In another area the peasants had revolted against their landlords and the local police. Some vagrants had spread the rumour among them that a time was near at hand when peasants would themselves become landlords and go about dressed in tailcoats, while landlords would have to clothe themselves in coarse-weave coats and be peasants—and an entire volost*—not realizing that, if this happened, there would be far too many landlords and captains of police—refused to pay any taxes at all. Coercive measures had to be applied. The poor prince was utterly distraught. And, in the midst of all this, the concessionaire Murazov sought an audience with him.

'Show him in,' said the prince.

The old man entered.

'So there's Chichikov for you! You stood up for him and took his side. Now he's embroiled in an affair that the most hard-bitten criminal wouldn't go near.'

'Permit me to inform you, Your Highness, that I am not fully aware of all the details of this business.'

'What we have here is forgery of a will—and a serious forgery! A public flogging is what he deserves.'

'Your Highness, I say this not to defend Chichikov, but the case has not been proved, after all: there still has to be an inquiry.'

'We have evidence. They've arrested the woman—the one who was dressed up as the old lady who died. I want you to be present when I interrogate her.' The prince rang and gave orders for the woman to be brought in.

Murazov fell silent.

'It's a most disgraceful business! And, to their shame, the town's leading officials, right up to the governor himself, are mixed up in it. He should not keep company with thieves and ne'er-do-wells!' said the prince heatedly.

'After all, the governor is one of the heirs: he has the right to make claims; as for all the others, latching on like that from all sides—that, Your Highness, is human nature. A rich woman has died, she failed to make sensible and fair dispositions, so the fortune-hunters are flocking in: that's human nature...'

'But why such vile deeds? The blackguards!' said the prince, seething with indignation. 'There's not one decent official among them: they're all scoundrels!'

'Your Highness! But who among us is really decent? All the officials of our town are only human beings: they have their merits and many of them are highly competent, but everyone can succumb to temptation.'

'Listen, Afanasy Vasilievich, tell me this: I know that you alone are an honest man, so why are you so eager to defend every manner of scoundrel?'

'Your Highness,' said Murazov, 'you may call them scoundrels but, whatever else they might be, the fact remains that they are God's creatures. How can you not defend a man when you know that half the evil deeds he does are the product of his coarseness and ignorance? For at every step we commit injustices, and at every moment of our lives we occasion the misfortunes of others, even without the intention of so doing. After all, Your Highness has himself also perpetrated a great injustice.'

'What!' exclaimed the prince in astonishment, quite taken aback by this unexpected revelation.

Murazov paused, fell silent a moment, as if gathering his thoughts, and finally said:

'Well, in the Derpennikov case,* for instance.'

'Afanasy Vasilievich, a crime committed against the fundamental laws of the state is tantamount to an act of treason against one's own land.'

'I do not mean to justify him. But is it really just to condemn a youth, who in his inexperience has been seduced and led astray by others, as harshly as one of those instigating the crime? For the same punishment has been meted out to Derpennikov as to some thieving guttersnipe, yet their crimes were not of the same order.'

'For Heaven's sake,' said the prince with pronounced agitation, 'do you know something more about this? If so, you must tell me. Just the other day I wrote directly to St Petersburg seeking clemency on his behalf.'

'No, Your Highness, I am not saying that I know something which you do not. Although, of course, there is one circumstance which would work in his favour, only he himself will not consent to its use, because it would entail the suffering of another. I am only wondering whether you might not have acted rather hastily on that occasion. Forgive me, Your Highness, I am judging by my own feeble understanding. On several occasions you have bidden me speak openly. Well, sir, when I was still an overseer, I had many workers of all kinds, good and bad... ⟨I also had to keep in mind⟩ a man's previous life, because, if you do not examine everything calmly, and if, from the very outset, you raise your voice at a man you will only succeed in frightening him and you will never get a true confession out of him; but when you talk to him with compassion, as brother to brother, he will willingly tell you everything and will not even seek clemency, and he will feel no bitterness towards anyone, for he clearly sees that it is not I who punish him, but the law.'

The prince grew pensive. At this moment a young officer entered and stood waiting respectfully, holding a portfolio. The cares of office and toil were stamped on his young and still fresh face. It was clear why he had been chosen for special duties. He was a member of that rare breed who throw themselves into their work *con amore*. Driven not by the flames of ambition, nor by a thirst for profit, nor a desire to emulate others, he applied himself to his duties simply because he was convinced that it was necessary for him to hold that post and no other, that he had been born for this work. To investigate, to scrutinize a complex affair, and having caught all its threads, then to disentangle it: this was his job. His labours, his endeavours, his sleepless nights were all abundantly recompensed if, at last, a case finally began to fall into place before him, if its secret springs were revealed, and if he felt that he could put it all across in a few succinct words, clearly and distinctly, so that it would be plain and obvious to any man. We could even say that the joy felt by a pupil when the import of an immensely difficult sentence is at last brought home to him and the real meaning of the thought of a great writer is revealed, is as nothing to the joy felt by this man when, before his eyes, a gravely entangled case was unravelled. On the other hand ⟨. . .⟩

[*The manuscript breaks off here and continues on a new page, in the middle of a sentence*]

⟨. . .⟩ with grain in the famine-stricken areas; I know this area better than the officials: I shall go in person to ascertain who needs what. And if you permit it, Your Highness, I shall also speak to the schismatics.* They will be more willing to talk with one of their own, a common man like themselves. And perhaps, God willing, I shall help you find a peaceful settlement with them. But officials will not be able to sort them out: they'll have to open an official correspondence and then they'll end up so bogged down in documents and paperwork that they'll no longer be able to see the wood for the trees. But I shall not take any money from you because—to tell you God's truth—I should be ashamed to think about my own profit at a time like this, when people are dying of hunger. I have some grain in store; in fact I've also sent to Siberia for more to be brought by next summer.'

'Only God can reward you for your services, Afanasy Vasilievich. But I shall not say a single word to you because—as you know yourself—words are powerless here... But permit me to say one thing regarding your own request. Tell me this: do I really have the right to turn a blind eye to this business, and would it be just, would it be honest for me to pardon scoundrels?'

'Your Highness, honest to God, you cannot call them that, especially as among ⟨them⟩ there are many who are entirely worthy people. The circumstances men find themselves in are intricate, Your Highness, very, very intricate. Sometimes a man seems to be guilty beyond doubt, but when you look more closely into the matter you find that it wasn't even him at all.'

'But what will they themselves say, if I drop the matter? As you know, there are those among them who, after this, will raise their noses still higher in the air and will even boast that they put the wind up me. They will be the first to lose their respect.'

'Your Highness, permit me to give you my opinion: gather them all together, tell them that you know about everything, and describe your own position to them exactly as you have been so good as to describe it here to me, and seek their advice: ask what would each of them have done in your place.'

'Do you imagine that they are capable of any more noble aspirations than double-dealing and lining their own pockets? Believe me, they will only laugh at me.'

'I do not think so, Your Highness. Every ⟨Russian⟩, even the very worst among us, still has his sense of justice. A Jew might laugh, but not a Russian. No, Your Highness, you have no need to hold anything back. Tell them everything, precisely as you told it to ⟨me⟩. As you know, they deride you as an ambitious man, a proud man, who in not prepared to listen to anything they say, who is utterly self-assured—so let them see everything as it really is. What is it to you? After all, your cause is just. Tell them as if you were making this confession not to them, but to God Himself.'

'Afanasy Vasilievich,' said the prince, pensively, 'I shall give this some thought, but in the mean while I thank you most sincerely for your advice.'

'But, Your Highness, please order Chichikov's release.'

'You tell that Chichikov to remove himself from here as soon as possible, and the further the better. Now that is someone I could never forgive.'

Murazov bowed and went from the prince directly to Chichikov. He found Chichikov already in fine spirits and totally relaxed, tucking into a very decent dinner, which had been served to him on china dishes from some very decent kitchen. From the very first sentences of their conversation the old man at once gathered that

Chichikov had already contrived to speak with some of the officials dealing with this labyrinthine case. He even detected the unseen hand of the artful jurisconsult.

'Now listen to me, Pavel Ivanovich,' he said, 'I have brought you freedom on the condition that you remove yourself at once from the town. Gather together all your goods and chattels and may God speed you on your way—do not delay for a single minute, because your case has become even worse. I know what's going on—I know that a certain person is giving you ideas; but let me tell you in confidence that yet another of his deeds is about to come to light, and no power on earth will save him now. He, of course, is glad to drag others down with him, to keep him company, but the whole business will soon be dragged out into the open. I left you in a good frame of mind—better than that in which I find you now. I am giving you this advice in all earnest. I mean it: there's more to life than property, which causes people to quarrel and commit murder. They believe it matters only to acquire property in this world without thinking of the next.

'Believe me, Pavel Ivanovich, until people renounce everything that makes them crush and devour one another on earth, and attend instead to their spiritual property—to put their spiritual house in order, they will never be able to set their earthly property in good order. Times of famine and poverty will set in, striking nations in their entirety and each individual separately.* That is plain to see. For, say what you will, the body depends upon the soul. How then can things be expected to proceed as they should? Think not about dead souls, but about your own living soul, and may God go with you along some different road! I shall also be leaving tomorrow. Make haste! Or else disaster will strike when I am no longer here.'

With these words the old man took his leave. Chichikov fell to thinking. The meaning of life once again loomed large before him. 'Murazov's right!' he said. 'It's time to follow a different road.' Saying this, he left the gaol. One sentry followed lugging his box, another his ⟨mattress⟩ and bed-linen. Selifan and Petrushka were overjoyed at their master's release.

'Well, my good fellows,' said Chichikov, addressing them graciously, 'we must pack and be on our way.'

'We'll whiz along, Pavel Ivanovich,' said Selifan. 'The road must be good and firm now: there's been enough snow. Honest, it's time we got out of this town. I'm that sick of it, I can't stand the sight of it any more.'

'Run along to the carriage-maker and tell him to put the carriage on runners,' said Chichikov, and himself headed for the town, but not with the intention of paying farewell calls. After all this brouhaha it would anyway have been most awkward—especially since a great number of highly disagreeable stories about him were circulating round town. He avoided all possible ⟨encounters⟩, and only called stealthily on the merchant from whom he had bought the cloth of Navarino smoke and flame, took another four arshins for a tailcoat and trousers and headed back to the same tailor. For double ⟨the fee⟩ the tailor agreed to redouble his zeal. He kept his underlings hard at work all night, busy with their needles, their flatirons, and their teeth—and the next day, albeit a little late, the suit was ready. The horses were all harnessed up. Chichikov still took the time to try on the coat. It was perfect, exactly like its predecessor. But, alas!—he noticed a bare patch on his head and murmured sadly to himself: 'Now why did I have to give way to such remorse? There surely was no cause to tear my hair.'

Having settled his account with the tailor he finally drove out of the town in a rather strange frame of mind. This was not the old Chichikov—no, this was but a ruin of the old Chichikov. His inner state could be compared to a structure which had been dismantled in order that from it a new structure might be assembled, but work on the new had not yet commenced because the final plans had not yet arrived from the architect and the workers had been left perplexedly twiddling their thumbs. An hour earlier old Murazov had departed on his way, riding together with Potapych in his bast-covered kibitka, and an hour after Chichikov's departure an order was issued that the prince, in view of his imminent departure for St Petersburg, wished to see every one of the officials without exception.

The entire official estate of the town, from the governor to the last titular councillor,* gathered in the large hall of the Governor-General's residence: heads of chancery, chiefs of staff, councillors, assessors, Kisloyedov, Krasnonosov, Samosvistov,* bribe-takers and bribe-refusers, rule-breakers, rule-benders and sticklers for the rules— all waited in a state of considerable agitation and anxiety for the Governor-General to make his entrance. The prince came out. He looked neither morose nor cheerful: his gaze was firm and so was his gait. The entire worthy assemblage bowed, many from the waist. Returning their courtesy with a slight bow, the prince began:

'Before departing for St Petersburg I thought it fit and proper to receive all of you and even in part to explain the reasons for my journey. A most scandalous business has been cooked up in our very midst. I trust that many of those present know to what I refer. This affair has led to the exposure of other, no less perfidious affairs, in which people whom I hitherto regarded as honest are implicated. I am even aware that the secret aim behind all this is to obfuscate everything so thoroughly that it will be quite impossible to sort matters out through the proper procedures. I even know the identity of the chief ⟨instigator⟩ and by whose subterfuge ⟨. . .⟩ although he has very skilfully concealed his involvement. I wish you to know, however, that I intend to deal with this not through any formal enquiry, following the proper procedures, but with a swift court martial, as in ⟨time⟩ of war, and I hope to receive His Majesty's authority when I set before him all the facts of the matter. In such a case, when it has become impossible to conduct proceedings by civil law, when cupboards full of ⟨documents⟩ catch fire, and, finally, when people attempt, with a mass of false testimony from outsiders and with hatched denunciations, to cast a veil over an affair which is shady enough as it is, I regard a court martial as the only solution and I wish to know your opinion.'

The prince paused, as if waiting for an answer. His listeners all stood still, with eyes downcast. Many were pale.

'I also know of one other affair, although its perpetrators are fully convinced that no one else could know about it. This will also be investigated but not through formal channels, because I myself shall be both plaintiff and petitioner and shall submit irrefutable testimony.'

Someone in the assemblage of officials started nervously; several of the more faint-hearted among them also looked uncomfortable.

'It stands to reason that the ringleaders should be stripped of their rank and property, the others should be dismissed from their posts. It also goes without saying that there will be many innocent persons among them and these will also suffer. What can be done? The affair is too perfidious and cries out for justice. Although I am only too aware that this will not even serve as a lesson for others, that others will appear to take the places of those dismissed, and the very ones who have hitherto been honest will become dishonest, and those deemed worthy of trust will deceive and betray—notwithstanding all this, I must act with severity because justice cries out to be done. I know I shall be accused of excessive severity, but I know too that those same people will... that they will also accuse me ⟨. . .⟩

[*The edge of the page is torn off in the manuscript and the rest of sentence is lost*]

⟨. . .⟩ I must therefore turn myself into an unfeeling instrument of justice, an axe, which must fall on the necks of ⟨the guilty⟩.'

An involuntary tremor ran across all the faces.

The prince was calm. His face exhibited neither anger, nor any inner agitation.

'Now this same man, who holds in his hands the destiny of many others, and whom all entreaties and pleas were powerless to move, this same man now ⟨falls⟩ at ⟨your⟩ feet and pleads with all of you. Everything will be forgotten, smoothed over, and pardoned; I shall myself intercede on everyone's behalf, if only my plea is granted. This is it.

'I know that it is not possible, by any devices, by any threats, by any punishments, to eradicate corruption: it is already too deeply rooted. The dishonest practice of taking bribes has become a compulsion, an obligation even for those who were not born to dishonesty. I know that for many it is now almost impossible to swim against the general tide. But now I am bound, as at a decisive and sacred moment, when the very safety of our fatherland is in jeopardy, when each and every citizen must endure everything and make every sacrifice, to turn in supplication at least to those in whose breast there still beats a Russian heart and ⟨for whom⟩ the word "nobility" still has some meaning. There is no purpose in debating here which of us is more guilty. Perhaps I am most guilty of all; perhaps I treated you too severely at the beginning; perhaps I was too suspicious and thrust aside those amongst you who genuinely wished to be of service to me, although I myself would probably have done exactly as you did.

'If they really cherished justice and the good of their land, they should not have taken umbrage at the haughty way in which I treated them, they should have suppressed the stirrings of ambition within them and sacrificed their personal pride. I could not have failed to notice their self-sacrifice and uplifting love of good, nor could I have failed, in the end, to accept their useful and wise advice. Surely it is more befitting for a subordinate to adapt to the character of his superior than for the superior to that of his subordinate? This, at least, is more logical, more straightforward, because subordinates have but one superior and a superior has hundreds of subordinates.

'But let us not concern ourselves for the moment with the apportionment of blame. The point is that we are called to save our land; that this our land is being laid waste not by the invasion of twenty alien tribes,* but by us ourselves; that, beside the lawful powers in the land, a new power has come into being, far mightier than any lawful government. It has laid down its own conditions; a value has been set on all things and those values have even become common knowledge. And no ruler, be he wiser than all other lawmakers and all other rulers, is capable of correcting evil, however he may strive to limit the activities of corrupt officials by appointing other officials to oversee them. All efforts will fail until each and every one of us realizes that, just as in times of insurrection the people armed themselves against their ⟨enemies⟩, so now must he also take up arms against injustice.

'As a Russian, as one bonded to you by kinship, by the common blood coursing through our veins, I now appeal to you. I appeal to those among you who have any understanding of the concept of nobility of thought. I invite you to recall the duty which stands before man at every stage of his life. I invite you to take a closer look at your own duty and the obligations placed upon you by your service on this earth, because that is something of which we are already dimly aware, but which we can scarcely ⟨. . .⟩ ⟨*At this point the manuscript breaks off.*⟩

APPENDIX

VARIANTS TO PART TWO

As explained in the introductory note to Part Two, (p. 257) below, the manuscript of this work contains two variant texts, or text 'strata', and I have followed the editors of the Academy edition in taking the later as more authoritative. In places the texts are largely the same, differing only in minor detail; in others, however, the differences are substantial and significant and, for the interested reader, I give some of those more significant variants below, marking the page on which, in this translation, the corresponding passage of the later layer occurs and the opening words of that passage. Ellipsis points in square brackets [. . .] mark omitted passages which are identical, or very close, to the corresponding passage in the later stratum.

p. 263 (Of the sciences he selected only those . . . greater strength of spirit):

He maintained that the thing man needed most was the science of life, and that, once having mastered this, he would then discover for himself what should be his principal object of study.

He made this same science of life the object of a special course of training to which only the most outstanding pupils were admitted. Those of little ability he released to join the government service after their first course, asserting that they need not be subjected to unnecessary suffering: for them it was enough if they had learnt to be patient, hard-working functionaries, free of arrogance and any sort of grand ideas. 'But with the bright ones, with the gifted ones I have to work long and hard,' he used to say.

Here they met a quite different Aleksandr Petrovich, who declared from the very start that, where hitherto he had demanded their mere wit, now he would demand the highest intelligence—not the intelligence which can make fun of a fool and hold him up to ridicule, but that which can suffer any insult, can suffer a fool—and feel no irritation. Now he started to demand of them what others demand from children. It was this that he called intelligence of the highest order. To be able, in the face of every possible disappointment, to preserve the sublime calm in which man should remain in perpetuity—that is what he called intelligence!

In this course Aleksandr Petrovich showed that he knew the science of life perfectly. Of the sciences he selected only those which could shape a person into a responsible citizen of his country. [. . .] In a word, he traced out before them a future that was far from roseate. [. . .] There was something sobering in their lives. Aleksandr Petrovich carried out all sorts of tests and experiments with them, subjecting them to the most wounding insults, delivered either by himself or by their own comrades, but— once they had fathomed his schooling—they became even more circumspect.

p. 264 (Aleksandr Petrovich's place was taken by a certain Fyodor Ivanovich . . . only for good conduct):

Aleksandr Petrovich's place was taken by a certain Fyodor Ivanovich, a good man and diligent, but with quite a different view of things. He fancied he saw something unbridled in the free and easy manner of the advanced course students. He began by enforcing certain rules of behaviour, demanding that the young men should maintain total silence, that on no account were they to walk other than in pairs. He even started measuring the distance between the pairs with a yardstick. At table, for the sake of better symmetry, he seated them according to height, and not intelligence, so that the dunces received the choicest pieces and the bright boys the leftovers.

p. 266 (He began to wish he had never left school . . . and the tears welled up in his eyes):

He suddenly remembered his schooldays as a time of bliss, now lost for ever, so elevated did the study of the sciences seem when compared to this wretched clerking. How superior that scholarly preparation for service had been to the service itself! The image of his incomparable, marvellous tutor, the irreplaceable Aleksandr Petrovich rose before him so vividly that the tears suddenly came flooding from his eyes.

p. 268 (But the uncle's arts of persuasion were wasted on his nephew):

Thus did the uncle, the actual state councillor, reason. He himself had never, in all the days of his life, walked along any other street than that which led to his place of service, where there were no fine public buildings; he noticed none of the people he encountered, whether generals or princes; he knew none of the temptations which in the capitals entice men wanting in abstinence, and had never in his life been to the theatre. He said all this with the sole purpose of reawakening the young man's ambition and exciting his imagination. In this, however, he failed: Tentetnikov obstinately stood his ground. Government departments and the capital had grown tedious to him.

Appendix

p. 270 (The bonnets, headscarves, kerchiefs ... their toil and their occupation):

Bonnets, headscarves, kerchiefs, homespun coats, beards of every kind—spade beards, forked beards and goatees, red, brown, and silvery white—filled the entire courtyard. The men roared: 'Father and benefactor, you've come at last!' The women wailed: 'You are the gold, the silver of our hearts!' Some, standing further off, even came to blows in their anxiety to push forward.

A decrepit old woman, as shrunken as a dried pear, slipped between the legs of the others, stepped up to the master and shrieked: 'Oh, you poor little dear, how scrawny you are! Those cursed German heathens have starved you to death!'

'Let him be, you fool woman!' the spade, forked, and goatee beards shouted at her. 'How dare you push yourself at him like that, you pock-marked old hag!' To this someone appended the sort of word which only a Russian peasant can hear without laughing.

The master also laughed, but nonetheless he was deeply moved. 'So much love! And for what?' he asked himself. 'For having never seen them, having never attended to their needs! From now on I solemnly pledge to share your toil and your activity! I shall do all in my power to make you what you should be, what you are destined to be by that good nature concealed within each and every one of you, so that your love for me shall be deserved, so that I shall indeed be your father and benefactor!'

p. 270 (He sacked the fool of a bailiff):

Now that he was on the spot he could see that the bailiff was an old woman and a fool with all the qualities of a useless manager, which is to say that he kept an accurate count of the chickens and eggs, of the wool yarn and linen which the peasant women brought in, but he did not know the first thing about sowing and harvesting, and to make matters still worse he suspected the peasants of plotting against his life.

p. 274 (But one century succeeds another ... uttering that word!):

But one century succeeds another: half a million stay-at-homes, lie-abeds, and marmots slumber on oblivious, and but rarely does Russia witness the birth of a man capable of uttering it, this all-powerful word.

pp. 274–5 (a daughter, a strange and most unusual creature ... paint her portrait):

a daughter, a strange, lovely creature, more like some fantastical vision than a woman. Sometimes a dream like this appears to a man, and from then on he is haunted all the days of his life by this vision; reality fades away altogether for him and he becomes quite incapable of any useful work. [. . .] She was more pretty than beautiful, more kind than clever; more graceful, more ethereal than any classical beauty. It was quite impossible to say which country had made its imprint on her, because it would be hard to find a profile like hers anywhere, except perhaps on the cameos of antiquity.

p. 275 (and she would readily throw him her purse . . . a moment's thought):

and, if he was poor, she would readily throw him her purse—no matter whether this was wise or foolish; should he be wounded, she would at once tear a strip from her own dress for a bandage!

p. 275 (This was precisely how it happened . . . His tedious life was brightened for a moment):

Andrei Ivanovich Tentetnikov would have been quite at a loss to say how it happened that from their very first meeting he felt as if he had known her always. [. . .] His dressing-gown was cast aside. It did not take him so long now to get out of bed, Mikhailo did not have to stand for hours with the basin in his hands. The windows in the rooms were thrown open and the owner of this picturesque estate often strolled down the dark, winding paths of his park and paused for hours at a time to admire the captivating views in the distance.

p. 276 (the Countess Boldyreva and the Princess Yuzyakina . . . the previous tsar):

The Countess Boldyreva and the Princess Yuzyakina: the one a widow, the other an old maid, both former ladies-in-waiting under the previous tsar, both gossips and scandal-mongers, not excessively enchanting in their amiability,

p. 280 (his boots were set out in a row . . . a calendar and two novels, both volume two):

his boots were set out in a row: boots that were not quite brand new, boots that were still brand new, boots with new toecaps, and patent-leather ankle-boots [. . .] On the table between the windows, the little box was placed. Then, on the writing table, facing the settee, his portfolio, a jar of eau de Cologne, sealing-wax, toothbrushes, a new calendar and two novels, both volume two.

p. 282 (and where the sky was darkened by great flocks of ravens, cawing as they flew hither and thither):

and here he was deafened by the cawing of crows, the chattering of daws, and crunking of rooks, which flew hither and thither in great flocks, darkening the sky; or else he went down to the water-meadows and the burst dams, to watch the water crashing down on the mill wheels with a deafening roar;

p. 283 (He enquired into everything, asking about this and that, and how the farm was doing, and all the while he thought to himself):

He enquired into everything, asking about this and that—discussing this and that, what sort of harvests might be expected, how the ploughing was progressing, what price wheat was fetching, what they charged in the spring and autumn for grinding the flour, and asking the name of each peasant—who was related to whom, and where he bought his cow, and what he fed his pig—in a word, everything. He also found out how many peasants had died. It transpired that not many had. Being a man of intelligence he at once noticed that Andrei Ivanovich's management of affairs was far from perfect. There was neglect, carelessness, thieving, and also widespread drunkenness. And he said to himself:

p. 283 (who had even learnt to play a musical instrument):

but educated and brought up like a gentlewoman—with an understanding of music, too, although, of course, music was not really the most important thing, but—if that was the custom—why go against the general opinion?

p. 283 (Petrushka bragged to Grigory about his travels far and wide):

Petrushka bragged to Grigory that he had been to Kostroma, Yaroslavl, Nizhny, and even Moscow;

p. 284 (and that he was moving with them in the round-dance):

and that he was moving with them in the round-dance. With a wave of his hand he would say: 'Cursed wenches!'

p. 290 (Everything about the general ... an impassioned zealot):

despite his kind heart the general was a scornful man. Generally speaking, he loved to be in command, loved adulation, loved to dazzle and impress with his intelligence,

p. 293 (And if she were to be depicted in marble . . . the work of a great master):

Although Chichikov knew her face from Andrei Ivanovich's drawings he gazed at her like one struck dumb, and only afterwards, when he had come to his senses, did he observe that she in fact had one substantial fault, namely, a lack of plumpness.

p. 293 (you, who have the kindest of souls . . . who you know to be a good-for-nothing):

'you have the kindest of souls and an uncommonly soft heart, but from the way you act a person might form quite a different opinion of you. Must you receive a man knowing full well that he is a good-for-nothing, simply because he has a glib tongue and is adept at fawning on you?'

p. 294 (At this point Chichikov deemed it appropriate to make a small contribution . . . 'We are not to blame in any way for all this.') [I quote this passage *in extenso* as it is one of the best known passages from Part Two, despite having been discarded by Gogol in subsequent editing]:

'Oh no, Your Excellency,' said Chichikov to Ulinka, with a slight bow of his head and an agreeable smile. 'According to Christian teaching it is precisely such men that we must love.'

And at this point he turned to the general and said with a smile, this time slightly roguish:

'Might I ask whether Your Excellency has heard the little story about "Try and love us when we're dirty; anyone can love us when we're nice and clean"?'

'No, I've not heard it.'

'Well, this is a most appropriate anecdote,' said Chichikov still with his roguish smile. 'Now, on the estate of Prince Gukzovsky, with whom Your Excellency is undoubtedly acquainted—'

'Don't know him.'

'There was a manager, a young man of German stock. His work often took him to town, on the matter of recruits and other business, and there, naturally, he would grease the palms of the law officers.' Here Chichikov, screwing up his eyes, showed by the expression on his face how palms were greased. 'They also took a liking to him, and wined and dined him. And so, one day at dinner with them, he said: "Well now, gentlemen, you must come and visit me some time, on the Prince's estate." They promised to visit him. Shortly after this assizes were held there on a case concerning the estates of Count Trekhmetyov, whom Your Excellency is also certain to know.'

'Don't know him.'

'As it transpired, the assizers did not carry out the investigation at all, but the entire crew turned off the road and made for the house of the Count's old steward, where they stayed for three days and three nights on end, doing nothing but play cards. The samovar and the grog pot, naturally enough, never left the table. In the end the old man grew tired of their company and, to get rid of them, suggested: "Gentlemen, you should call on the Prince's German manager: he lives near here and is expecting you."

'"Why not, indeed," they agreed, and just as they were, half drunk, unshaven, and groggy with sleep, they climbed on their carts and repaired to the German's house.

'Now I should tell you, Your Excellency, that the German had only just wed. He had married a young lady fresh from finishing school, a young, fragile thing' (here Chichikov's facial expression demonstrated fragility). 'The two of them were sitting together having tea, with never a care in the world, when suddenly the doors opened and in burst this ugly mob—'

'I can just imagine them—a splendid sight!' exclaimed the general with a laugh.

'The manager was quite dumbfounded and said: "What do you want?" "Aha," they cried, "it's like that, is it?" And they suddenly changed their tune completely... "We want to make a check up! How much vodka do you distil on the estate? Let's see your records." The German rushed to and fro in a panic. "Call the witnesses!" They grabbed hold of him, bound him, and the German spent the next year and a half in gaol.'

'Well I never!' said the general.

Ulinka clasped her hands.

'The wife petitioned, of course,' continued Chichikov. 'But what could a young, inexperienced woman do? Luckily she happened upon some kind people who advised her to make a deal with those assizers. The German got off with two thousand and the cost of a dinner for them. At this dinner, when they were already quite merry, and the German too, they said to him: "Aren't you ashamed of the rotten welcome you gave us that time? You only want to see us smart and clean-shaven and in our best bibs and tuckers. No, you must try to love us dirty, anyone can love us nice and clean,"'

The general guffawed heartily; Ulinka sighed.

'Papa, I do not understand how you can laugh!' she said angrily, her fair brow clouding over... 'That was the most dastardly act, for which they should all have been banished to I don't know where.'

'My dear, I am not condoning them at all,' said the general. 'But what can we do if it's funny? How does it go: "try to love us clean..."?'

'Dirty, Your Excellency,' corrected Chichikov.

'"Try and love us dirty, anyone can love us nice and clean." Ha, ha, ha, ha!'

And the general's body started to rock with laughter. Those shoulders that had once worn heavy epaulettes shook, just as if the heavy epaulettes pressed down on them still.

Chichikov also permitted himself an interjection of laughter, but out of respect to the general, he articulated it not as 'Ha, ha' but as 'He, he, he, he, he!' and his body also rocked with laughter, although his shoulders did not shake, because they had never worn heavy epaulettes.

'I can imagine, those unshaven assizers must have been a fine sight!' said the general, continuing to laugh.

'Indeed, Your Excellency, whichever way one looks at it... after a three-day vigil, playing cards and drinking, actually fasting too: they must have been pretty worn out!' said Chichikov, continuing to laugh.

Ulinka lowered herself into an armchair and placed a hand over her lovely eyes; as if annoyed that there was no one with whom she could share her indignation, she said: 'I don't know, I find the whole story extremely vexatious.'

Indeed, the feelings aroused in the hearts of the three persons assembled here in conversation were oddly contradictory. The first found the German's slowness and doltishness funny. The second found it funny because rogues had played a mischievous trick on someone. The third was sad because injustice had been allowed to go unpunished. There only lacked a fourth, who could have mused over these very words, which had occasioned laughter in one and sadness in another. What does it mean, he would have wondered, that even in his fall a sullied, degraded man should demand that he be loved? Is this some animal instinct? Or the feeble cry of a soul, choked by the oppressive weight of base passions, a voice that can still be heard through the hardening crust of loathsomeness, crying out: 'Brother, save me!' There was no fourth person, to whom the degraded soul of his brother would have seemed the most distressing thing of all.

'I don't know,' said Ulinka, removing her hand from her face, 'the whole story only vexes me.'

[. . .]

'How does it go?' he asked, rubbing his fat neck all round, 'try and love us clean...?'

'Dirty, Your Excellency.'

'Try and love us dirty, for anyone can love us nice and clean. Very good, very good!'

p. 296 ('There he goes again' . . . fretted Chichikov to himself):

Chichikov's situation was awkward in the extreme: before them stood the valet, his mouth hanging open and his eyes starting from his head.

'But Your Excellency, this laughter arises from another's lamentable predicament,' he said.

'Forgive me, brother!

p. 297 ('Eighty, Your Excellency'):

'Eighty, Your Excellency. But this is rather confidential, I would rather we...' Chichikov gave the general a significant look and at the same time glanced sideways at the valet. 'Yes—well now—Your Excellency... This, Your Excellency, is the sort of matter I would rather keep secret...'

'Of course, I understand perfectly. What an old fool! Imagine getting such foolhardy notions in your head at the age of eighty!

p. 298 ('If Colonel Koshkaryov is indeed off his rocker . . . a footman with his coarse physiognomy!'):

'No, no,' said Chichikov, finding himself once more surrounded by open fields and spaces, 'no, I shall not arrange my life like that. As soon as I finish everything successfully, God willing, and become a real man of property, a wealthy man, I shall proceed quite differently: I shall have a cook, and a house full of plenty, and the farming side will also be in good order. Not only will I make ends meet, I shall also put away a little sum each year for my descendants, if the good Lord should bestow fertility upon my wife... Hey you, blockhead!'

Selifan and Petrushka both looked round from the coach-box.

[. . .]

Seeing the direction in which this discussion was leading, Petrushka became fidgety. He wanted to swear that he hadn't even sampled the stuff, but this would be too shameless a lie.

'Nice carriage this, sir, to travel in,' said Selifan, turning round.

'What?'

'I was saying, Pavel Ivanovich, sir, that your honour's carriage is nice to travel in, sir, better, sir, than the chaise: it doesn't jolt.'

'Drive on! No one's asking for your opinion.'

Selifan lightly brushed the rounded haunches of the horses with his whip and addressed Petrushka:

'You know, they say old Koshkaryov got his peasants dressed up just like Germans; from a distance you wouldn't have known them, strutting around stork-fashion, just like Germans. And as for the women, he wouldn't let them wear their usual head-scarves or fancy head-dresses, but made them put on those German bonnets, just like the German women wear, those bonnet things, you know. One of those German bonnets.'

'I'd like to see you dressed up like a German with a bonnet on!' said Petrushka, giving Selifan a sideways look and chuckling. Heavens—how ugly he was with that grin! He did not appear to be smiling at all, but rather looked like a man who had caught cold and was trying to sneeze with a stuffed nose, but no sneeze came and the grimace of someone on the point of sneezing remained frozen on his face.

p. 301 (From within two young lads . . . wearing summer frock-coats):

Chichikov, with his usual genteelness, negotiated the doorway sideways, to permit his host to pass through together with him; but to no avail: his host would not have fitted, and anyway he was no longer there. Instead his voice could be heard shouting in the yard: 'What's with that Big Foma? Why isn't he here yet? Yemelian, you dunderhead, run along to that dolt of a cook and tell him to gut the sturgeon as fast as he can. The milt, roe, innards and bream can go into the soup and the carp can be used for the sauce. And crayfish, crayfish! Little Foma, you dunderhead, where's the crayfish, I said, crayfish!' And for a long time yet the words rang out: crayfish, crayfish.

'The good master is certainly going to great trouble,' said Chichikov, sitting down in an armchair and surveying the walls and corners of the room.

'Well here I am,' said the master, coming into the room followed by two youths clad in summer frock-coats.

p. 302 (He wasted no time in telling Chichikov . . . no future for them in the provinces):

He told their guest that the teaching was none too good in their school; that favour was shown to those boys whose mamas sent bigger presents; that the Ingermanland Hussar regiment was stationed in the town; that Captain Vetvitsky had a better horse than his own colonel, although Lieutenant Vyazemtsev was a far finer horseman.

pp. 305–6 (He kept topping up their glasses . . . once they moved to the capital):

It was the same thing with the wine. Having received the mortgage money Pyotr Petrovich had stocked up with provisions for ten years ahead. He kept topping up and topping up their glasses; what the guests did not finish he handed over to Aleksasha and Nikolasha, who knocked back glass after glass, but when they stood up from the table they were as steady as rocks, as if they had been drinking water.

pp. 307–8 (Not so much as a ripple disturbed the water . . . and their little Chichlings):

Not so much as a ripple disturbed the water. They drank tea and ate hot buns, as the boat glided beneath a succession of ropes stretched across the river to secure the nets. Before tea, their host undressed and dived into the river, where he splashed about yelling at the fishermen for half an hour or so, shouting orders to Big Foma and Kozma, and, when he had had his fill of shouting and fussing and getting chilled through in the water, he reappeared in the launch with a keen appetite and drank his tea with enviable gusto. In the meantime the sun had set. A glow remained in the skies. The shouts rang out more sonorously. The place of the fishermen was taken all along the banks by groups of bathing boys, and the air rang with their merry splashing and laughter. [. . .]

The moon rose and the darkness began to recede before its radiance; finally everything was illuminated: the lake and the cottages; the fires grew dimmer; the smoke from the chimneys became visible, silvery in the moonlight. Nikolasha and Aleksasha galloped past on two spirited colts, racing each other; the dust rose behind them as from a herd of rams. [. . .] Who could fail to be stirred by such an evening?

p. 309 ('And yet he's never gloomy . . . A tidy little sum.'):

'That is simply making a pig of oneself. Are you not uncomfortable, Platon Mikhailovich? The carriage was extremely comfortable before, and now suddenly it's uncomfortable. Petrushka, I suppose in your stupidity you went and repacked everything? What are all these boxes sticking out everywhere?'

Platonov chuckled.

'That I can explain,' he said. 'Pyotr Petrovich sent it in for us to eat on the road.'

'Yes sir,' said Petrushka, turning round from the box, 'orders was given to put it all in the carriage—liver pasties and pies and that.'

'That's right, Pavel Ivanovich, sir,' said Selifan, turning round from the box and beaming. 'A very decent gentleman. A hospitable landowner! He sent us each a glass of champagne! He did, I swear it, and he sent us down some dish from the table—a very good dish it was too, it tasted sort of delicate, you know. Such a decent gentleman as there's never been before.'

'Do you see? He has made us all content,' said Platonov.

p. 310 ('It's a pity I don't know much about these things . . . They call him a wizard'):

He works out exactly how much moisture is needed, and he plants the right number of trees; for him, everything performs two or three functions: the forest provides timber, fertilizes the fields with the rotting leaves, and keeps out the heat. That's his way with everything.'

p. 311 (The lady of the house herself came running out to greet them . . . lively and talkative):

The owner was not in; they were met by his wife, Platonov's sister, a beauty fair of face and hair, with an essentially Russian expression, just as good-looking and just as listless as her brother. It seemed she was little concerned about the concerns of others, either because the all-consuming industry of her husband left nothing for her to do, or because she belonged, by her very character, to that philosophical category of people who, possessed of feelings, and thoughts, and intelligence, somehow live only half-heartedly, looking at life with only half an eye, and when they see any distressing conflicts that greatly trouble everyone they say: 'Let them rant and rave, the fools! It's their funeral.'

pp. 312–13 ('This is what you had better do . . . As you say, sir'):

'Give your order then to accept it!' said the peasant with a bow.

'No, no, brother, I've already told you twenty times not to bring any more. I've got so much material piled up there's nowhere to put it.'

'But with you, Konstantin Fyodorovich, sir, everything is put to use. There isn't another master as clever as you anywhere in the world. You find a place for everything. So please give orders to accept.'

'Brother, what I need are hands; supply me with workers, not material.'

'Now that's one thing you'll never be short of. Whole villages will come to work: we're that poor in grain, we can't remember a year like it. What's really bad is that you don't want to take us for good, because we'd serve you in good faith, honest to God we would. With you there's all sorts of clever things to be learnt, Konstantin Fyodorovich. So please give orders to accept just this once.'

'But that's what you said last time too: and you've gone and brought some more.'

'This really is the last time, Konstantin Fyodorovich. If you don't take it no one will take it off me. So please, Your Honour, give orders to accept.'

'Listen, I'll take it this time, and that's only out of pity for you going to all this trouble for nothing. But if you bring me any more you can stand and whine at me for three weeks—I won't take it.'

'Yes, sir, Konstantin Fyodorovich; you can take my word for it, I swear I won't bring any more, I thank you most humbly.' The peasant departed, satisfied. He was lying, of course; he would bring some more: he'd take a chance.

p. 314 (Then Kostanzhoglo appeared ... other than Russian):

Kostanzhoglo's face was most remarkable. It betrayed his southern origins. The hair on his head and his eyebrows was dark and thick, his eyes glowed with an intense brightness. Every expression of his face was eloquent of intelligence, and bore no trace of lethargy. There was, however, a noticeable admixture of something splenetic and embittered. What, in point of fact, was his nationality? In Russia there are many Russians of non-Russian stock, who are yet true Russians. Kostanzhoglo did not delve into his origin, considering such activity pointless and irrelevant to running an estate. And, besides, he knew no language other than Russian.

p. 316 (He found the colonel ... most considerate of men):

Chichikov wondered if perhaps he had strayed into some provincial capital. The colonel himself was stiff and prim. There was a prudish arrogance in his triangular face. The sideburns ran down his cheeks in a thin string; his hair, coiffure, nose, lips, chin—everything looked as if it had just come out of a press. And yet, when he started to speak, he seemed a sensible sort of fellow.

p. 316 (while in Germany ... had even been able to play the fortepiano):

While in Germany, where he had been stationed in 1814, the miller's daughter had even able to play the fortepiano; had spoken French and dropped curtseys. With genuine compassion he described the depths of his neighbours' ignorance; how little they thought about their subjects; how they laughed when he tried to convince them that it was imperative to set up on an estate an inventorial office, offices for commissions, and even committees, as a safeguard against all kinds of theft, and to have every item recorded, and for the clerks, stewards, and bookkeepers to be properly educated people with university degrees;

pp. 318–19 (The books were on every subject ... *Social Productivity*):

There were such titles as: *Pig-breeding As a Science*. [. . .] *Propaedeutics to the Theory of Thought in Their Conjunctivity, Totality, and Essentiality and in Application to the Comprehension of the Organic Principles of the Reciprocal Bifurcation of Social Productivity*.

pp. 321–2 (It can indeed ... desires beyond his means to which he can aspire"):

'And not only that!...' Kostanzhoglo had not finished his speech: the bile had risen in him and now he was set on castigating his landowner neighbours. 'Now there's one smart fellow—and what do you think he's set up? A charity home, a stone building in the village! A Christian deed! But if you want to help your fellow man, then you should help him to fulfil his own duty and not tear him away from his Christian duty. Help the son nurse his ailing father in his own home, and don't give him the chance to shift the burden on to someone else's shoulders. Better give him the means to shelter his nearest and dearest in his home, give him the money, help him in every possible way, but do not shun him, or he will forget all his Christian duties altogether. There are Don Quixotes all over the place! Imagine spending 200 roubles a year for one person's keep in a charity home! I could keep ten men in my village for that money!' Kostanzhoglo spat in disgust.

Chichikov was not interested in the charity home: he wanted to pursue the subject of how any old rubbish could bring in profit. But Kostanzhoglo was angry now, the bile seethed within him, and the words came pouring out:

'And there's another Don Quixote of enlightenment: this one has set up schools! Of course, there's nothing more useful to a man than knowing how to read and write. But what do you think happened? The peasants came to me from his village. "Father," they said to me, "what's all this supposed to mean?" They told me: "Our sons have got quite out of hand, they don't want to help in the fields, they all want to be clerks, but we only need one clerk in the village." That was the upshot of it!'

Chichikov had no great need to hear about schools either, but Platonov took up the subject:

'Yet, just because we don't need clerks now, that's no reason to stop! They'll be needed later. You should work for posterity.'

'You at least, brother, should use your brains! What's all this worry about posterity? Everyone imagines himself another Peter the Great. Just look under your own feet and don't worry about posterity; see that you make your peasant contented and rich and that he has the time to study of his own free will and not with you standing over him with a stick in your hand, shouting "Study!" They start from the wrong end, that's what!... Just listen to this, I'll let you be the judge of this one yourself...' Here Kostanzhoglo moved closer to Chichikov and in order to get him to look more closely into the matter thrust his finger through the button-hole of his tailcoat. 'Well now, what could be clearer? Your peasants are there for you to guide them in their peasant lives. What is the essence of these lives? What is the essence of a peasant's work? Tilling the land? So make sure he's a good tiller. Clear? Oh no, there are these smart alecks who say: "He must be brought out of this state. He leads too harsh, too plain a life: he must be acquainted with luxury."

pp. 323–4 ('I do not mean that he should have no other calling . . . without falling into a rage'):

'Where tilling the land has formed the foundation of a social community there will be sufficiency and plenty; there is no poverty and no luxury, but there is sufficiency. Till the land, man is told, work and toil... It's all very simple. I tell my peasant: "Whoever you're working for, be it for me, yourself, or your neighbour, work properly. In your industry I am your first assistant. If you have no animals, here's a horse, here's a cow, here's a cart for you... I'm prepared to provide all you require, but you must work. I cannot abide the sight of disorderliness and poverty in your household. But above all things I will not tolerate idleness. The reason I am here over you is to make sure you work." Ha! They think they can increase incomes with their charity homes and factories! First think about how to make all your peasants rich, and then you will also be rich, without any factories, or any stupid notions.'

p. 332 (As for the rest . . . taking him to court, if they wished):

The remaining 10,000 he could obtain later, by mortgaging his souls. It was still impossible to mortgage all the souls he had bought, because as yet he lacked the lands on which they were to be resettled. Although he averred that he had such lands in Kherson province, these in fact existed mostly in his imagination. He did intend to buy such lands in Kherson province, because land could be purchased there very cheaply, and was even assigned gratis to anyone prepared to settle on it. His thoughts even turned on the necessity of making haste and buying whatever fugitive and dead souls he could from anyone, for the landowners were racing one another to mortgage their estates, and soon there might not remain a single unmortgaged nook or cranny in all Russia.

p. 340 (They were welcomed by Khlobuev's wife . . . even with their own governess):

Khlobuev introduced them to his wife. She was lovely to behold: this woman would have held her own in Moscow. Her dress was fashionable and in good taste. She liked to talk more about the town and the theatre which had been opened there. It was obvious that she was even less fond of the country than was her husband, and that she was more bored than Platonov when left on her own. Soon the room filled with children, little girls and boys. There were five of them. A sixth was borne in the nurse's arms. They were all handsome children. The boys and girls were dressed charmingly and with taste, they were playful and spirited. And for this reason it was all the sadder to look at them.

p. 340 (Chichikov decided to bargain . . . 'Let's make it twenty-five'):

'I say—thirty thousand! The estate is neglected, the peasants dead, and you ask thirty thousand? Make it twenty-five.'

'Pavel Ivanovich! I could mortgage it for twenty-five thousand, don't you see? Then I should get the twenty-five thousand and the estate would still be mine. The sole reason that I'm selling it is because I need the money urgently, but mortgaging would mean delays, and I would have to pay the clerks, and I've nothing to pay them with.'

p. 343 (I say, do me a favour . . . started from his head):

Good luck to him! Maybe he'll succeed! Good luck to the lot of them! I never was any good at grovelling, and it's too late to begin now: my back will no longer bend.'

'Fool!' thought Chichikov, 'I would have cosseted that sort of aunt as a wet-nurse cossets an infant child!'

'Talking is thirsty work, is it not?' said Khlobuev. 'Hey, Kiryushka! Bring us another bottle of champagne!'

'No, no, I shan't drink any more,' said Platonov.

'Nor shall I,' said Chichikov. And they both were adamant in their refusal.

'In that case, promise at least to be my guests in town: on the 8th of June I shall be giving a dinner for our local dignitaries.'

'My dear chap!' exclaimed Platonov. 'In a state like this, utterly ruined, and you're giving a dinner?'

'What can I do? I have to. It's my duty,' said Khlobuev. 'They have also entertained me.'

'What is to be done with him?' thought Platonov.

p. 343–4 (Khlobuev's house in town . . . splendidly provided for):

Such a one was Khlobuev. Only in Russia could a man lead such an existence. Without a copeck to his name, he received and entertained guests, and even set himself up as a patron of the arts, supporting all sorts of painters who flocked into the town, taking them under his own roof. Anyone glancing into his house while he was in town would have been quite unable to determine which of its occupants was the owner. [. . .] The next day some fellow, unknown to practically everyone in the house, would install himself with all his papers right in the drawing-room and turn it into his study, and this would not disturb or incommode anyone in the house, just as if it were the most natural thing on earth. The owner would appear in a cheerful, festive mood, with the air of a rich nobleman, and the gait of a man whose life is spent in abundance and contentment.

pp. 344–5 (He thought how, whatever else might have happened . . . he looked about him):

He enumerated, calculated, and pondered all the advantages of the estate he had bought. And however he looked at it, whichever way he turned the deal, he saw that in every event the purchase was advantageous. He could proceed by mortgaging the estate. He could proceed by mortgaging only the dead and fugitive peasants. He could proceed by first selling off all the best land in sections, and then mortgaging the rest. He could take over the management of the estate himself and became a landowner in Poponzhoglo's mould, following his advice as his neighbour and benefactor. He could even proceed by selling the estate back into private ⟨hands⟩ (if, of course, he decided not to take on the running of it himself), retaining ownership only of the fugitive and dead souls. Then he could see another advantage: he could slip away from this part of the country altogether and not pay back the money he had borrowed from Skudronzhoglo. In short, which-ever way he turned the matter in his mind he saw that in every event the purchase was advantageous.... and hum a little tune, and talk to himself, and trumpet a march through his fist held clenched against his mouth like a bugle, and even to utter aloud a few laudatory words and epithets addressed to himself, such as 'Clever Chops' and 'Smart Little Birdie'. But then, recalling that he was not alone, he suddenly fell silent, endeav-oured somehow or other to suppress this immoderate surge of exultation, and when Platonov, taking some of these noises to be remarks addressed to him, asked: 'What?' he answered: 'Nothing.'

p. 347 (And, full of mistrust . . . a person of the utmost respect-ability):

And, full of mistrust, he started surreptitiously to examine Chichikov and saw that he held himself in an extraordinarily decorous manner, still keeping his head inclined somewhat to one side and preserving a respect-fully affable facial expression, so that it was quite impossible to tell quite what sort of a fish this Chichikov was.

p. 350 ('Well, you see . . . to talk to such a man.'):

'Does that mean you would be prepared to let him have some other land?'

'I would, if he had not been so high-handed with me; but it appears he wants to go to court. Very well, let us see who wins. Although it is not all that clear on the map, but where are witnesses—old men are still alive who can remember.'

'Hm! stick-in-the-muds both of them, I can see,' thought Chichikov. And aloud he said:

'But it seems to me this matter can be resolved peaceably. Everything depends on the mediator. In writing...'

p. 351 (As he said this, he gazed ... it's all such a puzzle!):

What should he do? Lenitsyn found himself in an awkward position. He could not have foreseen that the opinion he had so recently voiced would be acted upon so quickly. The proposition was extremely unexpected. Of course, there could not be anything prejudicial for anyone in this course of action: the landowners would, in any case, have mortgaged these souls along with their living ones, which meant that the Treasury could not suffer any loss: the only difference was that now they would all be in the hands of one person, whereas before they were in various hands. Nevertheless he was at a loss. He was a stickler for the law and a businessman in the best sense of the word: no matter what bribes he was offered, he would never act dishonestly in any deal. But here he hesitated, not knowing what to call this deal: honest or dishonest? If anyone else had come to him with such a proposition he could have said: 'What rubbish! What nonsense! I have no wish to play such silly games like a fool.' But his guest had already such a favourable impression on him, they had found so much in common with regard to the progress of enlightenment and the sciences: so how could he refuse him? Lenitsyn was in a most difficult predicament.

p. 352 ('He certainly has a good aim ... You need land, do you not?'):

'He certainly has a good aim, the nasty little brat!'—'The lovely age of innocence!' he said aloud, when he had been wiped clean and the pleasant expression had returned to his face.

'You know, it's true,' said his host, turning to Chichikov, also with a pleasant smile, 'what could be more enviable than the age of infancy: no worries, no thoughts of the future...'

'A state for which we would exchange everything this very moment,' said Chichikov.

'Without thinking twice,' said Lenitsyn.

But, one thought, they were both lying: offer them such an exchange and they would both shoot out of the back door at once. Indeed, what sort of pleasure was it to sit in a wet-nurse's arms and ruin people's tailcoats! The young hostess and the first-born departed with the wet-nurse, because certain repairs had to be carried out on him too: in bestowing his favours on Chichikov he had not neglected himself. [. . .]

Lenitsyn reasoned thus: 'Why indeed should I not grant his request, if such is his desire?'

p. 353 (In this world . . . what they want) The opening passage of this chapter is quite different in the earlier 'stratum', so I quote it *in extenso*:

At the very time when Chichikov, sprawling on the divan in his new Persian dressing-gown of gold lamé, was haggling with the visiting contraband dealer of Jewish descent and a German accent, and the merchandise was already lying before them, to wit, a length of the very finest Dutch linen for shirts and two cardboard boxes containing the most excellent soap of top-class quality (this was the very same soap that he himself used to acquire when stationed in the Radzivilov customs; it did indeed have the property of imparting a remarkable tenderness and whiteness to the cheeks); at the very time when he, as a true connoisseur, was purchasing these products so essential to the cultured man, the quiet was shattered by the thunderous clatter of a carriage driving up, answered by the slight trembling of the windowpanes and the walls, and His Excellency Aleksei Ivanovich Lenitsyn entered.

'Might I ask Your Excellency to judge: what fine linen, what soap, and what a nice little thing I purchased yesterday!' Saying this Chichikov placed on his head a skull-cap, embroidered with gold thread and beads, and looked at once so full of dignity and majesty that he might be the Shah of Persia!

But His Excellency, without answering the question, said with a worried look:

'I have something serious to discuss with you.'

He looked noticeably upset. The esteemed merchant of the German accent was at once dispatched and they remained alone.

'Do you know what an unfortunate thing has happened? Another will by the old lady has come to light, drawn up five years ago. Half the estate is to be given to the monastery and the other half to be shared equally between her two wards, and not a bean for anyone else.'

Chichikov was dumbfounded.

'That will is rubbish: it carries no weight, it's countermanded by the second one.'

'But there's no mention in the second will that it countermands the first one.'

'That goes without saying: the later one countermands the earlier one.

The first will is quite invalid. I know exactly what the old lady wanted. I was with her at the time. Who signed it? Who were the witnesses?'

'It was witnessed properly, in court. The witnesses were the former common-law magistrate Burmilov and Khavanov.'

'Bad,' thought Chichikov. 'They say Khavanov is an honest man; Burmilov is an old bigot, he reads the gospels in church on holy days.'

'But it's rubbish, rubbish,' he said aloud, and at once felt equal to anything. 'I know best. I was at the old lady's side during her last minutes. I know it better than anyone. I am prepared to swear it on oath.'

These words and this decisive tone temporarily calmed Lenitsyn. In his agitation he had already begun to suspect that Chichikov might have done some fabricating with regard to the will. Now he reproached himself for harbouring such suspicions. The readiness to swear on oath was unchallenged proof that Chichikov was innocent. We do not know whether Pavel Ivanovich would in fact have had the courage to swear on oath, but he had the courage to say that he would.

'Do not worry, I shall discuss this matter with certain legal consultants. There need not be any involvement on your side; you must keep quite out of it. And now I can live in town as long as I wish.'

Chichikov at once called for his carriage and set off to see his legal consultant. This consultant was a man of uncommonly wide experience. He had been under investigation for the past fifteen years and he managed his case with such skill that it had been quite impossible to strip him of office. Everyone knew him, his exploits were such that he should already have been sent into exile six times over. He was under suspicion by one and all, but no convincing and proven evidence could be brought against him. There really was something mysterious about it, and he could have been rightfully called a magician if the story we are recounting had belonged to the dark ages of ignorance.

The legal consultant astounded Chichikov with the coldness of his mien and the griminess of his dressing-gown, presenting such a complete contrast to the fine mahogany furniture, the gold-domed clock, the chandelier, peeping through the muslin cover put on to protect it, and in general to everything around him, which bore the unmistakable stamp of dazzling European enlightenment.

Unabashed, however, by the sceptical air of the legal consultant, Chichikov explained the vexatious points of his case and offered the alluring prospect of the gratitude which would inevitably ensue upon good advice and sympathy.

The legal consultant responded to this by depicting the fickleness of all earthly things and also skilfully indicated that two birds in the bush were worth nothing: the bird in the hand was what he wanted.

There was nothing for it: the bird had to be put into the hand. The sceptical *froideur* of the philosophical legal consultant instantly vanished. It transpired that he was the most affable of men, the most talkative and the most agreeable in conversation, an equal to Chichikov himself in the adroitness of his turns of phrase.

'Allow me to suggest, instead of initiating lengthy legal proceedings, that you have probably not examined the actual will properly: there, I am sure, you will find a little codicil somewhere. Just take it home with you for a while. Although, of course, but if you ask certain officials nicely... I shall use my own influence too.'

'I understand,' thought Chichikov, and said:

'In point of fact it's true, I cannot quite remember whether there is a codicil there or not.' As if he had not written the will himself.

'The best thing would be for you to have a good look at it. I assure you, however,' the lawyer continued in the most good-natured tone, 'you need have no apprehensions, even if the worst possible thing should happen. Never despair of anything: there is no case which cannot be set to rights. Look at me: I am always calm. Whatever the charges raised against me my composure remains unshakable.'

The face of the lawyer-philosopher did indeed preserve an aspect of remarkable composure, so that Chichikov was very... [*the sentence is left unfinished in the msanuscript*]

'Of course, that is the most important thing,' he said. 'But all the same, you must agree that there can be such matters and cases, such actions and calumnies perpetrated by one's enemies and such complex predicaments that you'll forget what composure means!'

'Believe me, that is simply faint-heartedness,' answered the lawyer-philosopher with great calm and affability. 'Only try to ensure that every step in your case is backed by written records, and that nothing is left as spoken words. And as soon as you see that things are reaching an issue and that a decision is imminent, make every effort—not to justify and defend yourself—no, merely to confuse matters with new and extraneous issues.'

'You mean, in order—'

'To confuse them, confuse them, and nothing more,' answered the philosopher. 'Introduce other extraneous circumstances into your case, which in their turn would involve others, to complicate matters, and nothing more. And then let some St Petersburg official be called in and try to sort it out. Let him try, just let him try!' he repeated, gazing into Chichikov's eyes with pure delight, just as a teacher gazes at his pupil when explaining to him some alluring point of Russian grammar.

'Yes, it's all very well if you can find circumstances which can throw a veil of obscurity over things,' said Chichikov, also looking with delight into the eyes of the philosopher, like a pupil who has understood the alluring point being explained by his teacher.

'The circumstances can be found, they can be found! Believe me: frequent practice teaches the mind to be resourceful. First of all remember that people will help you. Many stand to gain from a complicated case, more officials will be needed and their remuneration will be higher... In a word, draw as many people as possible into the case. It doesn't matter that some will be involved for no reason: after all, it will be easy for them to justify themselves, they will have to answer inquiries, they will have to buy themselves... That's a bit of money coming in already... Believe me, the moment the situation becomes critical, the first rule is to spread confusion. Stir things up, create such a tangle that no one will understand a thing. Why am I so calm? Because I know: just let my affairs get worse and I will involve everyone—the governor, and the deputy governor, and the chief of police, and the government paymaster—I'll enmesh them all. I know all their backgrounds: who has a grievance against whom, who has fallen out with whom, and who wants to get even with whom. Now let them try to disentangle themselves, and while they are doing so others will be lining their pockets. After all, crayfish can only be caught in muddy water. Everybody is only waiting to spread a little fog.' Here the lawyer-philosopher gazed into Chichikov's eyes once again with the pure delight with which a teacher explains to a pupil the most alluring point in Russian grammar.

'No, this chap definitely knows his onions,' thought Chichikov, and he took leave of the legal consultant in the very best and most pleasant of spirits.

Completely reassured and mentally fortified he leapt with carefree adroitness into his carriage with the springy cushions, ordered Selifan to throw back the hood (he had driven to the consultant's with the hood drawn over and with the leather flaps closed) and sat back, exactly like a retired colonel of hussars or like Vishnepokromov himself—with one leg gracefully turned under the other, his new silk hat cocked slightly over one ear, and smiling at everyone he met. Selifan was told to make for the arcade. The merchants, visiting and local, who stood by the doors of their shops, respectfully doffed their hats, and Chichikov, not without dignity, slightly tipped his in response. Many of them were already known to him; as for the others, although they were visitors they were so enchanted by the dashing sight of a gentleman with such fine manners that they, too, greeted him like acquaintances. The fair in the town of Tfuslavl was unending. When the horse and agricultural fair was over the textile fair would begin for the enlightened populace. The merchants who arrived in carts counted on staying long enough to go back home in sleighs.

pp. 355–6 ('Let me see your black cloth," . . . also took off their hats):

'What are you buying here, my most esteemed friend?'

'Ah, what a pleasant encounter,' said the voice of the person whose arm had encircled his waist. This was Vishnepokromov. 'I was about to pass by the shop when I suddenly saw a familiar face—so, how could I deny myself the pleasure! I must say that the cloths this year are incomparably better. You must admit, it's disgraceful, outrageous! I was quite unable to find anything... I'm prepared to pay thirty roubles, forty roubles... take fifty even, but give me something good. To my mind, either you have a thing which is really first class, or you have nothing at all. Is that not so?'

'Indeed it is!' said Chichikov. 'Really, why should one toil if not to have something that is good?'

[. . .]

And the courteous merchant, holding out his hat as far out as his arm would stretch and, also leaning right forward, uttered:

'Our most humble respects to Afanasy Vasilievich!'

Printed on their faces was that canine servility, which to millionaires is displayed by people of a currish cast of mind.

p. 356 ('I wonder what it is they have to talk about?" . . . Settling his bill with the merchant, he left the shop):

'What glorious weather we're having, Afanasy Vasilievich,' said Chichikov.

'Yes indeed,' chimed in Vishnepokromov, 'isn't it remarkable?'

'Indeed, not bad at all, praise be to God. But we could do with a little rain for the crops.'

'We do, we do, we need it badly,' said Vishnepokromov, 'it's good for the hunting too.'

'Yes, a little spot of rain would be no bad thing,' said Chichikov, who had no need of any little rain, but how pleasant it was to agree with a man who owned millions.

And the old man bowed to them all once again and departed.

'It quite makes my head spin,' said Chichikov, 'to think that that man has ten million. It's quite beyond belief, really.'

'It's quite counter to the law, all the same,' said Vishnepokromov. 'Capital should not be concentrated in private hands. That's now discussed in treaties all over Europe. If you have the money—well, share it with others: entertain, give balls, create the sort of beneficial luxury which gives bread to tradesmen and craftsmen.'

'That I cannot understand,' said Chichikov. 'Ten million—and he lives like a simple peasant! After all, with ten million the devil knows what you could do. I mean, you could live the sort of life where you'd never have to mix with anyone but generals and princes.'

'Quite so' added the merchant. 'For all his estimable qualities Afanasy Vasilievich is sorely lacking in enlightenment. If a merchant has standing, he's no longer a merchant, in a sense he's already a negotiant. I, for example, would take a box at the theatre, and as for my daughter—no sir, I shall not give her in marriage to some mere colonel: it will have to be a general and nothing less. What's a colonel to me? My dinner must be prepared by a chef, and not some common cook-woman...'

'You're absolutely right!' said Vishnepokromov. 'With ten million there's nothing one can't do. Give me ten million, and see what I would do!'

'No,' thought Chichikov, 'you won't do anything very sensible with ten million. Now, if I had ten million, I would most definitely do something.'

'If only I had ten million now, after these terrible ordeals!' thought Khlobuev. 'I wouldn't make those mistakes now: experience teaches you the value of every single copeck.' And then, after a minute's thought he asked himself: 'Would I, in fact, order things more sensibly now?' And, with a wave of his hand he added: 'What the devil! I imagine I would blow the money just like before,' and he left the shop, curious to know what news Murazov had for him.

p. 358 (Honest to God, Afanasy Vasilievich, I've tried ... Murazov started to feel sorry for him):

'But what could I do, judge for yourself! I couldn't start as a chancellory scrivener. Perhaps you have forgotten that I have a family. I am forty years old, I already have a bad back, I have grown slothful; but they will not give me a more important office; after all, my record is none too good. I admit it myself: I would not accept an easy sinecure anyway. I may be worthless as a person, and an inveterate gambler, and everything you like, but I draw the line at bribes. I'm not going to join company with Krasnonosov and Samosvistov.'

'But still, if you'll forgive my saying so, I cannot understand how you can manage without following one road or another? How can you walk when there is no path; how can you go forward when there is no ground beneath your feet; how can you sail when your boat is not afloat? For what is life but a journey? Forgive me, Pyotr Petrovich, but those men of whom you speak, they are anyway following some path or other, they are doing their work. Well, let us suppose they might have strayed a bit, as happens with all us sinners; there is still the hope that they'll come back to the straight and narrow. He who walks cannot fail to arrive; there is always the hope that he'll find the road. But as for him who remains idle, what chance has he of getting on to any road? After all, the road will not come to us.'

'Believe me, Afanasy Vasilievich, I can see the absolute reasonableness of what you say, but I must tell you that any sort of activity has totally perished and died in me; I cannot see how I could be of any use to anyone in this world. I feel that I am a totally useless log. Before, when I was a little younger, I thought that money was all that mattered, that if I could only get my hands on a few hundred thousand I'd bring happiness to many: I'd help impoverished artists, and found libraries and useful institutions, I'd collect works of art. I am not lacking in taste and I know I could have managed things much better in many respects than our rich men who do it all so stupidly. But now I see that this, too, is a folly, and there is little sense in this too. No, Afanasy Vasilievich, I am no use for anything, not for anything at all, let me tell you. I am incapable of being of the slightest use.'

p. 361 (But let us leave Khlobuev a while and return to Chichikov):

'Now let me ask you,' said Murazov, 'what about this Chichikov and what sort of swindle is he up to?'

'I shall tell you some really fantastic things about Chichikov. The tricks he is up to... Do you know, Afanasy Vasilievich, that the will was quite false? The real will has been found, in which the entire estate goes to her wards.'

'What are you saying? And who fabricated the false will?'

'That's the whole point, that it's such a dirty business! They say it was Chichikov, and that the will was signed after her death: they dressed up some old woman in place of the deceased, and got her to sign it. In a word, the most scandalous business. They say thousands of petitions came from all over the place. Suitors are now flocking to Maria Yeremeevna; two of them, men of high office, are already fighting over her. That's the sort of business it is, Afanasy Vasilievich.'

'I've heard nothing of all this, but the business seems certainly none too clean. I must confess I find our Pavel Ivanovich Chichikov a most enigmatic fellow,' said Murazov.

'I also sent in a petition, just to remind them that there is a next of kin...'

'But let them all fight one another, for all I care,' thought Khlobuev, on his way out. 'Afanasy Vasilievich is no fool. He gave me this commission, no doubt, after careful thought. I just have to carry it out, that's all.' He started to think about the journey, at the same time as Murazov kept repeating to himself: 'That Pavel Ivanovich Chichikov really does intrigue me! To think, with his will power and perseverance, how much good he could do!'

EXPLANATORY NOTES

PART ONE

In his *Author's Confession*, Gogol records that the idea for *Dead Souls*—as with that for *The Government Inspector* before it—was given to him by Pushkin. The poet had urged Gogol to undertake a major work and even provided the plot, offering an idea he had been saving for a composition of his own. Gogol's anxiety to associate his idol Pushkin with the genesis of his works might suggest a lack of confidence on his own part, and I am tempted to take these accounts of Pushkin's involvement with a pinch of salt. Whatever its genesis, the story of his *Dead Souls*, with all its convolution and excursi into the devious workings of the human mind, is—and could only be—entirely Gogol's.

With or without the assistance of Pushkin, Gogol commenced work on *Dead Souls* in Russia, in mid-1835. On 12 November 1836 he wrote to the poet Zhukovsky from Switzerland about progress on his work, and here referred to *Dead Souls* for the first time as '*poema*', a long poem. Let the English reader not think that, in Russian, *poema* is a commonplace designation of a Russian work of some two or three hundred pages of prose, containing two or three mildly lyrical passages, but nothing resembling a rhyme or a line of verse (except for those in quotations). Over the ensuing years the designation has engaged the best minds of Gogolology, exciting what Fanger calls their 'pilpulistic speculation'. Commentators have ingeniously explained why this is, indeed, a poem, and not a novel or any other genre, and the curious reader should turn to them for an exploration of this subject. Gogol's contemporaries were similarly baffled by his choice of this epithet, which echoes Pushkin's choice, some twenty years earlier of 'novel in verse' (*roman v stikhakh*) for his poem *Eugene Onegin*. Hardly surprising, therefore, that the critic Senkovsky, when reviewing *Dead Souls* with ten other books, mostly worthy tomes of popular science—should greet them all as *poemy*.

The choice of this word—which is used for long poems, often of a narrative nature—also reinforces the view of *Dead Souls* as a latter-day, Russian *Divine Comedy*, conceived as forming three parts, with this, Part One, representing the voyage through Hell. There has been some debate about Gogol's real intentions to continue *Dead Souls* into second and third parts—the supposed Purgatory and Paradise—and for more on this see the introductory note to Part Two, below. But these intentions need not concern us here: my task has been to translate what Gogol actually wrote, and the inquiring reader may decide for himself whether, in his view, *Dead Souls* was intended to be a three-part, epic composition on the line of Dante's, or complete in itself, with the false promise of sequels—a promise Gogol himself was fooled into trying to fulfil, with his abortive Part Two.

The right to existence of Part One, at least, is undisputed. After a brisk start on the book in Russia, Gogol read the first few chapters to Pushkin, who was deeply depressed by what he heard and, after Gogol had finished reading, exclaimed despairingly: 'Lord, how sad this Russia of ours is!' Somewhat dismayed by Pushkin's reaction, Gogol decided to rework these chapters extensively and to revise the entire plan of the book. He continued work on its composition, mostly during his long sojourns in Switzerland, France, and Italy, over the years from 1835 to 1841.

At the end of 1841, the manuscript was ready and Gogol submitted it to the censor I. M. Snegiryov, an ethnographer and retired professor of Moscow University—and a personal friend—who supported its publication and foresaw no serious obstacle. Snegiryov's Moscow colleagues were not so easily pleased, however, and the book was sent to the censors in the capital, where strong objections were raised both to the title and to the 'Tale of Captain Kopeikin'. The latter was a cause of particular distress to Gogol, who declared that the loss of Kopeikin would create a hole in the work which could not be patched. Eventually, however, the work was passed with mostly minor excisions and changes—including to the title, which, on publication, read *The Adventures of Chichikov, or Dead Souls*. The Academy edition, on which this translation is based, has restored these excisions and the original title.

When *Dead Souls* was finally presented to the public on 21 May 1842, its impact on Russia was instant and dramatic: some claimed it as the apotheosis of Russia, others lambasted it as traitorous slander of the motherland. Thus, Konstantin Aksakov (Aksakov *fils*) hailed it as a Homeric epic; the influential critic Belinsky—while rejecting the comparison to Homer—called *Dead Souls* a 'purely Russian, national work, wrested from the inner sanctuary of popular life' and hailed its author as a 'national Russian poet in the broadest sense of the word'. In any age this would have been a sensational publication: every period in Russian history has claimed it as its own, and today it sits easily alongside works in the new canon of post-modern, post-Soviet literature. Its appearance on the Russian literary scene of the mid-nineteenth century, however, was all the more extraordinary when one recalls that, to that date, Russia—soon to become virtually synonymous with the epic novel—still lacked a true literature, it had not yet engendered a great work of prose, of substantial scope and dimensions. Many were to follow, but this was the first.

3 *small but rather handsome sprung chaise*: the names of the different varieties of carriages have particular importance to Gogol, as an impassioned taxonomist and collector of lists of names for the paraphernalia of Russian life, such as women's headgear, nicknames given to dogs, types of birdsong, country pies and pastries, and so on. As the modern reader may be less familiar with at least the names of carriages, some explanation of the terms as used in this translation—beside the generic term for carriage, *Kareta*—might be useful. The corresponding Russian word follows in brackets:

baggage-train (oboz): a train of large carts, used for the transport of freight, often on imperial commission, or for military supplies.

brake (lineika): a broad droshky, seating several passengers, usually fitted with coverlets.

britzka (brichka): a light, half-covered conveyance, with a removable calash top—usually of leather—and a space for reclining. The carriage of the type affected by bachelors, which drives through the gates of the inn in the town of NN, bearing Chichikov, is in fact a britzka, but for it I have preferred the more generic term 'chaise', as 'britzka' has an exotic ring to the English ear which the Russian *brichka* does not.

cabriolet (proletki): a light, fast carriage, with a folding hood, seating two and on four wheels (this, at least, is true of the Russian; the cabriolet was more likely to have only two wheels).

calèche (kolyaska): the vehicle featured in Gogol's story 'The Carriage'—first developed in Eastern Europe and known by many names in English—*galeche, gallesh, calesh*, etc., the calèche was a light carriage with a removable, folding hood; sometimes the word 'calash' is used for such a hood.

cart (telega, telezhka): plain, all-purpose vehicle, open and used for the transportation of goods and agricultural produce as well as people; the term has rather wider application in Russian, and can also refer, generically, to any carriage or conveyance.

chaise (brichka, kolyaska): a more general term, which applies to a variety of open carriages, sometimes with two and sometimes with four wheels, but of the lighter kind and often half-open or with removable hoods.

droshky (drozhki): a Russian-made, low four-wheeled carriage, without a top, and equipped with a narrow bench for a seat on which passengers sat astride or sideways; the droshky was commonly used for hire.

equipage (ekipazh): generic term for carriages intended specifically for the conveyance of people; in its narrower application, a gentleman's carriage of the larger kind, intended for riding out and with place for a coachman.

kibitka (kibitka): see 'trap', below.

landau (rydvan): the Russian word is derived from the German *Reitwagen*, which, like the landau, is a large, four-seater coach, with a seat for the coachman, well-sprung and usually covered; the Russian word has a somewhat wider application, and can also be used to refer to large, agricultural carts, as well as carriages for the conveyance of people.

rattle-trap (drebezzhalka): broken down old vehicle. The Russian—like the English—derives from the word for 'rattle'.

shandrydan (kolesosvistka): also a decrepit, noisy conveyance—the Russian word literally means 'wheel-whistler'.

tarantas (tarantass): a four-wheeled Russian carriage without springs on a long flexible wooden chassis, described by an early traveller to Siberia as a 'roofless, seatless, springless tumbril mounted on poles which connect two wooden axle-trees' (H. Landell, *Through Siberia*, 1882).

trap (kibitka): a light, covered vehicle, usually on two wheels.

troika (troika): a Russian vehicle—both on wheels and on runners for snow—drawn by three horses abreast (the *troika*, or 'threesome') and capable of great speed.

waggon (fura): large, usually covered, cart, used for the transport of loads and farm produce.

3 *staff-captain*: rank in the infantry, sapper, and artillery battalions of the Tsarist army, between lieutenant and captain.

Tula pin: the town of Tula, some two hundred versts to the south of Moscow, was, from the late sixteenth century, centre of the Russian armaments industry and known for the skill of its metalsmiths, celebrated in the short story 'Lefty', by Nikolai Semyonovich Leskov (1831–1895), and also, in modern times, by the Soviet premier Khrushchev in a memorable address, in February 1959, to the steelworkers of Tula.

4 *Karelian birch*: Karelia, now an autonomous republic within the Russian Federation, lies in the north-west of Russia, on the borders with Finland and, like much of the Russian north, is heavily wooded, including with the gracious birch.

6 *president of the chambers ... public prosecutor*: the chambers referred to here are, we presume, the *kazennaya palata*, or Imperial Revenue Chamber, an office in pre-Revolutionary Russia under the authority of the Ministry of Finance and responsible for the collection of taxes within the province and the settlement of judicial matters relating to taxes; as explained by Gogol in his notebooks, the Imperial Revenue Chamber 'keeps government contracts, commercial transactions and everything now dealt with by the Chamber of State Property, including the administration of state peasants, and quit-rent deeds, in return for the use of meadowlands, agricultural fields and fishing grounds; the central point for all payments from contractors'. It is this office which Chichikov visits in Chapter 7 to effect the transfer of his newly acquired souls. The public prosecutor was an official with functions rather more extensive than his title might suggest: as explained by Gogol in his notebooks, the public prosecutor was 'the keeper of the public coffers and guardian of the laws; his duty was to take action against any breach of law and order and all official business was submitted for his scrutiny ... In short, he was the eye of the law'.

Collegiate Councillor: collegiate councillor was a rank in the civil service system introduced by Peter the Great, of the sixth class and equivalent to the military rank of colonel; see the full Table of Ranks on p. xliv.

Pavel Ivanovich Chichikov: much has been written of the name bestowed on our nondescript hero; thus, his first name, somewhat less common than its English cognate Paul, might suggest the promise of a future, Pauline conversion to good; the surname, Chichikov, is perhaps derived from the Russian *chikhat*, 'to sneeze', and associates the name—like so many of Gogol's names—with the rhinological theme that runs through his works.

7 *twin-headed imperial eagle . . . 'Drinking Establishment'*: by a ruling introduced in August 1765 by Catherine the Great, which remained in effect until 1827, the state had a monopoly on the sale of liquor and establishments conducting such sale bore the imperial emblem, the twin-headed eagle, on their sign. With the liberalization of the liquor trade, which was 'farmed out' on a concession basis to entrepreneurs, such as the liquor concessionaire—*otkupshchik*—who features in this story, such hostelries became known simply as 'Drinking Establishments'. The eagle also featured in the signs of other state monopolies, such as apothecaries' shops.

8 *Mr Kotzebue*: August Friedrich Ferdinand von Kotzebue (1761–1819), a German dramatist whose plays were, at one time, very popular in Russia; the play referred to here is probably his *Spanier in Peru* (1797), an English version of which was prepared by Sheridan in 1799 under the title *Pizarro*; forced into voluntary exile from Germany in 1781, Kotzebue moved first to St Petersburg and then took up a position with the Russian civil service in Revel—modern-day Tallinn. He was assassinated as a Russian spy by a fanatical German student in 1819, when on a harmless fact-finding mission for Tsar Alexander to his native Germany.

St Anne . . . star: the order of St Anne, Second Class, was a cross worn on the lapel of a uniform jacket, hence the expression 'an Anna on your neck', which appears as the title of one of Chekhov's stories; the star is the order of St Stanislav, First Class, worn on a sash and awarded to higher ranks for services to the Empire.

liquor concessionaire: in his notebooks, Gogol describes in detail the operations of the *otkupshchik* (see also note to p. 7), whose position as virtual monopolist in the liquor trade gave him considerable power among the local citizenry; as Gogol remarks: 'The concessionaire gives bribes to everyone; they are all friendly with him and pleased with him . . . He gives bribes to all the police, municipal and rural, and all the police are in his pay.'

9 *'Your Excellency'*: according to the carefully defined system of forms of address, only officials of classes 3 and 4 could be addressed 'Your Excellency'—*'vashe prevoskhoditel'stvo'*, while mere state councillors, as here, were to be addressed 'Your Worship'—*'vashe vysokorodie'* (see the Table on p. xliii).

Boston: a card came, sometimes known as Boston whist and usually for four and played with two packs; the game was played for small stakes and it was therefore popular with the less prosperous members of the civil servant class; characterized by an extremely complicated system of scoring and payment for bids and a quaint nomenclature derived from the siege of Boston in the American War of Independence, from which it took its name.

9 *gendarmes*: a special corps of gendarmes was established in 1827 with, as its first general, Count Aleksandr Benckendorff, who, a year later, was appointed chief of Emperor Nicholas's hated Third Division, with responsibility for both regular and secret police.

12 *the most courteous and obliging landowner Manilov and the rather ungainly-looking Sobakevich*: Gogol's names usually carry some semantic baggage and these are no exception: thus, Manilov is derived from *manit'*—'to lure', and, lurking irresistibly in the background, *manilka*—one of many colloquial Russian terms for the female organ, with a suggestion also of *malina*—'raspberry', pointing to his saccharine nature; Sobakevich comes, quite simply, from *sobaka*—'dog'.

13 *versts*: the verst was a pre-Revolutionary measure of distance, slightly longer than a kilometre.

legendary giants . . . even in Russia: the Russian is *bogatyr*, the hero of folklore and legend, often of great stature and endowed with exceptional strength; numerous tales in Russian folklore recount the valorous deeds of *bogatyri*.

the landowner Nozdryov: the name Nozdryov continues the rhinological trend started by the hero's own surname, Chichikov: *nozdrya* is 'nostril'.

14 *imperial revenue chamber*: *kazennaya palata*—see note to p. 6.

16 *collegiate councillor . . . Aulic councillors . . . rank of general*: the collegiate councillor was sixth in order on the Petrine Table of Ranks, corresponding to the military rank of colonel; aulic councillors occupied the next rank down the table, corresponding to that of lieutenant colonel, while the equivalent of general was the lofty Actual Privy Councillor (see the Table on p. xliii).

17 *a priest walking by doffed his cap*: critics have observed that it was considered an ill omen for one's path to be crossed by a priest: while Chichikov attaches no significance to this encounter, by it the author may be suggesting that his hero's enterprise is likely to be ill-starred.

18 *English manner*: so-called English gardens, more natural and less formal in design, inspired by the garden design of such pioneers as Capability Brown, became popular in Russia at the end of the eighteenth century.

19 *shalloon*: closely woven woollen cloth named after Châlons-sur-Marne, the French town where it was originally made.

20 *bend the corner . . . two of diamonds*: in Russian cardplay, the corner represents a quarter of the stake and the corner is bent on a card that is played against the banker.

stationmaster: lowest—and most ill-treated—in the hierarchy of civil servants, the stationmaster, or postmaster, was responsible for the supervision of posting stations and held the 14th rank on the Petrine Table, that of collegiate registrar (see the Table on p. xliv).

21 *tax money*: the tax in question—*podat'*, a form of poll tax—was a tribute levied on all peasants and burghers in pre-Revolutionary Russia; the

podat' was considered by Lenin to have been one of the primary obstacles to the development of the Russian peasantry.

25 *Son of the Fatherland*: *Syn Otechestva* was a historical, political, and literary periodical, published between 1812 and 1844; it was influenced by the Decembrist movement and followed moderately liberal tendencies until 1825, when it took a strongly conservative direction. The journal was reissued as a liberal opposition publication in 1856. Its editors included Grech, the founding editor, and Bulgarin, a reactionary literary figure, who routinely attacked progressive writers, including Gogol.

26 *Themistoclus ... Alcides*: Alcides—another name for Hercules—is the subject of an eponymous fable by Krylov (see note to p. 232), illustrating the futility of strife, while Themistocles (527–460 BC) was an Athenian statesman and founder of the Greek fleet, veteran of the battle of Marathon and conqueror of the Persians at Salamis; needless to say, neither of these heroic names is common in Russian.

28 *census list*: the census, on the basis of which this list, the *revizskaya skazka*, was compiled, was conducted every 7 to 10 years, for the purpose of the computation of *podat'*, or poll tax; in modern times the Taganka theatre, under its director Yury Lyubimov, staged a theatrical interpretation of Gogol's work, called *Revizskaya skazka*, playing on two possible meanings of the term: the census list mentioned here and, in a literal translation: 'Fanciful tale about an inspector'—the *revizor* of the Government Inspector; the play had its première on 9 June 1978 and ran until 1984; the music was composed by Alfred Schnittke and conducted by Gennady Rozhdestvensky.

32 *Like a barque tossed on stormy seas*: it is interesting to see Chichikov's Romantic image echoed in Gogol's own description of his isolation and *déraciné* state after arriving in Rome in 1837: on 30 March, he writes to Pogodin, 'I am homeless, I am battered and tossed about by the waves...'

37 *allegiate consessor*: Selifan's spoonerism (the distortion is similar in the Russian) is of the rank 'collegiate assessor', eighth in the Table of Ranks (see the Table on p. xliii).

42 *Bobrov ... Pleshakov*: as usual with Gogol, to the Russian ear these names have a suggestive—and usually comic—force lost in translation—as Nabokov points out: 'The names Gogol invents are really nicknames which we surprise in the very act of turning into family names' (Nabokov, p. 43); thus, Bobrov is derived from *bobër*, 'beaver'; Svinin from *svinya*, 'pig'; Kanapatiev may come from *konopaty*, 'freckled', or *konopatit'*, 'to caulk', and also suggests, rather more obliquely, the *konoplya*, 'hemp', or 'neck-weed', another word for the *pen'ka* which the old lady is so anxious to sell her visitor later in the chapter; Trepakin—*trepat'*, 'to scutch, to strip' (among other things, the hemp mentioned above), also 'to prattle, to blather'; and Pleshakov—*pleshivy*, 'baldpated'.

43 *Field Marshal Kutuzov ... Emperor Paul*: Mikhail Iliaronovich Kutuzov (1745–1813) commanded the Russian armies during the Patriotic War of

1812–13 against Napoleon; Paul I reigned briefly, from 1796 to 1801, and was deposed in a coup conducted with the approval of his son and heir Alexander; during the coup he was strangled.

44 *watermelon rinds*: as remarked by Gogol's biographer V. V. Danilov, Gogol is here transposing a Ukrainian memory—watermelon rinds would have been a ubiquitous feature of all Ukrainian yards, but not likely in the more temperate Russian climate of Korobochka's estate.

46 *Korobochka ... Collegiate Secretary*: Mme Korobochka's name means nothing more nor less than 'little box', a not insignificant detail, in view of the importance of the little box which Chichikov carries around with him and in which he stows everything of interest, and, more generally, of boxes, containers, and compartments of all kinds in Gogol's world. The Russian writer Bely suggests that Chichikov's little box is a surrogate for his wife—a reading supported by the fact that Korobochka is the only woman among all the landowners he visits (although *korobochka*—perhaps deliberately, is not one of the numerous words Gogol uses for Chichikov's box: *larets*, *larchik*, *shkatulka*, *yashchik* and *yashchichek*). The rank held by the good lady's late husband lies tenth on the table, equivalent to that of Staff Captain.

assessor: the assessor was an elected official, who represented the local landed gentry on the district court (see note to p. 163); one of Chichikov's horses is called Assessor.

47 *Hemp perhaps? ... half a pood*: the hemp referred to here is the fibre extracted from the cannabis plant, *Cannabis sativa*, also used for cooking oil, for stockfeed, and, in infusion form, for medicinal purposes. Although used as a narcotic in Asian regions of the Russian empire, it is unlikely that Korobochka's crop would have been put to this use. In his notebooks, Gogol records that the going price for hemp was 1–2.5 roubles per pood; the pood was a pre-Revolutionary measure of weight, equal to slightly more than 36 pounds avoirdupois.

soul tax: *podat'*—see note to p. 21.

50 *dark blue banknotes*: blue was traditionally the colour of the five-rouble note, a tradition that survived through the Soviet era but ended with the collapse of the rouble in the 1990s; paper money remained in circulation in Russia, alongside coins, until 1843. Trade prices were calculated in banknotes, the rate of which fluctuated (in 1820 a paper rouble was equivalent to twenty-five copecks in silver coins). An imperial proclamation of 9 April 1812 required all payments to the Treasury to be made in banknotes; hence the anomalous preference expressed for paper money in some of the transactions described in *Dead Souls* despite its inferior value.

52 *official crested paper*: used for submission of petitions, registration of commercial transactions, contracts, etc. The paper came in different values, depending on the nature of the operation.

53 *Pyotr Saveliev Neuvazhai-Koryto*: this improbable name entered the Rus-

sian language as a designation of the common man, the Joe Bloggs of rustic Russia; although it perhaps would not be widely understood today, it occurs with that meaning in the writings of Chekhov, Hertzen, and Turgenev.

54 *yuletide*: the period in question—*svyatki*—extended from Christmas to Epiphany. In his notebooks, Gogol devotes several pages to an account of the various traditions followed in different parts of Russia and the Ukraine at this time of the year.

St Philip's fast: name given to the fast of Advent by country folk, as Advent begins after St Philip's day, on 14 November; traditionally, villagers in the central zone of Russia killed a fowl for St Philip's day.

55 *fashionable religion of Catholicism*: the Catholic faith enjoyed a certain vogue in Russia during the nineteenth century; moreover, and, from his letters and notebooks, it appears that Gogol was at one time drawn to the religion and, during his long sojourn in Rome, might even have entertained the possibility of conversion.

59 *Blokhin, Pochitaev, Mylnoy, Colonel Cherpakov*: these names may have a slight comic resonance to the Russian ear: Blokhin—in fact, a not uncommon name—suggests *blokha*—'flea'; Pochitaev is derived from *pochitat'*—'to respect'; Mylnoy means, quite simply, 'soapy', and Cherpakov comes from *cherpak*—'scoop', and recalls, among other uses, the popular Russian idiom for a futile exercise, 'to scoop water with a sieve'.

62 *Potseluev ... Kuvshinnikov*: here again, Gogol invents names with humorous connotations for the Russian reader: Potseluev suggests *potselui*, a kiss; Kuvshinnikov is derived from *kuvshin*, a jug (and foreshadows the 'jug-snouted'—*kuvshinnoe rylo*—Ivan Antonovich, the official to whom Chichikov is sent to formalize the transfer of his newly acquired souls, in Chapter 7). Among the names which follow, Mizhuev suggests *mizhevat'*—'peer', 'squint at', Khvostyryov *khvost*—'tail', with a suggestion also of *khvastat'sya*—'brag'; and Ponomaryov—a not uncommon surname—is derived from *ponomar'*—'sexton'.

63 *bezique or faro*: Gogol's ethnographic interest in popular pastimes extended also to games of hazard, and his notebooks contain lists of the names of card games and card-players' argot. The games referred to here—*gal'bik* and *banchishka*—have no exact equivalent in English; *banchishka*, or 'little bank', is a variation of the ubiquitous whist. Gambling was formally prohibited in Tsarist (as in Soviet) Russia but was widely practised in both eras.

Castor-oil Ivanovich: this odd insult sounds as odd in Russian: Nozdryov calls Chichikov *opodel'dok Ivanovich*, using the name of a camphor and soap-based liniment (*linimentum saponato-camphoratum*) known since Paracelsus by the name 'opodeldoc' and used for the relief of arthritis and rheumatic pain.

65 *Fenardi*: according to Russian commentators, Fenardi was a well-known

circus performer of the 1820s; I have been unable to confirm this, or to verify the spelling of his non-Russian name, so am forced to take this on trust.

67 *A silver twenty . . . a copper fifty*: the *dvugriveny*, or twenty-copeck coin, requested by the old lady, was a silver coin and, by Gogol's day, its value had risen to eighty copecks, while the *poltinnik*, or fifty-copeck piece, being made of copper, retained its face-value: hence the apparent discrepancy in these sums. Russian is particularly rich in colloquial terms for the different coins and denominations of banknotes that, over the years, have constituted its currency, and many of these terms appear in *Dead Souls*, but, in most cases, lack appropriate equivalents in English, whose own colloquial terms— 'bob', 'half-crown', etc.—are specific to English currency. Accordingly, I have had to use colourless terms like 'five-rouble note', 'copper coin', etc. The following terms—many of which are still current—occur: *grosh* (literally 'groat')—half-copeck coin, or, more loosely, 'penny'; *pyatak* (from *pyat'*, 'five')—a five-copeck piece, also *pyatak serebra*—a silver five-copeck piece; *grivna* (a unit of currency in Old Russia)—ten copecks; *dvugrivennyi, dvugrivennik* (from *dva*, 'two', and *grivna*)—a silver twenty-copeck piece; *chetvertak* (from *chetvert'*, 'quarter')—silver twenty-five-copeck coin (but *chetvertak raduzhny*—'rainbow-coloured quarter'—is a twenty-five rouble banknote); *poltina, poltinnik* (from *pol-*, 'half')—a fifty-copeck piece (thus the *poltina medi*— the 'half rouble in brass'—referred to by Plyushkin); *tselkovik* (from *tselyj*, 'whole')—a silver rouble; *sinyukha* (from *sinij*, 'dark blue', the colour of the note)—five-rouble note, *chervonets* (from *chervonny*, 'red')— a gold coin with a value of three roubles and, in Soviet times, the ten-rouble note (so-named because of its red colour); *krasnaya bumazhka* (literally 'little red paper', the colour of the note)—ten-rouble note; *ugol* (literally, 'corner') and *belen'kaya* (from *belyi*, 'white', the colour of the note)—twenty-five-rouble note; and *gosudarstvennaya* (literally, 'state note')—a two-hundred-rouble banknote.

68 *paltry collegiate registrars*: the rank of collegiate registrar stood 14th— and lowest—on the Petrine Table of Ranks; this was the rank held, for example, by the lowly stationmaster and by Gogol himself, during his brief career in the cadastral department (see the Table on p. xliv).

71 *shaggy . . . Headmistress*: included among Gogol's many taxonomic interests were the names given to dogs and terms used to describe their coats and other features; lists of such terms feature in his notebooks and furnish the raw material for passages such as this.

72 '*Marlboro' s'en va-t-en guerre*': satirical song about the Duke of Marlborough (1650–1722), who commanded the English forces in the War of the Spanish Succession (1701–14). The song acquired popularity in Russia during the Napoleonic wars, as Marlborough's unsuccessful campaign was identified with the similarly unsuccessful invasion of Russia by Napoleon.

74 *thumbsucker . . . (note by N. V. Gogol)*: the offensive word in question—

a daunting challenge for the translator—is *fetiuk*, the name of the letter Θ, which was used in words derived from the Greek but pronounced /f / and replaced in the orthographic reforms that followed the Revolution by Φ. The letter is considered offensive to men because its form suggests the female organ. In addition, the sound of the word *fetiuk* might suggest, by assonance, certain well-known Russian terms of abuse, such as *gavniuk* and *pizdiuk*. I hope that some of the sexual suggestion, as well as the aspersions against the victim's virility, are carried, albeit obliquely, by the English 'thumbsucker'.

84 *Suvorov*: Aleksandr Vasilievich Suvorov (1729–1800), Russian general with a long and distinguished military career, reaching through the Seven Years War, the Russo–Turkish war and the campaigns of 1768 and 1794. Suvorov fought the French in the anti-French coalition of 1798 and his reputation for valour largely rests on his achievement in escaping, through one of the most intrepid feats of military history, from almost certain rout by a much larger and surrounding French army, with his march through the St Gotthard. The scene of the storming of the unassailable fortress is considered by critics to be based on Suvorov's storm of the Bessarabian town of Izmail, in 1790, during the Russo–Turkish war. Nicknamed *General Vpered*—'General Forwards'—in Russian, Suvorov was identified in the popular imagination with the mad daring of the Russians.

87 *Nizhny Novgorod half-wit*: Nizhny Novgorod, renamed Gorky in the Soviet era and now Russia's third largest city, has been traditionally associated in the Russian popular imagination with the idea of provincial backwardness.

91 *German colonists*: large numbers of Germans moved to Russia in the late eighteenth and early nineteenth centuries, settling primarily in the Volga region; according to the 1989 census, there were over two million Germans in the territory of the USSR, making theirs the country's fifteenth largest ethnic group, outnumbering, for example, both the Estonians and the Latvians; emigration back to Germany in the late Soviet period and, to a much greater extent, after the collapse of the Union, has considerably reduced their numbers but sizable populations still remain in Russia and Kazakstan and there was even talk in the early 1990s of reconstituting the defunct Volga German Republic, which existed briefly in the 1920s.

planed walls: in his notebooks, Gogol defines a 'planed hut'—*izba vytesannaya*—as one in which the rough logs have been planed down to form a smooth wall.

92 *Mikhail Semyonovich*: in the Russian popular imagination, bears are always called Mikhail, or Misha.

Mavrocordato . . . Miaulis, Kanaris: Alexandros Mavrocordato, Andreas Miaulis, Theodoros Kolokotrinos, and Konstantinos Kanaris were all heroes of the Greek war of independence of 1821–9 and were popular figures in the *lubok*—the Russian chapbook literature of Gogol's day, in which they appeared more in caricature form than as portraits in the more conventional sense (and as they appear on the walls of Sobakevich's house).

Bagration: Prince Pyotr Ivanovich Bagration (1765–1812) was a Georgian general who served with valour and distinction in the Russian army, most notably in the Patriotic War of 1812 against Napoleon's invasion. He was mortally wounded in the battle of Borodino.

Bobelina: the Greek heroine Bobolina became popular in Russia in the early nineteenth century and was taken up by the authors of the *lubok* chapbooks, where, as Bobelina, she came to embody female strength and stature, a sort of Russian Amazon (although the historical Bobolina was remote from her chapbook alter-ego: she never bore arms, never dressed as a man and was not particularly martial in her appearance); following this mention by Gogol, the term entered the Russian language as a derogatory designation for oversized women.

94 *Gog and Magog*: the Biblical figures Gog and Magog (Rev. 20: 8–10) also feature in popular Russian folktales and chapbook literature.

95 *not a starched cap but a brightly coloured kerchief*: the starched, lace cap—*chepets*—was the headdress of gentlewomen, while peasant women would have worn *kosynki*, or kerchiefs.

96 *that Plyushkin*: Gogol's miser's name suggests most forcibly, of its many possible sources, *plyushch*—'ivy' and, possibly, *plesen'*—'mould'.

98 *the deathless Koshchei*: evil figure from Russian folktales, represented as an emaciated skeletal old man, rich and evil, who cannot be killed until his soul, buried somewhere far away, is found and destroyed.

100 *arshins*: Stepan Probka's height is actually put at 3 arshins and 1 vershok; the arshin, a pre-Revolutionary measure of height, was equivalent to 71 cm, while the vershok measured 4.45 cm, giving the doughty late peasant a height of 2.18 metres, over seven feet—and one belied by his name, which means, quite simply, 'cork'. The same stature is ascribed to the sergeant-at-arms in the 'Tale of Captain Kopeikin', in chapter 10. Of Sobakevich's other serfs, the following names are perhaps worthy of comment: Telyatnikov, from *tyelyatina*—'veal', with suggestions of stupidity and ineptitude (in Chapter 10 the postmaster describes himself as 'a lump of veal'); Sorokoplyokhin, from *soroka*—'magpie', with its connotations of empty chatter, and possibly also *sorok*—'forty', in combination with *opleukha*—'slap in the face'.

quit-rent: various forms of duty and taxation are encountered along the pages of *Dead Souls*, most of which have no equivalent in modern-day Russia. This obligation, the *obrok*, was a form of *métayage*, under which the serf paid some portion of his produce—or its monetary equivalent—to the feudal lord in return for use of the land. Quit-rent prevailed as the form of taxation for serfs on monastery and palace-owned land, while the corvée—*barshchina*—was more usually applied in private estates. Where, in the English feudal system, quit-rent was paid by freeholders in lieu of services, payment of the *obrok* did not imply that the serf's bondage was in any sense alleviated.

101 *Jacob's magpie*: reference to a Russian proverb: the magpie, as in English, represents a noisy, garrulous person (usually a woman).

102 *koulak*: derived from the Russian *kulak*—fist (hence the associated references to tight-fistedness), the word was used, generally as a term of opprobrium, in Tsarist times, to designate miserly merchants and village usurers of the peasant class; in Soviet times, it came to designate, with still greater opprobrium, a class of peasants who resisted enforced collectivization and who suffered severe reprisals under the authorities; thus, in his play *On the Rocks* (1934), George Bernard Shaw defines the koulak as an 'able, hardheaded, hardfisted farmer who was richer than his neighbours'.

103 *dog in me*: Sobakevich is apparently referring to his name, derived from the Russian word for dog—*sobaka*.

Vyatka carthorse: reference to the brightly coloured clay figurines, usually of domestic animals and persons, made in the Russian province of Vyatka and notable for their squat, thickset proportions; Vyatka, in the north-east of European Russia, was renamed Kirov in the Soviet era.

109 *almanac*: the publication in question, the *Adres-kalendar'*, contained a list of all the ranks of the Russian Empire and was published more or less on an annual basis.

Oh my youth! Oh my freshness!: As pointed out by commentators, this lyrical digression inspired such later works as Turgenev's prose poem 'O my youth! O my freshness', and even the Soviet poet Yesenin's 'I regret not, I call not, I weep not...' In its turn, Gogol's dithyramb is inspired by Zhukovsky's 'Song' of 1820, and by similar flights of reminiscence in Pushkin's *Eugene Onegin*.

110 *An old and spreading garden ... picturesque desolation*: We know from Gogol's biographers that the author was particularly attached to this scene (which, in turn, has attracted keen interest on the part of Gogol scholars) and contemporaries recall the intensity of feeling which Gogol imparted to this passage during his readings of the book to friends.

113 *well before the invasion of Moscow by the French*: this took place in 1812, in other words, some thirty years before the publication of this work.

115 *woodcraft market*: the market—*shchepnoi dvor*—in St Petersburg where artefacts of the woodworkers' trade were sold. The list of such artefacts which follows comes, like so many such lists in this work, from Gogol's notebooks.

118 *quit-rent*: see note to p. 100.

same quantity of linen: Gogol observes in his notebooks that country women were required, twice a year, to surrender a 25 arshin (approximately 2.5 metres) length of linen.

124 *Grigory Doezzhai-ne-Doedesh*: another typically Gogolian coinage, which sounds as improbable to the Russian ear as its awkward English translation.

129 *customary iron bar*: on Russian estates, watchmen were required periodically to sound rattles or to strike suspended iron bars to show that they were still awake.

130 *the great poet Schiller*: the youth described here is thought by commentators to be modelled on Gogol's school friend N. V. Kukolnik, a passionate devotee of Schiller's plays. It seems probable, too, that the 'universal poet' referred to at the beginning of the following chapter is Schiller, although Gogol himself was less enamoured of the German poet. A clue to this disparaging attitude is given by his use of the name 'Schiller' for the drunken, and nearly cuckolded, German craftsman in Nevsky Prospect.

Sennaya Square: noisy, commercial square in St Petersburg, which also served as the place of public executions; known in the Soviet era as *Ploshchad' Mira*—Peace Square—the original name (which may be translated, roughly, as Haymarket) has since been restored.

131 *from Ryazan, with bay horses*: Ryazan, home of the caligophilous lieutenant, who appears again at the end of the following chapter, is an ancient town and provisional centre, once capital of the Ryazan Principality and, in more modern times, a centre of commerce and industry with appropriately, an extensive shoe industry.

133 *For the judgement of our contemporaries . . . clowning of a fairground buffoon*: as noted by commentators, Gogol is responding here to criticism from, among others, the philosopher and publicist Petr Chaadaev, who dismissed the satirical humour of *The Government Inspector* and other comic writings by Gogol as such frivolous clowning.

134 *Torzhok*: ancient Russian town in Tver province, on the route from Moscow to St Petersburg, and twice sacked in history, first by Khan Baty and his Mongol Horde in 1238, and, some three centuries later, by the Polish armies; Torzhok was traditionally renowned for the quality of its leatherwork. As a curious aside, we might note that it was in Torzhok that Gogol's confessor—and, in the minds of many, the man most responsible for his final illness and manic depression—Father Matvey Konstantinovsky, reportedly healed himself by eating handfuls of rotten slime from the burial site of Saint Yulianiya, discovered beneath the sanctuary of the Torzhok parish church during restoration work.

performed two leaps, Scottish-fashion: Chichikov's agility with his feet recalls Scottish dancing, at that time enjoying a certain vogue in Russia—it is not, as some translations suggest, that his lack of trousers recalls Scottish attire.

137 *stove-bunk*: traditionally, in Russian houses, the stove was a large clay-brick structure in the centre of the room, sometimes tiled, and fitted with shelves and recesses on which people could sit and lie for warmth (and even sleep).

137 *Yeremei Karyakin, Nikita Volokita, his son Anton Volokita ... names*: Karyakin suggests 'sprawl, fall on all fours' (*na karyachki*), or 'recoil, fall back' (*karachit'sya*), 'spread one's legs wide', even 'swagger' (*karyachit'sya*—the word used by Gogol in his footnote on the 'gallinipper'—*koramora*—in Chapter 5), or 'gnarled wood' (*karyaga*), while Volokita has several direct denotations, including 'vagrant, wanderer', and also 'ladies' man, skirt-chaser'. The name which follows— Popov, a common Russian name—is derived from the Russian for priest (*pop*).

138 *Tsarevokokshaisk ... Vesyegonsk*: Tsarevokokshaisk—a town in Kazan province on the Lesser Kokshaga river, founded in 1584 and renamed first Krasnokokshaisk, and then Yoshkar Ola (which name it still bears) after the Revolution; Vesyegonsk—district centre in Tver province, founded in 1776; Gogol had originally put Volokolamsk but changed it to Vesyegonsk after hearing the writer M. P. Pogodin give a most unflattering account of his visit to the town.

139 *peas and wheat into the deep holds*: in his notebooks, Gogol records that peas were transported by barge along Russia's river system to supply the Russian fleet.

141 *Themis*: Greek goddess representing justice, wisdom, and good counsel (the name means 'order') and often depicted as holding the scales of justice in one hand.

146 *Trukhachevsky, Begushkin—all useless ballast on life's journey*: the name Trukhachevsky suggests *trukhly, trukhovy*—'rotten, mouldy', and, possibly, *strukhnut'*—'to be cowardly'; Begushkin is derived from *begat'*— 'to run' (including, presumably, away).

148 *Kherson province*: a province in the southern Ukraine, lying across the river Dnieper and a rich agricultural region in Gogol's day, as it is now.

publication in the Gazette: a form of stamp duty was levied for the publication of transfers of property, including serfs, in the *Supplements* to the *Senate Gazette*, published from 1838.

149 *measly twenty-five rouble note*: the value of paper money was subject to fluctuation and was usually well below its face value; in some parts of the Empire, especially provinces in the interior, paper money was not accepted as currency (see also note to p. 67 above).

dropped the -a off her name: Chichikov's accusation is actually slightly different—although with the same import—namely, that Sobakevich had ended her name with the 'hard sign', an orthographical mark formerly used to indicate any word ending in a consonant—and thus suggesting that it was a man's name (although the literary, and Church Slavonic, form of the woman's name was also spelt thus). (See above, p. 136.) There has been some debate about this alleged chicanery by Sobakevich and whether Sobakevich is in fact trying to dupe Chichikov, since—for all his roughness and obduracy in commercial transactions—out-and-out dishonesty is not in his character.

150 *gristle and cheeks of a nine-pood sturgeon*: in his notebooks, Gogol describes such a pie, made with the entire head of a sturgeon, together
with its gristle and cheeks, and with the pluck and belly of the fish; the
notebooks contain numerous such descriptions, and even recipes, for
pies, patties, and other dishes prepared by countryfolk.

152 *Kamarinsky laddy-o: Akh ty takoi i etakoi kamarinsky muzhik!*—a popular and humorous Russian song and dance, in 2/4 time, still widely sung
and danced today; its tune was used by the composer Glinka for his
work 'Kamarinskaya: Russian Fantasy for Orchestra'. The origin of
'Kamarinsky' (sometimes spelt 'Komarinsky') remains obscure, but it is
presumed to derive from a place-name.

three-field system of agriculture: under this system, arable land was divided into three fields which, respectively and in rotation, were sown
with winter wheat, spring wheat, and left to lie fallow.

verses which Werther writes to Charlotte: Goethe's *Die Leiden des jungen
Werthers* inspired various imitations by Russian writers, including a poem
by V. I. Tumansky entitled 'Werther to Charlotte (an hour before his
death)'. As there are no poems by Werther in Goethe's original, it is
possible that Tumansky's are the verses which Chichikov reads.

154 *frieze greatcoats*: uniform greatcoats—*shineli*—were worn by all those in
service, military or civilian, including, in tsarist Russia, functionaries,
seminarists, and even domestic servants. The quality of the cloth would
depend on the status of the wearer; thus, frieze coats would have been
the garb of the lower orders.

clearly a great amateur of boots: as recorded by his biographer Arnoldi,
Gogol was himself 'a great amateur of boots', always travelling with no
fewer than three or four pairs in his modest suitcase; here he pokes
gentle fun at his weakness and—like some modern film-makers—is perhaps also making a cameo appearance in his own work (we recall the
hack journalist Tryapichkin in *The Government Inspector*, who lives at
Gogol's own address in St Petersburg—97 Post Office Street). Interest-
ingly, Chichikov also appears to share this partiality for boots, as can be
seen from the description of his chattels in Chapter 1 of Part Two (pp.
280 and 389).

155 *Kamchatka*: peninsula in the Russian Far East, washed by the Sea of
Okhotsk and the Bering Sea, and known to Russians, from the eighteenth century, as a place of banishment.

156 *Little Russian provinces*: Little Russia—*Malorossiya*—at one time, all Eastern Slavs were loosely referred to as Russians (*russkie*). As the different
peoples diverged, a distinction was made between Little Russia
(*Malorossiya*—now the Ukraine) and Great Russia (*Velikorossiya*—Russia proper).

157 *Lancaster school of mutual instruction*: in the Lancaster method, named
after the English educationist Joseph Lancaster, the teacher gave instruction to the brightest pupils only, and these in turn taught the rest.

The Lancaster method was widely practised in Russia in the 1820s, particularly by the Decembrists as a means of promoting literacy among their rank-and-file soldiers.

157 *Zhukovsky's Lyudmila*: ballad by the Russian Romantic poet Vasily Andreevich Zhukovsky, published in 1808, a free adaptation of the macabre German ballad 'Leonore', written in 1773 by the poet Gottfried August Bürger (1747–94). (See also note to p. 109.)

158 *Young's Night Thoughts and Eckartshausen's Key to the Mysteries of Nature*: Young's *Night Thoughts* were widely read in nineteenth-century Russia and existed in a number of different translations. The postmaster was probably familiar with the version by Sergei Glinka, to judge by the title which he uses. Karl Eckartshausen, 1752–1803, was a German mystic, who published numerous articles and tracts on a wide range of literary, scientific and pedagogical subjects. His theosophical and alchemical writings, in particular, were popular among Masonic circles in the early nineteenth century.

Karamzin: Nikolai Karamzin (1766–1826), Russian author and historian. As a writer of fiction, he led the Russian Sentimental school and is best remembered for his short novel *Poor Liza*; his major historical work was *A History of the Russian State*

Moscow Gazette: oldest Russian newspaper, published continuously from 1756 to 1917 by Moscow University, initially, twice a week and, from 1859, daily. Always supported by the state, as a vehicle for its official announcements, the *Moscow Gazette* was the largest Russian newspaper until the mid-nineteenth century, and it grew increasingly conservative in its editorial policy. It was shut down by the Bolsheviks after the 1917 October Revolution.

161 *several sentiments . . . here*: Gogol indulges here in a light-hearted parody of Tatyana's letter to Onegin, in Pushkin's *Eugene Onegin*, and echoes can also be heard of Aleko's lament in another Pushkin poem, 'Gypsies'.

162 *Two turtle-doves . . . in tears*: incorrect quotation from the poem: 'Content with my fate...' by Karamzin (see note to p. 158 above). The correct version of the poem lacks the defects to which the author draws attention here. In the Russian it is the metre, rather than the rhyme, which is sacrificed to the speaker's immediate needs: in Karamzin's poem the remains are male and the poem ends with the words: 'He died in tears!'

163 *lower court*: a district court, the lowest administrative instance in the Russian juridical system, established in 1775. The court was headed by the captain of police and included two or three assessors from among the local gentry; it dealt with the enforcement of imperial edicts at the local level and the judicial resolution of minor disputes.

bon-bon card: cards containing a short poem or motto, placed inside confectionery wrapping, and presented at dances, were known as 'bon-bon cards'.

165 *Chipkhaikhilidzev . . . Monsieur Coucou, Perkhunovsky, Berebendovsky*: these

names also carry slightly ludicrous connotations. Chipkhaikhilidzev—a Russified Georgian name—is vaguely preposterous in Russian, as in English; Monsieur Coucou needs no gloss for the English reader; Perkhunovsky suggests *perkhota*—'tickle in the throat', *perkhot'*—'dandruff', as well as *perdun*—'farter'; Berebendovsky *beliberda*—'balderdash'.

168 *Zvonskys, Linskys, Lidins, Gryomins*: typical names from fiction—especially of the romantic variety—of that time; thus there is a Lidin in Pushkin's *Count Nilin* and a Gryomin in Bestuzhev-Marlinsky's *The Ordeal*.

171 *Simbirsk province*: province of Russia lying astride the middle course of the Volga; the provincial town of the same name was the birthplace of Vladimir Lenin, for which distinction it and the province were renamed Ulyanovsk during the Soviet era; for the location of this, and the other provinces which follow, see the map on p. xlv.

172 *Sofron Ivanovich Bespechny . . . Maklatura Aleksandrovna*: again, most of these names have a comic resonance to the Russian ear, in some cases, without carrying a direct semantic load, while others are more directly 'motivated': thus *bespechny* means 'insouciant'; Pobedonosny comes from *pobedonosets*—'victor', but with a suggestion of 'nose', less apparent in the more usual form of the name, Pobedonostsev; Perekroev suggests *perekroit'*—'rehash', 'redo', usually something laborious and wearisome; *maklatura* suggests both *maklachit'*—'to grasp, be greedy', and even *makulatura*—'maculature, scrap paper'; in general, their effect is one of provincial affectation.

178 *tarantass, or a calèche, or a britzka*: for an explanation of these carriages, see the note on p. 3.

bread loaves, calatches . . . egg-and-pickle pastie: here Gogol indulges his fondness for country cooking—or, at least, for the names which describe it; lists such as these defy the skills of the translator and a gloss of the original terms (with some assistance from Nabokov) might be of interest to readers who share Gogol's interest: *kalach*—calatch, a purse-shaped white roll; *kokurka*—bun with an egg or cheese stuffing; *skorodumok*—a kind of dumpling; *krendel*—a large roll, not unlike an American bagel, often in the shape of a capital B and richly flavoured and decorated; *pirog-kurnik*—a chicken pasty and *pirog-rassolnik*—(as defined by Gogol himself) 'a pie with a filling of chicken and buckwheat, mixed with pickle juice and chopped eggs'.

179 *St Nicholas on Nedotychki*: Russian churches are often popularly known by the name of their location—which may be a street, or river, or district—and this, presumably, is what is meant by 'Nedotychki'; the name has a slightly comic resonance in Russian, recalling the word *dotykat'*—to irritate by prodding, and the colloquial term *nedotyka*, variously a touchy, or a clumsy, person.

185 *Rinaldo Rinaldini*: hero of the novel about a robber chief, *Rinaldo Rinaldini* (1800), by the German writer—and brother-in-law to Goethe—

Christian August Vulpius (1762–1827), which was widely popular in early nineteenth-century Europe.

187 *She's . . . affected*: In the Academy edition, this remark is attributed to the merely pleasant lady, but it clearly belongs to the lady pleasant in all respects, as here.

191 *'hussar' . . . risen earlier*: Gogol's biographer P. A. Kulish writes that this episode owes its origins to an experience of the young Gogol, during his years at the Nezhin Lyceum.

192 *Polezhaev . . . embellishments*: names all suggestive of rest and sleep, thus: *polezhat'*, 'to have a lie-down, to nap'; *zavalit'sya* 'to collapse' or, in the anachronistic but precise modern equivalent, 'to crash'; *sopet'* 'to wheeze'; *khrapet'* 'to snore'.

500-rouble tureen of fish soup . . . spicy meat-pies: this extravagant claim recalls the 700-rouble watermelon in *The Government Inspector* and, below, the 100-rouble watermelon, and the cherries costing five roubles apiece, in *The Tale of Captain Kopeikin*. The links noted here underline the connection between these two tales of mistaken identity.

Sysoi Pafnutievich . . . Macdonald Karlovich: these two names are equally ludicrous in their different ways; thus, Sysoi and Pafnuty, although authentic Russian names, are both very uncommon and improbably so in combination; Macdonald and Karl, Scottish and German (there was a small influx of Scotsmen to Russia in the nineteenth century, primarily as industrialists and estate managers; for Germans, see the note to p. 90), make a similarly improbable pair.

195 *Solvychegodsk . . . Ustsysolsk*: Solvychegodsk—an ancient town and flourishing centre of commerce in Archangel province, in the Russian north, with important saltworks; Ustsysolsk—another northern town, renamed Syktyvkar in the Soviet era, when it served as capital of the Komi Autonomous Region (today the Republic of Komi); from the sixteenth century, an important centre of the Russian grain and fur trade.

196 *state peasants . . . Zadirailovo*: state peasants were peasants with individual liberty, who lived on state land and rendered service to the state; Vshivaya-Spes: another ludicrous name, literally meaning 'Lousy Arrogance'; Borovki suggests *borov*, or *borovok*, 'a hog', and the village's 'nickname' Zadirailovo—*zadirat'*, 'to quarrel, to brawl' (in consequence, presumably, of its inhabitants' pugilistic nature); the concupiscent policeman's name, Drobyazhkin, is cognate with *drobit'*—'to crush', suggesting that lechery was not his only failing.

200 *Praskushka . . . Petrushka*: Praskushka (diminutive of Praskovya) is a girl's name, Petrushka (diminutive of Pyotr) a boy's.

202 *they did not have the slightest idea who Captain Kopeikin was*: there are various identified sources for Captain Kopeikin (whose name, incidentally, is derived from the word *kopeika*—'copeck'), prominent among which are folktales and songs about the robber Kopeikin.

the campaign of 1812: reference to Napoleon's invasion of Russia.

203 *Krasny, or perhaps at Leipzig*: the clash at Krasny, near Smolensk, which continued for four bloody days from 3 to 6 November 1812, was one of the decisive battles of the 1812–14 campaign; in the battle at Leipzig, 4–7 October 1813, the combined armies of Russia, Prussia, Austria, and Sweden finally routed Napoleon's invading force.

Nevsky Prospect . . . Gorokhovaya Street . . . Liteinaya Street: all prominent streets in St Petersburg, which feature in Gogol's *Petersburg Tales*.

Semiramis: fabled Assyrian queen, credited with founding the city of Nineveh; attention should be drawn, at this point, to the particularly important function played by bridges in Gogol's work, particularly in the *Petersburg Tales*; suspension bridges, seen as a marvel of western genius, made their appearance in Russia in the early nineteenth century (the first was the Zeleny—'Green'—bridge in St Petersburg—subsequently renamed the Politseisky and then the Narodny) and contributed both to the allure and to the outlandish, 'alien' quality of Russia's northern capital.

Revel: former name for Tallinn, capital of Estonia; this is presumed by commentators to have been an inn kept by a native of that city.

205 *fourth and fifth class*: reference to the Petrine Table of Ranks; see p. xliii.

Palkin . . . London: the Palkin was an expensive restaurant in pre-Revolutionary St Petersburg; the London—a restaurant attached to the hotel of the same name on Nevsky Prospect.

206 *Milyutin shops*: fashionable food emporium, also on the city's main thoroughfare, Nevsky Prospect.

cherries—five roubles a piece, a monster watermelon . . . a hundred roubles for it: see note to p. 192.

208 *Ryazan forests*: the region of Ryazan, lying to the south-east of Moscow, is, to this day, heavily forested (see also note to p. 131).

209 *Napoleon in disguise*: preposterous though it appears, this theory has its foundations in fact; thus, the writer Vyazemsky describes how stationmasters sometimes kept a portrait of Napoleon hanging in their stations, to be able to recognize him should he turn up in disguise. In Gogol's story 'Old-World Landowners', the guest who visits the old couple mentions a secret plot hatched between the English and French to release Napoleon and turn him loose against the Russians.

210 *Moscow Gazette . . . Son of the Fatherland*: for *Moscow Gazette*, see the note to p. 158; for *Son of the Fatherland*, see the note to p. 25.

Antichrist . . . take possession of the entire world: the theme of Chichikov roaming about the world with sinister intent returns in Part Two, where, in the early version of the first chapter, he is compared to Mephistopheles, preying on the hapless landowners whom he deceives into selling him their dead souls.

apocalyptic numbers—during the war of 1812, when Napoleon's armies invaded Russia, some mystically inclined Russian patriots translated Napoleon's name into numerals, using the Old Church Slavonic system, whereby numbers were represented by letters, and arrived at 666, the number of the Beast (Rev. 13: 18).

211 *four poods, if not five*: i.e., between 144 and 180 pounds.

213 *Trukhmachovka*: this unattested place-name has connotations similar to those of the surname Trukhachevsky, in Chapter 7 (see note to p. 146).

having married the corn-chandler Mikhail to his own kinswoman: the degree of kinship in question is that of godparents to the same child—*kumovstvo*, or compaternity—and marriage between those thus related is prohibited in the Orthodox Church. The relationship occurs frequently in Gogol's work and, since the precise English term 'gossip' is, regrettably, no longer widely understood in that meaning today, for the Russian *kum* and *kuma* (also little understood in modern—at least, urban—Russia), I have had to resort to the more extensive notions of 'kinsman' and 'kinswoman'.

215 *future generations will also laugh one day*: as commentators have noted, this passage calls to mind the scene in *The Government Inspector* when the Mayor turns to the audience and asks: 'What are you laughing at?—You're laughing at yourselves!' *The Government Inspector* had its first performance in 1842, the year of the publication of *Dead Souls*.

La Duchesse de la Vallière: mistress of Louis XIV and uncrowned queen of festivities at the French court; it might be recalled that the good lady's portrait hangs, incongruously, in the home of Gogol's Ukrainian Philemon and Baucis, in the story 'Old-World Landowners' from the Mirgorod cycle; the novel which Chichikov is reading was by Mme de Genlis (1746–1830) and enjoyed great popularity in Russia; Chichikov, however, is still reading the book—and complaining that he is unable to finish it—in Chapter 3 of Part Two.

225 *they say it brings good luck*: according to a popular superstition, it was good luck for one's path to be crossed by a funeral procession. Critics have pointed out, however, that Gogol may be attaching quite another significance to this encounter, which should recall to Chichikov his own mortality and encourage him to re-examine his ways. Thus, the good luck presaged Chichikov by this encounter is perhaps not—as he would think—the success of his shady enterprise with the dead souls, but the possibility of moral transformation and rebirth created by its failure.

226 *The snows are white no more*: '*ne bely snegi*'—first words of a well-known Russian recruiting song, sung to the tune of a triumphant march.

229 *noblemen of hereditary lineage or through personal merit*: the names of hereditary noblemen were recorded in genealogical almanacs and their titles and privileges passed down to their heirs, while those who earned their titles through services to the Empire held such titles only for their own lifetimes.

232 *Solon*: Athenian statesman (638–559 BC), known as one of the Seven

Wise Men of Greece, who embodied the cardinal Geek virtue of moderation.

Krylov . . . If only they could play: the motto from the fable 'The Musicians' (or 'The Village Band', as translated by Bernard Pares, whose translation is used in the text), about discordant—but abstemious—musicians; the author, Ivan Krylov, 1768–1844, was a civil servant of undistinguished origins, whose close observation of Russian peasant speech and mores, as well as his critical view of the Russian authorities, inspired him to write a collection of fables, some based on models by La Fontaine and Aesop, but many entirely original, which have remained popular among Russians to this day.

233 *silver five-copeck piece*: see note to p. 67.

236 *Prince Khovansky*: interpretations of this reference differ, some commentators deriving it from the word *khovat'*, 'to slip something in', or 'to hide something stolen, to stash'; much more probable, however, is the derivation from a historical Prince A. N. Khovansky (1771–1857), director of the State Bank, whose signature was on all the banknotes issued.

238 *a commission was set up for the erection of some very substantial government building*: in the first version of this chapter, the reference is more specific, and concerns the construction of the Cathedral of Christ the Saviour in Moscow (torn down by Stalin to make room for an immense skyscraper to be topped by a huge statue of himself, but—when excavation of the foundation pit revealed faults in the ground which precluded the erection of such a tall building—converted into a vast outdoor swimming pool. In post-Soviet times the original cathedral has been rebuilt, as far as it could be reconstructed from drawings and photographs). In a celebrated scandal of the time, the commission set up in the early 1820s for the purpose of overseeing the construction of the original cathedral, the foundation stone of which was laid in October 1817, received huge bribes and in 1827 most of its members were subsequently charged and sentenced.

240 *position in the customs service*: as we learn from the surviving fragments of the final chapter of Part Two, Chichikov served in the Radzivilov office of the Russian customs service—an office which also makes an ignominious appearance in the story 'Taras Bulba', where its officers are depicted as using their powers to oppress the local citizenry; Radzivilov—a small town, now in the Ukraine and then in the Volynia province of Russia, on the Austrian frontier—was named after the Polish family Radziwill, and renamed Chervonoarmeisk in the Soviet era.

243 *Brabant lace*: lace from the Belgian province of Brabant, which led the world in the manufacture of lace from the sixteenth century; lace was first produced in Russia in only the eighteenth century, but on a very small scale and confined to convents and private households; it only started to be produced on anything like a commercial scale in the mid-nineteenth century.

246 *Board of Trustees*: a body which ran the Foundlings' Home in Moscow, where asylum was given to orphans and widows mainly of noble birth. The Board maintained its own bank, where money could be deposited for safekeeping and loans could be obtained against estates, serfs and other property. By an imperial decree of 3 July 1824, loans were granted at a rate of 200 roubles per soul for the central provinces and 150 roubles per soul for those in outlying areas.

epidemic fevers that had carried off the best workers: possible reference to the severe cholera epidemics which broke out first in Orenburg in 1829, spread to Tiflis (Tbilisi) and Astrakhan in 1830, and had spread through all Russia by the end of 1831.

247 *Tavrida and Kherson provinces*: Tavrida—also spelt Tauria—was the name introduced by the Tsarist authorities for the Crimean peninsula, after its annexation by Russia in 1783; the name was derived from the name of the ancient tribe of the southern Crimea, the Tauri, who inhabited the region known in ancient times as the Tauris Chersonese; Kherson province—see note to p. 148.

crossing himself, as Russians are wont to do: like adherents of other religions, Russians make the sign of the cross before embarking on an important, or risky, enterprise; the execution of this little ritual is carefully defined, however, and differs from other religions: thus, the thumb and two fingers, held in a group representing the Trinity, are brought to the forehead, the chest, the right, and then the left shoulder. As noted below (see note to p. 379), the Old Believers rejected the three-fingered technique as heresy and to this day continue to make the sign of the cross with two fingers only.

249 *passions not of man's choosing*: as noted by commentators, Gogol later—after falling under the influence of the teachings of the eighth-century mystic, Isaac of Nineveh, repudiated this idea. He even maintained that his unease about this passage and his growing conviction that inborn passions were an evil which man should, at all cost, extirpate from his soul, impeded his work on the continuation of *Dead Souls*.

250 *so-called patriots*: here, Gogol's apprehensions were not entirely frivolous: following the publication of *Dead Souls*, he was indeed accused of lack of patriotism, most significantly by the critic N. A. Polevoy.

251 *bogatyr*: see note to p. 13 above.

PART TWO

On a winter's night, 10–11 February 1852, in the house of Count A. P. Tolstoy, on Nikitsky Boulevard in Moscow, Gogol, his mind rendered unstable by religious introspection and his physical strength sapped by the attentions of his doctors, cast the completed manuscript of *Dead Souls*, Part Two, on the flames. This was the second burning of the ill-fated volume and the last literary immolation in a career which had seen, first, the unsold copies of his first published work, *Hanz Küchelgarten*, consigned to the flames, following a savaging by the critics, and, ten and more years later, an unfinished drama from Cossack history receive a similar fate, after Gogol's friend Zhukovsky fell asleep during a reading.

Following the excitement caused by the publication of Part One in 1841, rumours had started to circulate—supported even by announcements in the press—that the author was working on a sequel and that Part Two would appear soon. Despite repeated denials by Gogol himself, speculation continued, but documentary evidence suggests that, while the idea of Part Two was born and incubated during his work on Part One, and some initial sketch may have been prepared as early as 1841, work on this volume did not begin in earnest until late 1843—i.e., some two years after the appearance of Part One. He began writing in Nice and continued in Frankfurt in the autumn of 1844. Health problems impeded progress and, in general, the author remained discontent with the progress and shape of the book.

Finally, in 1845, during a paroxysm of illness, he burnt the chapters which he had completed by that time, considering them unsatisfactory. 'It was not easy to burn the fruits of five years' work,' he wrote in 1846, 'produced through such painful striving, in which each line was obtained through upheaval, in which there was much that constituted the best of my thinking and occupied my soul.' Yet burn them he did, in the belief that the content of the work would rise from the ashes regenerated, like a phoenix. Those reborn chapters were also destined not to survive, however, and all that remains today of this tortured work are five fragmentary chapters.

Some critics believe that Gogol's wish to destroy the text of Part Two should be honoured and that it should not be included in editions of *Dead Souls*. Thus, Susanne Fusso compellingly argues in her book *Designing Dead Souls* that *Dead Souls* is complete in Part One, that there was never meant to be a Part Two or Part Three, and that it is entirely consistent with Gogol's method to create the expectation of sequels, and even to break off his narratives in mid-story, or mid-sentence, and that he was only persuaded to embark on composition of the second part by the expectation of the Russian reading public. An ill-starred endeavour, he conceded finally that it was futile and destroyed what he had achieved.

Be that as it may, Gogol succumbed to his final illness and died, in a state of considerable mental agitation, without either completing the text or completely destroying the parts he had written. Whether he would have rewritten the second part and gone on to write a third, whether he could himself have restored what had survived, or have definitively destroyed all surviving traces, and have deliberately frustrated the expectations of a sequel he had aroused in his readers, we shall never know. The jury must remain out for ever on the question of *Dead Souls*, Part Two.

The fact remains that these chapters are from Gogol's hand and they represent his last literary endeavour and—with 'The *Dénouement* of *The Government Inspector*'—the only fiction he wrote during the period of his last religious *crise*. Towards the end of Part One, when describing his hero's

background and qualities, the author apologizes for the defects in his character, and warns the reader that 'there still remains a long road for them to
journey together hand in hand; two big parts still lie ahead'. The theme of
moral rebirth, broached in the surviving chapters of Part Two, is also indicated in Gogol's letters of this time, especially those to his close friend
Aleksandra Smirnova.

Generally critics praised images of less positive characters and deplored
those of Ulinka, Murazov, and Kostanzhoglo. But the radical Chernyshevsky—
while subscribing to the critical view of Tentetnikov's tutor, Kostanzhoglo
and Murazov, notes that, when on familiar ground, Gogol can be seen in his
former 'force and freshness', and he praises the righteousness and intensity of
Gogol's 'noble indignation'. Turgenev, who read the chapters of Part Two
before they were published, declared that, despite certain weaknesses, there
were passages 'that grip and astound the reader's soul at the same time'.
Indeed, there are many fine passages in these fragmentary chapters, representative of Gogol at his quirky best, and I certainly believe that the reader
should be allowed to decide for himself whether or not this sequel was
intended to be written.

The compositional history of Part Two is particularly complex, largely
because no final text has come down to us. All that survives are notebooks
containing drafts of some five chapters, in several versions. After the first
burning, Gogol recommended work on the second part of his 'poem' at the
end of December 1848, upon his return to Moscow from a pilgrimage to the
Holy Land. This followed a period of some three or four years' absence from
Dead Souls, but during this same period he made a number of acquaintances
who would serve as prototypes of characters in Part Two, notably Betrishchev
and Tentetnikov.

By 1849 work on this part was well advanced and Gogol gave his first
reading in Kaluga in June–July 1849. His biographer Arnoldi describes in
detail one of these readings, and recounts many episodes which are now lost.
Clearly the work he read on this occasion was in some sort of complete state
(he read daily, from 12 to 2, for some days on end). He continued working on
the text at the house of his friends, the Aksakovs, and in Abramtsevo, and a
revised version of the first and second chapters was read to the Aksakovs in
early 1850. Aksakov's reaction was one of rapture—especially about Chapter
2, prompting him to compare its author to Homer.

A revised version of Chapters 3 and 4 was read to the Aksakovs in mid-
1850, and, at about this same time, certain revisions were made to the last
chapter to bring it into line with the first four chapters—but this chapter was
not completed. In late 1850, in his home at Vasilievka, and subsequently in
Odessa, Gogol made further improvements to the text.

Of the five notebooks that have come down to us, four—containing the
first four chapters of Part Two—belong to the version burnt in 1852. The
fifth—continuing the fragment of the final chapter—belongs to a much earlier version, presumably that which he burnt in 1844. These notebooks are
heavily edited in the author's own hand: often, entire passages have been
crossed out and written anew in the space between the lines. Editors have

done a remarkable job in reconstructing two separate text 'strata', an earlier version, and a later, incorporating the Moscow revisions of 1849–50 and the later Odessa revisions.

From the memoirs of contemporaries, who attended readings of Part Two, we know of a number of chapters and episodes in the plot that have not survived. Father Matvei Konstantinovsky, Gogol's confessor, recalls seeing a number of chapters, including the description of a priest 'with shades of Catholicism, so that the resulting figure was not entirely an Orthodox priest. I objected to the publication of these notebooks,' continues Konstantinovsky, quite unabashed, 'and even besought him to destroy them'. Evidence of other missing chapters was provided by the editor of the first published edition of Part Two, S. P. Shevyryov, in his note to the end of Chapter 2, also reproduced here.

The surviving chapters were first published in 1855, by Shevyryov, as a supplement to the second collected works. For this translation, I have followed the editors of the Academy edition in taking the later version as more authoritative, although where the text of the earlier version differs substantially—and in a way that I consider significant—I have included the passages in question in the Appendix which immediately follows the text of Part Two. Where the text of the earlier version of Volume 2 of *Dead Souls* differs substantially, the variant passage, marked between the symbol † is provided in the appendix following this text.

259 *Tremalakhansk district*: coinage by Gogol, presumed to be derived from the French *très mal*, placing this district in the same category as Pushkin's village Goryukhino and Nekrasov's Neelovo, Gorelovo, etc.—place names similarly derived from words for sorrow and misfortune.

262 *a wonder among pedagogues, Aleksandr Petrovich*: contemporaries questioned Gogol about this figure, and Gogol admitted that he was based on a real-life prototype, without specifying whom. It is thought to have been his Nezhin teacher N. G. Belousov. More open to question, however, is the extent to which Aleksandr Petrovich really represents an ideal to Gogol, and critics have shown the wide divergence between Aleksandr Petrovich's concept of education and that promulgated by Gogol himself in his articles on the subject. A possible further clue to Tentetnikov's gullibility and readiness to accept the eccentric Aleksandr Ivanovich as an ideal is given by his name, which suggests the Ukrainian *tenditniy*, 'tender', 'refined'.

264 *Fedka*: diminutives of Russian names formed with the suffix *-ka* often have a derogatory force.

265 *Actual State Councillor Onufry Ivanovich*: civil rank equivalent to the military rank of Major General, placed fourth on the Table (see p. xliii).

267 *commissionaire's list of all those who had called to pay him their respects*: refers to the custom in government offices in accordance with which, on important holidays, junior employees recorded their congratulations to their superiors by entering their names in a book kept by the

commissionaire and, in due course, passed on to the recipient for his scrutiny.

270 *bonnets, headscarves, kerchiefs*: there are frequent references to the different types of bonnets, scarves, and other headgear worn by Russian women in Gogol's day, which, like so much of the paraphernalia of his world, lack direct equivalents in English and have had to be paraphrased. The terms encountered in *Dead Souls* include: *povoinik*—kerchief worn by married women, usually of the peasant class; *kokoshnik*—stiff, fan-shaped headdress (the word derives from a Slavonic word for chicken, reflecting its similarity to a cock's-comb), made of card and attached to a cap, worn by women—including unmarried girls—of the peasant and merchant classes; *kika* (*kichka*)—complex headdress of married women, worn on festive occasions, with a wimple and forming two horn-like points at the sides, sometimes decorated with beads at the back; *soroka*—strictly speaking, part of the *kika*, a linen or calico scarf with embroidered designs in front; *chepets*—starched bonnet or cap, often embroidered with gold thread, worn by women of the higher classes; and *povyazka*—more general term for a headscarf, sometimes also forming part of more complex headdresses.

corvée: the tax in question—*barshchina*—took the form of unpaid labour due by a serf to his feudal lord; the corvée was the main form of taxation for estate serfs, while quit-rent—*obrok*—was rendered by palace and monastery serfs (see note to p. 100).

272 *the quail taps . . . a skylark trills*: among Gogol's many lists of names and words for things is a list of the different types of bird noises, which include all the forms rendered here.

far from the vile highroads: in his letters, both to his mother and to friends, Gogol displays a strong aversion to the construction of highroads, complaining in particular about plans to build one which was to pass right through the village in which he was staying at the time.

273 *Varvar Nikolaevich Vishnepokromov*: the name Vishnepokromov comes from the word *vishnepokromoi*, which, as recorded by Gogol in his notebooks, describes the coat of a dove with a cherry-coloured border on its wings; there is perhaps an irony in this association of doves with fire-breathing colonels.

277 *fastened round the waist with a handkerchief*: improbably large handkerchiefs feature elsewhere in Gogol's works too; a notable example is the handkerchief in which Akaky Akakievich wraps his new overcoat, in the story of that name.

279 *Voltaire ⟨chair⟩*: (the word chair, absent in the manuscript, is supplied) the Voltaire chair, or *fauteuil Voltaire*, is a padded armchair, with a low seat and a high, curved back; the chair appeared after the Restoration; some commentators prefer to see this as a reference to an eighteenth-century English cabinet-maker Walter (this name would have been identical to Voltaire in Russian transliteration).

blew his nose more loudly than Andrei Ivanovich had ever heard any nose blown before: a recent edition of *Dead Souls* provides additional text from a manuscript copy of these chapters held in the archives of the Pushkin House in St Petersburg: there, the text continues: 'A male borzoi hound, which had crept under the divan, was so startled that he deemed it his duty to go up to the gentleman, sniff at him between the skirts of his tailcoat and sit down before him, staring directly into his eyes, in the expectation of something else equally startling...'

283 *State councillor . . . respected rank*: fifth in the Table of Ranks—equivalent to the military rank of Brigadier.

thirty thousand versts: it is perhaps no coincidence that this distance is more or less the circumference of the earth.

284 *the Akulka*: a girl's name, diminutive of Akulina; it might be recalled that one of Sobakevich's serf girls is called Akulka.

eyes as round as turnips: this unlikely sounding simile was collected by Gogol and duly recorded in his notebooks, where he glosses its meaning as '(1) almond eyes, (2) languorous eyes'.

'boyars, show us your bridegroom': traditional song sung by the girls during village courtship rituals, such as that being enacted in the scene described here. Corresponding songs are sung by the boys.

291 *Imperial Revenue Chamber*: For an explanation of this office, see the note to p. 6.

Aulic Council: this institution, the *nadvorny sud*, functioned as the highest judicial instance in the province.

297 *And martial laughter once again reverberated through the martial apartments*: The end of the chapter is missing. In the first edition of the second volume of *Dead Souls*, published in 1855, the editor, S. P. Shevyryov, comments: 'Missing here is the reconciliation between General Betrishchev and Tentetnikov; dinner at the general's and their conversation about the 1812 campaign; Ulinka's betrothal to Tentetnikov; her praying and weeping at her mother's graveside; the conversation of the betrothed couple in the garden. Chichikov departs on a commission from General Betrishchev to his relatives, to give news of the daughter's betrothal, and he calls on one of these relatives, Colonel Koshkaryov.' Shevyryov had privileged knowledge of the content of Part Two: in 1851, Gogol had read him the first six chapters, ready for publication, and a seventh, in almost final form.

Another biographer, Arnoldi, gives the following detailed account of the rest of the chapter: 'Chichikov stayed for dinner. At table they were joined, besides Ulinka, by two more people: an English miss, serving as her governess, and some Spaniard or Portuguese, who had been living with Betrishchev in his estate since time immemorial and for no immediately apparent purpose. The former was a maiden of middle years, an insipid creature, very plain, with a large, thin nose and extraordinarily rapid eyes. She held herself upright, remained silent for entire days on end and spent her time darting her eyes from side to side and gazing about her with a stupid, inquiring look. The Portuguese, as far as I recall, was called Ekspanton, Khsintendon or something like that; I do remember quite clearly, however, that the general's entire household simply called him: "Eskadron". He also remained silent all the time, but after dinner was supposed to play chess with the general. Nothing out of the ordinary occurred after dinner. The general was in high spirits and cracked jokes with Chichikov, who ate his dinner with great relish. Ulinka was pensive and her features only became animated when she heard Tentetnikov's name mentioned.

'After dinner, the general sat down to play chess with the Spaniard and, as he moved his pieces, kept repeating: "Try loving us clean..." "Dirty, Your Excellency," Chichikov would correct him. "Yes," the general would repeat, "try loving us dirty, the Good Lord Himself loves us nice and clean." Five minutes later he would start getting it wrong again and would say: "Try loving us clean", and Chichikov would have to correct him and once again the general, laughing, would repeat: "Try loving us dirty, the Good Lord Himself loves us nice and clean."

'After several games with the Spaniard, the general invited Chichikov to play one or two games and here Chichikov demonstrated remarkable skill. He played very well, causing the general no end of bother with his moves and still managed to lose; the general was very pleased that he had beaten such a strong opponent and his heart warmed still further to Chichikov as a result. On taking his farewell of his guest, he urged him to call again soon and to bring Tentetnikov with him.

'Returning to Tentetnikov's estate, Chichikov describes to him Ulinka's sadness, the general's regret not to see him again, assures him of the general's genuine remorse and intention, in order to put an end to the misunderstanding once and for all, to visit him and seek his forgiveness. All this is Chichikov's invention.

'But Tentetnikov, in love as he is with Ulinka, is of course delighted by the opening this provides and announces that, if this is indeed how things stand, he will not make the general do that but is prepared to call on him himself the very next day, to avert his own visit. Chichikov approves of this plan and they agree to travel together the next day to General Betrishchev's estate. That same evening Chichikov confesses to Tentetnikov that he told a lie, telling Betrishchev that Tentetnikov was writing a history of generals. Tentetnikov fails to understand why Chichikov had to do that and is at a loss as to what to do if the general starts talking to him about this history. Chichikov admits that he himself does not understand how his tongue ran away with him like that; but the die is now cast and he therefore earnestly entreats him—if he is not prepared to lie—then at least to say nothing, but in any event not to deny the story, so that he does not compromise Chichikov in the general's eyes.

'This is followed by their journey to the general's village, Tentetnikov's meeting with Betrishchev and Ulinka and, finally, the dinner. The description of this dinner,' observes Arnoldi, 'was, in my opinion, the best passage in Part Two. The general sat in the middle, with Tentetnikov on his right, Chichikov on his left, Ulinka beside Chichikov, the Spaniard beside Tentetnikov, and the English miss between the Spaniard and Ulinka; the entire company seemed content and in high spirits. The general was happy to have made his peace with Tentetnikov and to be able to converse with a man writing the history of the generals of Russia; Tentetnikov was happy that Ulinka was sitting almost across the table from him and that from time to time their eyes would meet; Ulinka was happy that the man she loved was with them once again and that he and her father were on good terms once more, and, finally, Chichikov was happy with his function of peacemaker in this highborn and rich family.

'The English miss darted her eyes about with gay abandon, the Spaniard gazed at his plate and only lifted his eyes when new dishes were borne into the room. Picking out the choicest piece, he would keep his eyes fixed on it while the dish went the rounds of all the diners or until it landed on someone else's plate.

'After the second course, the general raised the topic of Tentetnikov's literary undertaking and touched on the subject of 1812. Chichikov's heart sank as he waited for Tentetnikov's reply. Tentetnikov extricated himself with great skill. He replied that it was not for him to write the history of the campaign, of its individual battles and personalities involved in this war, that 1812 was remarkable not for these heroic events, that there were, besides him, many historians of that time; but that the era had to be considered from a different angle: what was important about it, in his opinion, was how the entire nation had risen as one man in defence of Russia; how all quarrels, intrigues, and petty feuds had been set aside for that period; how all estates of society had joined together in a united feeling of love for their country, how each citizen had hastened to offer up his very last possessions and to sacrifice everything for the salvation of the greater cause; that was what had been important in that war and it was that which he wished to describe in a single, vivid picture, with all the details of these invisible achievements and these lofty—but secret—sacrifices!

'Tentetnikov spoke for some time and with enthusiasm, and, as he did so, he was suffused with a feeling of love for Russia. Betrishchev listened to him in rapture, and, for the first time, he heard such warm, living words enter his ears. A tear, like a bright jewel of the purest liquid, hung on his grey whiskers.

'The general was fine to behold; but what of Ulinka? She had eyes only for Tentetnikov, she seemed to lap up greedily his every word; she was intoxicated by his speeches, as by music; she loved him, she was proud of him! The Spaniard's head sank ever deeper into his plate; the English miss gazed at everyone with a stupid expression, with no idea what was going on. When Tentetnikov finished and silence reigned once more, they were all in a state of elation...

'Chichikov, wishing to have his say, broke the silence. "Yes," he said, "there were terrible frosts in 1812!"

'"We're not talking of frosts," said the general, giving him a severe look. Chichikov was embarrassed. The general stretched out his hand to Tentetnikov and thanked him warmly; but Tentetnikov was already entirely happy to see the look of approval in Ulinka's eyes. The history of generals was forgotten. The day passed quietly and agreeably for everyone...

'After this,' continues Arnoldi, 'I do not recall the order in which the chapters followed; I only remember that, after this day, Ulinka decided to have a serious talk with her father about Tentetnikov. Before embarking on this serious talk, one evening, she visited her mother's grave and, in her prayers, sought further strengthening of her resolve. After this prayer, she entered her father's study, knelt before him, and begged his consent and blessing for her marriage to Tentetnikov. The general hesitated for a long while before finally agreeing. Tentetnikov was summoned and informed of the general's decision. This occurred several days after the reconciliation. On receiving the general's consent, Tentetnikov, beside himself with happiness, left Ulinka for a moment and ran into the garden. He needed to be alone for a moment, he was suffocating with happiness!...

'Here Gogol had two marvellous lyrical pages. On a hot summer's day, at the height of noon, Tentetnikov stands in the lush, shady garden amidst a deep, all-prevailing silence. The garden was painted with the brush of a true master, each branch on the trees, the scorching heat, the grasshoppers in the grass, the insects, and finally all the feelings surging through Tentetnikov, loving and loved in return! I vividly recall,' continues Arnoldi, 'that this description was particularly fine, with so much strength, bright colour, and poetry, that it quite took my breath away. Gogol read magnificently! In an excess of feeling, from a surfeit of joy, Tentetnikov weeps and at once vows to devote his entire life to his bride. At this moment Chichikov appears at the end of the path. Tentetnikov rushes to meet him and thanks him.

'"You are my benefactor, I owe my happiness to you; how can I thank you?... To give you my life would be insufficient recompense..."

'A new idea at once enters Chichikov's head: "I did nothing for you, it was sheer chance," he answers, "I am very happy, but it would be easy for you to thank me!"

'"How, how?" repeats Tentetnikov. "Tell me quickly, I shall do everything."

'Here Chichikov tells him about his imaginary uncle, about how he needs, at least on paper, three hundred souls. "But why should they be dead ones?" asks Tentetnikov, not quite grasping exactly what Chichikov is after. "I'll give you all my three hundred souls on paper and you can show your uncle that you've fulfilled his condition, and afterwards, when you've been given his estate, we can destroy the transfer papers."

'Chichikov was thunderstruck! "What—you're not afraid to do this?... You're not afraid that I might deceive you... that I might abuse your trust?"

'But Tentetnikov does not let him finish. "What?" he exclaims. "I should doubt you, to whom I owe more than my own life?" Hereupon they embrace and the matter is decided between them.

'Chichikov slept sweetly that night. The following day, in the general's house, there is a discussion on how best to inform the general's relations about his daughter's betrothal, whether by letter or in some other fashion, or whether they should call on them in person. It is apparent that Betrishchev is very anxious about how Princess Zyuzyukina and his other blue-blooded relations will take the news. Here too Chichikov proves to be of great service: he offers to travel round the estates of all the general's relations and to inform them about Ulinka and Tentetnikov's betrothal. Naturally, with an eye to his own advantage—in other words, the acquisition of "dead souls".

'His offer is gratefully accepted. "What could be better?" reflects the general, "he's clever, and respectable; he will know how to present the news of this wedding in such a way that everyone is pleased."

'For the purpose of this journey the general offers Chichikov a two-seater calèche of foreign manufacture and Tentetnikov provides a fourth horse. Chichikov is to set off in a few days' time. From this moment on everyone in General Betrishchev's house starts to regard him as one of the family.

'On his return to Tentetnikov's, Chichikov at once summons Selifan and Petrushka and instructs them to prepare for the journey. Selifan has grown utterly indolent on Tentetnikov's estate, taking to the bottle and completely neglecting his coachman's duties. The horses have been left entirely without care. Petrushka, on the other hand, has spent all his time pursuing the village girls. When the general's lightweight calèche, almost brand-new, is brought from the general's and Selifan sees that he will sit on a broad coachman's seat and drive a team of four, all his coachman's instincts are reawakened in him and he starts inspecting the vehicle with close attention and an expert's eye, asking the general's men for various spare bolts and spanners such as did not even exist. Chichikov also looked forward to the journey with relish: he thought how he would lie back on the soft, springy cushions and how the team of four would fly ahead with this feather-light calèche.'

Gogol's close friend Aleksandra Smirnova told an earlier biographer, Panteleimon Kulish, that the surviving fragments did not include 'a description of Vorony-Dryannoy's village, from which Chichikov moves to Kostanzhoglo's. Nor is there a word about Chegranov's estate, which is run by a young man recently graduated from the university. Here Platonov, Chichikov's apathetic companion, is fascinated by a portrait, and later they meet the portrait's flesh-and-blood original at the house of General Betrishchev's brother, and a love affair begins, from which Chichikov seeks to extract the utmost profit, as he does from all situations, whatever they may be'.

Finally, we learn about Tentetnikov's subsequent fate from an account told by Shevyryov to Prince D. A. Obolensky: 'While Tentetnikov, roused from his apathy by Ulinka's influence, is in a state of bliss as her intended husband, he is arrested and sent to Siberia; this arrest has to do with the composition he was preparing on Russia and with his friendship with a student of dangerous liberal tendencies, who has dropped out of his course' (this student is thought to be modelled on the critic Belinsky). 'Departing from his village and taking his leave of the peasants, Tentetnikov delivers a farewell address (which, according to Shevyryov, was a remarkable work of art). Ulinka follows Tentetnikov to Siberia—there they are married, and so forth.'

300 *Venus de Medici*: famous statue, presumed to be a first-century BC Roman copy of a Greek original, found in 1680 in the villa of the emperor Hadrian at Tivoli and acquired by the Medici family, whence its name. The statue, which represented the ideal of the 'modest Venus'—as opposed to her 'natural' or 'celestial' hypostases—was greatly admired in Russia and many copies were made; in addition, Gogol may have seen the statue itself in his travels in Italy. In Fielding's novel *Sophia Western*, the heroine, as she enters the ball in a famous scene, is compared to the Venus de Medici (or 'Medicis', as Fielding spells it).

301 *Petukh, Pyotr Petrovich*: the name Petukh means, quite simply, 'cock', with similar associations to those brought by the English bird.

a full arshin: a pre-Revolutionary measure of length, equivalent to 28 inches.

303 *a fearsome monster of a hound, called Yarb*: In Gogol's world, even dogs have interesting names. Yarb is named after Iarbas, king of the Numidian Gaetulians, who first sells Dido the land on which she builds Carthage and then woos her; she escapes his embraces when she immolates herself. A slightly different version of the story is told by Virgil, in Book IV of the *Aeneid*, and it is perhaps not coincidental that the mad Colonel Koshkaryov, later in this chapter, would have his serfs read Virgil's *Georgics* as they walk behind the plough. Later, we meet another dog, called Azor—named after the pilot of Jason's *Argo*: the two dogs, we might note, belong to brothers called Platonov.

304 *dessiatines*: a dessiatine is a pre-Revolutionary measure of area, equivalent to about two and a half acres, or slightly more than a hectare.

307 *No, you shall stop the night here, and tomorrow after an early luncheon you may set off on your travels*: critics have observed that Petukh has his protoype in Storchenko, the insistent host in the story 'Ivan Fyodorovich Shponka and his Aunt', from the Dikanka tales. There is often a suggestion of disapproval in Gogol's depiction of prandial hospitality, foreshadowing his own asceticism and self-denial at the end of his life.

309 *Murazov—it's no problem for him*: Murazov is thought to be based, at least, partly on the concessionaire Bernadaki, a man of great wealth and extensive knowledge of the length and breadth of Russia, whom Gogol came to know and admire in Marienbad. Aspects of Bernadaki may also be seen in Tentetnikov. Commentators have pointed out the ambiguity

in Murazov's image, a clue to which is provided by his oriental name, derived from the Persian *mirza*, with its connotations—at least, to the ninteteenth-century Russian ear—of shadiness.

310 *Konstantin Fyodorovich Kostanzhoglo! I shall be delighted to make his acquaintance. It will be most instructive to get to know such a man*: Kostanzhoglo's name evolved through many variants, Skudronzhoglo, Poponzhoglo, Gobronzhoglo, and Berdanzhoglo, the last of which (as well as the Greek–Turkish origin of the name) gives a clue as to his partial prototype, the concessionaire Bernadaki (see the previous note).

311 *no jardins anglais here*: for the popularity of English gardens in Russia, see the note to p. 18.

316 *Benjamin Franklin's book about lightning conductors . . . Chemical Analysis of the Soil*: the work by Benjamin Franklin (1706–90) intended here is probably *Experiments and Observations on Electricity*, 1751, a compilation of his letters on scientific matters, which was translated into a number of European languages and widely read throughout Europe; Franklin was elected an honorary member of the Russian Academy of Sciences in 1789, one year before his death. *Chemical Analysis of the Soil* is thought by commentators to refer to a work by the German chemist Justus Liebig (1803–73), among other things, the discoverer of chloroform, whose books on the role of chemistry in agriculture were translated into Russian in 1842 and who gave his name both to Liebig extract of beef and to the Liebig condenser, familiar to many generations of science students.

318 *Office for Incoming Reports and Depositions . . . Office for the Submission of Reports . . . Commission for the Submission of Reports*: the names of Koshkaryov's offices metamorphose, with each mention, as if they have a life of their own.

320 *Moscow Gazette*: see note to p. 158.

321 *Frenchman in 1812*: reference to Napoleon's invasion of Russia.

322 *as in the fable . . . lifting the lid*: reference to Krylov's (see note to p. 232) well-known fable *Larchik*—'A Little Box', the moral of which, after the mechanic has failed, with all his ingenuity, to open the box, reads, in Pares's translation: 'And why not raise the lid? He never tried that way! | There was a box that opened of itself.'

323 *"In the sweat of thy brow shalt thou till the land"*: Paraphrased from Gen. 3: 19: 'In the sweat of thy face shalt thou eat bread, till thou return unto the ground.'

324 *what best to undertake* [. . .]: An entire sheet of the manuscript is missing here. The first edition of Volume Two of *Dead Souls* (1855) contains the note: 'Here there is a hiatus in Kostanzhoglo's conversation with Chichikov. We must presume that Kostanzhoglo suggests to Chichikov that he purchase the estate of his neighbour, the landowner Khlobuev.'

329 *commissionaire*: under the system of *otkup*, the sale of liquor was exercised by private individuals on a licence basis; another such *otkupshchik*, or concessionaire, appears in Part One—see the note to p. 8.

333 *Khlobuev's*: Khlobuev's real-life prototype is thought to be the poet Pushkin's friend P. V. Nashchokin, who was recommended by Gogol as a tutor to the concessionaire Bernadaki's children (for Bernadaki, see the note to p. 309).

335 *Gubernia Secretary*: low-ranking official, tenth on the Table (see p. xliii) and equivalent to the military rank of second lieutenant.

339 *Trishka's caftan ... elbows*: reference to the fable 'Trishka's caftan' by Krylov (see note to p. 232), illustrating the futility of remedying one defect by creating another; in the fable, Trishka attempts to patch his old coat by cutting cloth from its sleeves, then has to cut off its flaps and tails to lengthen the sleeves.

342 *kvass*: humble—but excellent—beverage, generally made from fermented old bread, and slightly alcoholic; in Part One, the braggart Nozdryov disparagingly compares the governor's champagne to kvass.

348 *lipec*: alcoholic drink, similar to mead, made from fermented honey with the addition of spices; the honey is from the blossom of the lime, or linden tree (*lipa*)—hence the name *lipec*.

Little Russia ... Poltava: Little Russia—see note to p. 156; Poltava—ancient Ukrainian town, centre of the Cossack settlement and site of the famous battle of Poltava in 1709, in which Peter the Great defeated the combined armies of Charles X of Sweden and the Cossack hetman Mazepa. Gogol himself hailed from Poltava province.

349 *Red Hill festivities*: celebrated by Russian countryfolk on the Sunday of St Thomas's week (the first week following Easter): a time when weddings were usually celebrated. In his notebooks, Gogol describes in detail the various activities and traditions associated with this day.

350 ⟨. . .⟩: the pages which follow are missing in the manuscript. The first edition of Part Two of Dead Souls (1855) contains the note: 'Here there is a hiatus which, it may be surmised, contains an account of Chichikov setting off to visit the landowner Lenitsyn.'

352 *You need land, do you not*: The chapters which follow are lost, and only fragments remain. Some episodes from these missing chapters have been recorded by Gogol's contemporaries—see, for example, the note to p. 297.

353 *Final Chapter*: taken from an earlier edition than the other chapters. For an explanation of the exegesis of this and other chapters of Part Two, see the account on pp. 436–7.

Hambs furniture: Ernst Hambs (1805–49) was the proprietor of a fashionable furniture store in St Petersburg.

koulaks: see note on p. 102.

355 *Navarino smoke-grey shot with flame-red*: Navarino—Italian name for the

Greek port Pylos, site of a major sea battle in 1827, at which the Egyptian and Turkish fleets were routed by a combined Russian, French, and English fleet.

358 *as the ant says ... "Now you're free to dance out there"*: reference to a well-known fable by Ivan Krylov, 'The Dragonfly and the Ant', here in Pares' translation, better known to English-speakers as 'The Ant and the Grasshopper' (and to the French—via La Fontaine—as 'The Cicada and the Ant'); for Krylov, see note to p. 232.

363 *Kammerherr at court*: courtier's rank, one of a system of courtiers' ranks introduced by Catherine II and incorporated into the Petrine Table of Ranks; the Kammerherr was equivalent to the 4th rank on the Table, that of Actual Councillor, or the military rank of Major General; by the time of Gogol's writing, the Kammerherr was a purely honorary rank, awarded to civilians, and, as his insignia of office, the holder wore a gold key on a blue ribbon hanging from the left waist button on his tailcoat.

372 *the kingdom suffers violence it is written*: paraphrased from Matt. 11: 12: 'the kingdom of heaven suffereth violence, and the violent take it by force'.

373 *Samosvistov*: a name suggestive of waste and idleness, from *samo-*, 'self', and *svistet'*, 'to whistle'.

376 *volost*: pre-Revolutionary administrative unit, comprising a group of hamlets under the control of a single village headman.

378 *Derpennikov case*: As this chapter is from an earlier version than those which precede it, this name had not yet evolved to the form it has in the later version (and that used in the previous chapters), Tentetnikov.

379 *schismatics*: the schismatics—or *raskolniki*—were a large sect which separated from the Russian Orthodox Church in the seventeenth century in protest against reforms introduced by Patriarch Nikon, both to the liturgy and to forms of worship. The reforms were designed to bring the Russian Church back in line with its Greek parent, but they enraged large numbers of the faithful, led by Archpriest Avvakum, who declared the reforms heretical and denounced Peter the Great as Antichrist. The schismatics established a number of break-away churches, collectively known as the Old Believers, which flourished in remoter parts of the Russian North and East. There are large numbers of Old Believers to this day, both in Russia itself and abroad, particularly in Canada and Argentina. The anathema on all the Old Believer sects was finally lifted by the Patriarch in 1971.

381 *Times of famine and poverty will set in, striking nations in their entirety and each individual separately*: this is thought by commentators to contain a submerged reference to Acts 11: 28–9: 'there should be great dearth throughout the earth . . .'.

382 *titular councillor*: ninth in order on the Table of Ranks (see p. xliii) and equivalent to the military rank of captain.

382 *Kisloedov, Krasnonosov, Samosvistov*: as usual, these names have a comic resonance, lost in English. Thus, Kisloedov suggests *kisly*—'sour', and *-ed-*—'eater'; Krasnonosov *krasny*—'red', and *nos*—'nose'; for Samosvistov, see note to p. 373.

385 *twenty alien tribes*: reference to the multi-national invading force of Napoleon.

*The
Oxford
World's
Classics
Website*

www.worldsclassics.co.uk

- Information about new titles
- Explore the full range of Oxford World's Classics
- Links to other literary sites and the main OUP webpage
- Imaginative competitions, with bookish prizes
- Peruse the Oxford World's Classics Magazine
- Articles by editors
- Extracts from Introductions
- A forum for discussion and feedback on the series
- Special information for teachers and lecturers

www.worldsclassics.co.uk

American Literature

British and Irish Literature

Children's Literature

Classics and Ancient Literature

Colonial Literature

Eastern Literature

European Literature

History

Medieval Literature

Oxford English Drama

Poetry

Philosophy

Politics

Religion

The Oxford Shakespeare

A complete list of Oxford Paperbacks, including Oxford World's Classics, Oxford Shakespeare, Oxford Drama, and Oxford Paperback Reference, is available in the UK from the Academic Division Publicity Department, Oxford University Press, Great Clarendon Street, Oxford OX2 6DP.

In the USA, complete lists are available from the Paperbacks Marketing Manager, Oxford University Press, 198 Madison Avenue, New York, NY 10016.

Oxford Paperbacks are available from all good bookshops. In case of difficulty, customers in the UK can order direct from Oxford University Press Bookshop, Freepost, 116 High Street, Oxford OX1 4BR, enclosing full payment. Please add 10 per cent of published price for postage and packing.